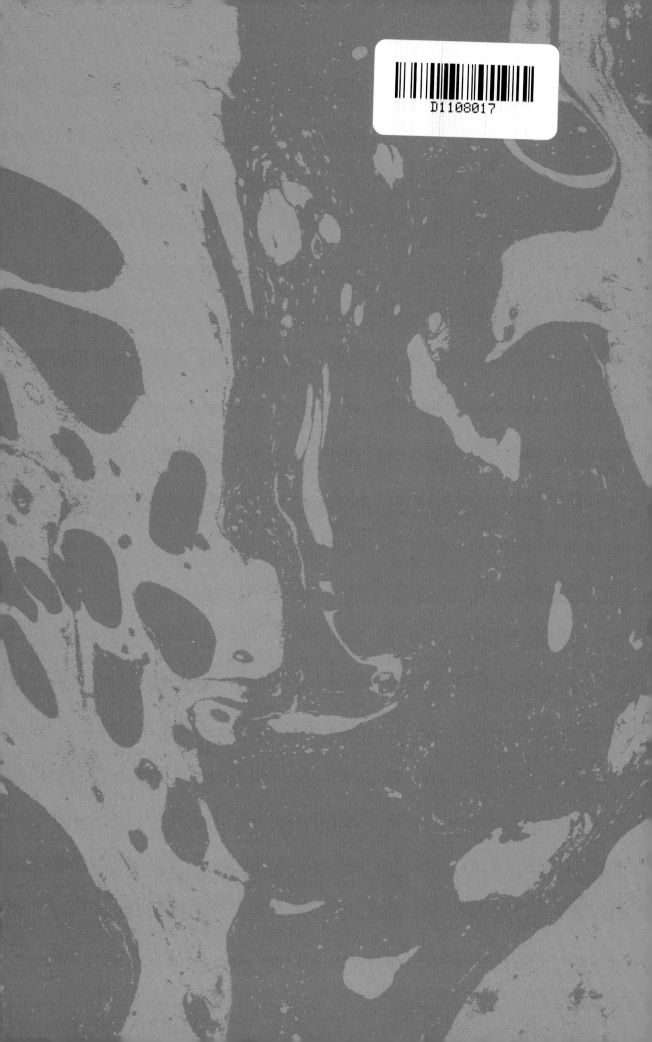

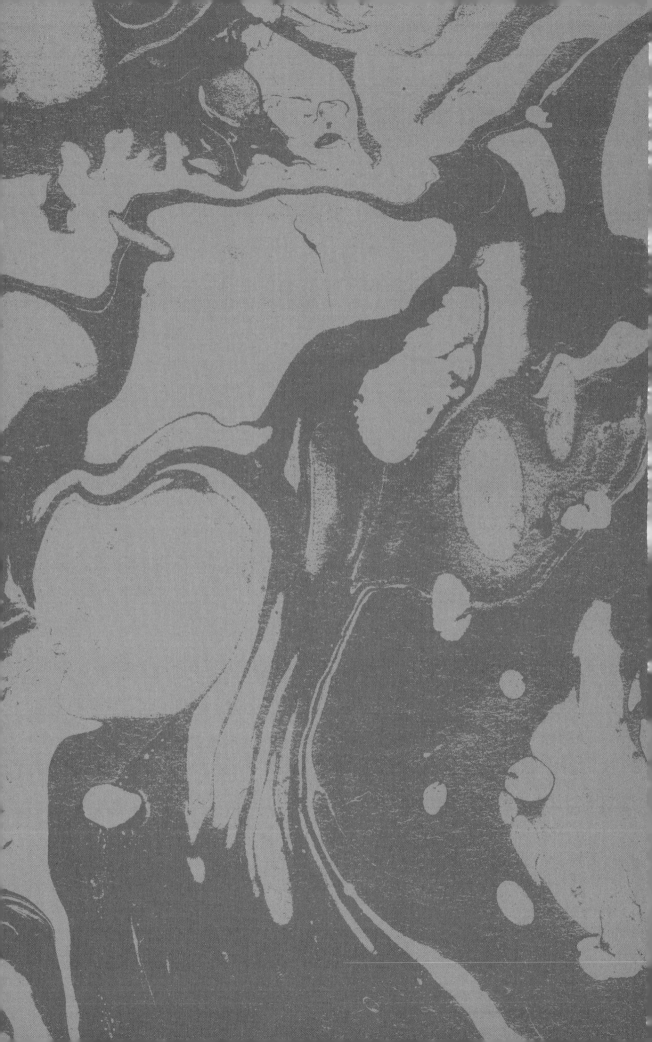

OBLIVION SONG

CREATED BY
ROBERT KIRKMAN
AND
LORENZO DE FELICI

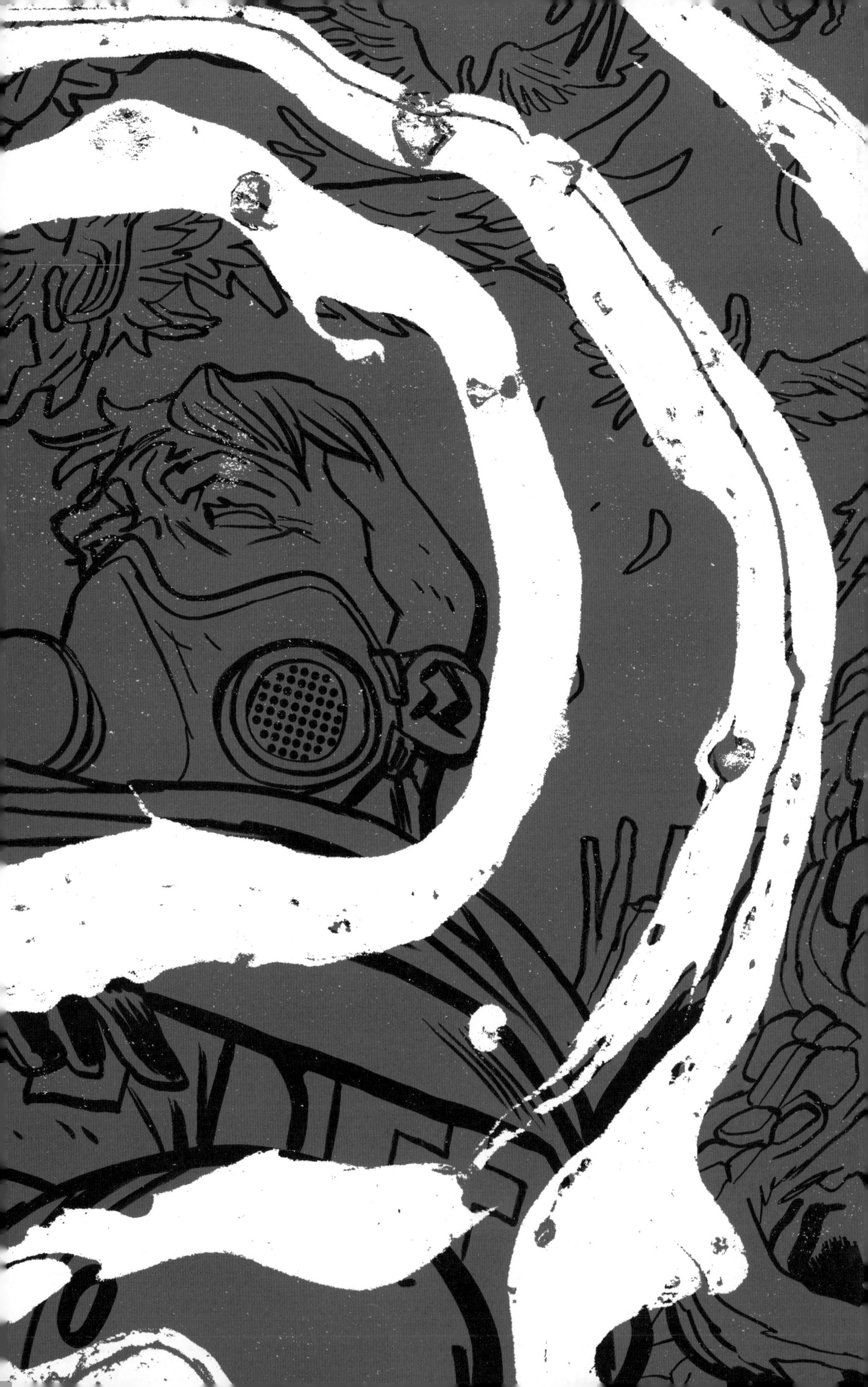

ROBERT KIRKMAN
WRITER/CREATOR

LORENZO DE FELICI
ARTIST/CREATOR

ANNALISA LEONI
COLORIST

RUS WOOTON
LETTERER

SEAN MACKIEWICZ
EDITOR

ANDRES JUAREZ
LOGO & COLLECTION DESIGN

CARINA TAYLOR
PRODUCTION

FOR SKYBOUND ENTERTAINMENT

ROBERT KIRKMAN *Chairman* • DAVID ALPERT *CEO* • SEAN MACKIEWICZ *SVP, Editor-in-Chief*
SHAWN KIRKHAM *SVP, Business Development* • BRIAN HUNTINGTON *VP of Online Content*
ANDRES JUAREZ *Art Director* • ARUNE SINGH *Director of Brand, Editorial* • ALEX ANTONE *Senior Editor*
AMANDA LaFRANCO *Editor* • JON MOISAN *Editor* • CARINA TAYLOR *Graphic Designer*
DAN PETERSEN *Sr. Director of Operations & Events*
Foreign Rights & Licensing Inquiries: contact@skybound.com
SKYBOUND.COM

IMAGE COMICS, INC.

TODD MCFARLANE *President* • JIM VALENTINO *Vice President* • MARC SILVESTRI *Chief Executive
Officer* • ERIK LARSEN *Chief Financial Officer* • ROBERT KIRKMAN *Chief Operating Officer* •
ERIC STEPHENSON *Publisher / Chief Creative Officer* • NICOLE LAPALME *Controller* • LEANNA
CAUNTER *Accounting Analyst* • SUE KORPELA *Accounting & HR Manager* • MARLA EIZIK *Talent
Liaison* • JEFF BOISON *Director of Sales & Publishing Planning* • DIRK WOOD *Director of International
Sales & Licensing* • ALEX COX *Director of Direct Market Sales* • CHLOE RAMOS *Book Market & Library Sales
Manager* • EMILIO BAUTISTA *Digital Sales Coordinator* • JON SCHLAFFMAN *Specialty Sales Coordinator* • KAT
SALAZAR *Director of PR & Marketing* • DREW FITZGERALD *Marketing Content Associate* • HEATHER DOORNINK
Production Director • DREW GILL *Art Director* • HILARY DILORETO *Print Manager* TRICIA RAMOS *Traffic
Manager* • MELISSA GIFFORD *Content Manager* • ERIKA SCHNATZ *Senior Production Artist* • RYAN BREWER
Production Artist • DEANNA PHELPS *Production Artist* • IMAGECOMICS.COM

OBLIVION SONG BOOK ONE.
Second Printing. ISBN: 978-1-5343-1688-1

CHAPTER

ONE

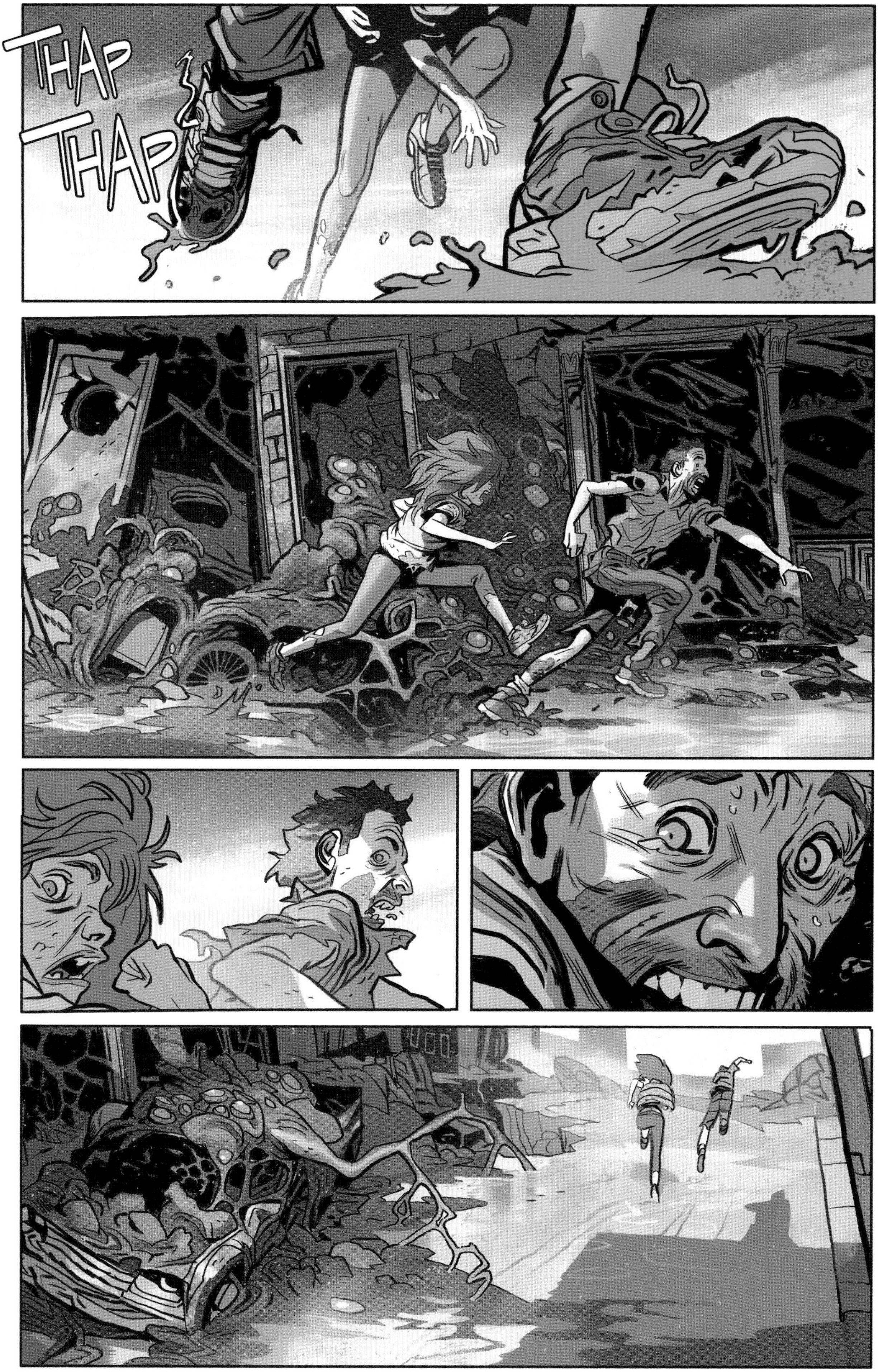
THAP
THAP

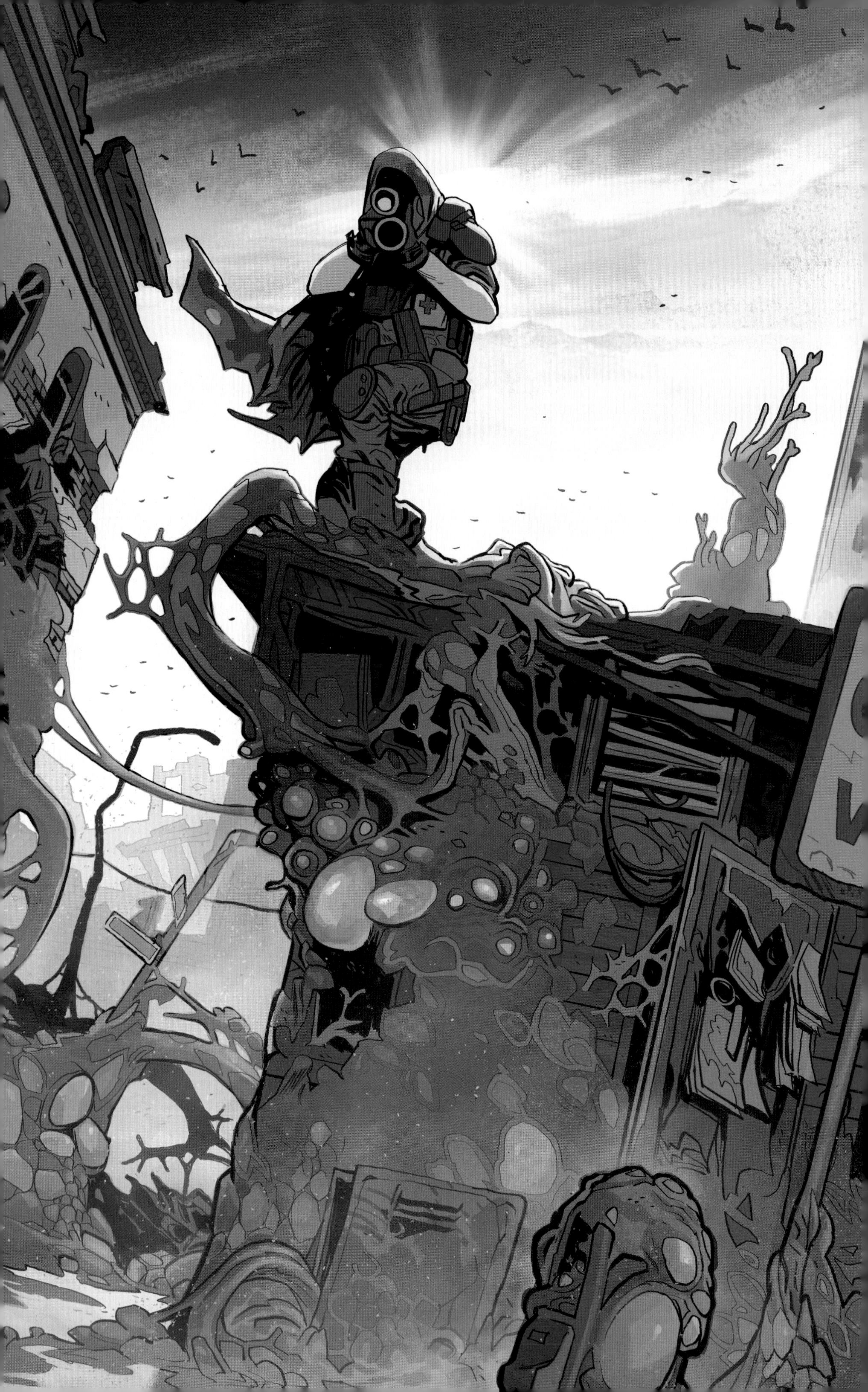

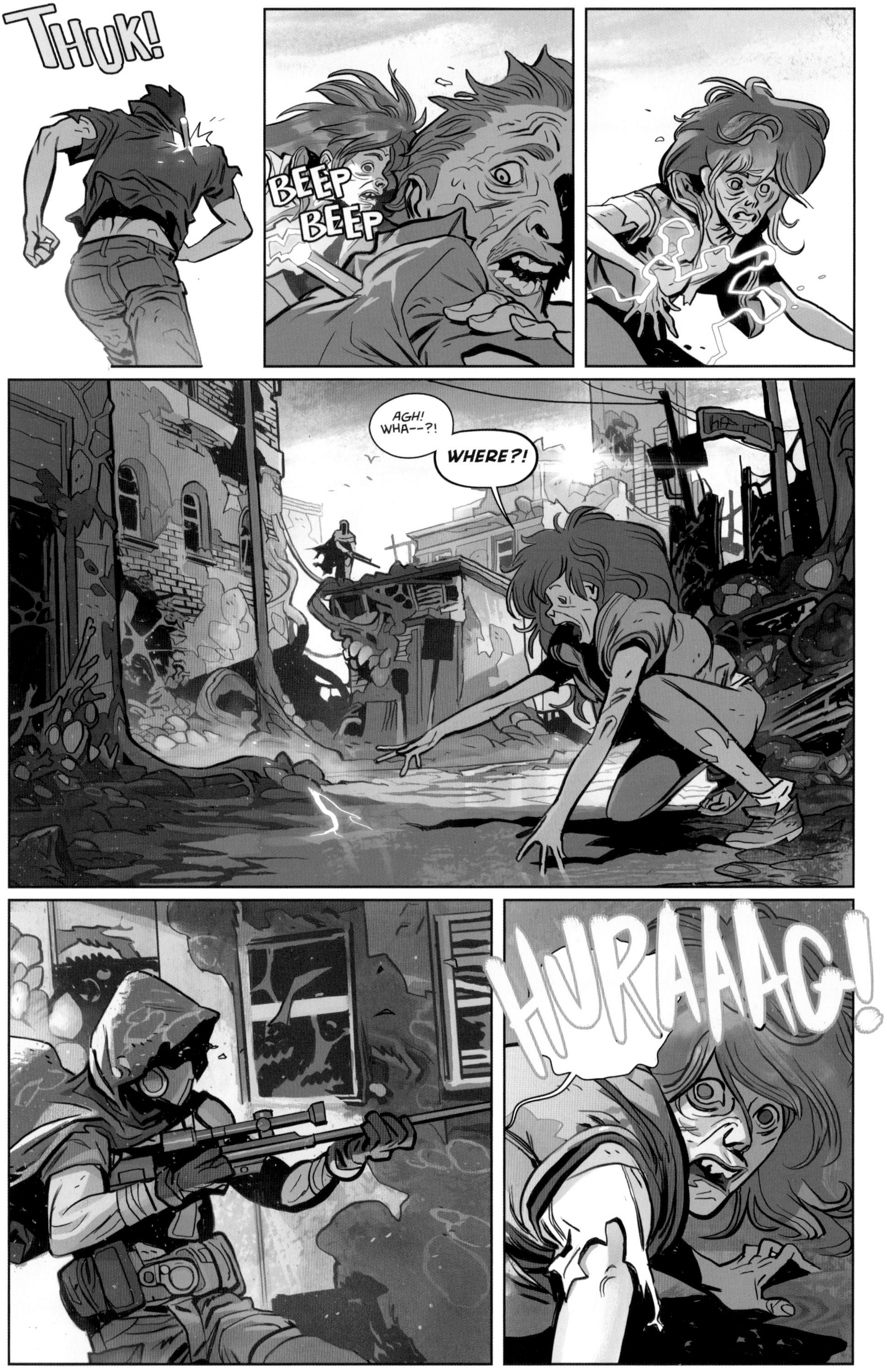
THUK!
BEEP BEEP
AGH! WHA--?!
WHERE?!
HURAAAG!

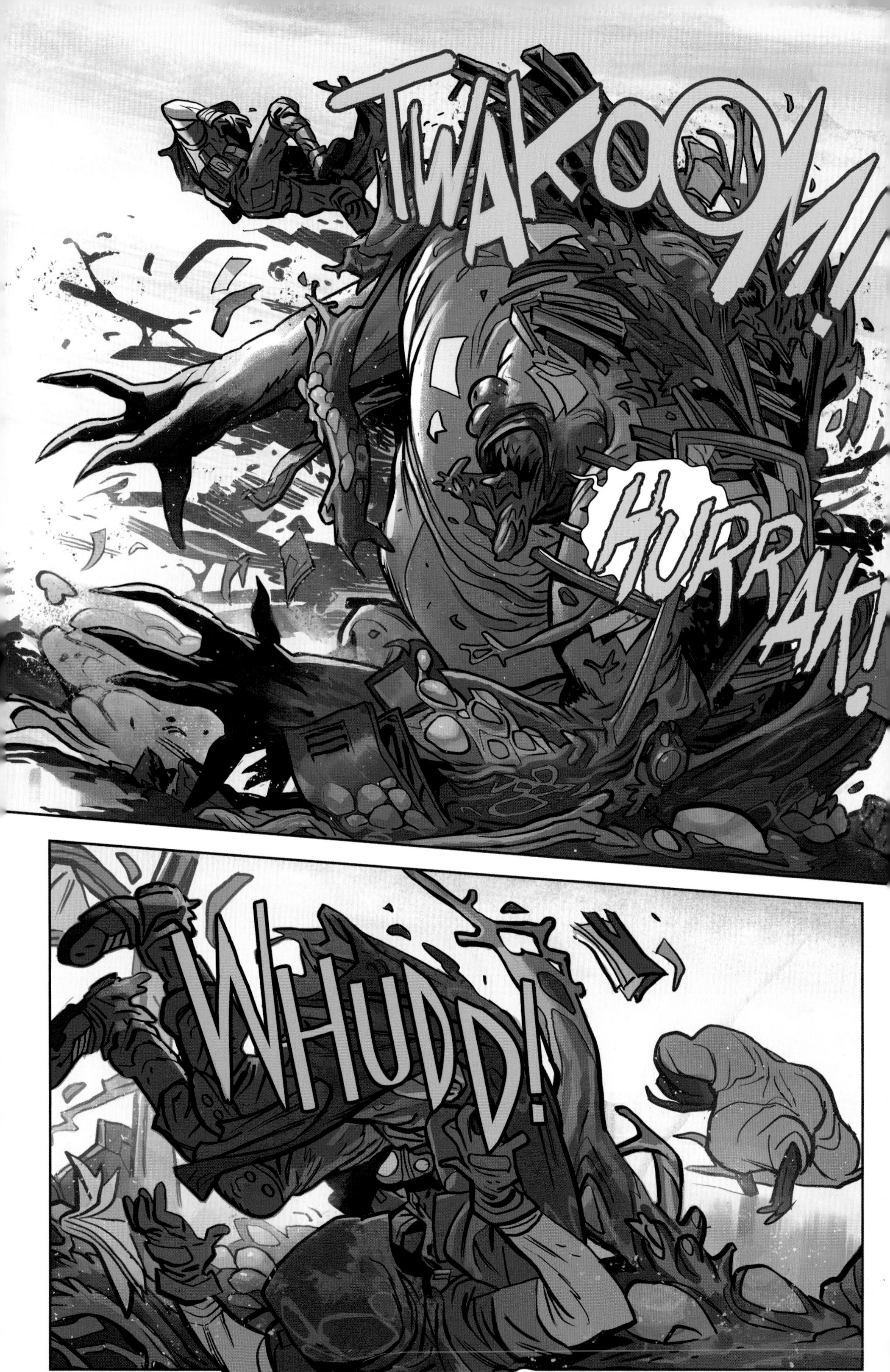
TWAKOOM!!
HURRAK!
WHUDD!

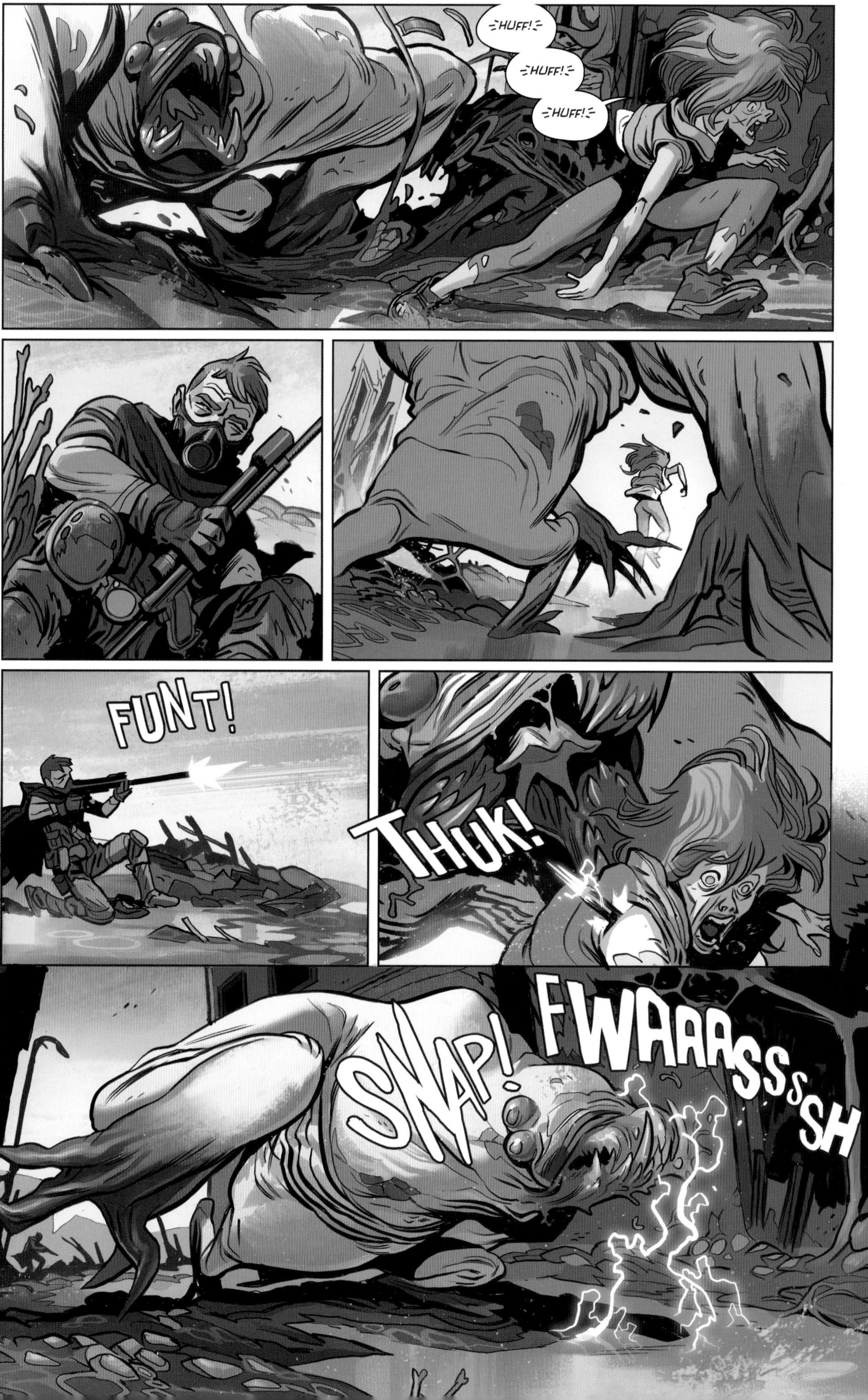
HUFF!
HUFF!
HUFF!
FUNT!
THUK!
SNAP!
FWAAASSSSH

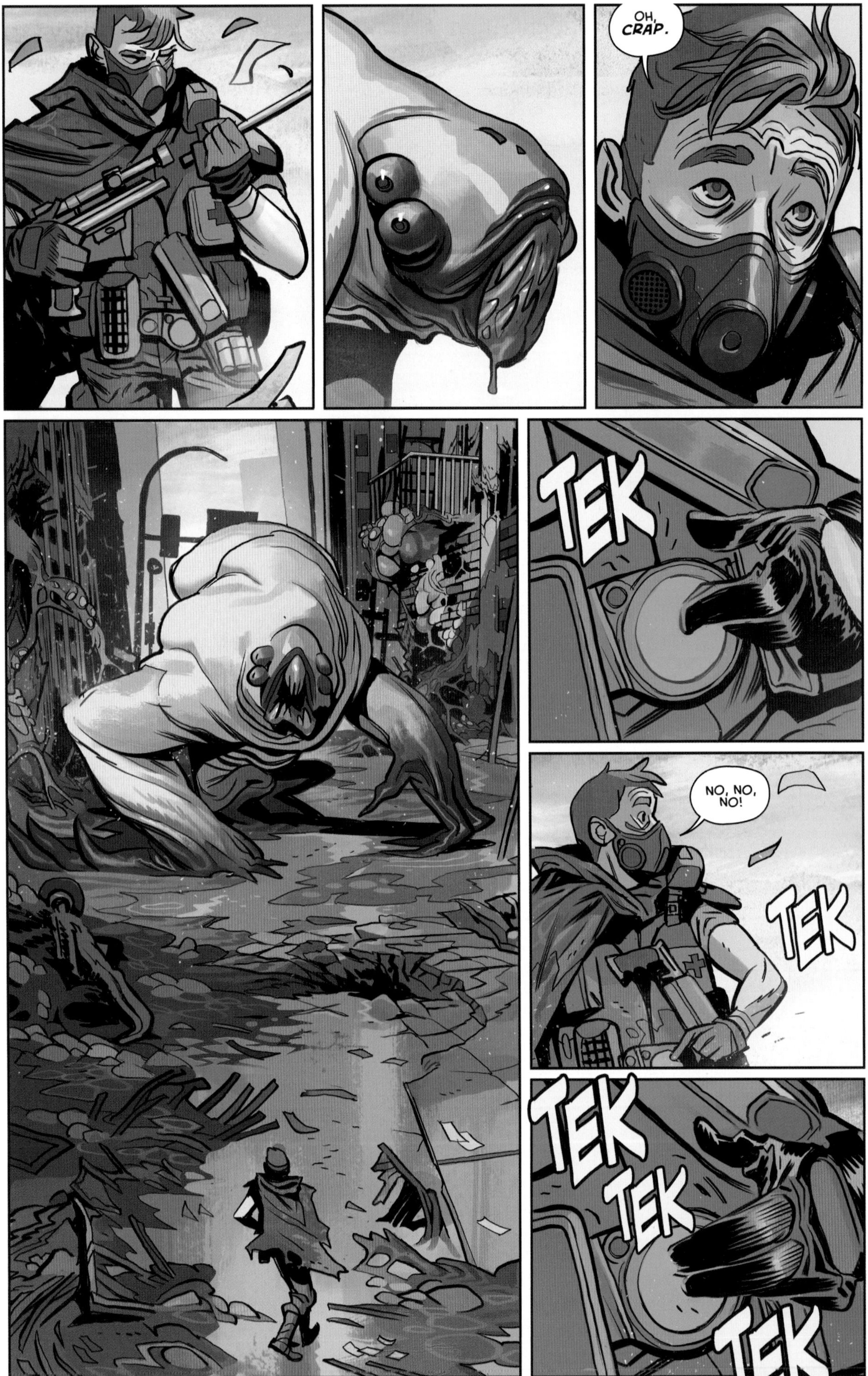
OH, CRAP.
TEK
NO, NO, NO!
TEK
TEK
TEK
TEK

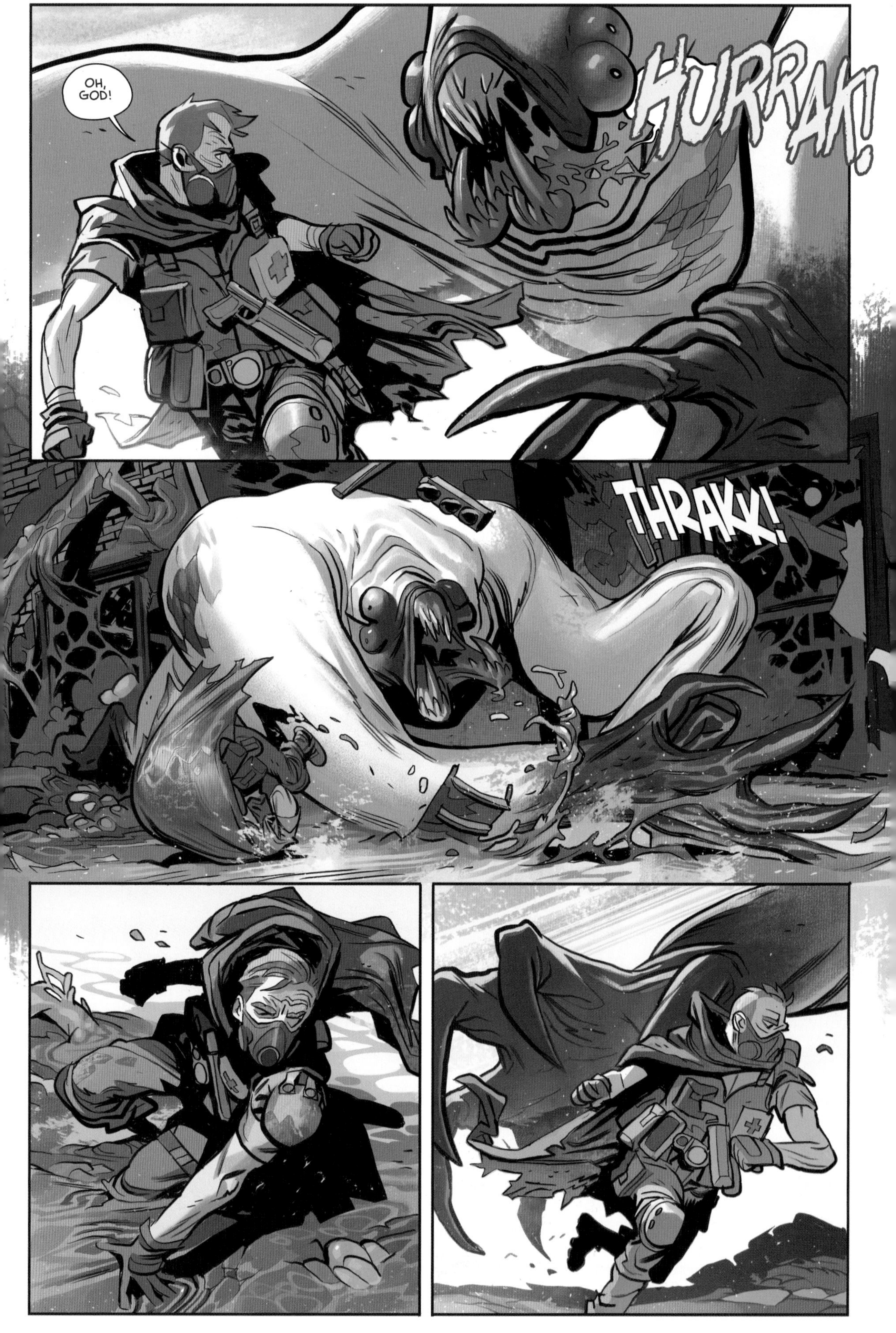
OH, GOD!
HURRAK!
THRAKK!

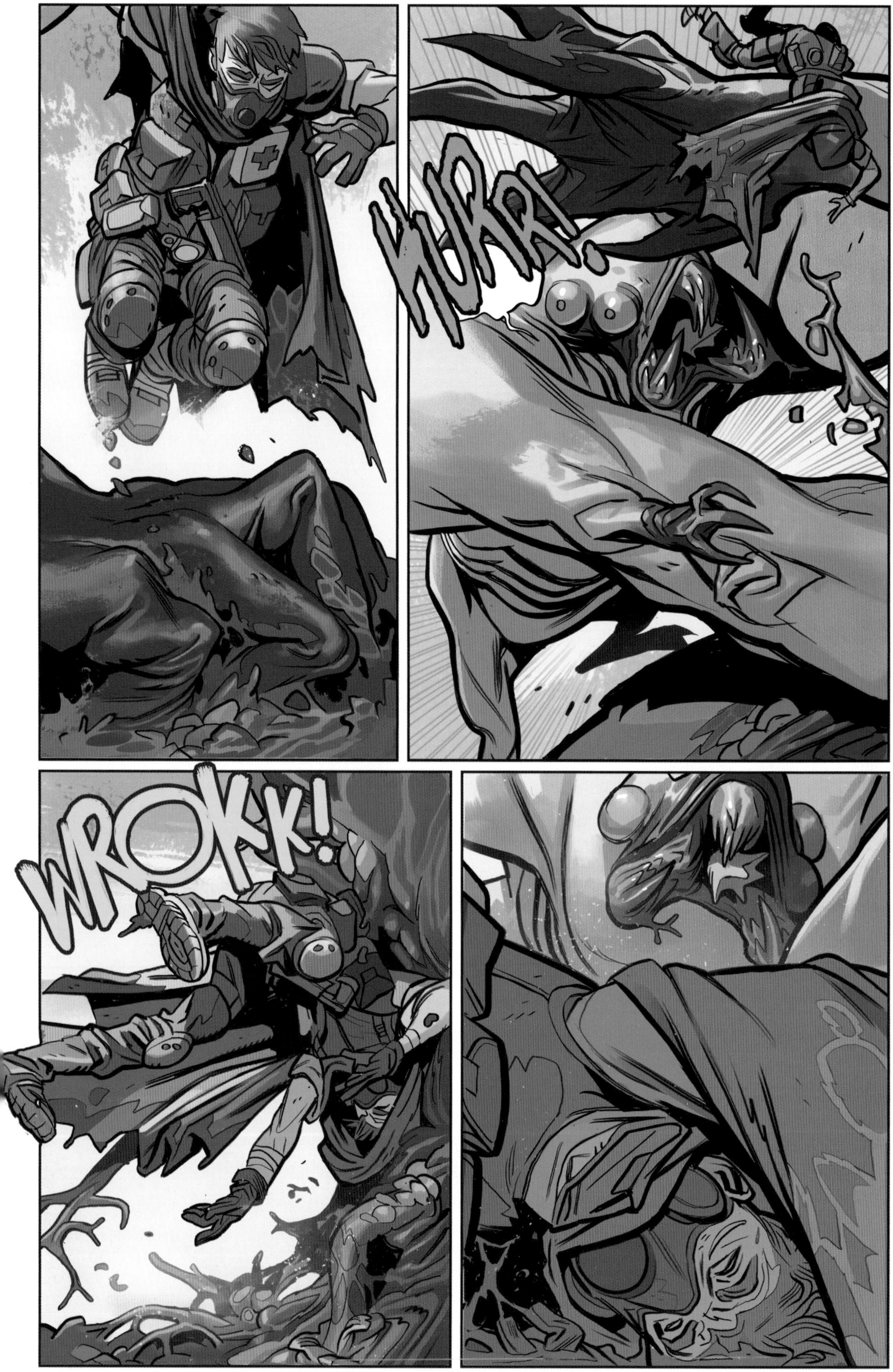
HURR!
WROKK!

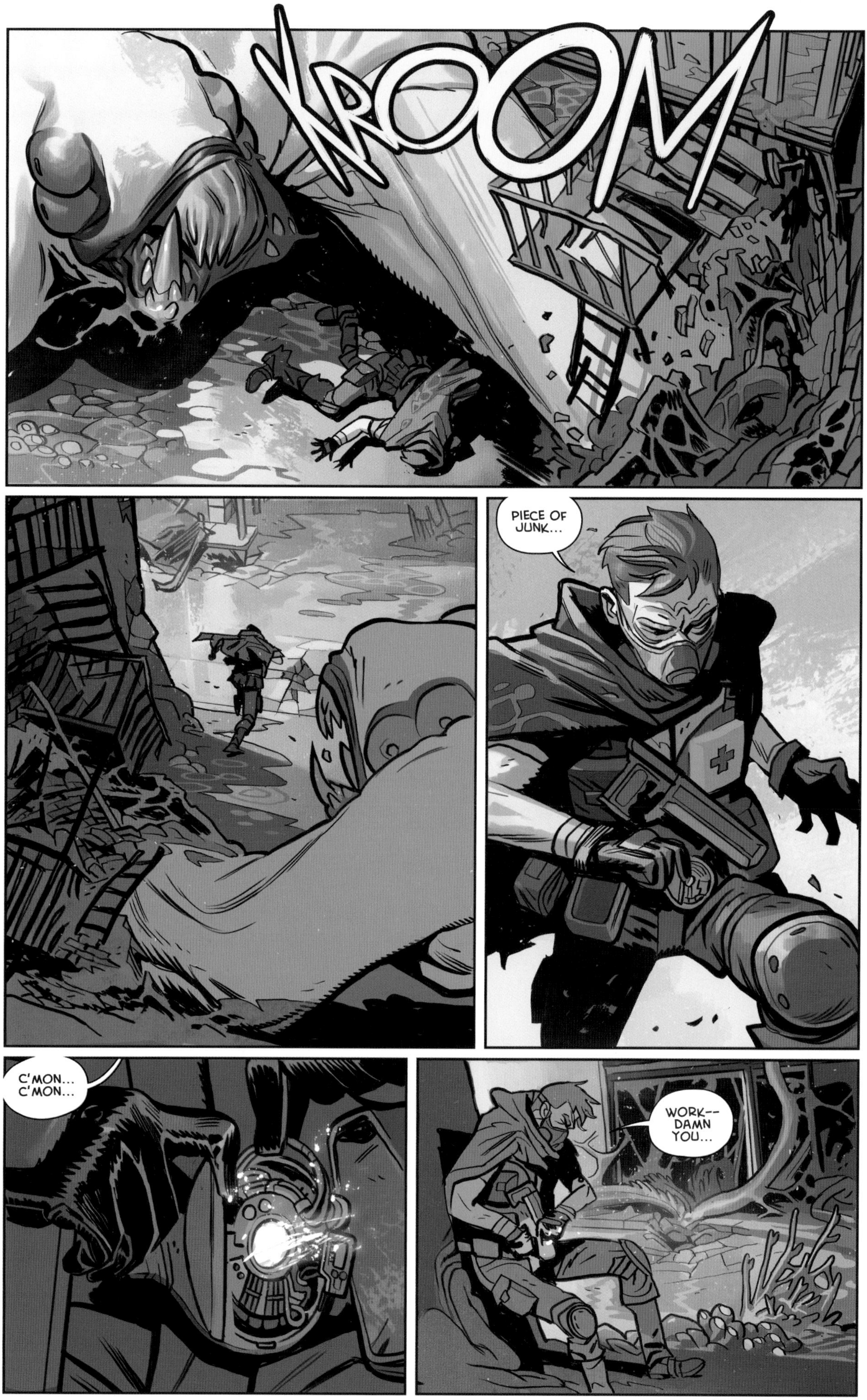
KROOM
PIECE OF JUNK...
C'MON... C'MON...
WORK-- DAMN YOU...

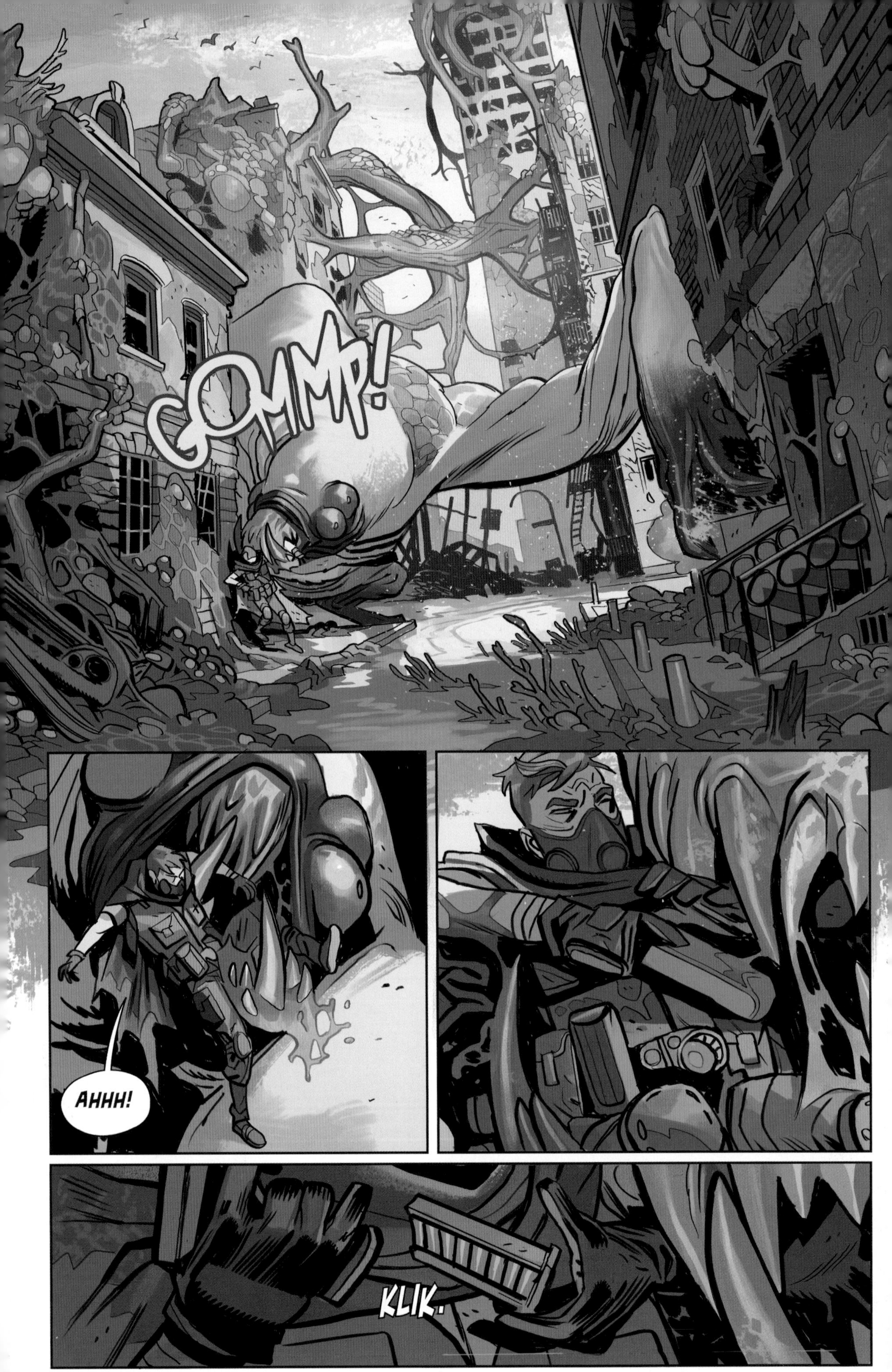
GOMMP!
AHHH!
KLIK.

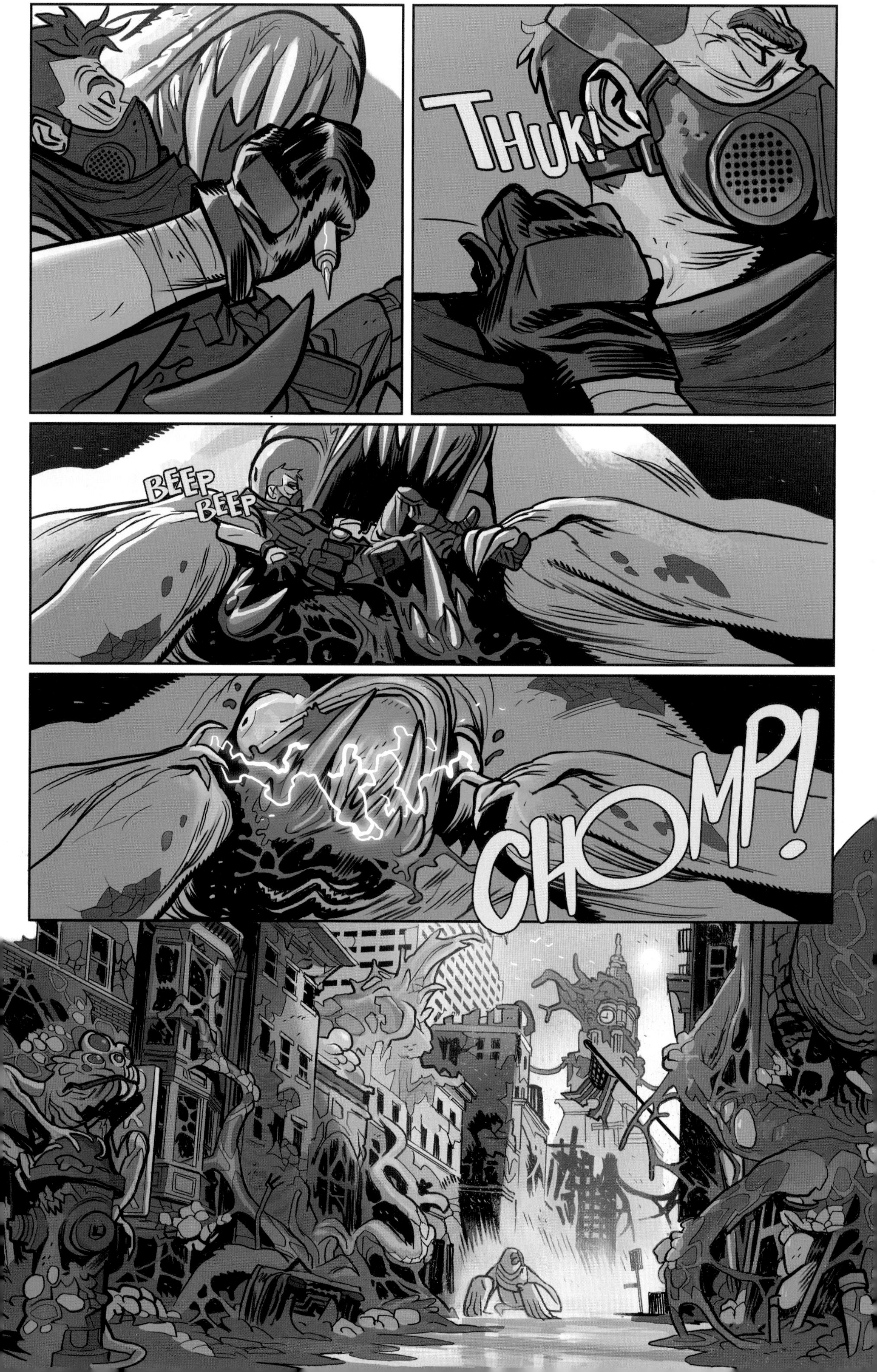
THUK!
BEEP
BEEP
CHOMP!

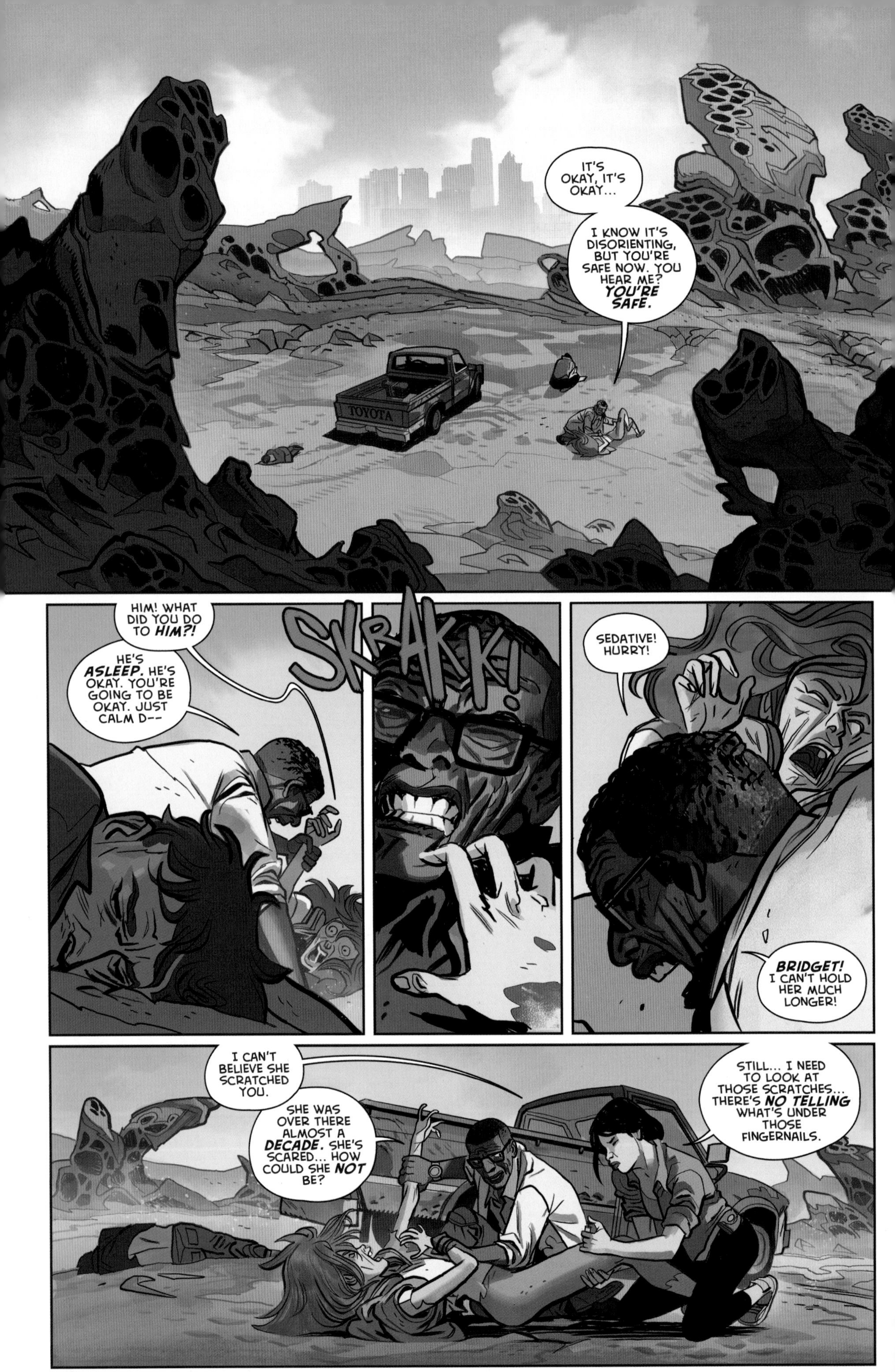
IT'S OKAY, IT'S OKAY...
I KNOW IT'S DISORIENTING, BUT YOU'RE SAFE NOW. YOU HEAR ME? YOU'RE SAFE.
TOYOTA
HIM! WHAT DID YOU DO TO HIM?!
HE'S ASLEEP. HE'S OKAY. YOU'RE GOING TO BE OKAY. JUST CALM D--
SKRAKK!
SEDATIVE! HURRY!
BRIDGET! I CAN'T HOLD HER MUCH LONGER!
I CAN'T BELIEVE SHE SCRATCHED YOU.
SHE WAS OVER THERE ALMOST A DECADE. SHE'S SCARED... HOW COULD SHE NOT BE?
STILL... I NEED TO LOOK AT THOSE SCRATCHES... THERE'S NO TELLING WHAT'S UNDER THOSE FINGERNAILS.

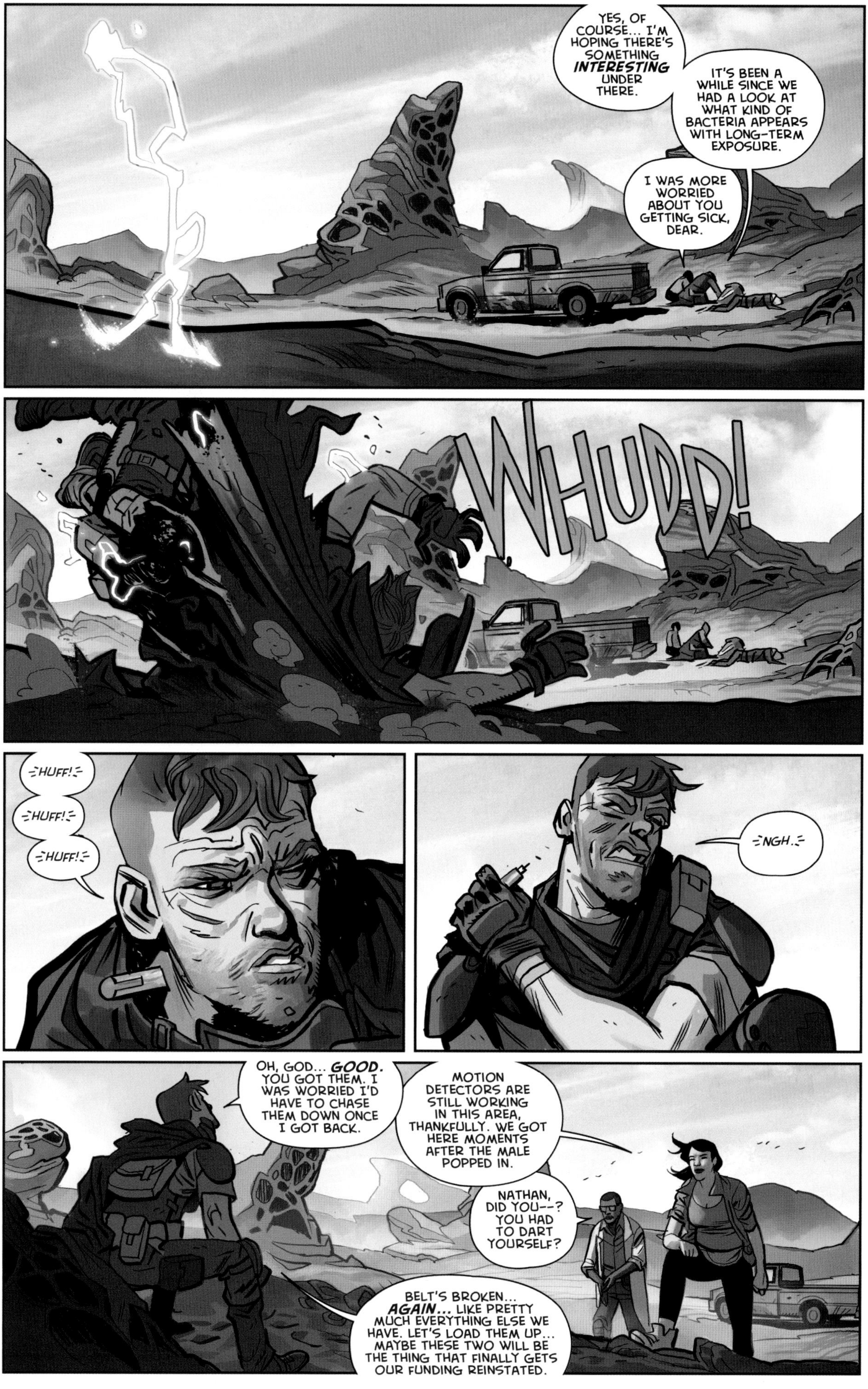
YES, OF COURSE... I'M HOPING THERE'S SOMETHING **INTERESTING** UNDER THERE.
IT'S BEEN A WHILE SINCE WE HAD A LOOK AT WHAT KIND OF BACTERIA APPEARS WITH LONG-TERM EXPOSURE.
I WAS MORE WORRIED ABOUT YOU GETTING SICK, DEAR.
WHUDD!
HUFF!
HUFF!
HUFF!
NGH.
OH, GOD... **GOOD.** YOU GOT THEM. I WAS WORRIED I'D HAVE TO CHASE THEM DOWN ONCE I GOT BACK.
MOTION DETECTORS ARE STILL WORKING IN THIS AREA, THANKFULLY. WE GOT HERE MOMENTS AFTER THE MALE POPPED IN.
NATHAN, DID YOU--? YOU HAD TO DART YOURSELF?
BELT'S BROKEN... **AGAIN...** LIKE PRETTY MUCH EVERYTHING ELSE WE HAVE. LET'S LOAD THEM UP... MAYBE THESE TWO WILL BE THE THING THAT FINALLY GETS OUR FUNDING REINSTATED.

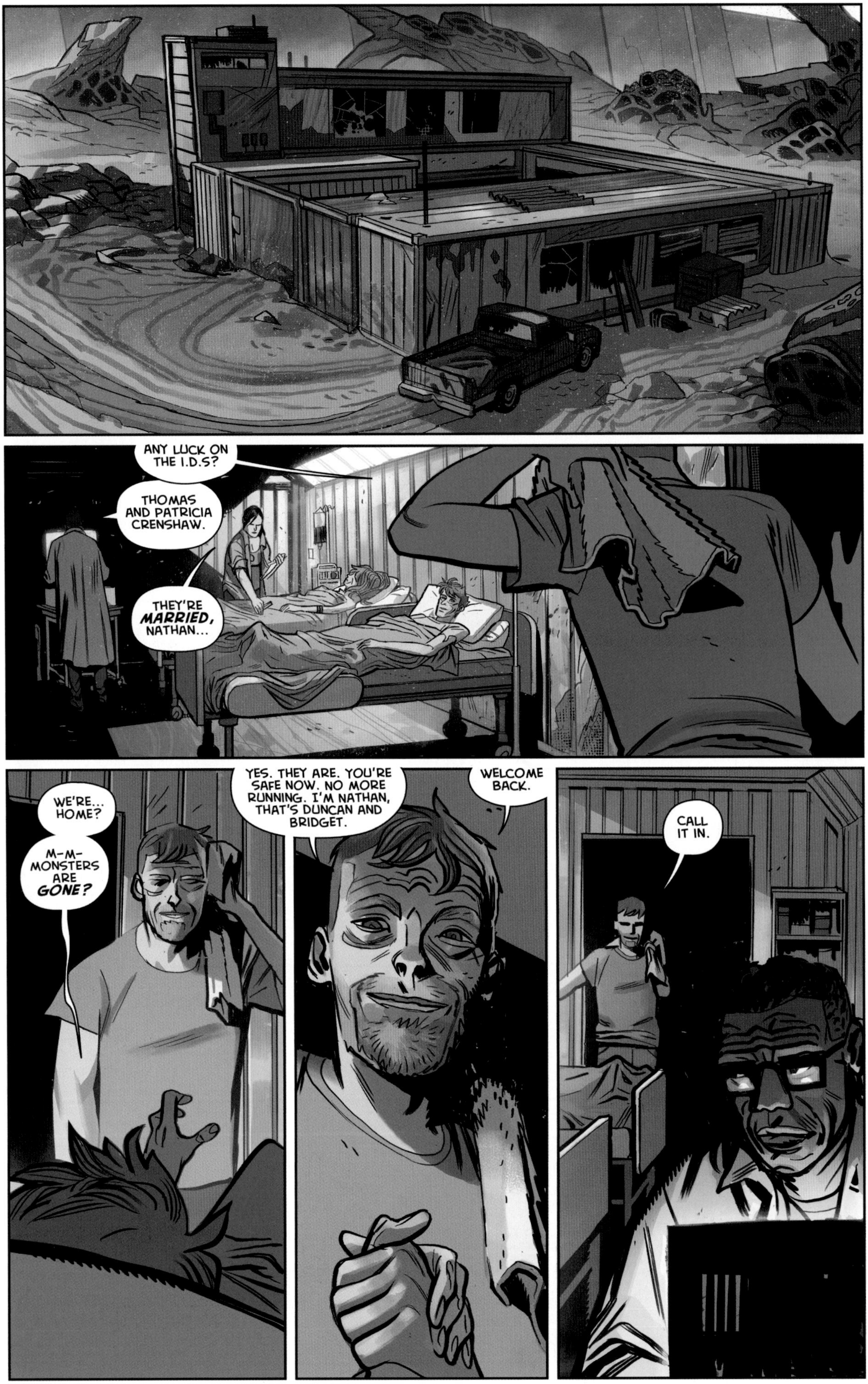
ANY LUCK ON THE I.D.S?
THOMAS AND PATRICIA CRENSHAW.
THEY'RE *MARRIED,* NATHAN...
WE'RE... HOME?
M-M-MONSTERS ARE *GONE?*
YES. THEY ARE. YOU'RE SAFE NOW. NO MORE RUNNING. I'M NATHAN, THAT'S DUNCAN AND BRIDGET.
WELCOME BACK.
CALL IT IN.

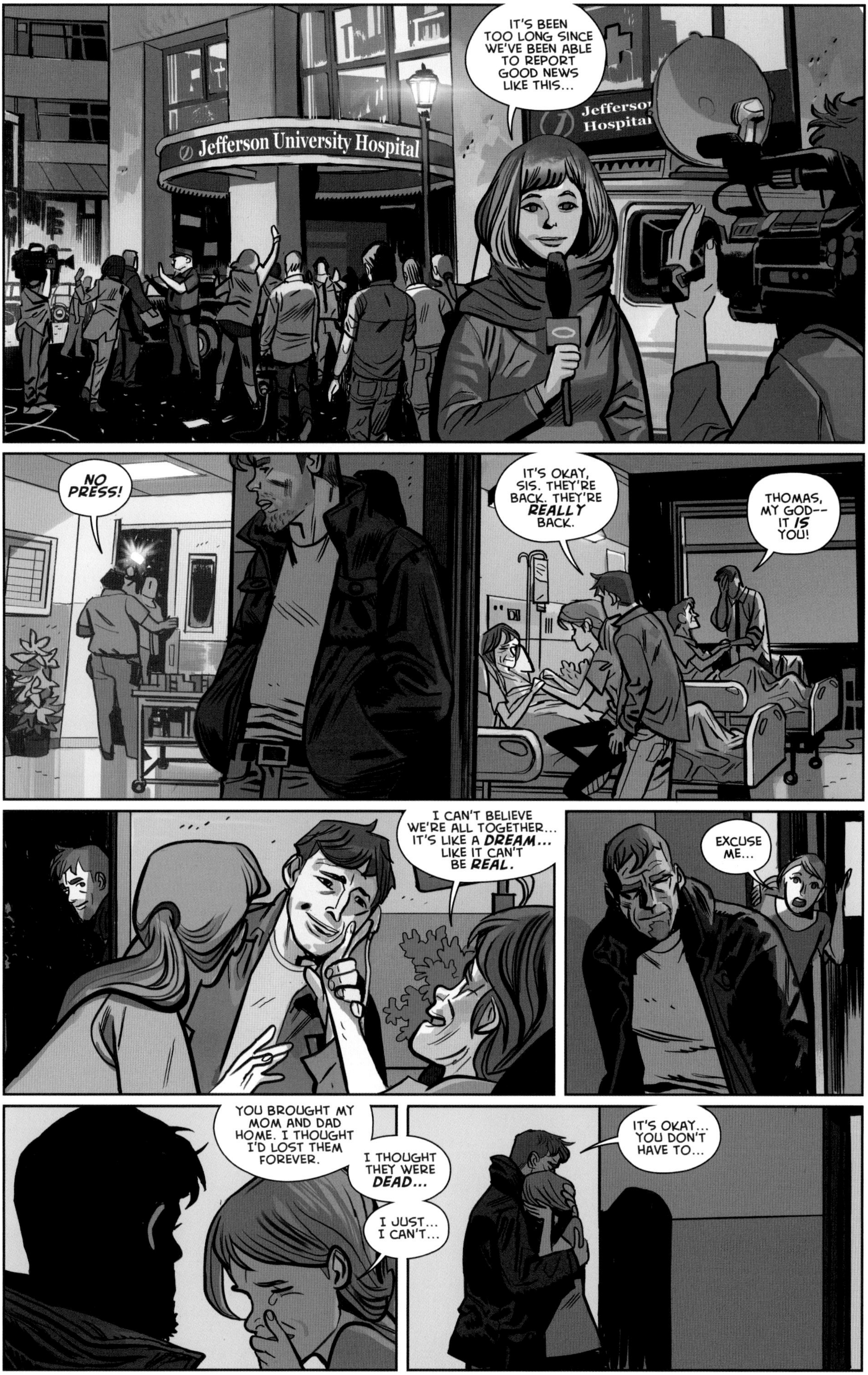
Jefferson University Hospital
IT'S BEEN TOO LONG SINCE WE'VE BEEN ABLE TO REPORT GOOD NEWS LIKE THIS...
Jefferson Hospital
NO PRESS!
IT'S OKAY, SIS. THEY'RE BACK. THEY'RE REALLY BACK.
THOMAS, MY GOD-- IT IS YOU!
I CAN'T BELIEVE WE'RE ALL TOGETHER... IT'S LIKE A DREAM... LIKE IT CAN'T BE REAL.
EXCUSE ME...
YOU BROUGHT MY MOM AND DAD HOME. I THOUGHT I'D LOST THEM FOREVER.
I THOUGHT THEY WERE DEAD...
I JUST... I CAN'T...
IT'S OKAY... YOU DON'T HAVE TO...

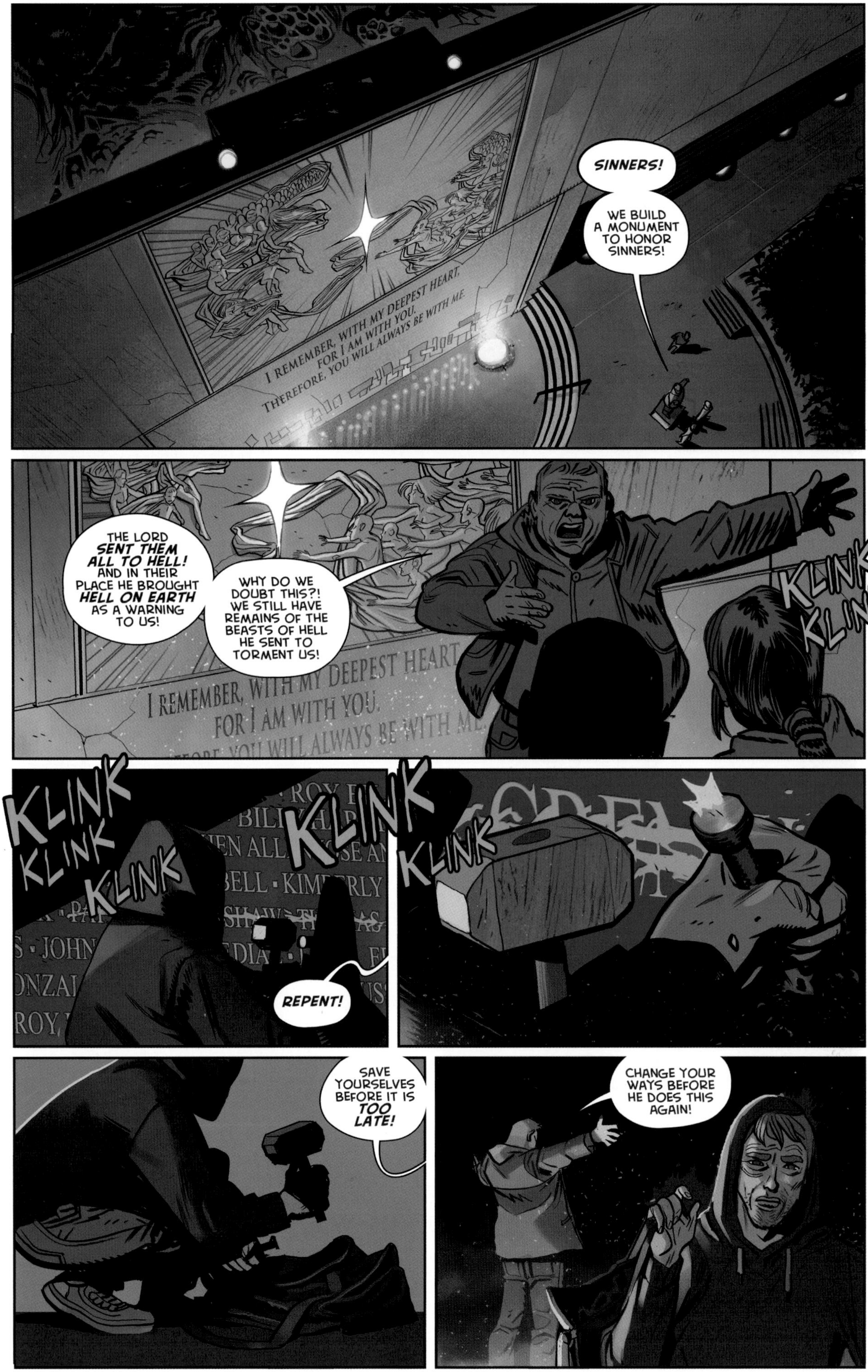
I REMEMBER, WITH MY DEEPEST HEART,
FOR I AM WITH YOU.
THEREFORE, YOU WILL ALWAYS BE WITH ME.
SINNERS!
WE BUILD A MONUMENT TO HONOR SINNERS!
THE LORD SENT THEM ALL TO HELL! AND IN THEIR PLACE HE BROUGHT HELL ON EARTH AS A WARNING TO US!
WHY DO WE DOUBT THIS?! WE STILL HAVE REMAINS OF THE BEASTS OF HELL HE SENT TO TORMENT US!
I REMEMBER, WITH MY DEEPEST HEART
FOR I AM WITH YOU.
KLINK KLINK
KLINK KLINK KLINK
REPENT!
KLINK KLINK
SAVE YOURSELVES BEFORE IT IS TOO LATE!
CHANGE YOUR WAYS BEFORE HE DOES THIS AGAIN!

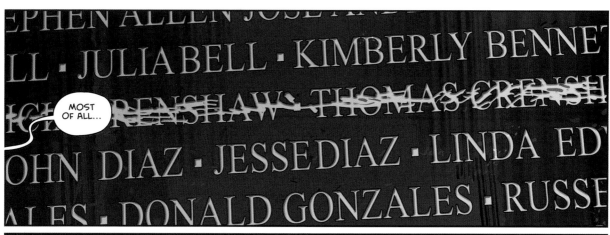

MOST OF ALL...

FEAR THE *RETURNED!* WHY HAVE THEY BEEN ALLOWED TO COME BACK?!

WHAT DEAL DID *THEY* MAKE WITH THE DEVIL?!

AND WHAT KIND OF *EVIL* COULD THEY HAVE BROUGHT BACK WITH THEM?!

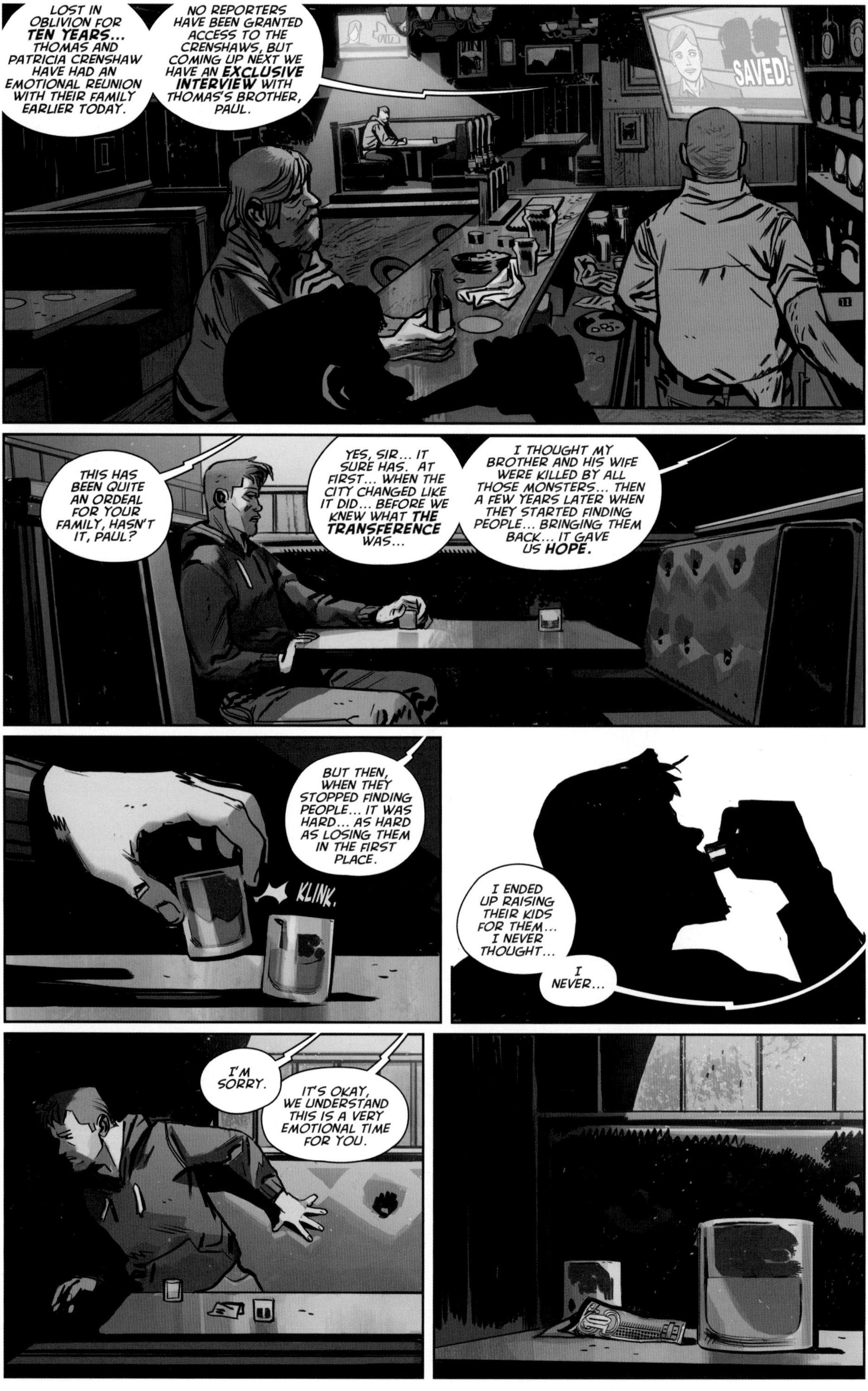
LOST IN OBLIVION FOR TEN YEARS... THOMAS AND PATRICIA CRENSHAW HAVE HAD AN EMOTIONAL REUNION WITH THEIR FAMILY EARLIER TODAY.
NO REPORTERS HAVE BEEN GRANTED ACCESS TO THE CRENSHAWS, BUT COMING UP NEXT WE HAVE AN EXCLUSIVE INTERVIEW WITH THOMAS'S BROTHER, PAUL.
SAVED!
THIS HAS BEEN QUITE AN ORDEAL FOR YOUR FAMILY, HASN'T IT, PAUL?
YES, SIR... IT SURE HAS. AT FIRST... WHEN THE CITY CHANGED LIKE IT DID... BEFORE WE KNEW WHAT THE TRANSFERENCE WAS...
I THOUGHT MY BROTHER AND HIS WIFE WERE KILLED BY ALL THOSE MONSTERS... THEN A FEW YEARS LATER WHEN THEY STARTED FINDING PEOPLE... BRINGING THEM BACK... IT GAVE US HOPE.
BUT THEN, WHEN THEY STOPPED FINDING PEOPLE... IT WAS HARD... AS HARD AS LOSING THEM IN THE FIRST PLACE.
KLINK.
I ENDED UP RAISING THEIR KIDS FOR THEM... I NEVER THOUGHT...
I NEVER...
I'M SORRY.
IT'S OKAY, WE UNDERSTAND THIS IS A VERY EMOTIONAL TIME FOR YOU.

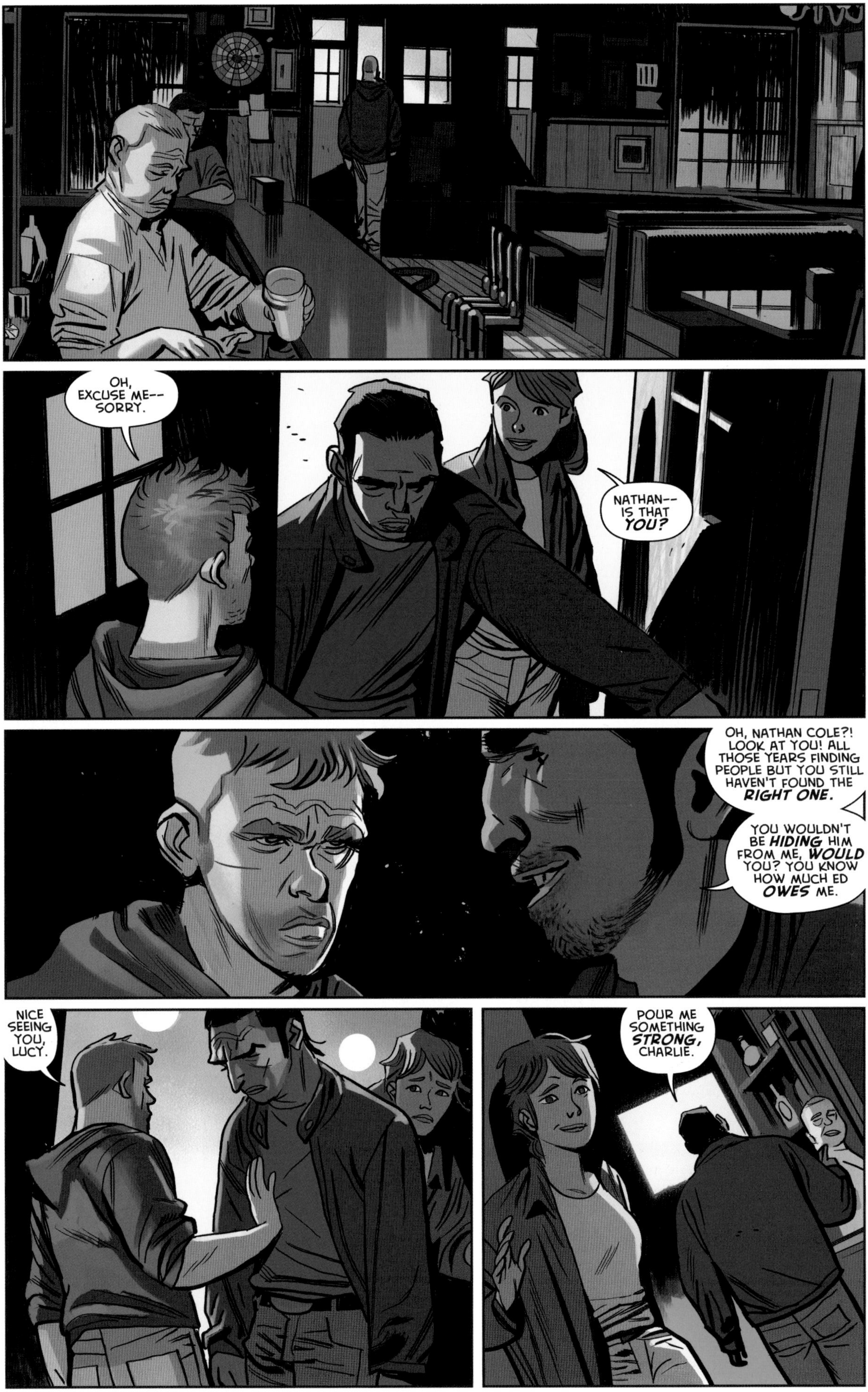
OH, EXCUSE ME-- SORRY.
NATHAN-- IS THAT YOU?
OH, NATHAN COLE?! LOOK AT YOU! ALL THOSE YEARS FINDING PEOPLE BUT YOU STILL HAVEN'T FOUND THE RIGHT ONE.
YOU WOULDN'T BE HIDING HIM FROM ME, WOULD YOU? YOU KNOW HOW MUCH ED OWES ME.
NICE SEEING YOU, LUCY.
POUR ME SOMETHING STRONG, CHARLIE.

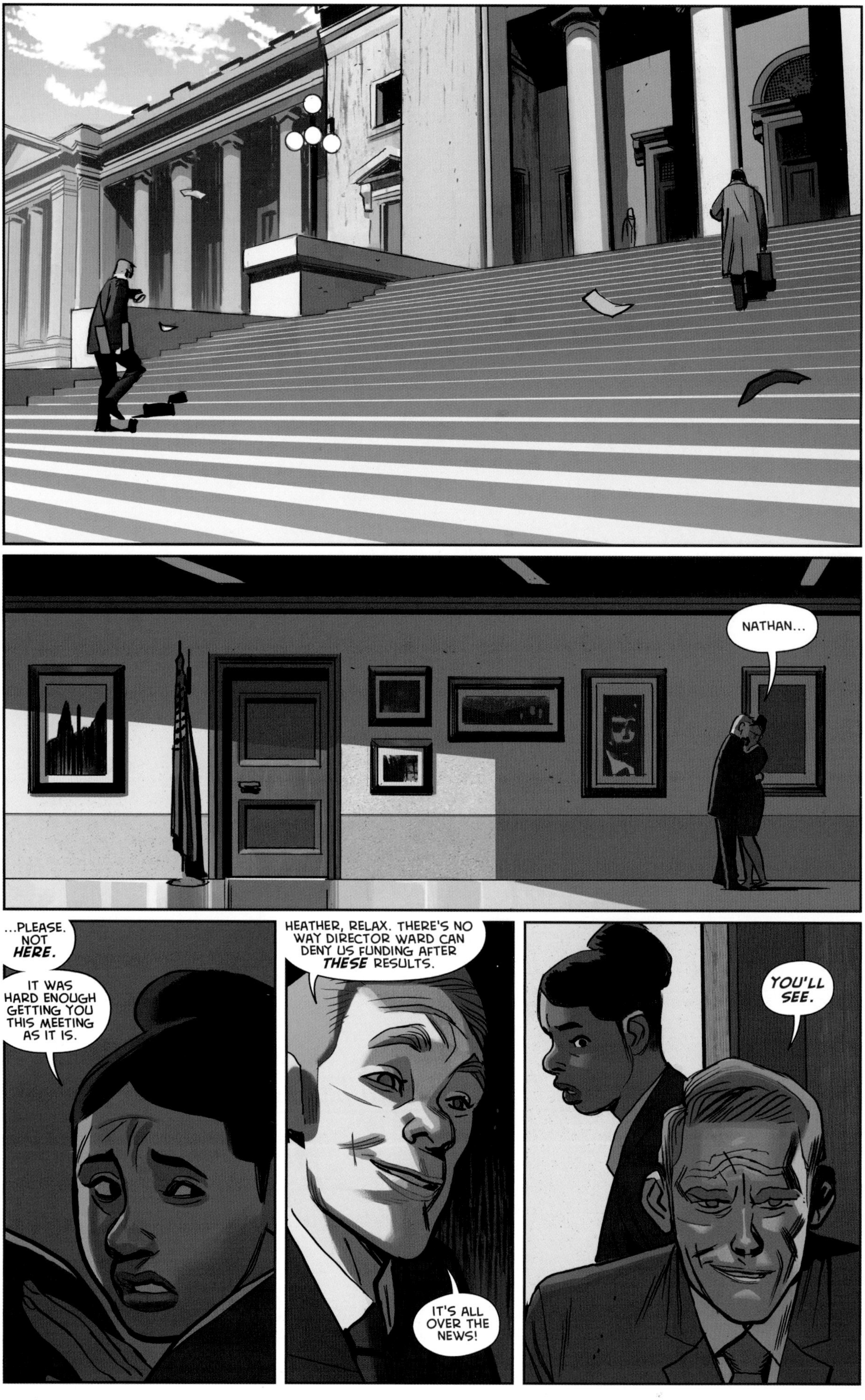
NATHAN...
...PLEASE. NOT HERE.
IT WAS HARD ENOUGH GETTING YOU THIS MEETING AS IT IS.
HEATHER, RELAX. THERE'S NO WAY DIRECTOR WARD CAN DENY US FUNDING AFTER THESE RESULTS.
IT'S ALL OVER THE NEWS!
YOU'LL SEE.

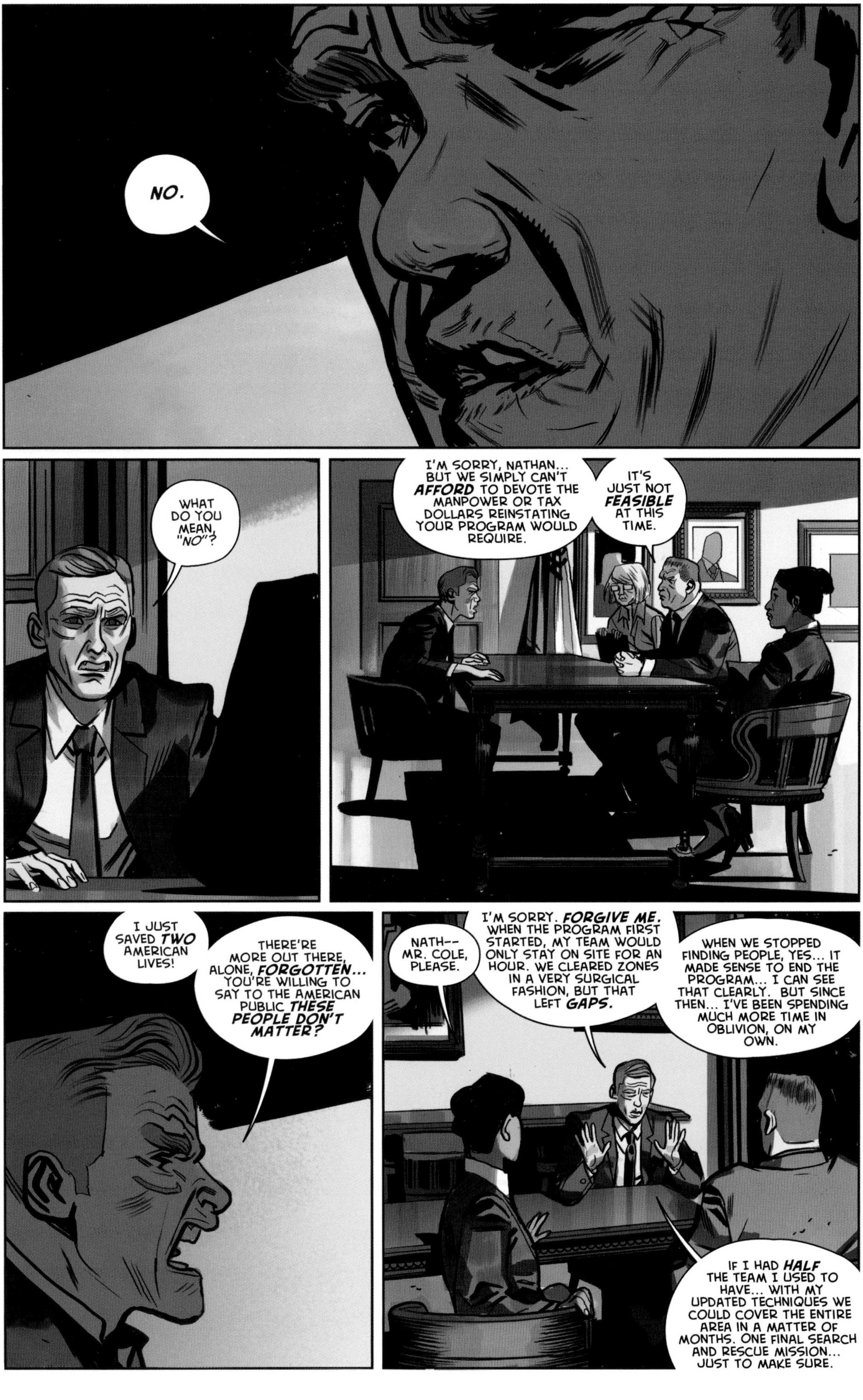
NO.
WHAT DO YOU MEAN, "NO"?
I'M SORRY, NATHAN... BUT WE SIMPLY CAN'T AFFORD TO DEVOTE THE MANPOWER OR TAX DOLLARS REINSTATING YOUR PROGRAM WOULD REQUIRE.
IT'S JUST NOT FEASIBLE AT THIS TIME.
I JUST SAVED TWO AMERICAN LIVES!
THERE'RE MORE OUT THERE, ALONE, FORGOTTEN... YOU'RE WILLING TO SAY TO THE AMERICAN PUBLIC THESE PEOPLE DON'T MATTER?
NATH-- MR. COLE, PLEASE.
I'M SORRY. FORGIVE ME. WHEN THE PROGRAM FIRST STARTED, MY TEAM WOULD ONLY STAY ON SITE FOR AN HOUR. WE CLEARED ZONES IN A VERY SURGICAL FASHION, BUT THAT LEFT GAPS.
WHEN WE STOPPED FINDING PEOPLE, YES... IT MADE SENSE TO END THE PROGRAM... I CAN SEE THAT CLEARLY. BUT SINCE THEN... I'VE BEEN SPENDING MUCH MORE TIME IN OBLIVION, ON MY OWN.
IF I HAD HALF THE TEAM I USED TO HAVE... WITH MY UPDATED TECHNIQUES WE COULD COVER THE ENTIRE AREA IN A MATTER OF MONTHS. ONE FINAL SEARCH AND RESCUE MISSION... JUST TO MAKE SURE.

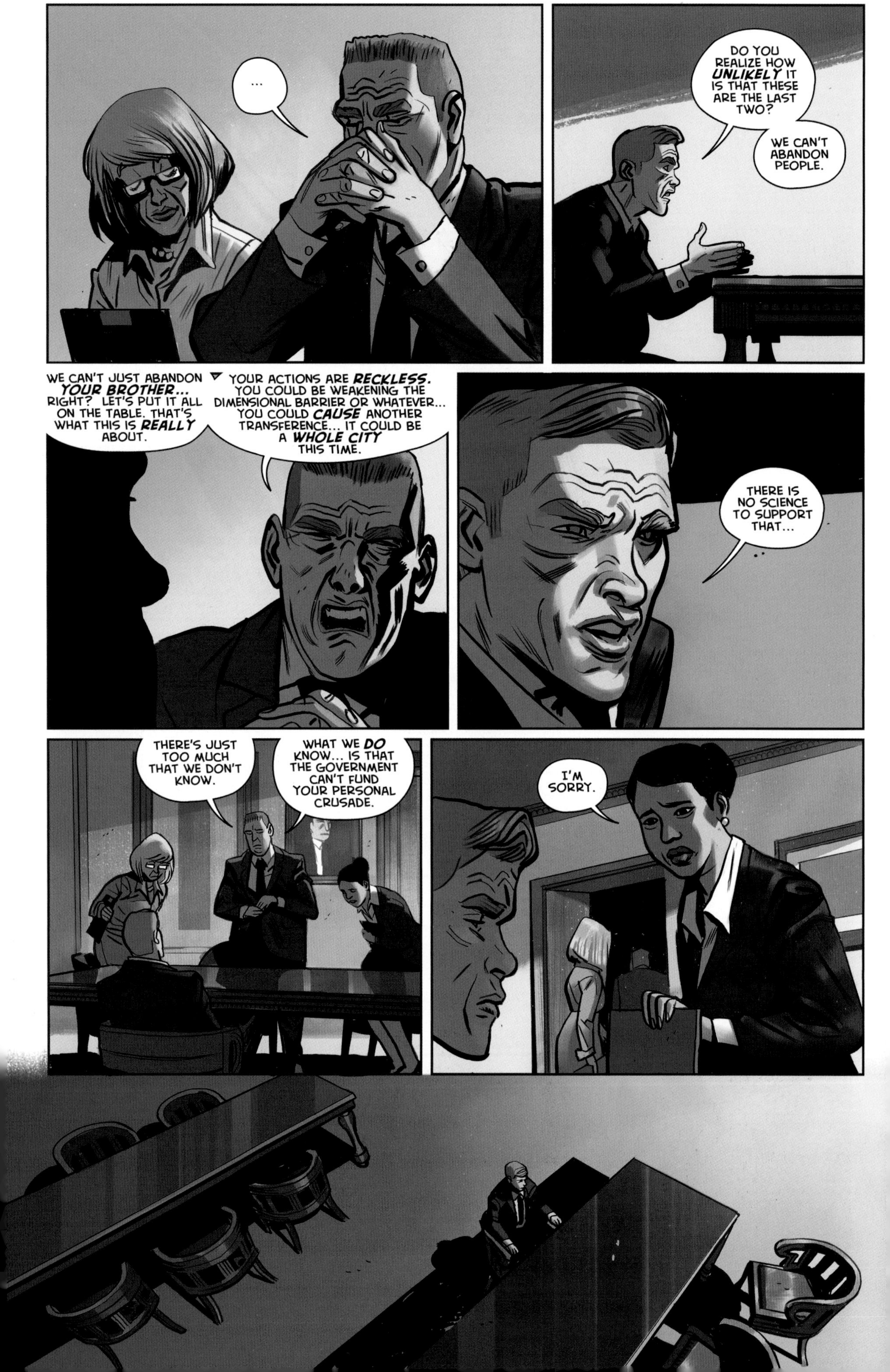
...
DO YOU REALIZE HOW UNLIKELY IT IS THAT THESE ARE THE LAST TWO?
WE CAN'T ABANDON PEOPLE.
WE CAN'T JUST ABANDON YOUR BROTHER... RIGHT? LET'S PUT IT ALL ON THE TABLE. THAT'S WHAT THIS IS REALLY ABOUT.
YOUR ACTIONS ARE RECKLESS. YOU COULD BE WEAKENING THE DIMENSIONAL BARRIER OR WHATEVER... YOU COULD CAUSE ANOTHER TRANSFERENCE... IT COULD BE A WHOLE CITY THIS TIME.
THERE IS NO SCIENCE TO SUPPORT THAT...
THERE'S JUST TOO MUCH THAT WE DON'T KNOW.
WHAT WE DO KNOW... IS THAT THE GOVERNMENT CAN'T FUND YOUR PERSONAL CRUSADE.
I'M SORRY.

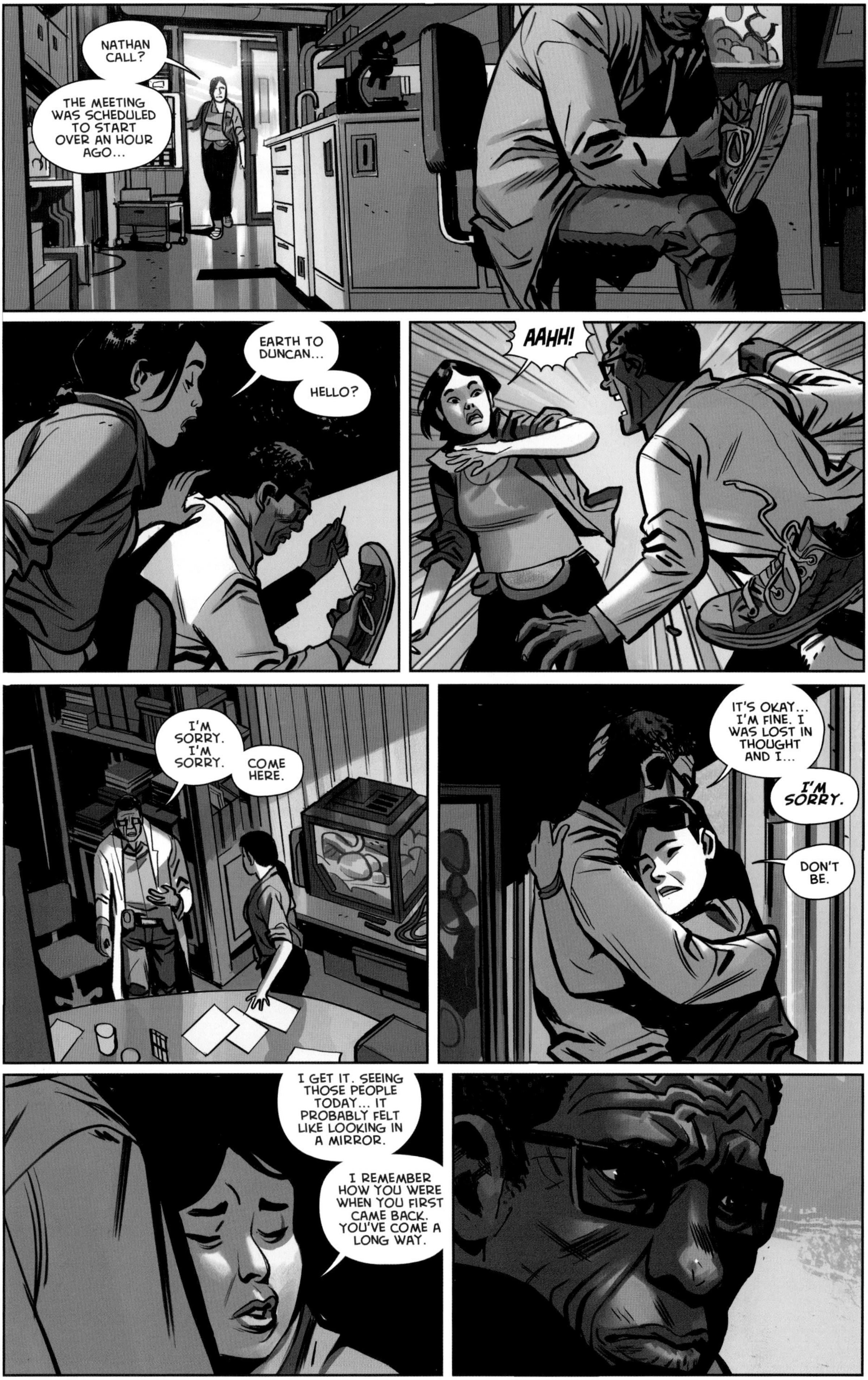
NATHAN CALL?
THE MEETING WAS SCHEDULED TO START OVER AN HOUR AGO...
EARTH TO DUNCAN...
HELLO?
AAHH!
I'M SORRY. I'M SORRY.
COME HERE.
IT'S OKAY... I'M FINE. I WAS LOST IN THOUGHT AND I...
I'M SORRY.
DON'T BE.
I GET IT. SEEING THOSE PEOPLE TODAY... IT PROBABLY FELT LIKE LOOKING IN A MIRROR.
I REMEMBER HOW YOU WERE WHEN YOU FIRST CAME BACK. YOU'VE COME A LONG WAY.

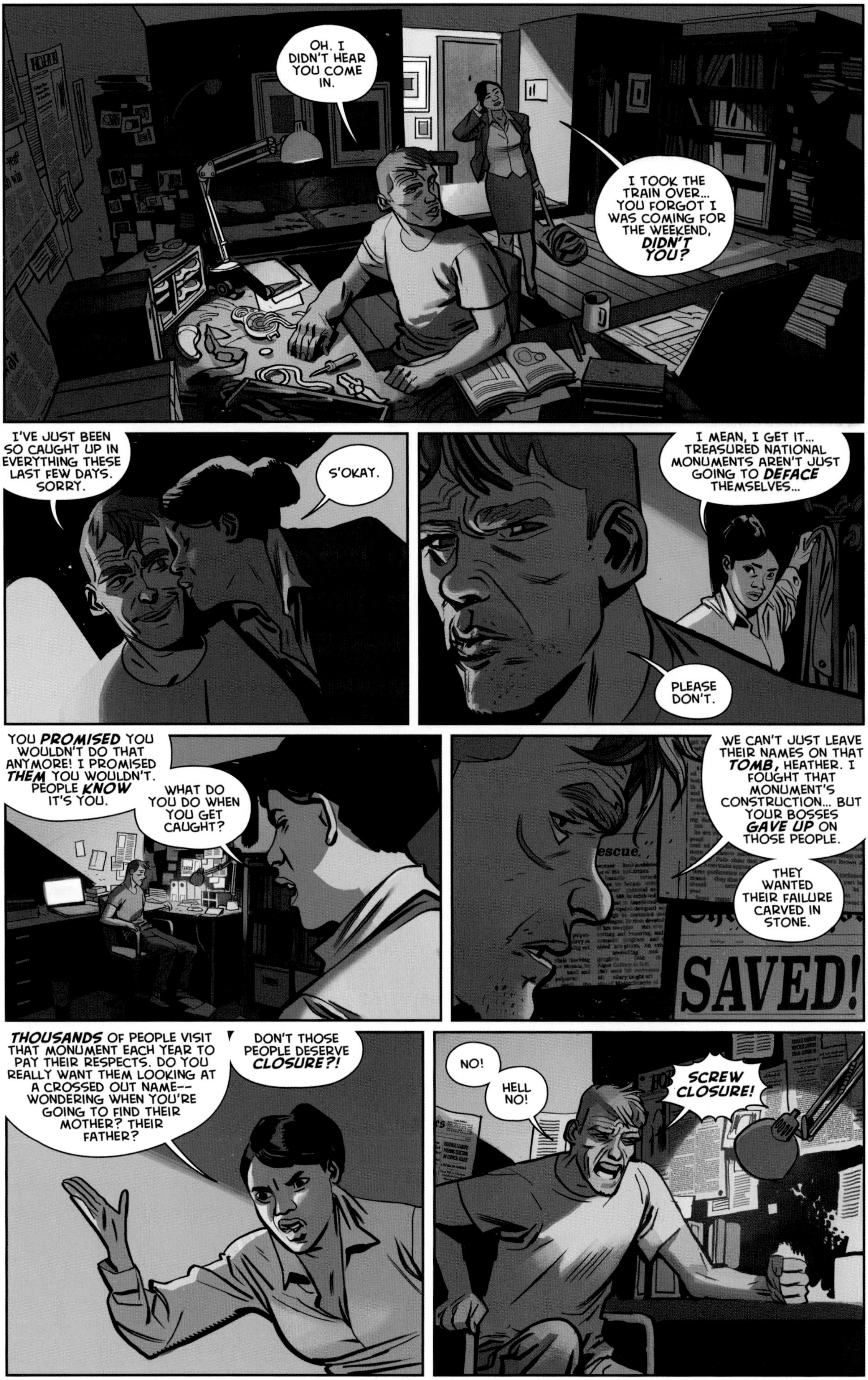
OH. I DIDN'T HEAR YOU COME IN.
I TOOK THE TRAIN OVER... YOU FORGOT I WAS COMING FOR THE WEEKEND, ***DIDN'T YOU?***
I'VE JUST BEEN SO CAUGHT UP IN EVERYTHING THESE LAST FEW DAYS. SORRY.
S'OKAY.
I MEAN, I GET IT... TREASURED NATIONAL MONUMENTS AREN'T JUST GOING TO ***DEFACE*** THEMSELVES...
PLEASE DON'T.
YOU ***PROMISED*** YOU WOULDN'T DO THAT ANYMORE! I PROMISED ***THEM*** YOU WOULDN'T. PEOPLE ***KNOW*** IT'S YOU.
WHAT DO YOU DO WHEN YOU GET CAUGHT?
WE CAN'T JUST LEAVE THEIR NAMES ON THAT ***TOMB***, HEATHER. I FOUGHT THAT MONUMENT'S CONSTRUCTION... BUT YOUR BOSSES ***GAVE UP*** ON THOSE PEOPLE.
THEY WANTED THEIR FAILURE CARVED IN STONE.
SAVED!
THOUSANDS OF PEOPLE VISIT THAT MONUMENT EACH YEAR TO PAY THEIR RESPECTS. DO YOU REALLY WANT THEM LOOKING AT A CROSSED OUT NAME-- WONDERING WHEN YOU'RE GOING TO FIND THEIR MOTHER? THEIR FATHER?
DON'T THOSE PEOPLE DESERVE ***CLOSURE?!***
NO!
HELL NO!
SCREW CLOSURE!

I **WANT** THOSE PEOPLE TO SEE THOSE LINES THROUGH THOSE NAMES! I WANT THEM TO ASK, "WHY HAVEN'T THEY FOUND **MY** MOM?" I WANT THEM TO ASK, "WHY AREN'T THEY EVEN TRYING ANYMORE?!"

YOU THINK THESE PEOPLE SHOULD HAVE CLOSURE? WITH THEIR LOVED ONES **OVER THERE**... SURVIVING... HOPING THAT SOMEONE IS COMING, SOMEONE IS TRYING TO FIND THEM.

I WON'T GIVE UP ON **THEM**!

YOU MEAN YOU WON'T GIVE UP ON **EDWARD**!

NOT YOU, TOO.

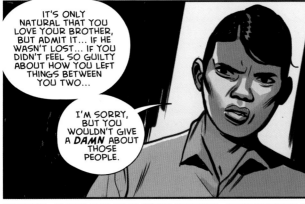

IT'S ONLY NATURAL THAT YOU LOVE YOUR BROTHER, BUT ADMIT IT... IF HE WASN'T LOST... IF YOU DIDN'T FEEL SO GUILTY ABOUT HOW YOU LEFT THINGS BETWEEN YOU TWO...

I'M SORRY, BUT YOU WOULDN'T GIVE A **DAMN** ABOUT THOSE PEOPLE.

...

YOU'RE NOT SOME **HERO** STANDING UP FOR THE LITTLE GUY. YOU SEE HOW DANGEROUS AND FUTILE WHAT YOU'RE DOING IS... YOU SEE WHY MY DEPARTMENT **REFUSES** TO GET INVOLVED AGAIN.

YOU JUST CAN'T LET GO. STOP PRETENDING THIS ISN'T **ALL ABOUT YOU**!

PLEASE G--

I'M **ALREADY LEAVING**!

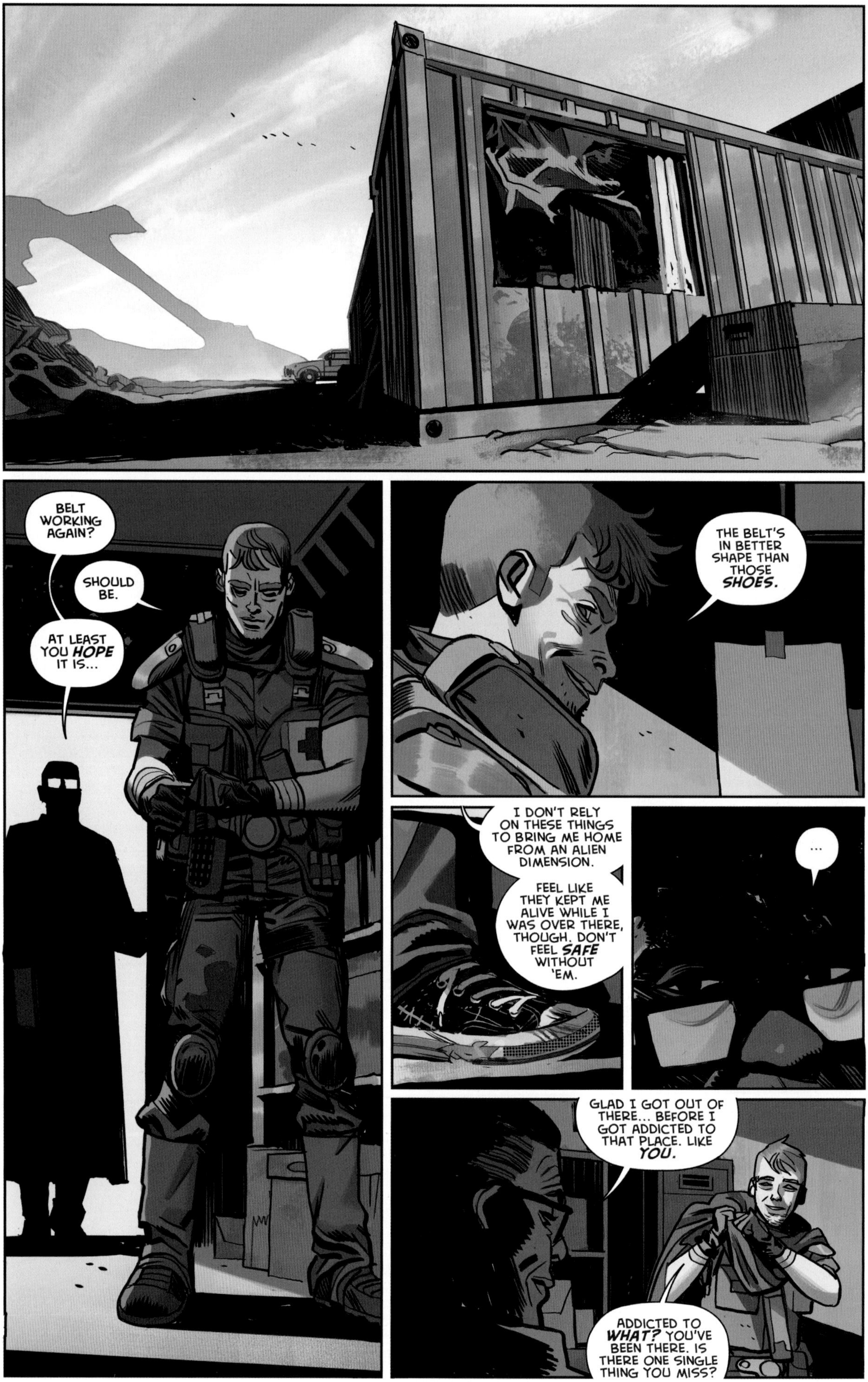

BELT WORKING AGAIN?
SHOULD BE.
AT LEAST YOU HOPE IT IS...
THE BELT'S IN BETTER SHAPE THAN THOSE SHOES.
I DON'T RELY ON THESE THINGS TO BRING ME HOME FROM AN ALIEN DIMENSION.
FEEL LIKE THEY KEPT ME ALIVE WHILE I WAS OVER THERE, THOUGH. DON'T FEEL SAFE WITHOUT 'EM.
...
GLAD I GOT OUT OF THERE... BEFORE I GOT ADDICTED TO THAT PLACE. LIKE YOU.
ADDICTED TO WHAT? YOU'VE BEEN THERE. IS THERE ONE SINGLE THING YOU MISS?

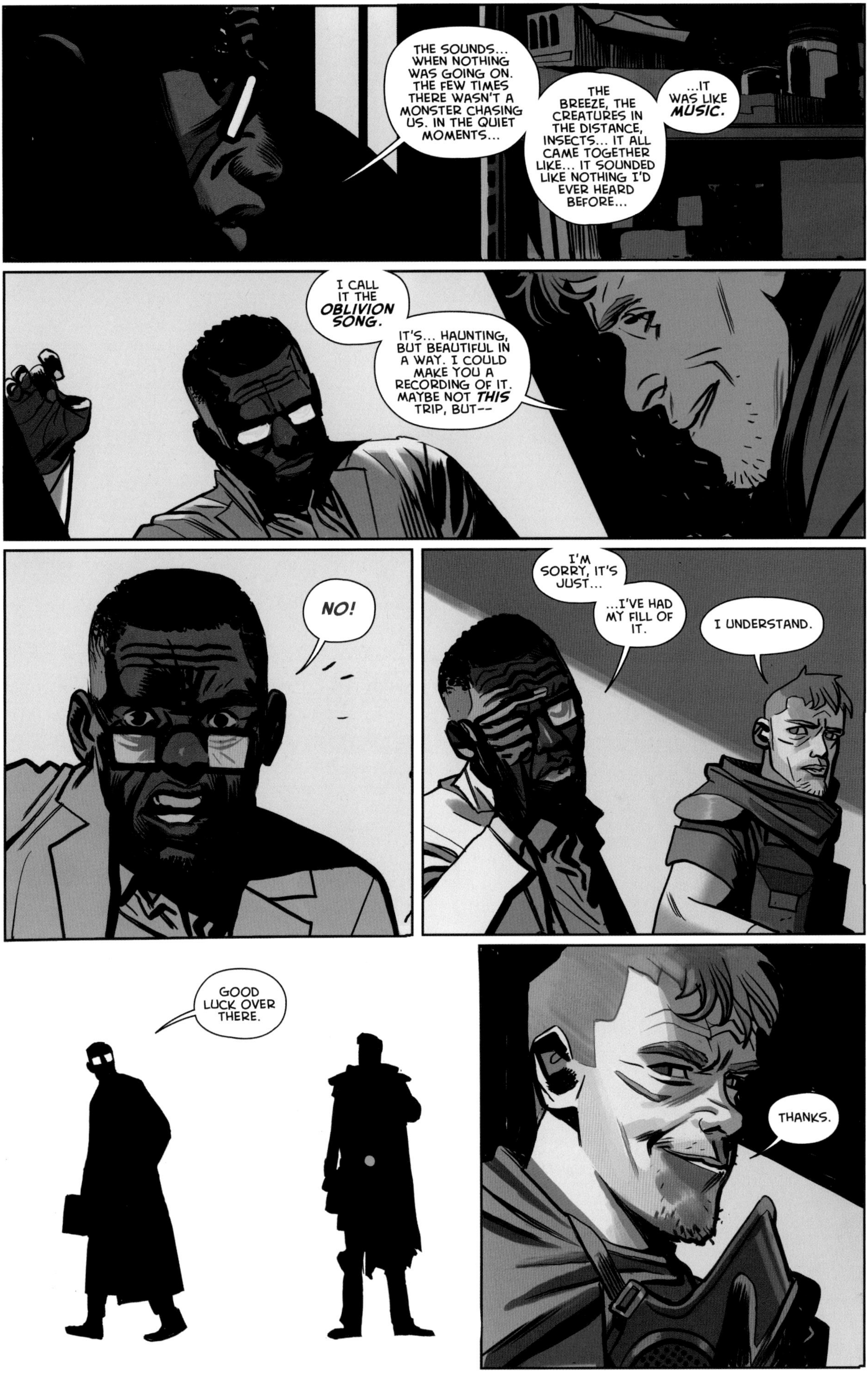
THE SOUNDS... WHEN NOTHING WAS GOING ON. THE FEW TIMES THERE WASN'T A MONSTER CHASING US. IN THE QUIET MOMENTS...
THE BREEZE, THE CREATURES IN THE DISTANCE, INSECTS... IT ALL CAME TOGETHER LIKE... IT SOUNDED LIKE NOTHING I'D EVER HEARD BEFORE...
...IT WAS LIKE MUSIC.
I CALL IT THE OBLIVION SONG.
IT'S... HAUNTING, BUT BEAUTIFUL IN A WAY. I COULD MAKE YOU A RECORDING OF IT. MAYBE NOT THIS TRIP, BUT--
NO!
I'M SORRY, IT'S JUST...
...I'VE HAD MY FILL OF IT.
I UNDERSTAND.
GOOD LUCK OVER THERE.
THANKS.

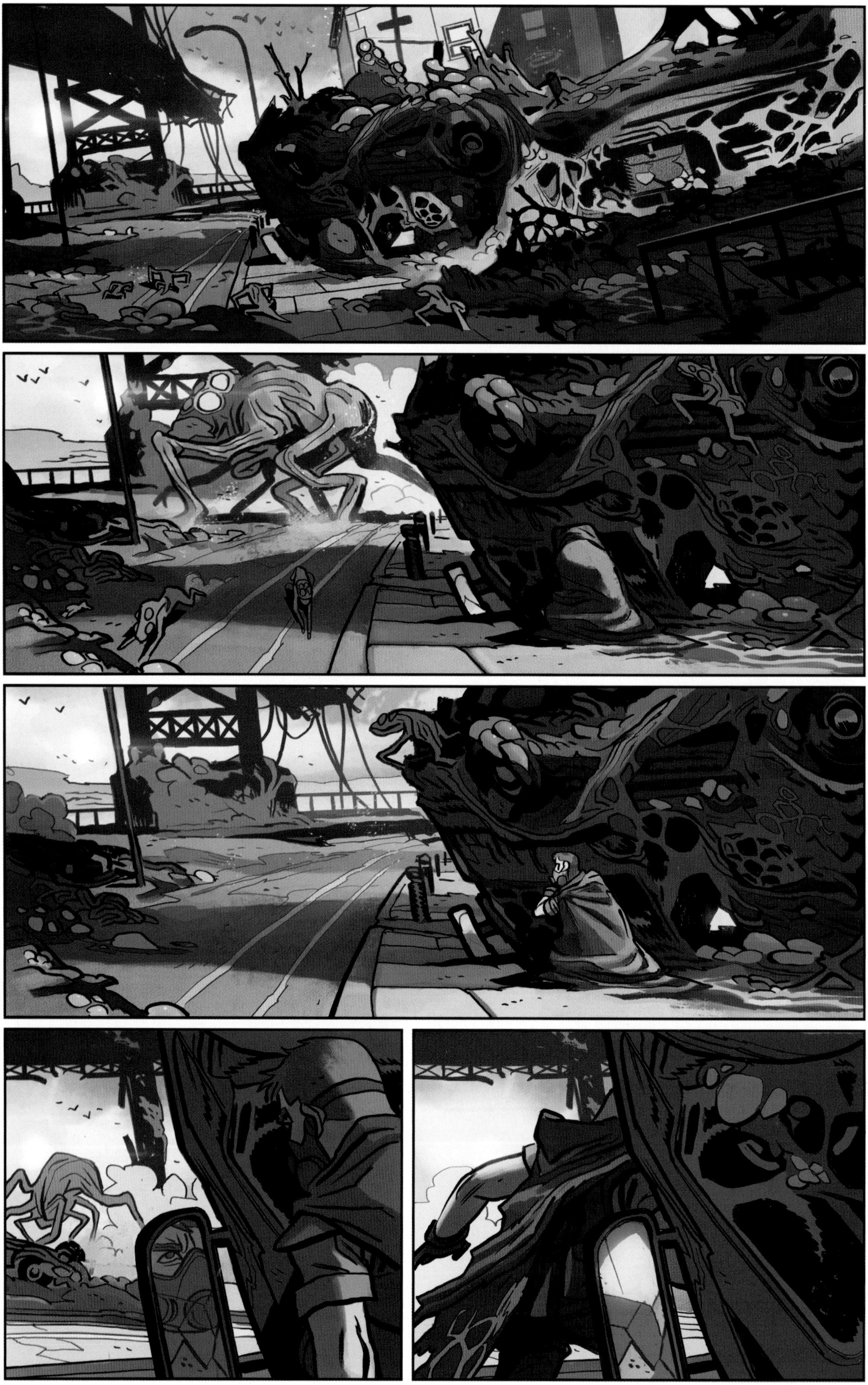

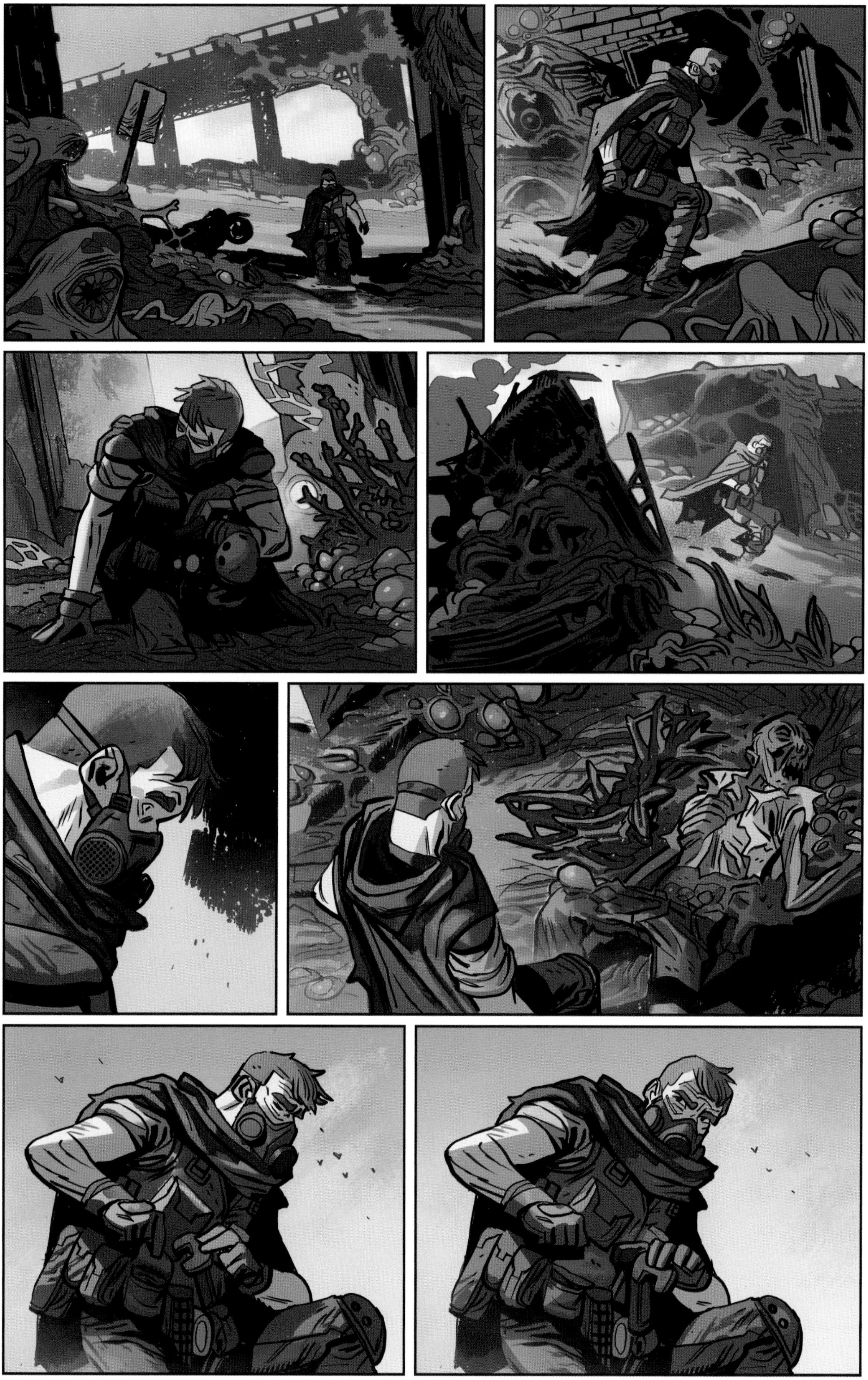

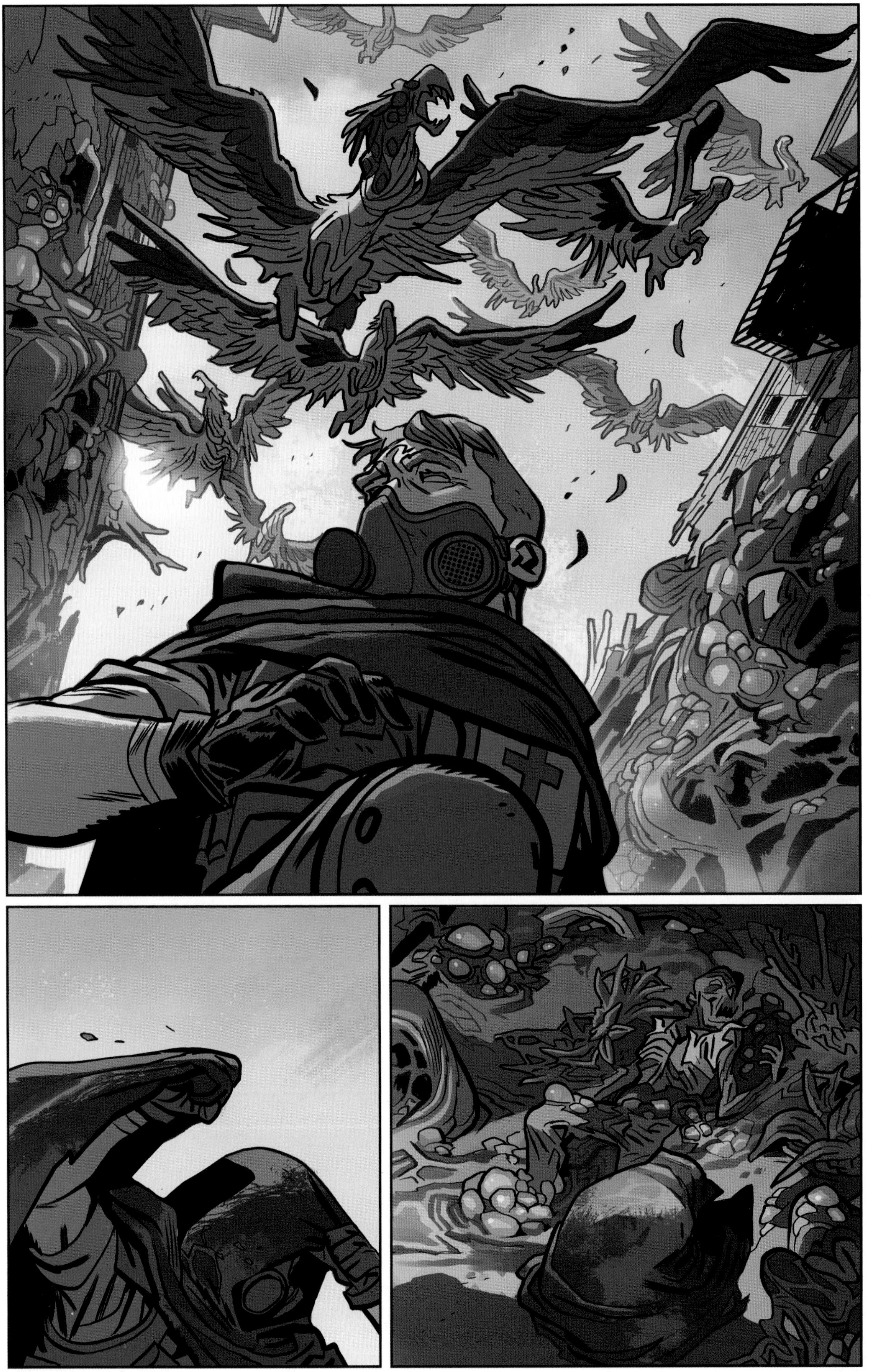

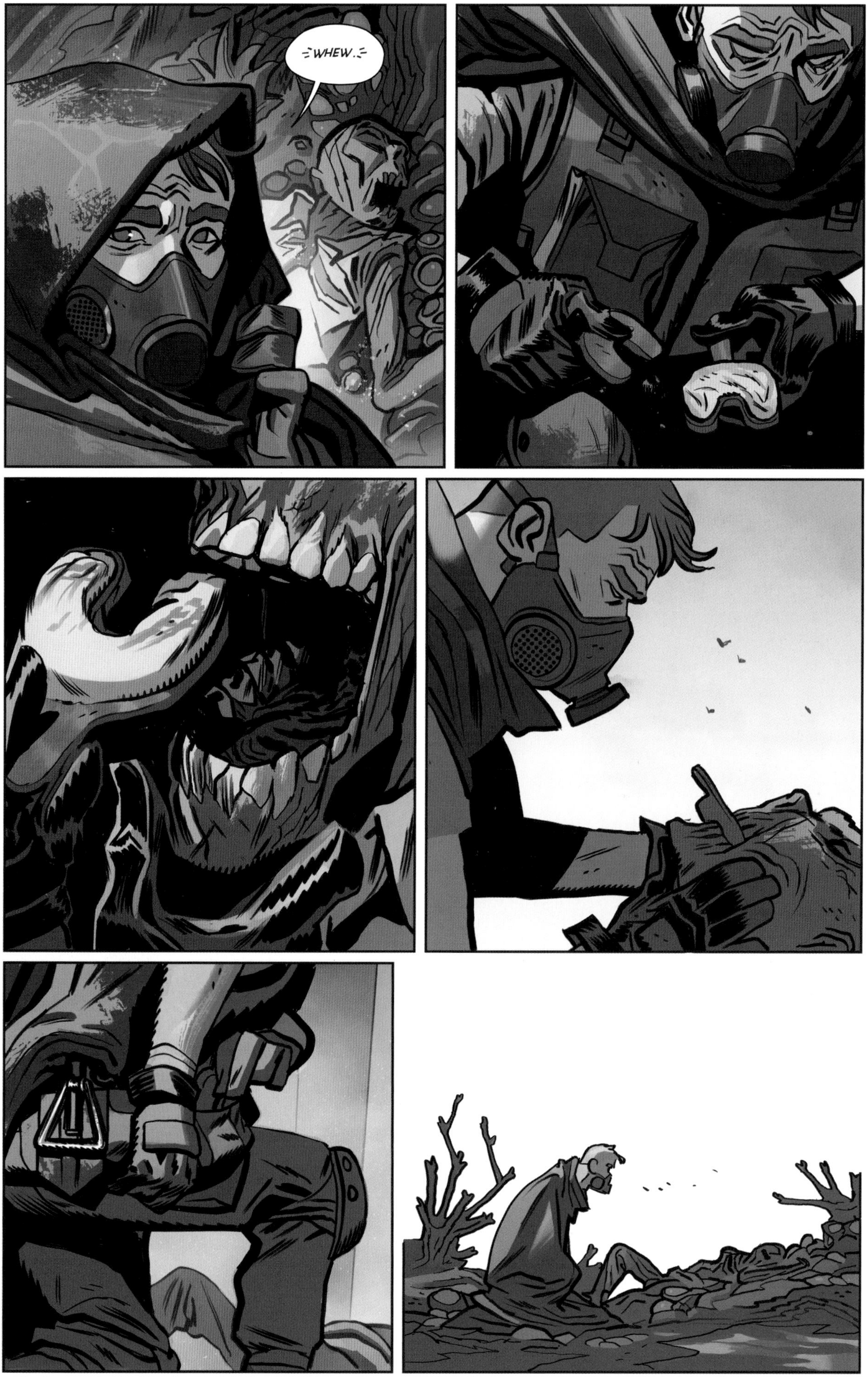
WHEW.

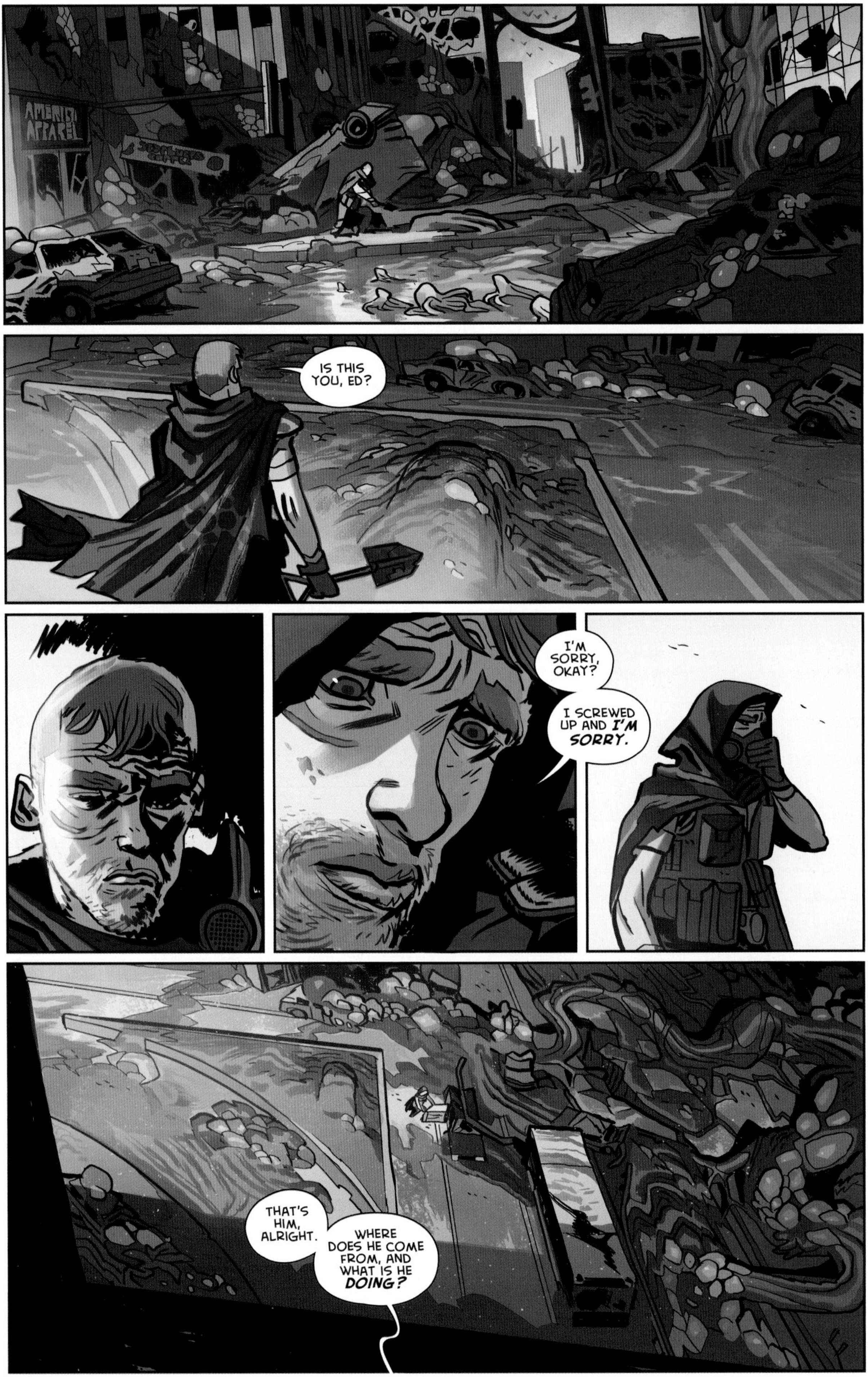
AMERICAN APPAREL
IS THIS YOU, ED?
I'M SORRY, OKAY?
I SCREWED UP AND I'M SORRY.
THAT'S HIM, ALRIGHT.
WHERE DOES HE COME FROM, AND WHAT IS HE DOING?

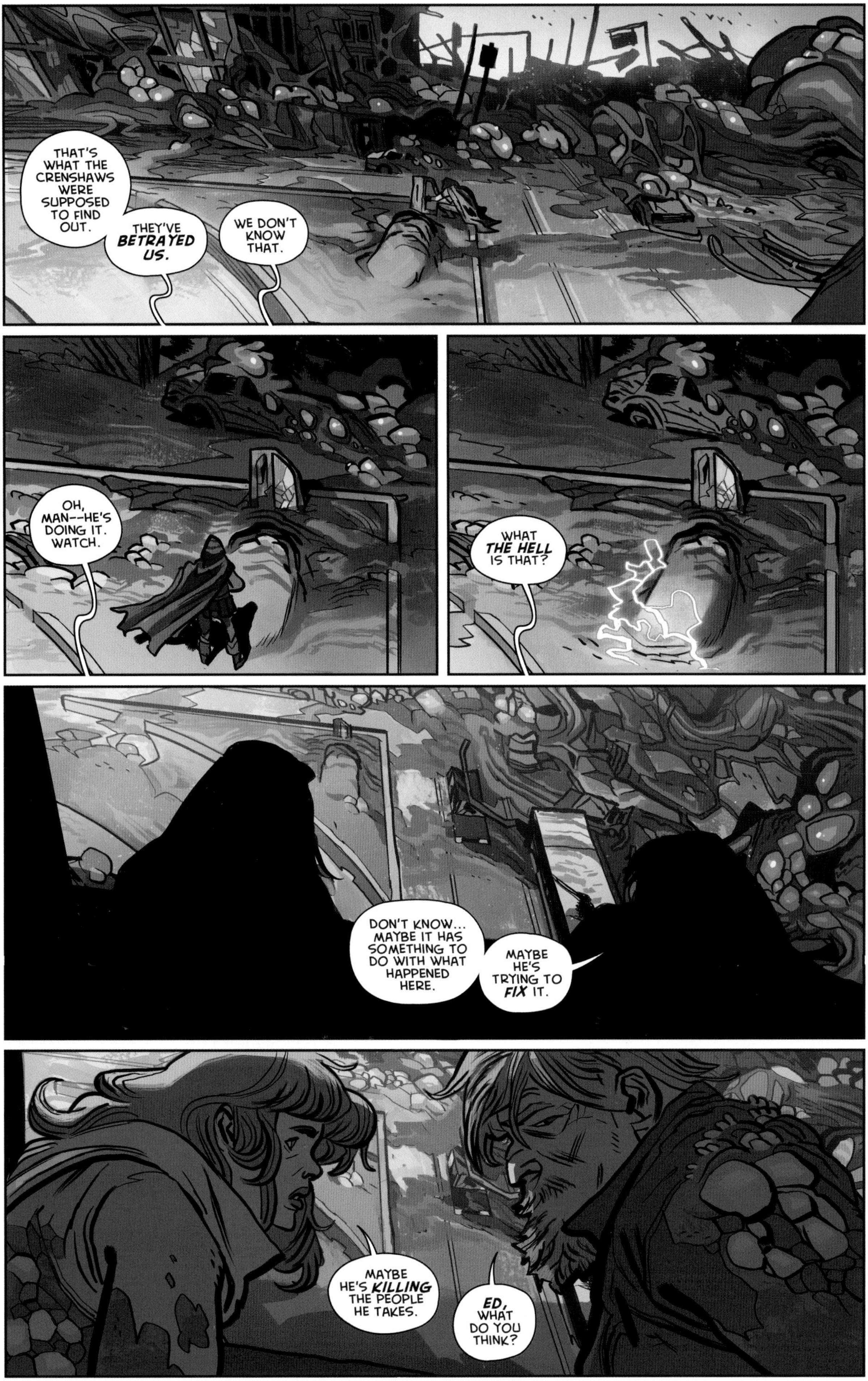
THAT'S WHAT THE CRENSHAWS WERE SUPPOSED TO FIND OUT.
THEY'VE BETRAYED US.
WE DON'T KNOW THAT.
OH, MAN--HE'S DOING IT. WATCH.
WHAT THE HELL IS THAT?
DON'T KNOW... MAYBE IT HAS SOMETHING TO DO WITH WHAT HAPPENED HERE.
MAYBE HE'S TRYING TO FIX IT.
MAYBE HE'S KILLING THE PEOPLE HE TAKES.
ED, WHAT DO YOU THINK?

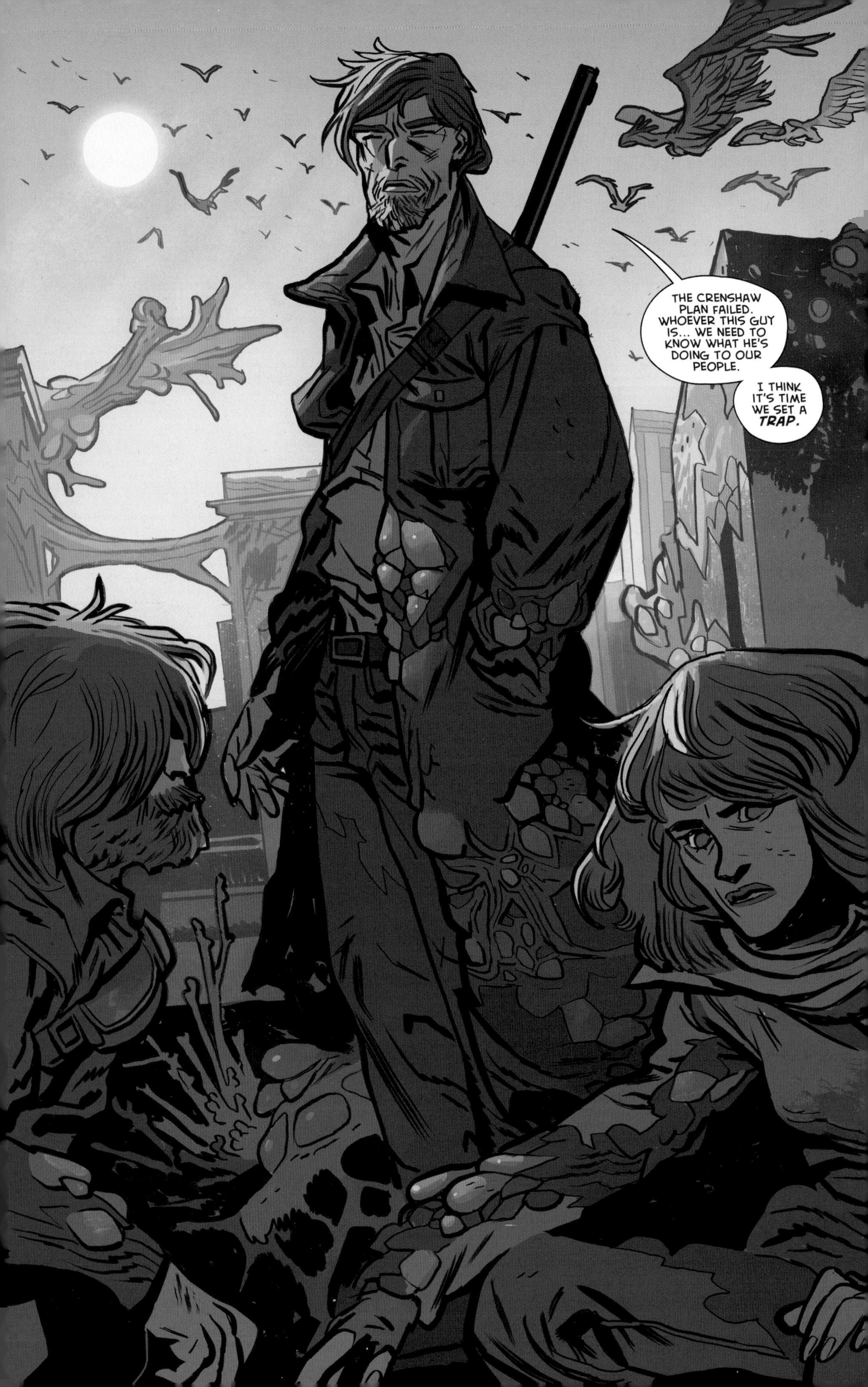
THE CRENSHAW PLAN FAILED. WHOEVER THIS GUY IS... WE NEED TO KNOW WHAT HE'S DOING TO OUR PEOPLE.
I THINK IT'S TIME WE SET A TRAP.

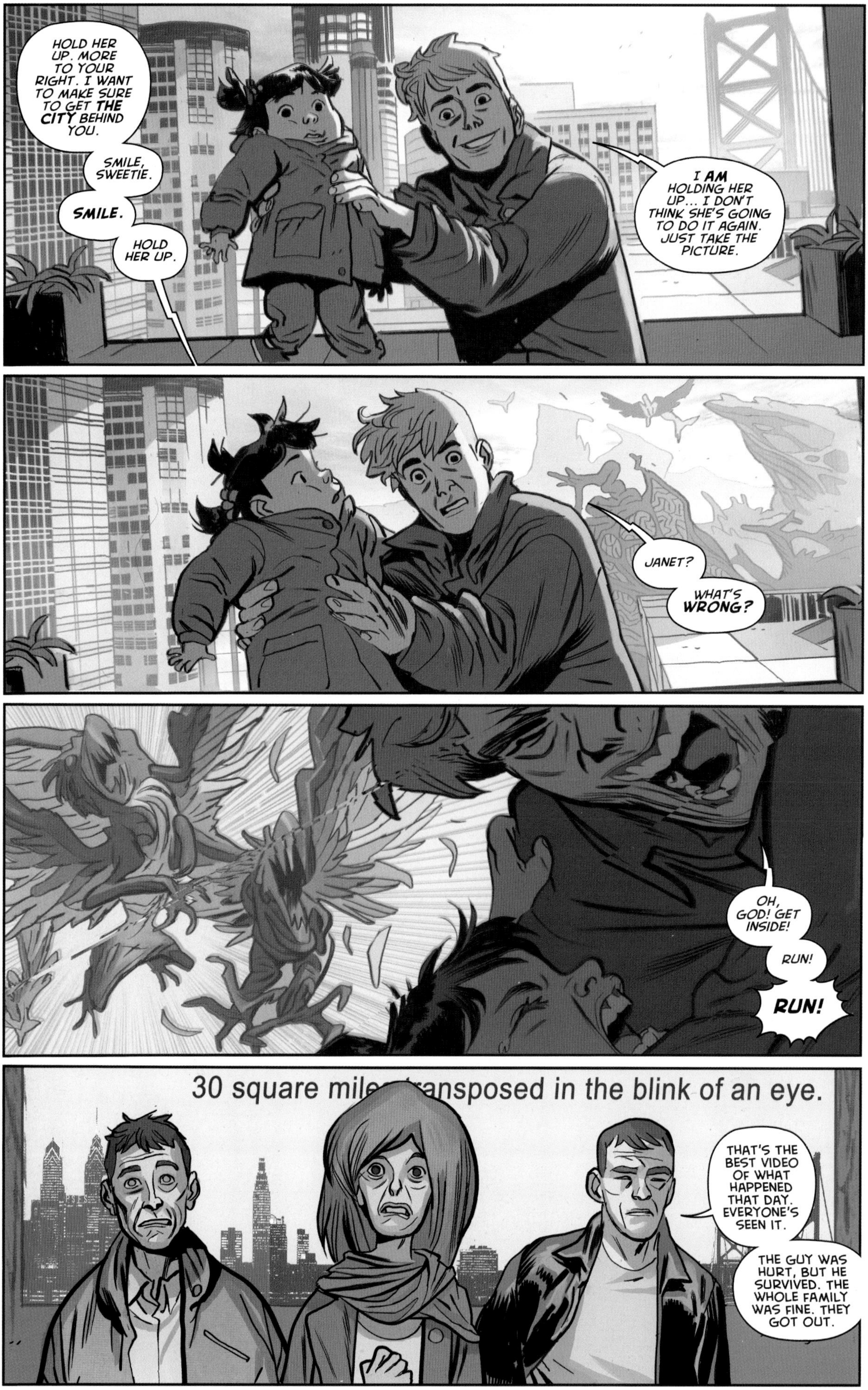
HOLD HER UP. MORE TO YOUR RIGHT. I WANT TO MAKE SURE TO GET THE CITY BEHIND YOU.
SMILE, SWEETIE.
SMILE.
HOLD HER UP.
I AM HOLDING HER UP... I DON'T THINK SHE'S GOING TO DO IT AGAIN. JUST TAKE THE PICTURE.
JANET?
WHAT'S WRONG?
OH, GOD! GET INSIDE!
RUN!
RUN!
30 square miles transposed in the blink of an eye.
THAT'S THE BEST VIDEO OF WHAT HAPPENED THAT DAY. EVERYONE'S SEEN IT.
THE GUY WAS HURT, BUT HE SURVIVED. THE WHOLE FAMILY WAS FINE. THEY GOT OUT.

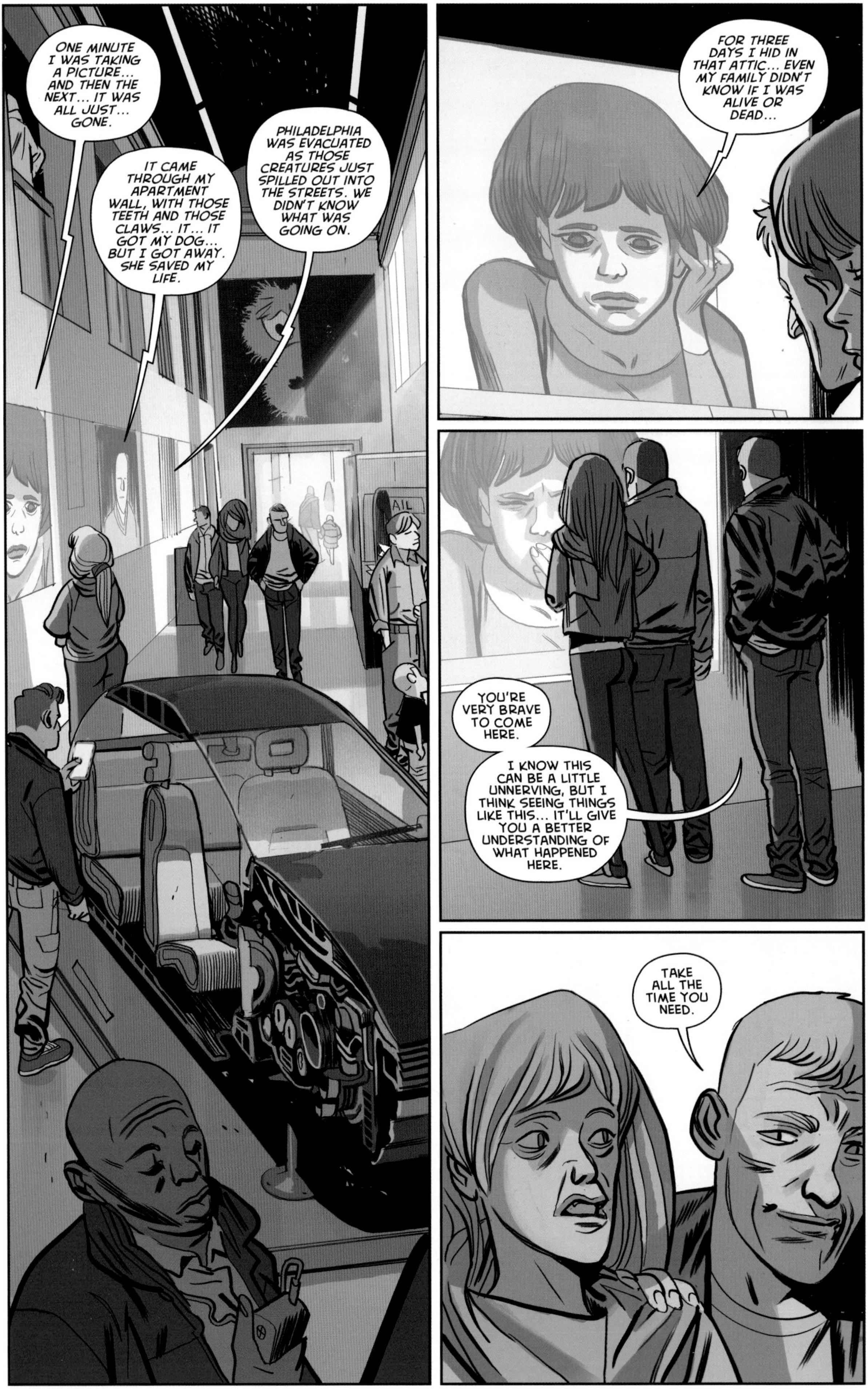

ONE MINUTE I WAS TAKING A PICTURE... AND THEN THE NEXT... IT WAS ALL JUST... GONE.
IT CAME THROUGH MY APARTMENT WALL, WITH THOSE TEETH AND THOSE CLAWS... IT... IT GOT MY DOG... BUT I GOT AWAY. SHE SAVED MY LIFE.
PHILADELPHIA WAS EVACUATED AS THOSE CREATURES JUST SPILLED OUT INTO THE STREETS. WE DIDN'T KNOW WHAT WAS GOING ON.
FOR THREE DAYS I HID IN THAT ATTIC... EVEN MY FAMILY DIDN'T KNOW IF I WAS ALIVE OR DEAD...
YOU'RE VERY BRAVE TO COME HERE.
I KNOW THIS CAN BE A LITTLE UNNERVING, BUT I THINK SEEING THINGS LIKE THIS... IT'LL GIVE YOU A BETTER UNDERSTANDING OF WHAT HAPPENED HERE.
TAKE ALL THE TIME YOU NEED.

PEOPLE HERE... IT WAS *YEARS* BEFORE WE KNEW WHAT HAD ACTUALLY HAPPENED. TO US... MAYBE THESE MONSTERS *WERE* THE PEOPLE MISSING.

MAYBE THIS NEW TERRAIN HAD SOMEHOW *CRUSHED* WHAT WAS HERE BEFORE.

ANOTHER DIMENSION? THE POSSIBILITY THOSE PEOPLE WERE STILL OUT THERE... IT WAS AN *INSANE* IDEA.

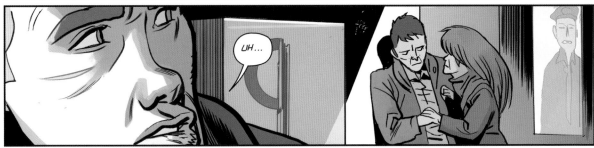

UH...

I'M SORRY, I KNOW THIS IS A LOT TO TAKE IN ALL AT ONCE.

WE'LL BE FINE.

DON'T WORRY ABOUT--

--US.

THAT THING'S STUFFED... IT'S NOT GOING ANYWHERE. DON'T WORRY.

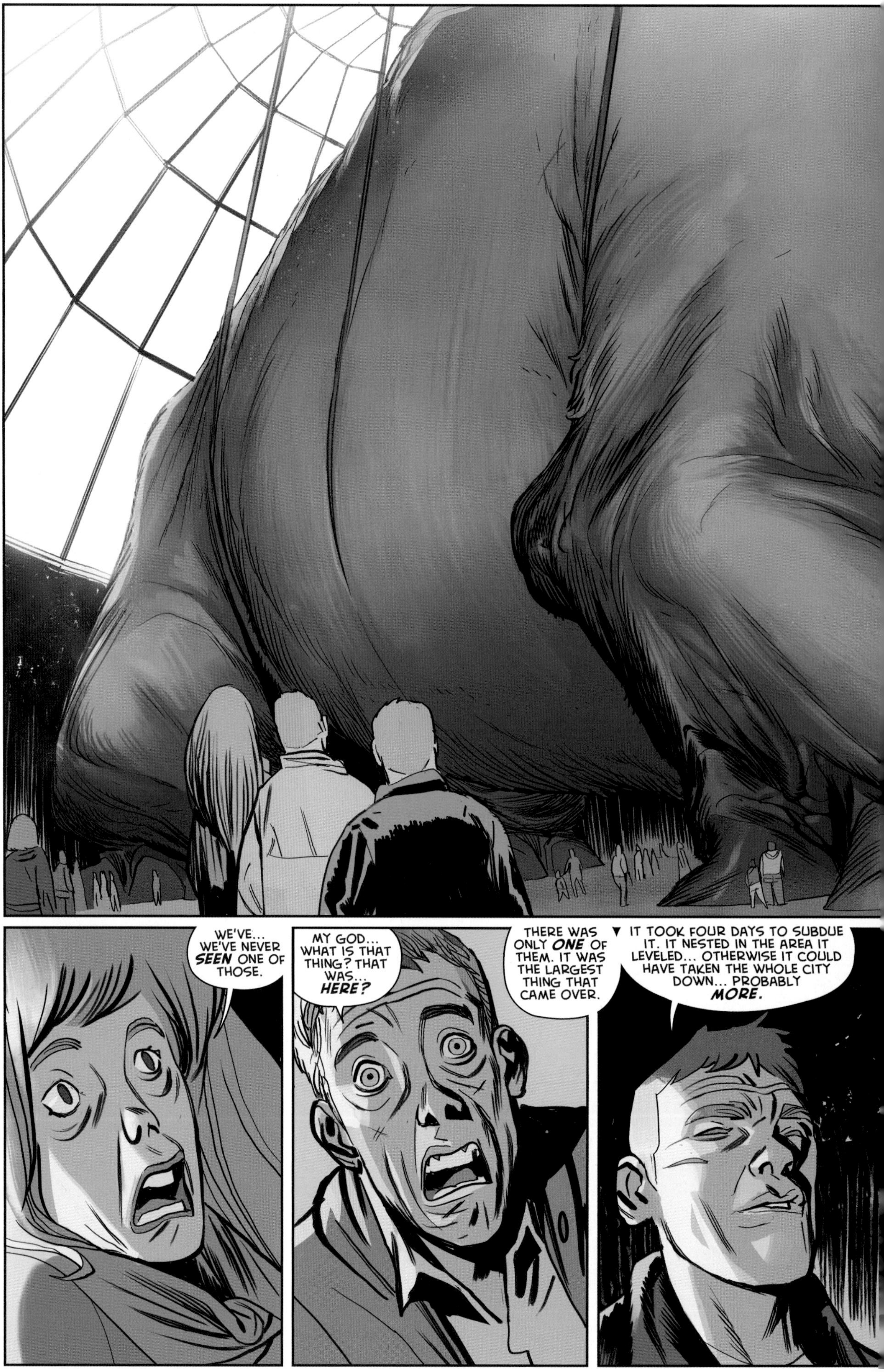
WE'VE... WE'VE NEVER SEEN ONE OF THOSE.
MY GOD... WHAT IS THAT THING? THAT WAS... HERE?
THERE WAS ONLY ONE OF THEM. IT WAS THE LARGEST THING THAT CAME OVER.
IT TOOK FOUR DAYS TO SUBDUE IT. IT NESTED IN THE AREA IT LEVELED... OTHERWISE IT COULD HAVE TAKEN THE WHOLE CITY DOWN... PROBABLY MORE.

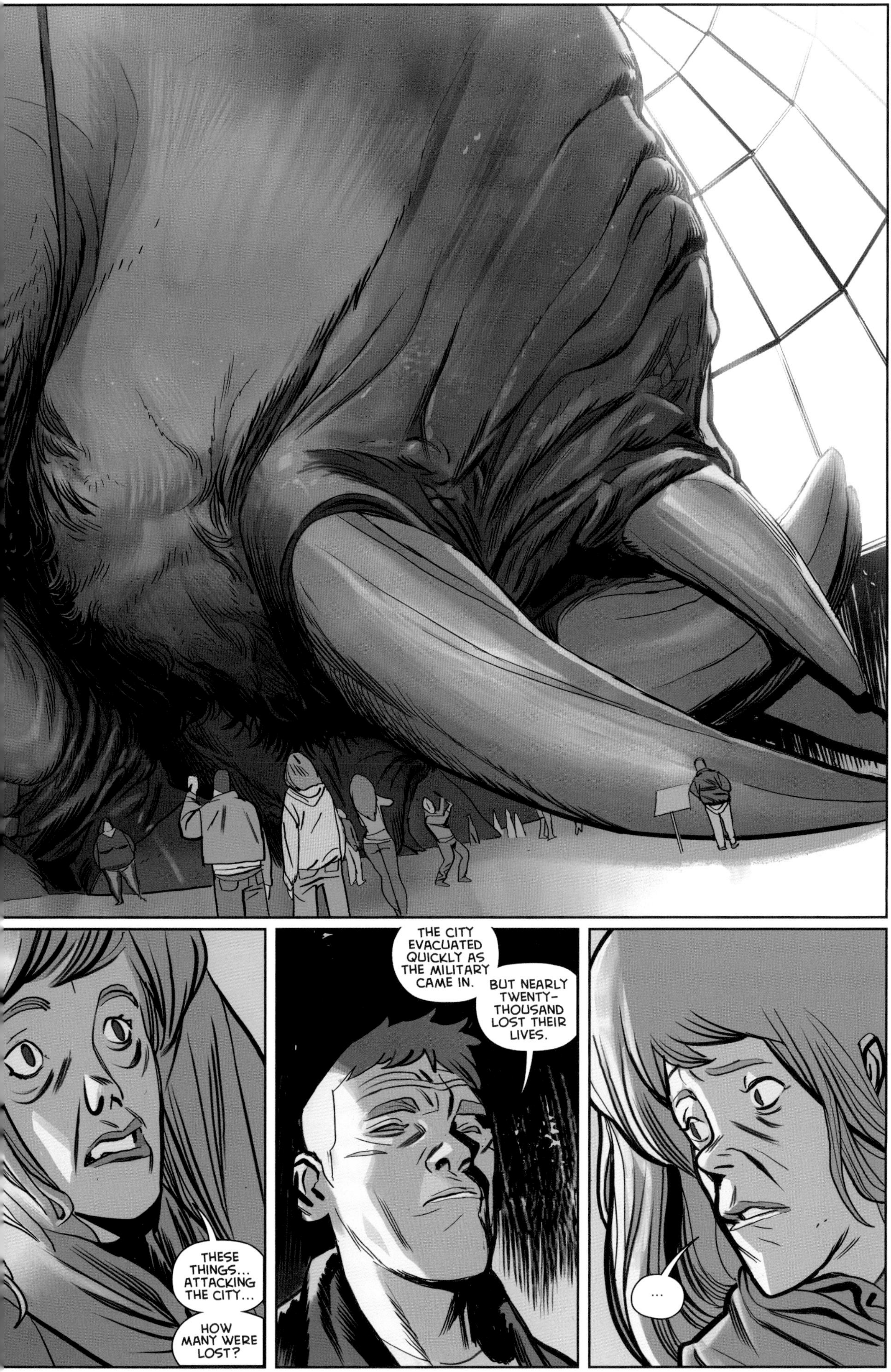
THESE THINGS... ATTACKING THE CITY...
HOW MANY WERE LOST?
THE CITY EVACUATED QUICKLY AS THE MILITARY CAME IN.
BUT NEARLY TWENTY-THOUSAND LOST THEIR LIVES.
...

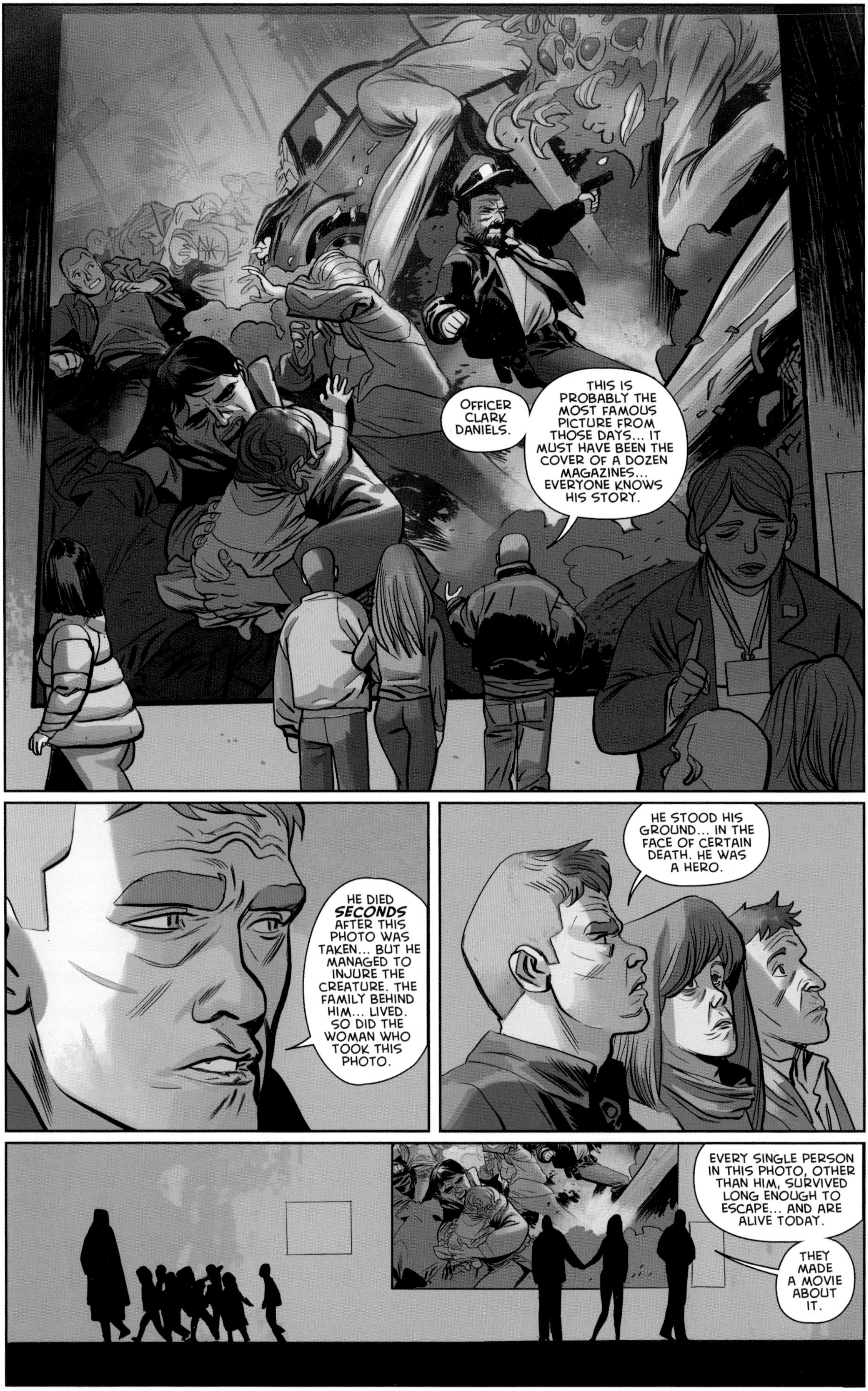
OFFICER CLARK DANIELS.
THIS IS PROBABLY THE MOST FAMOUS PICTURE FROM THOSE DAYS... IT MUST HAVE BEEN THE COVER OF A DOZEN MAGAZINES... EVERYONE KNOWS HIS STORY.
HE DIED **SECONDS** AFTER THIS PHOTO WAS TAKEN... BUT HE MANAGED TO INJURE THE CREATURE. THE FAMILY BEHIND HIM... LIVED. SO DID THE WOMAN WHO TOOK THIS PHOTO.
HE STOOD HIS GROUND... IN THE FACE OF CERTAIN DEATH. HE WAS A HERO.
EVERY SINGLE PERSON IN THIS PHOTO, OTHER THAN HIM, SURVIVED LONG ENOUGH TO ESCAPE... AND ARE ALIVE TODAY.
THEY MADE A MOVIE ABOUT IT.

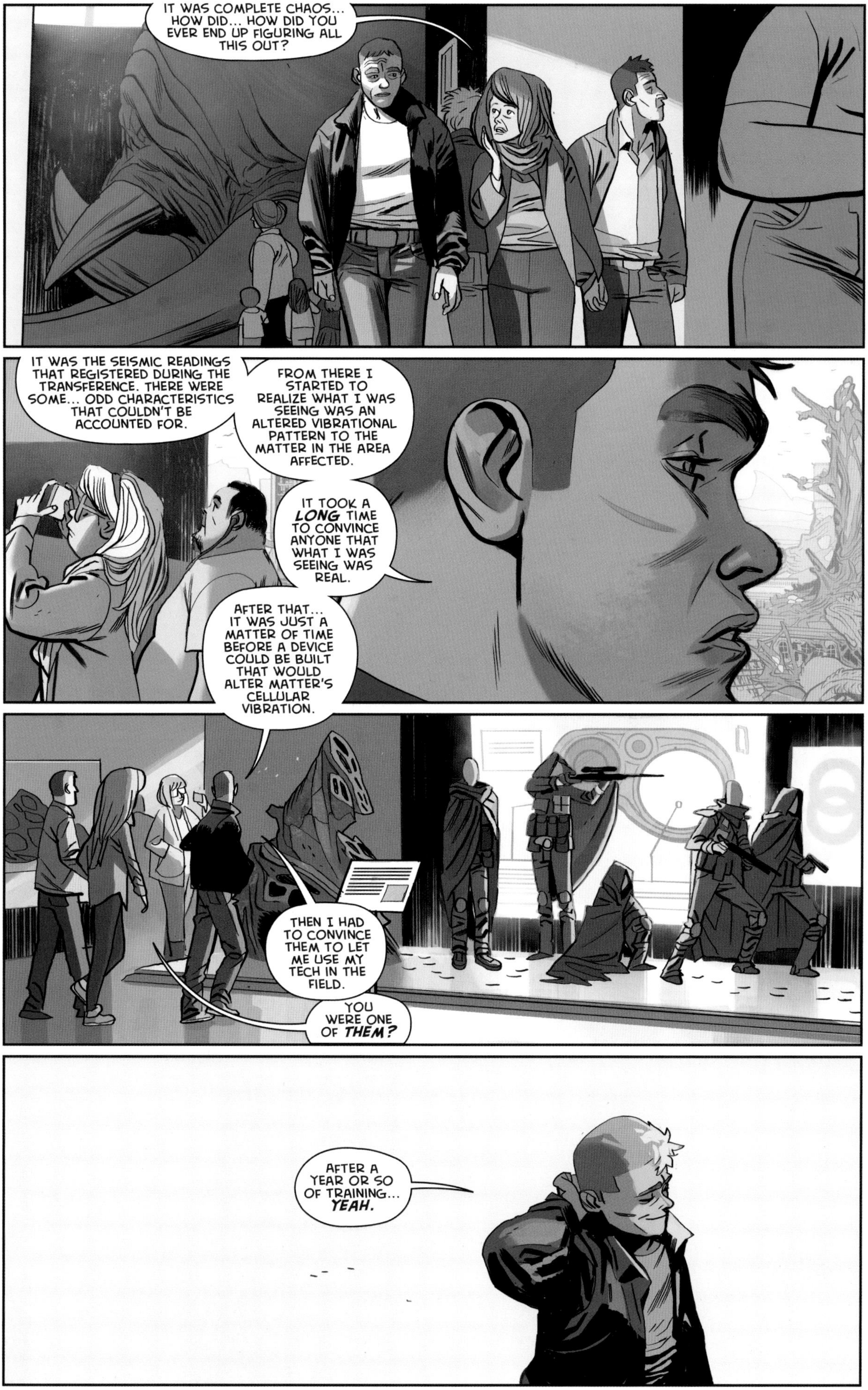
IT WAS COMPLETE CHAOS... HOW DID... HOW DID YOU EVER END UP FIGURING ALL THIS OUT?
IT WAS THE SEISMIC READINGS THAT REGISTERED DURING THE TRANSFERENCE. THERE WERE SOME... ODD CHARACTERISTICS THAT COULDN'T BE ACCOUNTED FOR.
FROM THERE I STARTED TO REALIZE WHAT I WAS SEEING WAS AN ALTERED VIBRATIONAL PATTERN TO THE MATTER IN THE AREA AFFECTED.
IT TOOK A LONG TIME TO CONVINCE ANYONE THAT WHAT I WAS SEEING WAS REAL.
AFTER THAT... IT WAS JUST A MATTER OF TIME BEFORE A DEVICE COULD BE BUILT THAT WOULD ALTER MATTER'S CELLULAR VIBRATION.
THEN I HAD TO CONVINCE THEM TO LET ME USE MY TECH IN THE FIELD.
YOU WERE ONE OF THEM?
AFTER A YEAR OR SO OF TRAINING... YEAH.

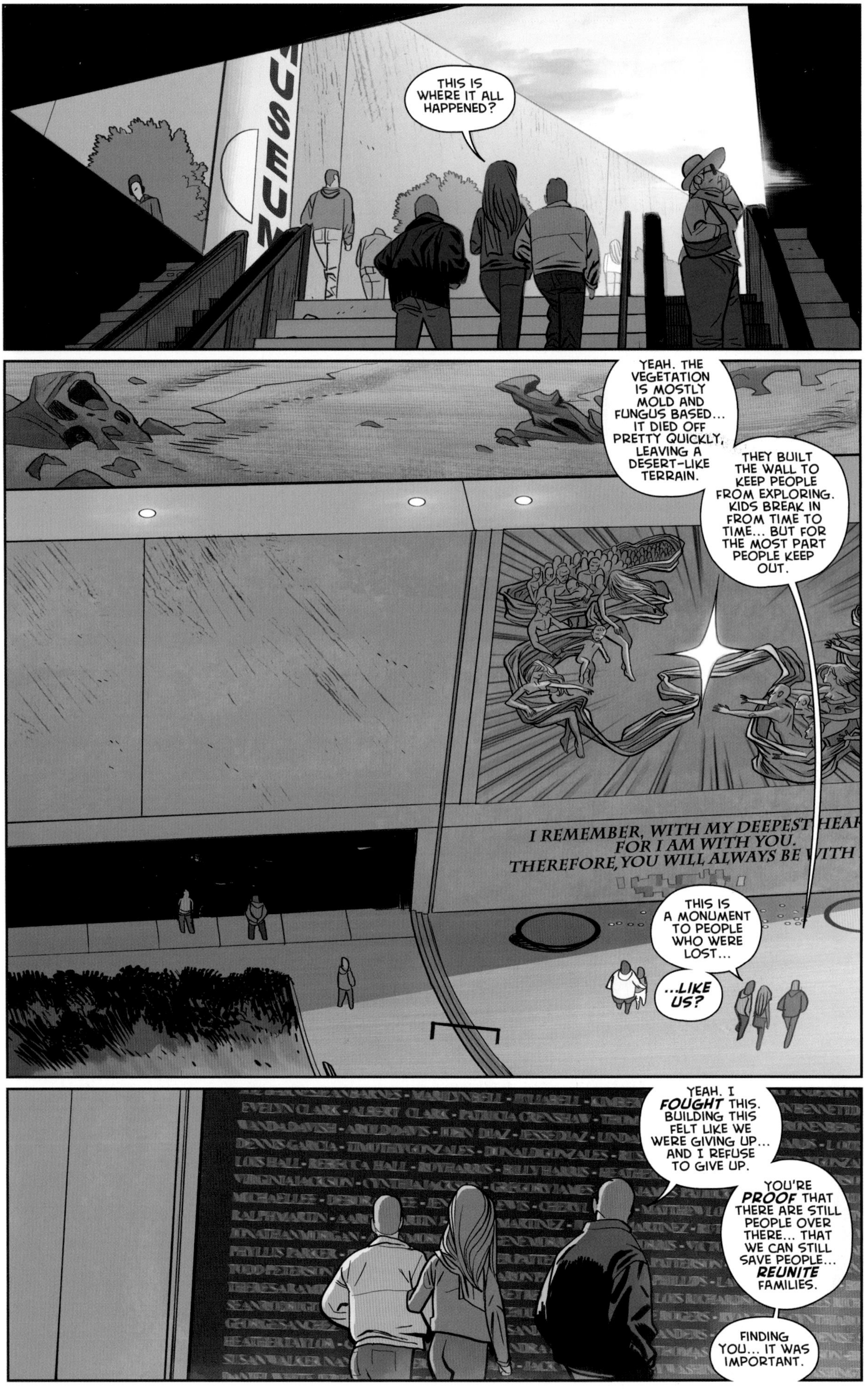
THIS IS WHERE IT ALL HAPPENED?
YEAH. THE VEGETATION IS MOSTLY MOLD AND FUNGUS BASED... IT DIED OFF PRETTY QUICKLY, LEAVING A DESERT-LIKE TERRAIN.
THEY BUILT THE WALL TO KEEP PEOPLE FROM EXPLORING. KIDS BREAK IN FROM TIME TO TIME... BUT FOR THE MOST PART PEOPLE KEEP OUT.
I REMEMBER, WITH MY DEEPEST HEAR
FOR I AM WITH YOU.
THEREFORE, YOU WILL ALWAYS BE WITH
THIS IS A MONUMENT TO PEOPLE WHO WERE LOST...
...LIKE US?
YEAH. I FOUGHT THIS. BUILDING THIS FELT LIKE WE WERE GIVING UP... AND I REFUSE TO GIVE UP.
YOU'RE PROOF THAT THERE ARE STILL PEOPLE OVER THERE... THAT WE CAN STILL SAVE PEOPLE... REUNITE FAMILIES.
FINDING YOU... IT WAS IMPORTANT.

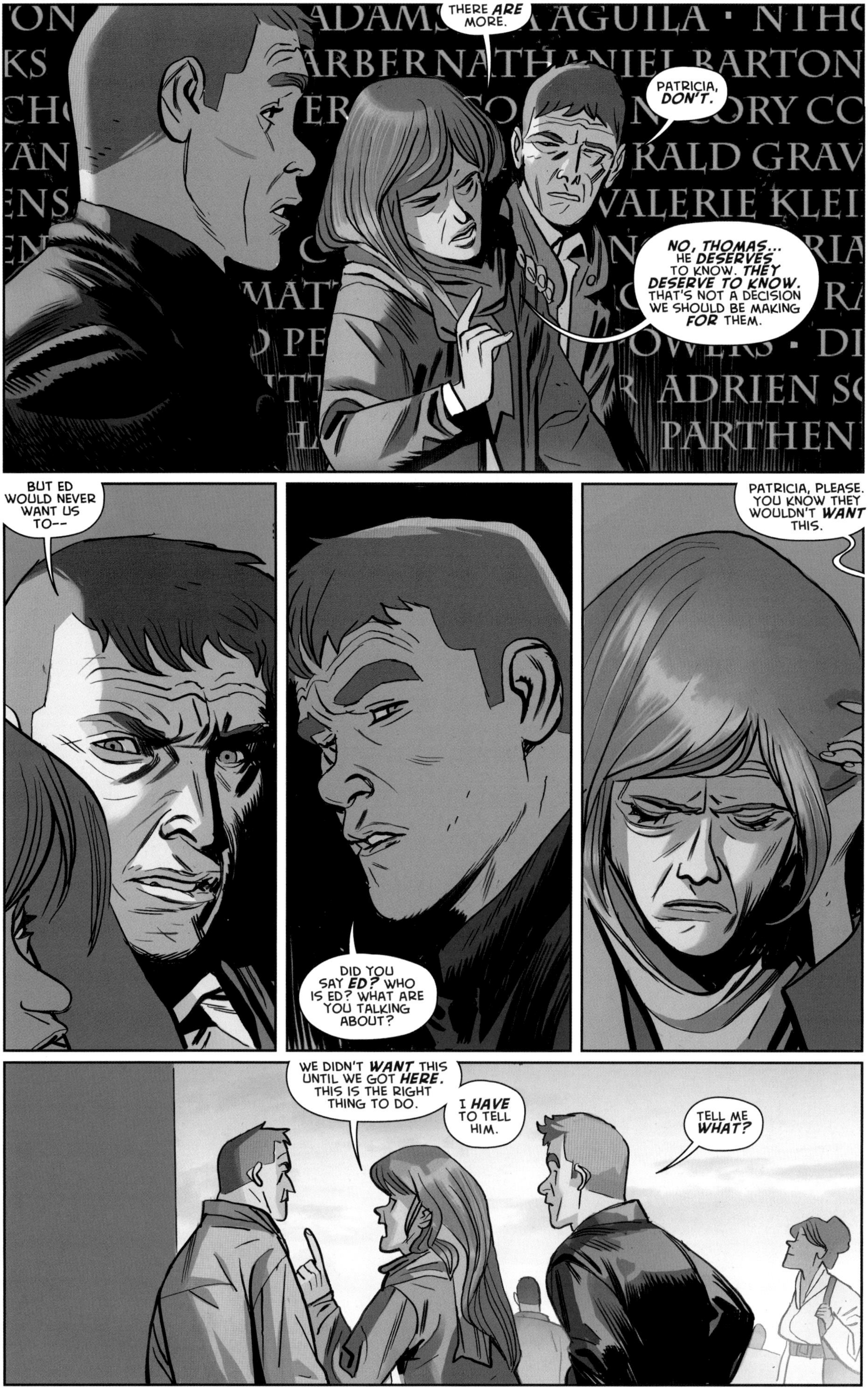
THERE **ARE** MORE.
PATRICIA, **DON'T.**
NO, THOMAS... HE **DESERVES** TO KNOW. **THEY DESERVE TO KNOW.** THAT'S NOT A DECISION WE SHOULD BE MAKING **FOR** THEM.
BUT ED WOULD NEVER WANT US TO--
DID YOU SAY **ED?** WHO IS ED? WHAT ARE YOU TALKING ABOUT?
PATRICIA, PLEASE. YOU KNOW THEY WOULDN'T **WANT** THIS.
WE DIDN'T **WANT** THIS UNTIL WE GOT **HERE.** THIS IS THE RIGHT THING TO DO.
I **HAVE** TO TELL HIM.
TELL ME **WHAT?**

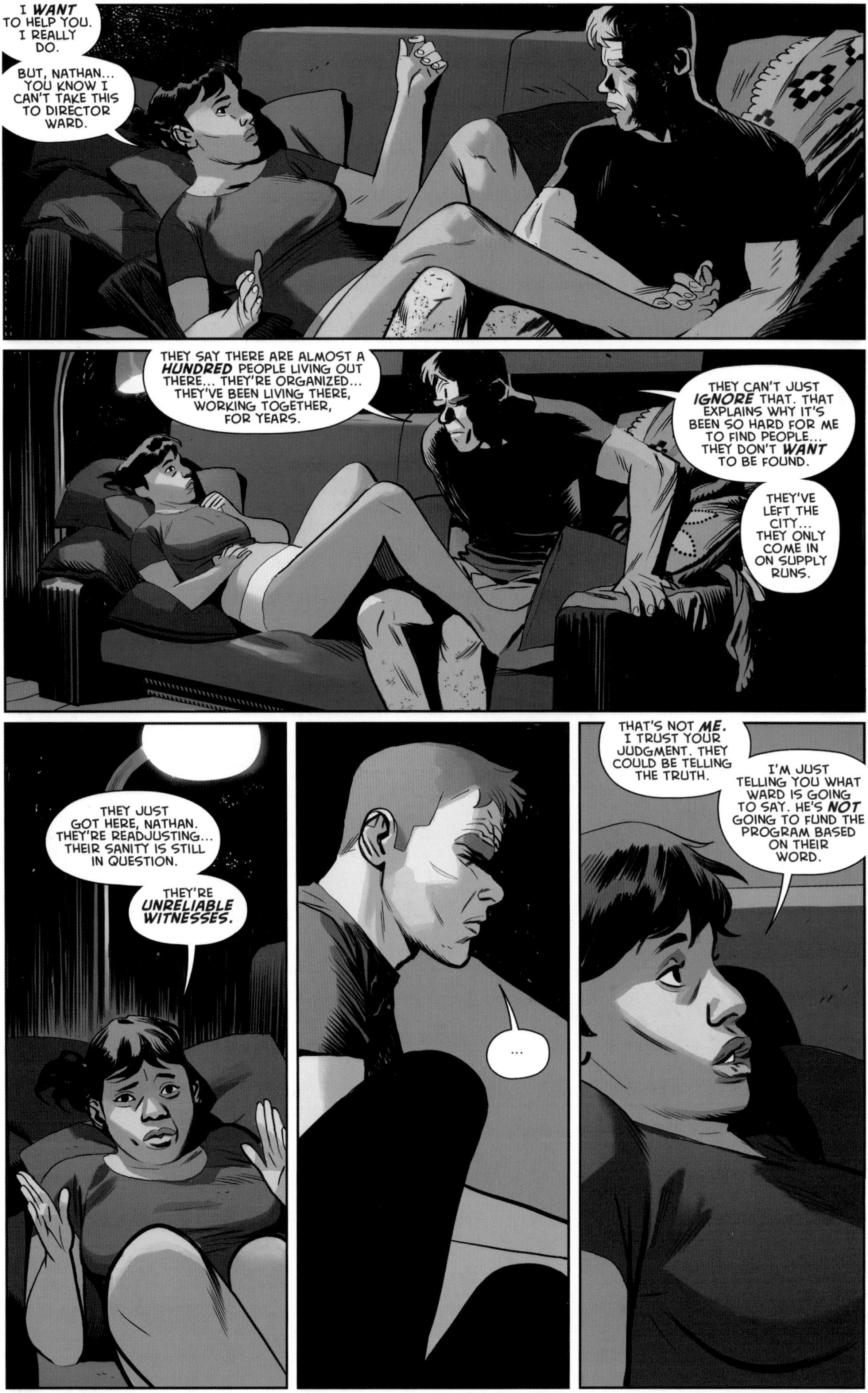
I WANT TO HELP YOU. I REALLY DO.
BUT, NATHAN... YOU KNOW I CAN'T TAKE THIS TO DIRECTOR WARD.
THEY SAY THERE ARE ALMOST A HUNDRED PEOPLE LIVING OUT THERE... THEY'RE ORGANIZED... THEY'VE BEEN LIVING THERE, WORKING TOGETHER, FOR YEARS.
THEY CAN'T JUST IGNORE THAT. THAT EXPLAINS WHY IT'S BEEN SO HARD FOR ME TO FIND PEOPLE... THEY DON'T WANT TO BE FOUND.
THEY'VE LEFT THE CITY... THEY ONLY COME IN ON SUPPLY RUNS.
THEY JUST GOT HERE, NATHAN. THEY'RE READJUSTING... THEIR SANITY IS STILL IN QUESTION.
THEY'RE UNRELIABLE WITNESSES.
...
THAT'S NOT ME. I TRUST YOUR JUDGMENT. THEY COULD BE TELLING THE TRUTH.
I'M JUST TELLING YOU WHAT WARD IS GOING TO SAY. HE'S NOT GOING TO FUND THE PROGRAM BASED ON THEIR WORD.

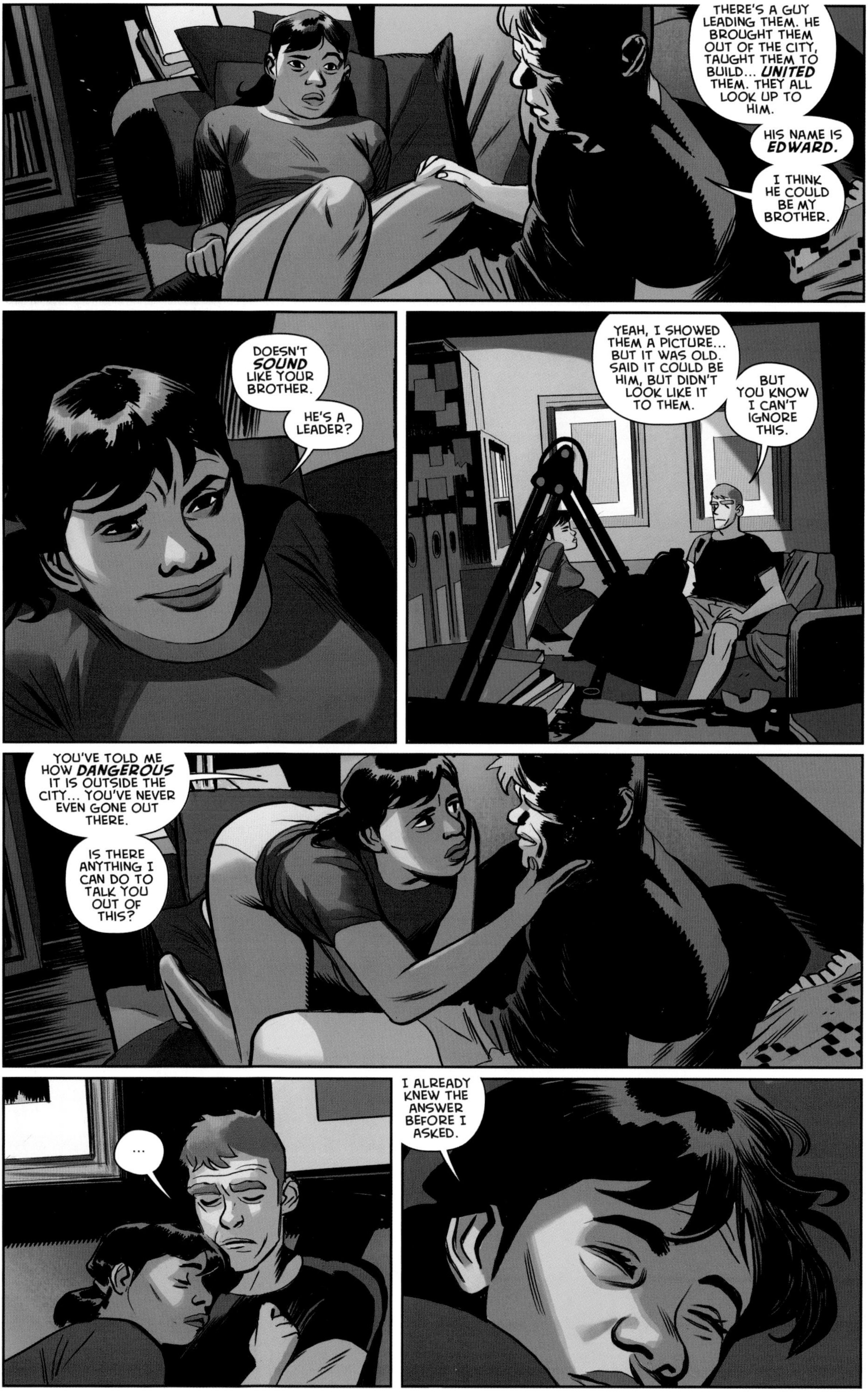
THERE'S A GUY LEADING THEM. HE BROUGHT THEM OUT OF THE CITY, TAUGHT THEM TO BUILD... UNITED THEM. THEY ALL LOOK UP TO HIM.
HIS NAME IS EDWARD.
I THINK HE COULD BE MY BROTHER.
DOESN'T SOUND LIKE YOUR BROTHER.
HE'S A LEADER?
YEAH, I SHOWED THEM A PICTURE... BUT IT WAS OLD. SAID IT COULD BE HIM, BUT DIDN'T LOOK LIKE IT TO THEM.
BUT YOU KNOW I CAN'T IGNORE THIS.
YOU'VE TOLD ME HOW DANGEROUS IT IS OUTSIDE THE CITY... YOU'VE NEVER EVEN GONE OUT THERE.
IS THERE ANYTHING I CAN DO TO TALK YOU OUT OF THIS?
...
I ALREADY KNEW THE ANSWER BEFORE I ASKED.

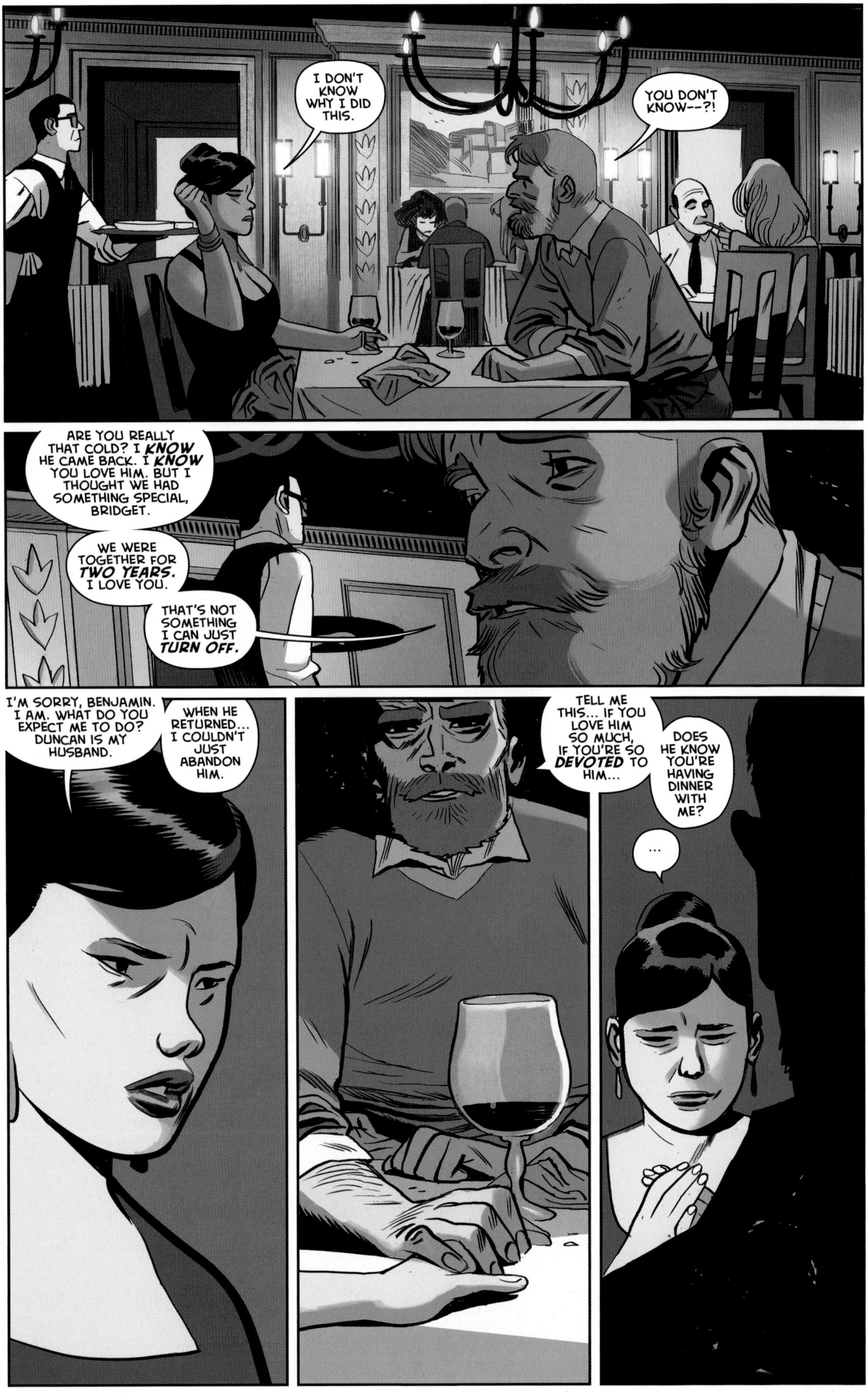
I DON'T KNOW WHY I DID THIS.
YOU DON'T KNOW--?!
ARE YOU REALLY THAT COLD? I KNOW HE CAME BACK. I KNOW YOU LOVE HIM. BUT I THOUGHT WE HAD SOMETHING SPECIAL, BRIDGET.
WE WERE TOGETHER FOR TWO YEARS. I LOVE YOU.
THAT'S NOT SOMETHING I CAN JUST TURN OFF.
I'M SORRY, BENJAMIN. I AM. WHAT DO YOU EXPECT ME TO DO? DUNCAN IS MY HUSBAND.
WHEN HE RETURNED... I COULDN'T JUST ABANDON HIM.
TELL ME THIS... IF YOU LOVE HIM SO MUCH, IF YOU'RE SO DEVOTED TO HIM...
DOES HE KNOW YOU'RE HAVING DINNER WITH ME?
...

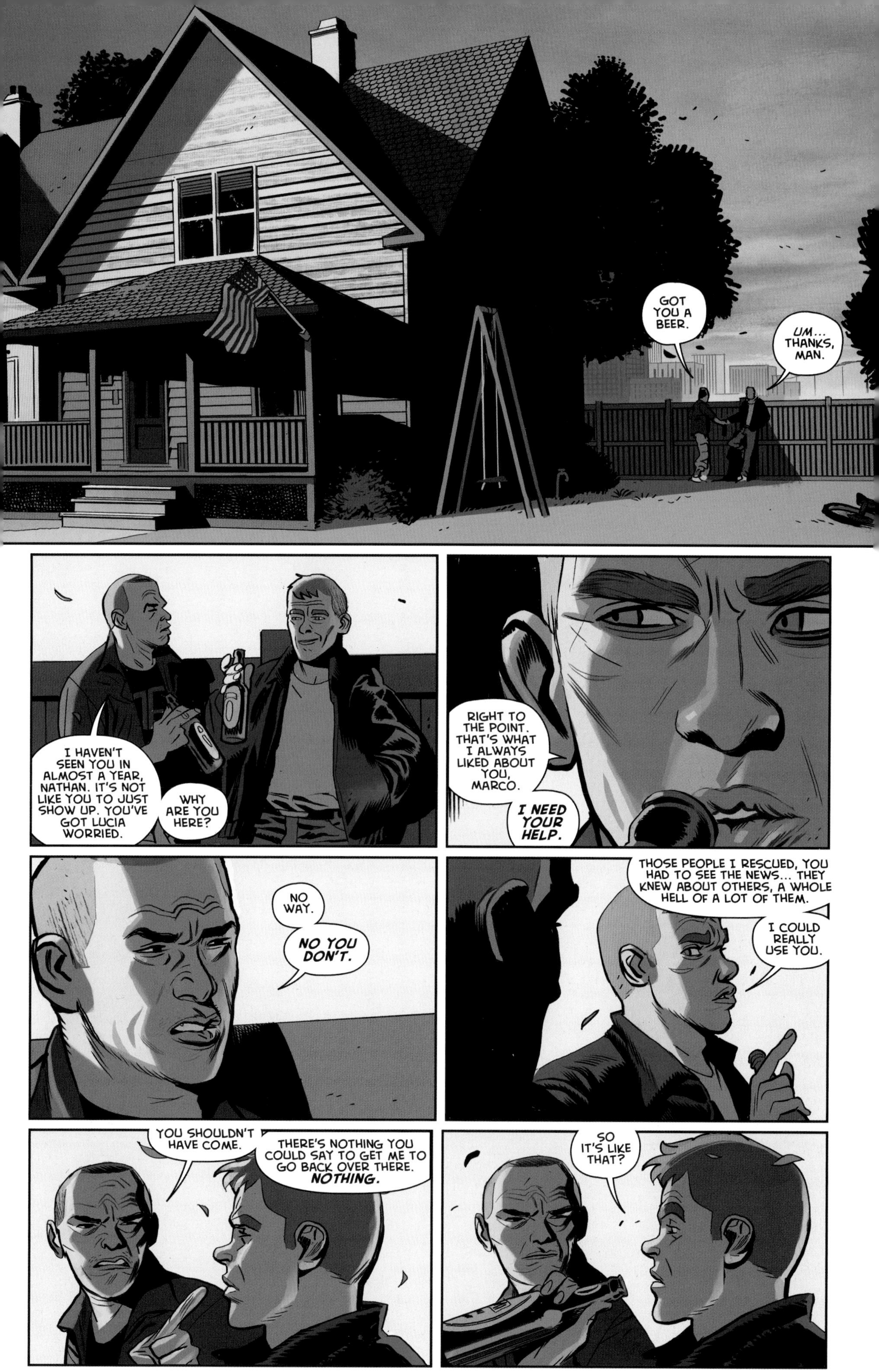
GOT YOU A BEER.
UM... THANKS, MAN.
I HAVEN'T SEEN YOU IN ALMOST A YEAR, NATHAN. IT'S NOT LIKE YOU TO JUST SHOW UP. YOU'VE GOT LUCIA WORRIED.
WHY ARE YOU HERE?
RIGHT TO THE POINT. THAT'S WHAT I ALWAYS LIKED ABOUT YOU, MARCO.
I NEED YOUR HELP.
NO WAY.
NO YOU DON'T.
THOSE PEOPLE I RESCUED, YOU HAD TO SEE THE NEWS... THEY KNEW ABOUT OTHERS, A WHOLE HELL OF A LOT OF THEM.
I COULD REALLY USE YOU.
YOU SHOULDN'T HAVE COME.
THERE'S NOTHING YOU COULD SAY TO GET ME TO GO BACK OVER THERE. NOTHING.
SO IT'S LIKE THAT?

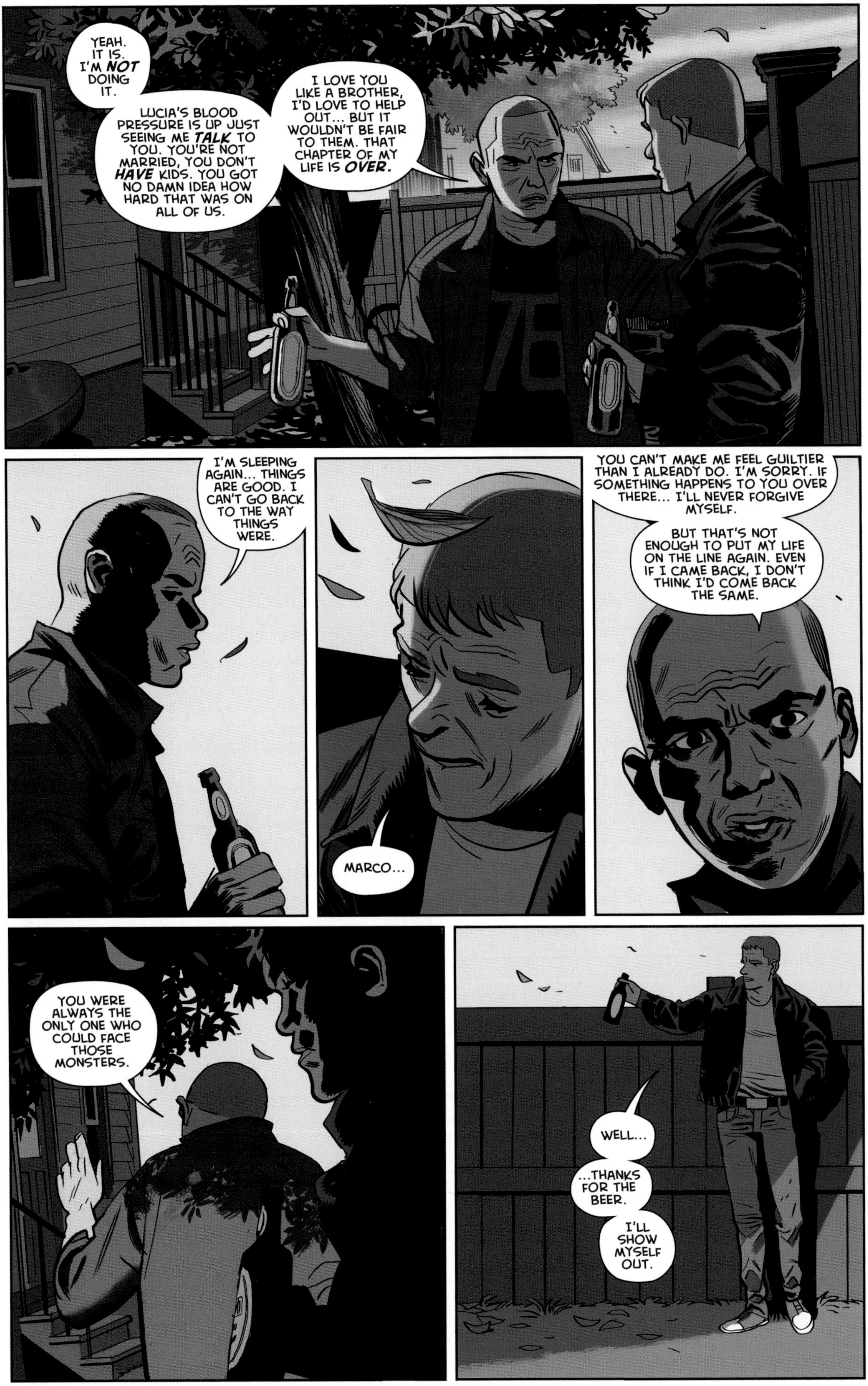
YEAH. IT IS. I'M NOT DOING IT.
LUCIA'S BLOOD PRESSURE IS UP JUST SEEING ME TALK TO YOU. YOU'RE NOT MARRIED, YOU DON'T HAVE KIDS. YOU GOT NO DAMN IDEA HOW HARD THAT WAS ON ALL OF US.
I LOVE YOU LIKE A BROTHER, I'D LOVE TO HELP OUT... BUT IT WOULDN'T BE FAIR TO THEM. THAT CHAPTER OF MY LIFE IS OVER.
I'M SLEEPING AGAIN... THINGS ARE GOOD. I CAN'T GO BACK TO THE WAY THINGS WERE.
MARCO...
YOU CAN'T MAKE ME FEEL GUILTIER THAN I ALREADY DO. I'M SORRY. IF SOMETHING HAPPENS TO YOU OVER THERE... I'LL NEVER FORGIVE MYSELF.
BUT THAT'S NOT ENOUGH TO PUT MY LIFE ON THE LINE AGAIN. EVEN IF I CAME BACK, I DON'T THINK I'D COME BACK THE SAME.
YOU WERE ALWAYS THE ONLY ONE WHO COULD FACE THOSE MONSTERS.
WELL...
...THANKS FOR THE BEER.
I'LL SHOW MYSELF OUT.

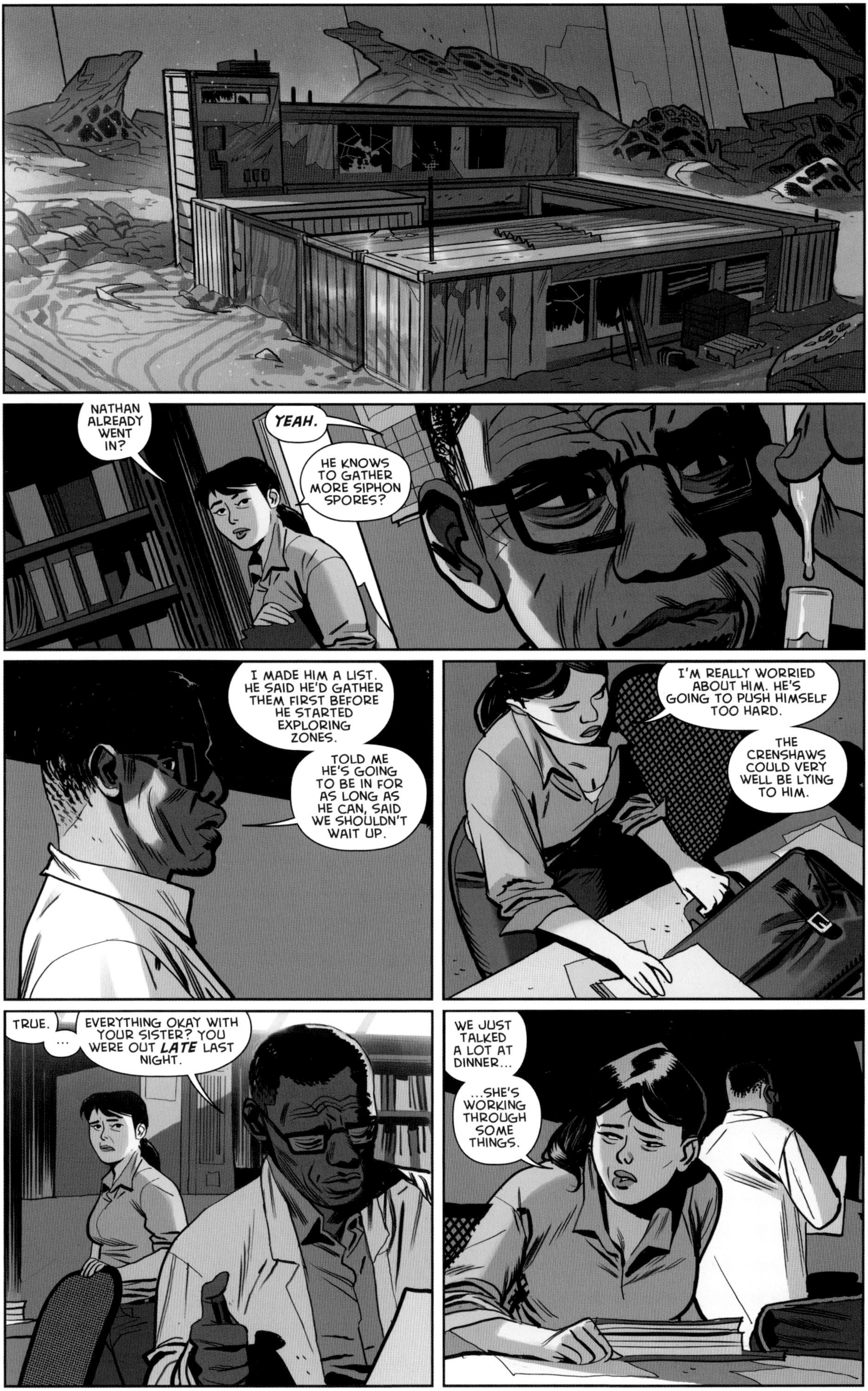
NATHAN ALREADY WENT IN?
YEAH.
HE KNOWS TO GATHER MORE SIPHON SPORES?
I MADE HIM A LIST. HE SAID HE'D GATHER THEM FIRST BEFORE HE STARTED EXPLORING ZONES.
TOLD ME HE'S GOING TO BE IN FOR AS LONG AS HE CAN, SAID WE SHOULDN'T WAIT UP.
I'M REALLY WORRIED ABOUT HIM. HE'S GOING TO PUSH HIMSELF TOO HARD.
THE CRENSHAWS COULD VERY WELL BE LYING TO HIM.
TRUE.
...
EVERYTHING OKAY WITH YOUR SISTER? YOU WERE OUT LATE LAST NIGHT.
WE JUST TALKED A LOT AT DINNER...
...SHE'S WORKING THROUGH SOME THINGS.

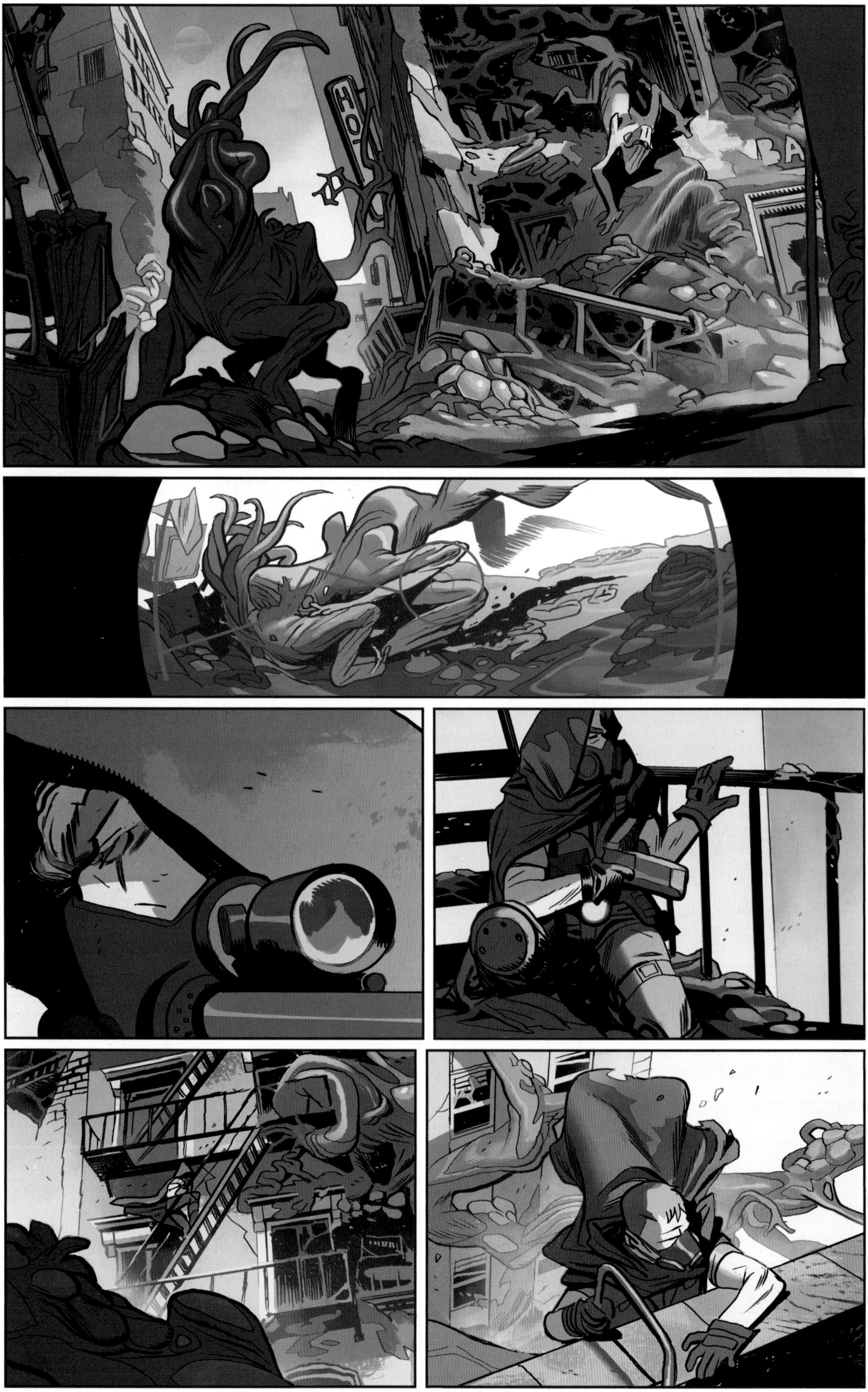
HO
BA

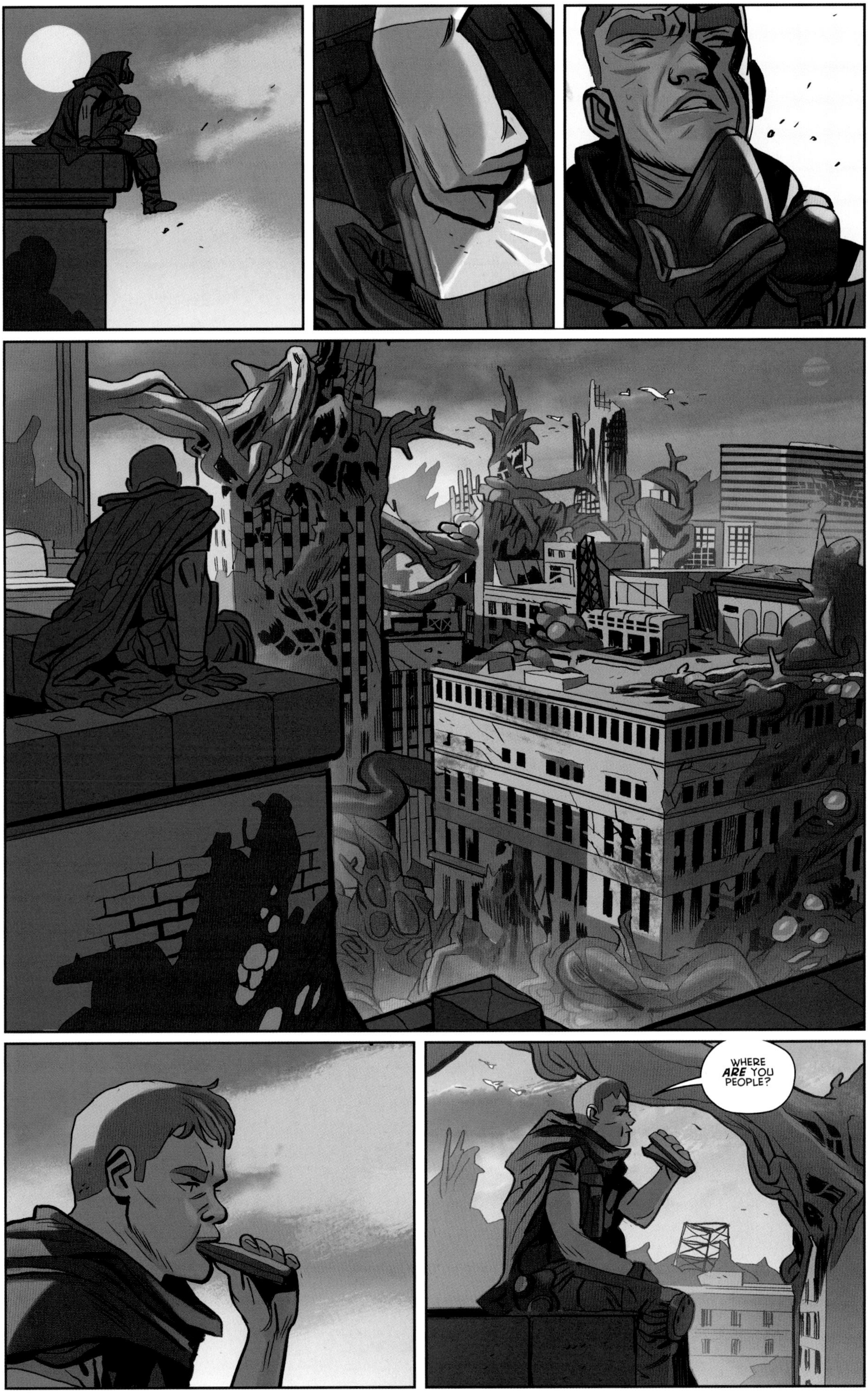
WHERE ARE YOU PEOPLE?

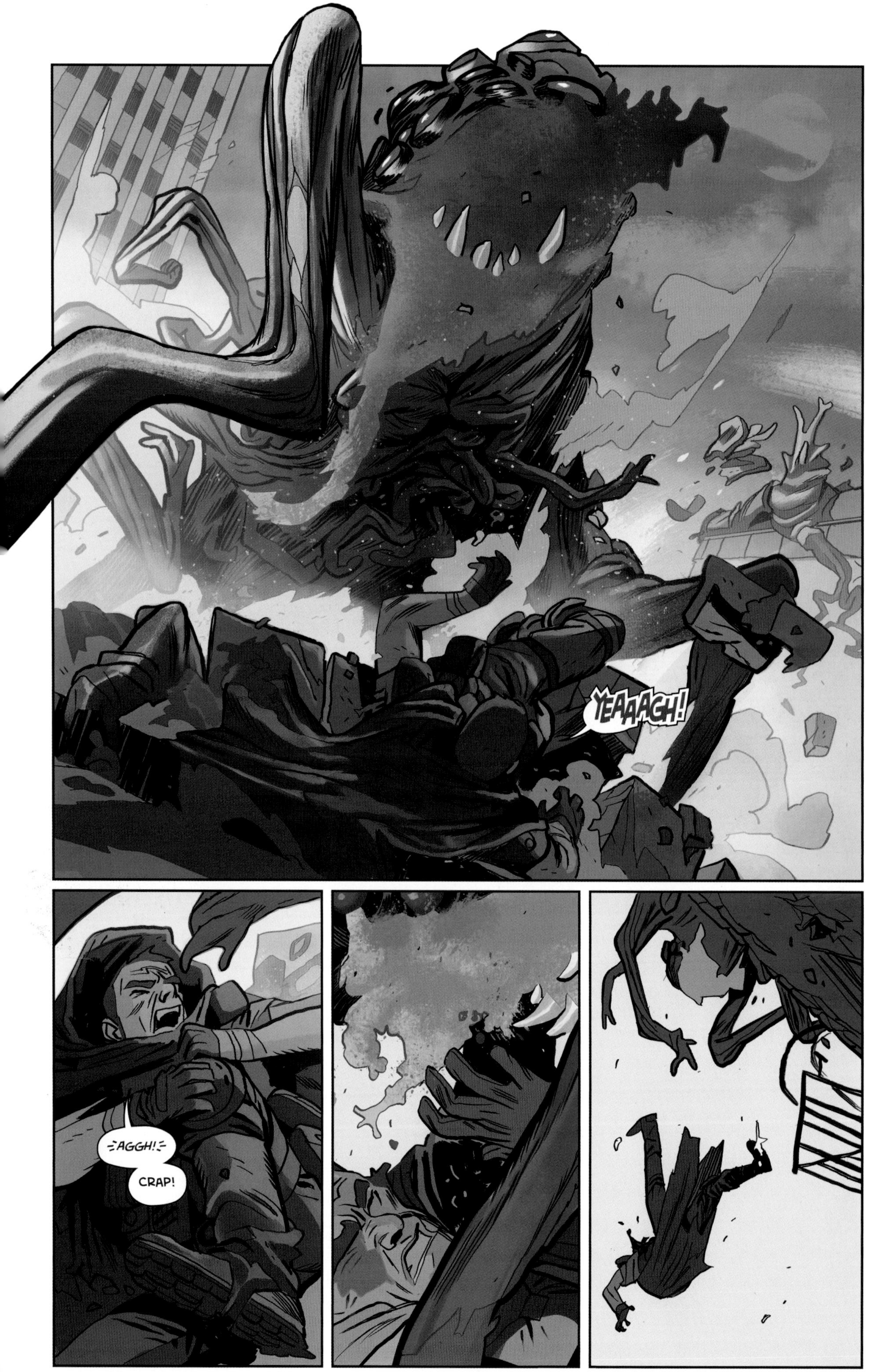
YEAAAGH!
AGGH!
CRAP!

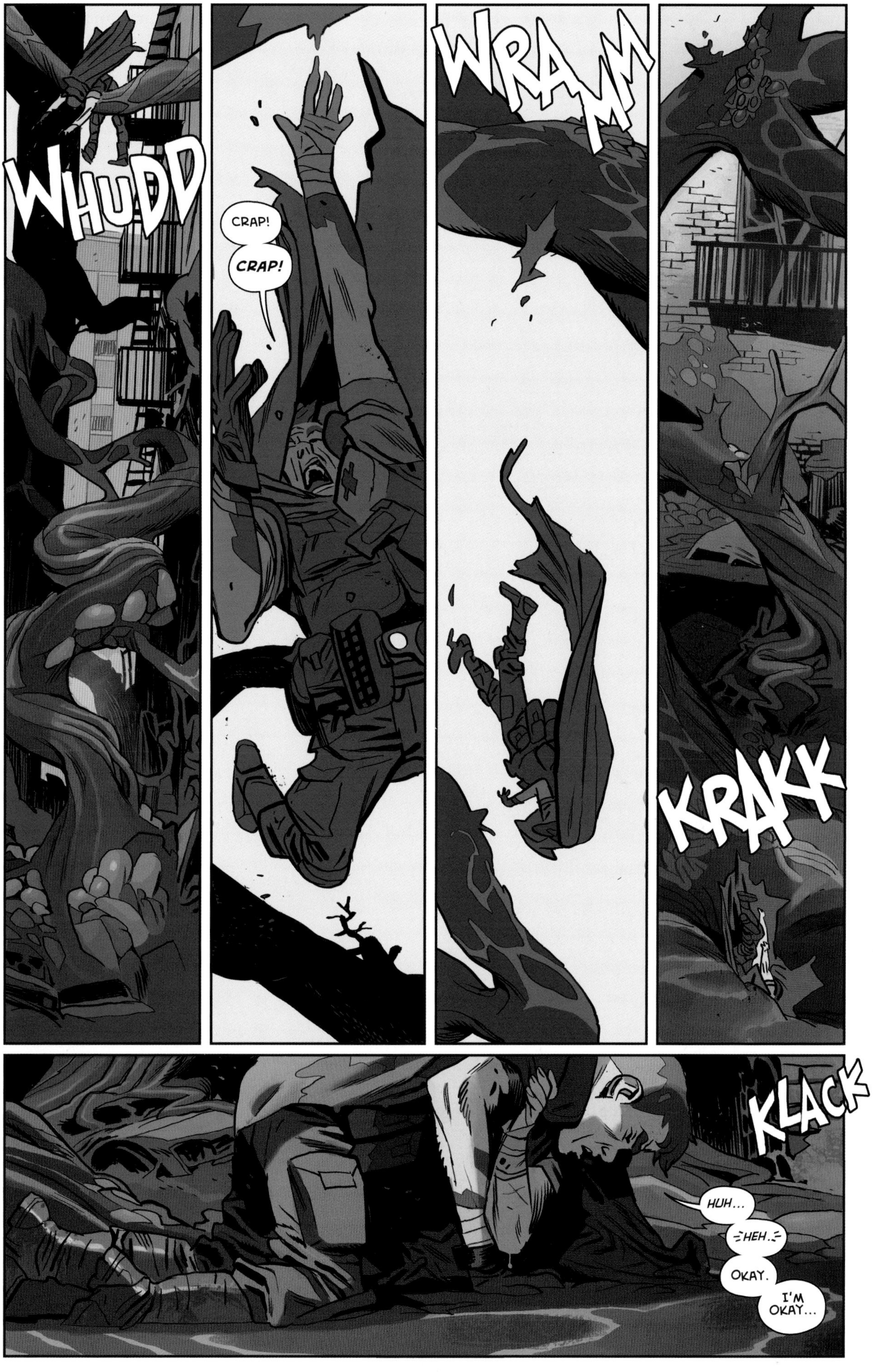
WHUDD
CRAP!
CRAP!
WRAMM
KRAKK
KLACK
HUH...
HEH..
OKAY.
I'M OKAY...

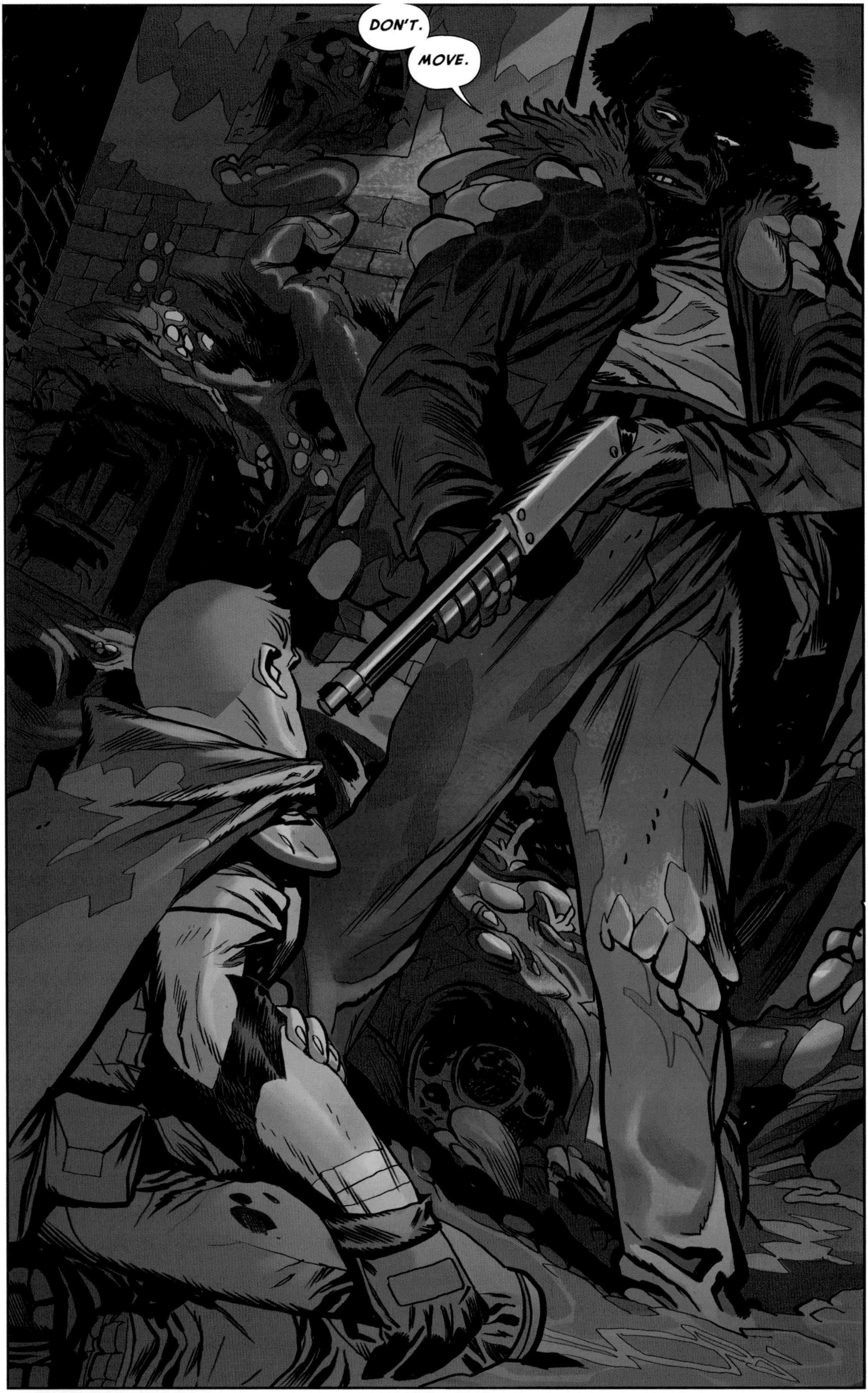
DON'T.
MOVE.

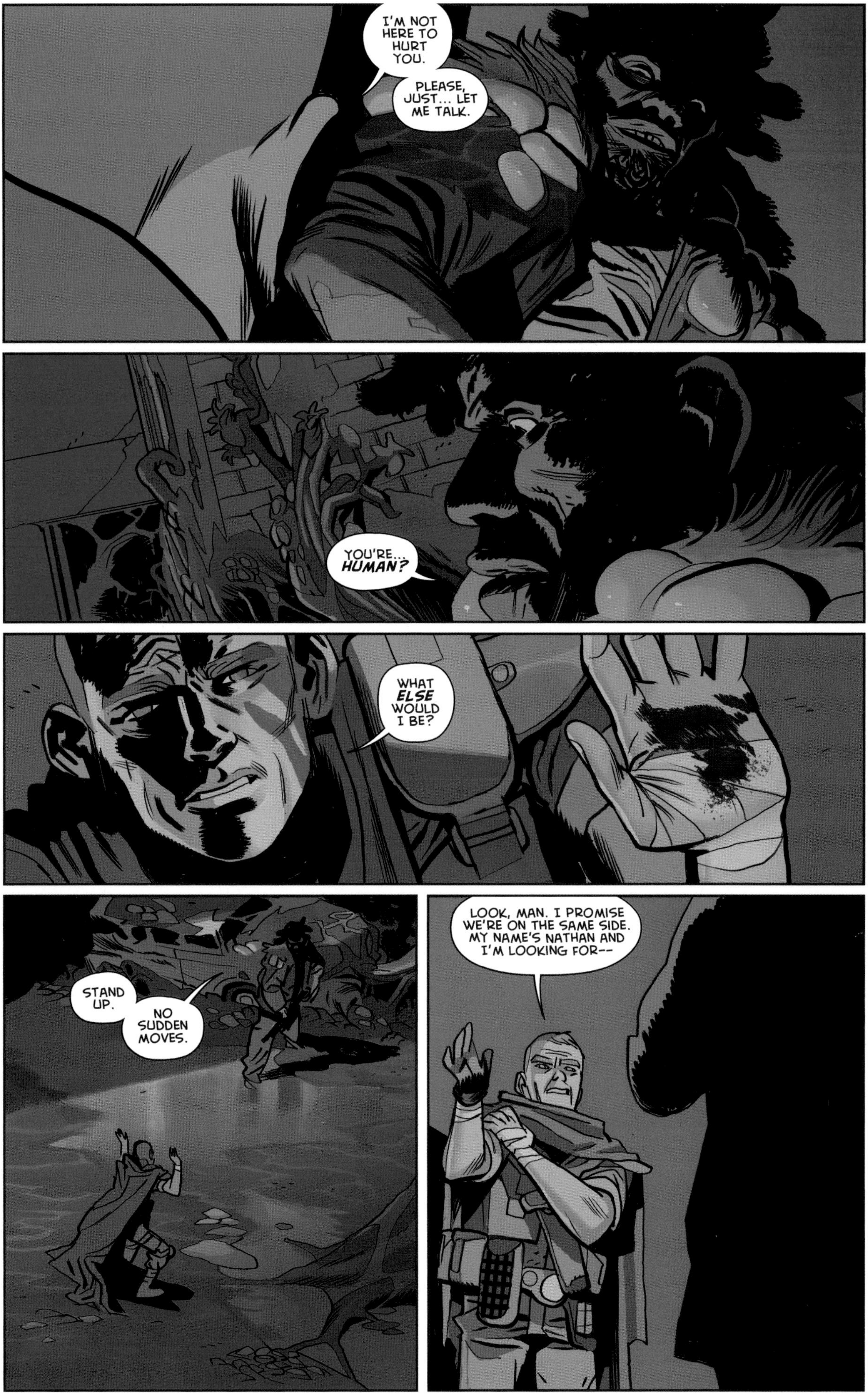
I'M NOT HERE TO HURT YOU.
PLEASE, JUST... LET ME TALK.
YOU'RE... *HUMAN?*
WHAT *ELSE* WOULD I BE?
STAND UP.
NO SUDDEN MOVES.
LOOK, MAN. I PROMISE WE'RE ON THE SAME SIDE. MY NAME'S NATHAN AND I'M LOOKING FOR--

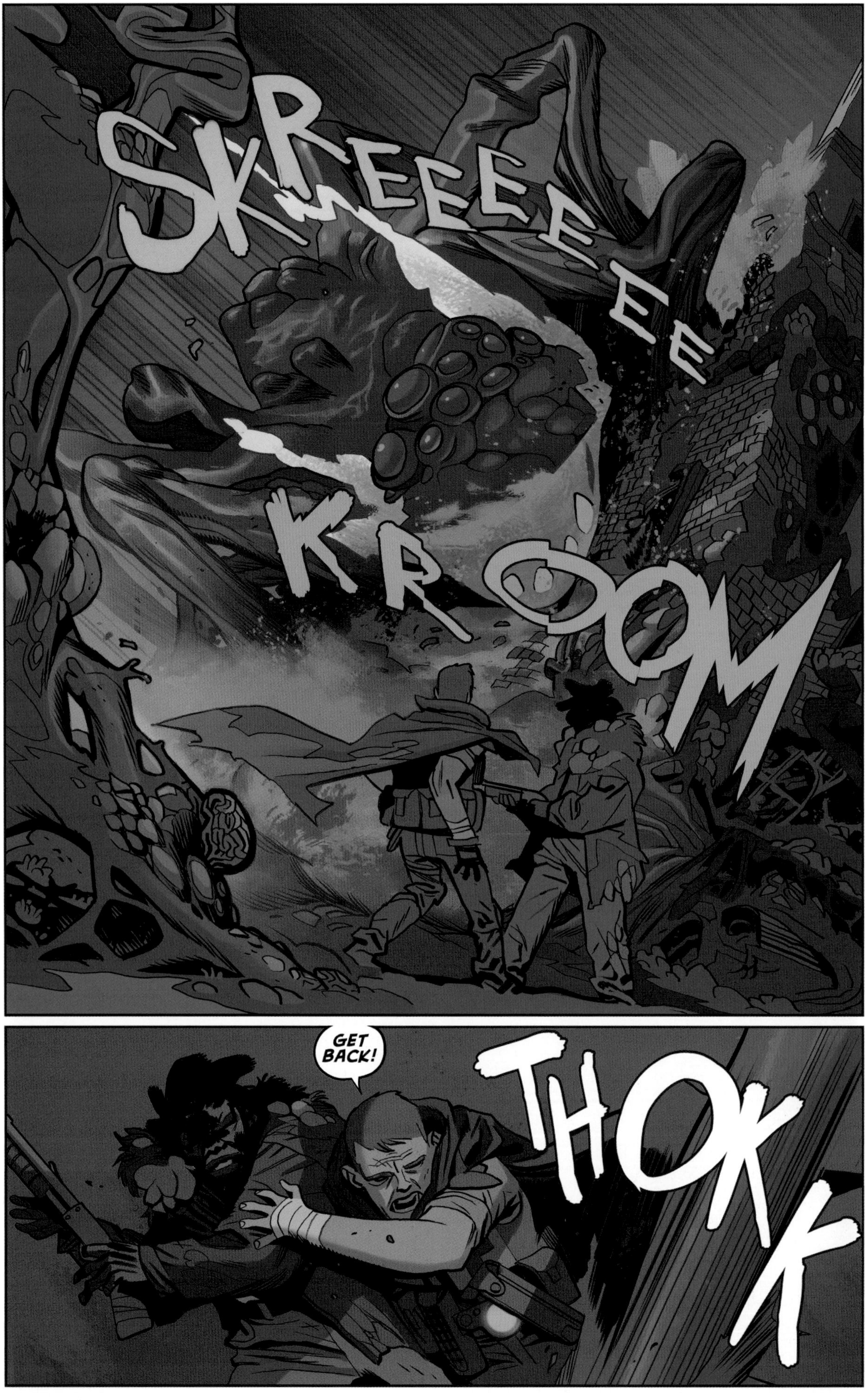
SKREEEEEEE
KROOM
GET BACK!
THOKK

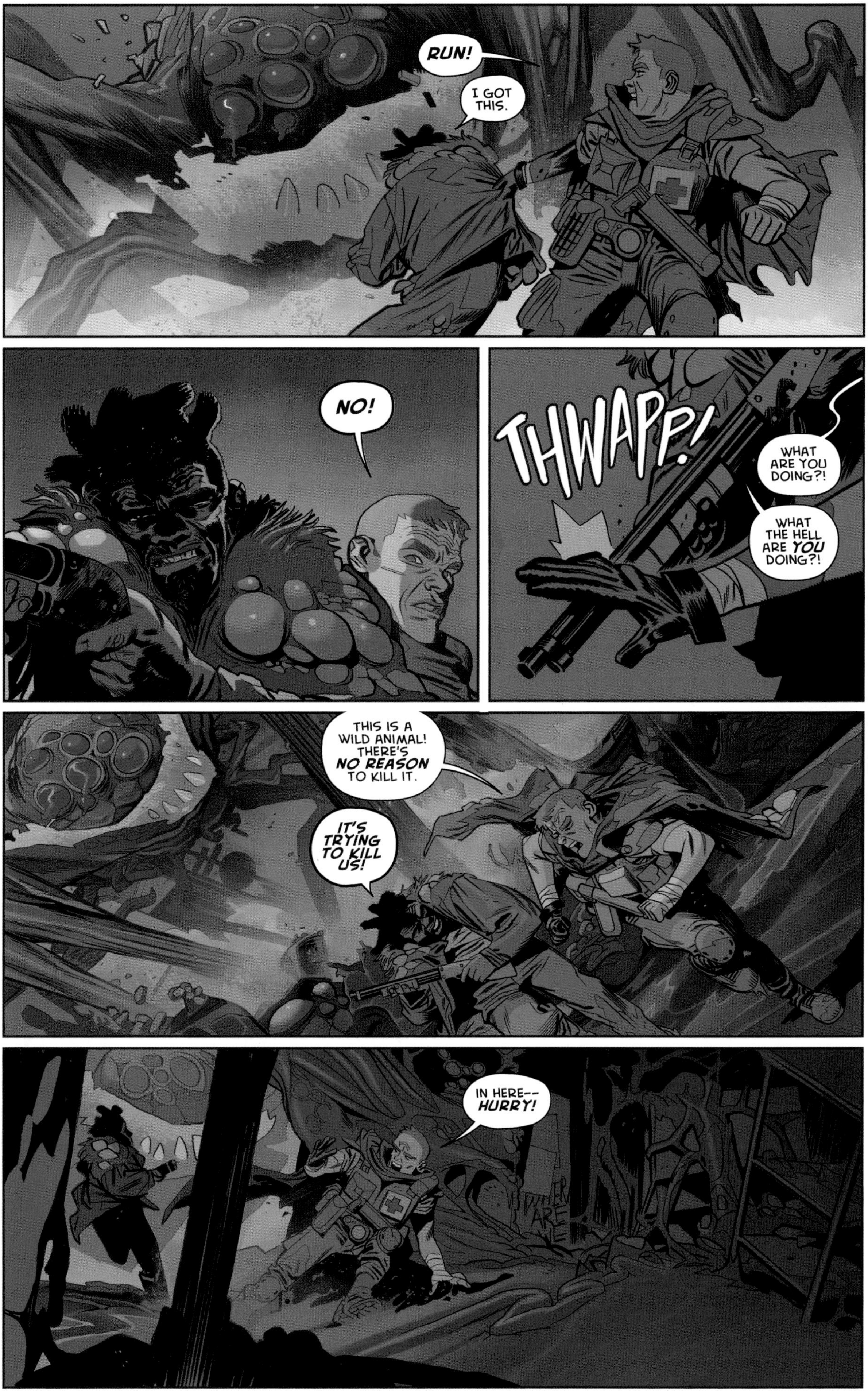
RUN!
I GOT THIS.
NO!
THWAPP!
WHAT ARE YOU DOING?!
WHAT THE HELL ARE YOU DOING?!
THIS IS A WILD ANIMAL! THERE'S NO REASON TO KILL IT.
IT'S TRYING TO KILL US!
IN HERE-- HURRY!

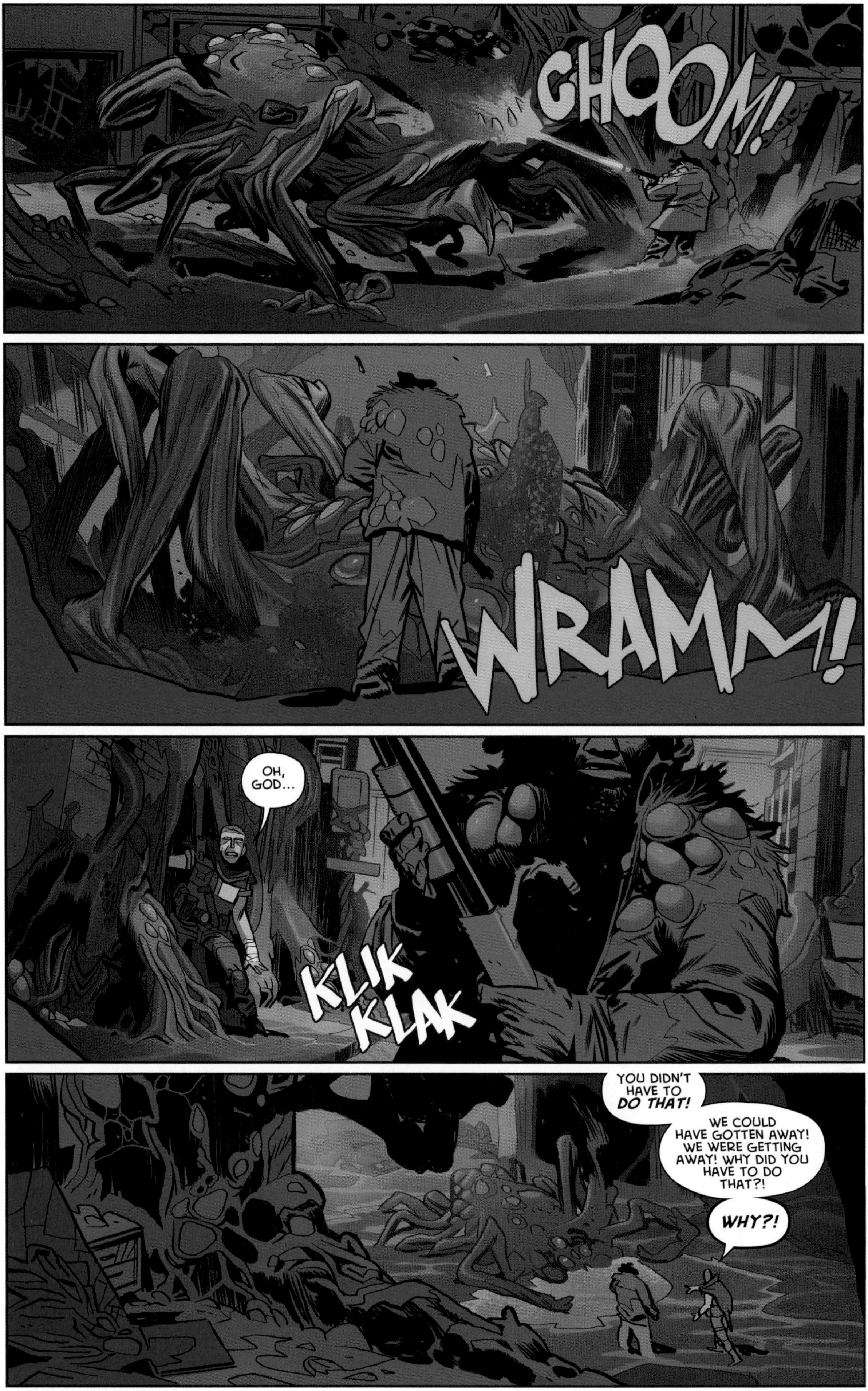
GHOOM!
WRAMM!
OH, GOD...
KLIK KLAK
YOU DIDN'T HAVE TO *DO THAT!*
WE COULD HAVE GOTTEN AWAY! WE WERE GETTING AWAY! WHY DID YOU HAVE TO DO THAT?!
WHY?!

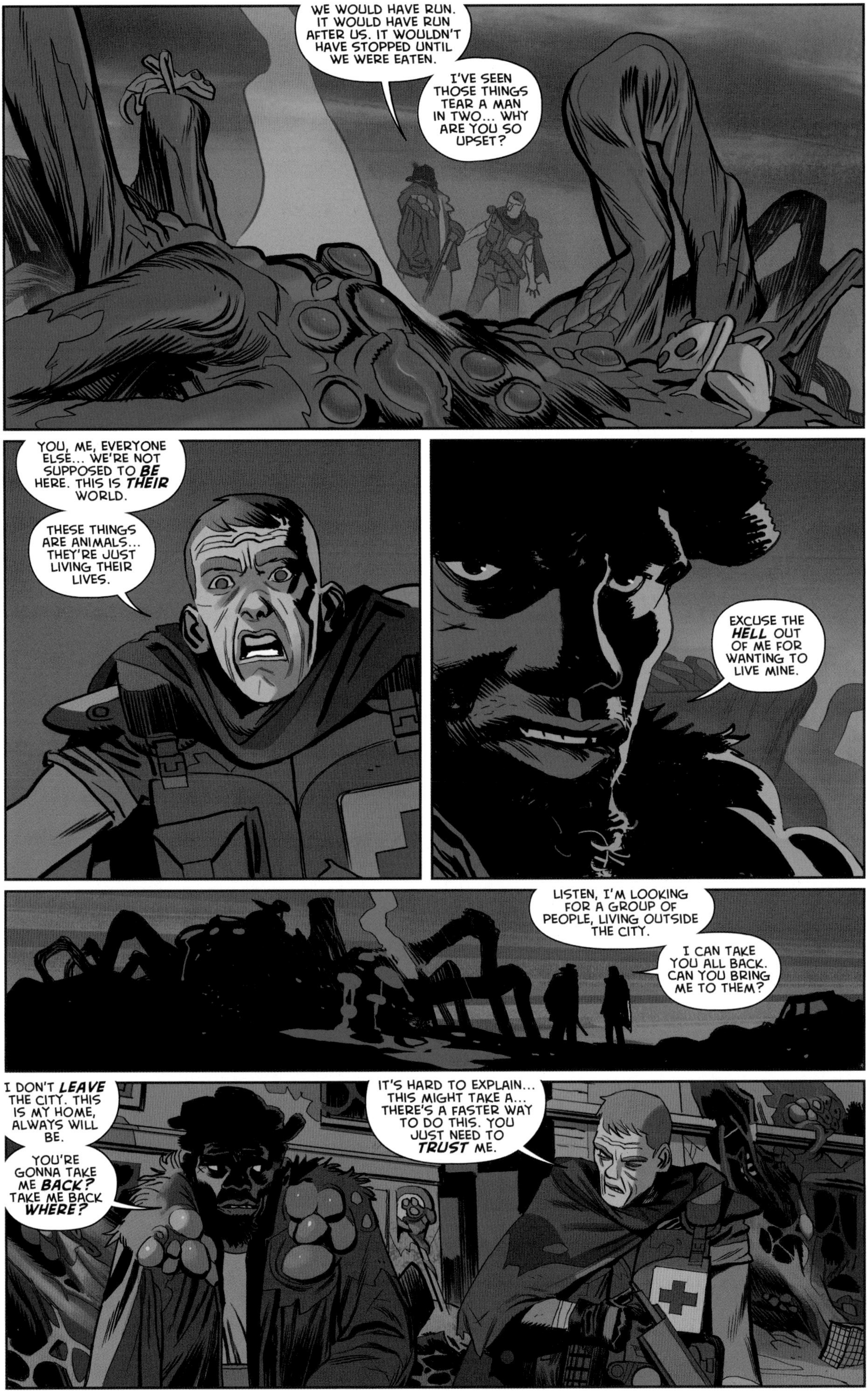
WE WOULD HAVE RUN. IT WOULD HAVE RUN AFTER US. IT WOULDN'T HAVE STOPPED UNTIL WE WERE EATEN.
I'VE SEEN THOSE THINGS TEAR A MAN IN TWO... WHY ARE YOU SO UPSET?
YOU, ME, EVERYONE ELSE... WE'RE NOT SUPPOSED TO ***BE*** HERE. THIS IS ***THEIR*** WORLD.
THESE THINGS ARE ANIMALS... THEY'RE JUST LIVING THEIR LIVES.
EXCUSE THE ***HELL*** OUT OF ME FOR WANTING TO LIVE MINE.
LISTEN, I'M LOOKING FOR A GROUP OF PEOPLE, LIVING OUTSIDE THE CITY.
I CAN TAKE YOU ALL BACK. CAN YOU BRING ME TO THEM?
I DON'T ***LEAVE*** THE CITY. THIS IS MY HOME, ALWAYS WILL BE.
YOU'RE GONNA TAKE ME ***BACK?*** TAKE ME BACK ***WHERE?***
IT'S HARD TO EXPLAIN... THIS MIGHT TAKE A... THERE'S A FASTER WAY TO DO THIS. YOU JUST NEED TO ***TRUST*** ME.

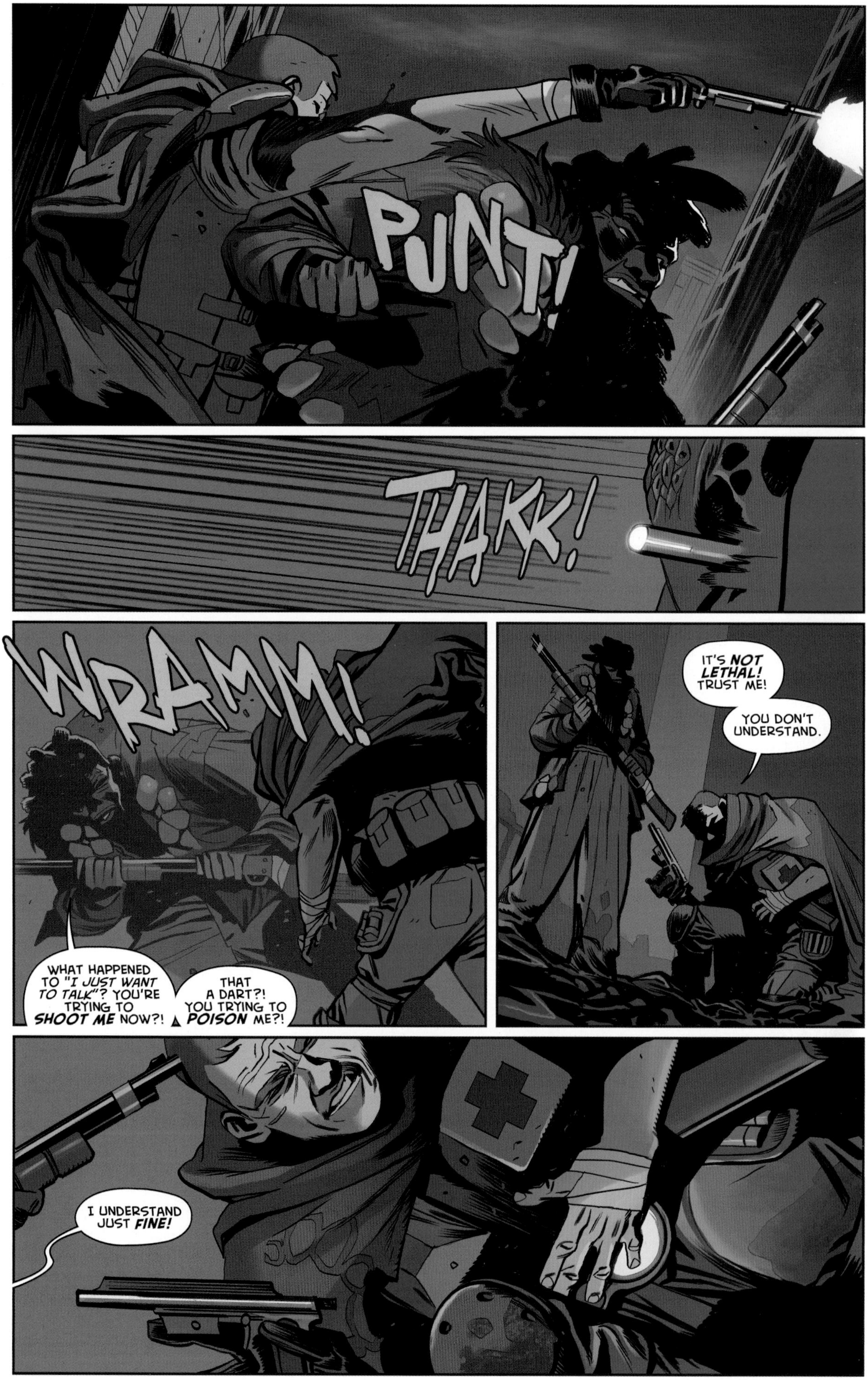
PUNT!
THAKK!
WRAMM!
WHAT HAPPENED TO "I JUST WANT TO TALK"? YOU'RE TRYING TO SHOOT ME NOW?!
THAT A DART?! YOU TRYING TO POISON ME?!
IT'S NOT LETHAL! TRUST ME!
YOU DON'T UNDERSTAND.
I UNDERSTAND JUST FINE!

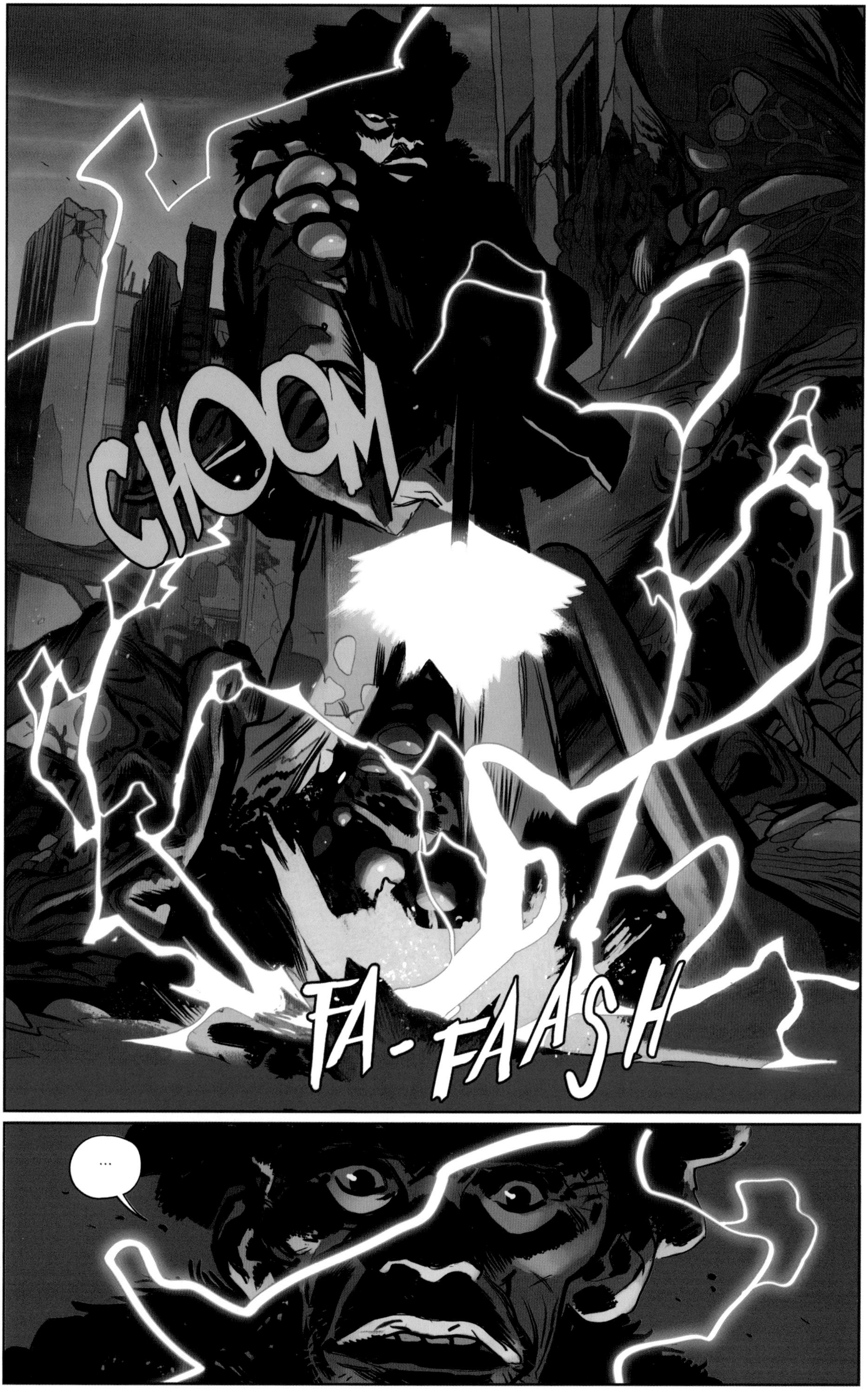
CHOOM
FA-FAASH
...

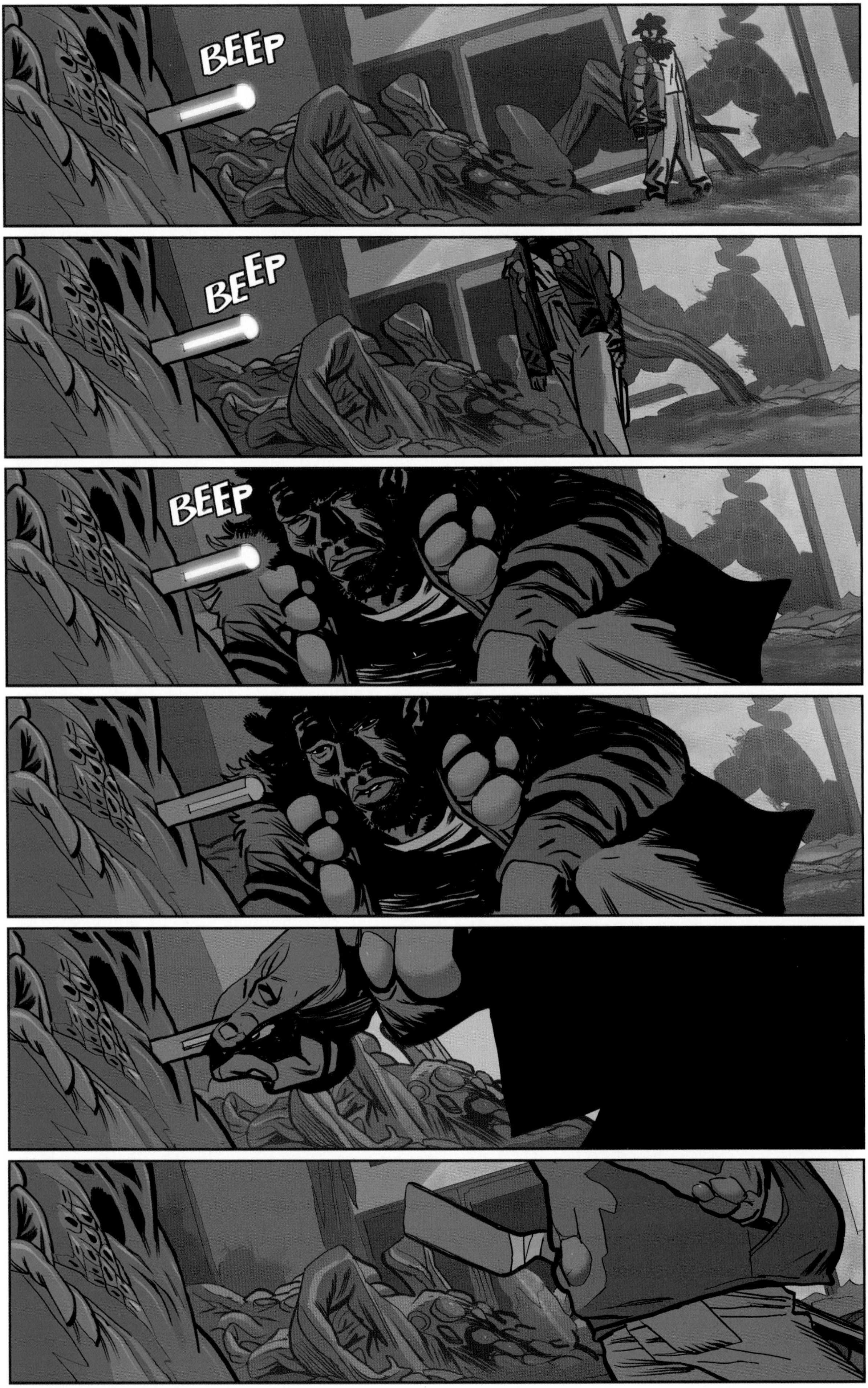
BEEP
BEEP
BEEP

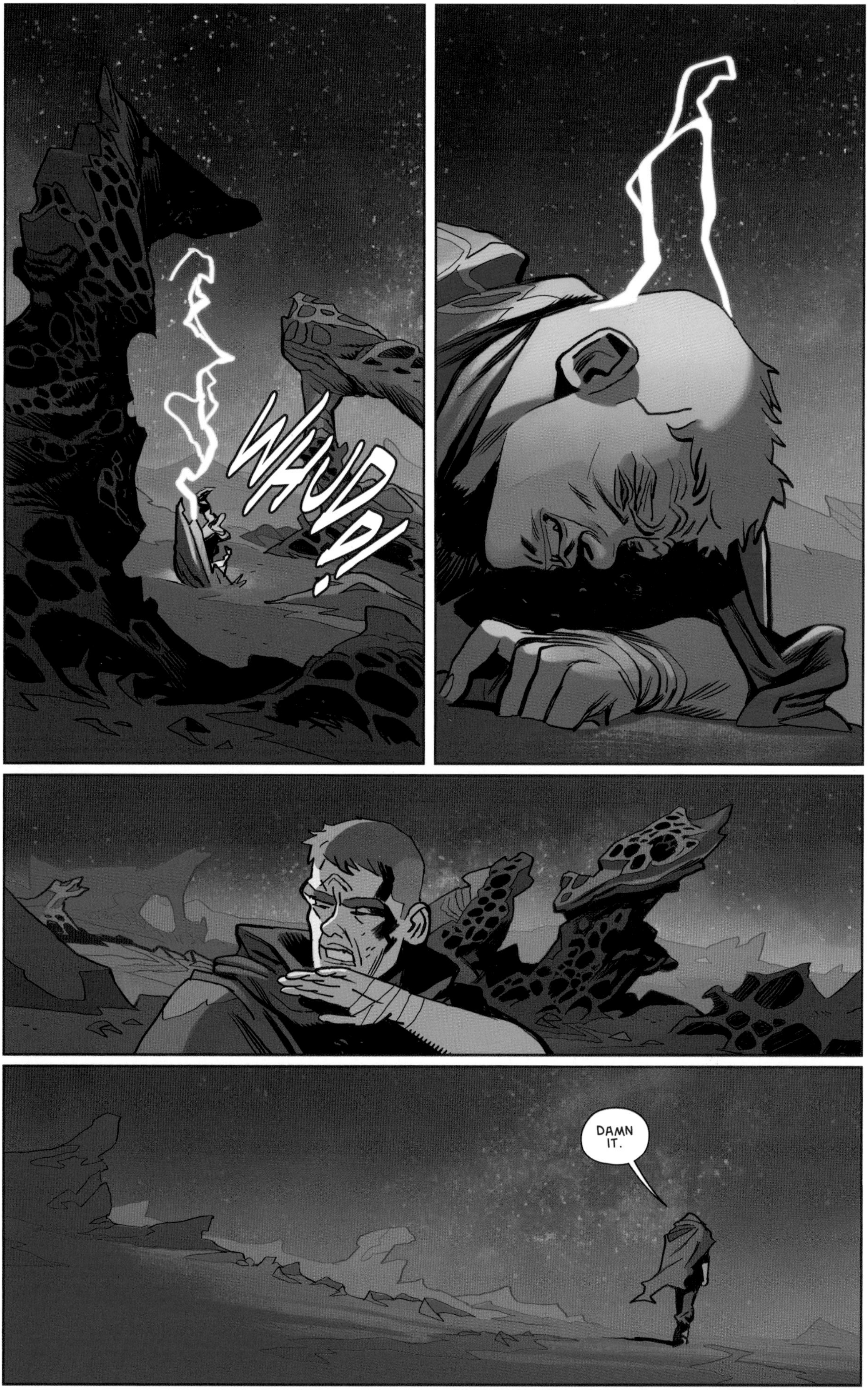
WHUDD!
DAMN IT.

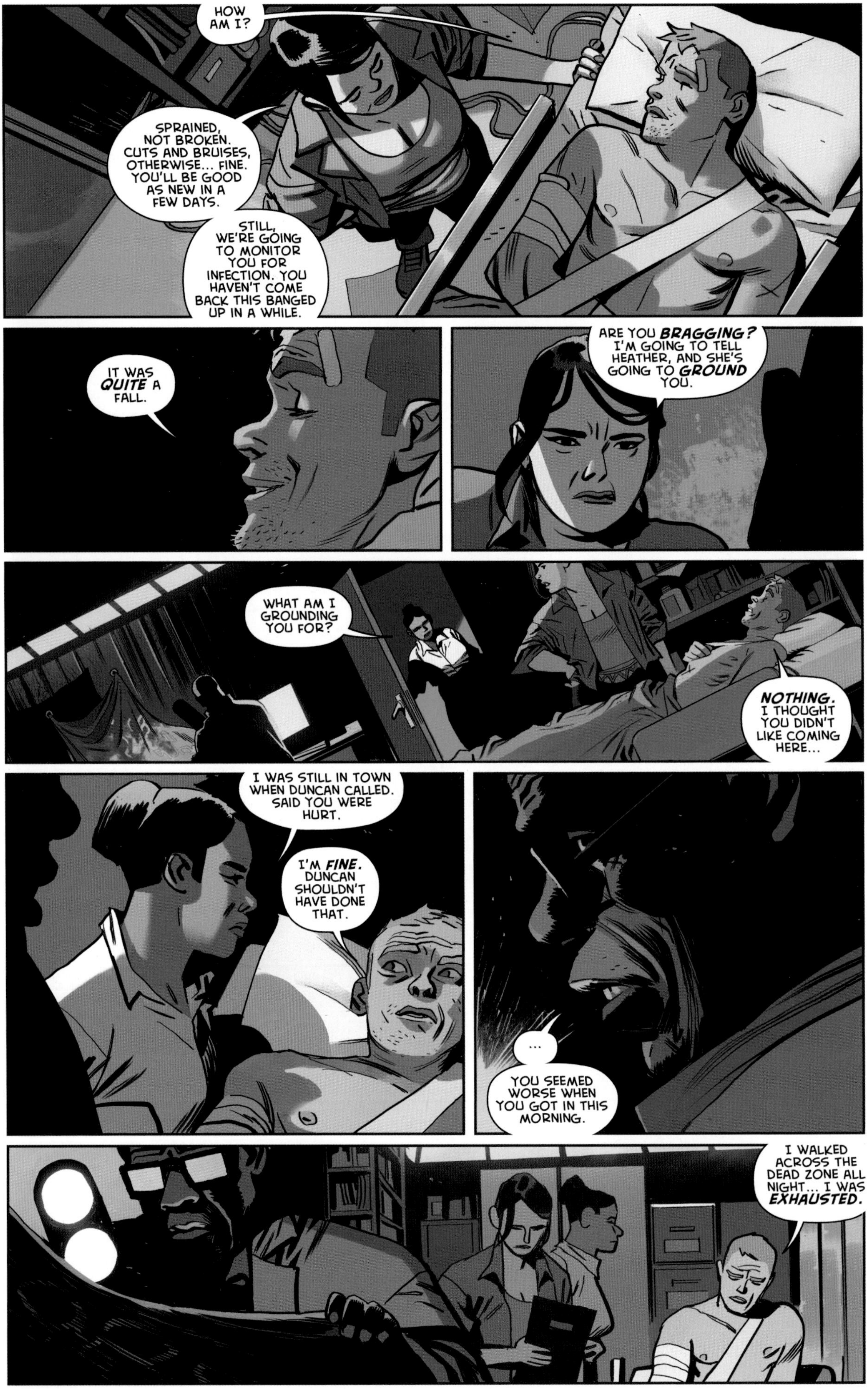

HOW AM I?
SPRAINED, NOT BROKEN. CUTS AND BRUISES, OTHERWISE... FINE. YOU'LL BE GOOD AS NEW IN A FEW DAYS.
STILL, WE'RE GOING TO MONITOR YOU FOR INFECTION. YOU HAVEN'T COME BACK THIS BANGED UP IN A WHILE.
IT WAS QUITE A FALL.
ARE YOU BRAGGING? I'M GOING TO TELL HEATHER, AND SHE'S GOING TO GROUND YOU.
WHAT AM I GROUNDING YOU FOR?
NOTHING. I THOUGHT YOU DIDN'T LIKE COMING HERE...
I WAS STILL IN TOWN WHEN DUNCAN CALLED. SAID YOU WERE HURT.
I'M FINE. DUNCAN SHOULDN'T HAVE DONE THAT.
...
YOU SEEMED WORSE WHEN YOU GOT IN THIS MORNING.
I WALKED ACROSS THE DEAD ZONE ALL NIGHT... I WAS EXHAUSTED.

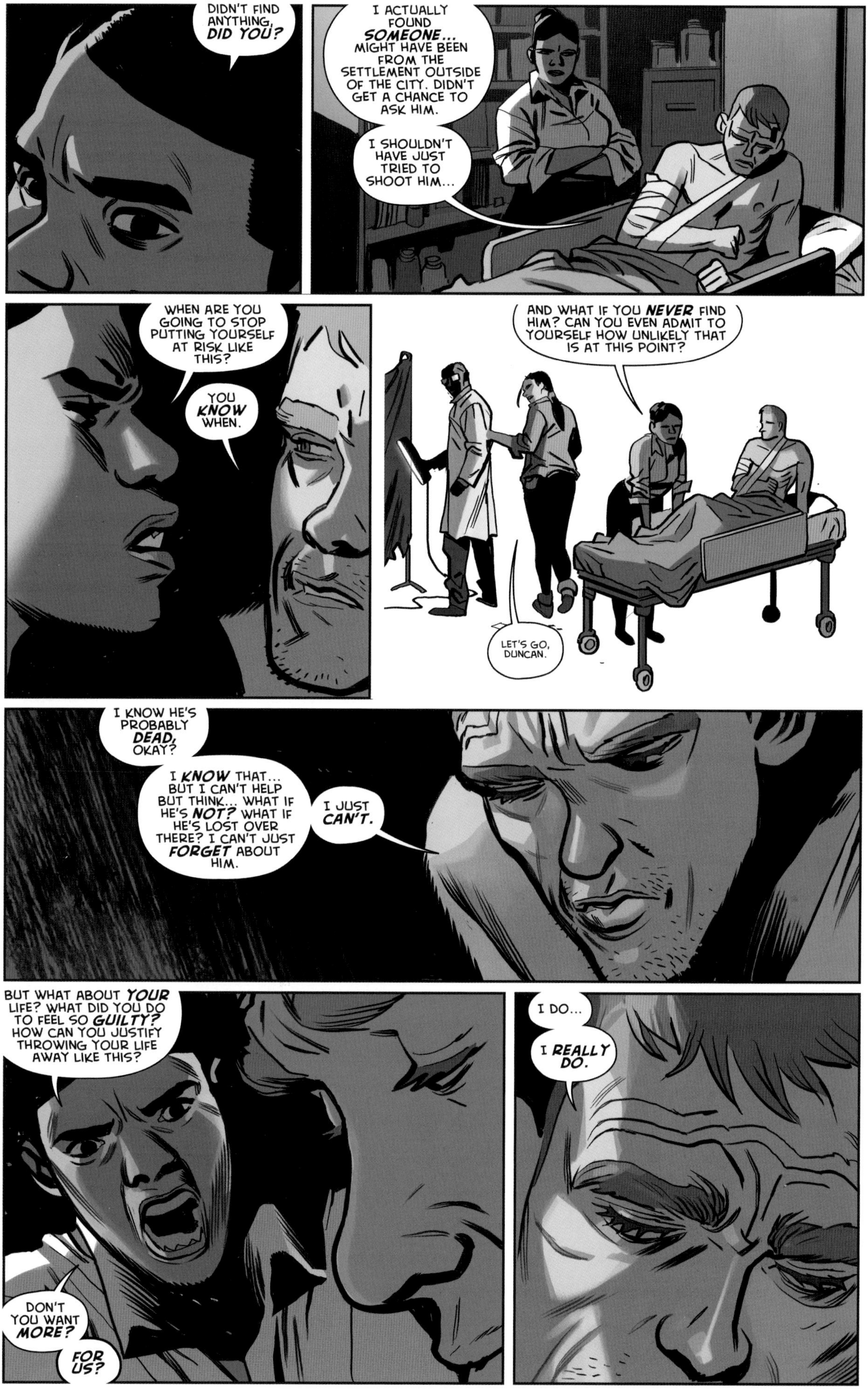
DIDN'T FIND ANYTHING, DID YOU?
I ACTUALLY FOUND SOMEONE... MIGHT HAVE BEEN FROM THE SETTLEMENT OUTSIDE OF THE CITY. DIDN'T GET A CHANCE TO ASK HIM.
I SHOULDN'T HAVE JUST TRIED TO SHOOT HIM...
WHEN ARE YOU GOING TO STOP PUTTING YOURSELF AT RISK LIKE THIS?
YOU KNOW WHEN.
AND WHAT IF YOU NEVER FIND HIM? CAN YOU EVEN ADMIT TO YOURSELF HOW UNLIKELY THAT IS AT THIS POINT?
LET'S GO, DUNCAN.
I KNOW HE'S PROBABLY DEAD, OKAY?
I KNOW THAT... BUT I CAN'T HELP BUT THINK... WHAT IF HE'S NOT? WHAT IF HE'S LOST OVER THERE? I CAN'T JUST FORGET ABOUT HIM.
I JUST CAN'T.
BUT WHAT ABOUT YOUR LIFE? WHAT DID YOU DO TO FEEL SO GUILTY? HOW CAN YOU JUSTIFY THROWING YOUR LIFE AWAY LIKE THIS?
DON'T YOU WANT MORE?
FOR US?
I DO...
I REALLY DO.

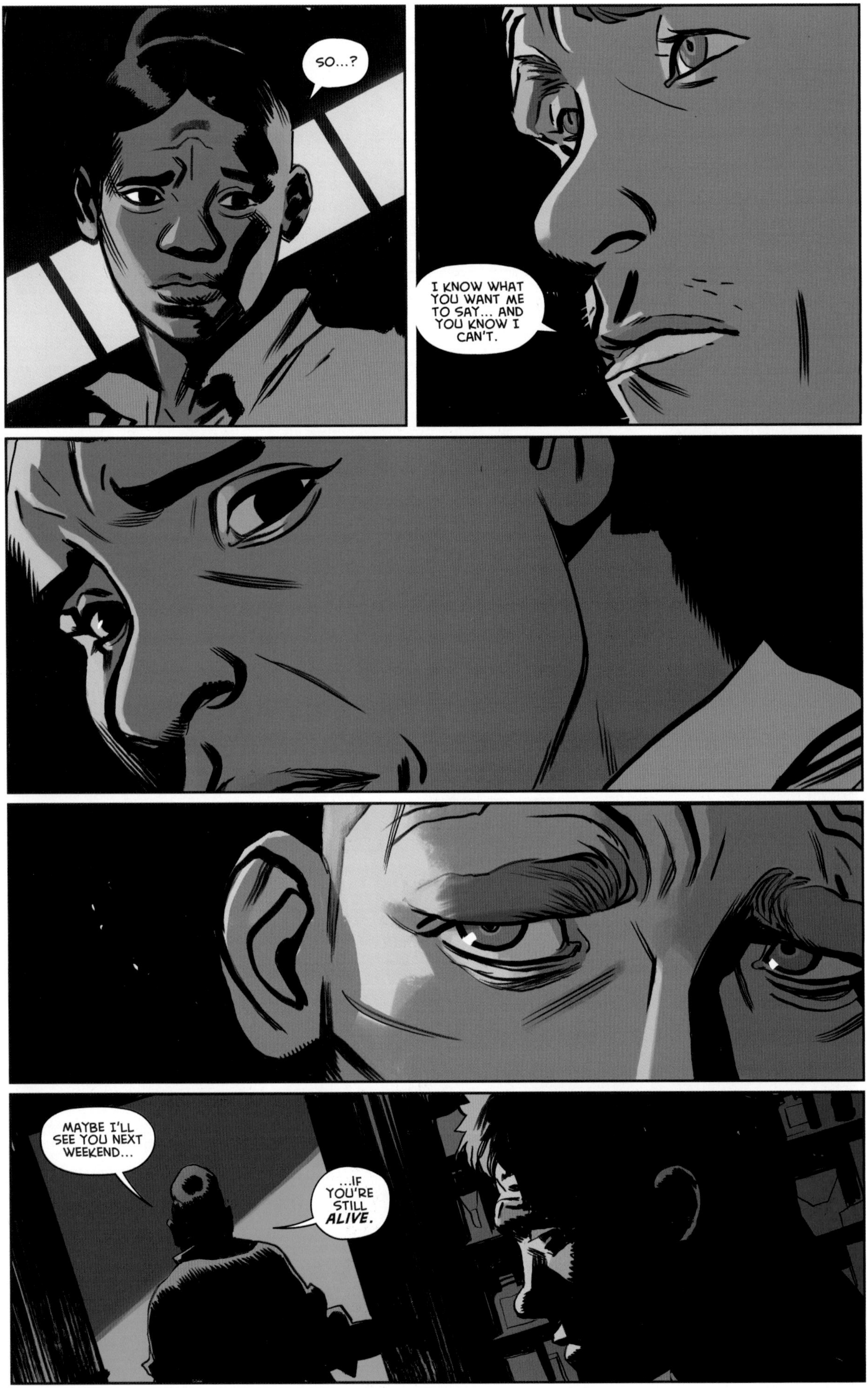
SO...?
I KNOW WHAT YOU WANT ME TO SAY... AND YOU KNOW I CAN'T.
MAYBE I'LL SEE YOU NEXT WEEKEND...
...IF YOU'RE STILL *ALIVE*.

MAYBE IT *IS* TIME TO QUIT.

WHAT?

TRUTH OF THE MATTER IS... EVEN IF YOU SAVE PEOPLE, IT'S NOT REALLY THE PEOPLE THEY *WERE* YOU'RE SAVING. THE CRENSHAWS ARE FINDING OUT JUST HOW HARD IT IS TO COME BACK HERE.

SPEAKING FROM EXPERIENCE... I DON'T KNOW HOW I'D READJUST IF IT HAD TAKEN YOU ANOTHER YEAR TO FIND ME.

NOW YOU'VE GOT PEOPLE LIVING OUTSIDE THE CITY... IN THE WILDS OF OBLIVION? WHO ARE *THEY* NOW? THEY'RE GOING TO COME BACK AND GET DAY JOBS? DROP THEIR KIDS OFF AT SCHOOL?

YOU MIGHT AS WELL TEACH A WOLF TO DRIVE A CAR.

YOU DON'T BELIEVE THAT. THE CRENSHAWS ARE DOING FINE.

LOOK AT YOU. *YOU'RE* OKAY.

I'M GETTING BY... BUT I AM *NOT* OKAY.

IF THE CRENSHAWS SAY THESE PEOPLE DON'T *WANT* TO COME BACK... *LEAVE THEM*.

YOU'VE GIVEN ENOUGH OF YOUR LIFE TO THIS. IT'S NOT YOUR CROSS TO BEAR. YOU DON'T OWE ANYONE ANYTHING.

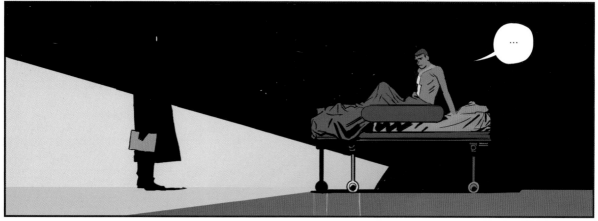

...

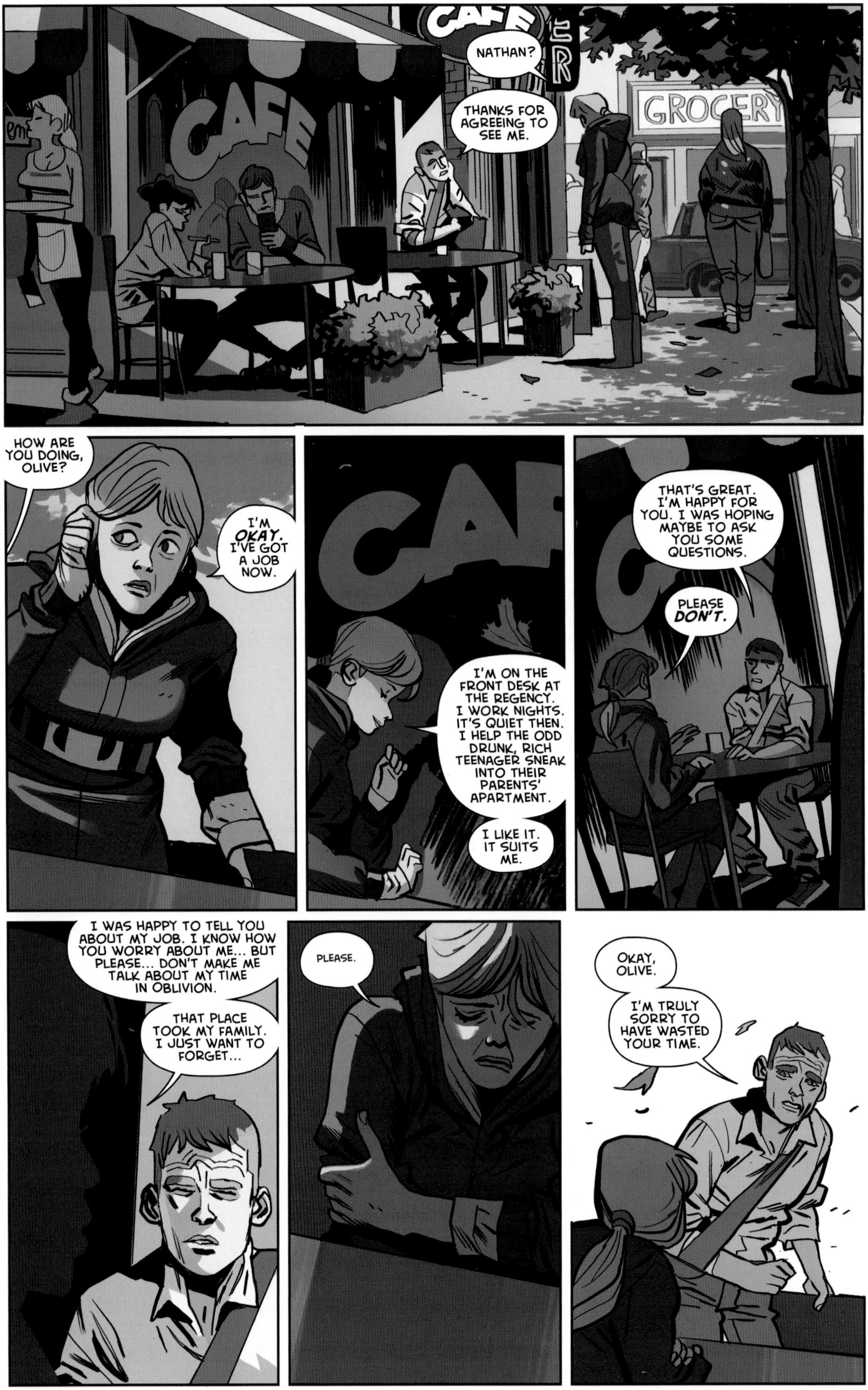
CAFE
GROCERY
NATHAN?
THANKS FOR AGREEING TO SEE ME.
HOW ARE YOU DOING, OLIVE?
I'M *OKAY*. I'VE GOT A JOB NOW.
I'M ON THE FRONT DESK AT THE REGENCY. I WORK NIGHTS. IT'S QUIET THEN. I HELP THE ODD DRUNK, RICH TEENAGER SNEAK INTO THEIR PARENTS' APARTMENT.
I LIKE IT. IT SUITS ME.
THAT'S GREAT. I'M HAPPY FOR YOU. I WAS HOPING MAYBE TO ASK YOU SOME QUESTIONS.
PLEASE *DON'T*.
I WAS HAPPY TO TELL YOU ABOUT MY JOB. I KNOW HOW YOU WORRY ABOUT ME... BUT PLEASE... DON'T MAKE ME TALK ABOUT MY TIME IN OBLIVION.
THAT PLACE TOOK MY FAMILY. I JUST WANT TO FORGET...
PLEASE.
OKAY, OLIVE.
I'M TRULY SORRY TO HAVE WASTED YOUR TIME.

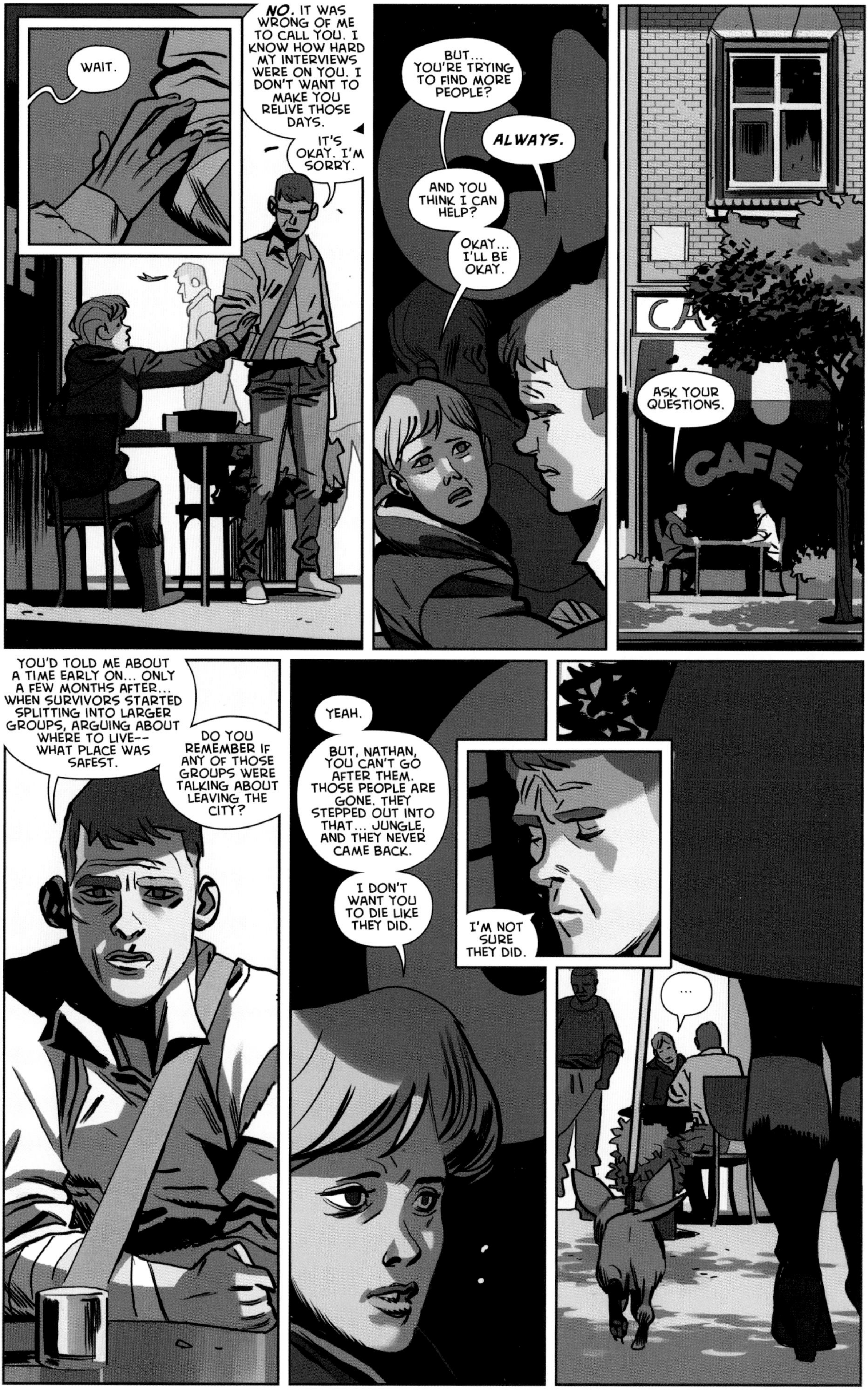
WAIT.
NO. IT WAS WRONG OF ME TO CALL YOU. I KNOW HOW HARD MY INTERVIEWS WERE ON YOU. I DON'T WANT TO MAKE YOU RELIVE THOSE DAYS.
IT'S OKAY. I'M SORRY.
BUT... YOU'RE TRYING TO FIND MORE PEOPLE?
ALWAYS.
AND YOU THINK I CAN HELP?
OKAY... I'LL BE OKAY.
CA
ASK YOUR QUESTIONS.
CAFE
YOU'D TOLD ME ABOUT A TIME EARLY ON... ONLY A FEW MONTHS AFTER... WHEN SURVIVORS STARTED SPLITTING INTO LARGER GROUPS, ARGUING ABOUT WHERE TO LIVE-- WHAT PLACE WAS SAFEST.
DO YOU REMEMBER IF ANY OF THOSE GROUPS WERE TALKING ABOUT LEAVING THE CITY?
YEAH.
BUT, NATHAN, YOU CAN'T GO AFTER THEM. THOSE PEOPLE ARE GONE. THEY STEPPED OUT INTO THAT... JUNGLE, AND THEY NEVER CAME BACK.
I DON'T WANT YOU TO DIE LIKE THEY DID.
I'M NOT SURE THEY DID.
...

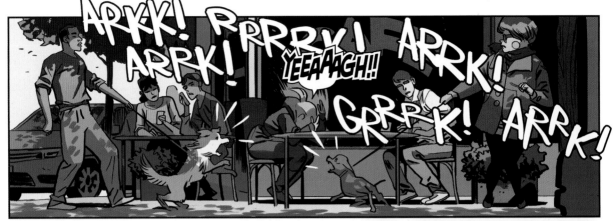

ARKK! RRRRK! ARRK!

ARRK! *YEEAAACH!!* ARRK!

GRRRK! ARRK!

MISTY! HEEL! MISTY!

BAD DOG!

IT'S JUST DOGS, OLIVE. YOU'RE OKAY.

IT'S JUST DOGS.

I'M SORRY. I'M SORRY.

IT'S *OKAY.* DON'T APOLOGIZE.

I'M STILL NOT GOOD WITH... NOISES... THEY... IT'S JUST SO HARD TO BELIEVE I'M *HERE*... AND I'M *SAFE.*

DO YOU UNDERSTAND? I WAS IN THAT NIGHTMARE FOR SO LONG.

IS IT SOMETIMES *HARDER*... BEING *HERE?*

WHAT? NO.

NEVER. I'VE *NEVER* THOUGHT THAT. READJUSTING... IT'S BEEN DIFFICULT. IT'S TAKEN YEARS, AND I'M STILL NOT DONE.

BUT MY HARDEST DAY HERE IS NOTHING COMPARED TO THAT PLACE.

WHY WOULD YOU *SAY* THAT?

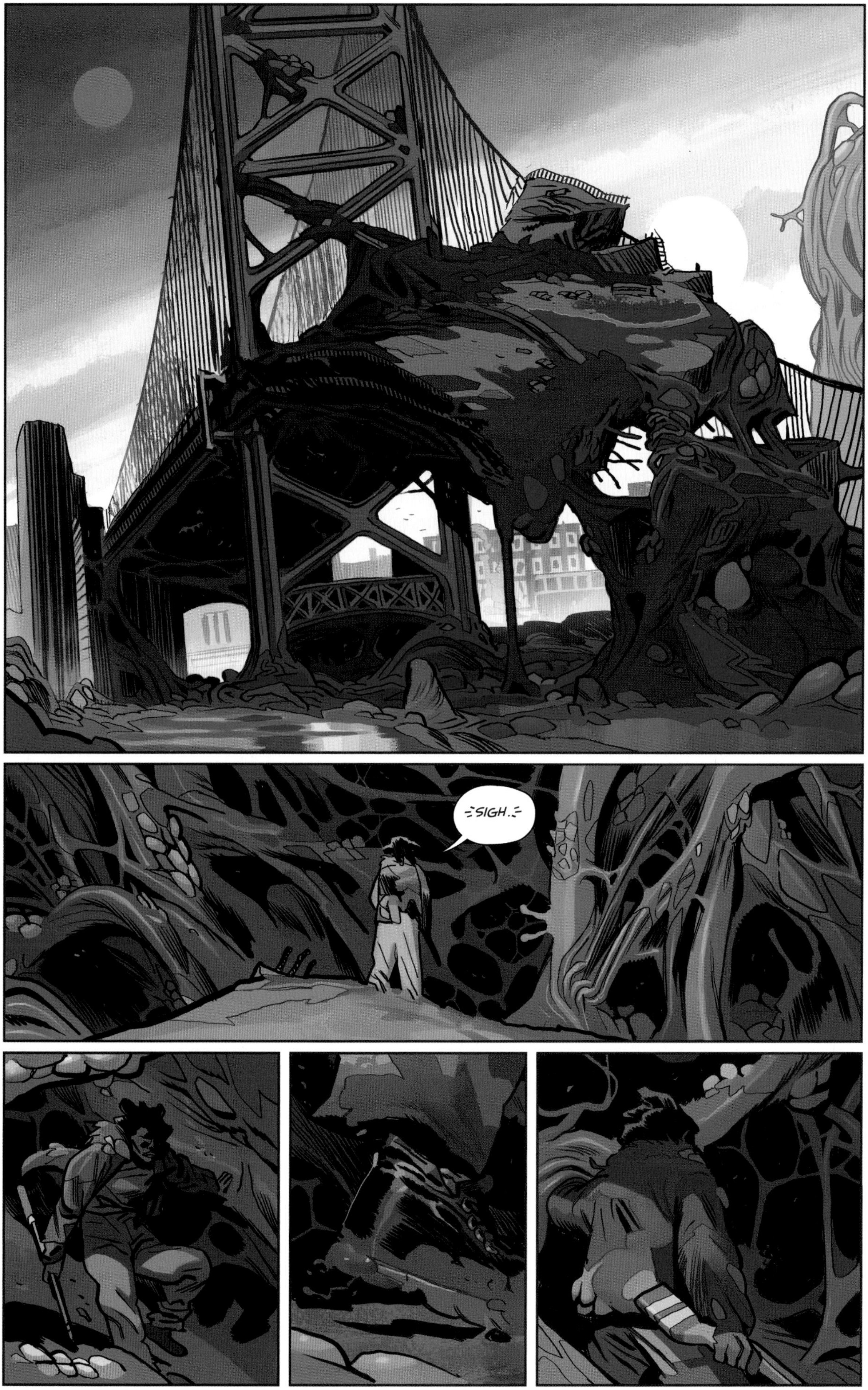
SIGH.

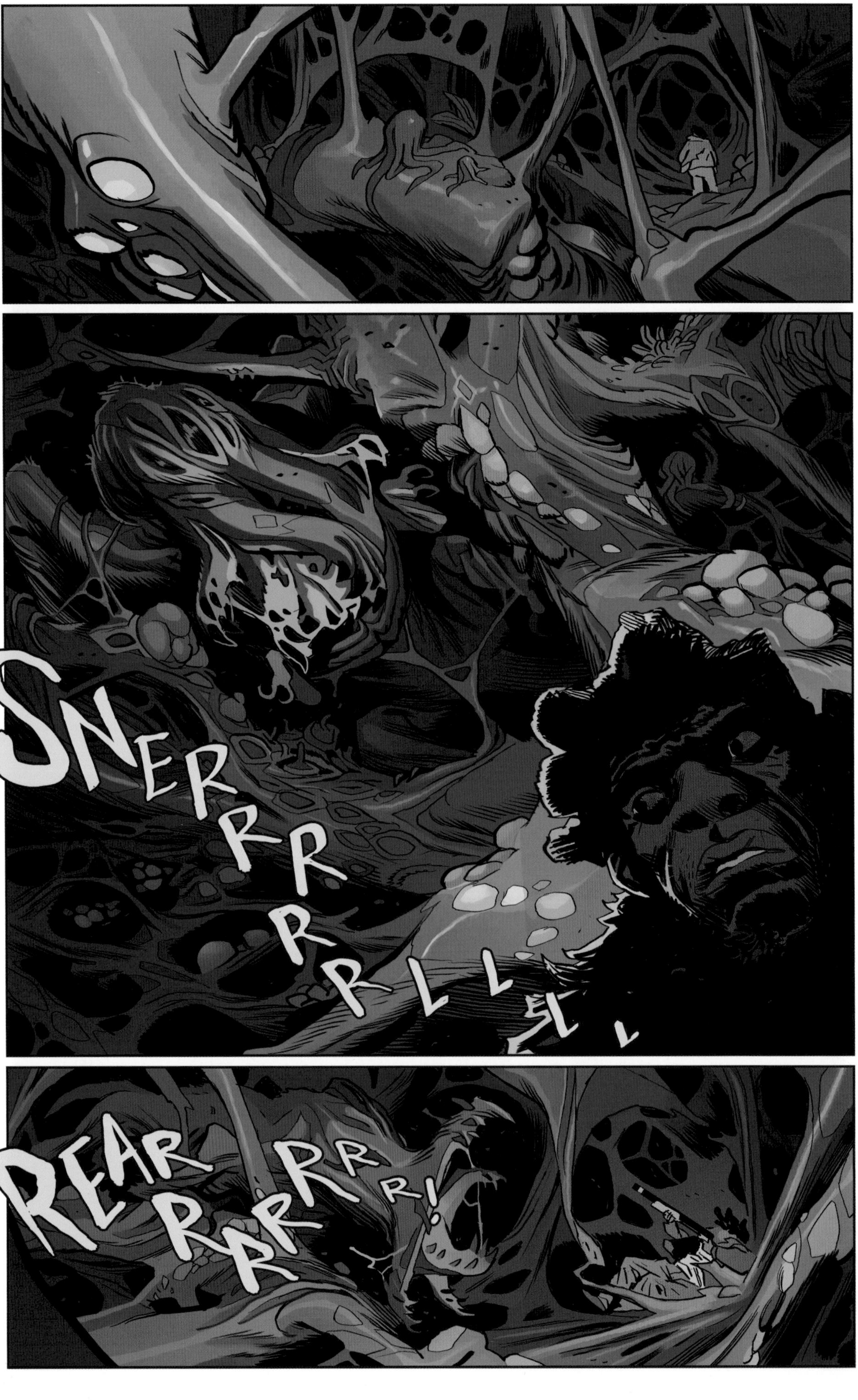
SNERRRRRLLLLL
REARRRRRRRI!

WRAKK

GRRRWGLLL

≡NNGH!≡

PPKOW PKOW PKOW

SKREEEEE

WHUMP

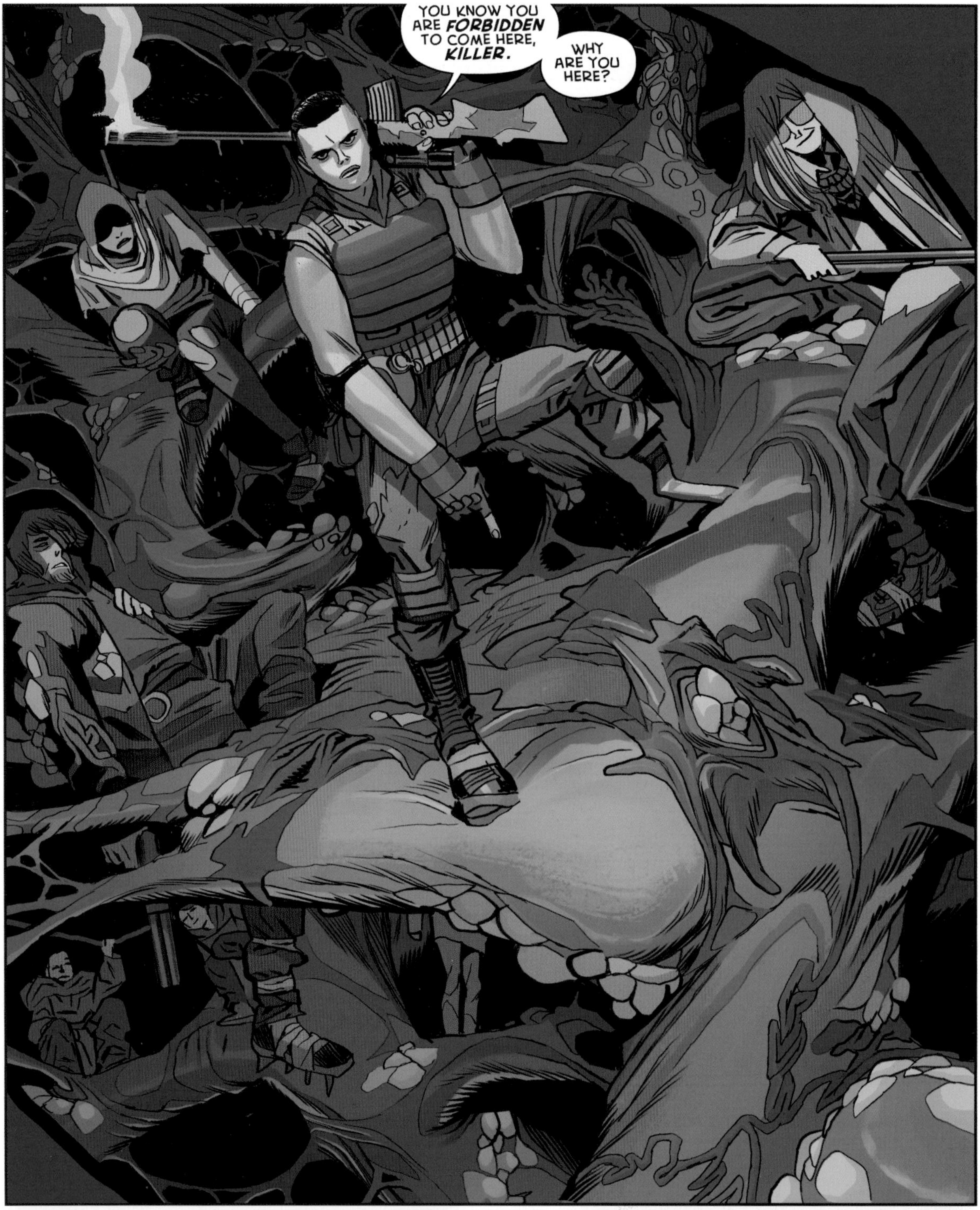
YOU KNOW YOU ARE FORBIDDEN TO COME HERE, KILLER.
WHY ARE YOU HERE?

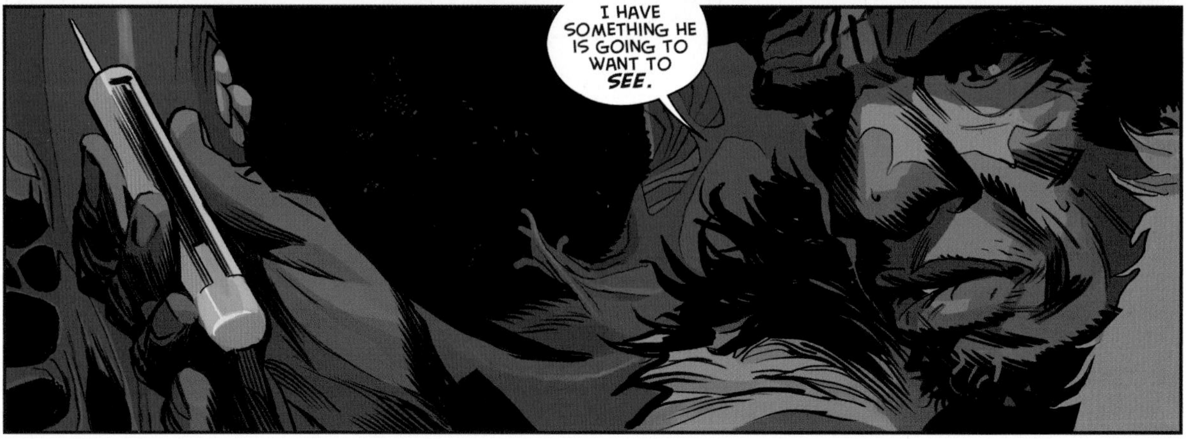
I HAVE SOMETHING HE IS GOING TO WANT TO SEE.

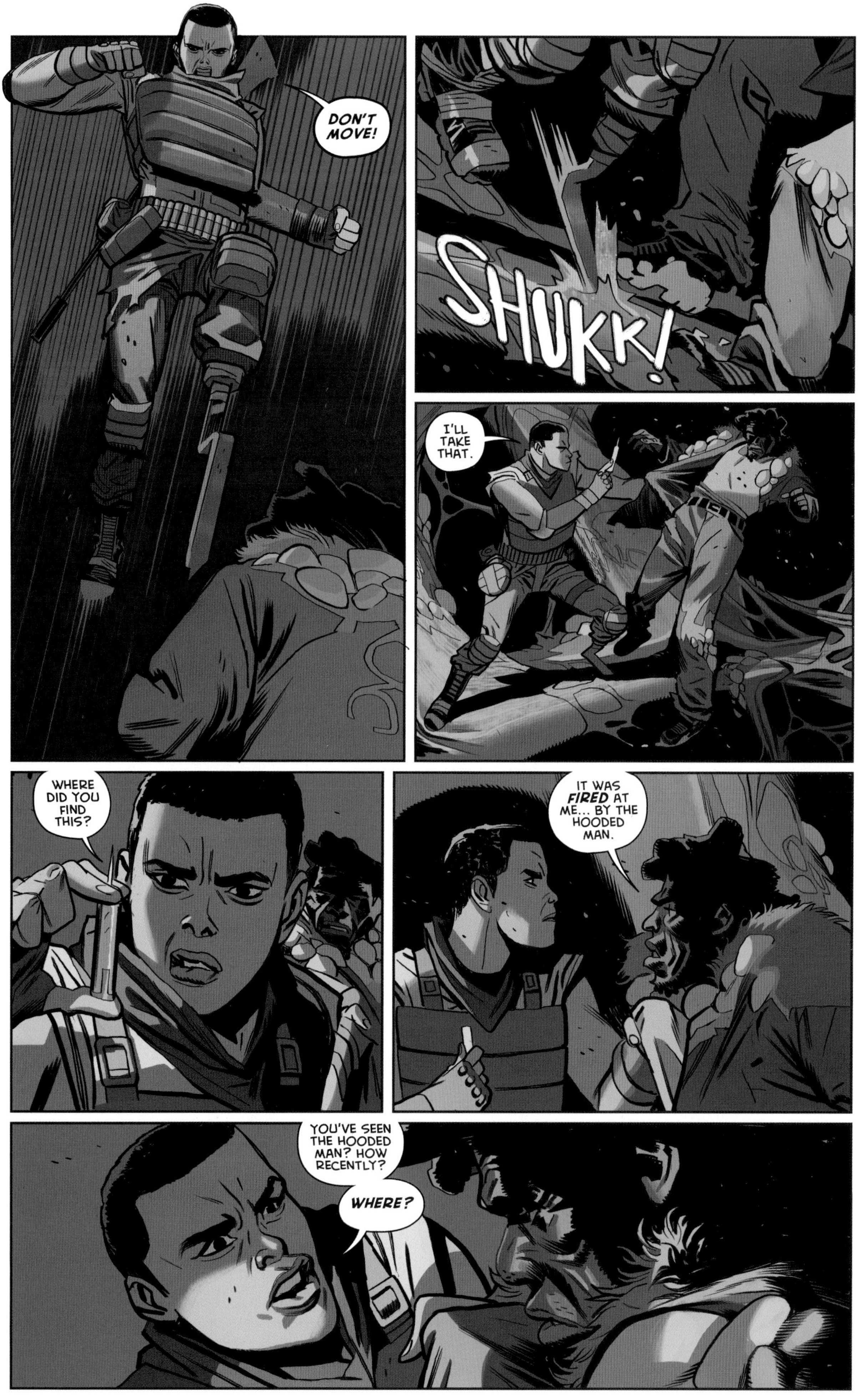
DON'T MOVE!
SHUKK!
I'LL TAKE THAT.
WHERE DID YOU FIND THIS?
IT WAS FIRED AT ME... BY THE HOODED MAN.
YOU'VE SEEN THE HOODED MAN? HOW RECENTLY?
WHERE?

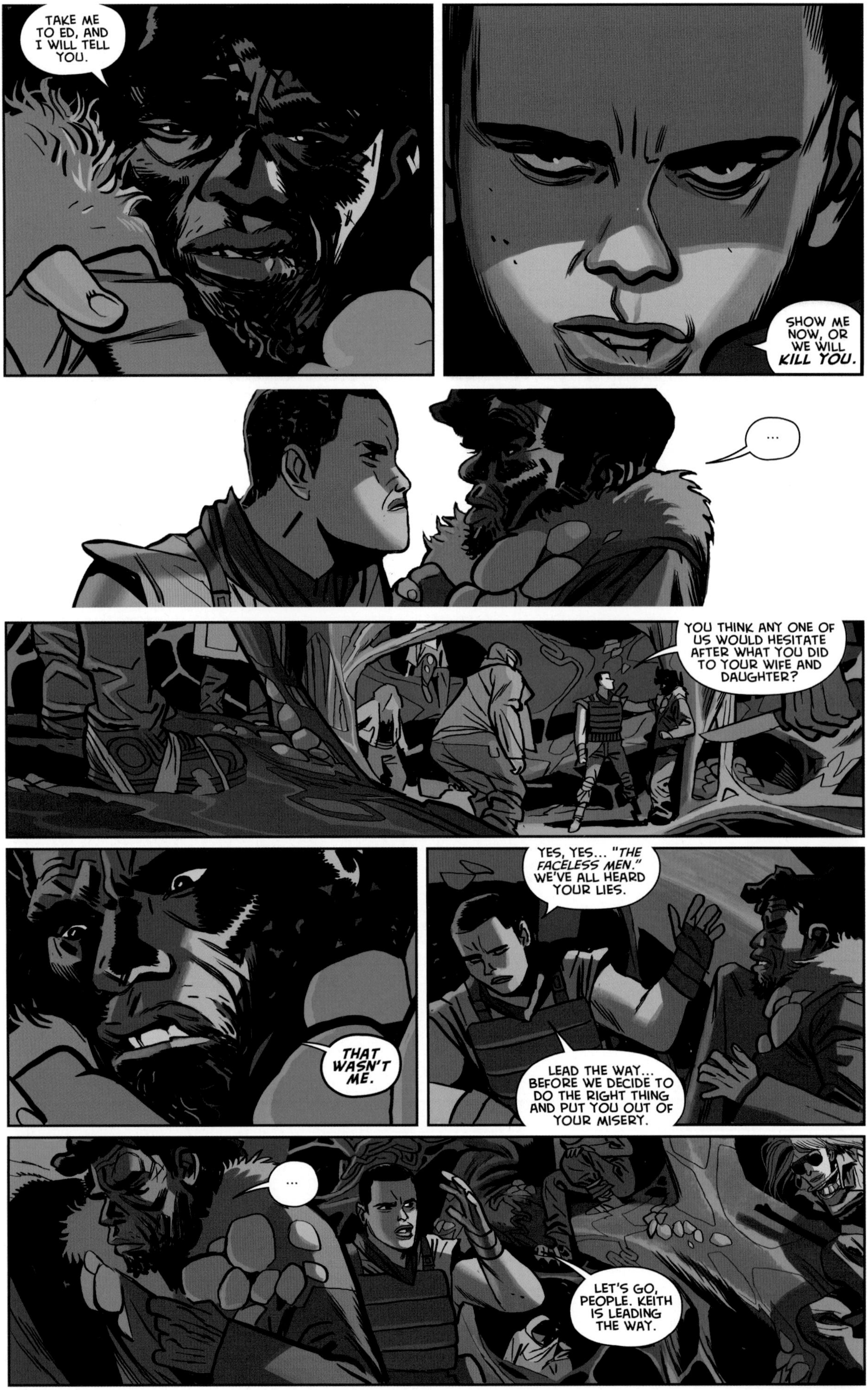
TAKE ME TO ED, AND I WILL TELL YOU.
SHOW ME NOW, OR WE WILL KILL YOU.
...
YOU THINK ANY ONE OF US WOULD HESITATE AFTER WHAT YOU DID TO YOUR WIFE AND DAUGHTER?
THAT WASN'T ME.
YES, YES... "THE FACELESS MEN." WE'VE ALL HEARD YOUR LIES.
LEAD THE WAY... BEFORE WE DECIDE TO DO THE RIGHT THING AND PUT YOU OUT OF YOUR MISERY.
...
LET'S GO, PEOPLE. KEITH IS LEADING THE WAY.

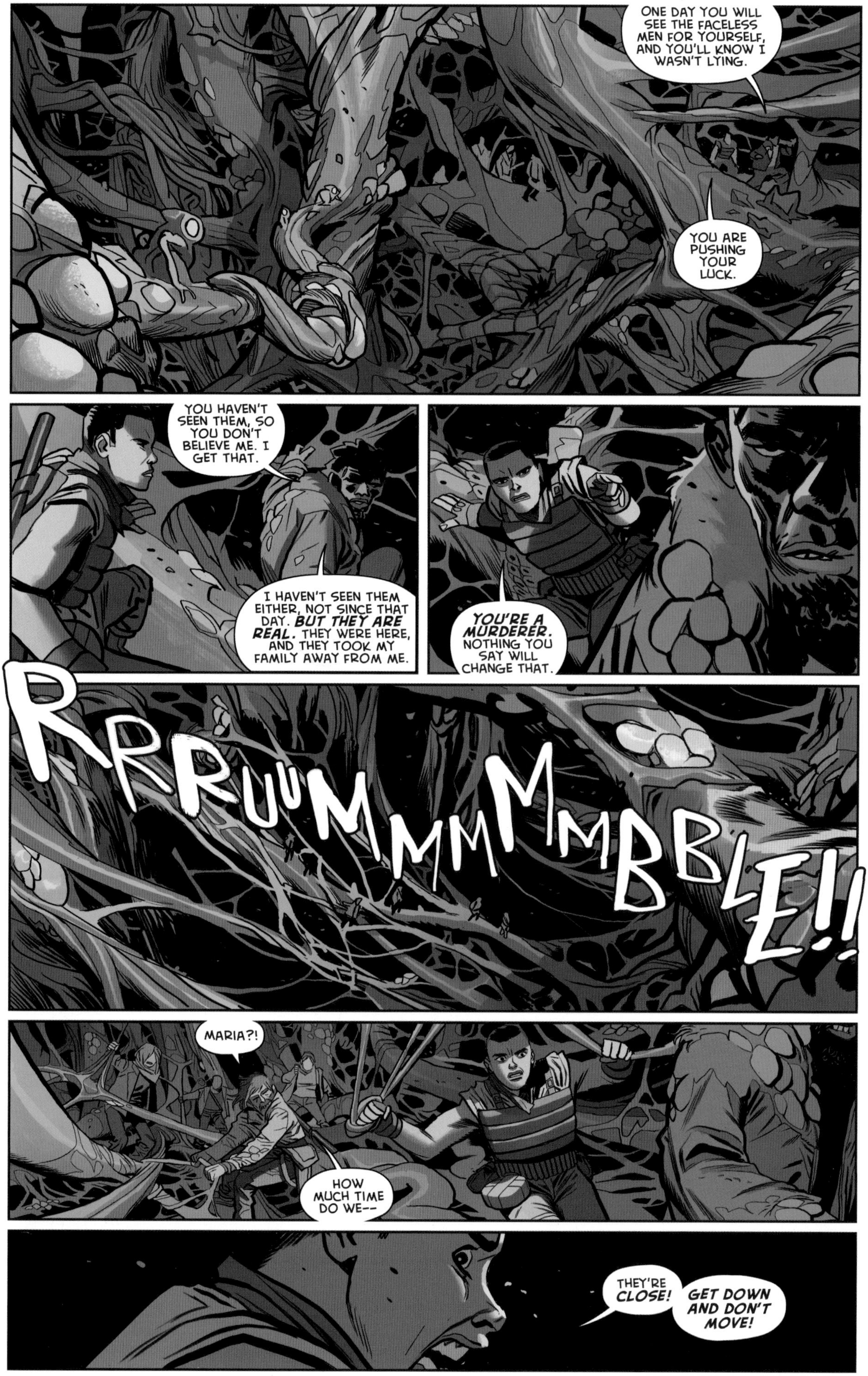
ONE DAY YOU WILL SEE THE FACELESS MEN FOR YOURSELF, AND YOU'LL KNOW I WASN'T LYING.
YOU ARE PUSHING YOUR LUCK.
YOU HAVEN'T SEEN THEM, SO YOU DON'T BELIEVE ME. I GET THAT.
I HAVEN'T SEEN THEM EITHER, NOT SINCE THAT DAY. BUT THEY ARE REAL. THEY WERE HERE, AND THEY TOOK MY FAMILY AWAY FROM ME.
YOU'RE A MURDERER. NOTHING YOU SAY WILL CHANGE THAT.
RRRUUMMMMMBBLE!!
MARIA?!
HOW MUCH TIME DO WE--
THEY'RE CLOSE!
GET DOWN AND DON'T MOVE!

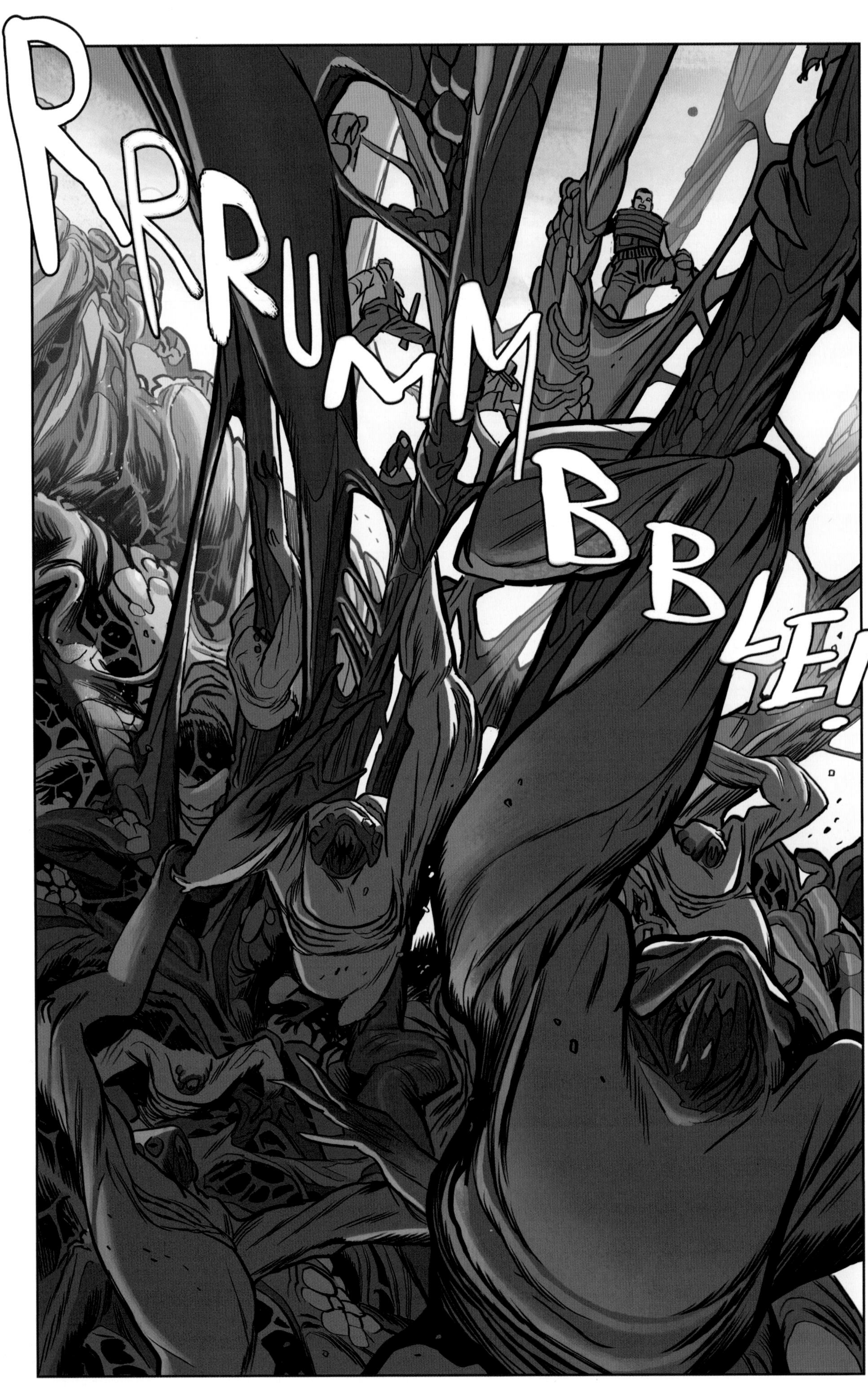
RRRUMMBBLE!

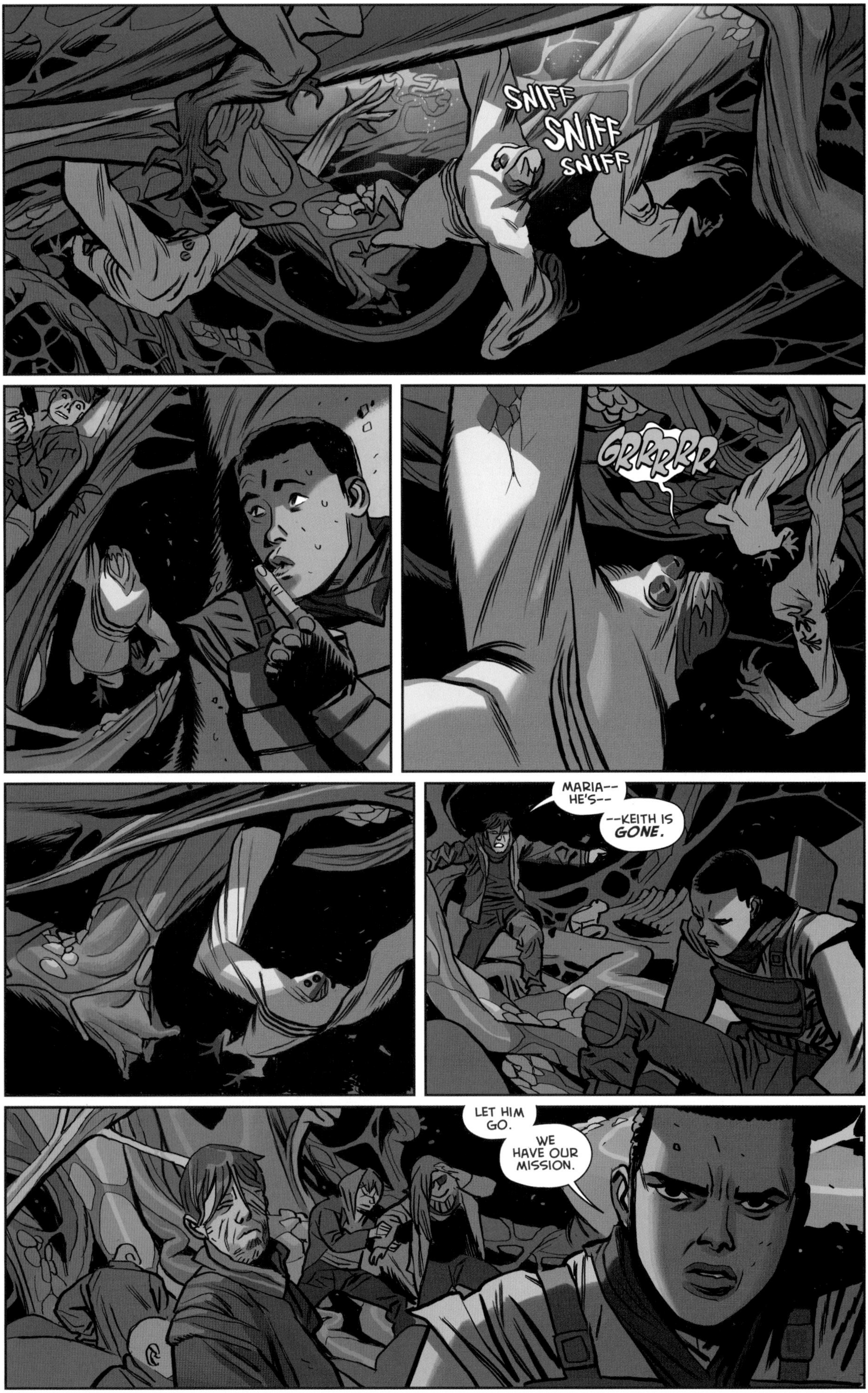
SNIFF
SNIFF
SNIFF
GRRRRR.
MARIA-- HE'S--
--KEITH IS GONE.
LET HIM GO.
WE HAVE OUR MISSION.

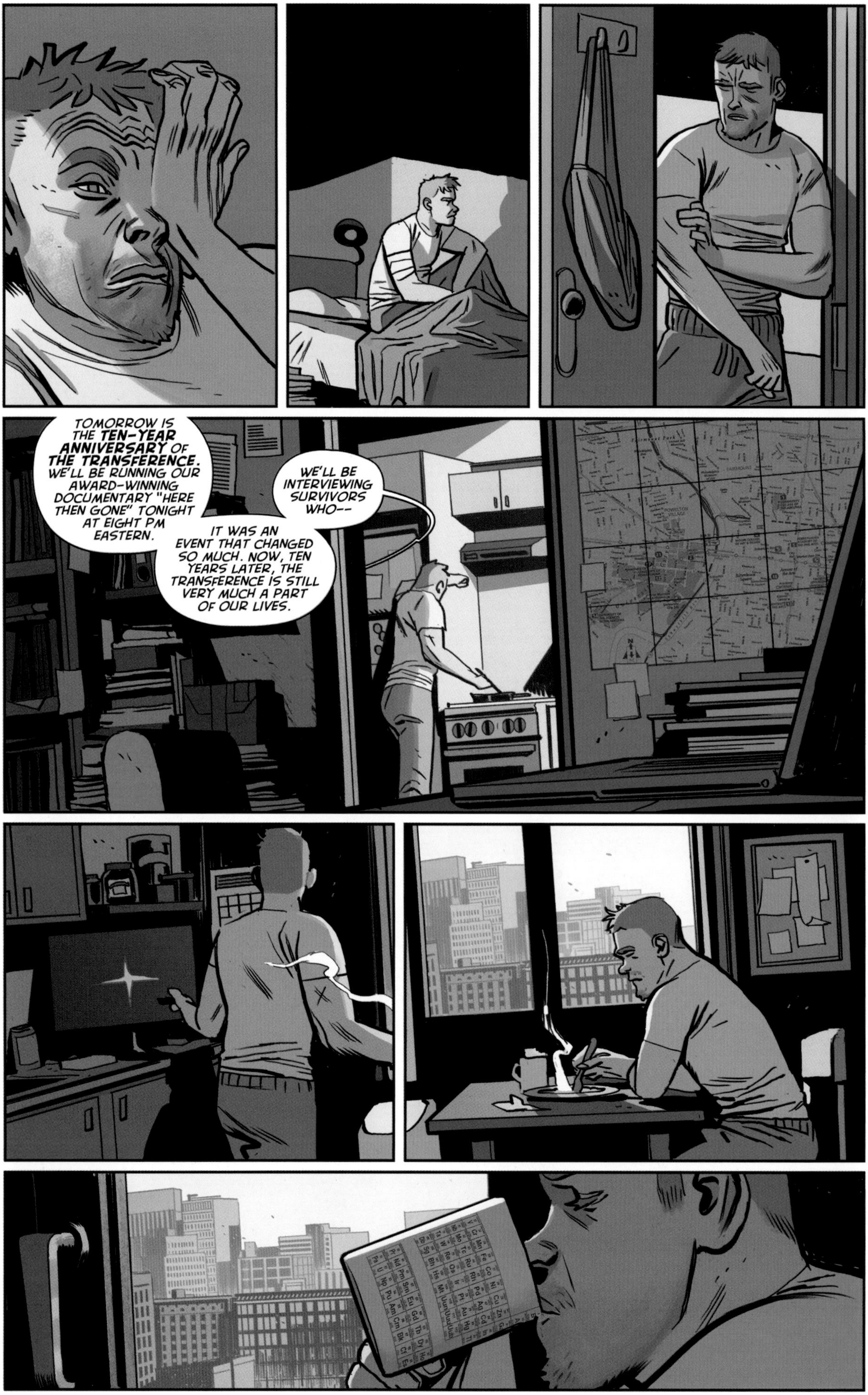
TOMORROW IS THE **TEN-YEAR ANNIVERSARY** OF **THE TRANSFERENCE**. WE'LL BE RUNNING OUR AWARD-WINNING DOCUMENTARY "HERE THEN GONE" TONIGHT AT EIGHT PM EASTERN.
WE'LL BE INTERVIEWING SURVIVORS WHO--
IT WAS AN EVENT THAT CHANGED SO MUCH. NOW, TEN YEARS LATER, THE TRANSFERENCE IS STILL VERY MUCH A PART OF OUR LIVES.

TAXI
1-4
6-2

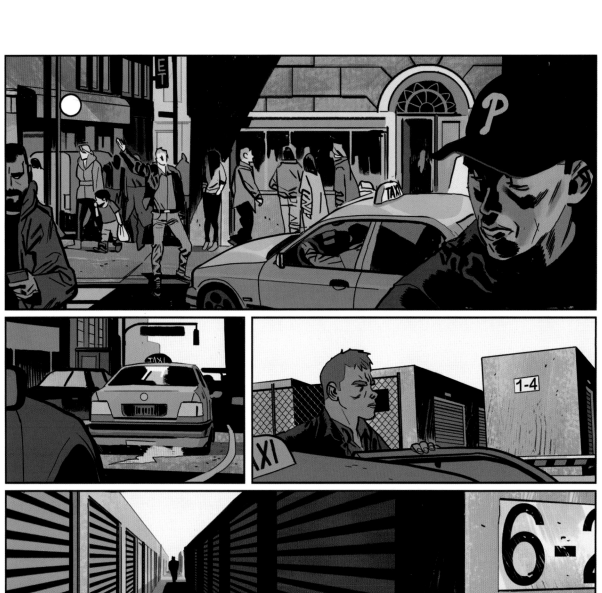

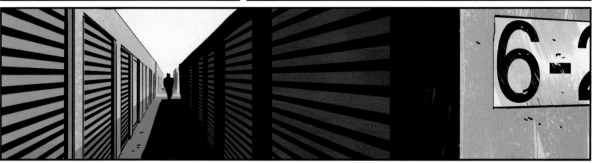

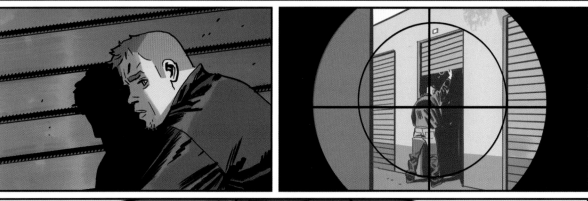

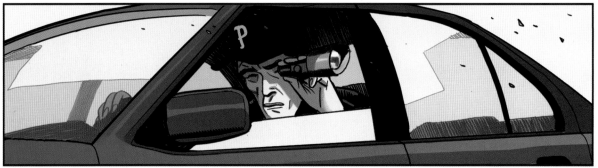

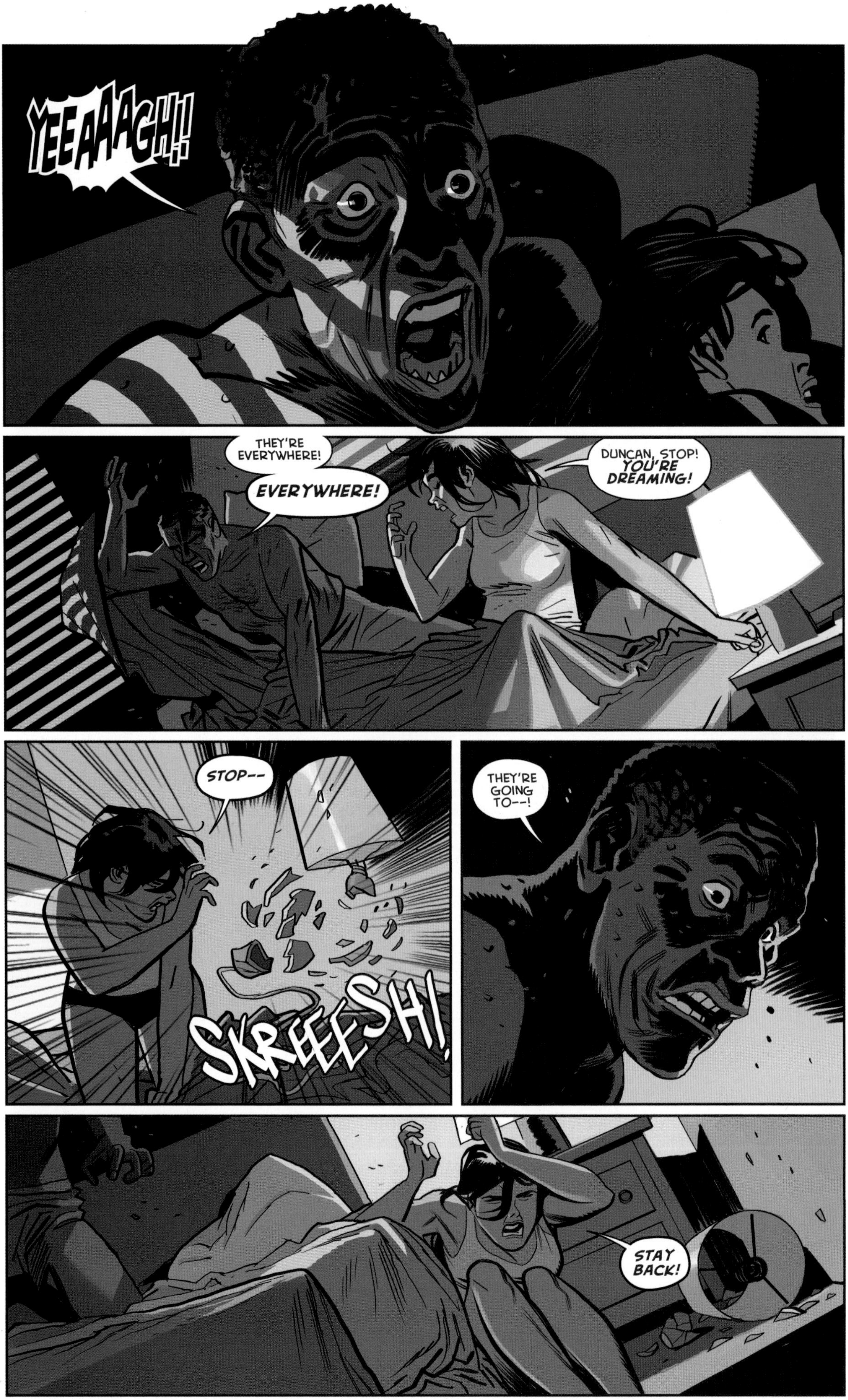

YEEAAAGH!!
THEY'RE EVERYWHERE!
EVERYWHERE!
DUNCAN, STOP! YOU'RE DREAMING!
STOP--
SKREEESH!
THEY'RE GOING TO--!
STAY BACK!

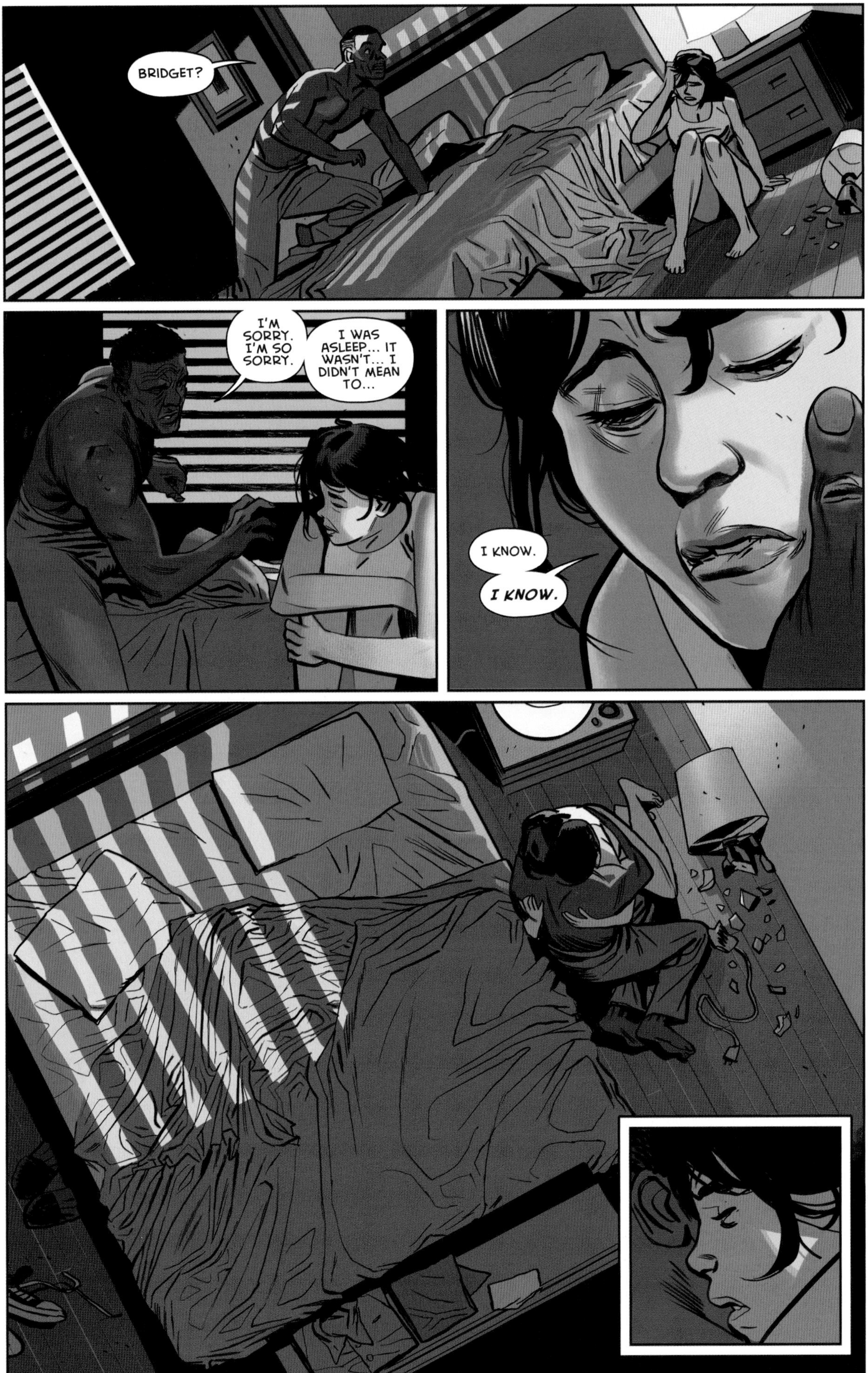
BRIDGET?
I'M SORRY. I'M SO SORRY.
I WAS ASLEEP... IT WASN'T... I DIDN'T MEAN TO...
I KNOW.
I KNOW.

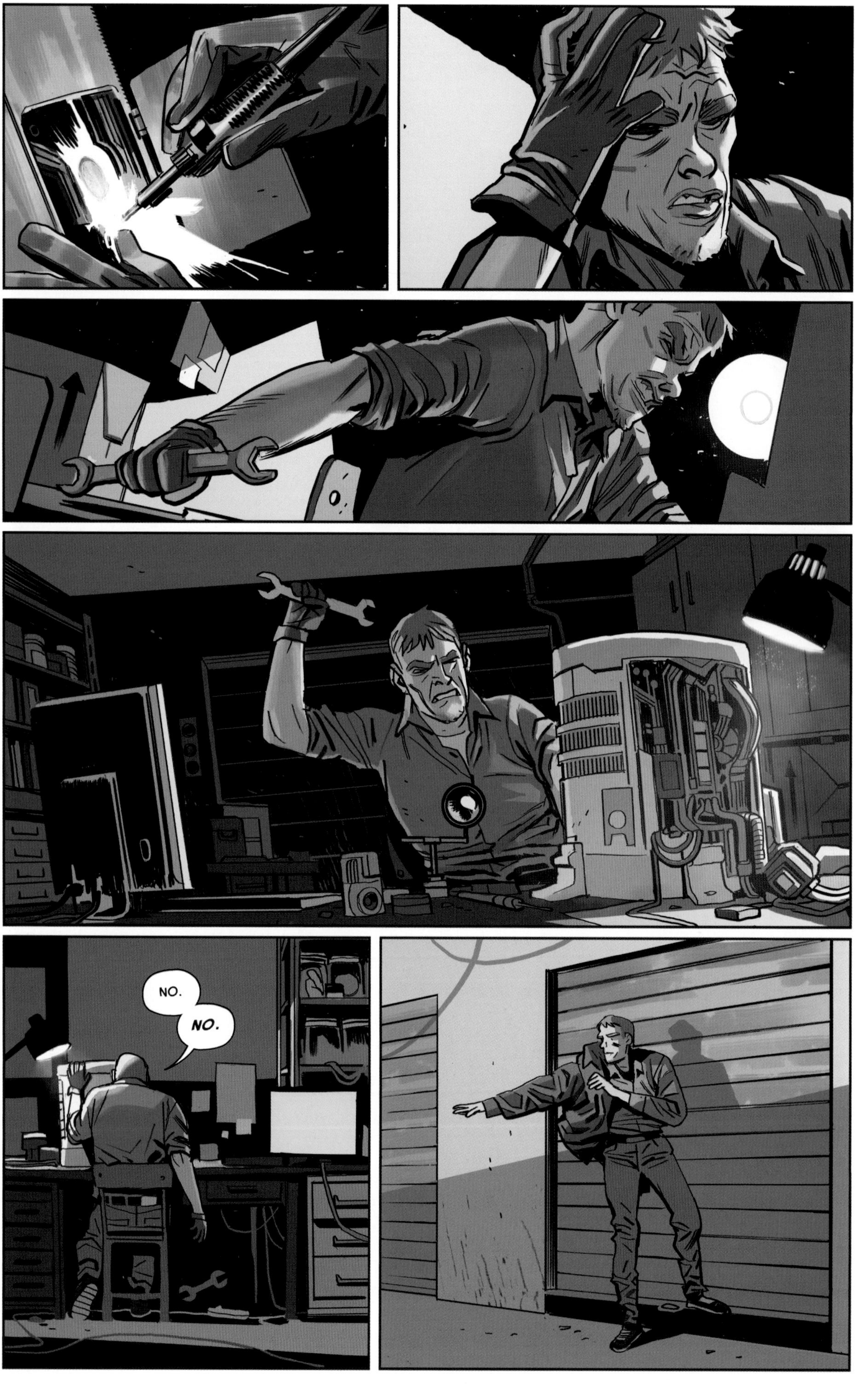
NO.
NO.

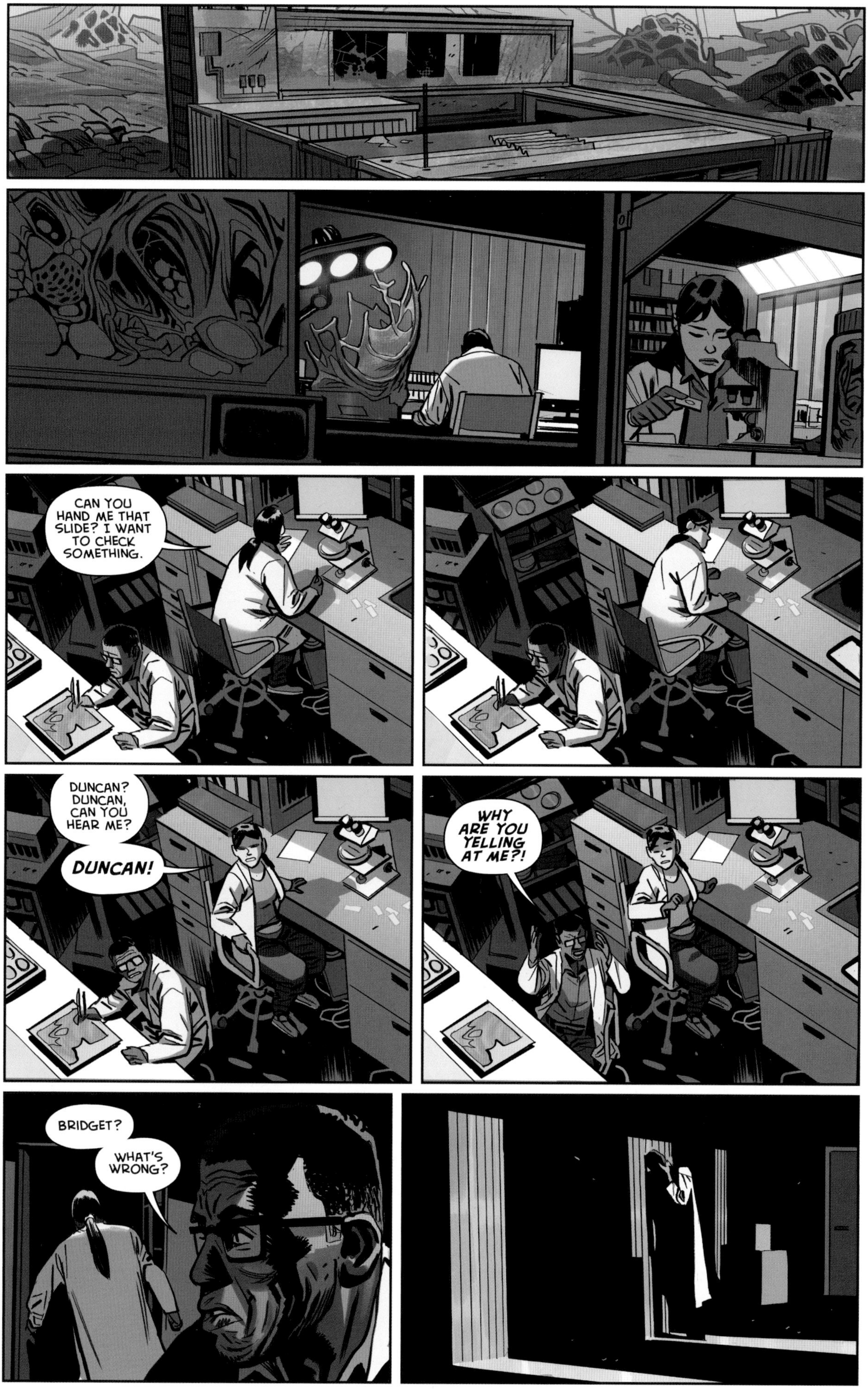
CAN YOU HAND ME THAT SLIDE? I WANT TO CHECK SOMETHING.
DUNCAN? DUNCAN, CAN YOU HEAR ME?
DUNCAN!
WHY ARE YOU YELLING AT ME?!
BRIDGET?
WHAT'S WRONG?

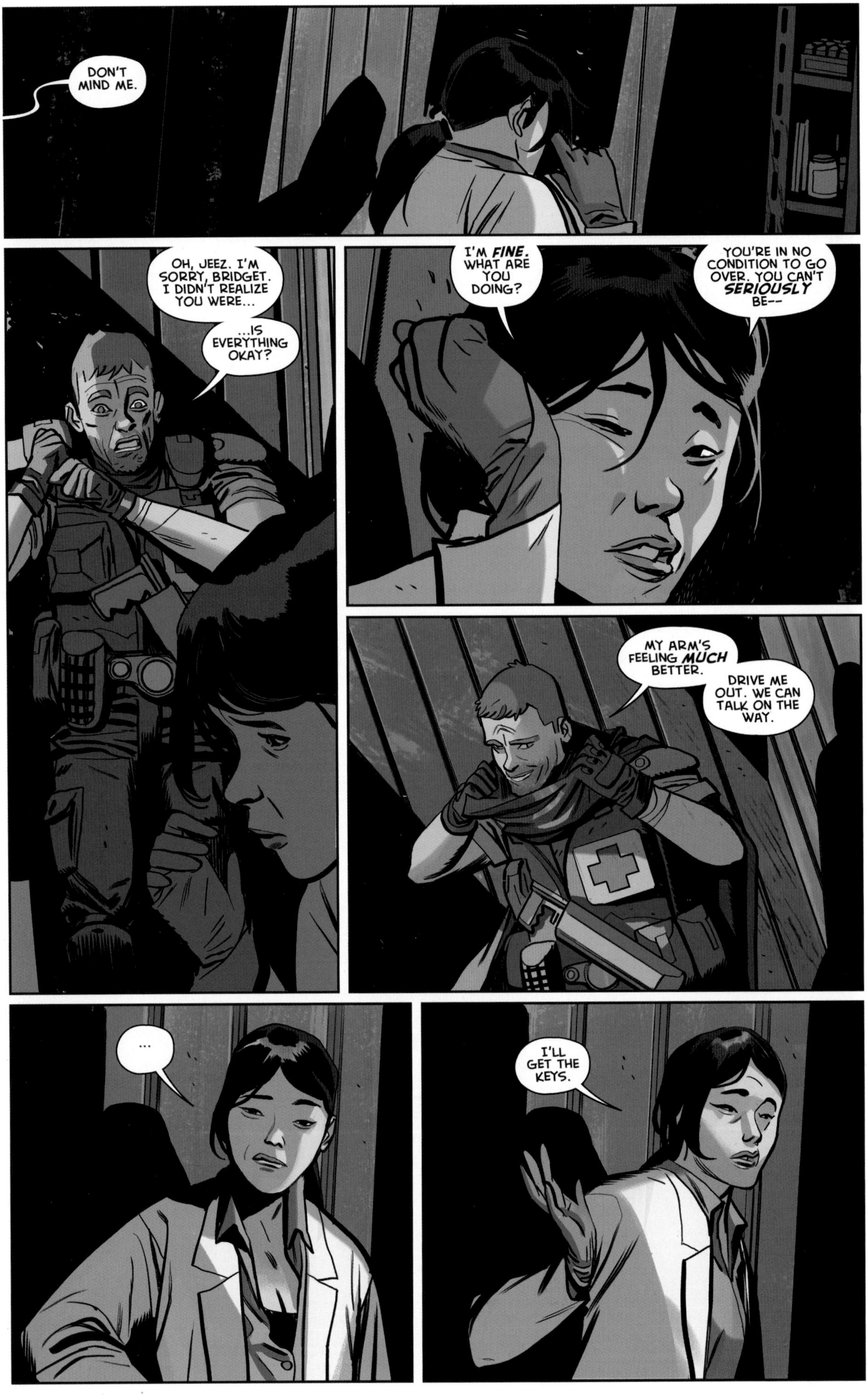
DON'T MIND ME.
OH, JEEZ. I'M SORRY, BRIDGET. I DIDN'T REALIZE YOU WERE...
...IS EVERYTHING OKAY?
I'M FINE. WHAT ARE YOU DOING?
YOU'RE IN NO CONDITION TO GO OVER. YOU CAN'T SERIOUSLY BE--
MY ARM'S FEELING MUCH BETTER.
DRIVE ME OUT. WE CAN TALK ON THE WAY.
...
I'LL GET THE KEYS.

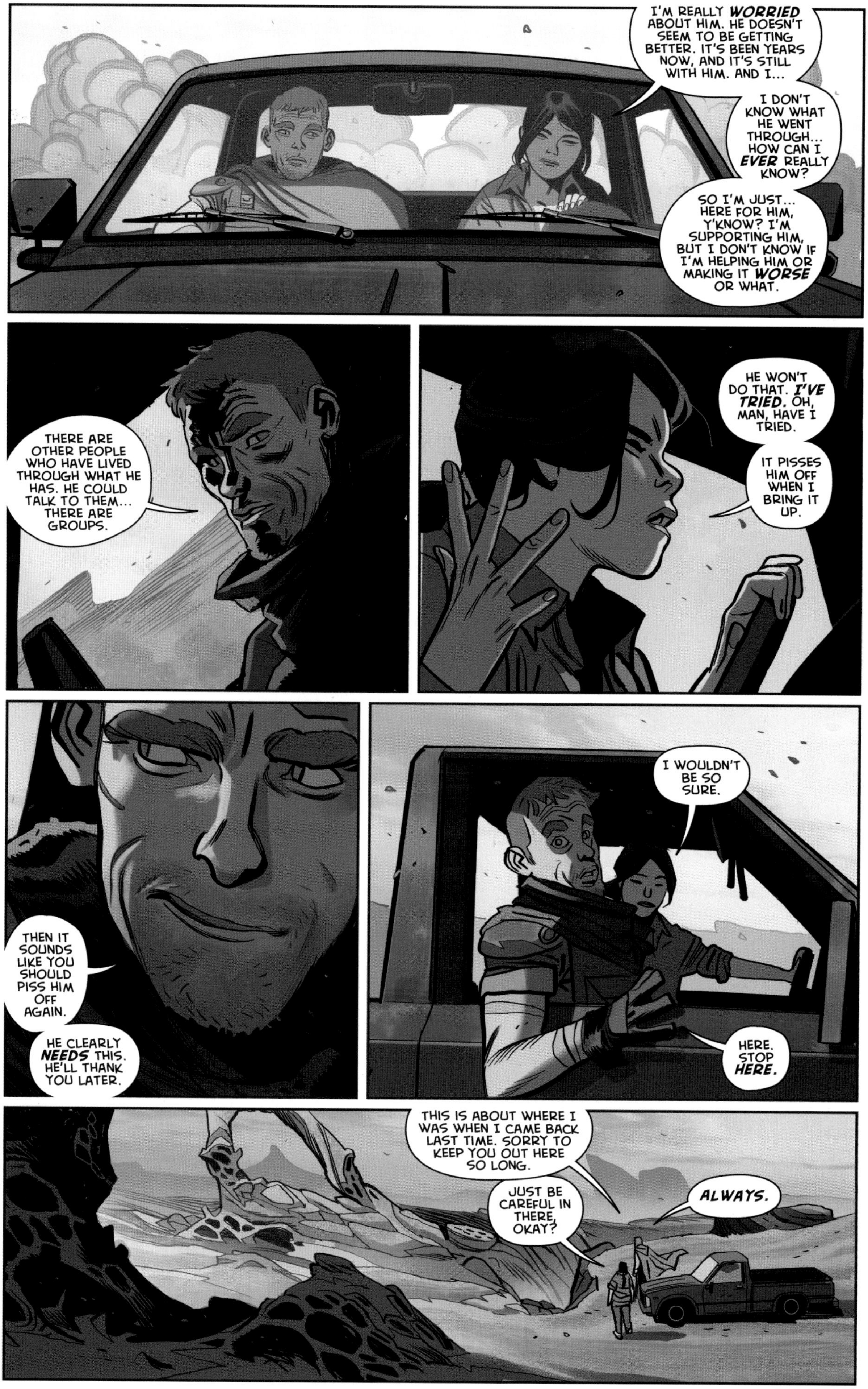
I'M REALLY WORRIED ABOUT HIM. HE DOESN'T SEEM TO BE GETTING BETTER. IT'S BEEN YEARS NOW, AND IT'S STILL WITH HIM. AND I...
I DON'T KNOW WHAT HE WENT THROUGH... HOW CAN I EVER REALLY KNOW?
SO I'M JUST... HERE FOR HIM, Y'KNOW? I'M SUPPORTING HIM, BUT I DON'T KNOW IF I'M HELPING HIM OR MAKING IT WORSE OR WHAT.
THERE ARE OTHER PEOPLE WHO HAVE LIVED THROUGH WHAT HE HAS. HE COULD TALK TO THEM... THERE ARE GROUPS.
HE WON'T DO THAT. I'VE TRIED. OH, MAN, HAVE I TRIED.
IT PISSES HIM OFF WHEN I BRING IT UP.
THEN IT SOUNDS LIKE YOU SHOULD PISS HIM OFF AGAIN.
HE CLEARLY NEEDS THIS. HE'LL THANK YOU LATER.
I WOULDN'T BE SO SURE.
HERE. STOP HERE.
THIS IS ABOUT WHERE I WAS WHEN I CAME BACK LAST TIME. SORRY TO KEEP YOU OUT HERE SO LONG.
JUST BE CAREFUL IN THERE, OKAY?
ALWAYS.

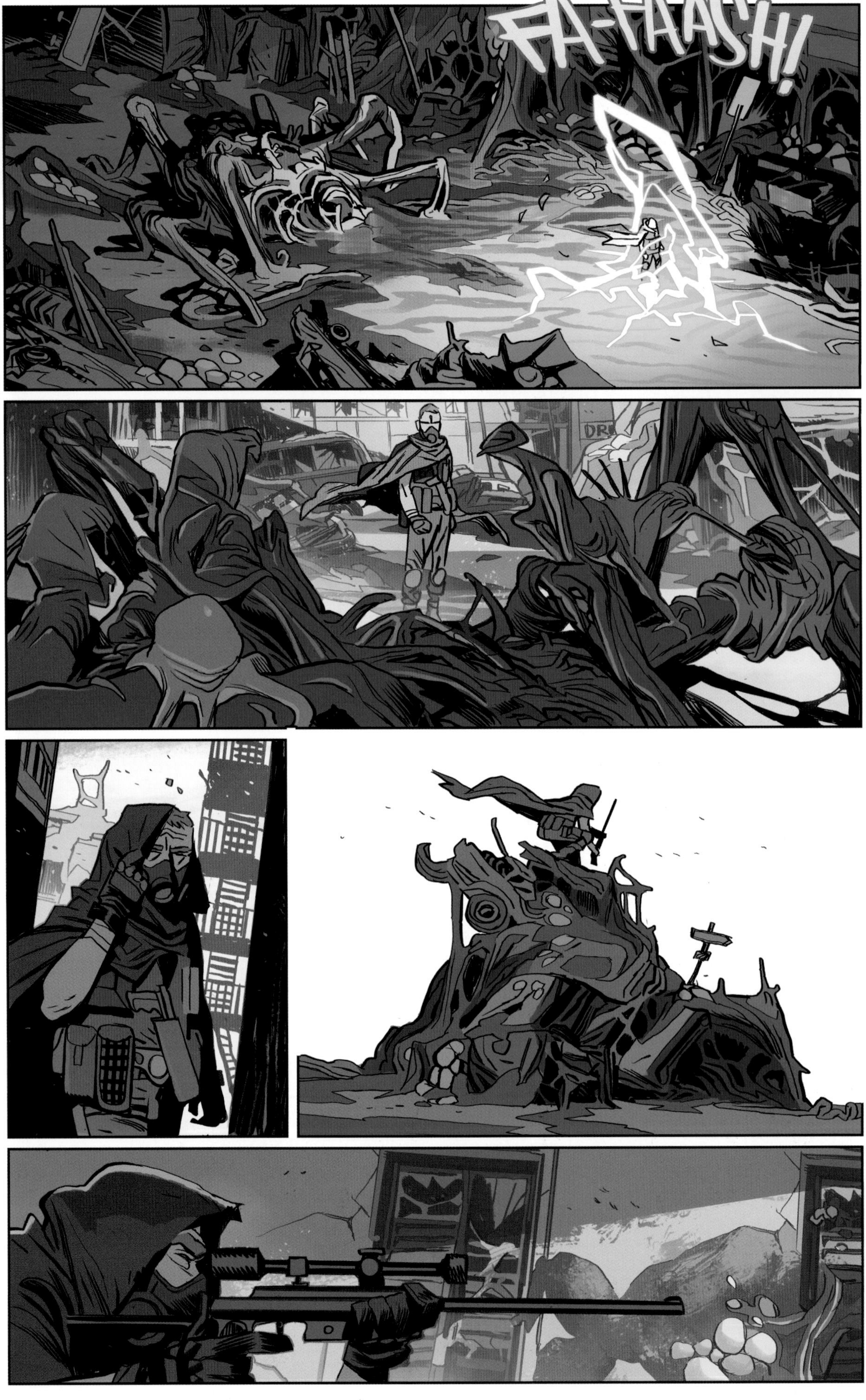
FA-FAASH!

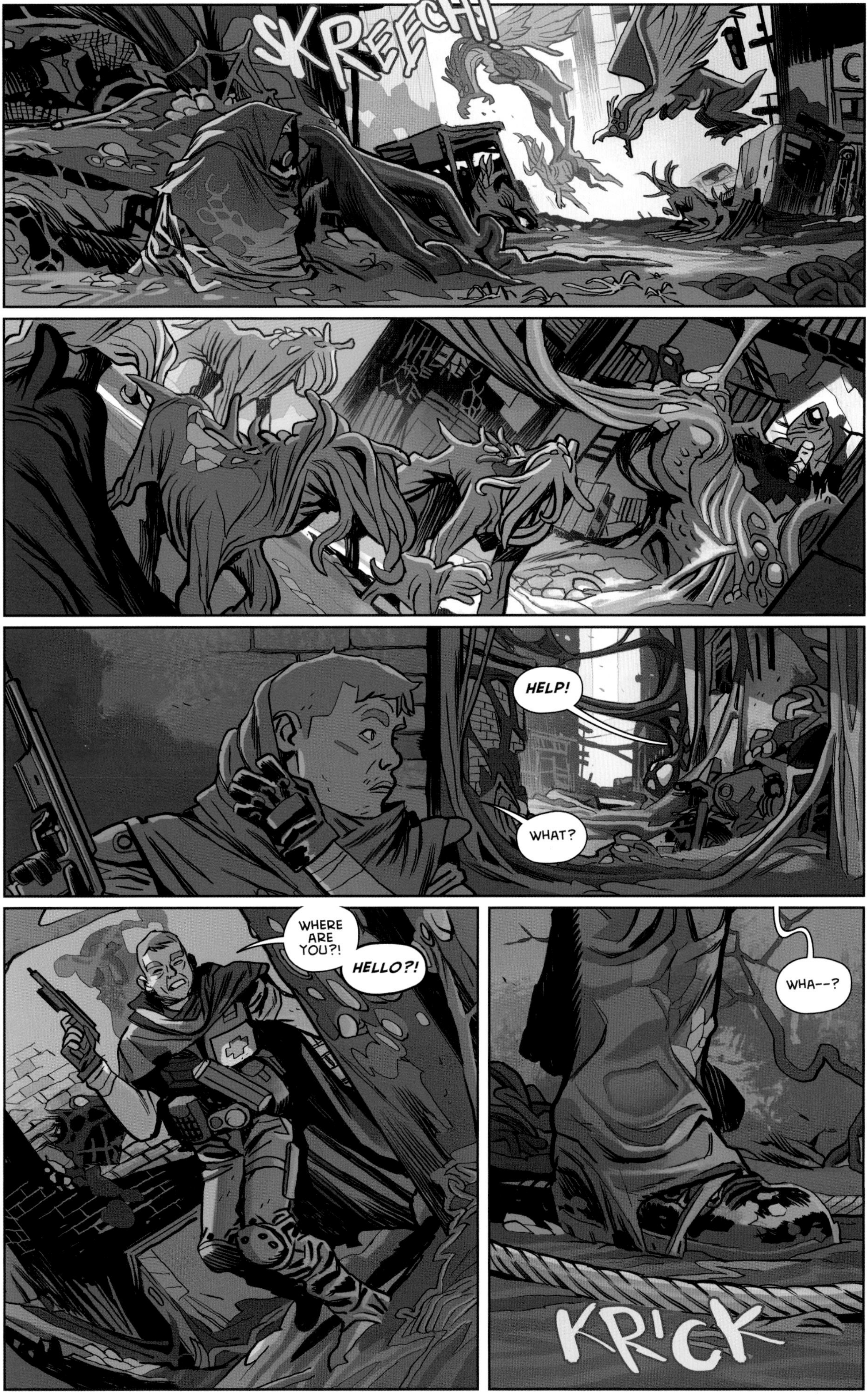
SKREECH!
HELP!
WHAT?
WHERE ARE YOU?!
HELLO?!
WHA--?
KRICK

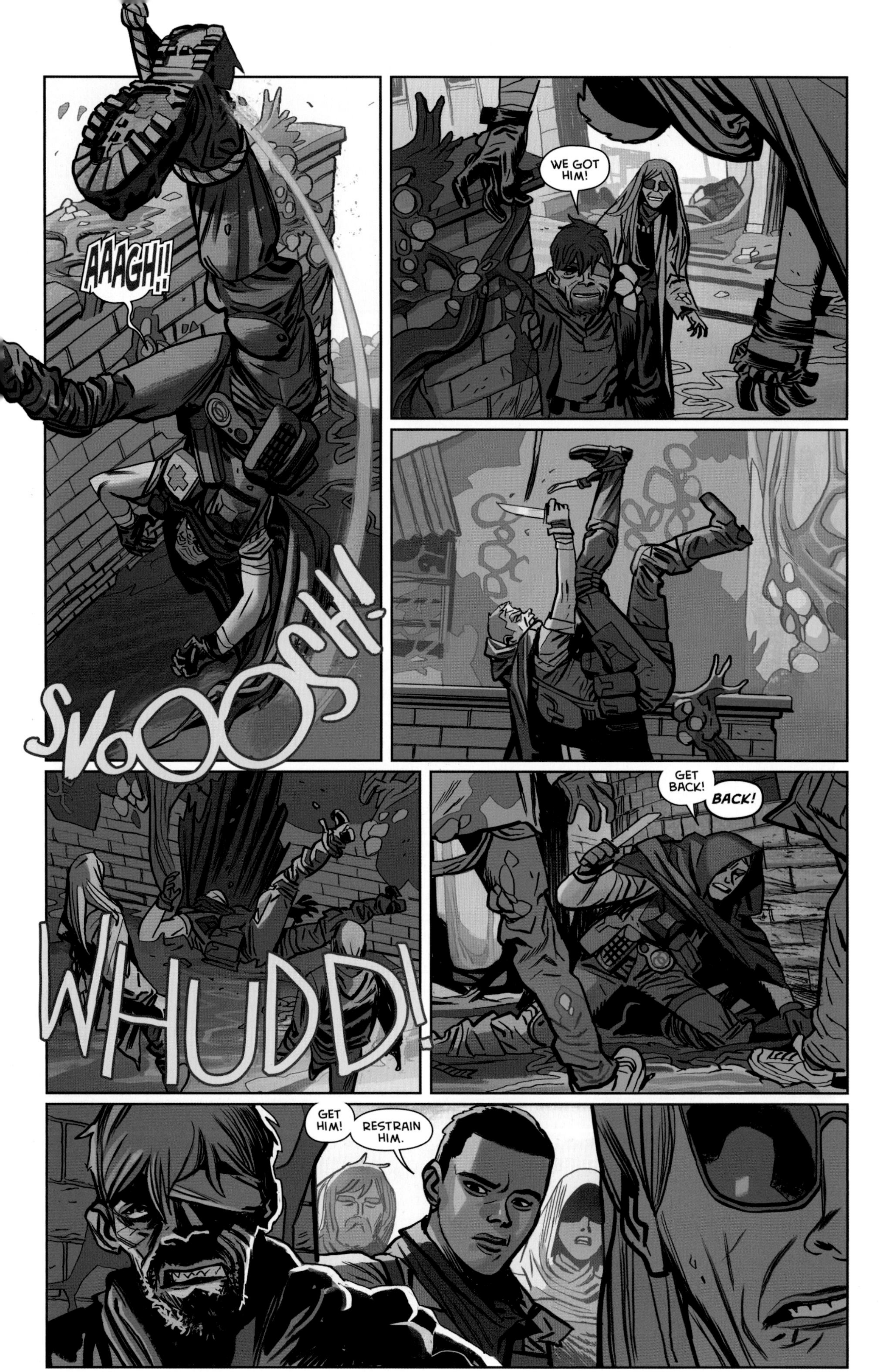
AAAGH!!
SVOOOSH!
WE GOT HIM!
WHUDD!
GET BACK!
BACK!
GET HIM!
RESTRAIN HIM.

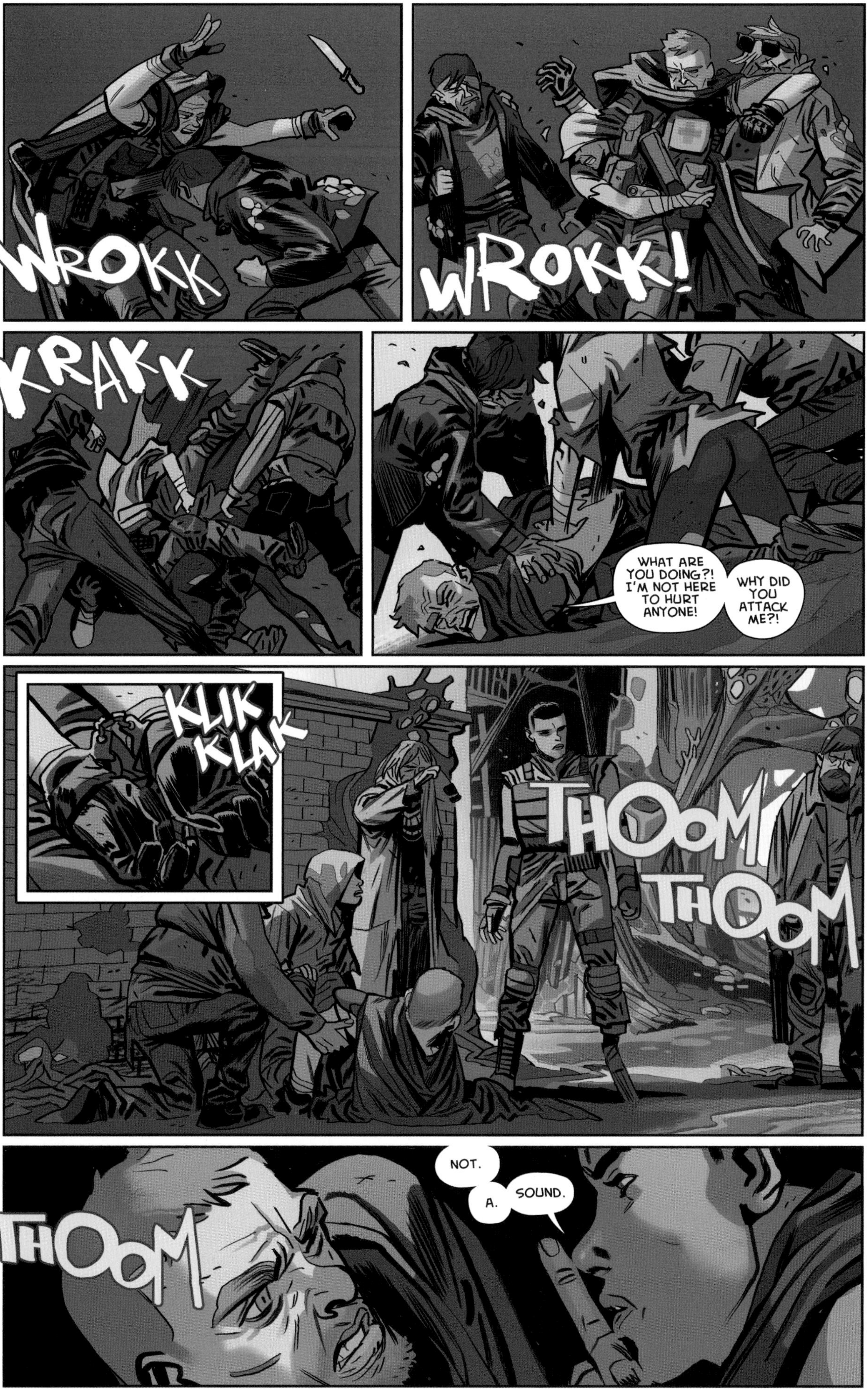
WROKK
WROKK!
KRAKK
WHAT ARE YOU DOING?! I'M NOT HERE TO HURT ANYONE!
WHY DID YOU ATTACK ME?!
KLIK KLAK
THOOM
THOOM
THOOM
NOT.
A.
SOUND.

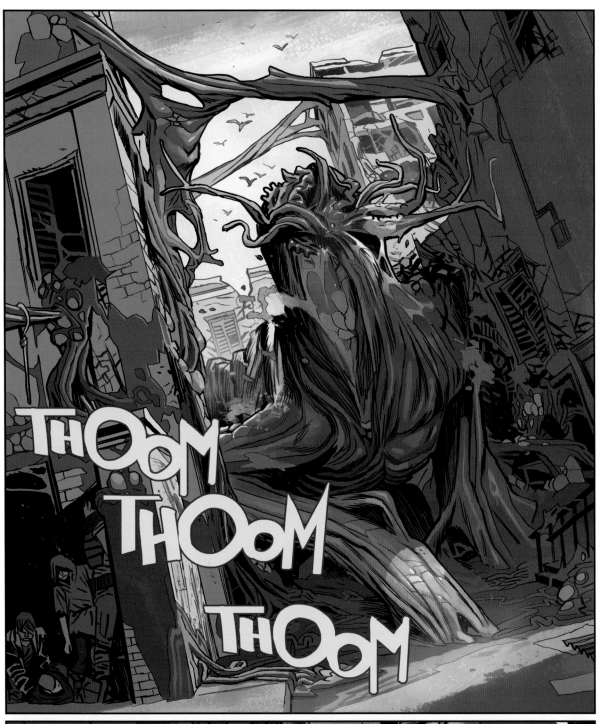

THOOM
THOOM
THOOM

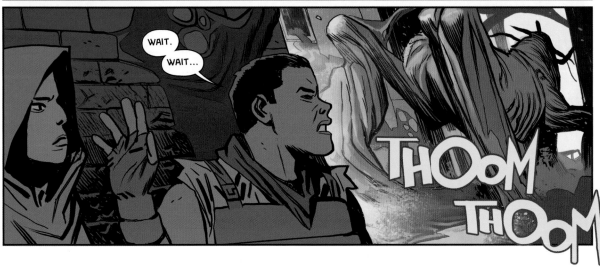

WAIT. WAIT...

THOOM
THOOM

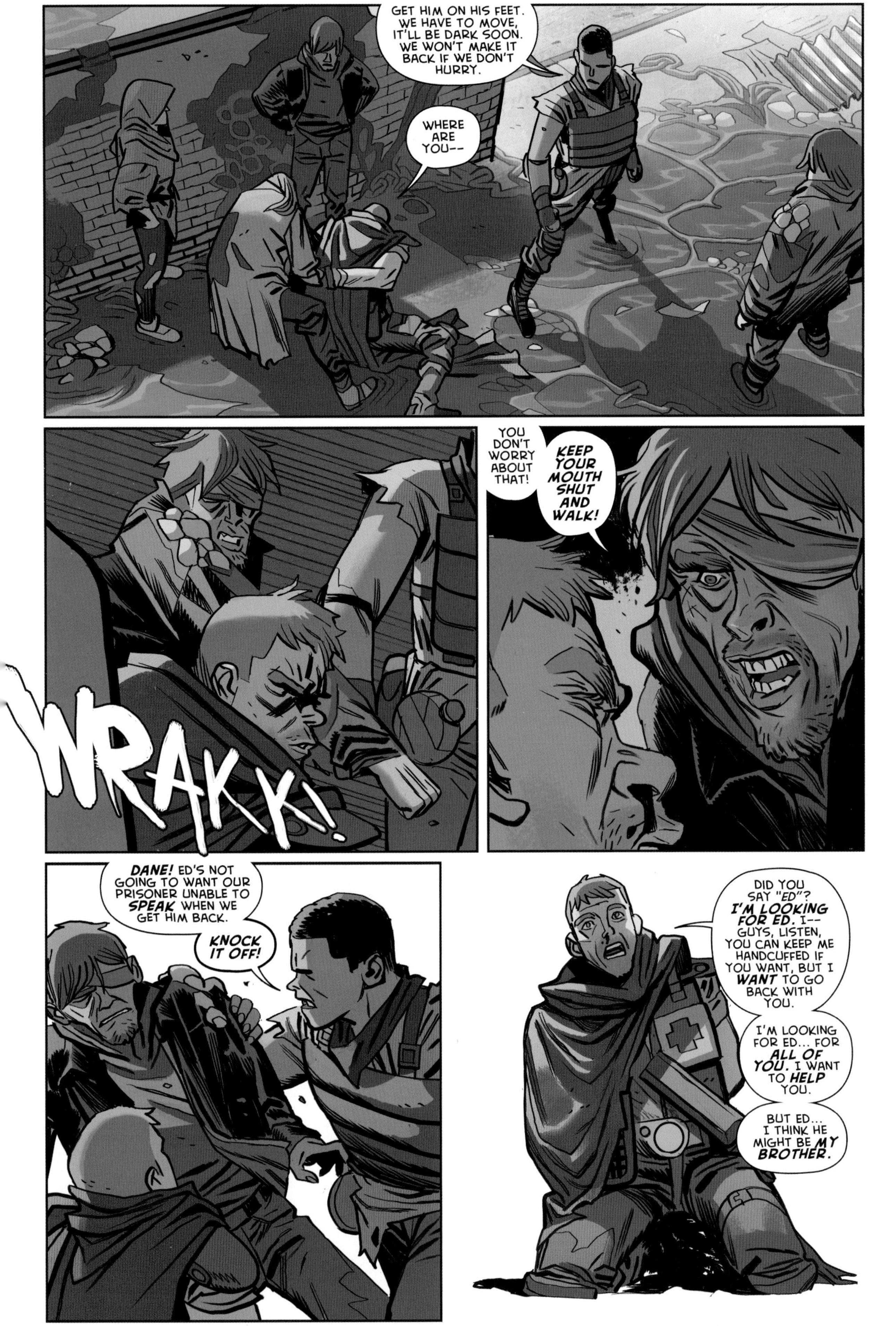
GET HIM ON HIS FEET. WE HAVE TO MOVE, IT'LL BE DARK SOON. WE WON'T MAKE IT BACK IF WE DON'T HURRY.
WHERE ARE YOU--
WRAKK!
YOU DON'T WORRY ABOUT THAT!
KEEP YOUR MOUTH SHUT AND WALK!
DANE! ED'S NOT GOING TO WANT OUR PRISONER UNABLE TO SPEAK WHEN WE GET HIM BACK.
KNOCK IT OFF!
DID YOU SAY "ED"? I'M LOOKING FOR ED. I-- GUYS, LISTEN, YOU CAN KEEP ME HANDCUFFED IF YOU WANT, BUT I WANT TO GO BACK WITH YOU.
I'M LOOKING FOR ED... FOR ALL OF YOU. I WANT TO HELP YOU.
BUT ED... I THINK HE MIGHT BE MY BROTHER.

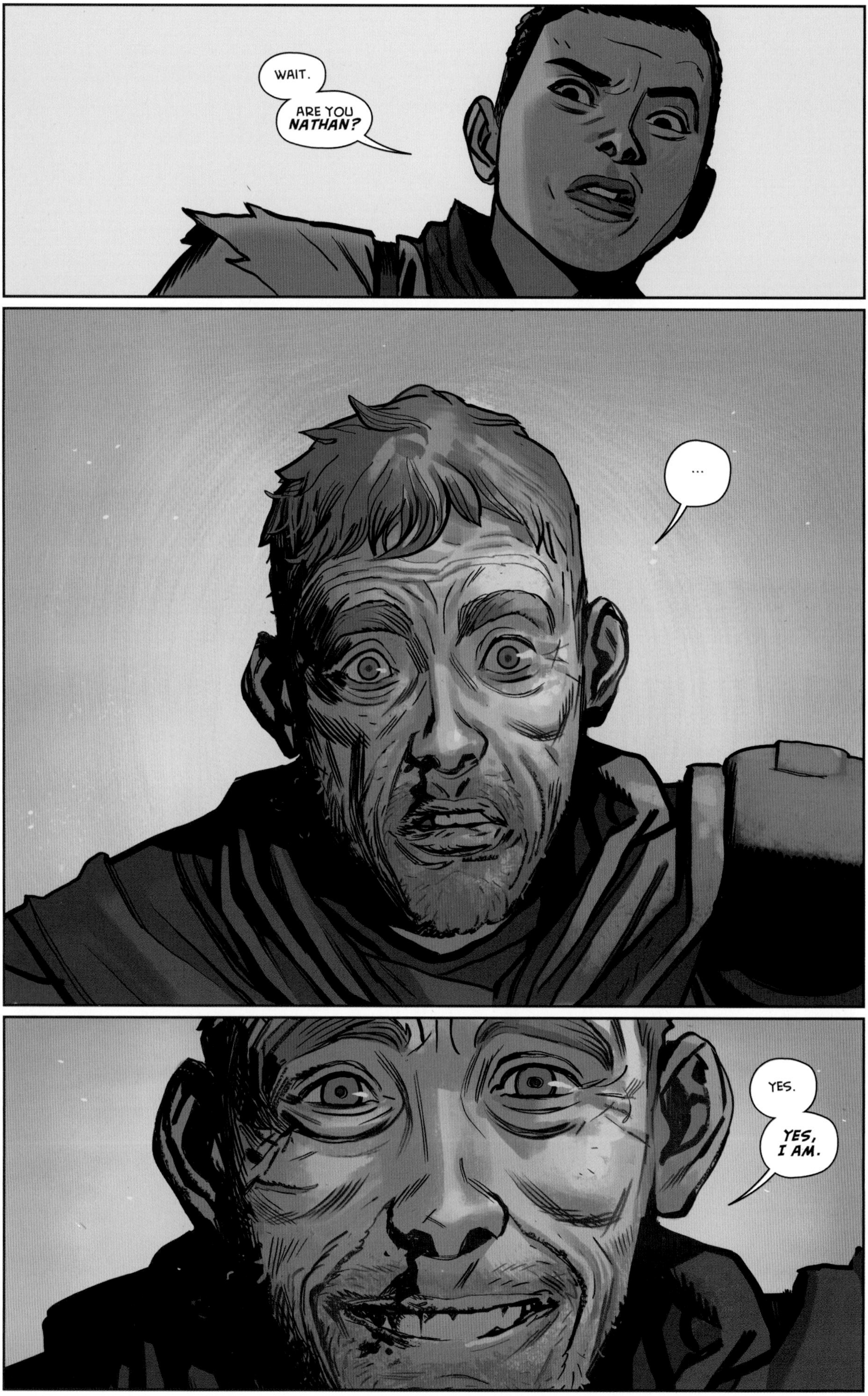
WAIT.
ARE YOU *NATHAN?*
...
YES.
YES, I AM.

HOLD UP.

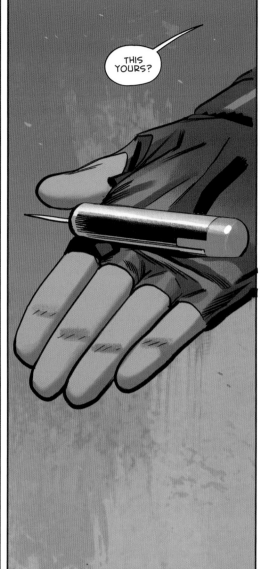

THIS YOURS?

YES. THAT'S AN ALIGNMENT DART. IT REALIGNS THE FREQUENCY OF YOUR MOLECULES TO PLACE YOU BACK IN THE PROPER DIMENSION AND--

JUST TELL IT TO YOUR BROTHER.

YOU'VE GOT A LOT OF EXPLAINING TO DO.

LEAD THE WAY.

EVERYONE... KEEP EYES ON THIS ONE. NO SURPRISES.

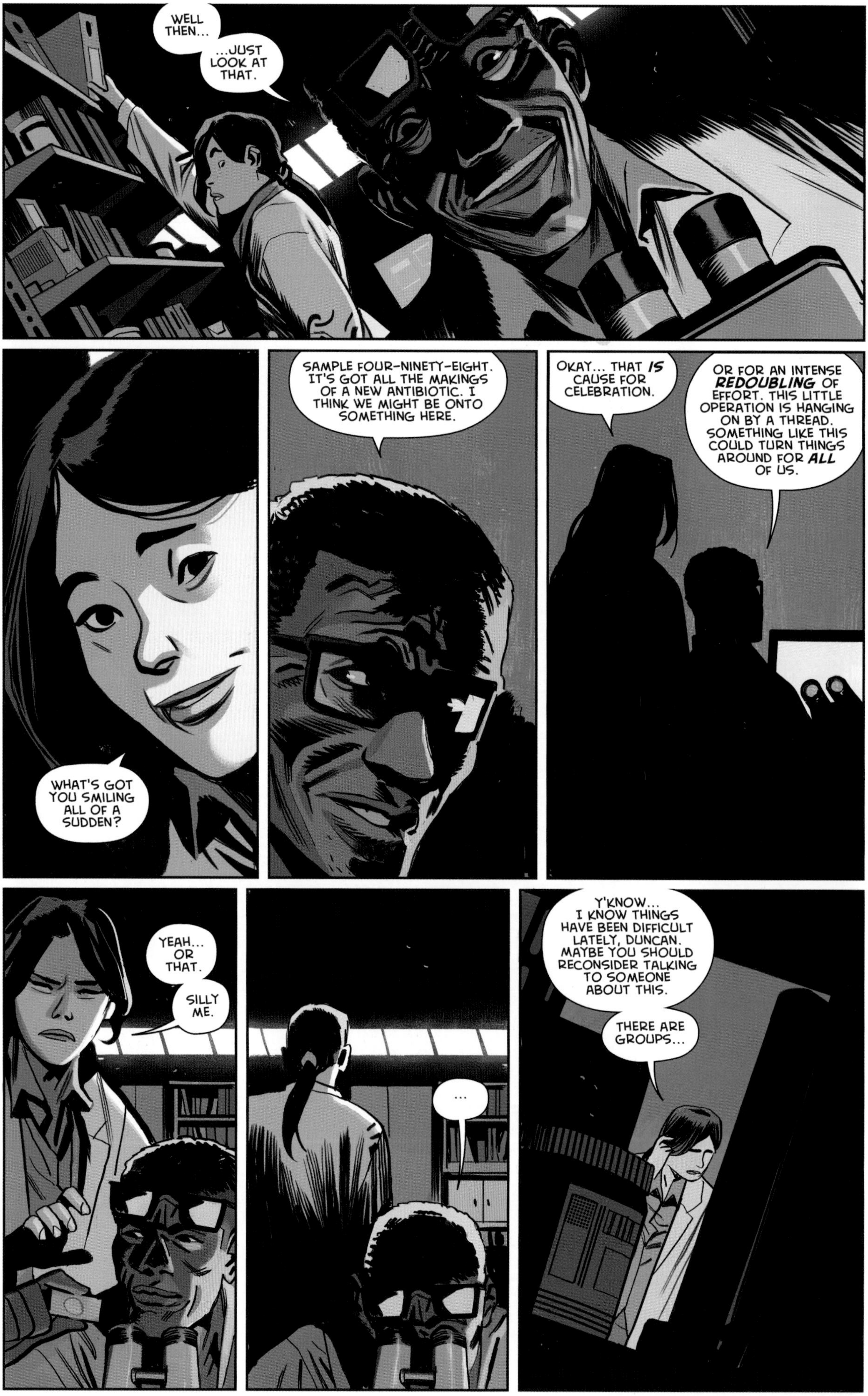
WELL THEN...
...JUST LOOK AT THAT.
WHAT'S GOT YOU SMILING ALL OF A SUDDEN?
SAMPLE FOUR-NINETY-EIGHT. IT'S GOT ALL THE MAKINGS OF A NEW ANTIBIOTIC. I THINK WE MIGHT BE ONTO SOMETHING HERE.
OKAY... THAT *IS* CAUSE FOR CELEBRATION.
OR FOR AN INTENSE ***REDOUBLING*** OF EFFORT. THIS LITTLE OPERATION IS HANGING ON BY A THREAD. SOMETHING LIKE THIS COULD TURN THINGS AROUND FOR ***ALL*** OF US.
YEAH... OR THAT.
SILLY ME.
...
Y'KNOW... I KNOW THINGS HAVE BEEN DIFFICULT LATELY, DUNCAN. MAYBE YOU SHOULD RECONSIDER TALKING TO SOMEONE ABOUT THIS.
THERE ARE GROUPS...

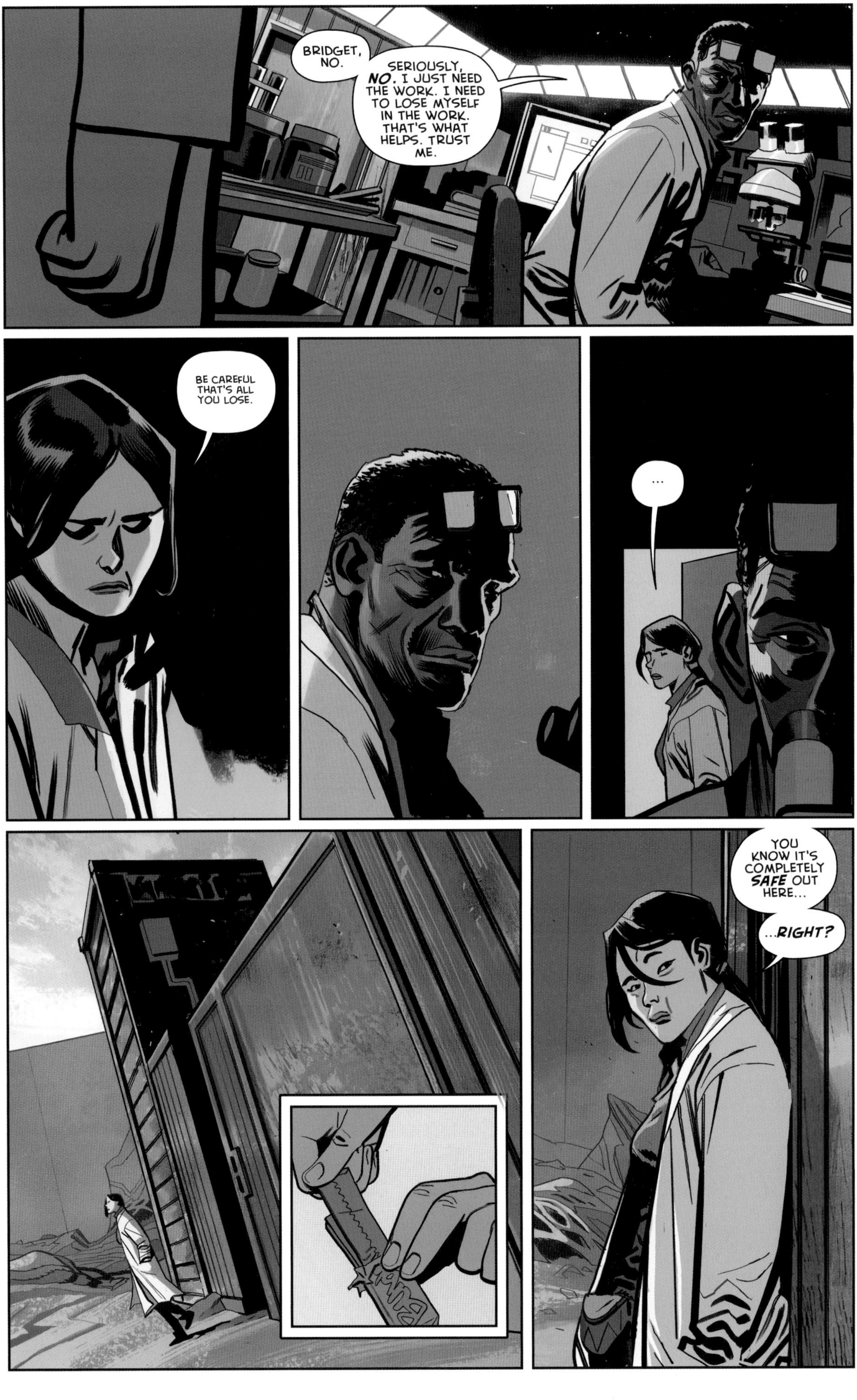
BRIDGET, NO.
SERIOUSLY, NO. I JUST NEED THE WORK. I NEED TO LOSE MYSELF IN THE WORK. THAT'S WHAT HELPS. TRUST ME.
BE CAREFUL THAT'S ALL YOU LOSE.
...
YOU KNOW IT'S COMPLETELY SAFE OUT HERE...
...RIGHT?

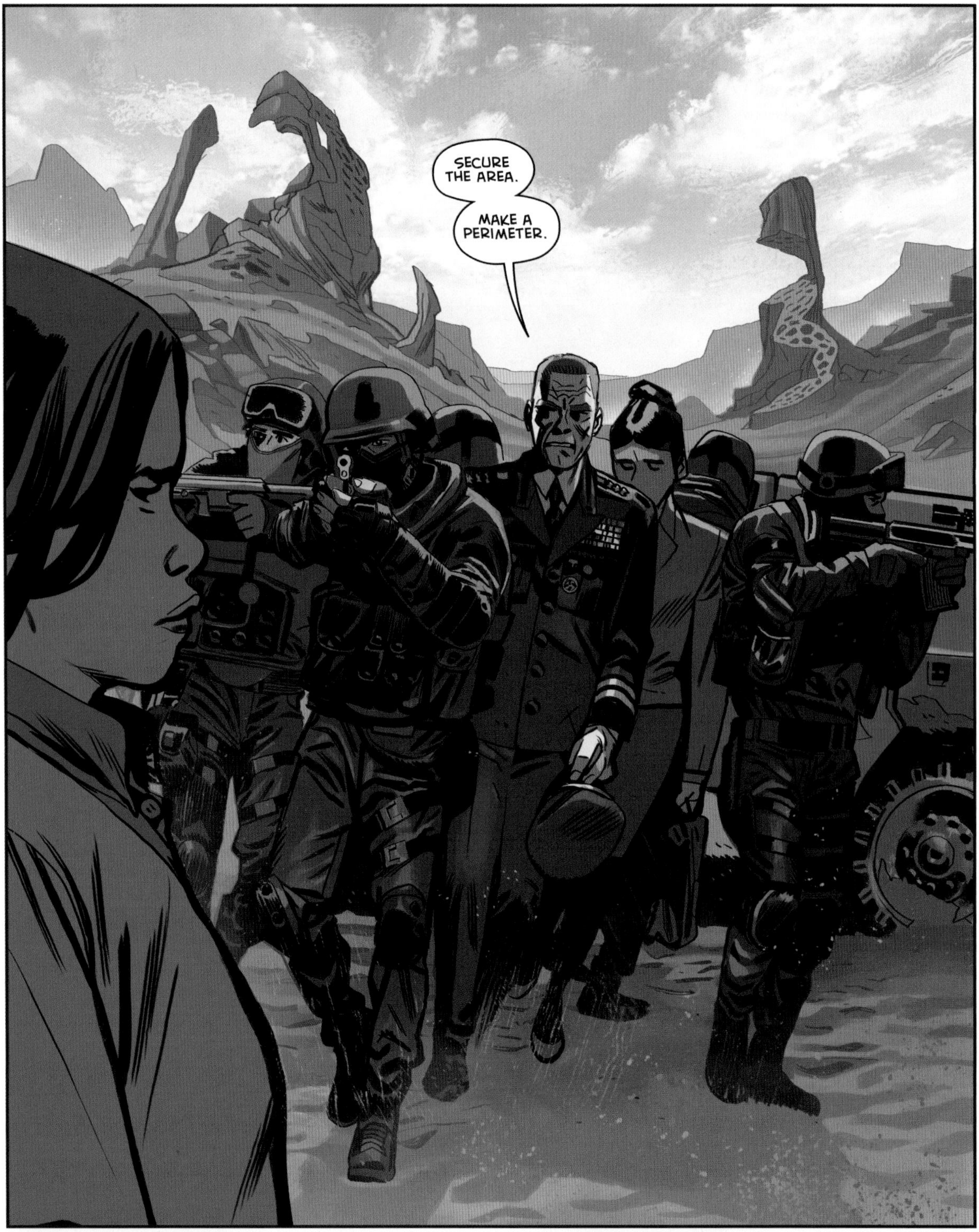
SECURE THE AREA.
MAKE A PERIMETER.

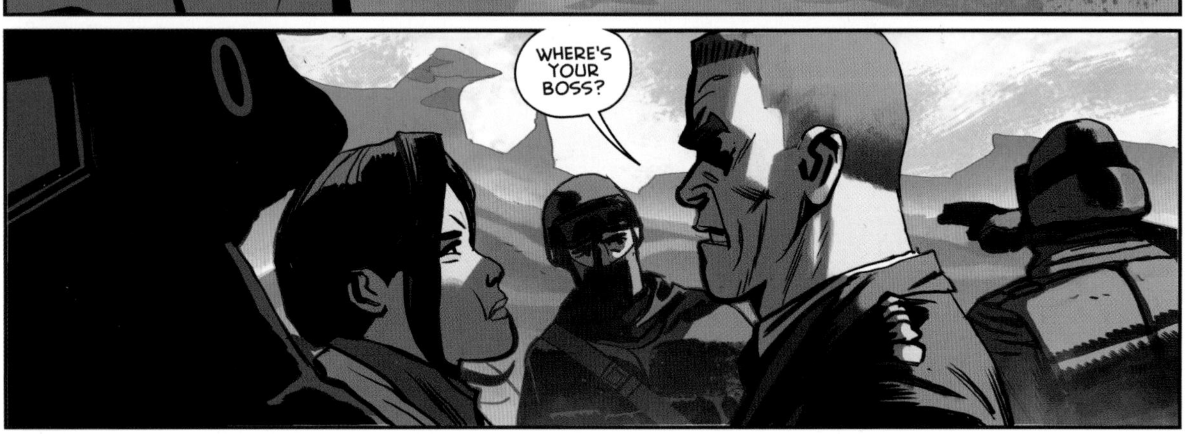
WHERE'S YOUR BOSS?

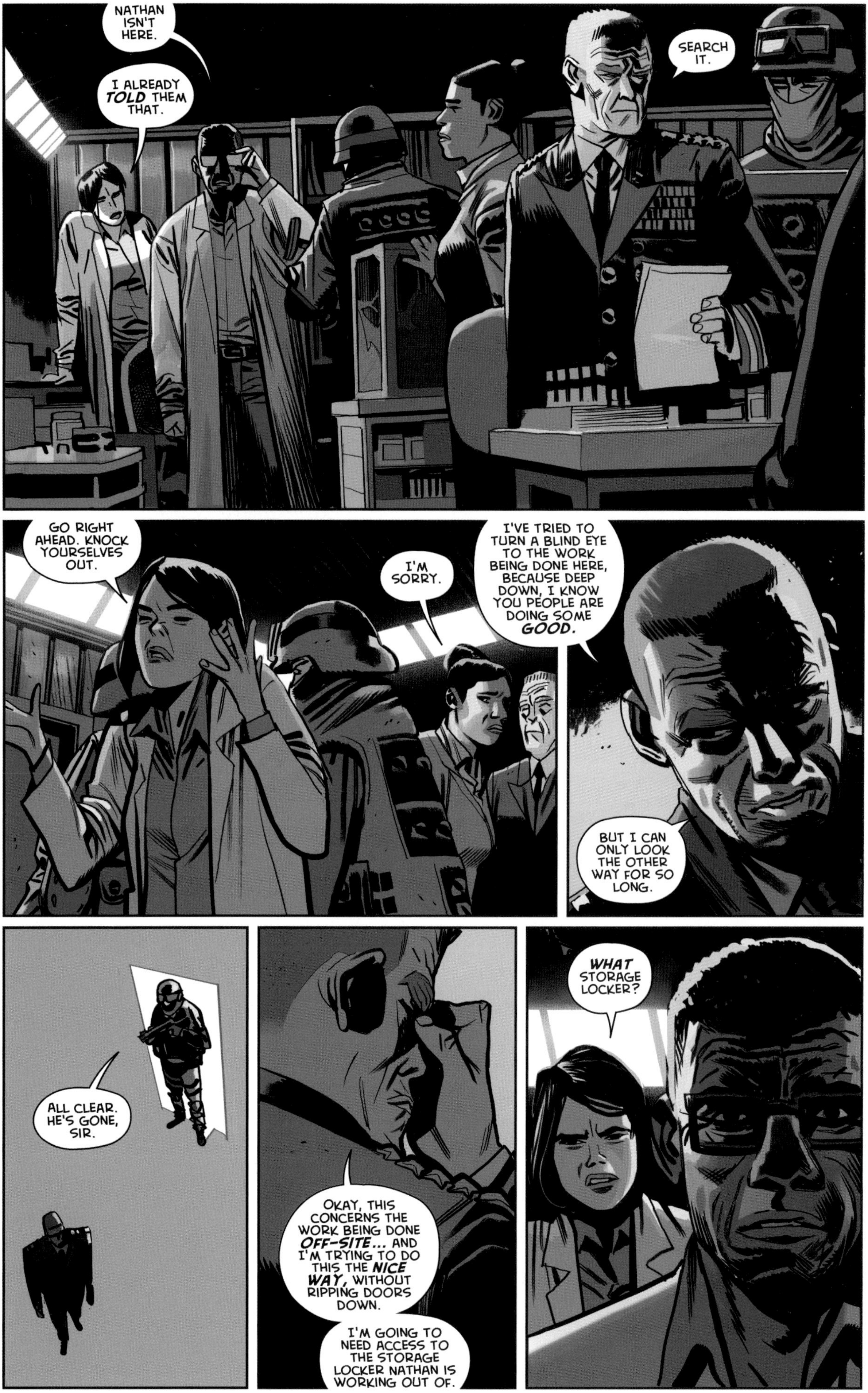
NATHAN ISN'T HERE.
I ALREADY TOLD THEM THAT.
SEARCH IT.
GO RIGHT AHEAD. KNOCK YOURSELVES OUT.
I'M SORRY.
I'VE TRIED TO TURN A BLIND EYE TO THE WORK BEING DONE HERE, BECAUSE DEEP DOWN, I KNOW YOU PEOPLE ARE DOING SOME GOOD.
BUT I CAN ONLY LOOK THE OTHER WAY FOR SO LONG.
ALL CLEAR. HE'S GONE, SIR.
OKAY, THIS CONCERNS THE WORK BEING DONE OFF-SITE... AND I'M TRYING TO DO THIS THE NICE WAY, WITHOUT RIPPING DOORS DOWN.
I'M GOING TO NEED ACCESS TO THE STORAGE LOCKER NATHAN IS WORKING OUT OF.
WHAT STORAGE LOCKER?

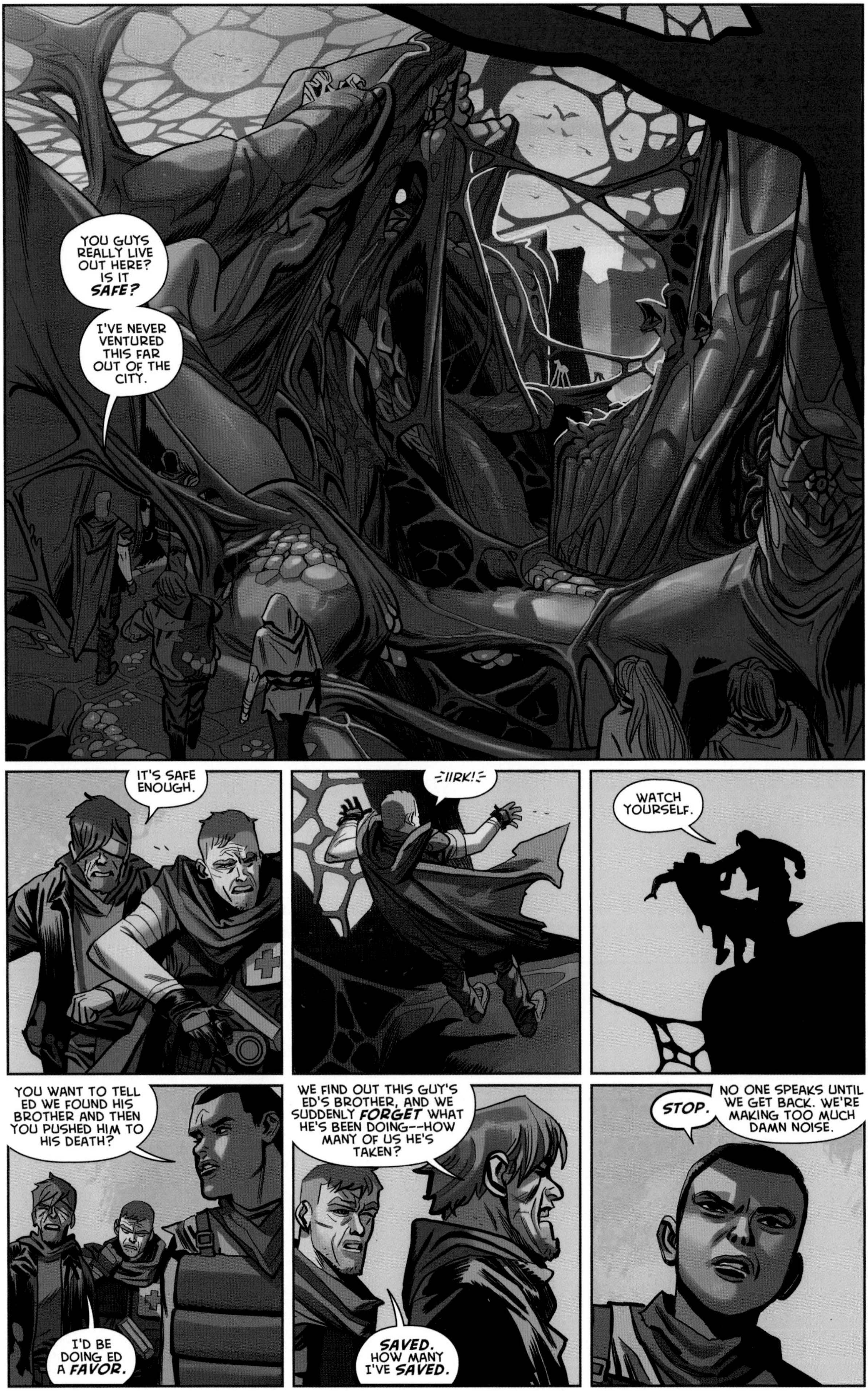

YOU GUYS REALLY LIVE OUT HERE? IS IT SAFE?
I'VE NEVER VENTURED THIS FAR OUT OF THE CITY.
IT'S SAFE ENOUGH.
=IIRK!=
WATCH YOURSELF.
YOU WANT TO TELL ED WE FOUND HIS BROTHER AND THEN YOU PUSHED HIM TO HIS DEATH?
I'D BE DOING ED A FAVOR.
WE FIND OUT THIS GUY'S ED'S BROTHER, AND WE SUDDENLY FORGET WHAT HE'S BEEN DOING--HOW MANY OF US HE'S TAKEN?
SAVED. HOW MANY I'VE SAVED.
STOP.
NO ONE SPEAKS UNTIL WE GET BACK. WE'RE MAKING TOO MUCH DAMN NOISE.

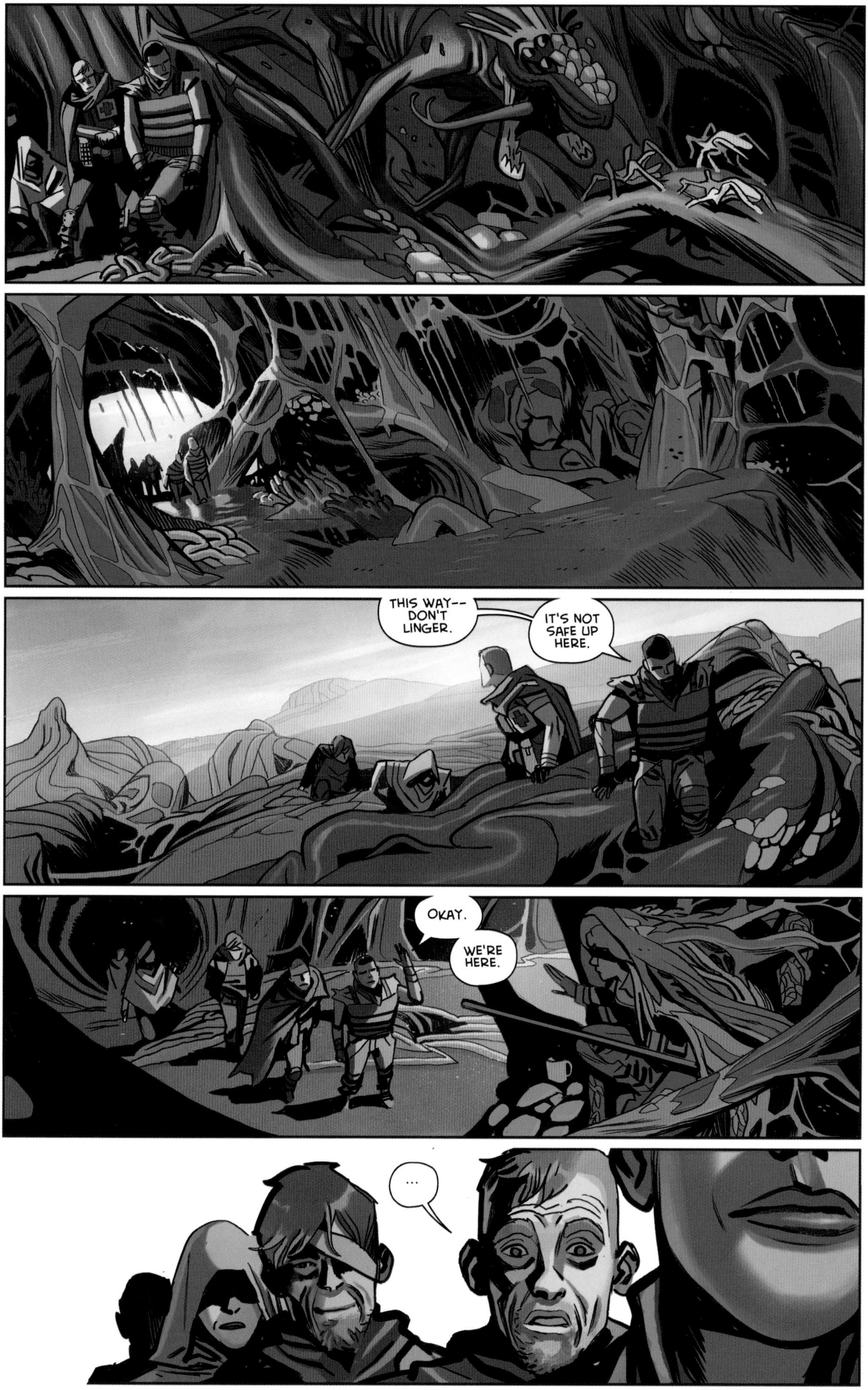
THIS WAY-- DON'T LINGER.
IT'S NOT SAFE UP HERE.
OKAY.
WE'RE HERE.
...

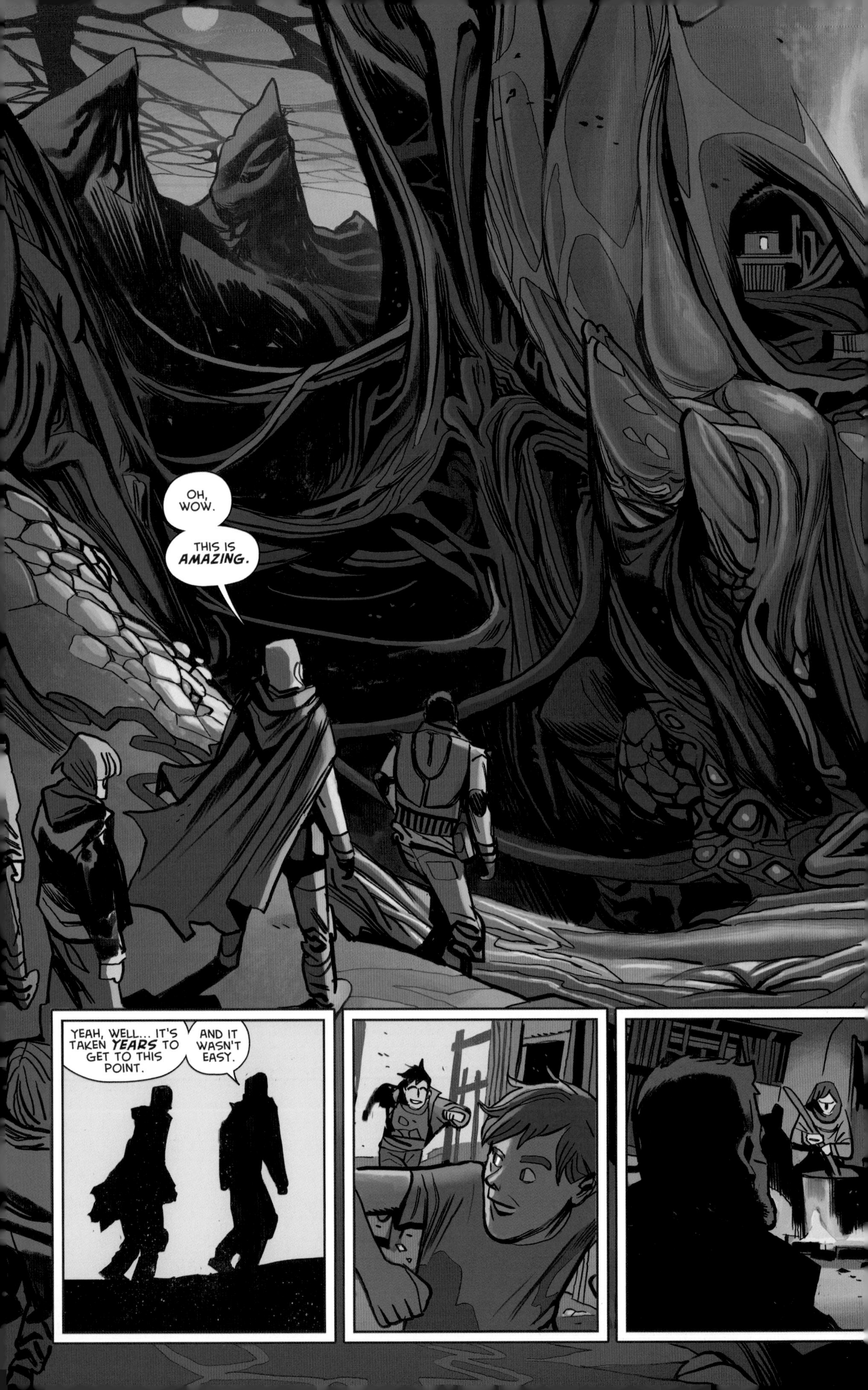
OH, WOW.
THIS IS AMAZING.
YEAH, WELL... IT'S TAKEN YEARS TO GET TO THIS POINT.
AND IT WASN'T EASY.

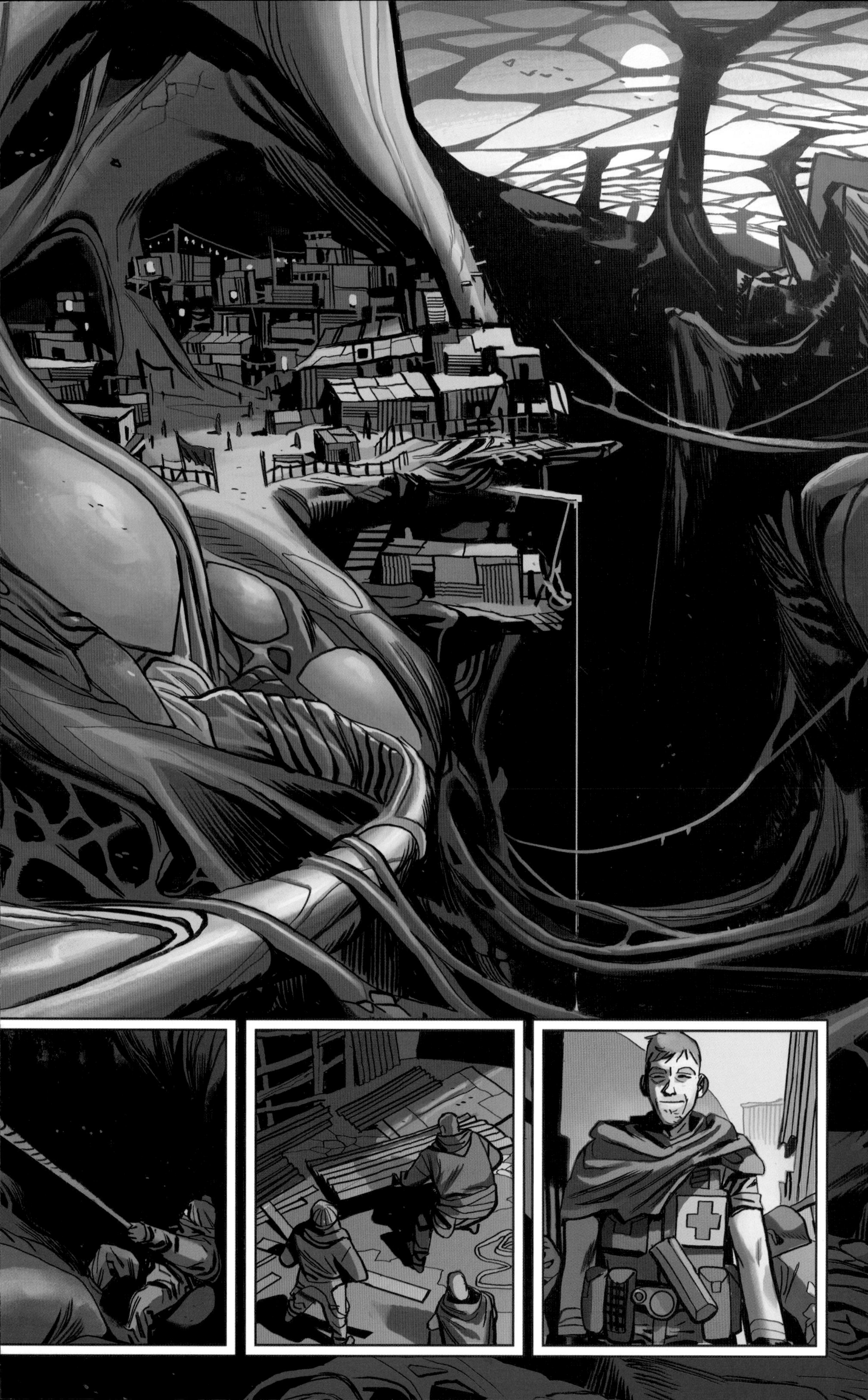

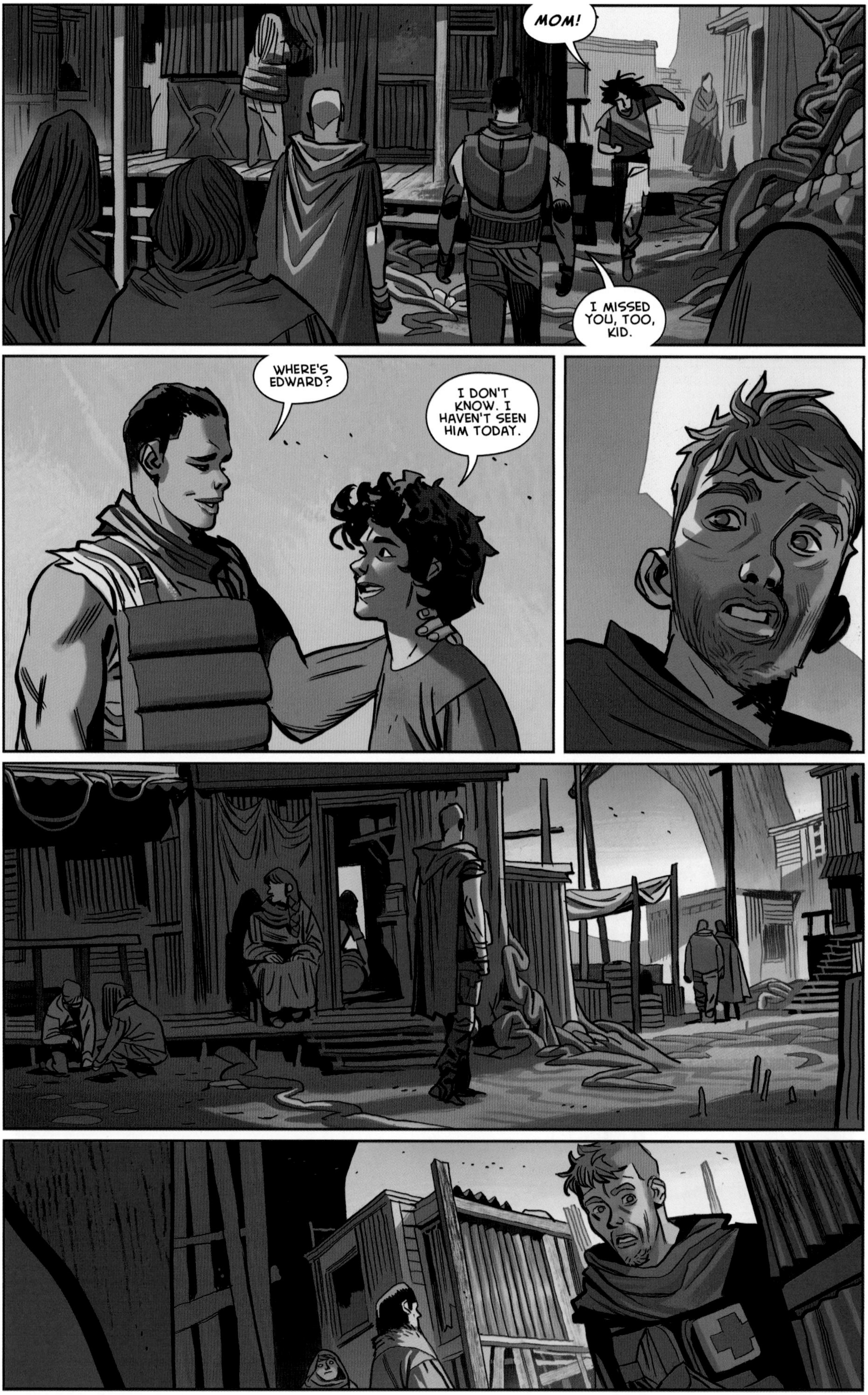
MOM!
I MISSED YOU, TOO, KID.
WHERE'S EDWARD?
I DON'T KNOW. I HAVEN'T SEEN HIM TODAY.

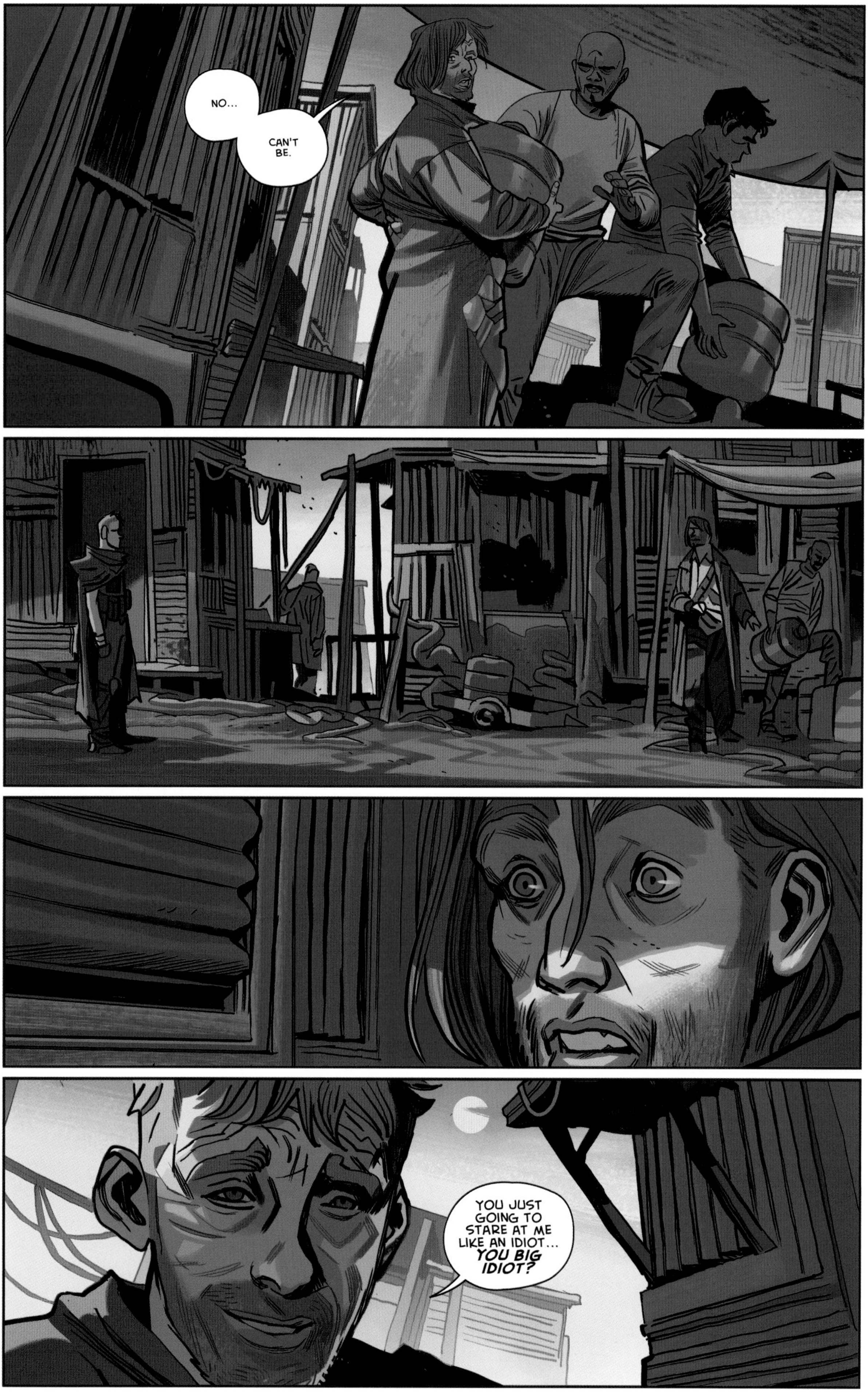
NO...
CAN'T BE.
YOU JUST GOING TO STARE AT ME LIKE AN IDIOT... ***YOU BIG IDIOT?***

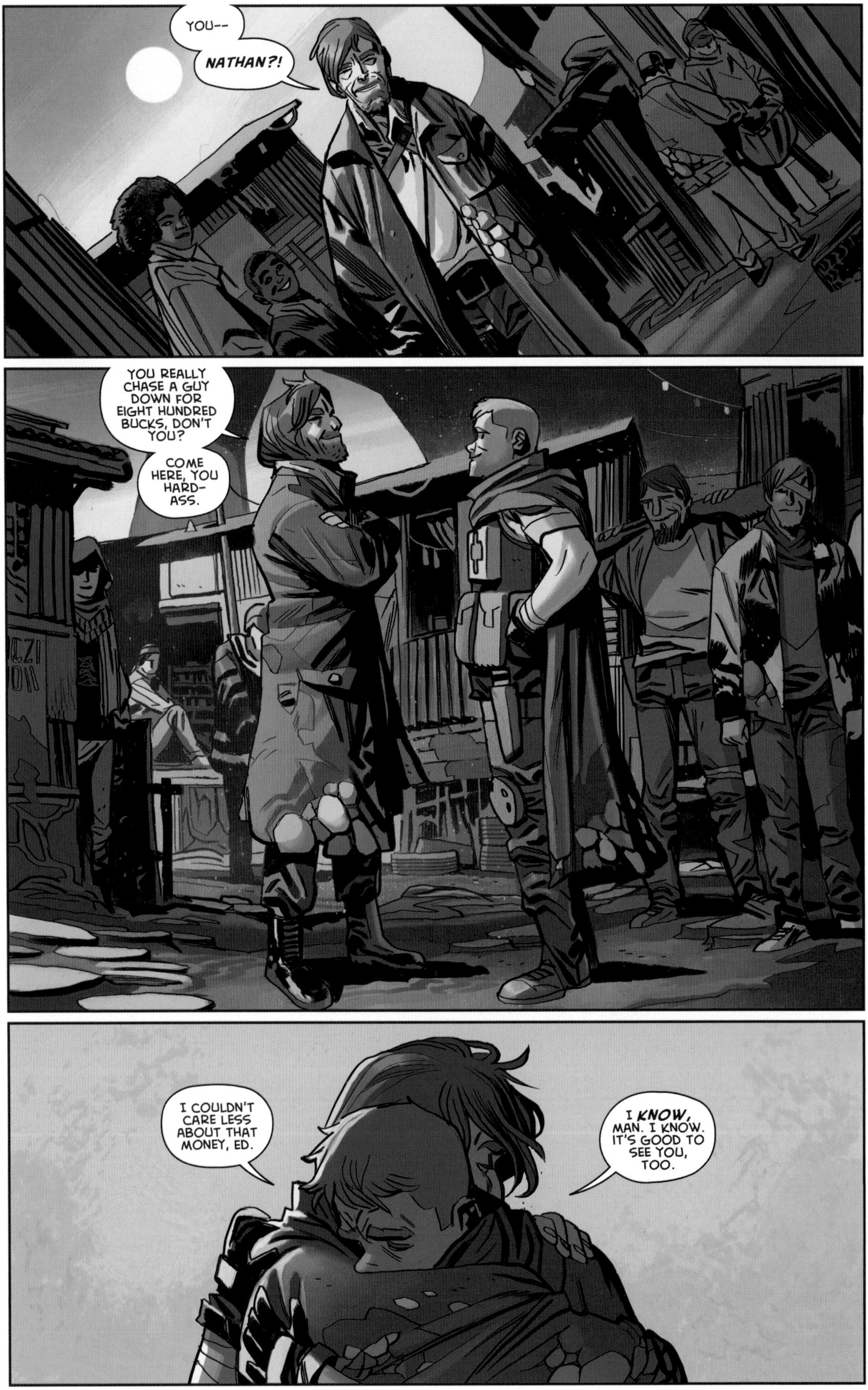
YOU--
NATHAN?!
YOU REALLY CHASE A GUY DOWN FOR EIGHT HUNDRED BUCKS, DON'T YOU?
COME HERE, YOU HARD-ASS.
I COULDN'T CARE LESS ABOUT THAT MONEY, ED.
I KNOW, MAN. I KNOW. IT'S GOOD TO SEE YOU, TOO.

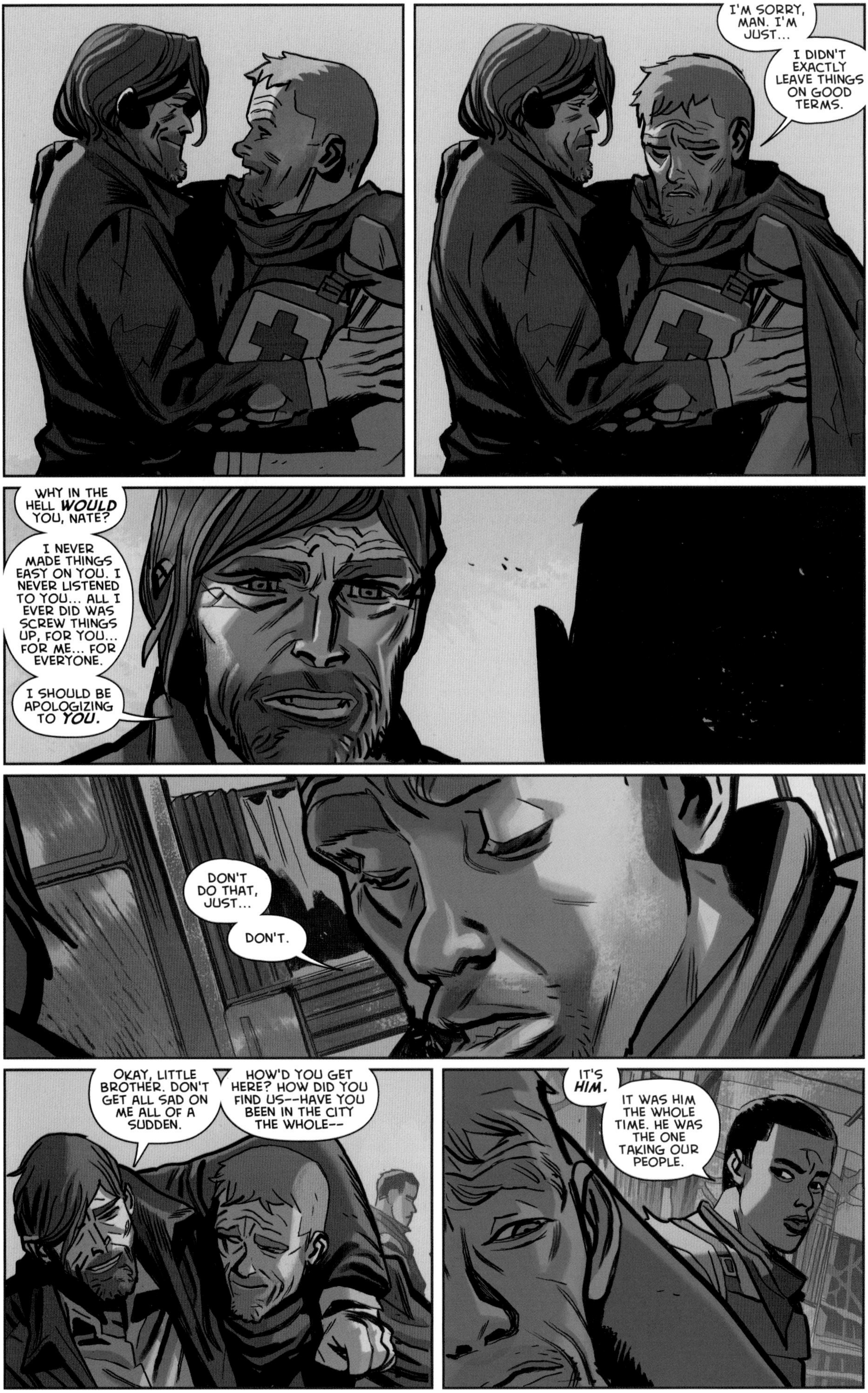
I'M SORRY, MAN. I'M JUST...
I DIDN'T EXACTLY LEAVE THINGS ON GOOD TERMS.
WHY IN THE HELL *WOULD* YOU, NATE?
I NEVER MADE THINGS EASY ON YOU. I NEVER LISTENED TO YOU... ALL I EVER DID WAS SCREW THINGS UP, FOR YOU... FOR ME... FOR EVERYONE.
I SHOULD BE APOLOGIZING TO *YOU.*
DON'T DO THAT, JUST...
DON'T.
OKAY, LITTLE BROTHER. DON'T GET ALL SAD ON ME ALL OF A SUDDEN.
HOW'D YOU GET HERE? HOW DID YOU FIND US--HAVE YOU BEEN IN THE CITY THE WHOLE--
IT'S *HIM.*
IT WAS HIM THE WHOLE TIME. HE WAS THE ONE TAKING OUR PEOPLE.

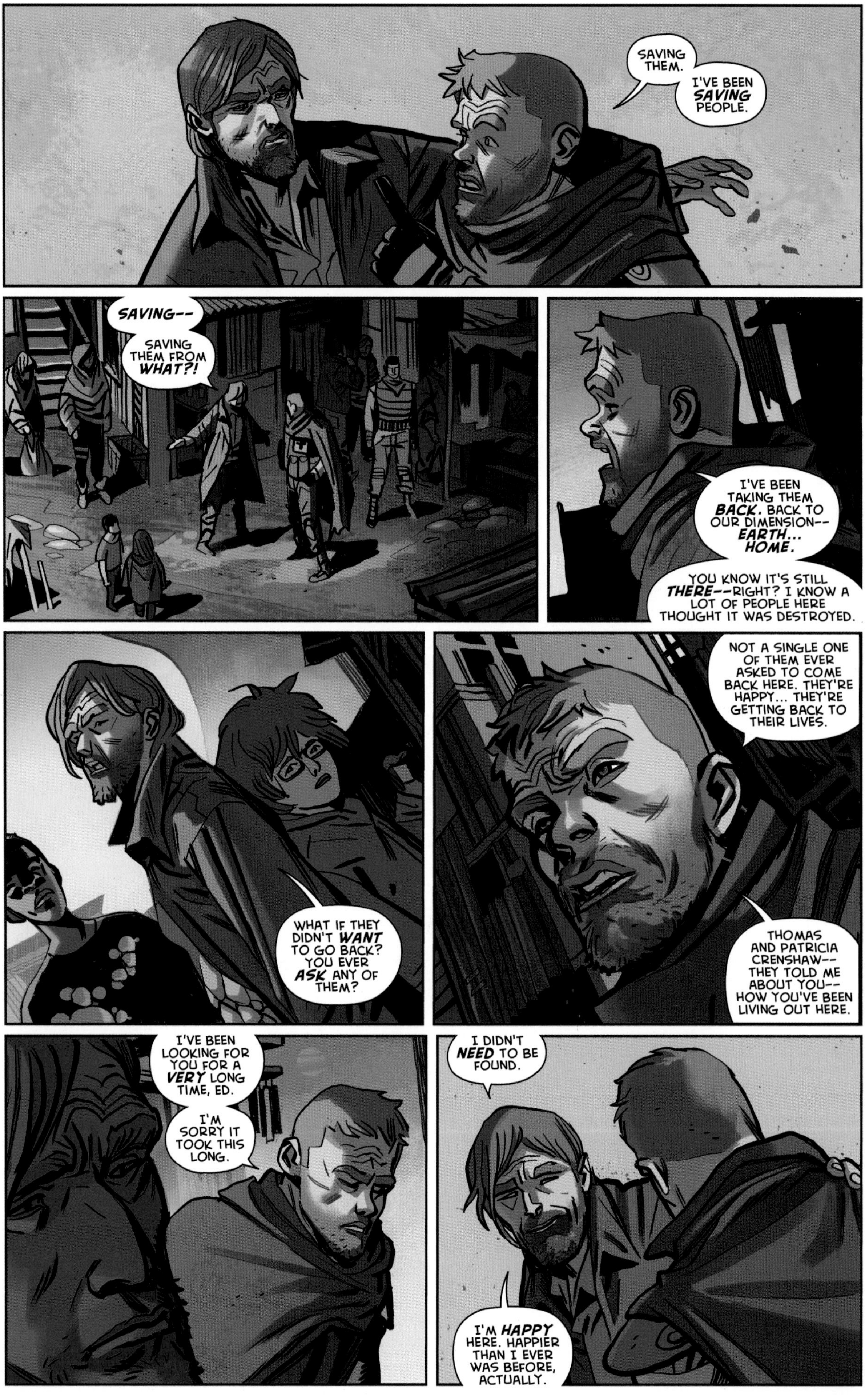
SAVING THEM.
I'VE BEEN SAVING PEOPLE.
SAVING--
SAVING THEM FROM WHAT?!
I'VE BEEN TAKING THEM BACK. BACK TO OUR DIMENSION-- EARTH... HOME.
YOU KNOW IT'S STILL THERE--RIGHT? I KNOW A LOT OF PEOPLE HERE THOUGHT IT WAS DESTROYED.
WHAT IF THEY DIDN'T WANT TO GO BACK? YOU EVER ASK ANY OF THEM?
NOT A SINGLE ONE OF THEM EVER ASKED TO COME BACK HERE. THEY'RE HAPPY... THEY'RE GETTING BACK TO THEIR LIVES.
THOMAS AND PATRICIA CRENSHAW-- THEY TOLD ME ABOUT YOU-- HOW YOU'VE BEEN LIVING OUT HERE.
I'VE BEEN LOOKING FOR YOU FOR A VERY LONG TIME, ED.
I'M SORRY IT TOOK THIS LONG.
I DIDN'T NEED TO BE FOUND.
I'M HAPPY HERE. HAPPIER THAN I EVER WAS BEFORE, ACTUALLY.

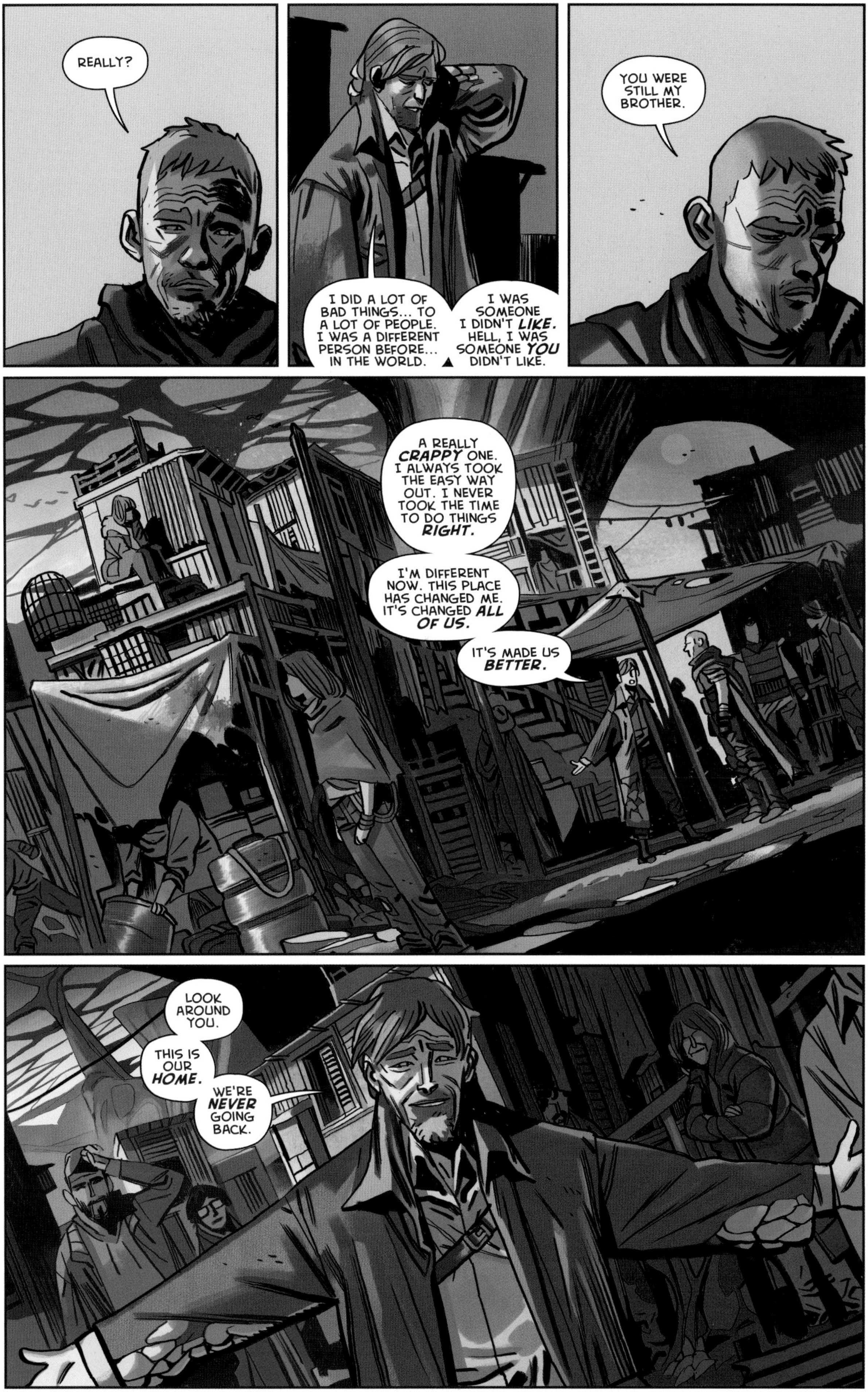
REALLY?
I DID A LOT OF BAD THINGS... TO A LOT OF PEOPLE. I WAS A DIFFERENT PERSON BEFORE... IN THE WORLD.
I WAS SOMEONE I DIDN'T *LIKE.* HELL, I WAS SOMEONE *YOU* DIDN'T LIKE.
YOU WERE STILL MY BROTHER.
A REALLY *CRAPPY* ONE. I ALWAYS TOOK THE EASY WAY OUT. I NEVER TOOK THE TIME TO DO THINGS *RIGHT.*
I'M DIFFERENT NOW. THIS PLACE HAS CHANGED ME. IT'S CHANGED *ALL OF US.*
IT'S MADE US *BETTER.*
LOOK AROUND YOU.
THIS IS OUR *HOME.*
WE'RE *NEVER* GOING BACK.

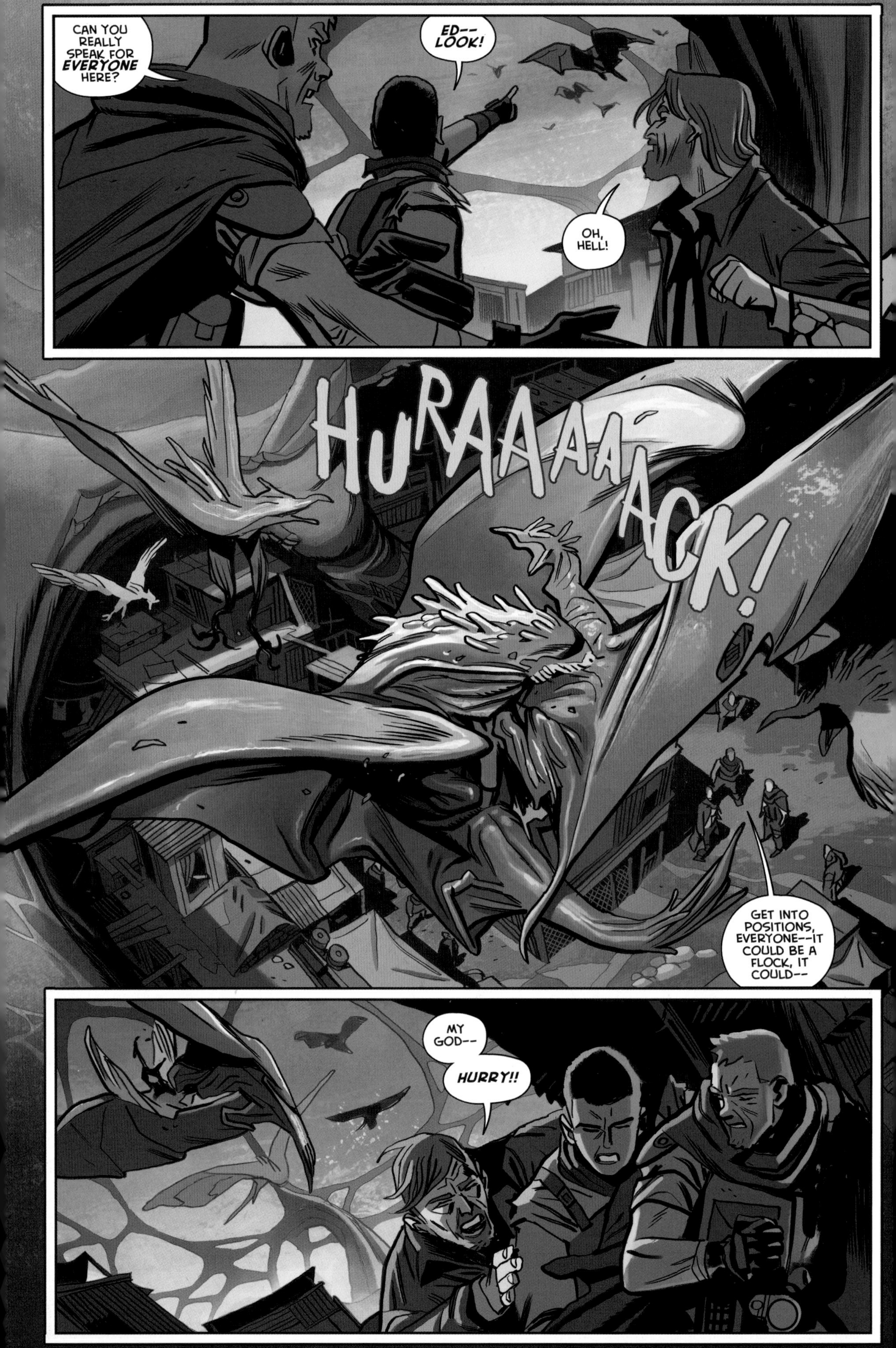
CAN YOU REALLY SPEAK FOR *EVERYONE* HERE?
ED-- LOOK!
OH, HELL!
HURAAAAACK!
GET INTO POSITIONS, EVERYONE--IT COULD BE A FLOCK, IT COULD--
MY GOD--
HURRY!!

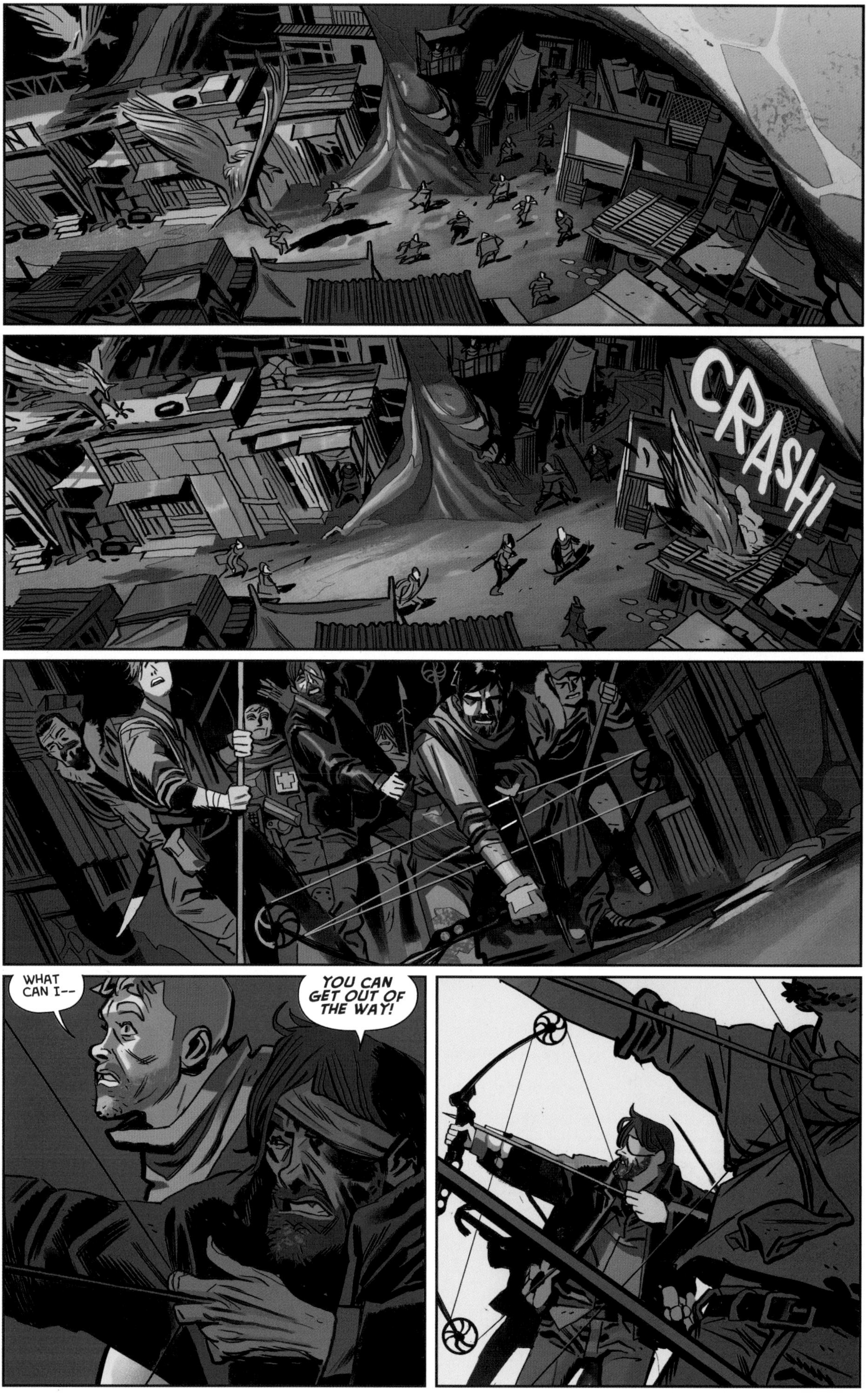
CRASH!
WHAT CAN I--
YOU CAN GET OUT OF THE WAY!

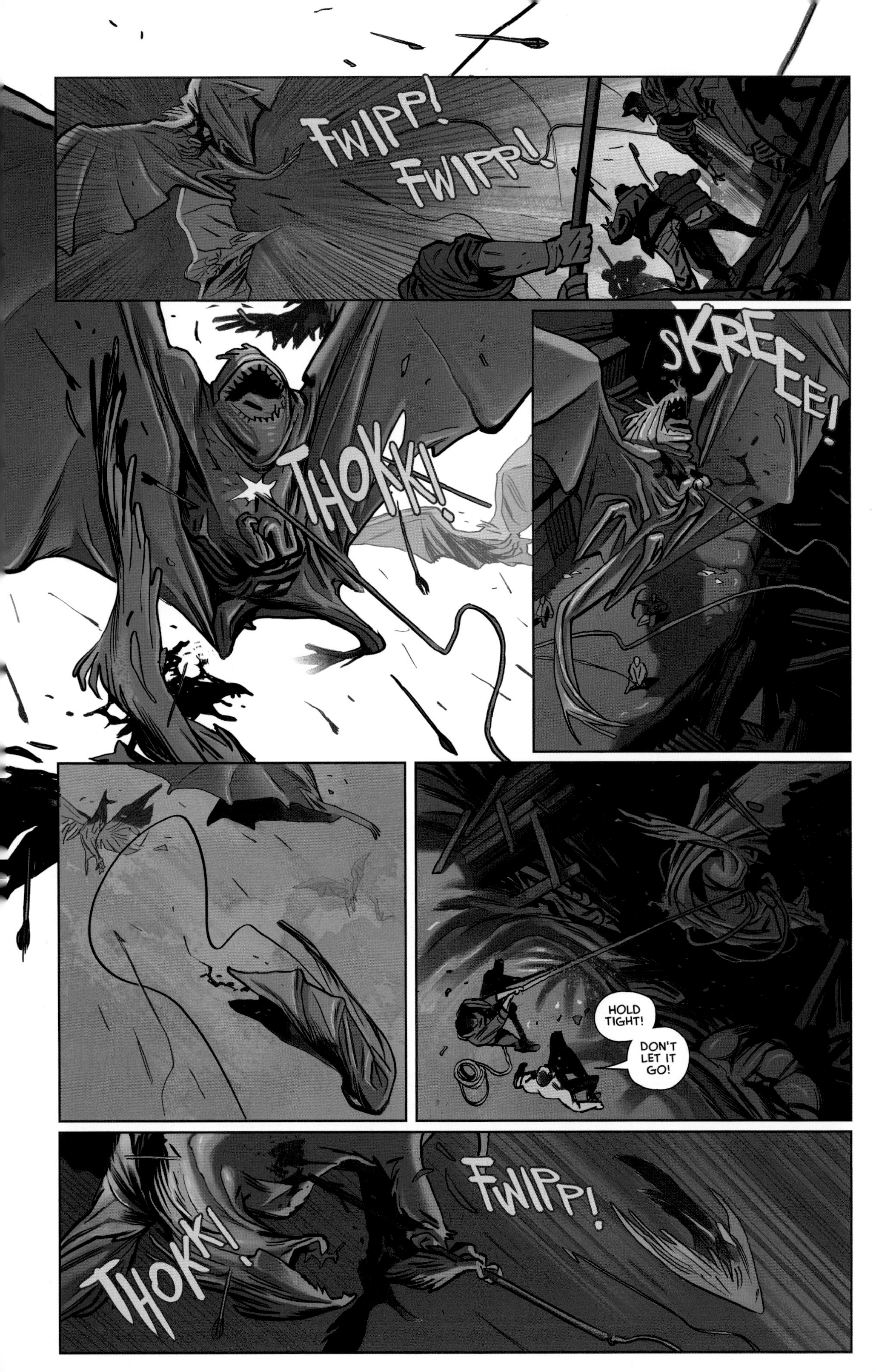
FWIPP!
FWIPP!
THOKK!
SKREEEE!
HOLD TIGHT!
DON'T LET IT GO!
FWIPP!
THOKK!

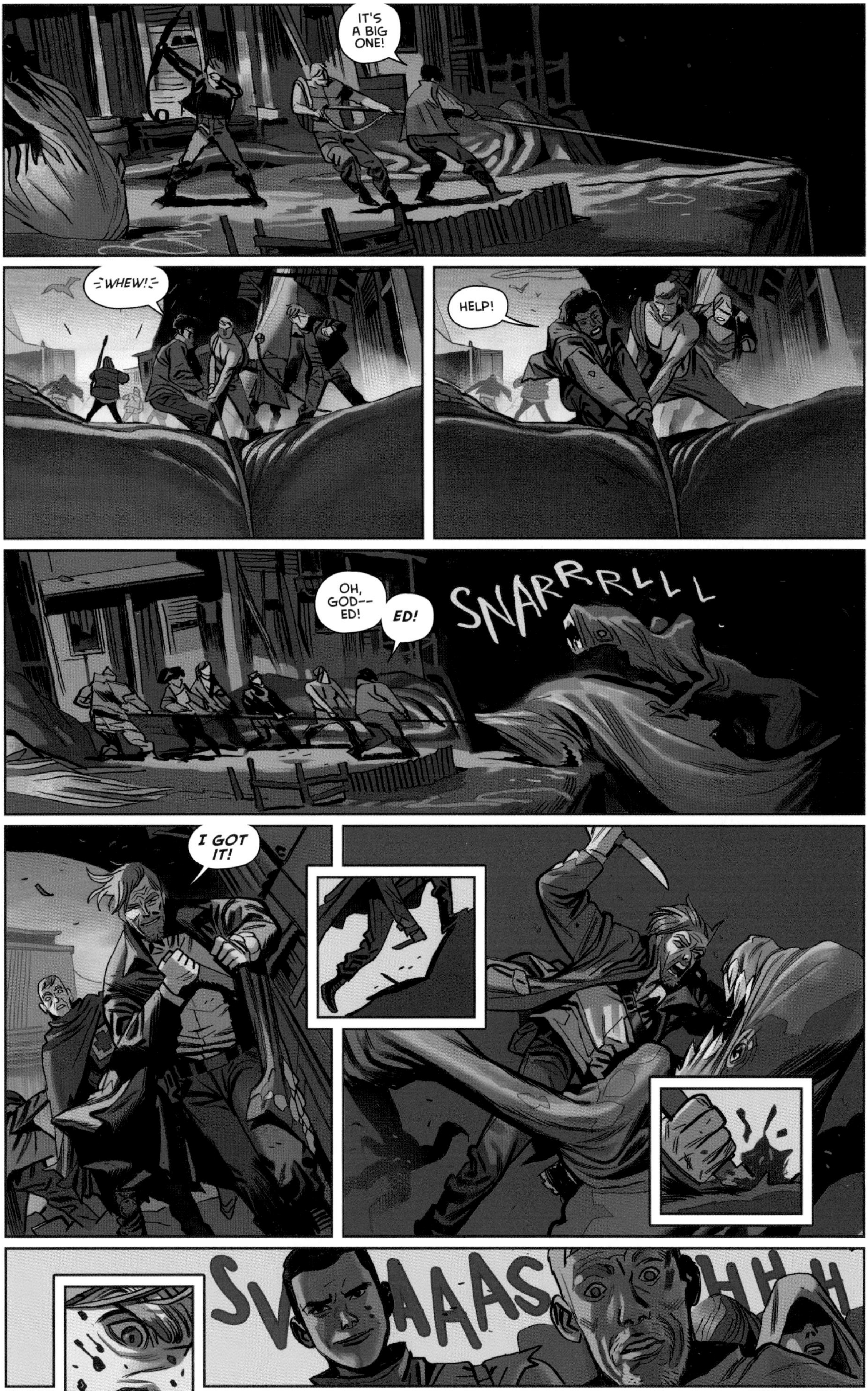
IT'S A BIG ONE!
WHEW!
HELP!
OH, GOD-- ED!
ED!
SNARRRLLL
I GOT IT!
SVAAASHHH

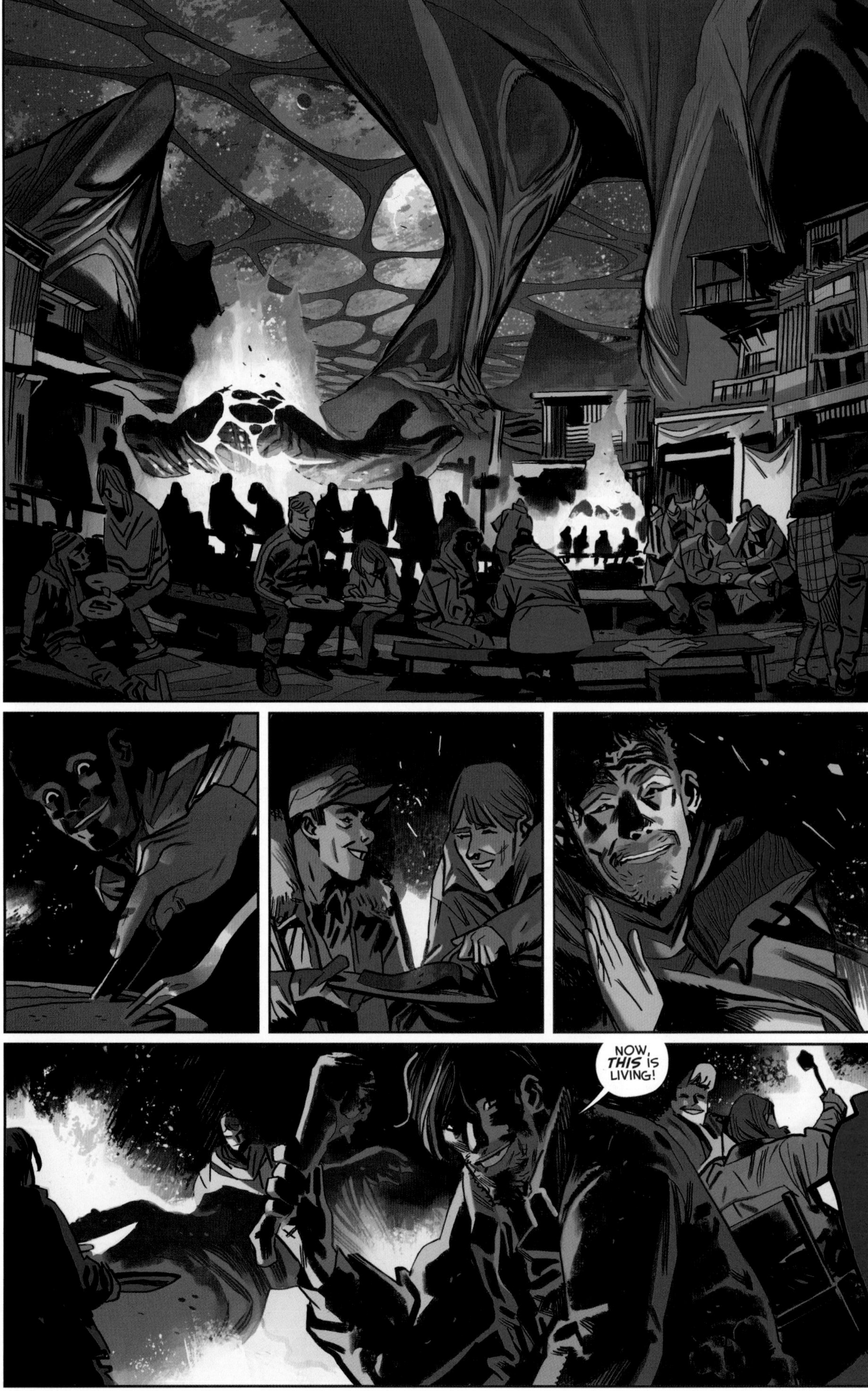
NOW, THIS IS LIVING!

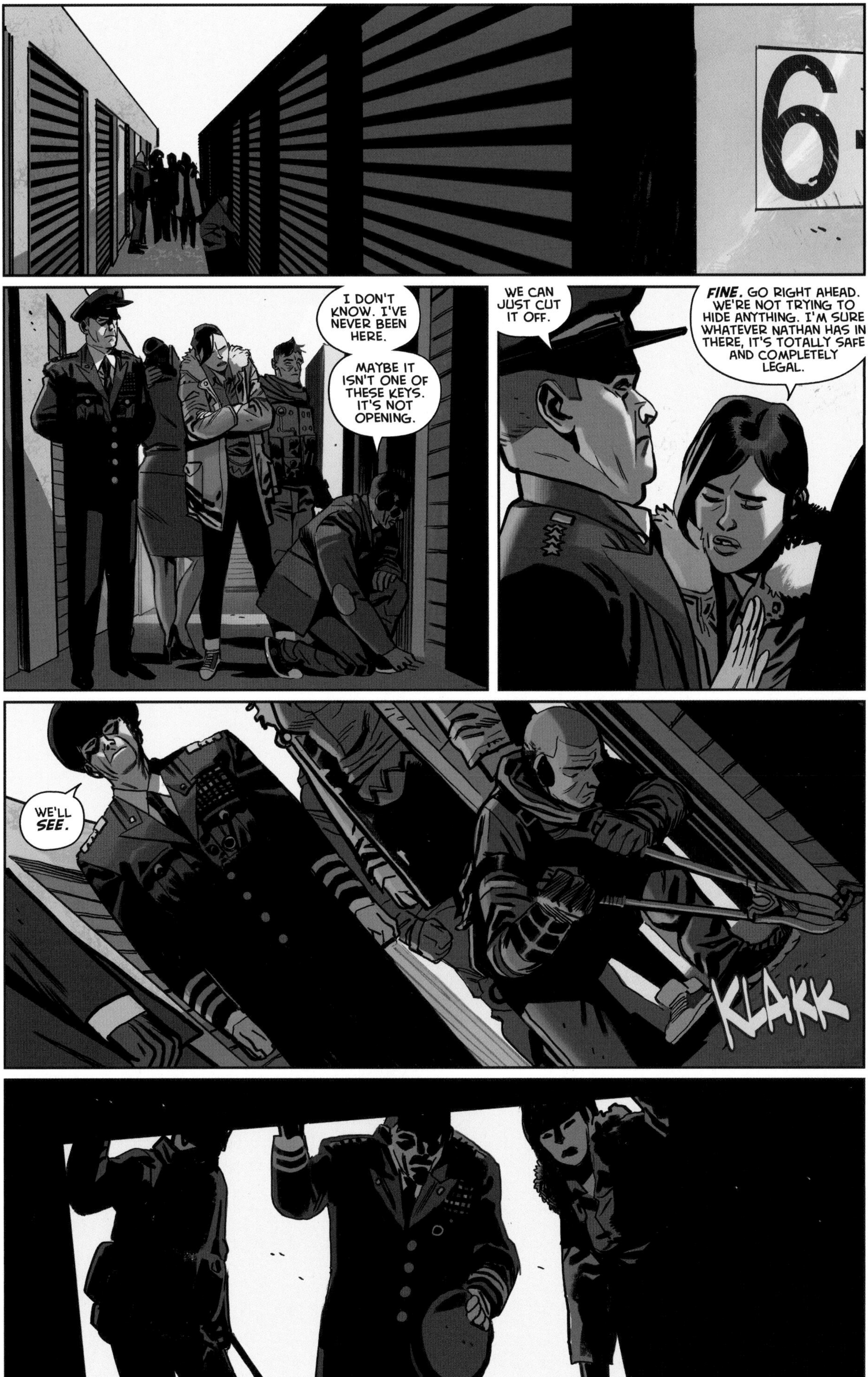
6
I DON'T KNOW. I'VE NEVER BEEN HERE.
MAYBE IT ISN'T ONE OF THESE KEYS. IT'S NOT OPENING.
WE CAN JUST CUT IT OFF.
FINE. GO RIGHT AHEAD. WE'RE NOT TRYING TO HIDE ANYTHING. I'M SURE WHATEVER NATHAN HAS IN THERE, IT'S TOTALLY SAFE AND COMPLETELY LEGAL.
WE'LL SEE.
KLAKK

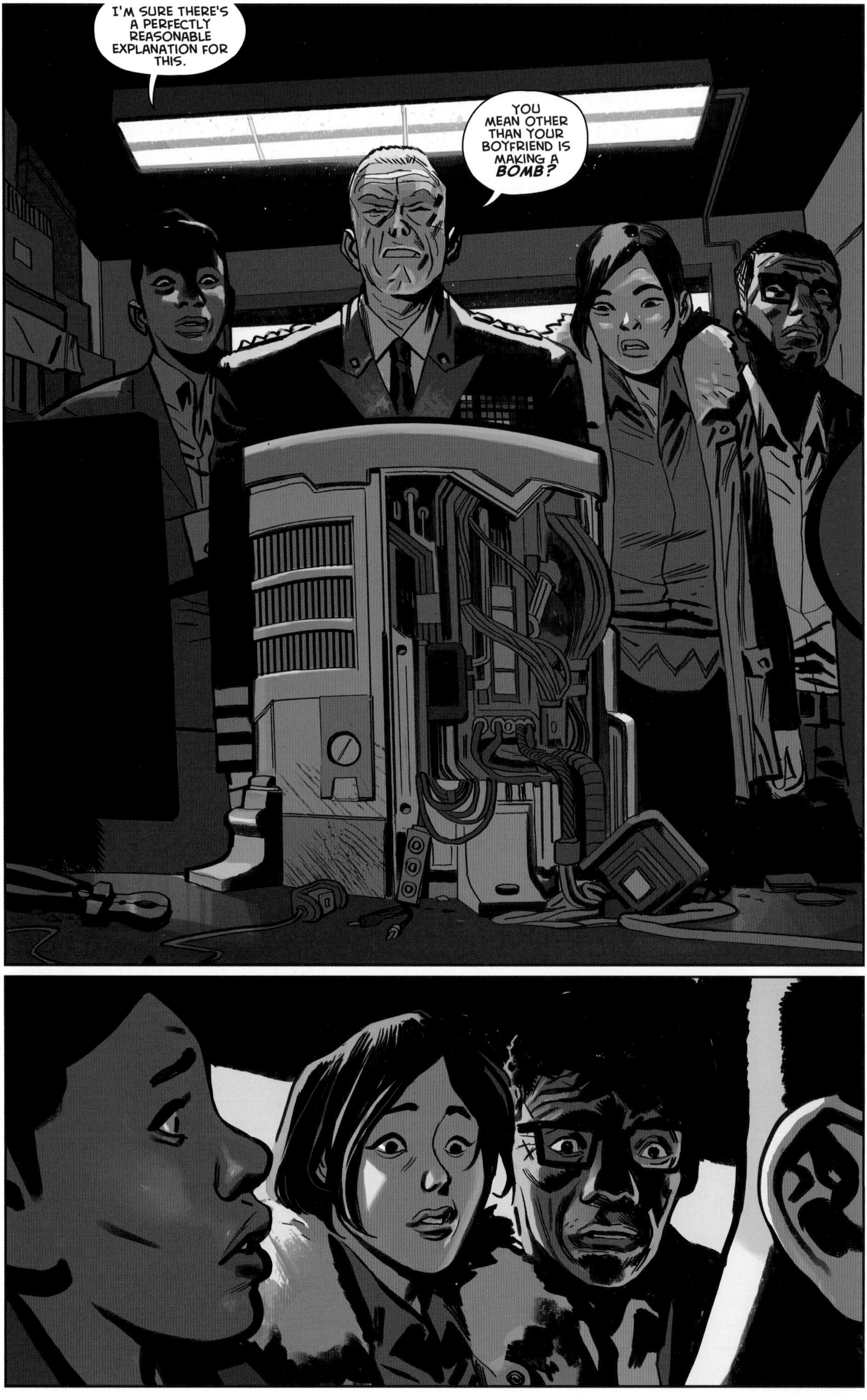
I'M SURE THERE'S A PERFECTLY REASONABLE EXPLANATION FOR THIS.
YOU MEAN OTHER THAN YOUR BOYFRIEND IS MAKING A **BOMB?**

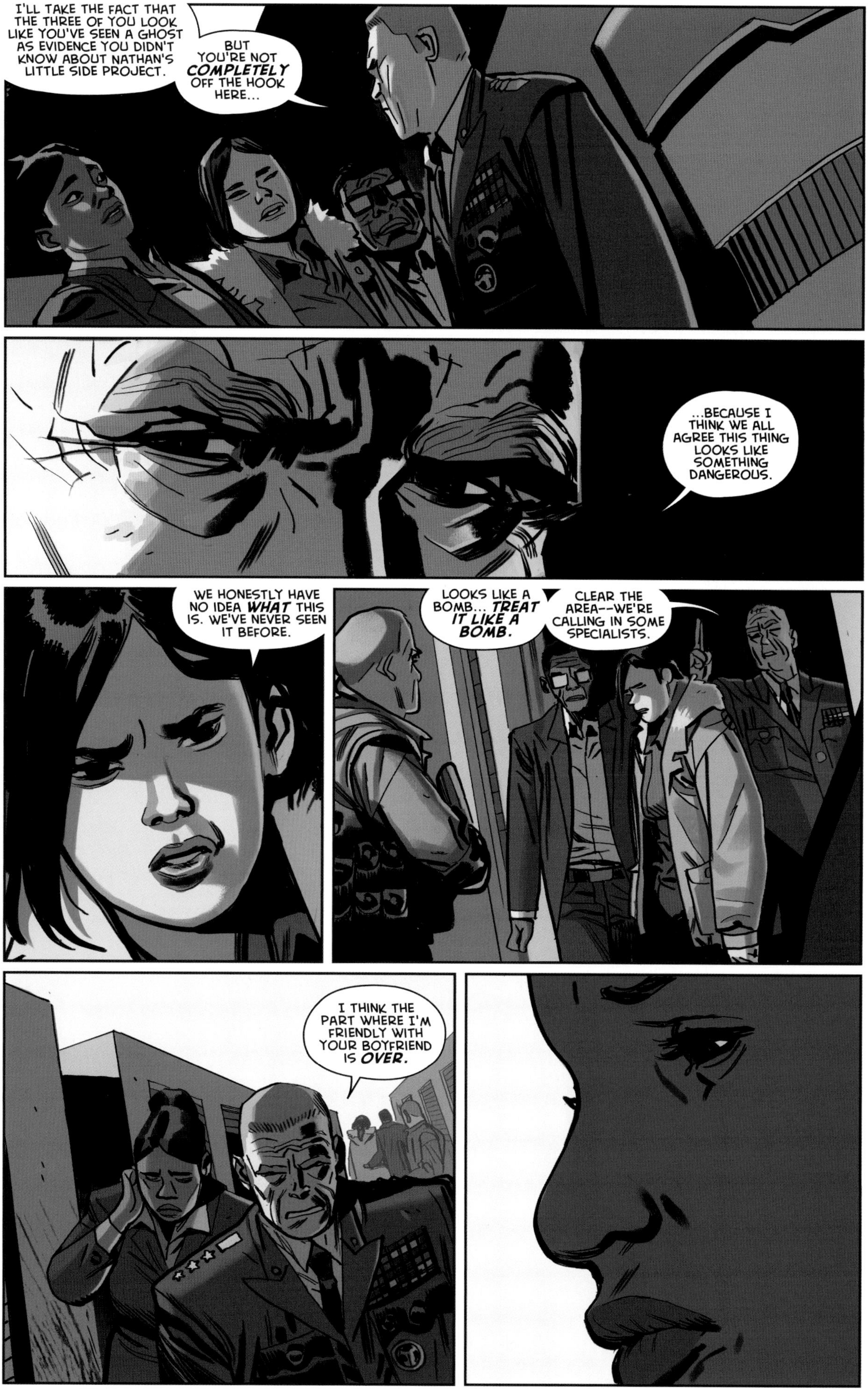
I'LL TAKE THE FACT THAT THE THREE OF YOU LOOK LIKE YOU'VE SEEN A GHOST AS EVIDENCE YOU DIDN'T KNOW ABOUT NATHAN'S LITTLE SIDE PROJECT.
BUT YOU'RE NOT *COMPLETELY* OFF THE HOOK HERE...
...BECAUSE I THINK WE ALL AGREE THIS THING LOOKS LIKE SOMETHING DANGEROUS.
WE HONESTLY HAVE NO IDEA *WHAT* THIS IS. WE'VE NEVER SEEN IT BEFORE.
LOOKS LIKE A BOMB... *TREAT IT LIKE A BOMB.*
CLEAR THE AREA--WE'RE CALLING IN SOME SPECIALISTS.
I THINK THE PART WHERE I'M FRIENDLY WITH YOUR BOYFRIEND IS *OVER.*

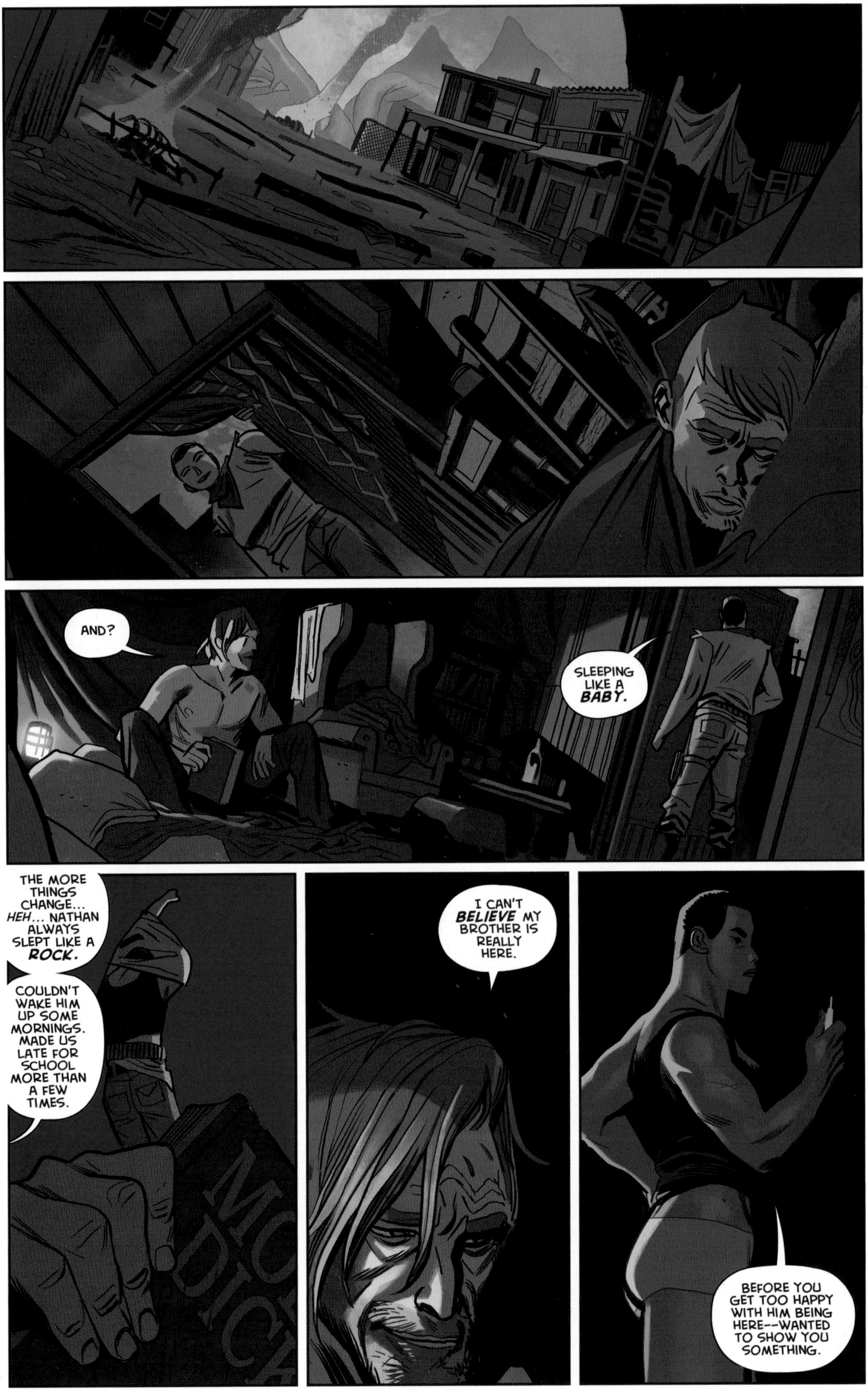
AND?
SLEEPING LIKE A *BABY.*
THE MORE THINGS CHANGE... *HEH*... NATHAN ALWAYS SLEPT LIKE A **ROCK.**
COULDN'T WAKE HIM UP SOME MORNINGS. MADE US LATE FOR SCHOOL MORE THAN A FEW TIMES.
I CAN'T ***BELIEVE*** MY BROTHER IS REALLY HERE.
BEFORE YOU GET TOO HAPPY WITH HIM BEING HERE--WANTED TO SHOW YOU SOMETHING.

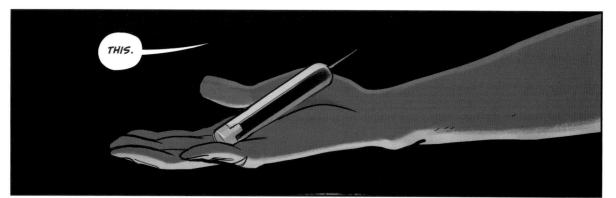

THIS.

WHAT IS IT?

GOT IT FROM *KEITH*. THEY HAD A RUN-IN--YOUR BROTHER TRIED TO SHOOT HIM WITH IT. IT'S WHAT SENDS PEOPLE BACK, APPARENTLY.

THAT'S WHAT HE'S BEEN SHOOTING OUR PEOPLE WITH.

THIS LITTLE THING? I CAN'T EVEN BEGIN TO IMAGINE HOW THIS WORKS.

I KNEW MY BROTHER WAS A SCIENTIST-- *BUT THIS*-- HE MUST BE A DAMN *GENIUS*.

MY BROTHER AND I... WE'VE ALWAYS HAD A *COMPLICATED* RELATIONSHIP, BUT HE'S NEVER GIVEN ME REASON NOT TO TRUST HIM.

DO YOU *TRUST* HIM?

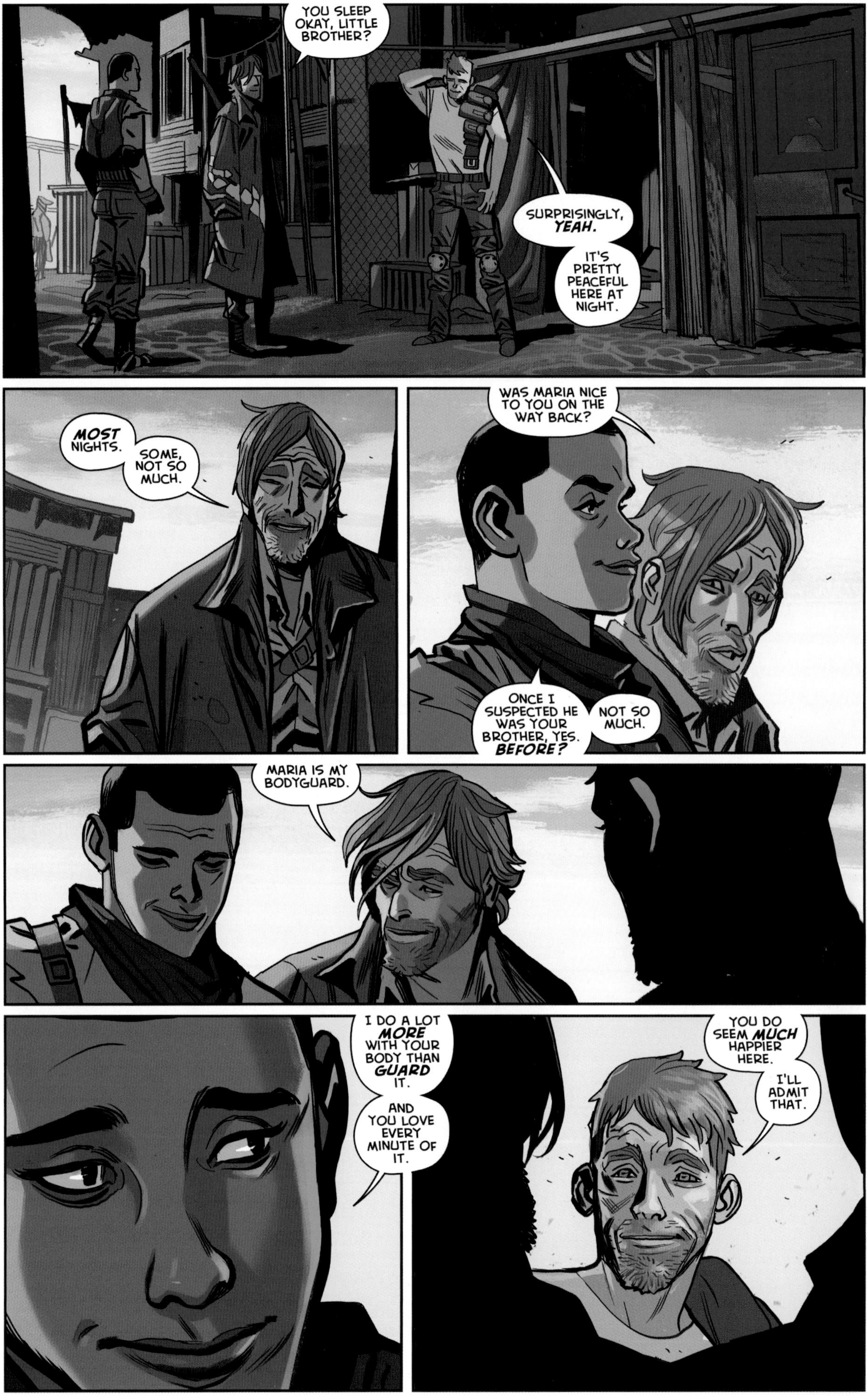

YOU SLEEP OKAY, LITTLE BROTHER?
SURPRISINGLY, YEAH.
IT'S PRETTY PEACEFUL HERE AT NIGHT.
MOST NIGHTS.
SOME, NOT SO MUCH.
WAS MARIA NICE TO YOU ON THE WAY BACK?
NOT SO MUCH.
ONCE I SUSPECTED HE WAS YOUR BROTHER, YES. BEFORE?
MARIA IS MY BODYGUARD.
I DO A LOT MORE WITH YOUR BODY THAN GUARD IT.
AND YOU LOVE EVERY MINUTE OF IT.
YOU DO SEEM MUCH HAPPIER HERE.
I'LL ADMIT THAT.

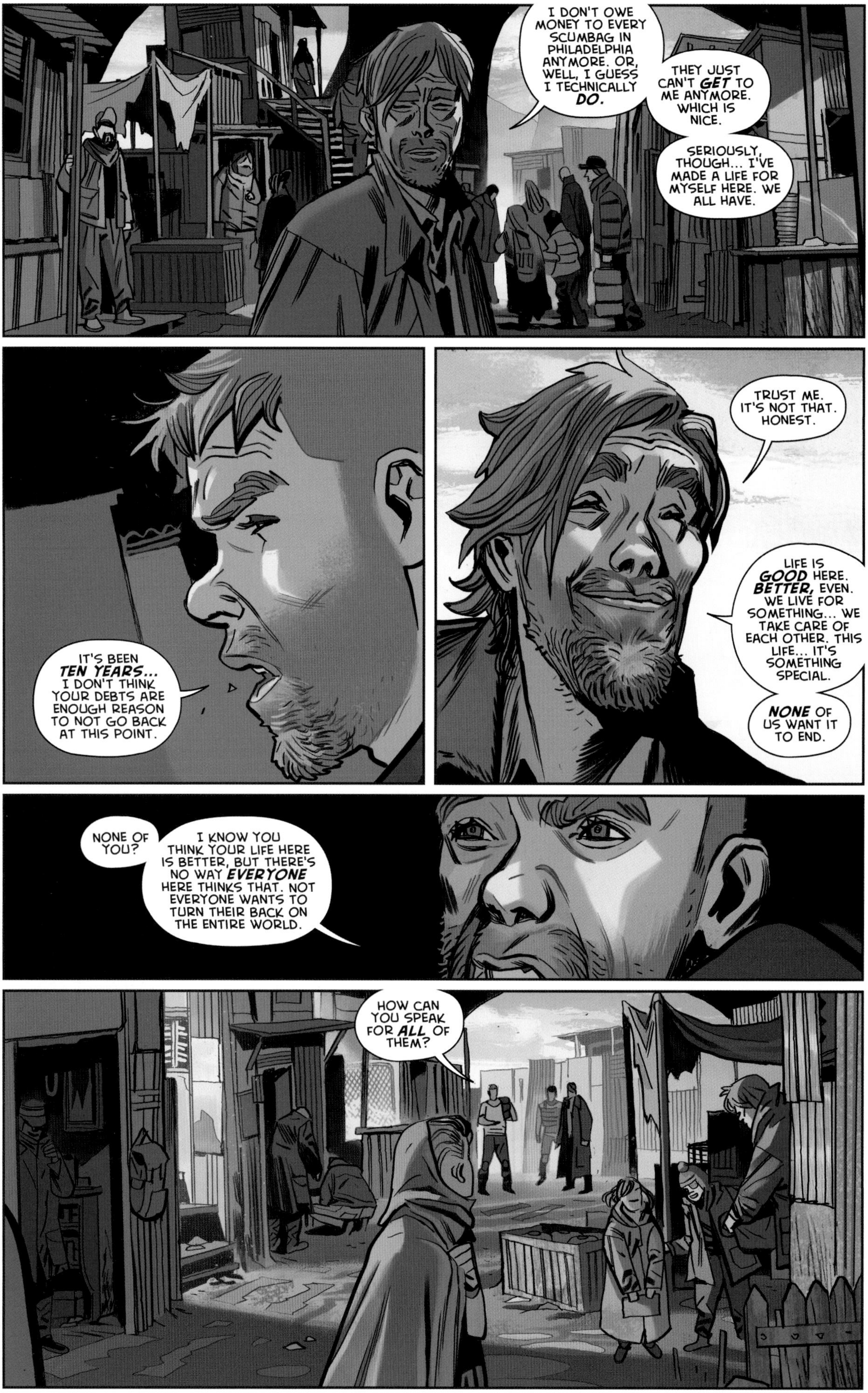
I DON'T OWE MONEY TO EVERY SCUMBAG IN PHILADELPHIA ANYMORE. OR, WELL, I GUESS I TECHNICALLY DO.
THEY JUST CAN'T GET TO ME ANYMORE. WHICH IS NICE.
SERIOUSLY, THOUGH... I'VE MADE A LIFE FOR MYSELF HERE. WE ALL HAVE.
IT'S BEEN TEN YEARS... I DON'T THINK YOUR DEBTS ARE ENOUGH REASON TO NOT GO BACK AT THIS POINT.
TRUST ME. IT'S NOT THAT. HONEST.
LIFE IS GOOD HERE. BETTER, EVEN. WE LIVE FOR SOMETHING... WE TAKE CARE OF EACH OTHER. THIS LIFE... IT'S SOMETHING SPECIAL.
NONE OF US WANT IT TO END.
NONE OF YOU?
I KNOW YOU THINK YOUR LIFE HERE IS BETTER, BUT THERE'S NO WAY EVERYONE HERE THINKS THAT. NOT EVERYONE WANTS TO TURN THEIR BACK ON THE ENTIRE WORLD.
HOW CAN YOU SPEAK FOR ALL OF THEM?

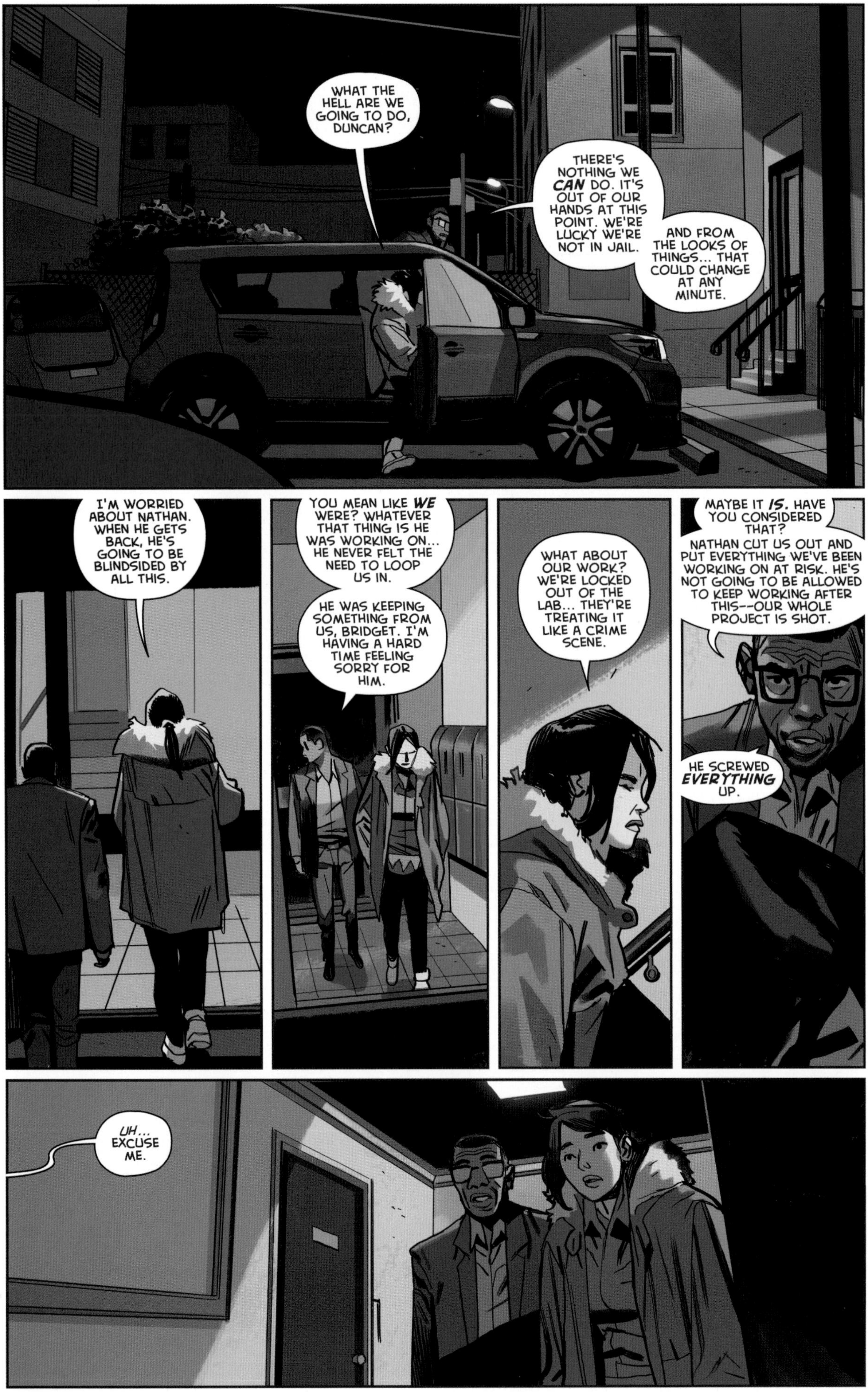

WHAT THE HELL ARE WE GOING TO DO, DUNCAN?
THERE'S NOTHING WE CAN DO. IT'S OUT OF OUR HANDS AT THIS POINT. WE'RE LUCKY WE'RE NOT IN JAIL.
AND FROM THE LOOKS OF THINGS... THAT COULD CHANGE AT ANY MINUTE.
I'M WORRIED ABOUT NATHAN. WHEN HE GETS BACK, HE'S GOING TO BE BLINDSIDED BY ALL THIS.
YOU MEAN LIKE WE WERE? WHATEVER THAT THING IS HE WAS WORKING ON... HE NEVER FELT THE NEED TO LOOP US IN.
HE WAS KEEPING SOMETHING FROM US, BRIDGET. I'M HAVING A HARD TIME FEELING SORRY FOR HIM.
WHAT ABOUT OUR WORK? WE'RE LOCKED OUT OF THE LAB... THEY'RE TREATING IT LIKE A CRIME SCENE.
MAYBE IT IS. HAVE YOU CONSIDERED THAT?
NATHAN CUT US OUT AND PUT EVERYTHING WE'VE BEEN WORKING ON AT RISK. HE'S NOT GOING TO BE ALLOWED TO KEEP WORKING AFTER THIS--OUR WHOLE PROJECT IS SHOT.
HE SCREWED EVERYTHING UP.
UH... EXCUSE ME.

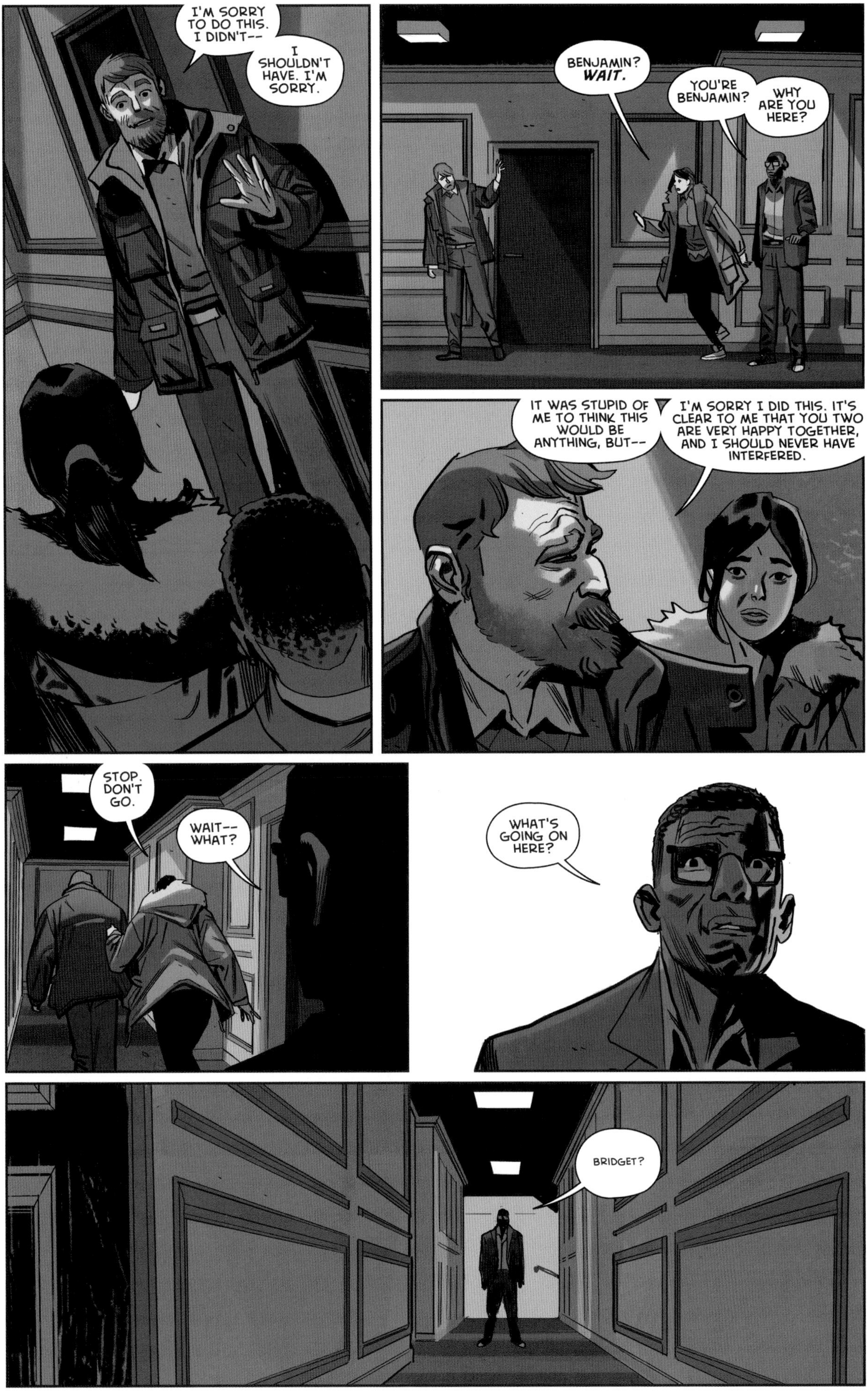

I'M SORRY TO DO THIS. I DIDN'T--
I SHOULDN'T HAVE. I'M SORRY.
BENJAMIN? WAIT.
YOU'RE BENJAMIN?
WHY ARE YOU HERE?
IT WAS STUPID OF ME TO THINK THIS WOULD BE ANYTHING, BUT--
I'M SORRY I DID THIS. IT'S CLEAR TO ME THAT YOU TWO ARE VERY HAPPY TOGETHER, AND I SHOULD NEVER HAVE INTERFERED.
STOP. DON'T GO.
WAIT-- WHAT?
WHAT'S GOING ON HERE?
BRIDGET?

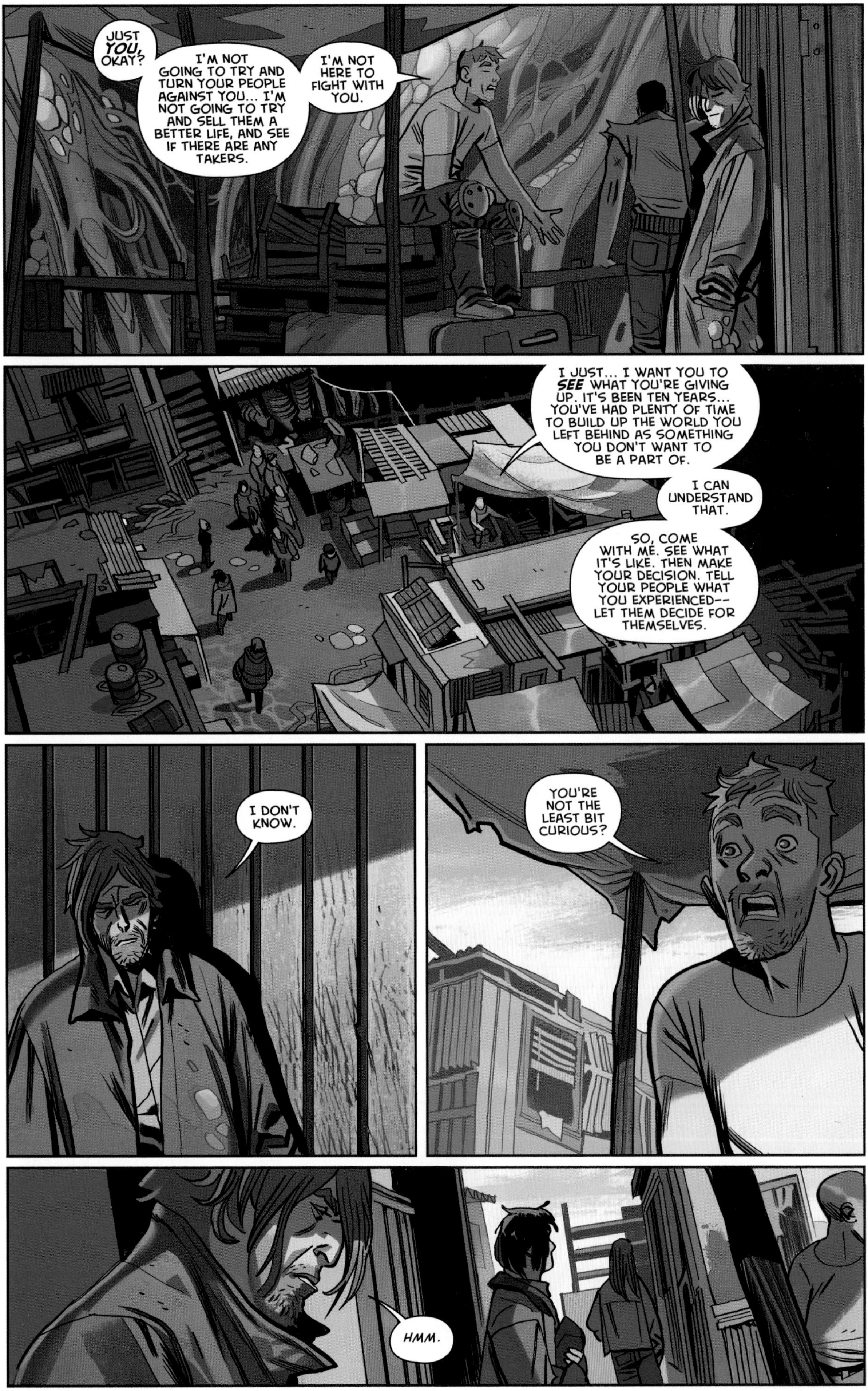
JUST *YOU*, OKAY?
I'M NOT GOING TO TRY AND TURN YOUR PEOPLE AGAINST YOU... I'M NOT GOING TO TRY AND SELL THEM A BETTER LIFE, AND SEE IF THERE ARE ANY TAKERS.
I'M NOT HERE TO FIGHT WITH YOU.
I JUST... I WANT YOU TO *SEE* WHAT YOU'RE GIVING UP. IT'S BEEN TEN YEARS... YOU'VE HAD PLENTY OF TIME TO BUILD UP THE WORLD YOU LEFT BEHIND AS SOMETHING YOU DON'T WANT TO BE A PART OF.
I CAN UNDERSTAND THAT.
SO, COME WITH ME. SEE WHAT IT'S LIKE. THEN MAKE YOUR DECISION. TELL YOUR PEOPLE WHAT YOU EXPERIENCED-- LET THEM DECIDE FOR THEMSELVES.
I DON'T KNOW.
YOU'RE NOT THE LEAST BIT CURIOUS?
HMM.

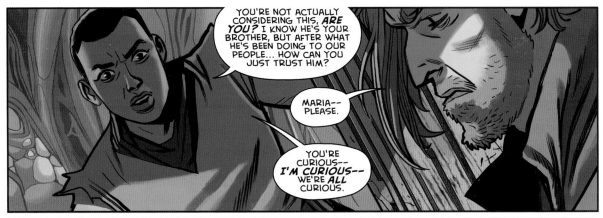

YOU'RE NOT ACTUALLY CONSIDERING THIS, *ARE YOU?* I KNOW HE'S YOUR BROTHER, BUT AFTER WHAT HE'S BEEN DOING TO OUR PEOPLE... HOW CAN YOU JUST TRUST HIM?

MARIA-- PLEASE.

YOU'RE CURIOUS-- *I'M CURIOUS*-- WE'RE *ALL* CURIOUS.

THEN THAT'S *WHY* I SHOULD GO. FOR OUR PEOPLE. SO THEY CAN *KNOW.*

WOULD YOU WANT TO STAY HERE... NOT KNOWING... NEVER KNOWING IF THERE'S A BETTER LIFE OUT THERE FOR YOU? FOR YOUR SON?

NO.

OF COURSE NOT.

OKAY THEN.

THIS.

THAT'S ONE OF MY DARTS.

DOES IT STILL WORK?

YEAH, IT'S STILL ACTIVE. BE CAREFUL WITH IT.

YOU KEEP *THIS.*

JUST IN CASE.

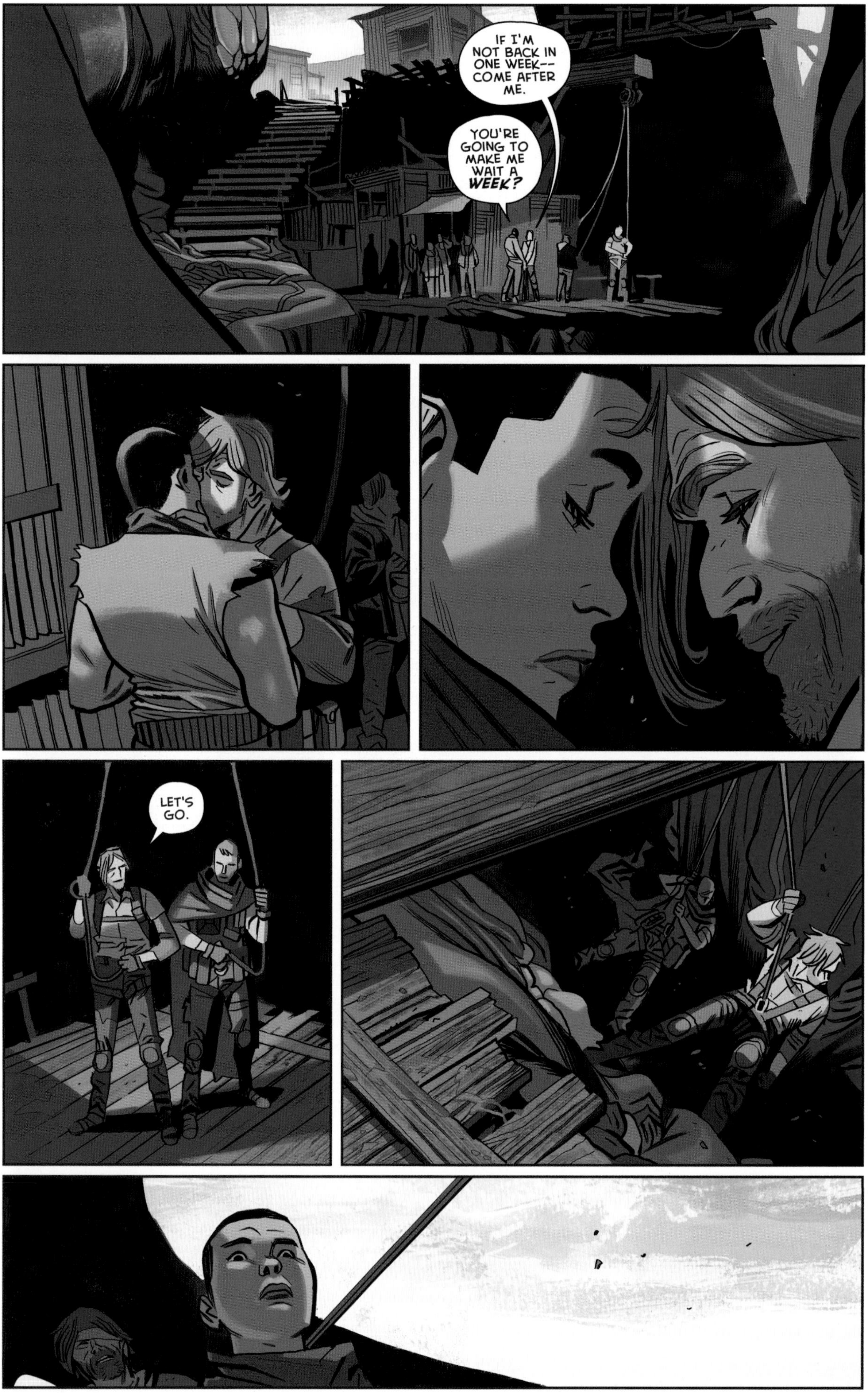
IF I'M NOT BACK IN ONE WEEK-- COME AFTER ME.
YOU'RE GOING TO MAKE ME WAIT A *WEEK?*
LET'S GO.

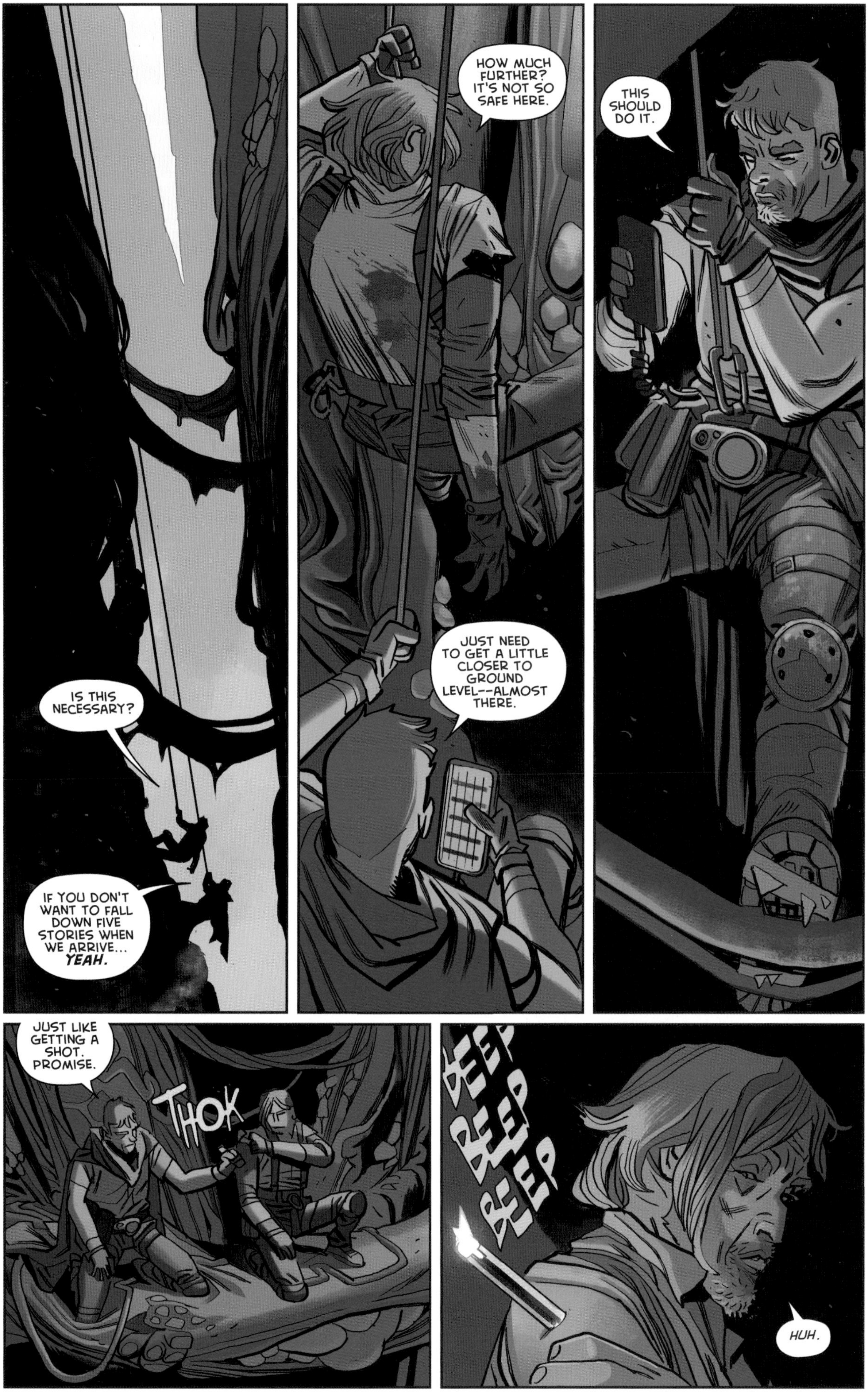
IS THIS NECESSARY?
IF YOU DON'T WANT TO FALL DOWN FIVE STORIES WHEN WE ARRIVE... **YEAH.**
HOW MUCH FURTHER? IT'S NOT SO SAFE HERE.
JUST NEED TO GET A LITTLE CLOSER TO GROUND LEVEL--ALMOST THERE.
THIS SHOULD DO IT.
JUST LIKE GETTING A SHOT. PROMISE.
THOK
BEEP BEEP BEEP
HUH.

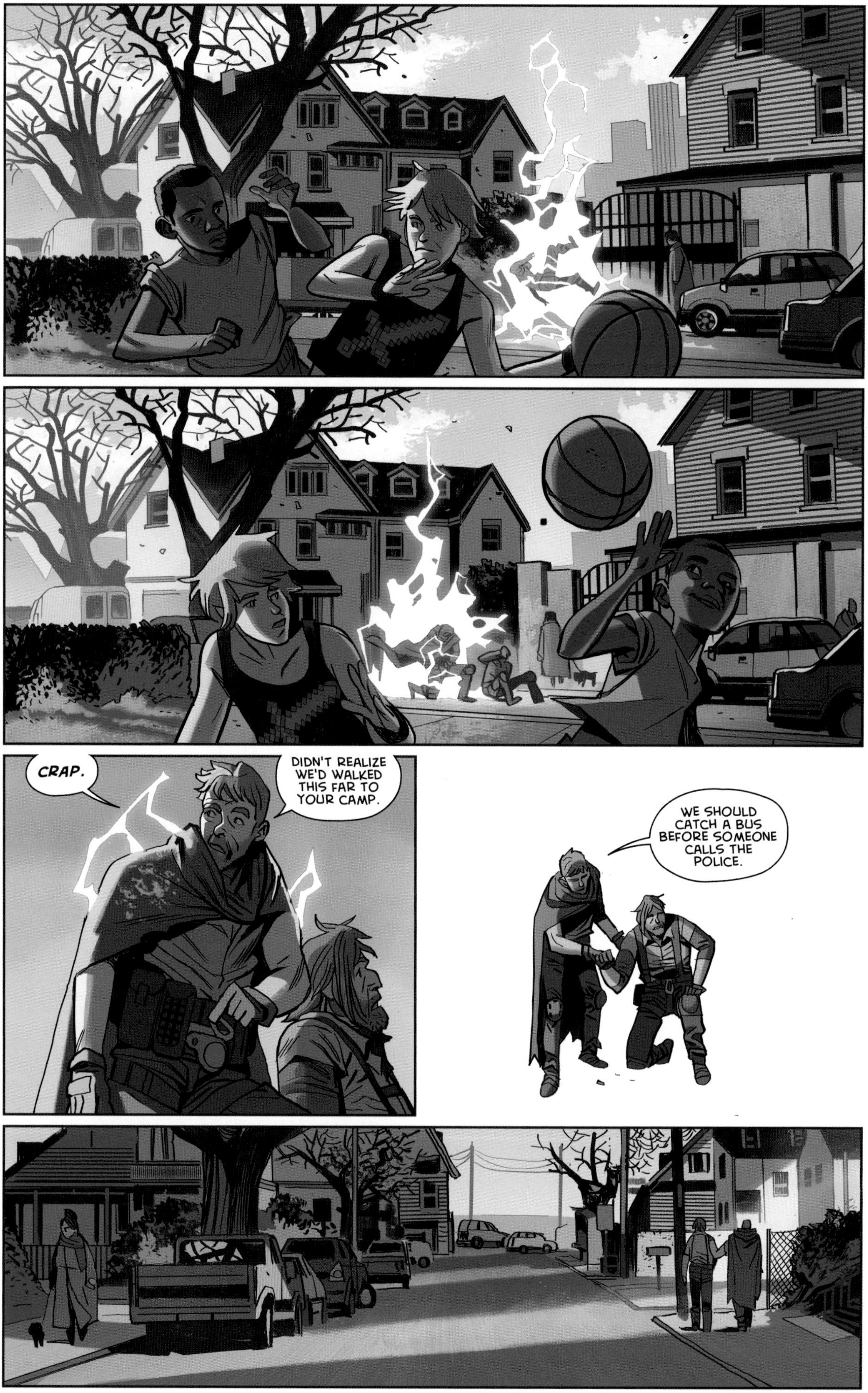
CRAP.
DIDN'T REALIZE WE'D WALKED THIS FAR TO YOUR CAMP.
WE SHOULD CATCH A BUS BEFORE SOMEONE CALLS THE POLICE.

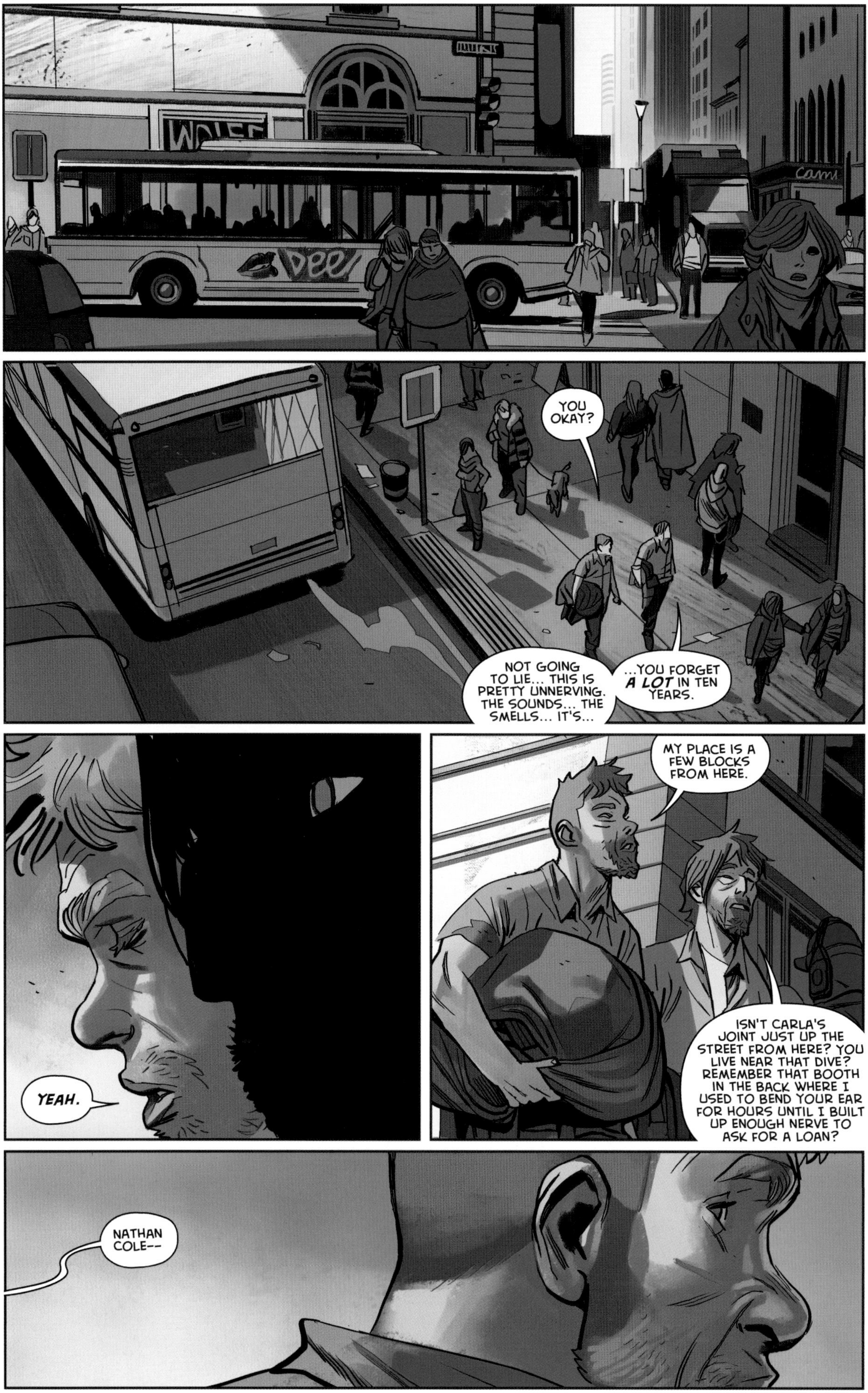
YOU OKAY?
NOT GOING TO LIE... THIS IS PRETTY UNNERVING. THE SOUNDS... THE SMELLS... IT'S...
...YOU FORGET *A LOT* IN TEN YEARS.
YEAH.
MY PLACE IS A FEW BLOCKS FROM HERE.
ISN'T CARLA'S JOINT JUST UP THE STREET FROM HERE? YOU LIVE NEAR THAT DIVE? REMEMBER THAT BOOTH IN THE BACK WHERE I USED TO BEND YOUR EAR FOR HOURS UNTIL I BUILT UP ENOUGH NERVE TO ASK FOR A LOAN?
NATHAN COLE--

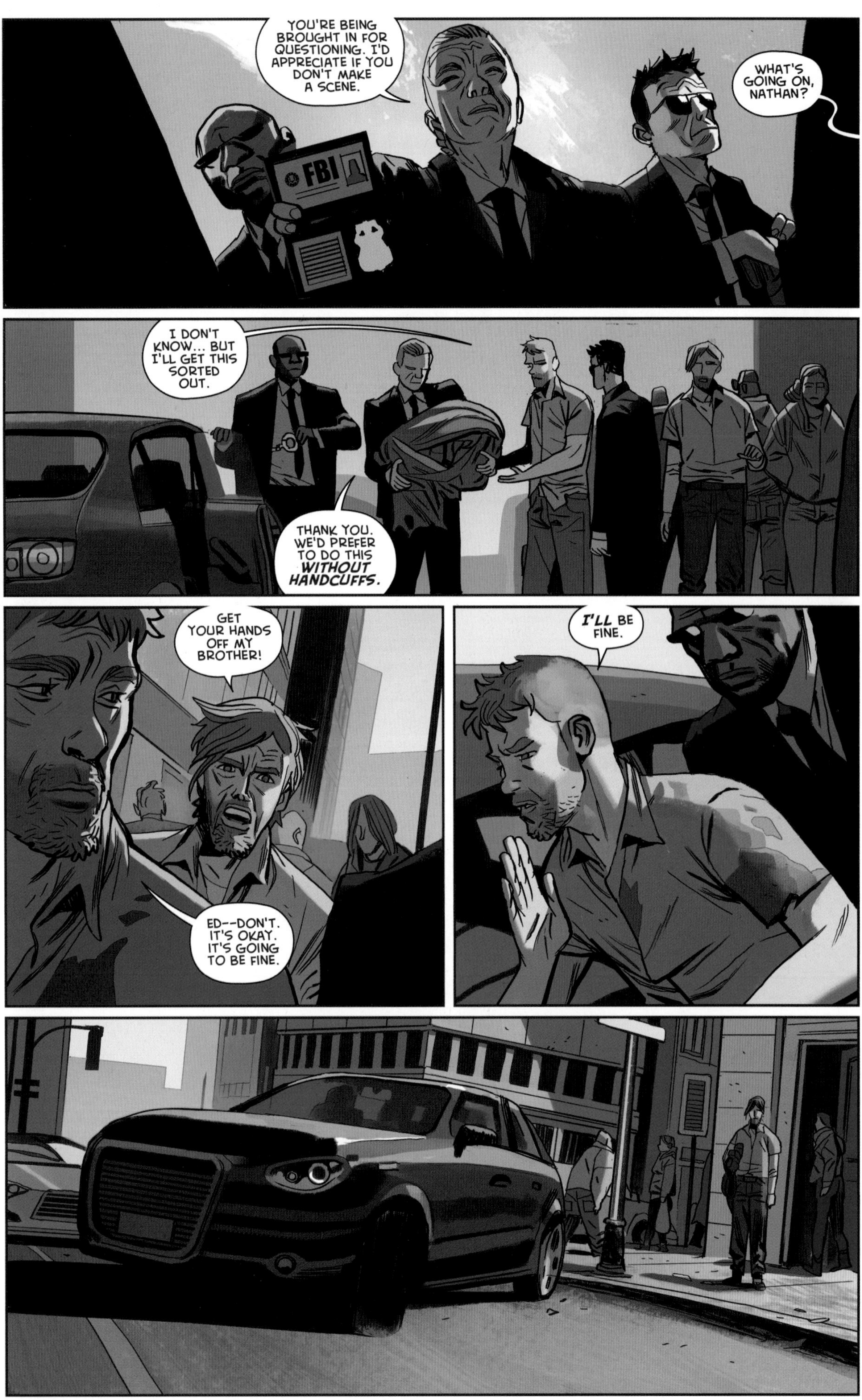
YOU'RE BEING BROUGHT IN FOR QUESTIONING. I'D APPRECIATE IF YOU DON'T MAKE A SCENE.
WHAT'S GOING ON, NATHAN?
I DON'T KNOW... BUT I'LL GET THIS SORTED OUT.
THANK YOU. WE'D PREFER TO DO THIS WITHOUT HANDCUFFS.
GET YOUR HANDS OFF MY BROTHER!
ED--DON'T. IT'S OKAY. IT'S GOING TO BE FINE.
I'LL BE FINE.
FBI

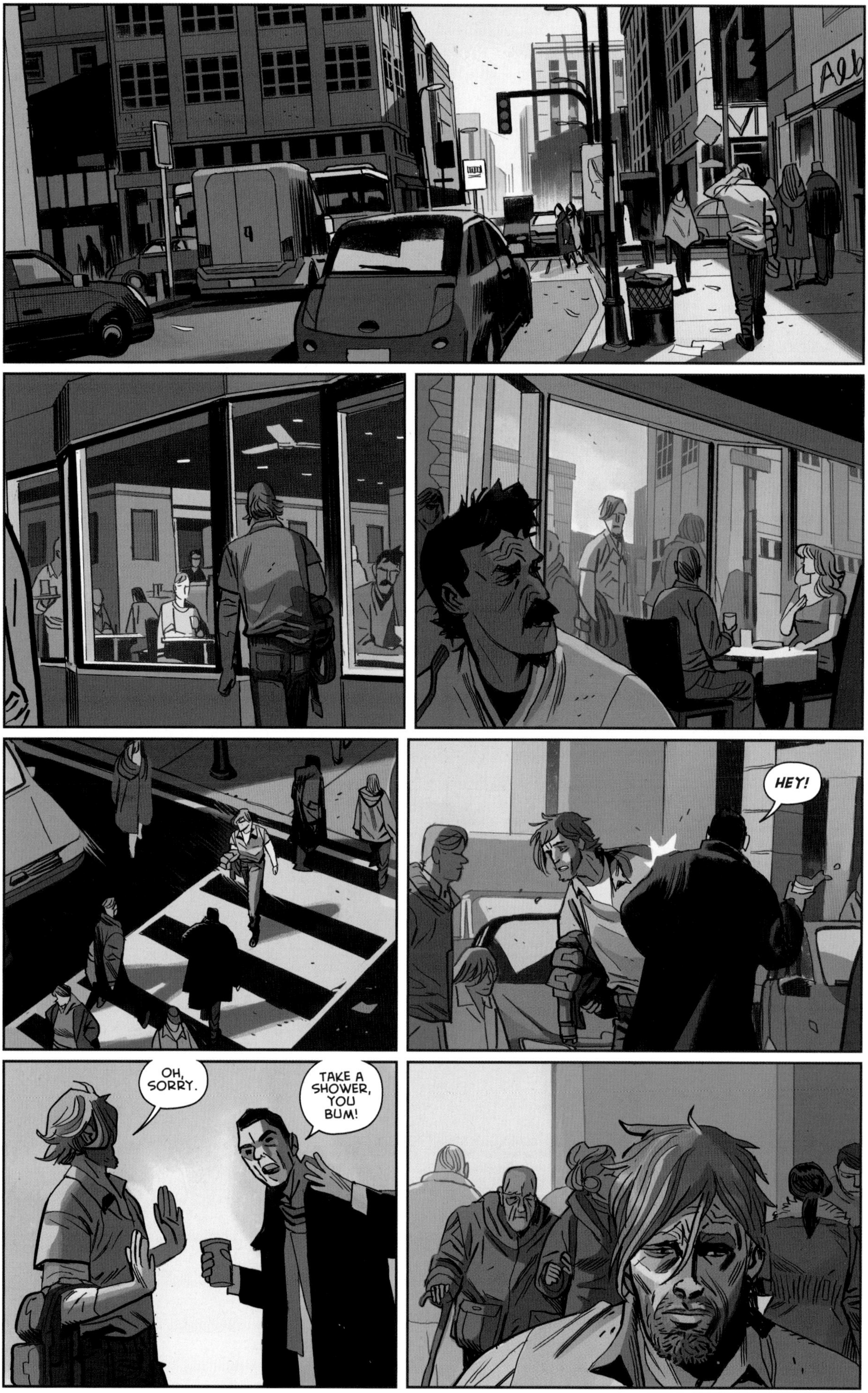
HEY!
OH, SORRY.
TAKE A SHOWER, YOU BUM!

REMIND ME
NEVER TO
PISS YOU
OFF...

THIS IS **SERIOUS**,
NATHAN. THIS IS... I
DON'T EVEN KNOW
WHAT TO SAY.

THEY
FOUND THAT...
DEVICE YOU'RE
WORKING ON IN
YOUR STORAGE
LOCKER.

OH.

IS THAT THING... THEY'RE SAYING
IT HAS SOMETHING TO DO WITH
THE **TRANSFERENCE**...

BUT THAT
CAN'T BE,
CAN--?

YEAH.

...

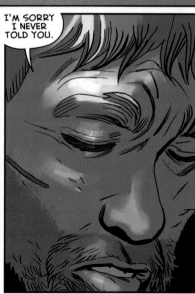

I'M SORRY
I NEVER
TOLD YOU.

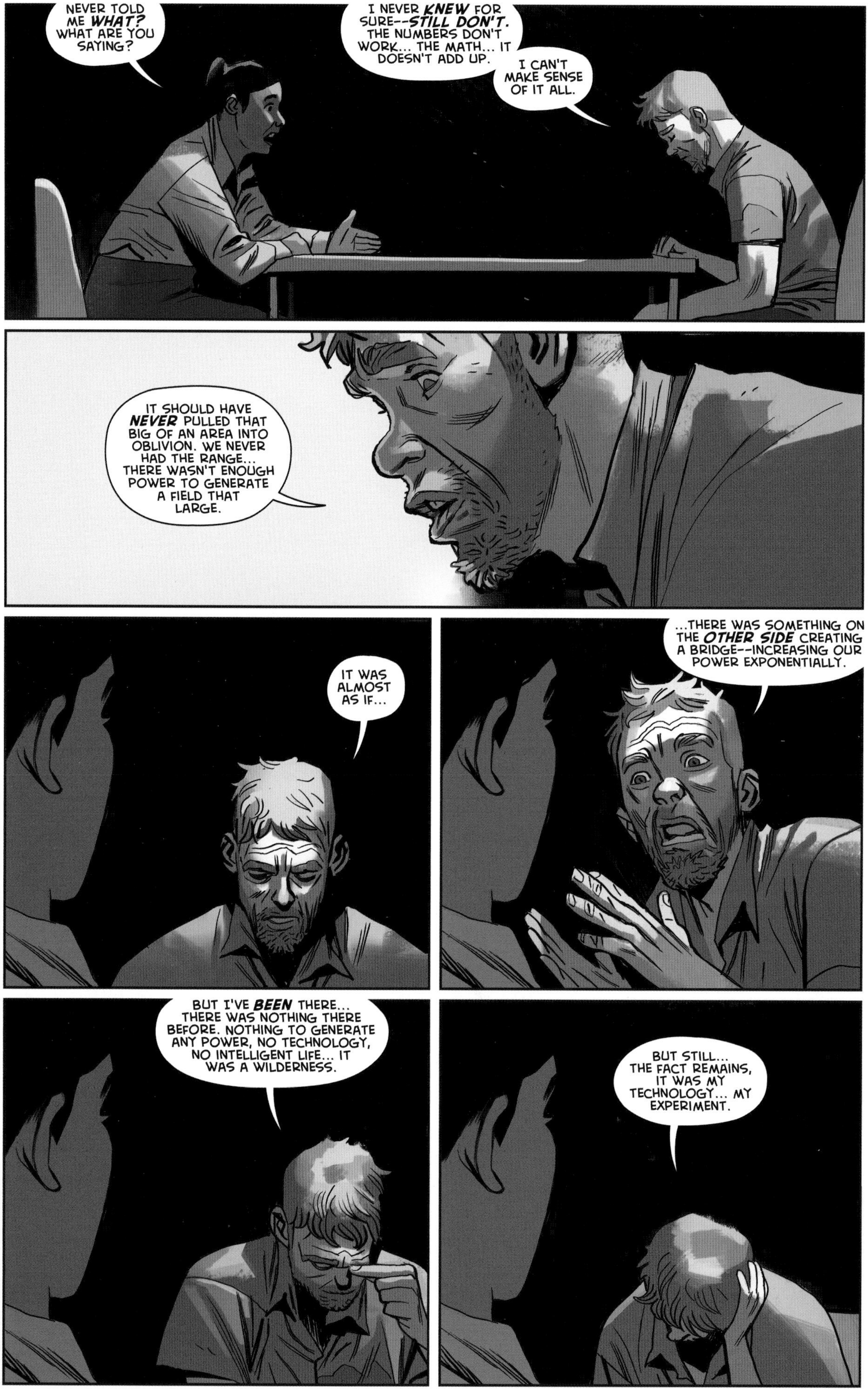
NEVER TOLD ME WHAT? WHAT ARE YOU SAYING?
I NEVER KNEW FOR SURE--STILL DON'T. THE NUMBERS DON'T WORK... THE MATH... IT DOESN'T ADD UP.
I CAN'T MAKE SENSE OF IT ALL.
IT SHOULD HAVE NEVER PULLED THAT BIG OF AN AREA INTO OBLIVION. WE NEVER HAD THE RANGE... THERE WASN'T ENOUGH POWER TO GENERATE A FIELD THAT LARGE.
IT WAS ALMOST AS IF...
...THERE WAS SOMETHING ON THE OTHER SIDE CREATING A BRIDGE--INCREASING OUR POWER EXPONENTIALLY.
BUT I'VE BEEN THERE... THERE WAS NOTHING THERE BEFORE. NOTHING TO GENERATE ANY POWER, NO TECHNOLOGY, NO INTELLIGENT LIFE... IT WAS A WILDERNESS.
BUT STILL... THE FACT REMAINS, IT WAS MY TECHNOLOGY... MY EXPERIMENT.

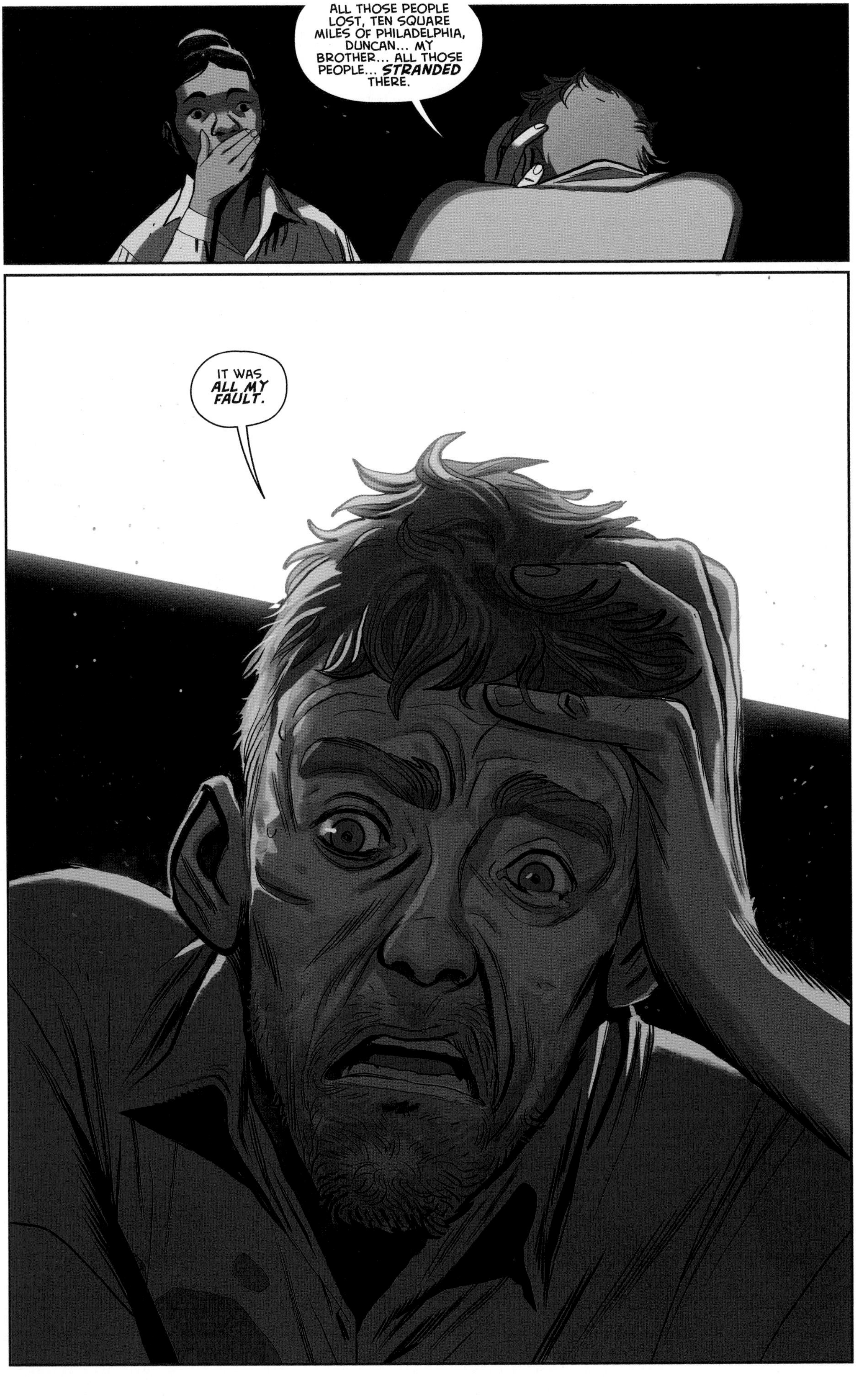
ALL THOSE PEOPLE LOST, TEN SQUARE MILES OF PHILADELPHIA, DUNCAN... MY BROTHER... ALL THOSE PEOPLE... STRANDED THERE.
IT WAS ALL MY FAULT.

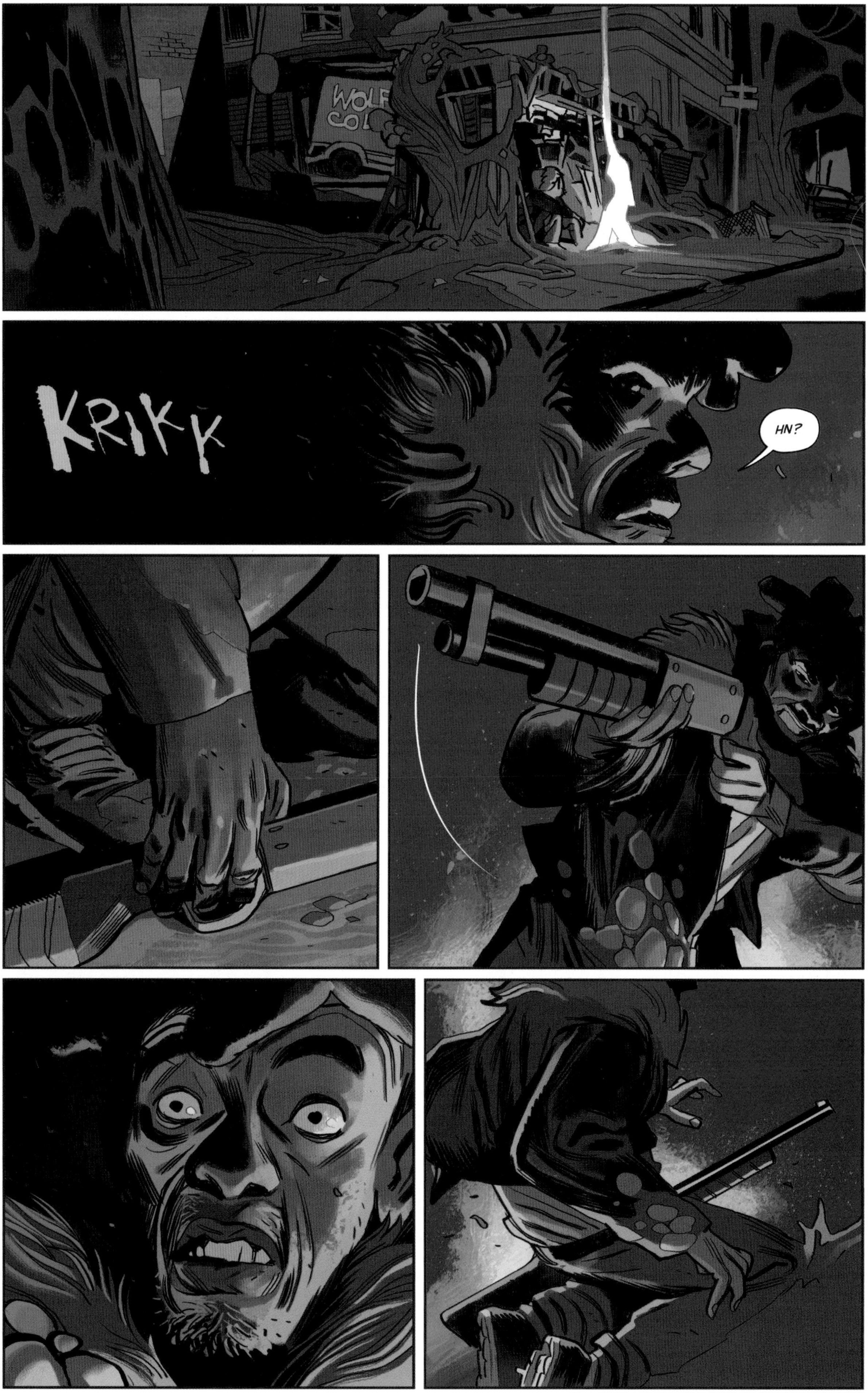
KRIKK
HN?

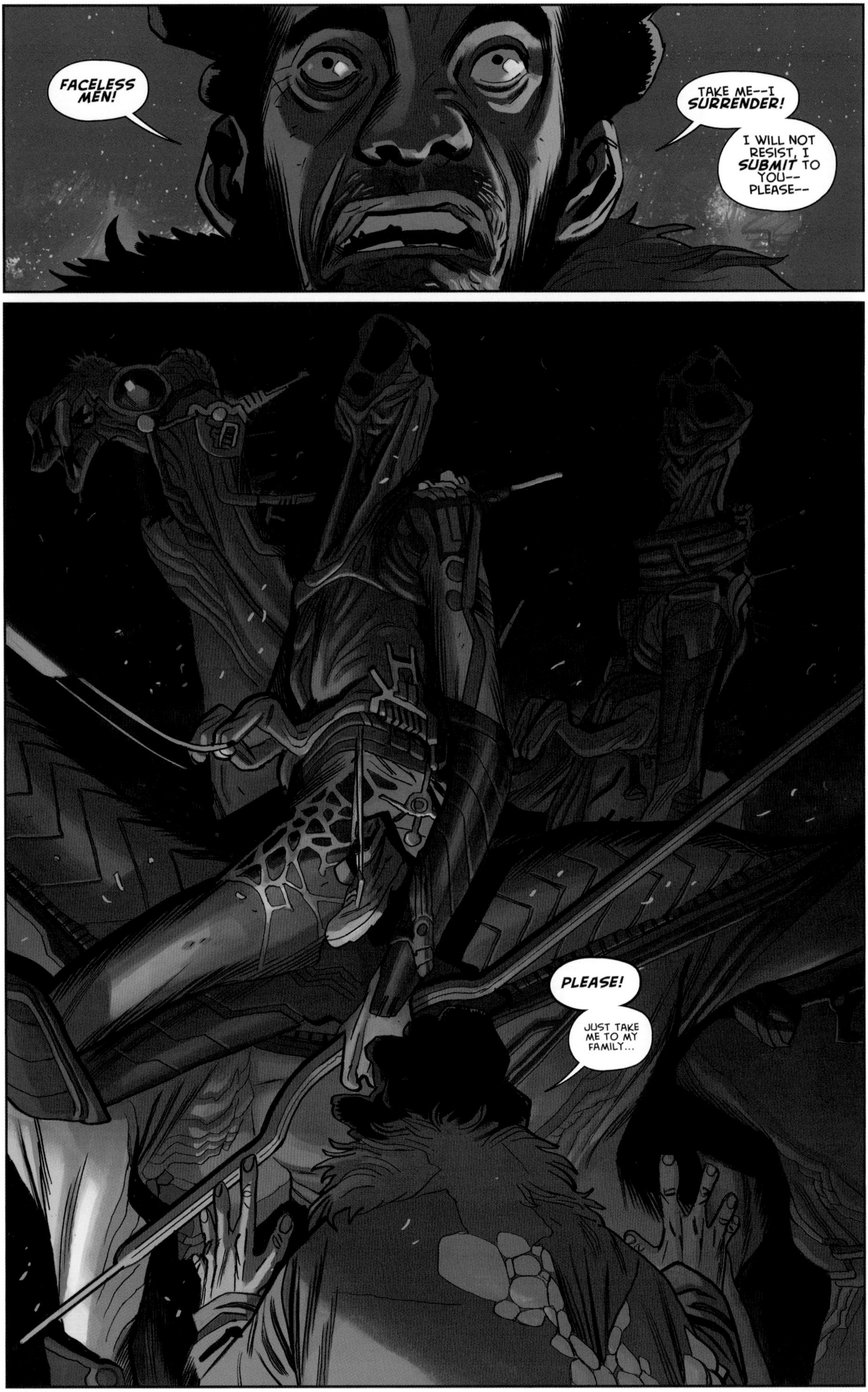
FACELESS MEN!
TAKE ME--I SURRENDER!
I WILL NOT RESIST, I SUBMIT TO YOU-- PLEASE--
PLEASE!
JUST TAKE ME TO MY FAMILY...

CHAPTER

TWO

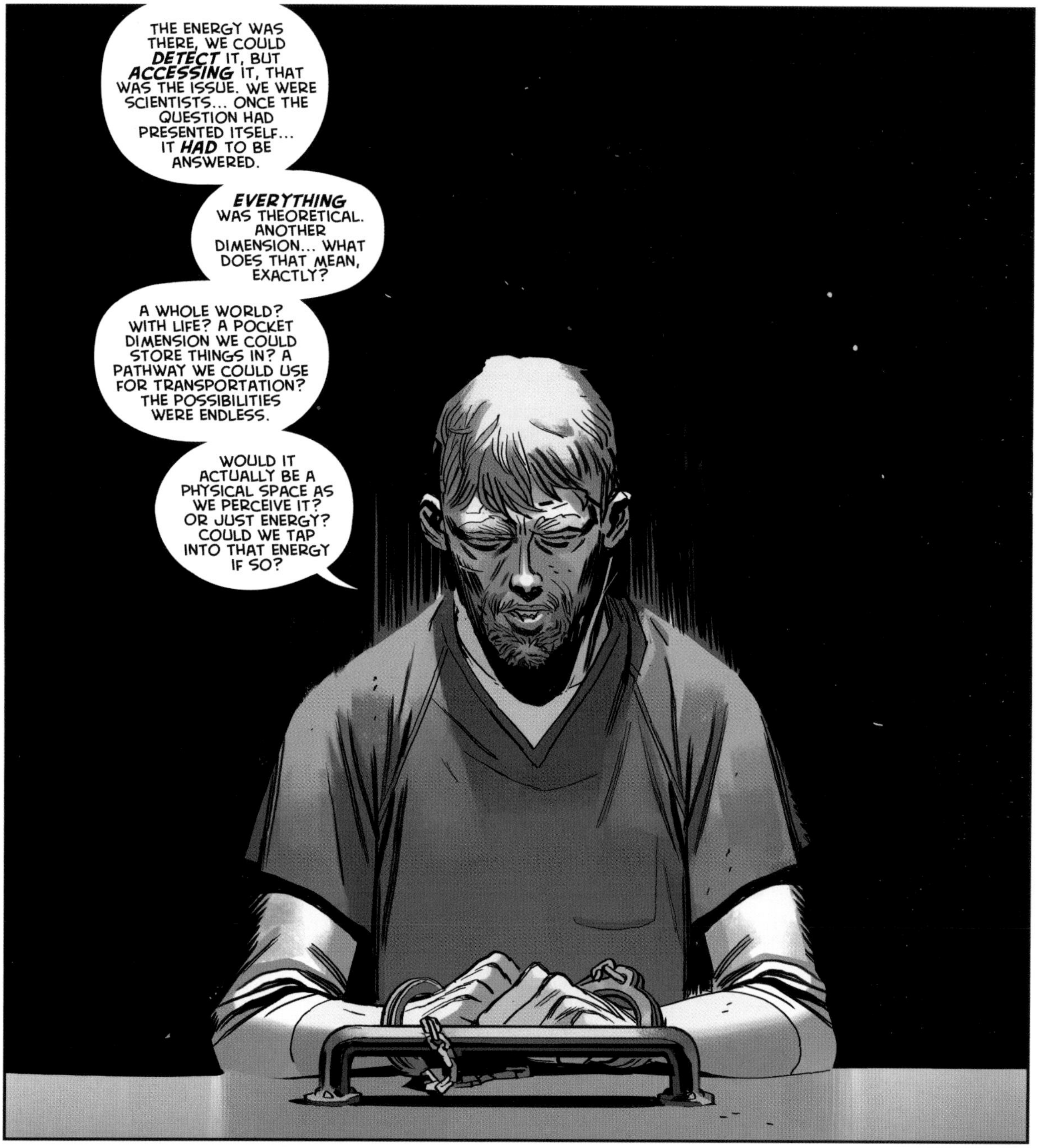
THE ENERGY WAS THERE, WE COULD DETECT IT, BUT ACCESSING IT, THAT WAS THE ISSUE. WE WERE SCIENTISTS... ONCE THE QUESTION HAD PRESENTED ITSELF... IT HAD TO BE ANSWERED.
EVERYTHING WAS THEORETICAL. ANOTHER DIMENSION... WHAT DOES THAT MEAN, EXACTLY?
A WHOLE WORLD? WITH LIFE? A POCKET DIMENSION WE COULD STORE THINGS IN? A PATHWAY WE COULD USE FOR TRANSPORTATION? THE POSSIBILITIES WERE ENDLESS.
WOULD IT ACTUALLY BE A PHYSICAL SPACE AS WE PERCEIVE IT? OR JUST ENERGY? COULD WE TAP INTO THAT ENERGY IF SO?

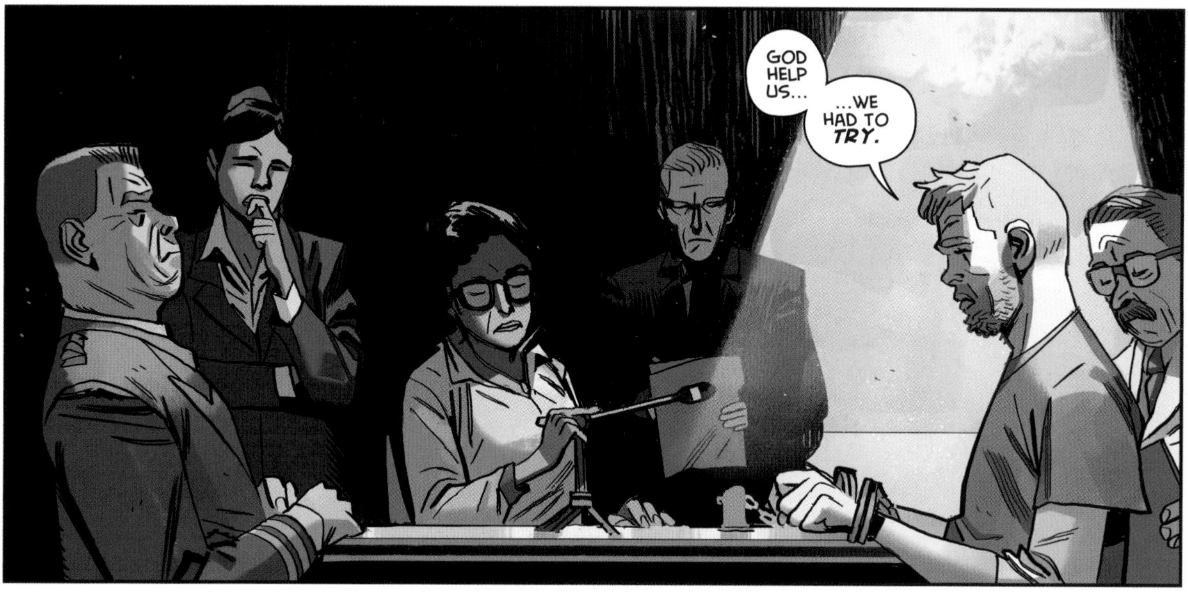
GOD HELP US...
...WE HAD TO TRY.

WE WERE AN INDEPENDENT THINK TANK, FUNDED BY GRANTS... WE STRUGGLED TO HOLD THINGS TOGETHER, BUT WE MADE IT ALL WORK.

WE BELIEVED IN IT. OUR WORK WAS MORE IMPORTANT THAN ANYTHING ELSE IN OUR LIVES.

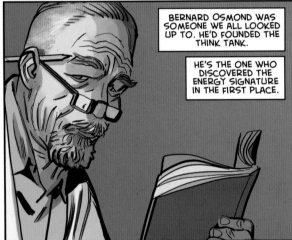

BERNARD OSMOND WAS SOMEONE WE ALL LOOKED UP TO. HE'D FOUNDED THE THINK TANK.

HE'S THE ONE WHO DISCOVERED THE ENERGY SIGNATURE IN THE FIRST PLACE.

HIS DAUGHTER MARIE KEPT EVERYTHING RUNNING.

SHE SOMEHOW SPENT HALF THE DAY APPLYING FOR GRANTS AND STILL WORKED CIRCLES AROUND THE REST OF US.

LESLIE MCKINLEY WAS THE REAL ROCK STAR OF THE BUNCH. SHE'D GOTTEN HER DOCTORATE IN THEORETICAL PHYSICS AT AGE FIFTEEN.

SHE WAS WORKING ON HER NINTH DEGREE AT THE TIME, AND SHE STILL WASN'T OLD ENOUGH TO DRINK.

KATHERINE JONAS HAD A MIND TO RIVAL EINSTEIN.

SHE COULD USE THOUGHT EXERCISES TO EXPLORE AND SOLVE ALMOST EVERY ROADBLOCK WE ENCOUNTERED. IT WAS REMARKABLE.

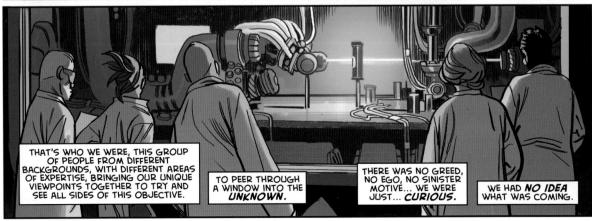

THAT'S WHO WE WERE, THIS GROUP OF PEOPLE FROM DIFFERENT BACKGROUNDS, WITH DIFFERENT AREAS OF EXPERTISE, BRINGING OUR UNIQUE VIEWPOINTS TOGETHER TO TRY AND SEE ALL SIDES OF THIS OBJECTIVE.

TO PEER THROUGH A WINDOW INTO THE *UNKNOWN*.

THERE WAS NO GREED, NO EGO, NO SINISTER MOTIVE... WE WERE JUST... *CURIOUS*.

WE HAD *NO IDEA* WHAT WAS COMING.

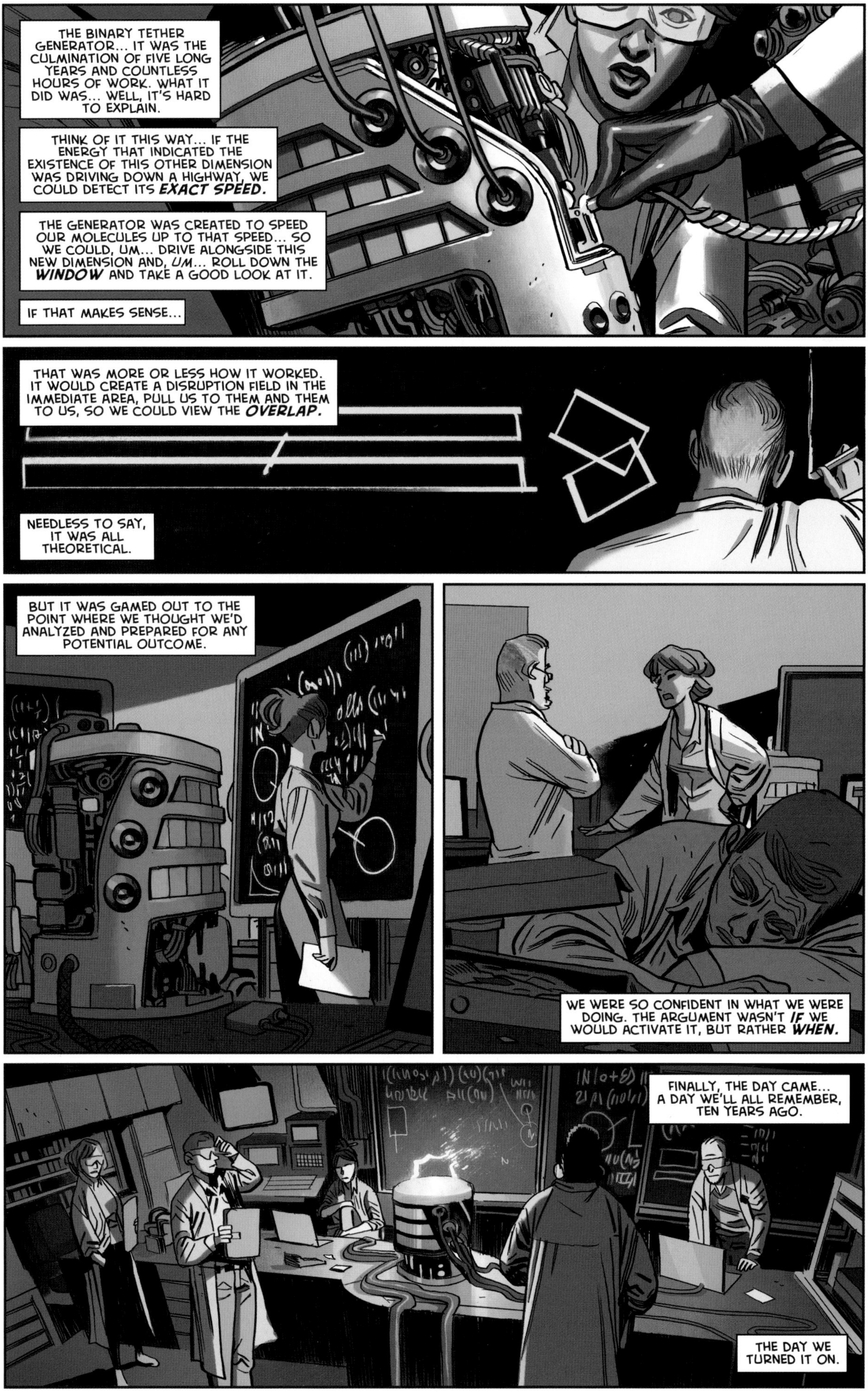
THE BINARY TETHER GENERATOR... IT WAS THE CULMINATION OF FIVE LONG YEARS AND COUNTLESS HOURS OF WORK. WHAT IT DID WAS... WELL, IT'S HARD TO EXPLAIN.
THINK OF IT THIS WAY... IF THE ENERGY THAT INDICATED THE EXISTENCE OF THIS OTHER DIMENSION WAS DRIVING DOWN A HIGHWAY, WE COULD DETECT ITS EXACT SPEED.
THE GENERATOR WAS CREATED TO SPEED OUR MOLECULES UP TO THAT SPEED... SO WE COULD, UM... DRIVE ALONGSIDE THIS NEW DIMENSION AND, UM... ROLL DOWN THE WINDOW AND TAKE A GOOD LOOK AT IT.
IF THAT MAKES SENSE...
THAT WAS MORE OR LESS HOW IT WORKED. IT WOULD CREATE A DISRUPTION FIELD IN THE IMMEDIATE AREA, PULL US TO THEM AND THEM TO US, SO WE COULD VIEW THE OVERLAP.
NEEDLESS TO SAY, IT WAS ALL THEORETICAL.
BUT IT WAS GAMED OUT TO THE POINT WHERE WE THOUGHT WE'D ANALYZED AND PREPARED FOR ANY POTENTIAL OUTCOME.
WE WERE SO CONFIDENT IN WHAT WE WERE DOING. THE ARGUMENT WASN'T IF WE WOULD ACTIVATE IT, BUT RATHER WHEN.
FINALLY, THE DAY CAME... A DAY WE'LL ALL REMEMBER, TEN YEARS AGO.
THE DAY WE TURNED IT ON.

THE POWER WENT OUT.

AT FIRST IT SEEMED LIKE ALL THE DEVICE DID WAS KNOCK OUT A PORTION OF THE CITY'S ELECTRICAL GRID.

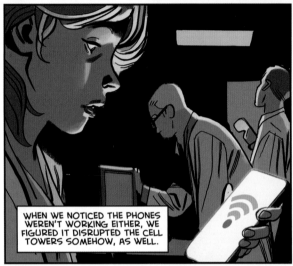

WHEN WE NOTICED THE PHONES WEREN'T WORKING EITHER, WE FIGURED IT DISRUPTED THE CELL TOWERS SOMEHOW, AS WELL.

POWER, PHONES, EVERYTHING WAS JUST... *DEAD.* EVEN THE WATER TO OUR BUILDING WASN'T WORKING.

EVENTUALLY WE NOTICED PEOPLE WERE STARTING TO GATHER OUTSIDE--SO WE JOINED THEM.

IN THOSE FIRST FEW MOMENTS WE DIDN'T NOTICE ANYTHING HAD CHANGED. THE STREET LOOKED THE SAME... THE AIR SMELLED THE SAME, AT FIRST. PEOPLE CAME OUTSIDE BECAUSE OF THE POWER OUTAGE. IT SEEMED... NORMAL, SAVE FOR *ONE* LARGE DETAIL...

...THE SKY WASN'T RIGHT.

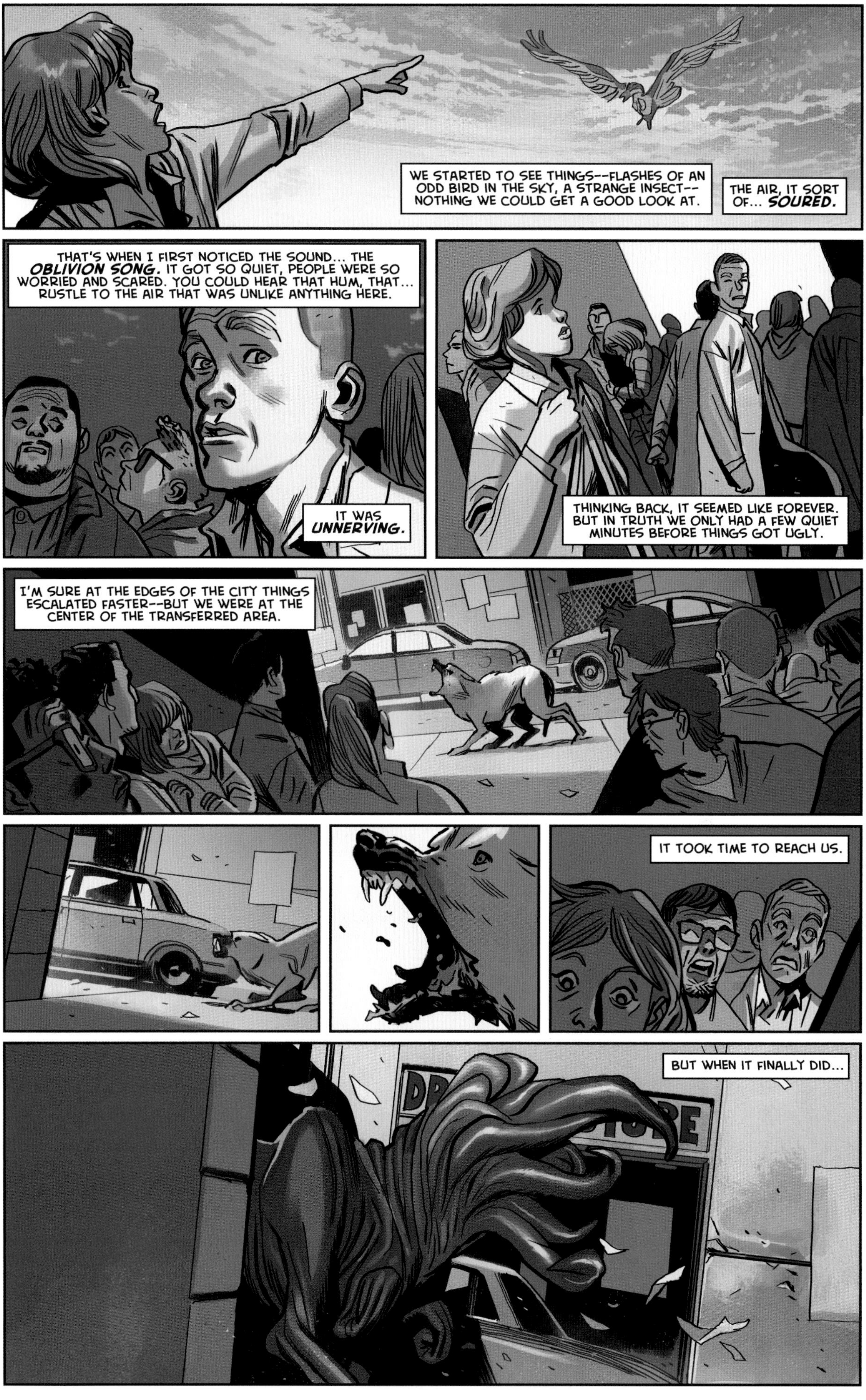
WE STARTED TO SEE THINGS--FLASHES OF AN ODD BIRD IN THE SKY, A STRANGE INSECT-- NOTHING WE COULD GET A GOOD LOOK AT.
THE AIR, IT SORT OF... SOURED.
THAT'S WHEN I FIRST NOTICED THE SOUND... THE OBLIVION SONG. IT GOT SO QUIET, PEOPLE WERE SO WORRIED AND SCARED. YOU COULD HEAR THAT HUM, THAT... RUSTLE TO THE AIR THAT WAS UNLIKE ANYTHING HERE.
IT WAS UNNERVING.
THINKING BACK, IT SEEMED LIKE FOREVER. BUT IN TRUTH WE ONLY HAD A FEW QUIET MINUTES BEFORE THINGS GOT UGLY.
I'M SURE AT THE EDGES OF THE CITY THINGS ESCALATED FASTER--BUT WE WERE AT THE CENTER OF THE TRANSFERRED AREA.
IT TOOK TIME TO REACH US.
BUT WHEN IT FINALLY DID...

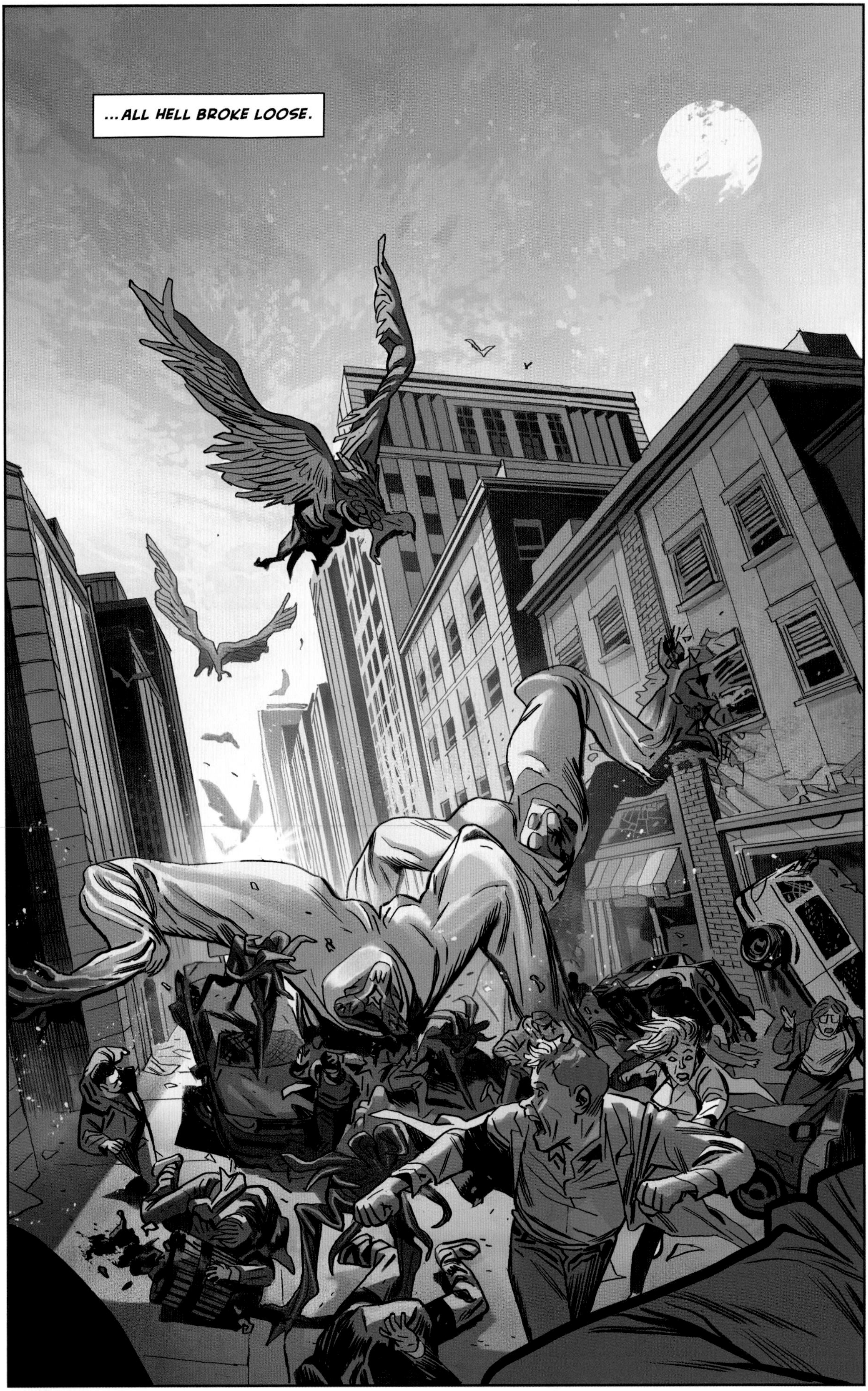
...ALL HELL BROKE LOOSE.

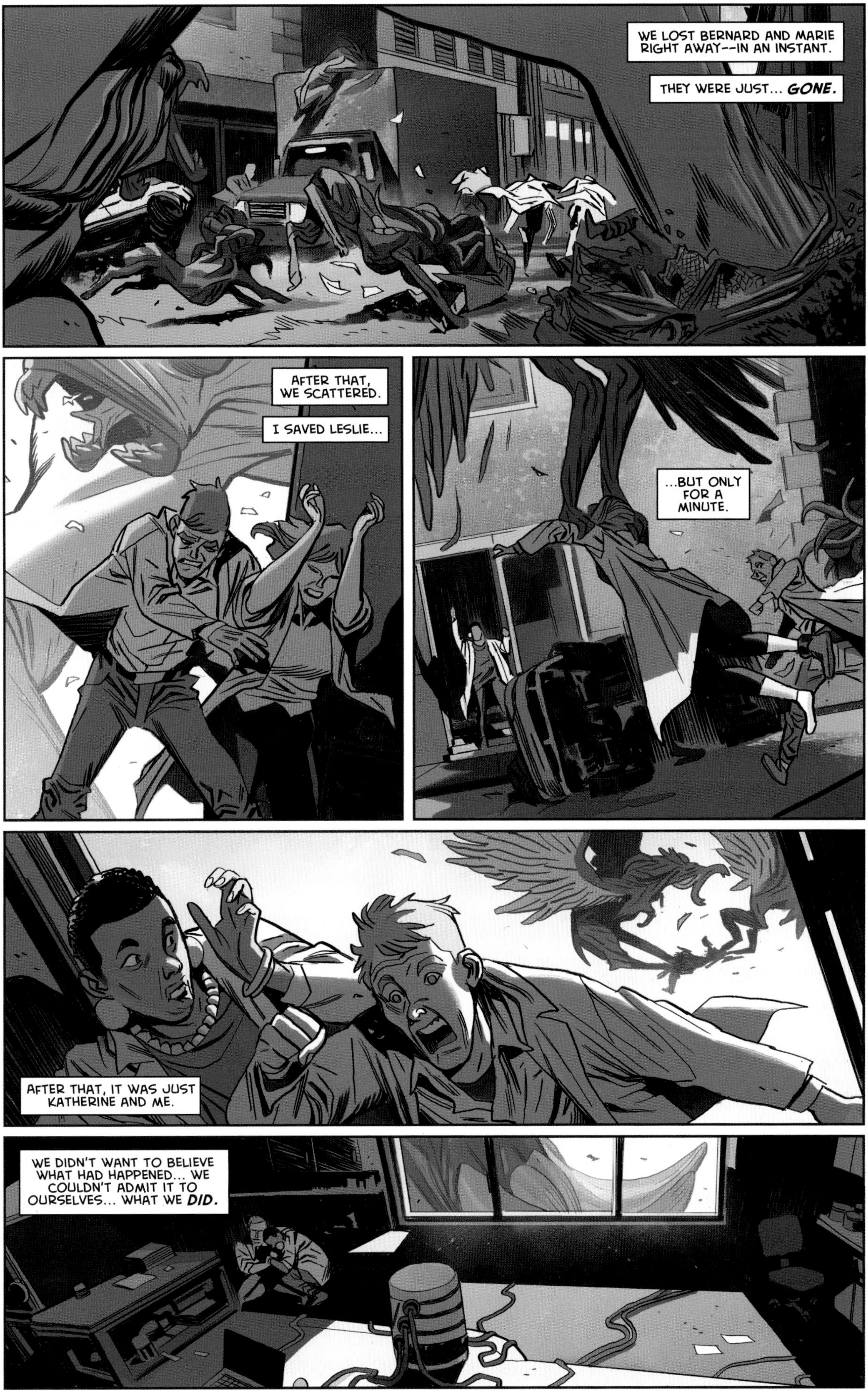
WE LOST BERNARD AND MARIE RIGHT AWAY--IN AN INSTANT.
THEY WERE JUST... GONE.
AFTER THAT, WE SCATTERED.
I SAVED LESLIE...
...BUT ONLY FOR A MINUTE.
AFTER THAT, IT WAS JUST KATHERINE AND ME.
WE DIDN'T WANT TO BELIEVE WHAT HAD HAPPENED... WE COULDN'T ADMIT IT TO OURSELVES... WHAT WE DID.

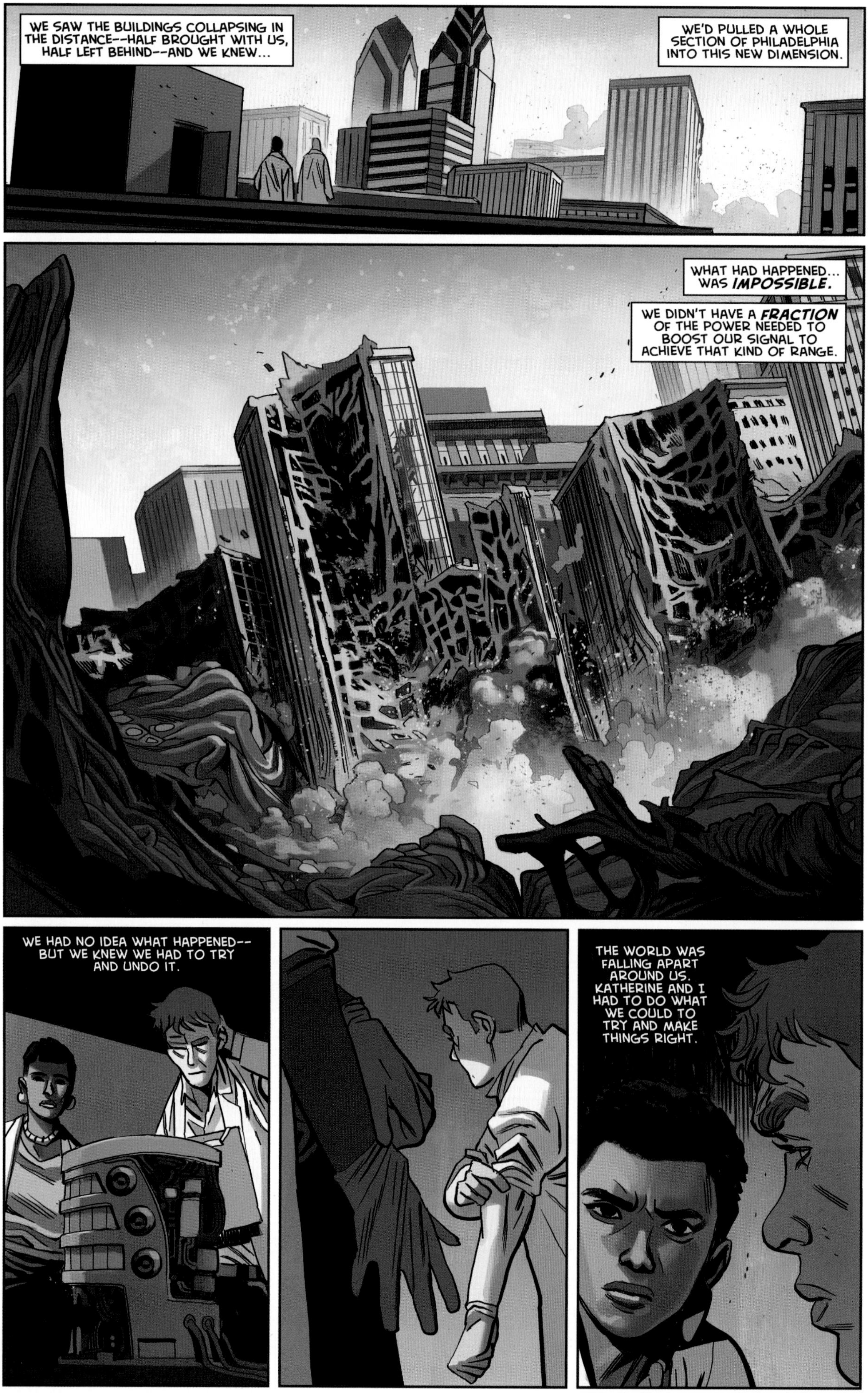
WE SAW THE BUILDINGS COLLAPSING IN THE DISTANCE--HALF BROUGHT WITH US, HALF LEFT BEHIND--AND WE KNEW...
WE'D PULLED A WHOLE SECTION OF PHILADELPHIA INTO THIS NEW DIMENSION.
WHAT HAD HAPPENED... WAS IMPOSSIBLE.
WE DIDN'T HAVE A FRACTION OF THE POWER NEEDED TO BOOST OUR SIGNAL TO ACHIEVE THAT KIND OF RANGE.
WE HAD NO IDEA WHAT HAPPENED-- BUT WE KNEW WE HAD TO TRY AND UNDO IT.
THE WORLD WAS FALLING APART AROUND US. KATHERINE AND I HAD TO DO WHAT WE COULD TO TRY AND MAKE THINGS RIGHT.

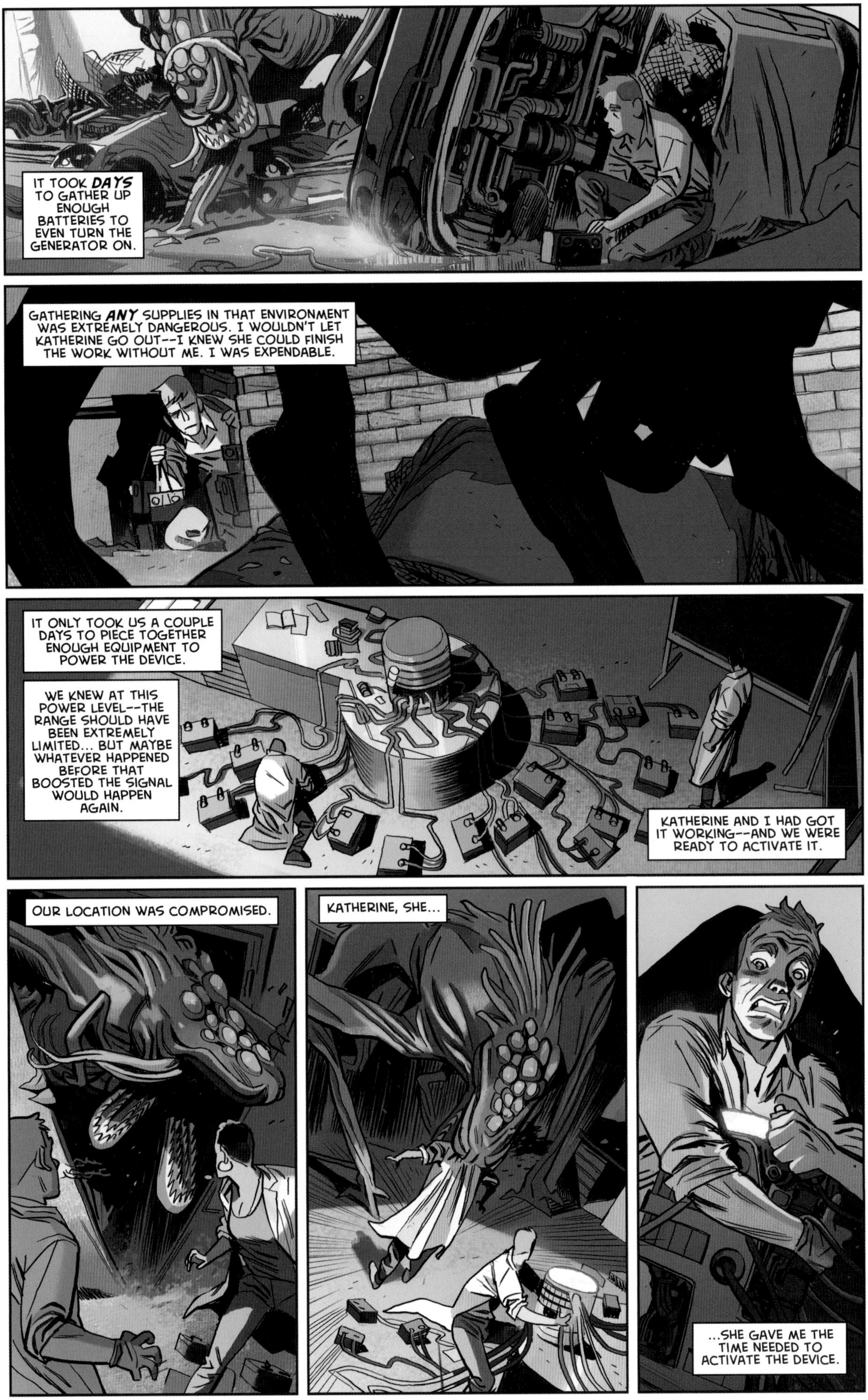
IT TOOK DAYS TO GATHER UP ENOUGH BATTERIES TO EVEN TURN THE GENERATOR ON.
GATHERING ANY SUPPLIES IN THAT ENVIRONMENT WAS EXTREMELY DANGEROUS. I WOULDN'T LET KATHERINE GO OUT--I KNEW SHE COULD FINISH THE WORK WITHOUT ME. I WAS EXPENDABLE.
IT ONLY TOOK US A COUPLE DAYS TO PIECE TOGETHER ENOUGH EQUIPMENT TO POWER THE DEVICE.
WE KNEW AT THIS POWER LEVEL--THE RANGE SHOULD HAVE BEEN EXTREMELY LIMITED... BUT MAYBE WHATEVER HAPPENED BEFORE THAT BOOSTED THE SIGNAL WOULD HAPPEN AGAIN.
KATHERINE AND I HAD GOT IT WORKING--AND WE WERE READY TO ACTIVATE IT.
OUR LOCATION WAS COMPROMISED.
KATHERINE, SHE...
...SHE GAVE ME THE TIME NEEDED TO ACTIVATE THE DEVICE.

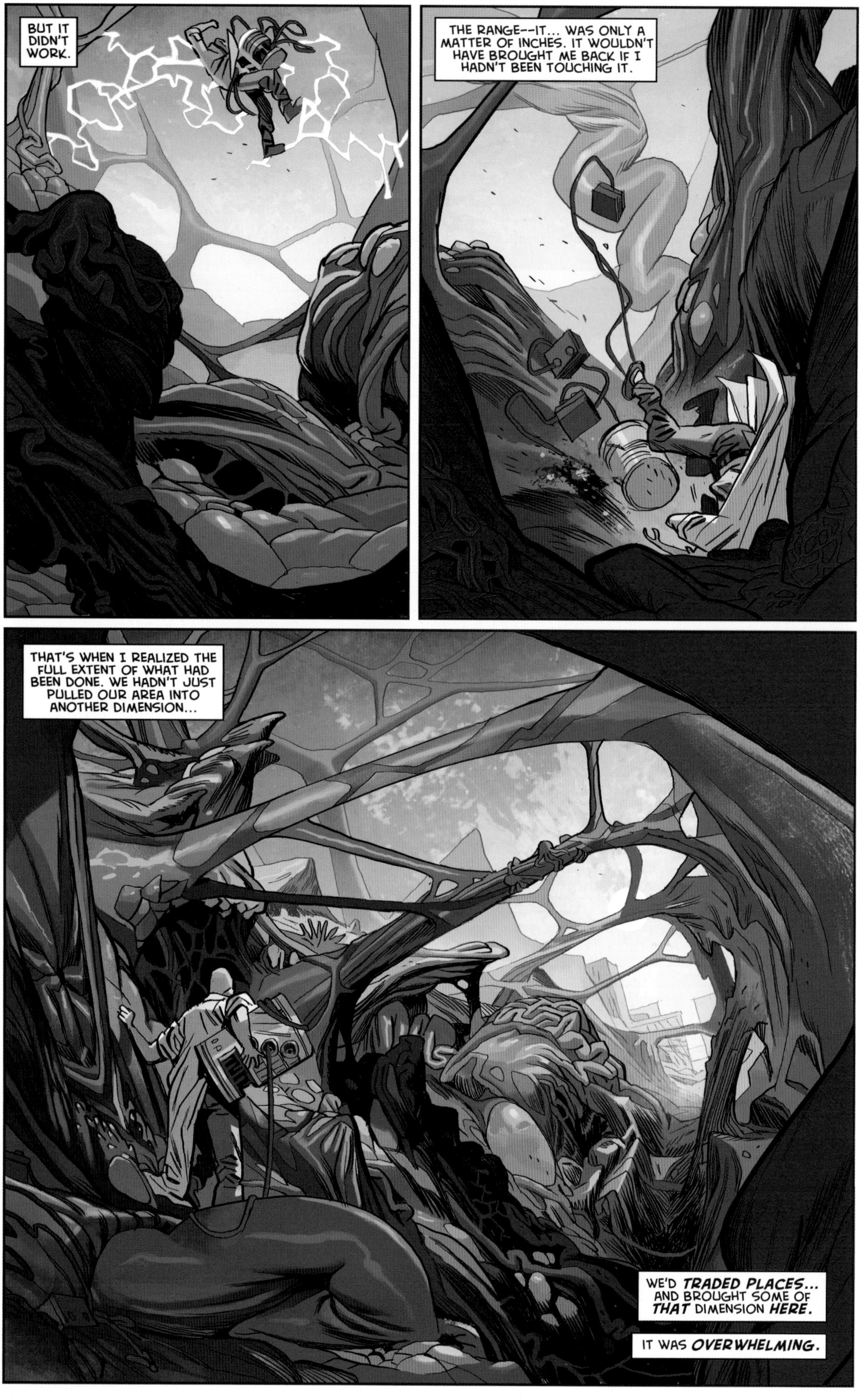
BUT IT DIDN'T WORK.
THE RANGE--IT... WAS ONLY A MATTER OF INCHES. IT WOULDN'T HAVE BROUGHT ME BACK IF I HADN'T BEEN TOUCHING IT.
THAT'S WHEN I REALIZED THE FULL EXTENT OF WHAT HAD BEEN DONE. WE HADN'T JUST PULLED OUR AREA INTO ANOTHER DIMENSION...
WE'D TRADED PLACES... AND BROUGHT SOME OF THAT DIMENSION HERE.
IT WAS OVERWHELMING.

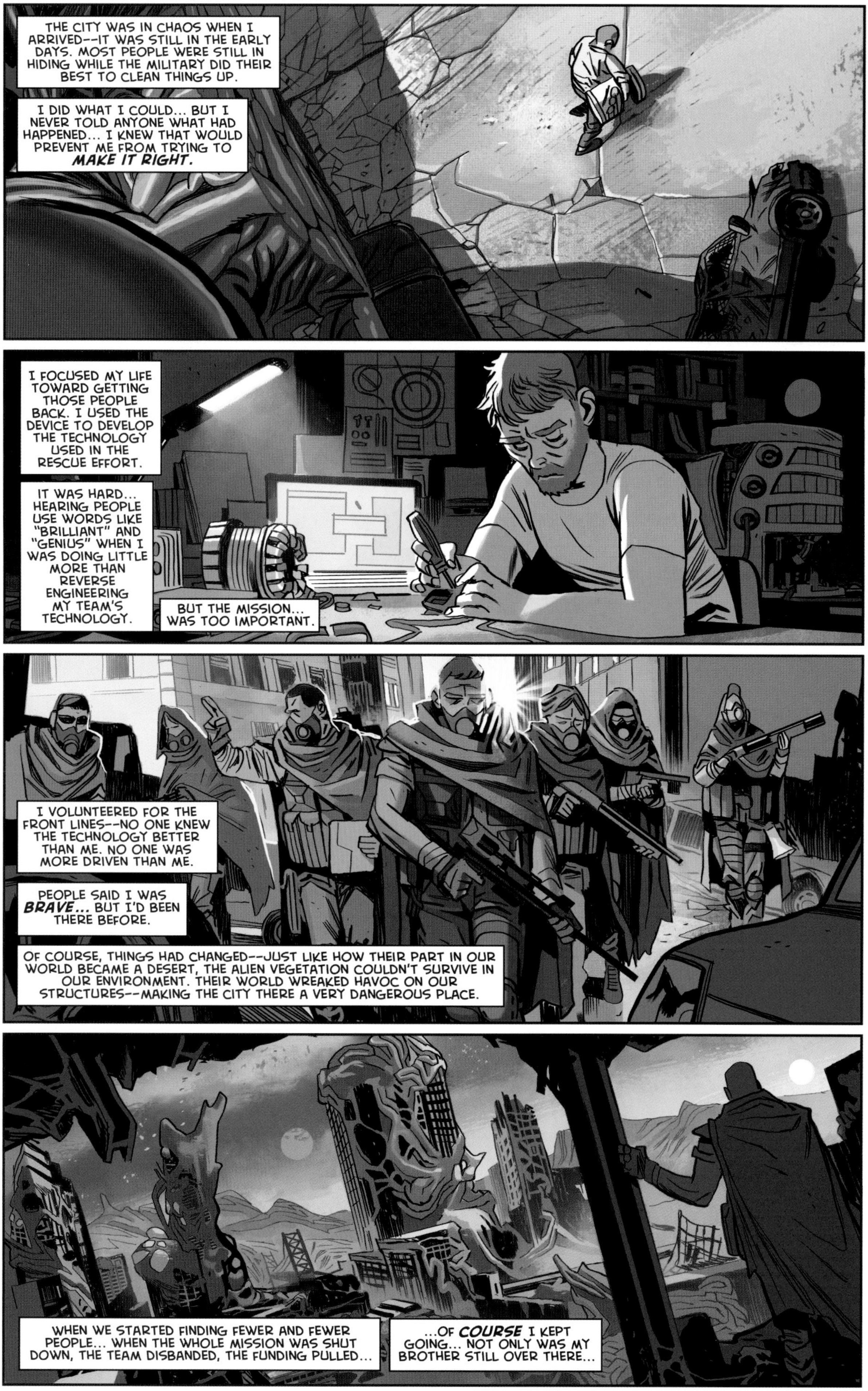
THE CITY WAS IN CHAOS WHEN I ARRIVED--IT WAS STILL IN THE EARLY DAYS. MOST PEOPLE WERE STILL IN HIDING WHILE THE MILITARY DID THEIR BEST TO CLEAN THINGS UP.
I DID WHAT I COULD... BUT I NEVER TOLD ANYONE WHAT HAD HAPPENED... I KNEW THAT WOULD PREVENT ME FROM TRYING TO *MAKE IT RIGHT.*
I FOCUSED MY LIFE TOWARD GETTING THOSE PEOPLE BACK. I USED THE DEVICE TO DEVELOP THE TECHNOLOGY USED IN THE RESCUE EFFORT.
IT WAS HARD... HEARING PEOPLE USE WORDS LIKE "BRILLIANT" AND "GENIUS" WHEN I WAS DOING LITTLE MORE THAN REVERSE ENGINEERING MY TEAM'S TECHNOLOGY.
BUT THE MISSION... WAS TOO IMPORTANT.
I VOLUNTEERED FOR THE FRONT LINES--NO ONE KNEW THE TECHNOLOGY BETTER THAN ME. NO ONE WAS MORE DRIVEN THAN ME.
PEOPLE SAID I WAS *BRAVE...* BUT I'D BEEN THERE BEFORE.
OF COURSE, THINGS HAD CHANGED--JUST LIKE HOW THEIR PART IN OUR WORLD BECAME A DESERT, THE ALIEN VEGETATION COULDN'T SURVIVE IN OUR ENVIRONMENT. THEIR WORLD WREAKED HAVOC ON OUR STRUCTURES--MAKING THE CITY THERE A VERY DANGEROUS PLACE.
WHEN WE STARTED FINDING FEWER AND FEWER PEOPLE... WHEN THE WHOLE MISSION WAS SHUT DOWN, THE TEAM DISBANDED, THE FUNDING PULLED...
...OF *COURSE* I KEPT GOING... NOT ONLY WAS MY BROTHER STILL OVER THERE...

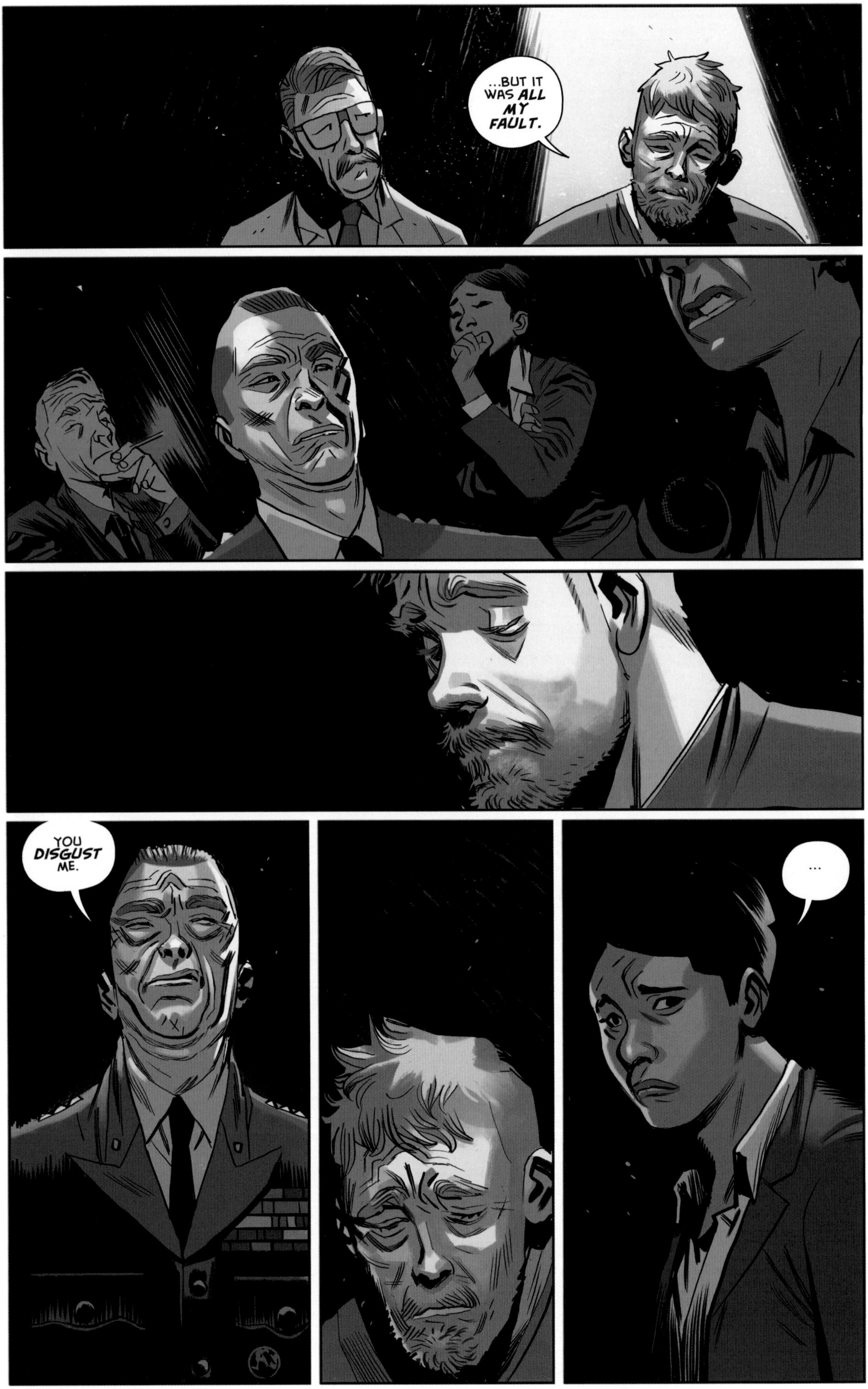
...BUT IT WAS ALL MY FAULT.
YOU DISGUST ME.
...

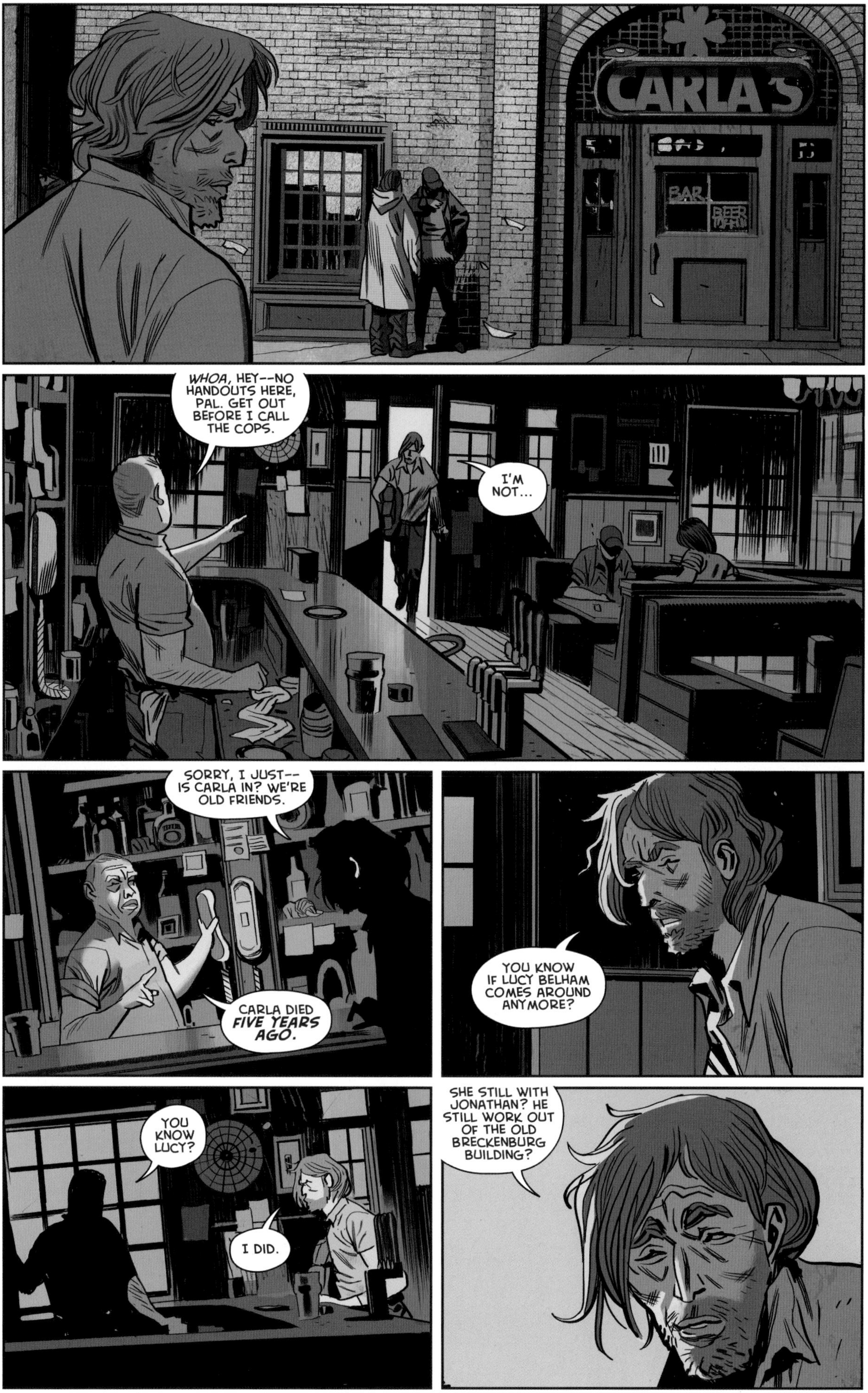
CARLA'S
BAR
BEER
WHOA, HEY--NO HANDOUTS HERE, PAL. GET OUT BEFORE I CALL THE COPS.
I'M NOT...
SORRY, I JUST--IS CARLA IN? WE'RE OLD FRIENDS.
CARLA DIED ***FIVE YEARS AGO.***
YOU KNOW IF LUCY BELHAM COMES AROUND ANYMORE?
YOU KNOW LUCY?
I DID.
SHE STILL WITH JONATHAN? HE STILL WORK OUT OF THE OLD BRECKENBURG BUILDING?

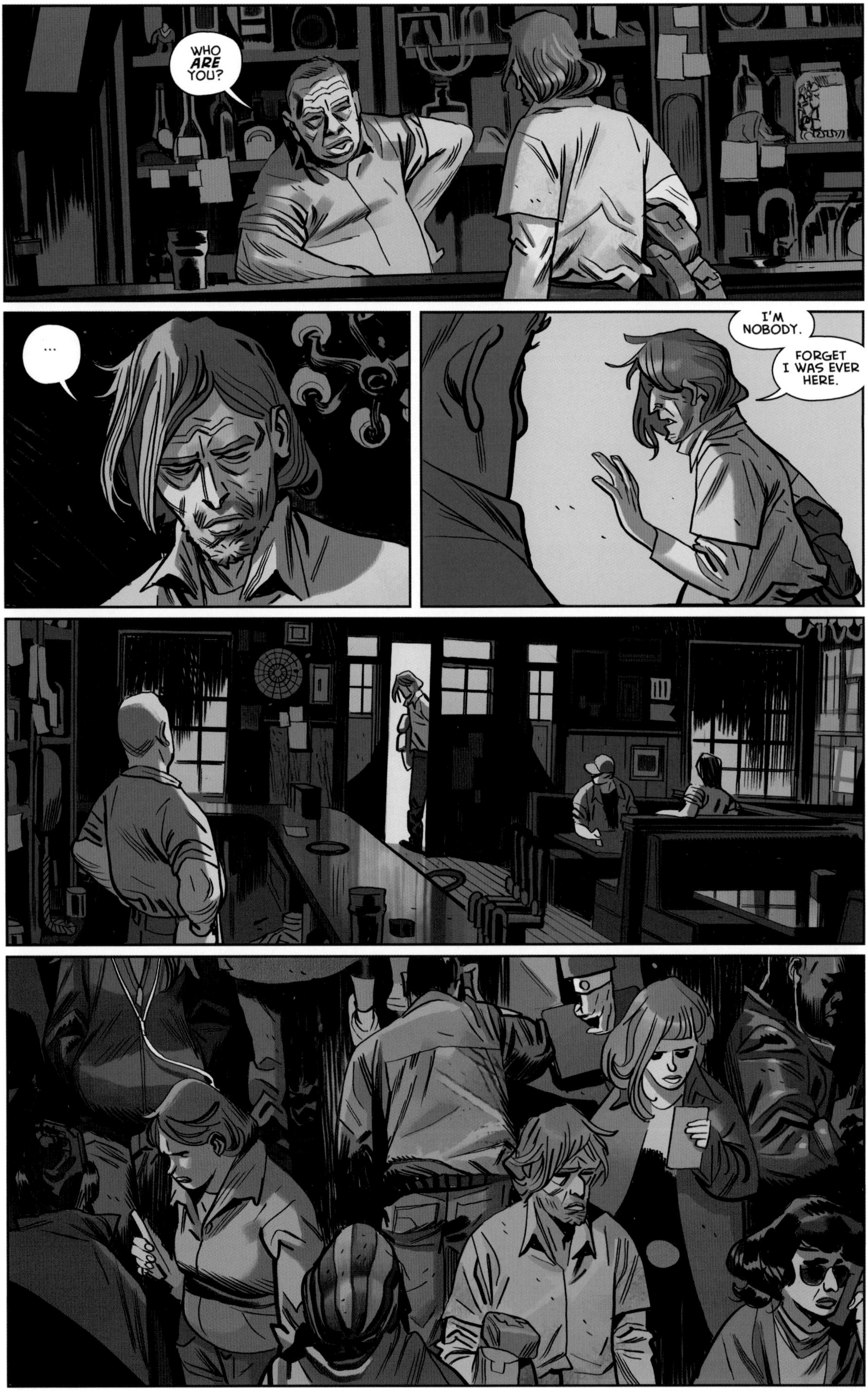
WHO *ARE* YOU?
...
I'M NOBODY.
FORGET I WAS EVER HERE.

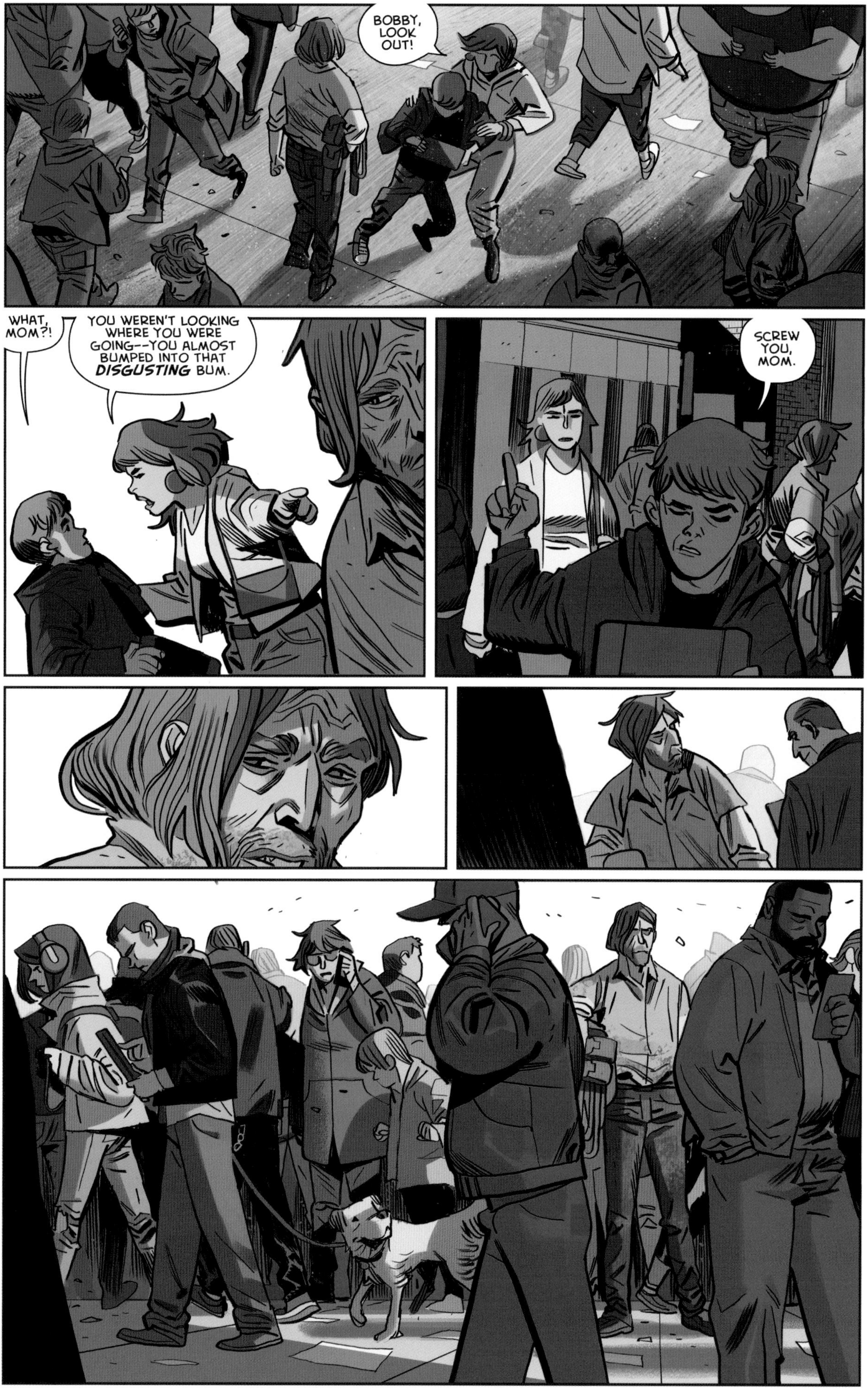
BOBBY, LOOK OUT!
WHAT, MOM?!
YOU WEREN'T LOOKING WHERE YOU WERE GOING--YOU ALMOST BUMPED INTO THAT DISGUSTING BUM.
SCREW YOU, MOM.

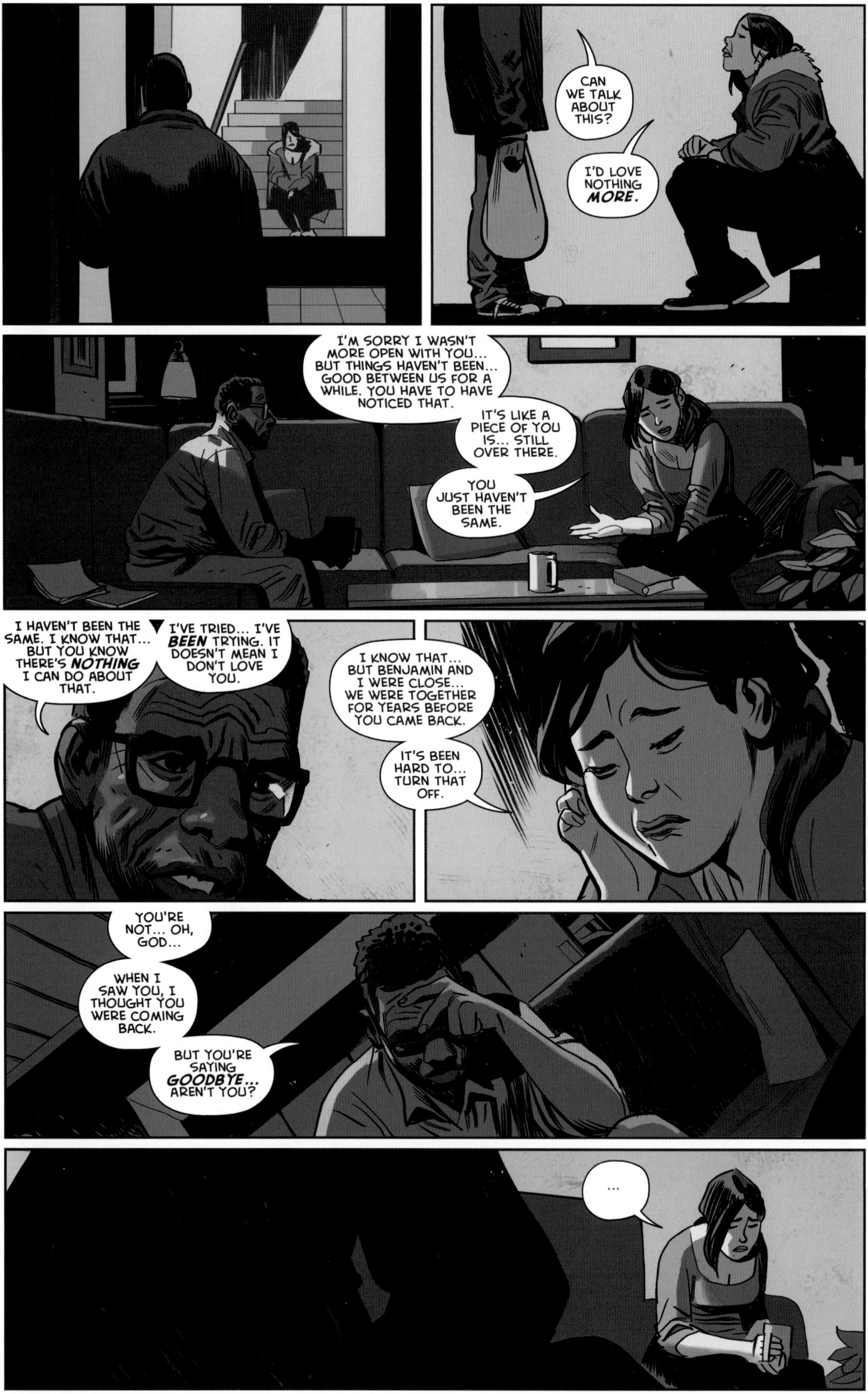
CAN WE TALK ABOUT THIS?
I'D LOVE NOTHING MORE.
I'M SORRY I WASN'T MORE OPEN WITH YOU... BUT THINGS HAVEN'T BEEN... GOOD BETWEEN US FOR A WHILE. YOU HAVE TO HAVE NOTICED THAT.
IT'S LIKE A PIECE OF YOU IS... STILL OVER THERE.
YOU JUST HAVEN'T BEEN THE SAME.
I HAVEN'T BEEN THE SAME. I KNOW THAT... BUT YOU KNOW THERE'S NOTHING I CAN DO ABOUT THAT.
I'VE TRIED... I'VE BEEN TRYING. IT DOESN'T MEAN I DON'T LOVE YOU.
I KNOW THAT... BUT BENJAMIN AND I WERE CLOSE... WE WERE TOGETHER FOR YEARS BEFORE YOU CAME BACK.
IT'S BEEN HARD TO... TURN THAT OFF.
YOU'RE NOT... OH, GOD...
WHEN I SAW YOU, I THOUGHT YOU WERE COMING BACK.
BUT YOU'RE SAYING GOODBYE... AREN'T YOU?
...

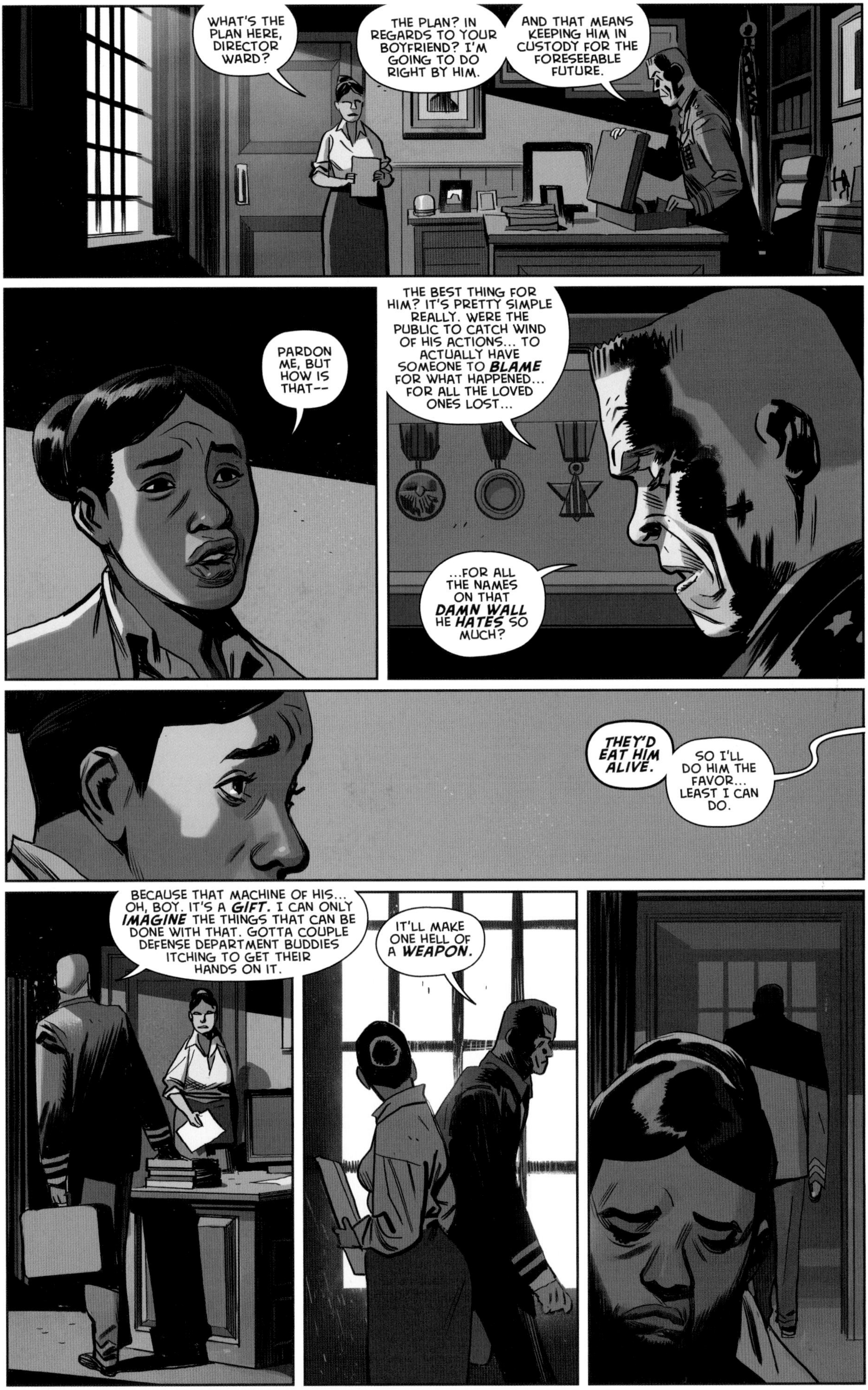
WHAT'S THE PLAN HERE, DIRECTOR WARD?
THE PLAN? IN REGARDS TO YOUR BOYFRIEND? I'M GOING TO DO RIGHT BY HIM.
AND THAT MEANS KEEPING HIM IN CUSTODY FOR THE FORESEEABLE FUTURE.
PARDON ME, BUT HOW IS THAT--
THE BEST THING FOR HIM? IT'S PRETTY SIMPLE REALLY. WERE THE PUBLIC TO CATCH WIND OF HIS ACTIONS... TO ACTUALLY HAVE SOMEONE TO BLAME FOR WHAT HAPPENED... FOR ALL THE LOVED ONES LOST...
...FOR ALL THE NAMES ON THAT DAMN WALL HE HATES SO MUCH?
THEY'D EAT HIM ALIVE.
SO I'LL DO HIM THE FAVOR... LEAST I CAN DO.
BECAUSE THAT MACHINE OF HIS... OH, BOY. IT'S A GIFT. I CAN ONLY IMAGINE THE THINGS THAT CAN BE DONE WITH THAT. GOTTA COUPLE DEFENSE DEPARTMENT BUDDIES ITCHING TO GET THEIR HANDS ON IT.
IT'LL MAKE ONE HELL OF A WEAPON.

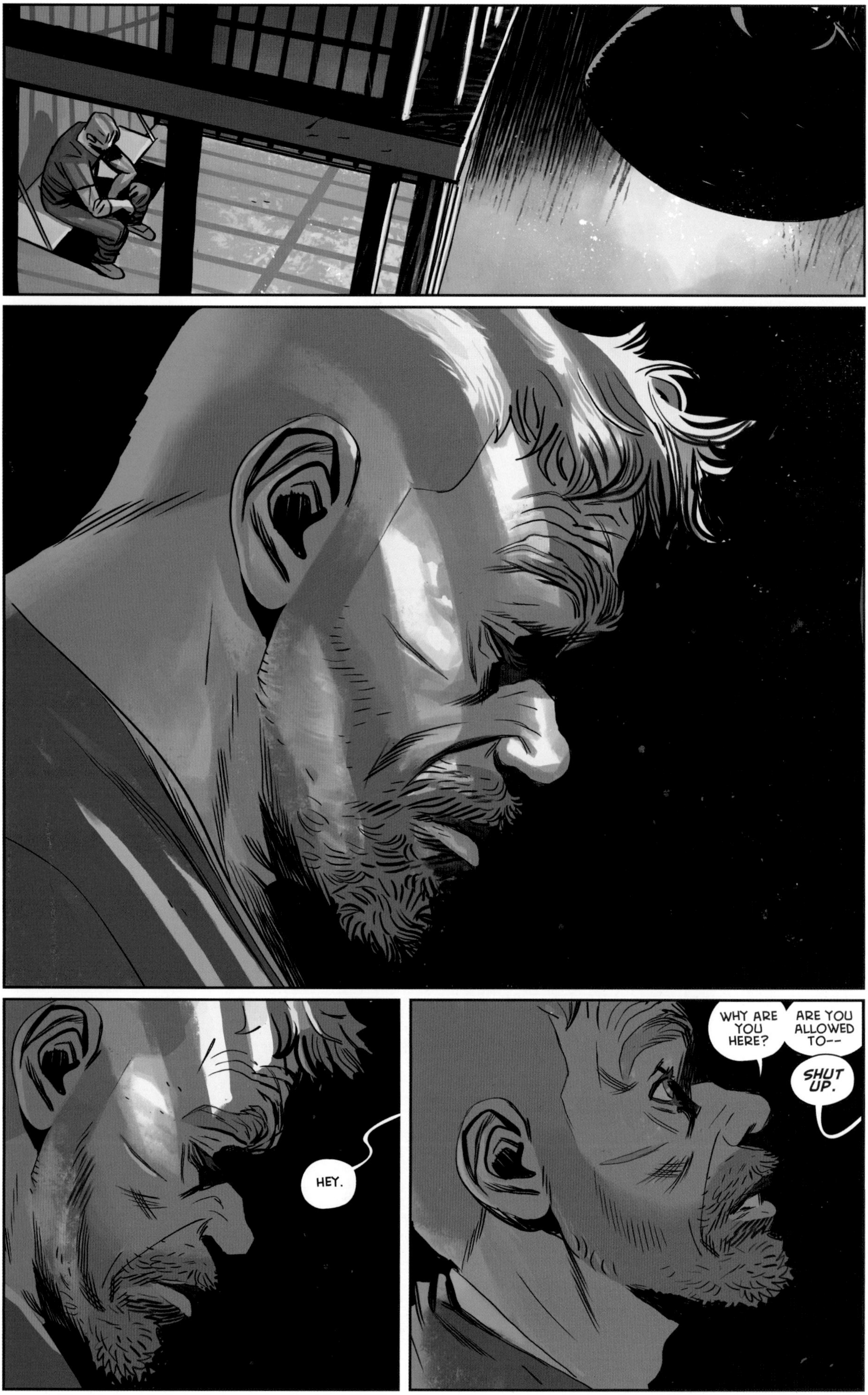
HEY.
WHY ARE YOU HERE?
ARE YOU ALLOWED TO--
SHUT UP.

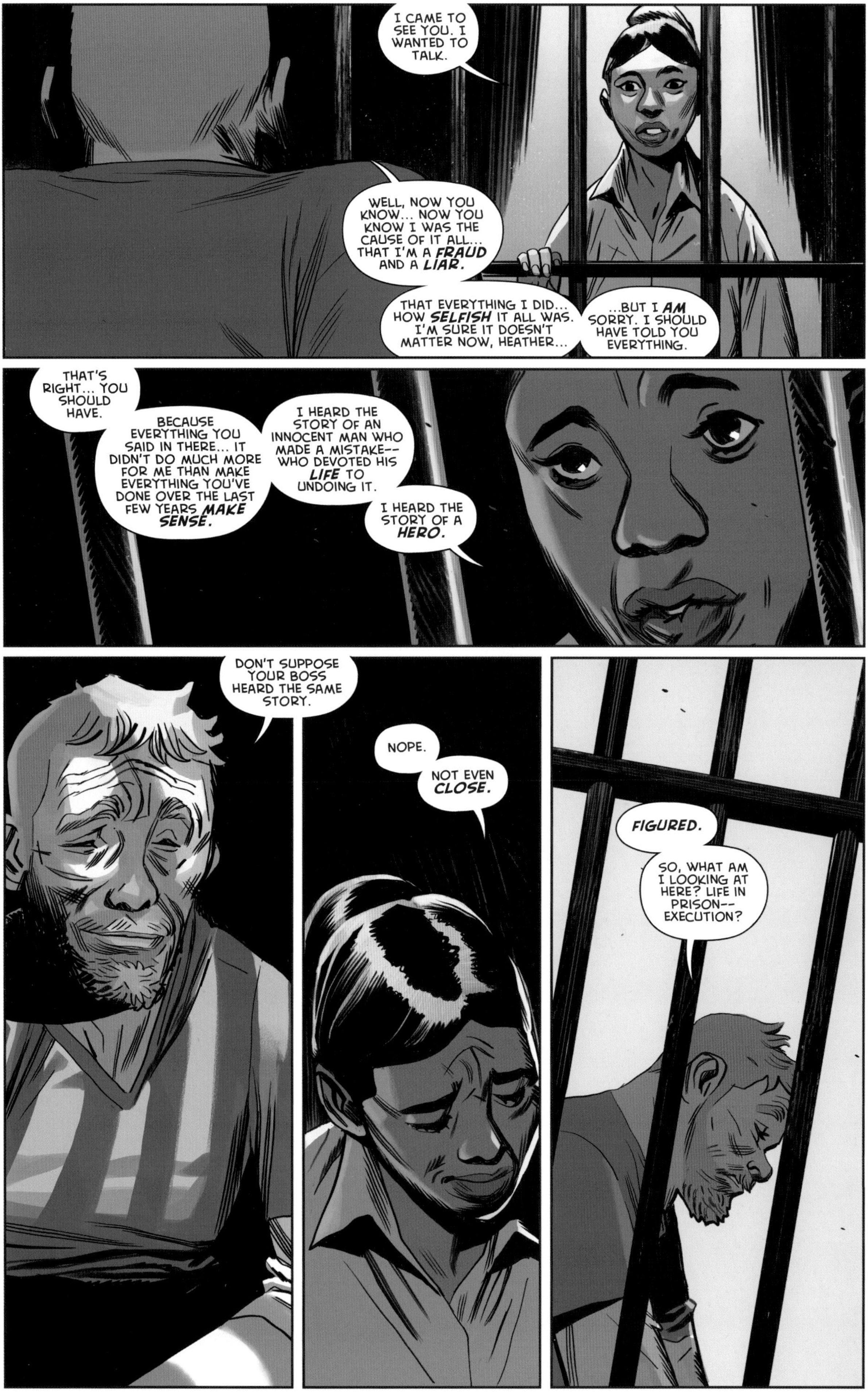
I CAME TO SEE YOU. I WANTED TO TALK.
WELL, NOW YOU KNOW... NOW YOU KNOW I WAS THE CAUSE OF IT ALL... THAT I'M A FRAUD AND A LIAR.
THAT EVERYTHING I DID... HOW SELFISH IT ALL WAS. I'M SURE IT DOESN'T MATTER NOW, HEATHER...
...BUT I AM SORRY. I SHOULD HAVE TOLD YOU EVERYTHING.
THAT'S RIGHT... YOU SHOULD HAVE.
BECAUSE EVERYTHING YOU SAID IN THERE... IT DIDN'T DO MUCH MORE FOR ME THAN MAKE EVERYTHING YOU'VE DONE OVER THE LAST FEW YEARS MAKE SENSE.
I HEARD THE STORY OF AN INNOCENT MAN WHO MADE A MISTAKE-- WHO DEVOTED HIS LIFE TO UNDOING IT.
I HEARD THE STORY OF A HERO.
DON'T SUPPOSE YOUR BOSS HEARD THE SAME STORY.
NOPE.
NOT EVEN CLOSE.
FIGURED.
SO, WHAT AM I LOOKING AT HERE? LIFE IN PRISON-- EXECUTION?

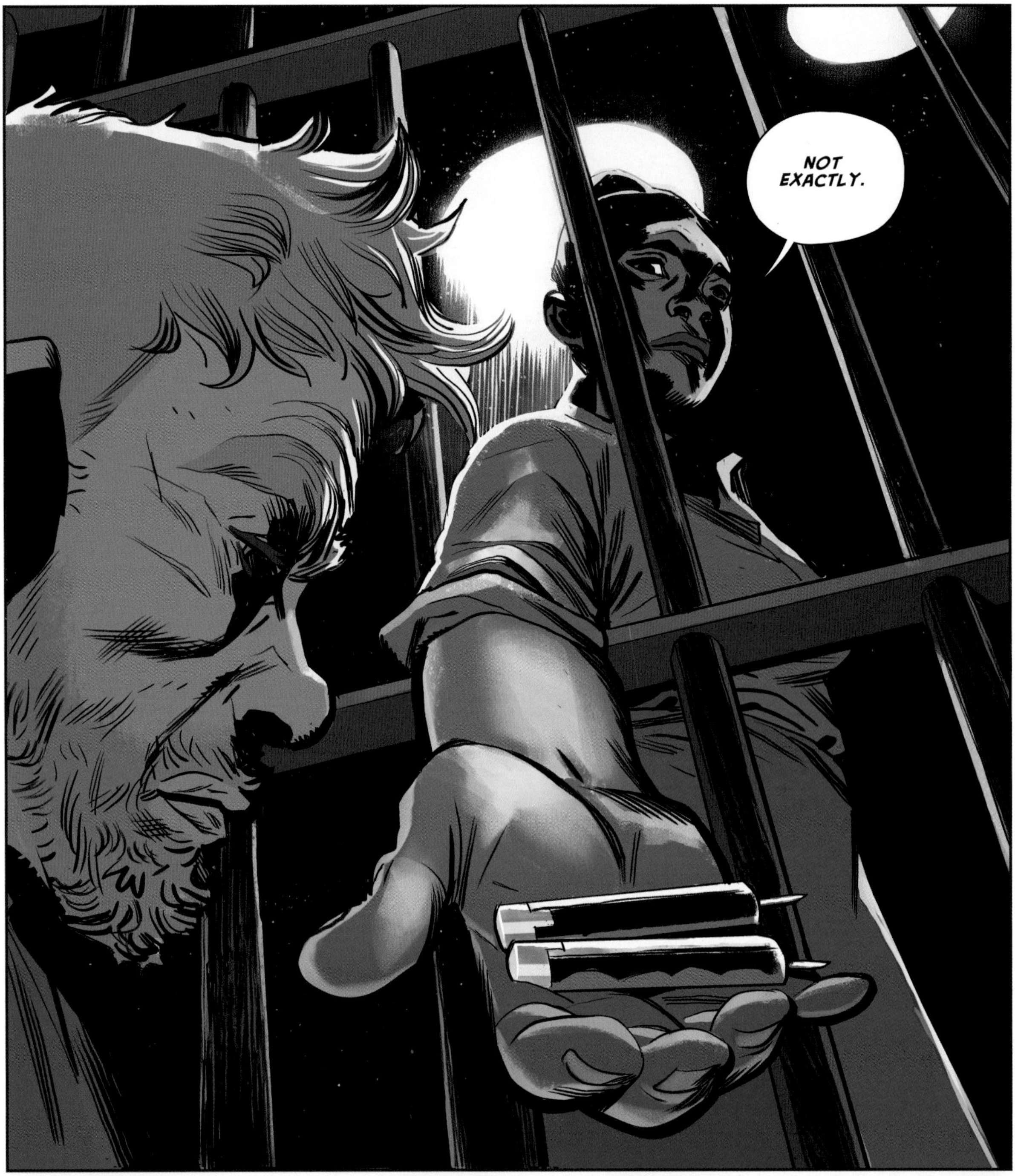
NOT EXACTLY.

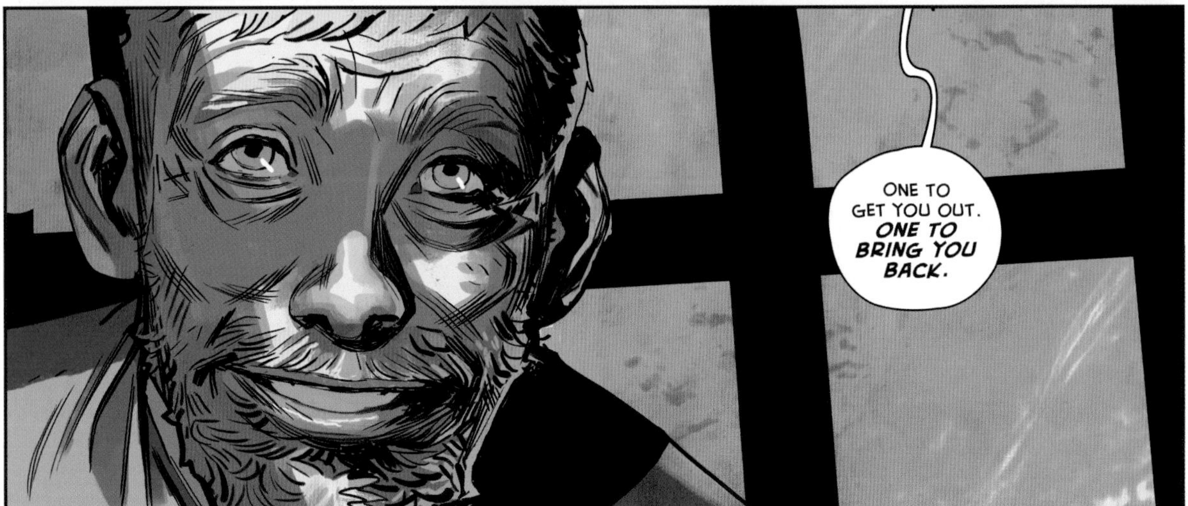
ONE TO GET YOU OUT. ONE TO BRING YOU BACK.

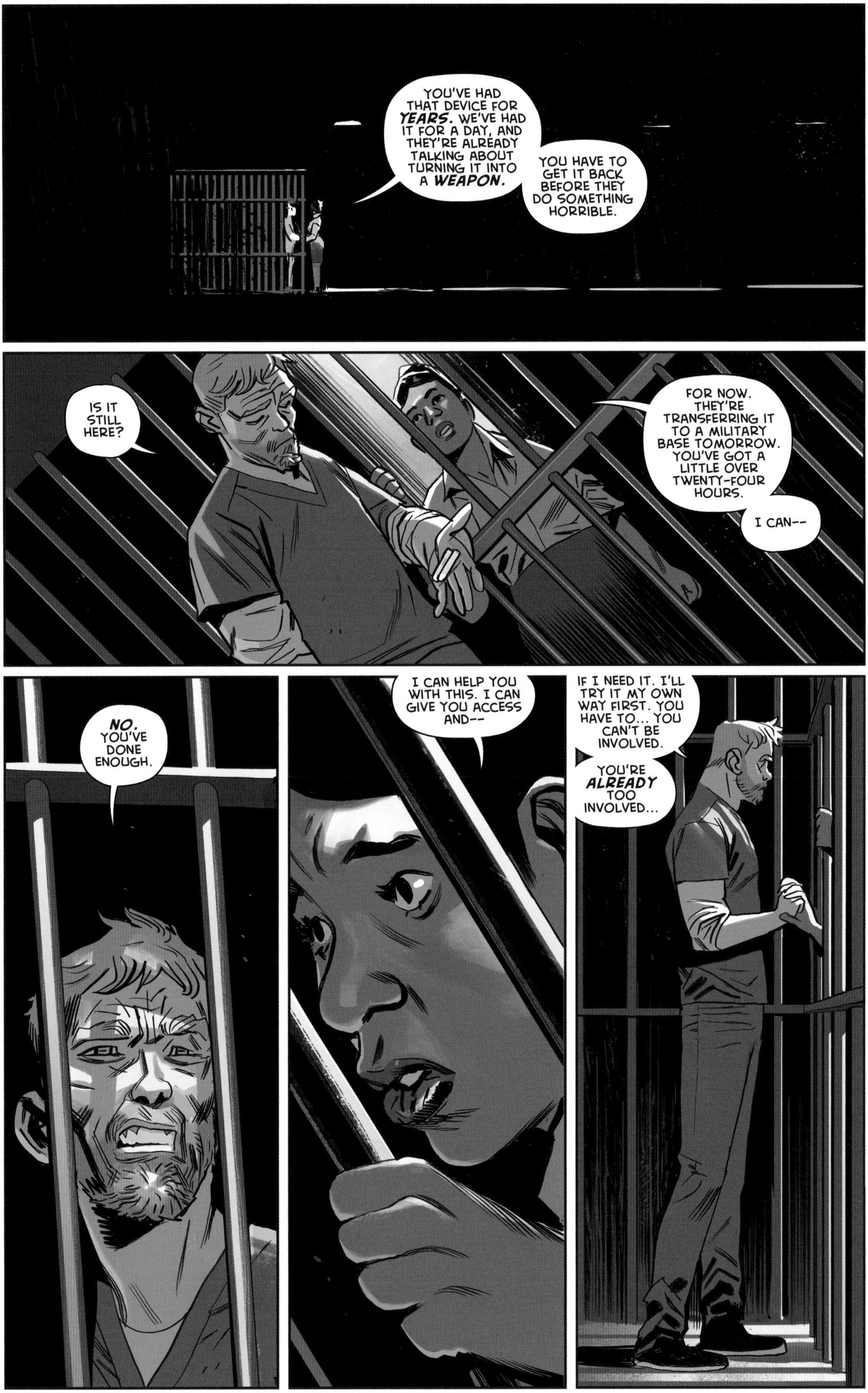
YOU'VE HAD THAT DEVICE FOR YEARS. WE'VE HAD IT FOR A DAY, AND THEY'RE ALREADY TALKING ABOUT TURNING IT INTO A WEAPON.
YOU HAVE TO GET IT BACK BEFORE THEY DO SOMETHING HORRIBLE.
IS IT STILL HERE?
FOR NOW. THEY'RE TRANSFERRING IT TO A MILITARY BASE TOMORROW. YOU'VE GOT A LITTLE OVER TWENTY-FOUR HOURS.
I CAN--
NO. YOU'VE DONE ENOUGH.
I CAN HELP YOU WITH THIS. I CAN GIVE YOU ACCESS AND--
IF I NEED IT. I'LL TRY IT MY OWN WAY FIRST. YOU HAVE TO... YOU CAN'T BE INVOLVED.
YOU'RE ALREADY TOO INVOLVED...

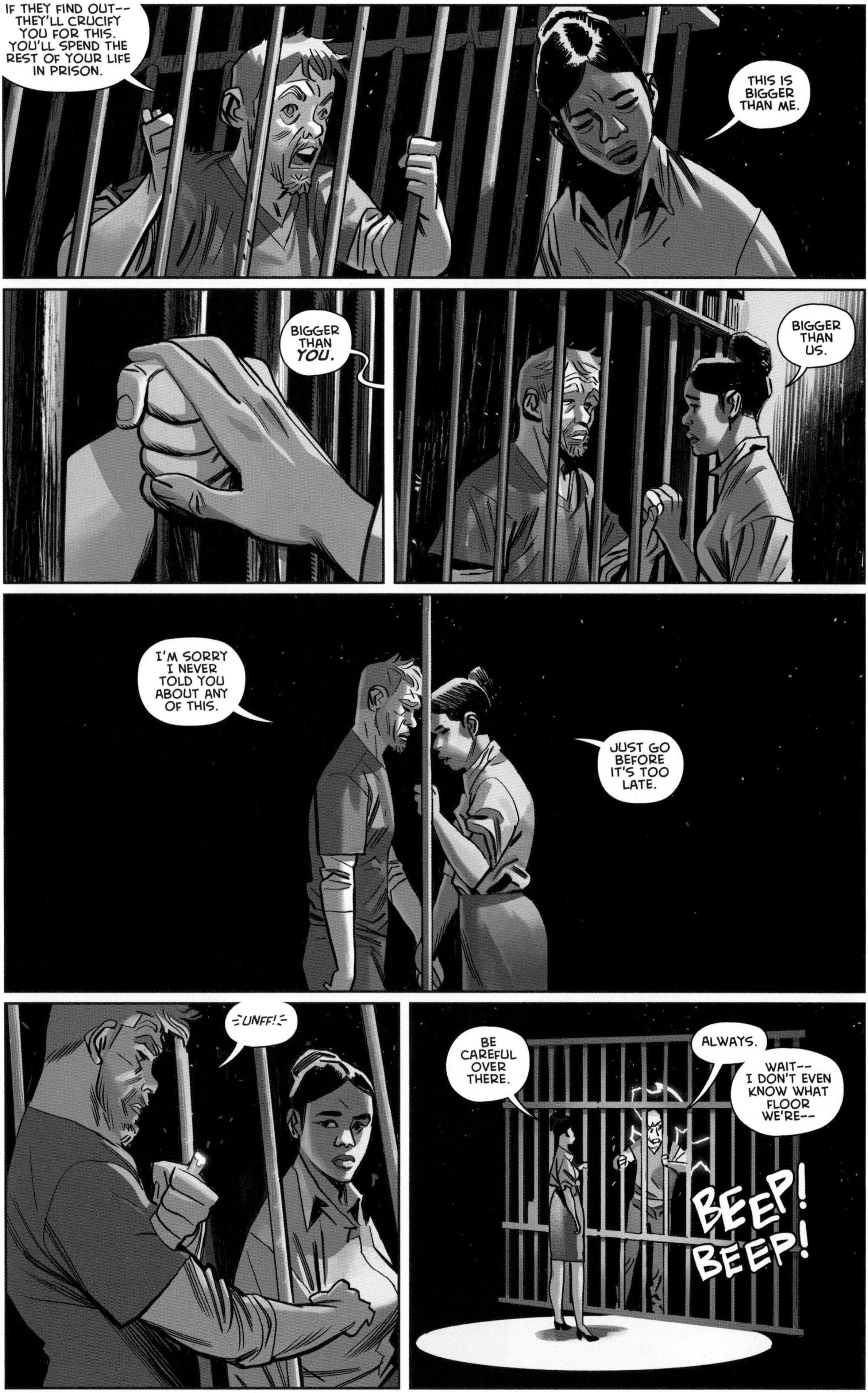
IF THEY FIND OUT-- THEY'LL CRUCIFY YOU FOR THIS. YOU'LL SPEND THE REST OF YOUR LIFE IN PRISON.
THIS IS BIGGER THAN ME.
BIGGER THAN *YOU.*
BIGGER THAN US.
I'M SORRY I NEVER TOLD YOU ABOUT ANY OF THIS.
JUST GO BEFORE IT'S TOO LATE.
UNFF!
BE CAREFUL OVER THERE.
ALWAYS.
WAIT-- I DON'T EVEN KNOW WHAT FLOOR WE'RE--
BEEP! BEEP!

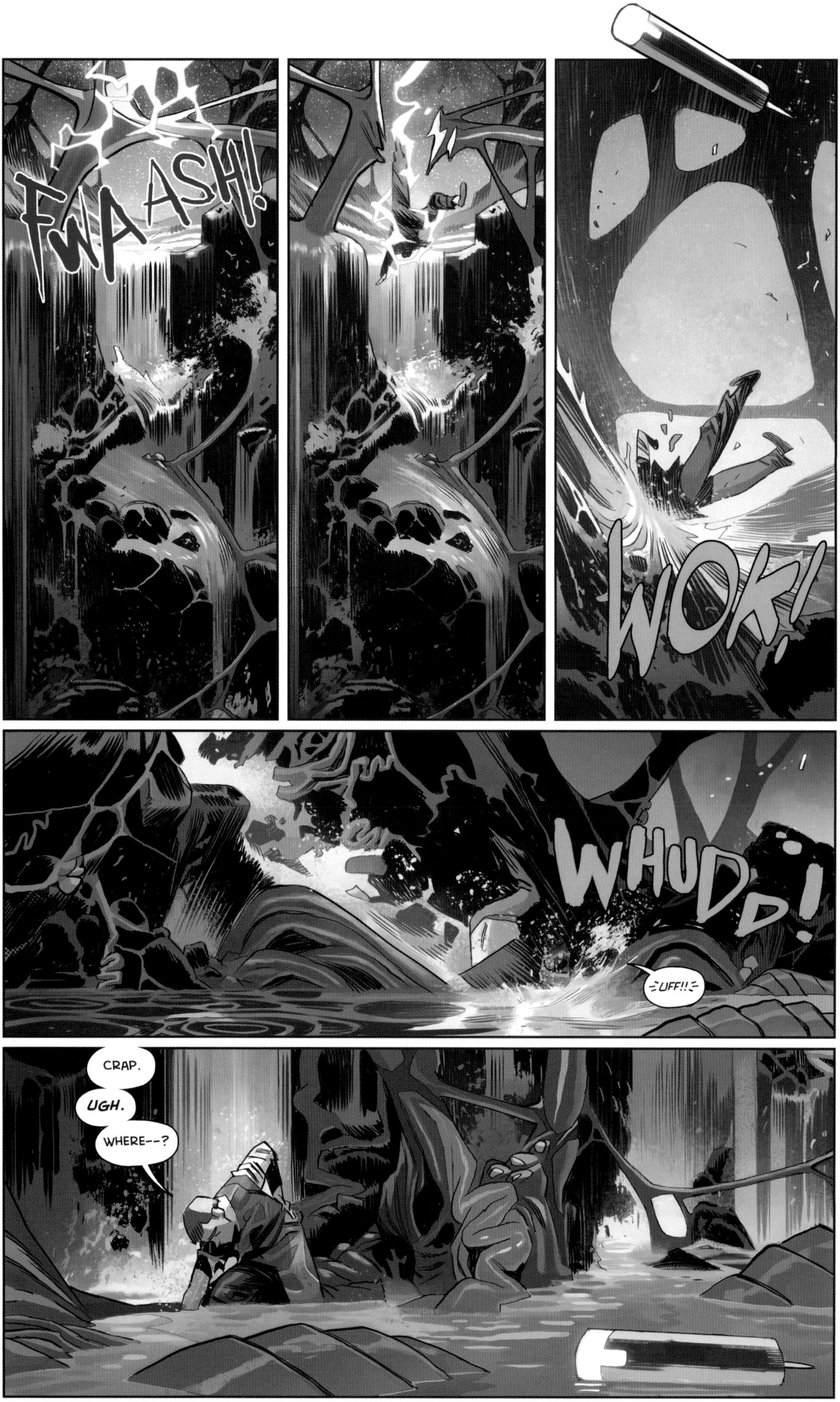
FWAASH!
WOK!
WHUDD!
UFF!!
CRAP.
UGH.
WHERE--?

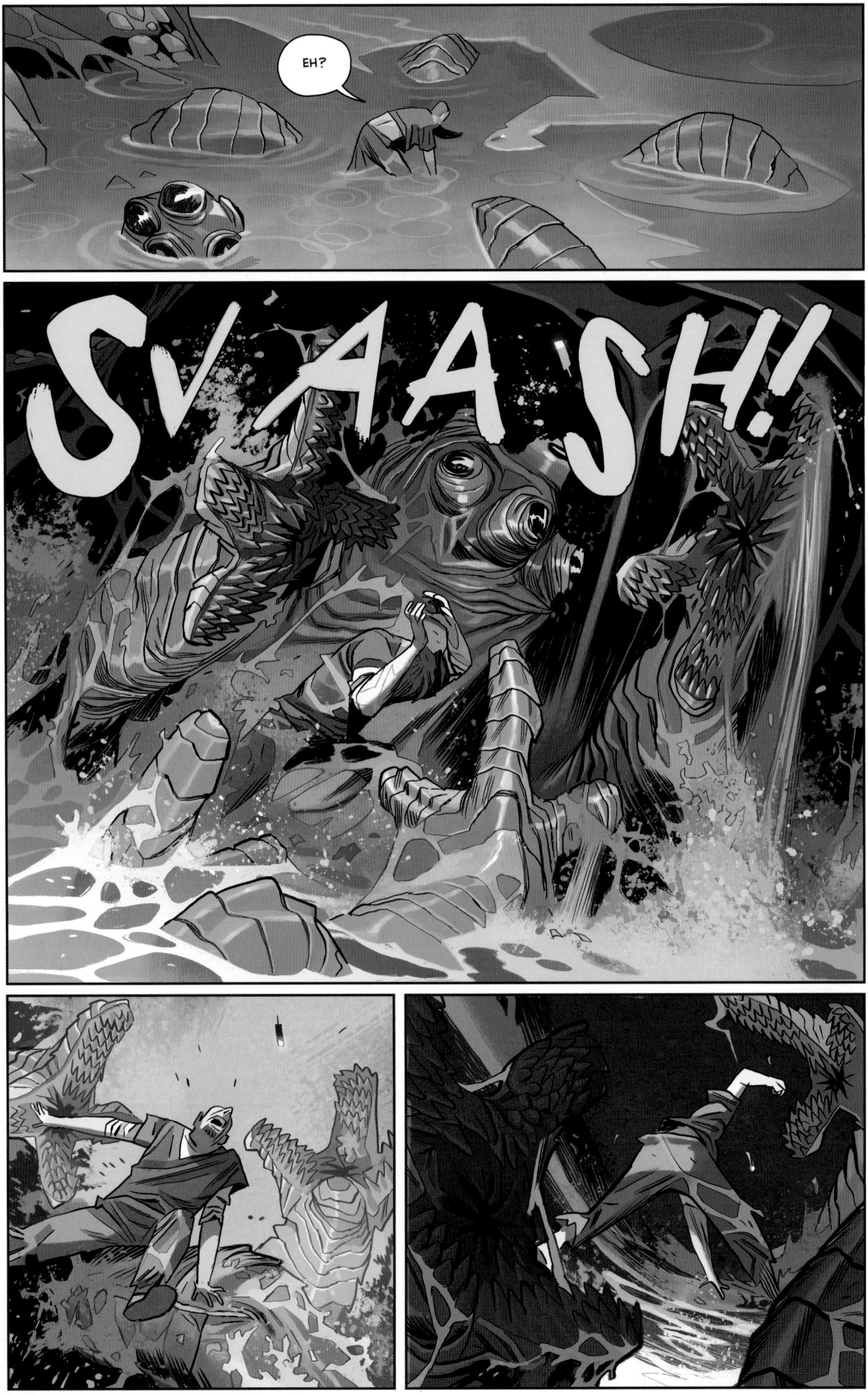
EH?
SWAASH!

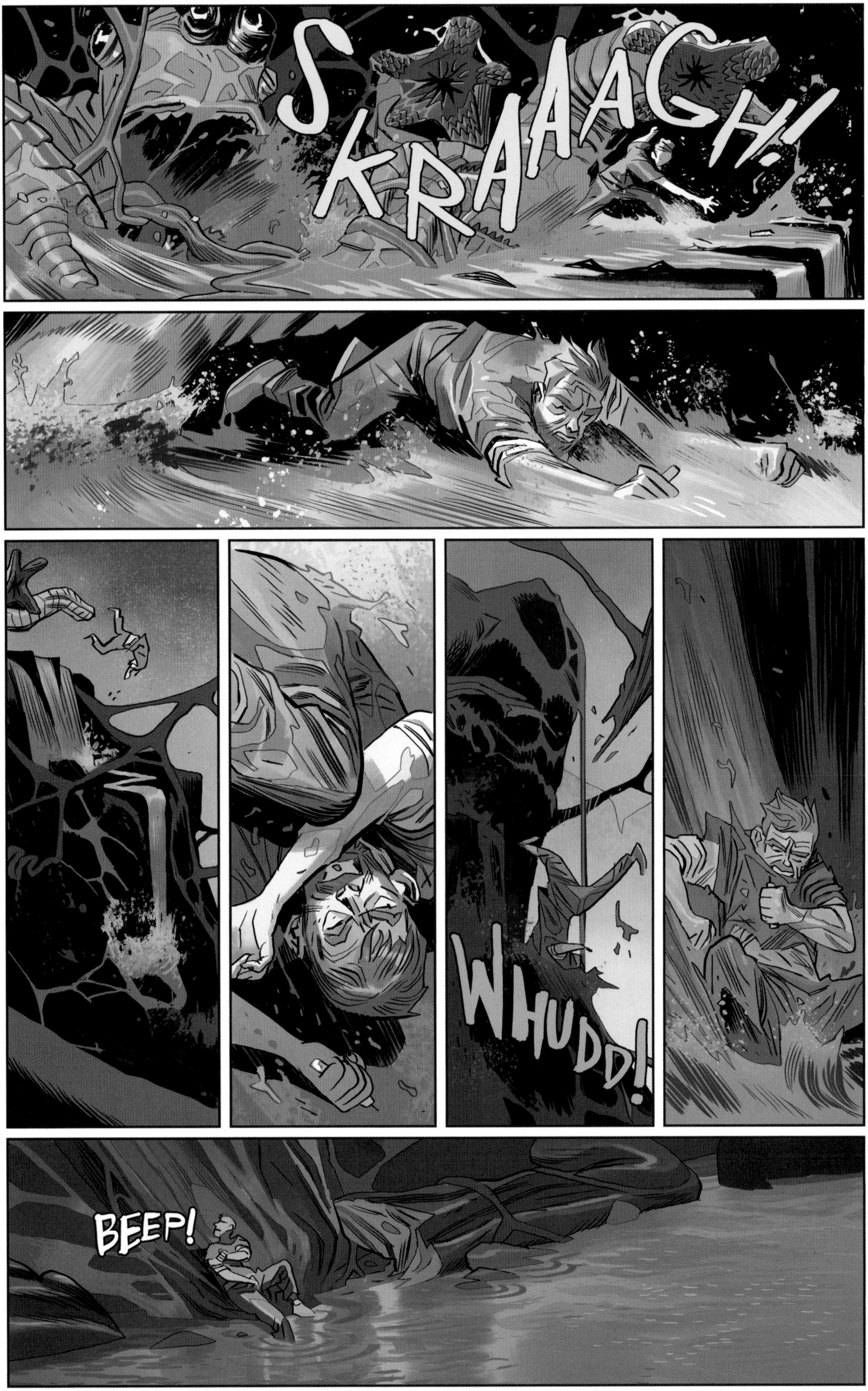
SKRAAAAGH!
WHUDD!
BEEP!

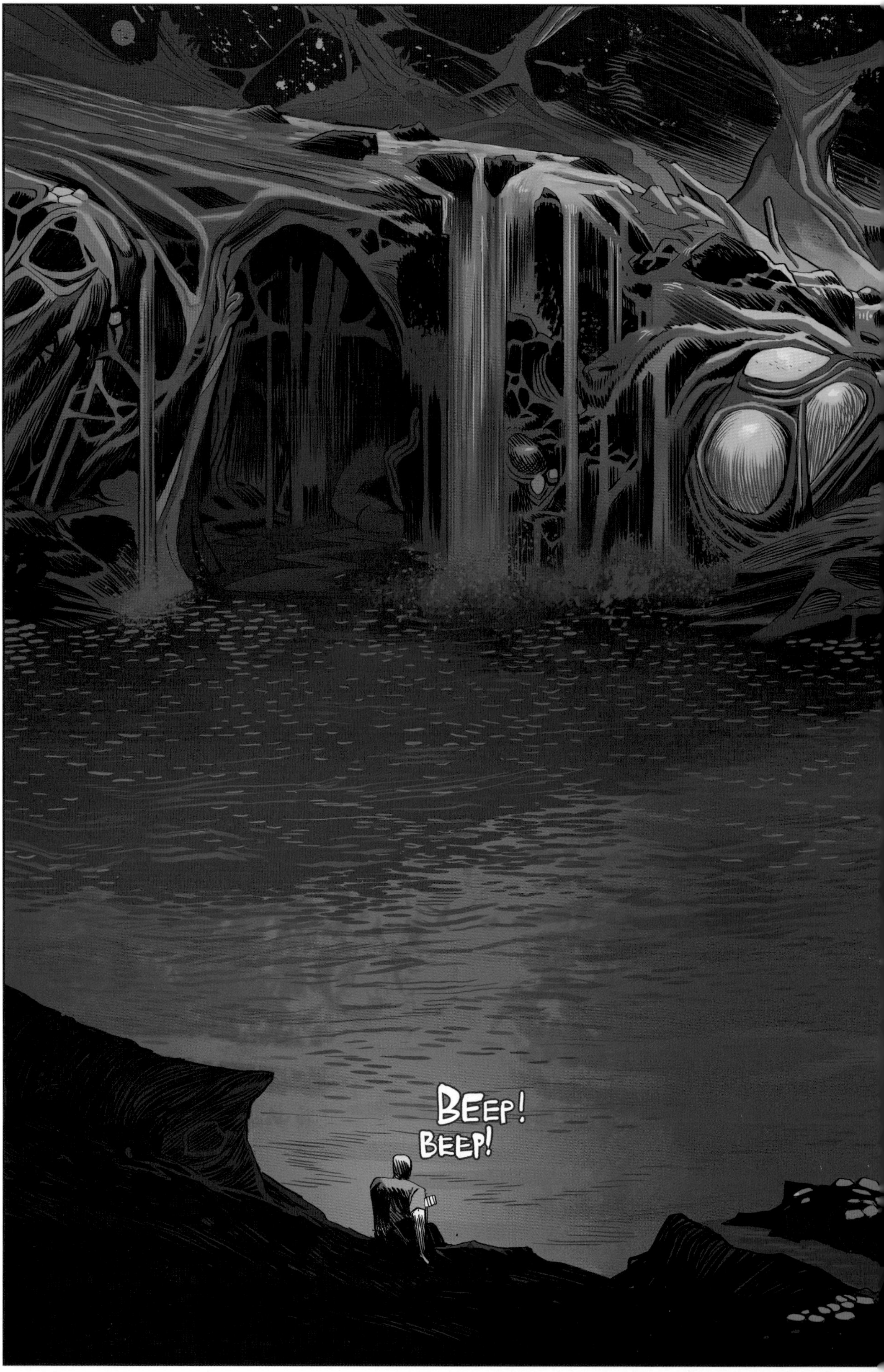
BEEP!
BEEP!

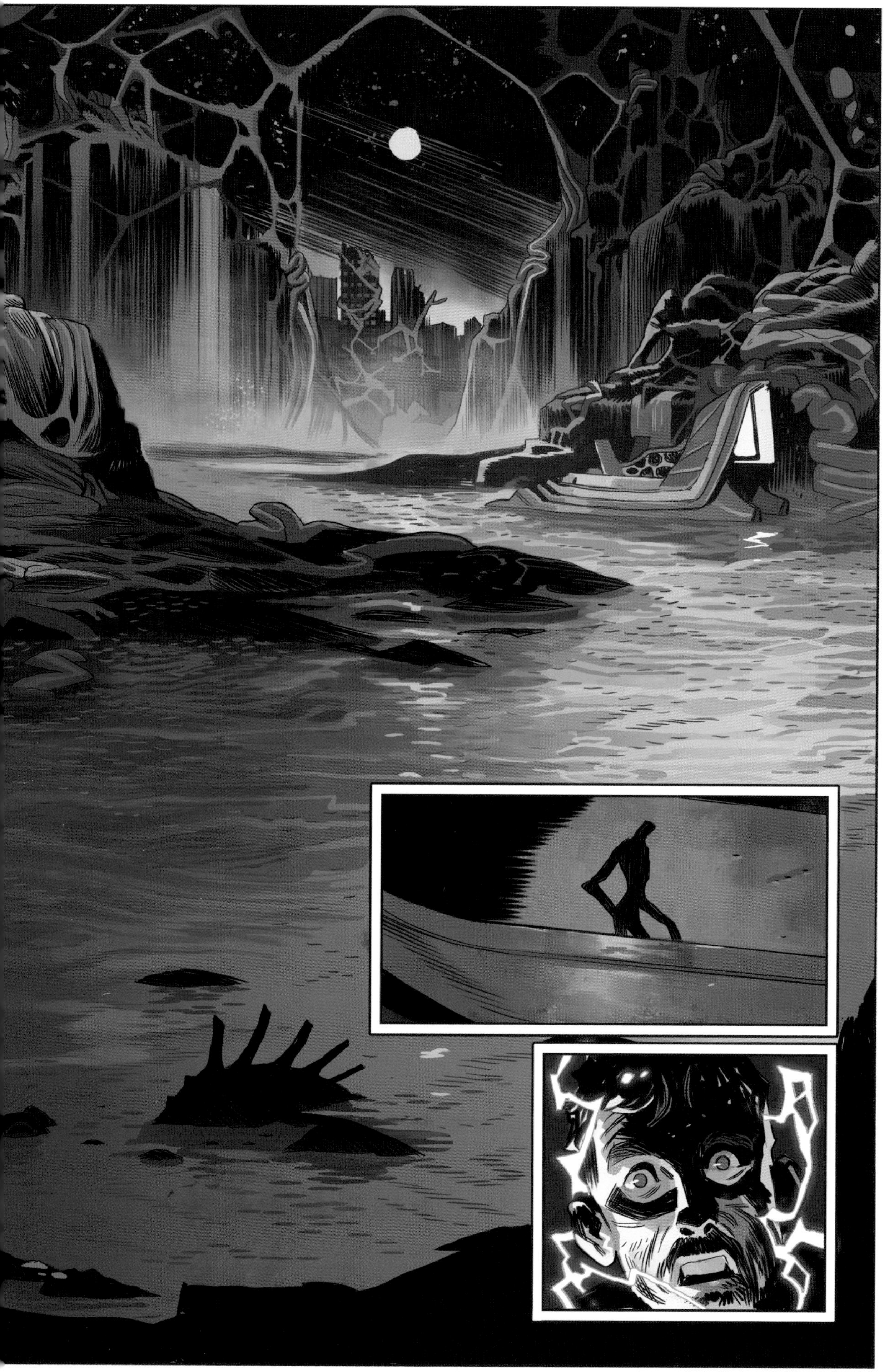

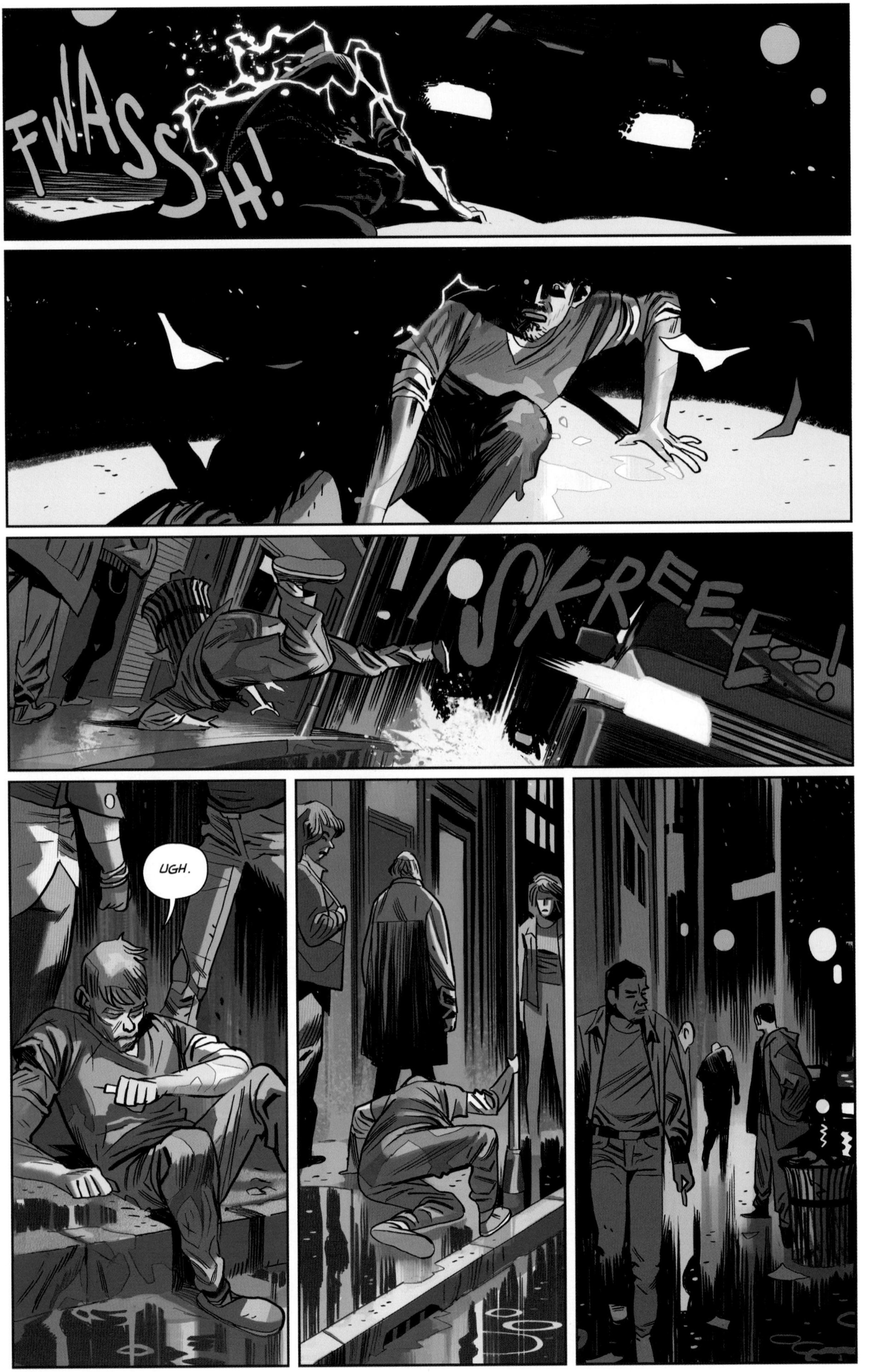
FWASSH!
SKREEEE--!
UGH.

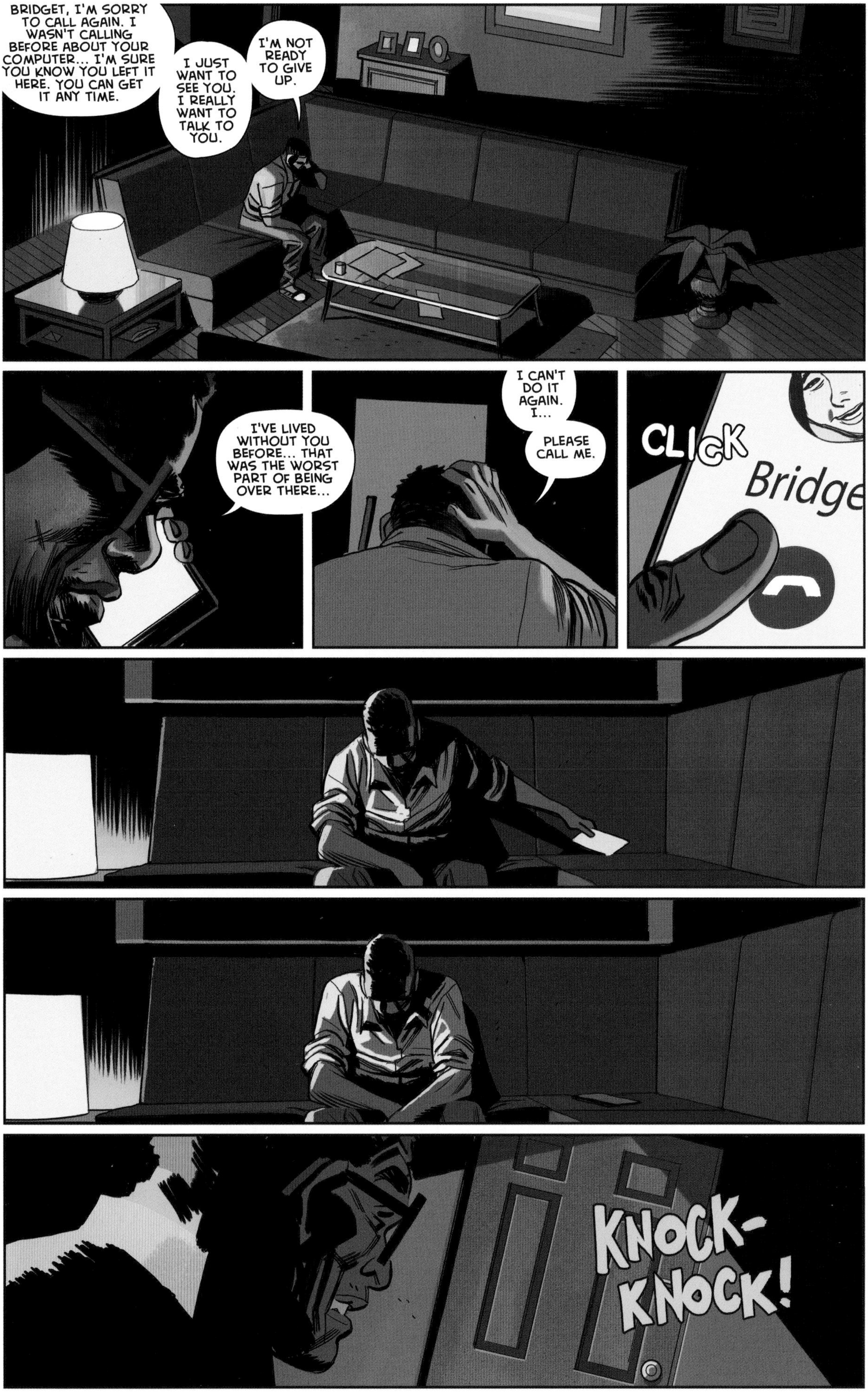
BRIDGET, I'M SORRY TO CALL AGAIN. I WASN'T CALLING BEFORE ABOUT YOUR COMPUTER... I'M SURE YOU KNOW YOU LEFT IT HERE. YOU CAN GET IT ANY TIME.
I JUST WANT TO SEE YOU. I REALLY WANT TO TALK TO YOU.
I'M NOT READY TO GIVE UP.
I'VE LIVED WITHOUT YOU BEFORE... THAT WAS THE WORST PART OF BEING OVER THERE...
I CAN'T DO IT AGAIN. I...
PLEASE CALL ME.
CLICK
Bridge
KNOCK-KNOCK!

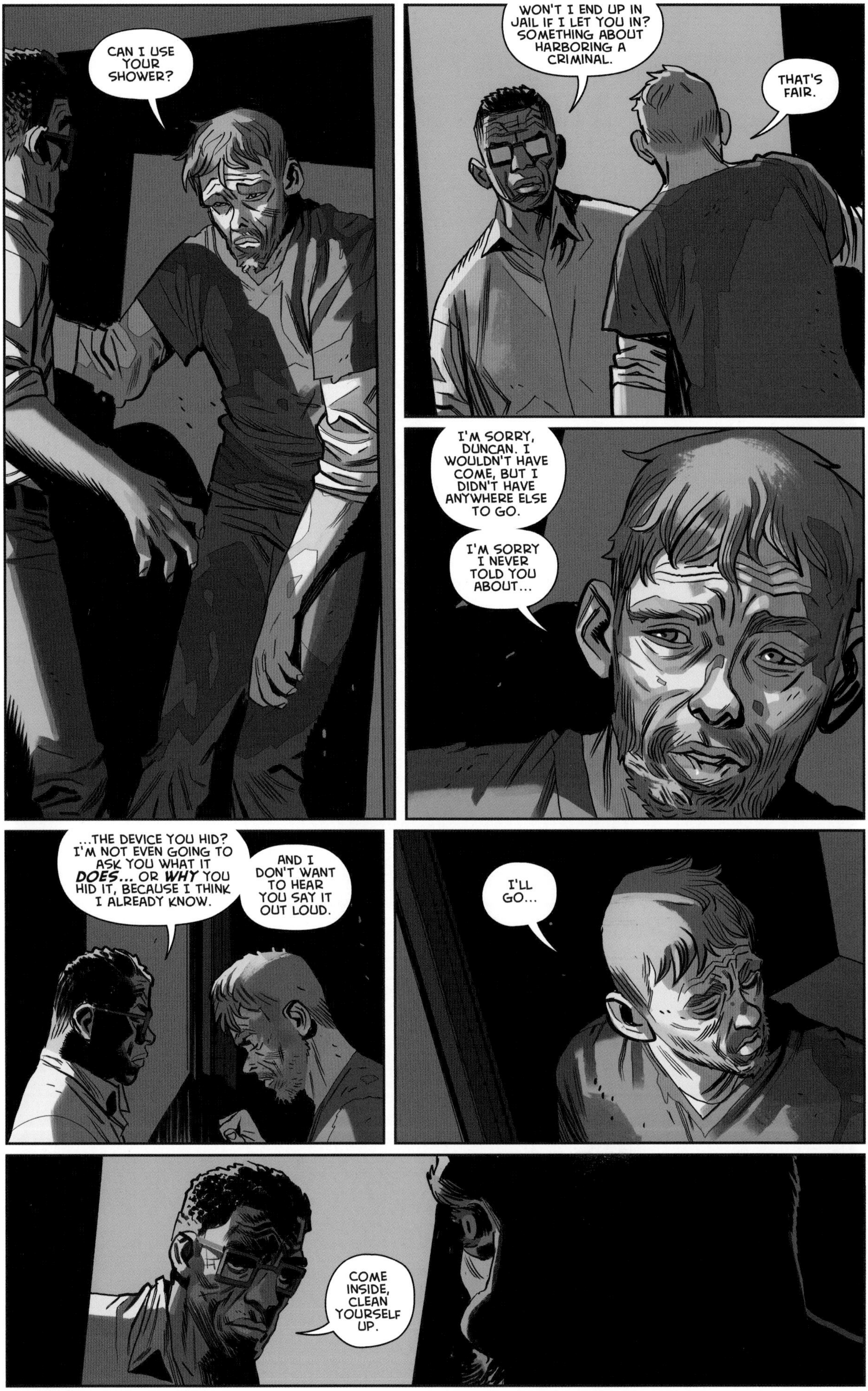
CAN I USE YOUR SHOWER?
WON'T I END UP IN JAIL IF I LET YOU IN? SOMETHING ABOUT HARBORING A CRIMINAL.
THAT'S FAIR.
I'M SORRY, DUNCAN. I WOULDN'T HAVE COME, BUT I DIDN'T HAVE ANYWHERE ELSE TO GO.
I'M SORRY I NEVER TOLD YOU ABOUT...
...THE DEVICE YOU HID? I'M NOT EVEN GOING TO ASK YOU WHAT IT DOES... OR WHY YOU HID IT, BECAUSE I THINK I ALREADY KNOW.
AND I DON'T WANT TO HEAR YOU SAY IT OUT LOUD.
I'LL GO...
COME INSIDE, CLEAN YOURSELF UP.

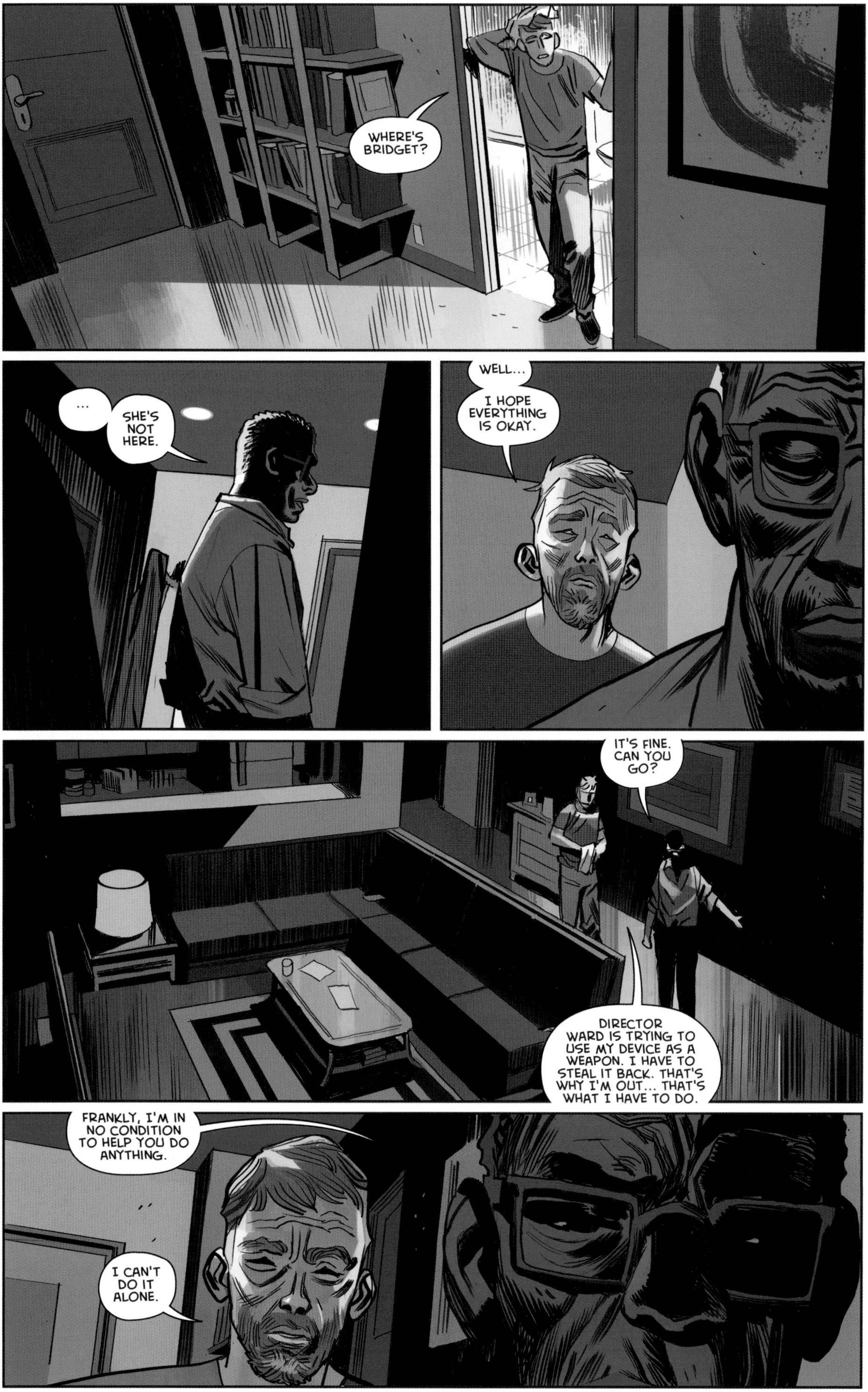
WHERE'S BRIDGET?
...
SHE'S NOT HERE.
WELL...
I HOPE EVERYTHING IS OKAY.
IT'S FINE. CAN YOU GO?
DIRECTOR WARD IS TRYING TO USE MY DEVICE AS A WEAPON. I HAVE TO STEAL IT BACK. THAT'S WHY I'M OUT... THAT'S WHAT I HAVE TO DO.
FRANKLY, I'M IN NO CONDITION TO HELP YOU DO ANYTHING.
I CAN'T DO IT ALONE.

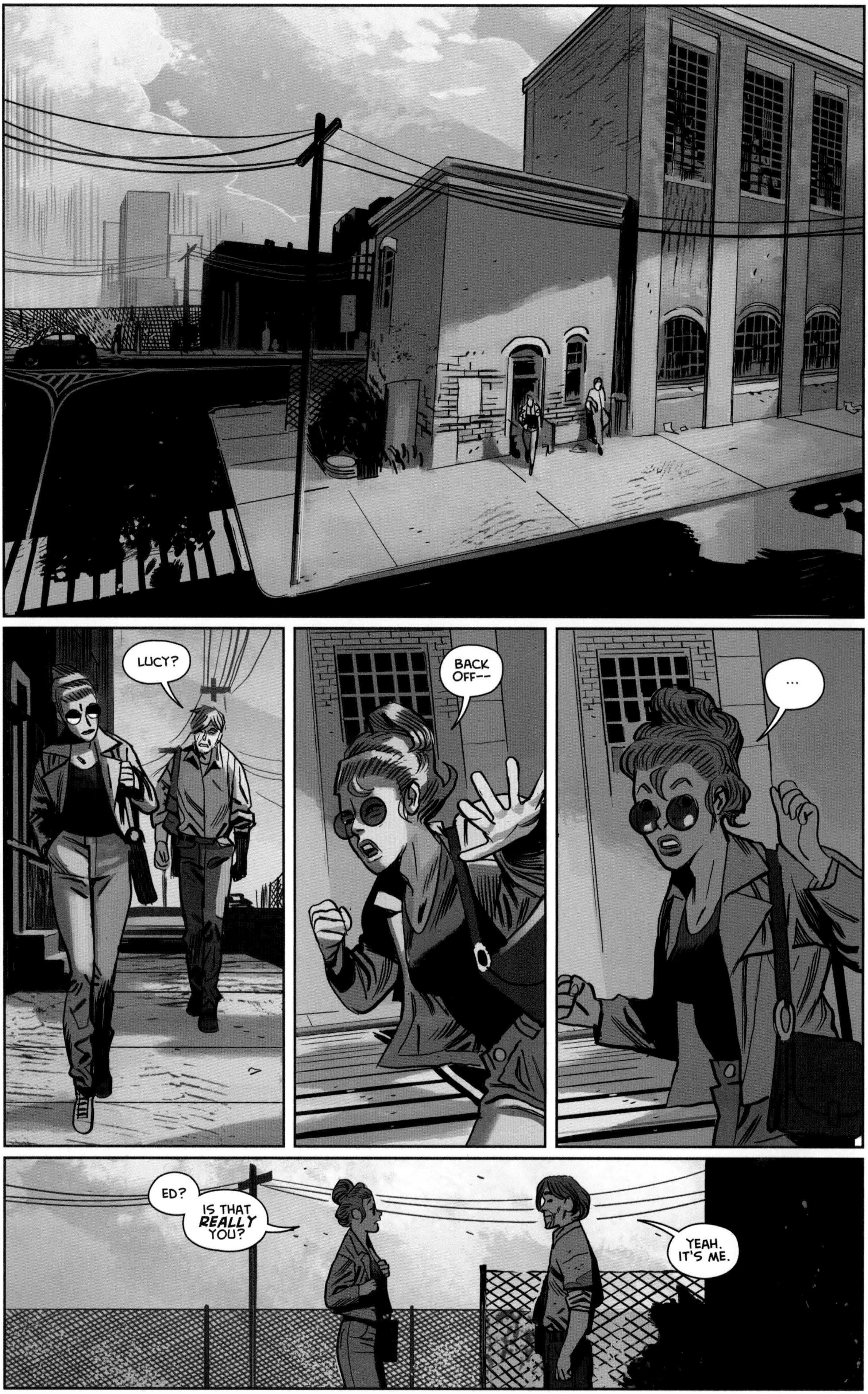
LUCY?
BACK OFF--
...
ED? IS THAT REALLY YOU?
YEAH. IT'S ME.

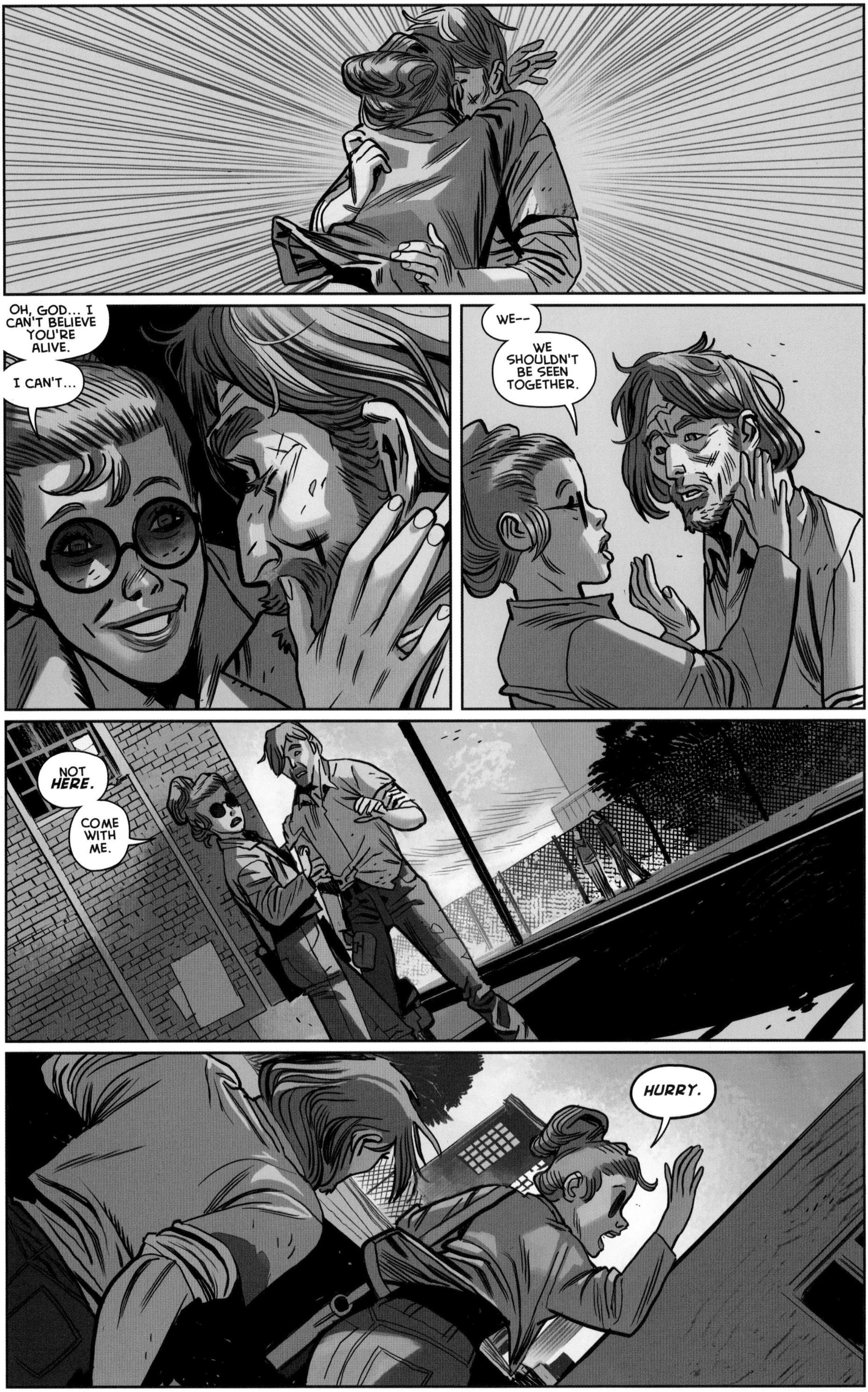
OH, GOD... I CAN'T BELIEVE YOU'RE ALIVE.
I CAN'T...
WE--
WE SHOULDN'T BE SEEN TOGETHER.
NOT *HERE.*
COME WITH ME.
HURRY.

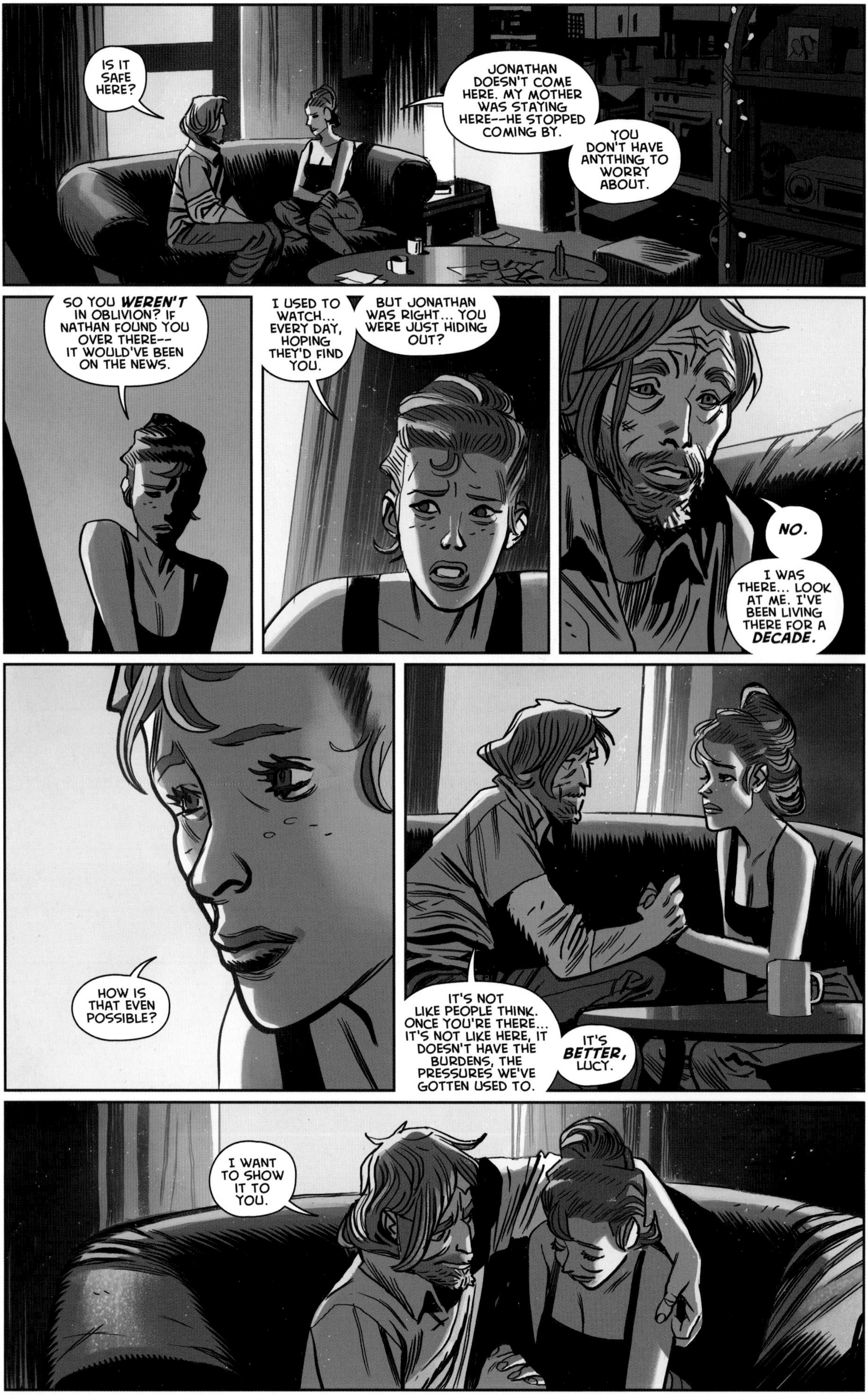
IS IT SAFE HERE?
JONATHAN DOESN'T COME HERE. MY MOTHER WAS STAYING HERE--HE STOPPED COMING BY.
YOU DON'T HAVE ANYTHING TO WORRY ABOUT.
SO YOU **WEREN'T** IN OBLIVION? IF NATHAN FOUND YOU OVER THERE-- IT WOULD'VE BEEN ON THE NEWS.
I USED TO WATCH... EVERY DAY, HOPING THEY'D FIND YOU.
BUT JONATHAN WAS RIGHT... YOU WERE JUST HIDING OUT?
NO.
I WAS THERE... LOOK AT ME. I'VE BEEN LIVING THERE FOR A **DECADE.**
HOW IS THAT EVEN POSSIBLE?
IT'S NOT LIKE PEOPLE THINK. ONCE YOU'RE THERE... IT'S NOT LIKE HERE, IT DOESN'T HAVE THE BURDENS, THE PRESSURES WE'VE GOTTEN USED TO.
IT'S **BETTER,** LUCY.
I WANT TO SHOW IT TO YOU.

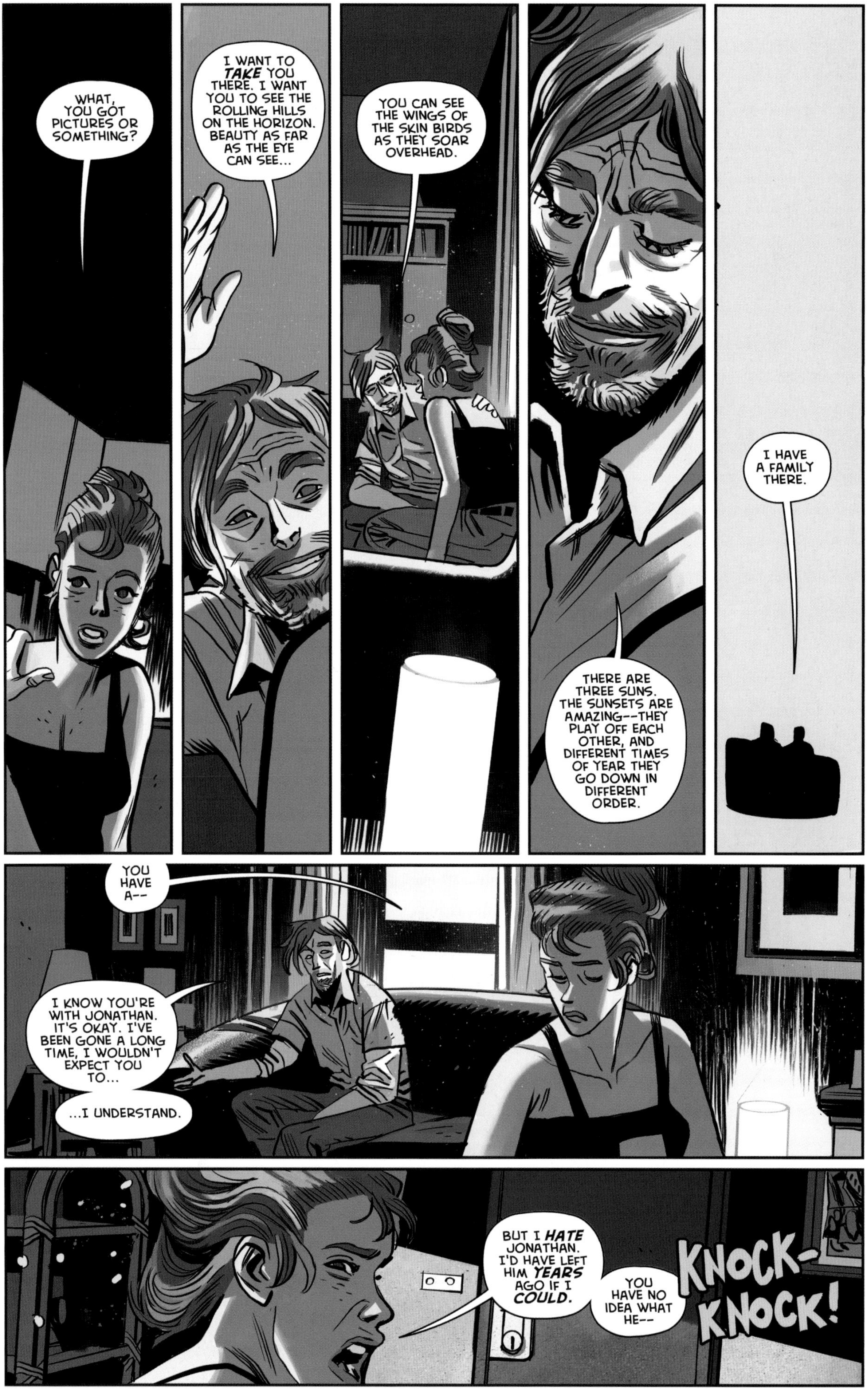
WHAT, YOU GOT PICTURES OR SOMETHING?
I WANT TO *TAKE* YOU THERE. I WANT YOU TO SEE THE ROLLING HILLS ON THE HORIZON. BEAUTY AS FAR AS THE EYE CAN SEE...
YOU CAN SEE THE WINGS OF THE SKIN BIRDS AS THEY SOAR OVERHEAD.
THERE ARE THREE SUNS. THE SUNSETS ARE AMAZING--THEY PLAY OFF EACH OTHER, AND DIFFERENT TIMES OF YEAR THEY GO DOWN IN DIFFERENT ORDER.
I HAVE A FAMILY THERE.
YOU HAVE A--
I KNOW YOU'RE WITH JONATHAN. IT'S OKAY. I'VE BEEN GONE A LONG TIME, I WOULDN'T EXPECT YOU TO...
...I UNDERSTAND.
BUT I *HATE* JONATHAN. I'D HAVE LEFT HIM *YEARS* AGO IF I *COULD*.
YOU HAVE NO IDEA WHAT HE--
KNOCK-KNOCK!

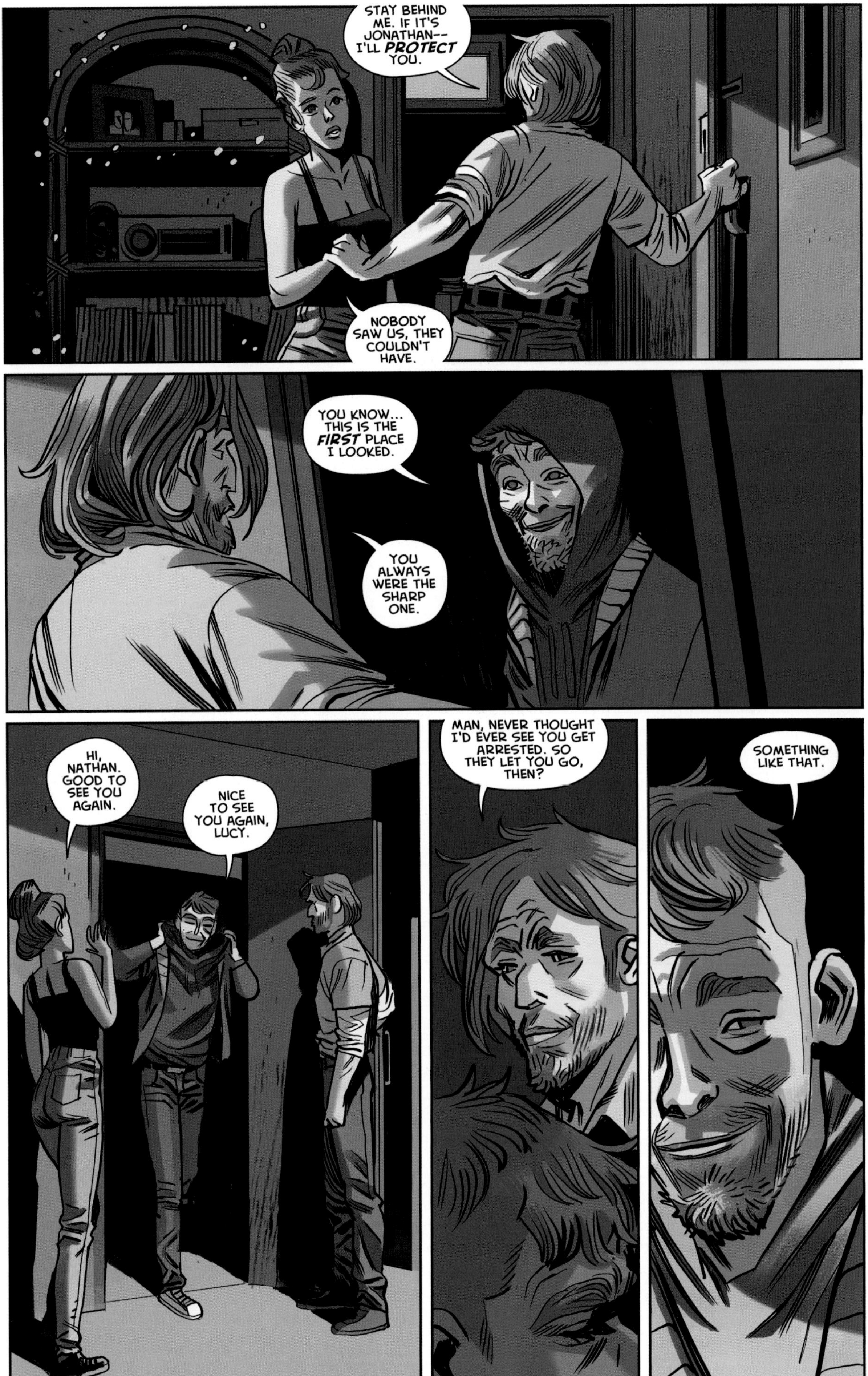
STAY BEHIND ME. IF IT'S JONATHAN-- I'LL PROTECT YOU.
NOBODY SAW US, THEY COULDN'T HAVE.
YOU KNOW... THIS IS THE FIRST PLACE I LOOKED.
YOU ALWAYS WERE THE SHARP ONE.
HI, NATHAN. GOOD TO SEE YOU AGAIN.
NICE TO SEE YOU AGAIN, LUCY.
MAN, NEVER THOUGHT I'D EVER SEE YOU GET ARRESTED. SO THEY LET YOU GO, THEN?
SOMETHING LIKE THAT.

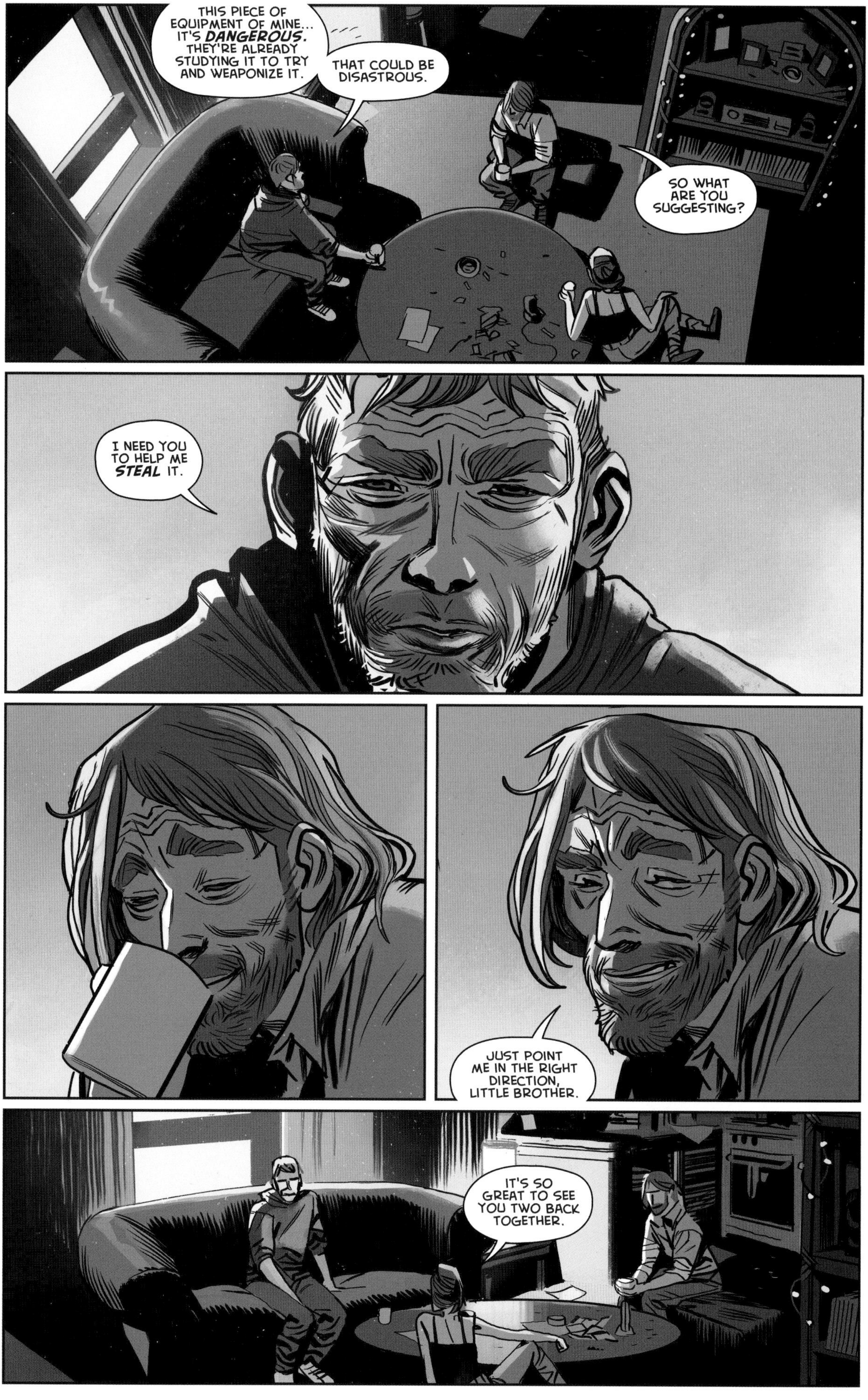
THIS PIECE OF EQUIPMENT OF MINE... IT'S DANGEROUS. THEY'RE ALREADY STUDYING IT TO TRY AND WEAPONIZE IT.
THAT COULD BE DISASTROUS.
SO WHAT ARE YOU SUGGESTING?
I NEED YOU TO HELP ME STEAL IT.
JUST POINT ME IN THE RIGHT DIRECTION, LITTLE BROTHER.
IT'S SO GREAT TO SEE YOU TWO BACK TOGETHER.

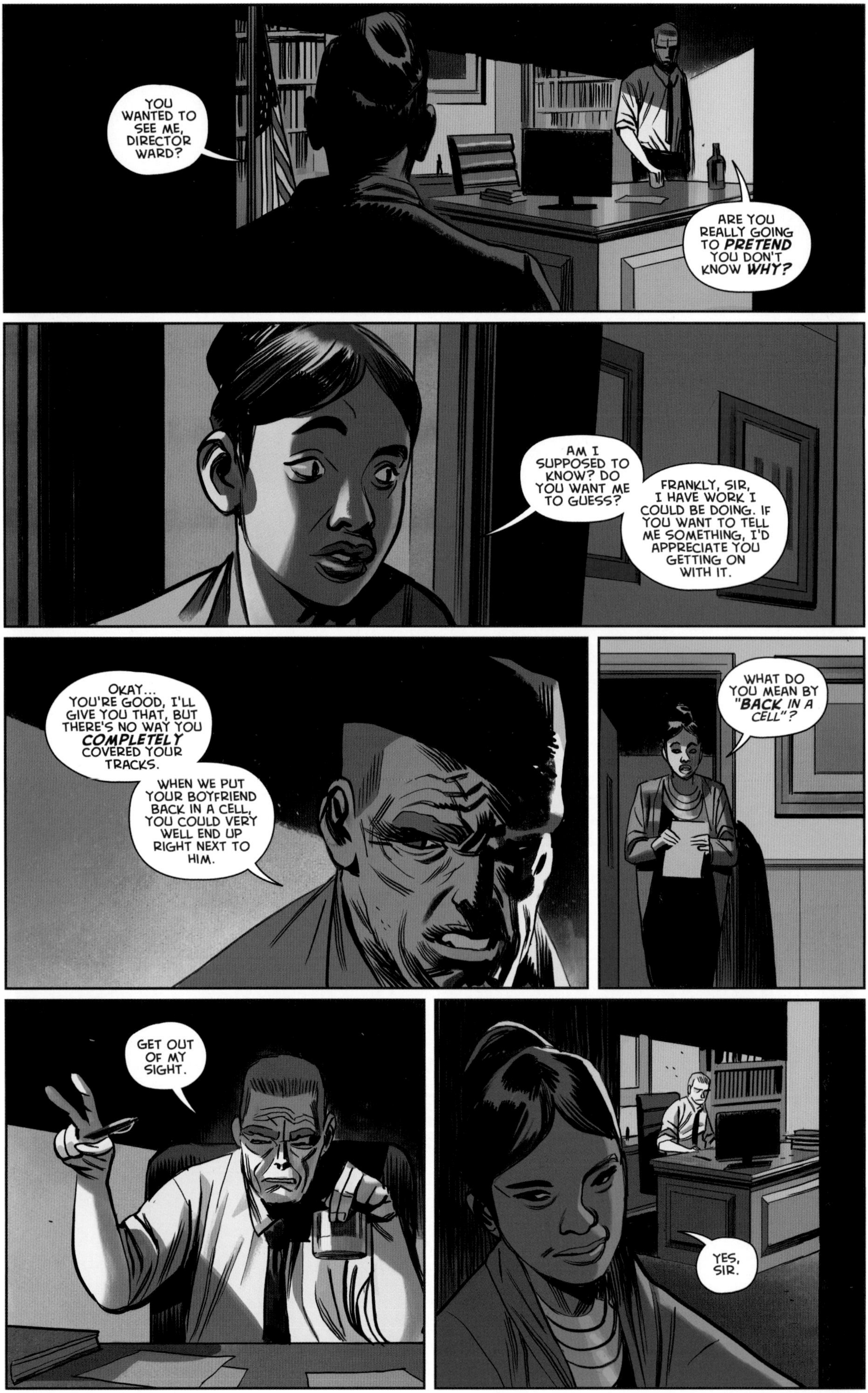
YOU WANTED TO SEE ME, DIRECTOR WARD?
ARE YOU REALLY GOING TO PRETEND YOU DON'T KNOW WHY?
AM I SUPPOSED TO KNOW? DO YOU WANT ME TO GUESS?
FRANKLY, SIR, I HAVE WORK I COULD BE DOING. IF YOU WANT TO TELL ME SOMETHING, I'D APPRECIATE YOU GETTING ON WITH IT.
OKAY... YOU'RE GOOD, I'LL GIVE YOU THAT, BUT THERE'S NO WAY YOU COMPLETELY COVERED YOUR TRACKS.
WHEN WE PUT YOUR BOYFRIEND BACK IN A CELL, YOU COULD VERY WELL END UP RIGHT NEXT TO HIM.
WHAT DO YOU MEAN BY "BACK IN A CELL"?
GET OUT OF MY SIGHT.
YES, SIR.

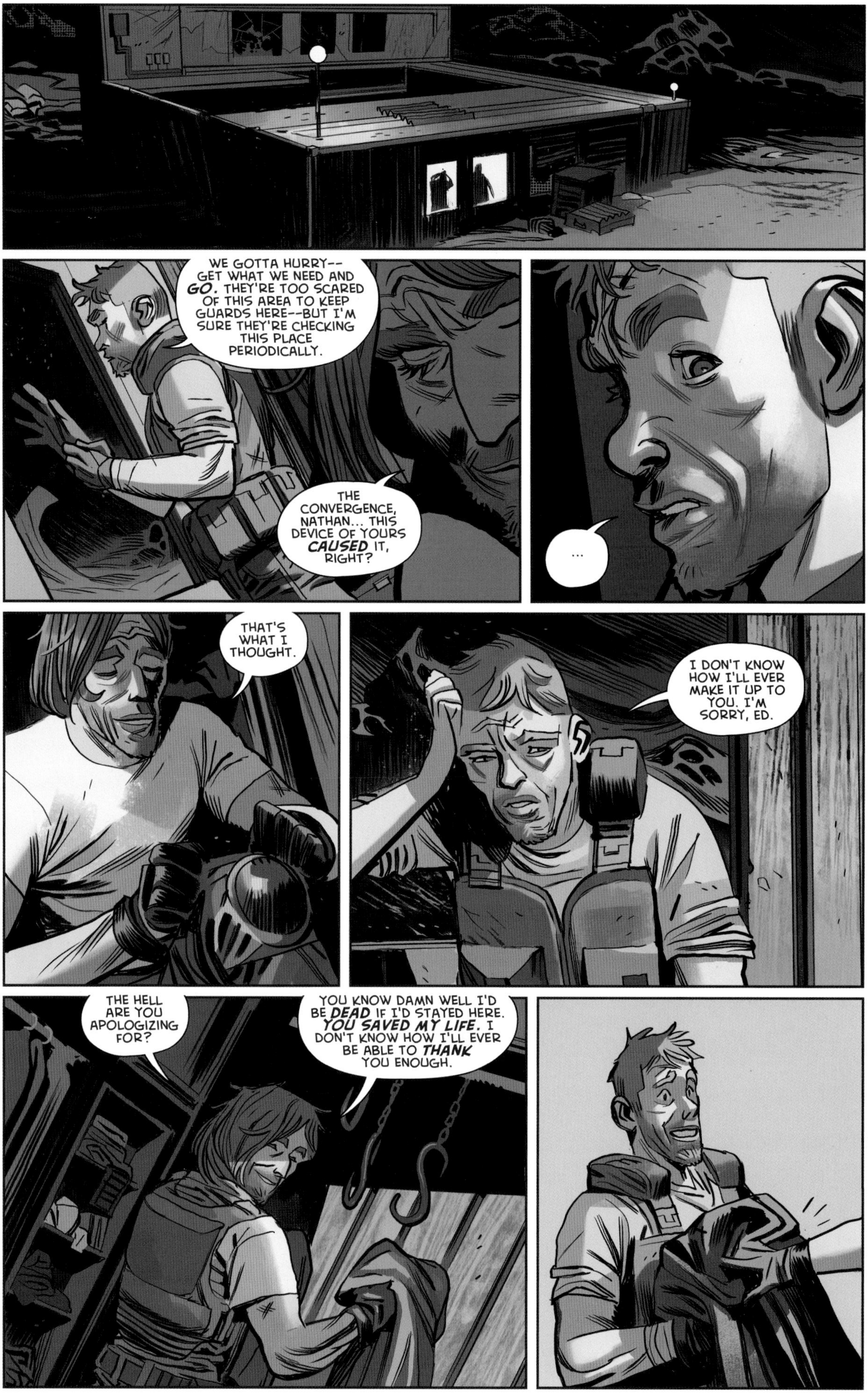
WE GOTTA HURRY-- GET WHAT WE NEED AND GO. THEY'RE TOO SCARED OF THIS AREA TO KEEP GUARDS HERE--BUT I'M SURE THEY'RE CHECKING THIS PLACE PERIODICALLY.
THE CONVERGENCE, NATHAN... THIS DEVICE OF YOURS CAUSED IT, RIGHT?
...
THAT'S WHAT I THOUGHT.
I DON'T KNOW HOW I'LL EVER MAKE IT UP TO YOU. I'M SORRY, ED.
THE HELL ARE YOU APOLOGIZING FOR?
YOU KNOW DAMN WELL I'D BE DEAD IF I'D STAYED HERE. YOU SAVED MY LIFE. I DON'T KNOW HOW I'LL EVER BE ABLE TO THANK YOU ENOUGH.

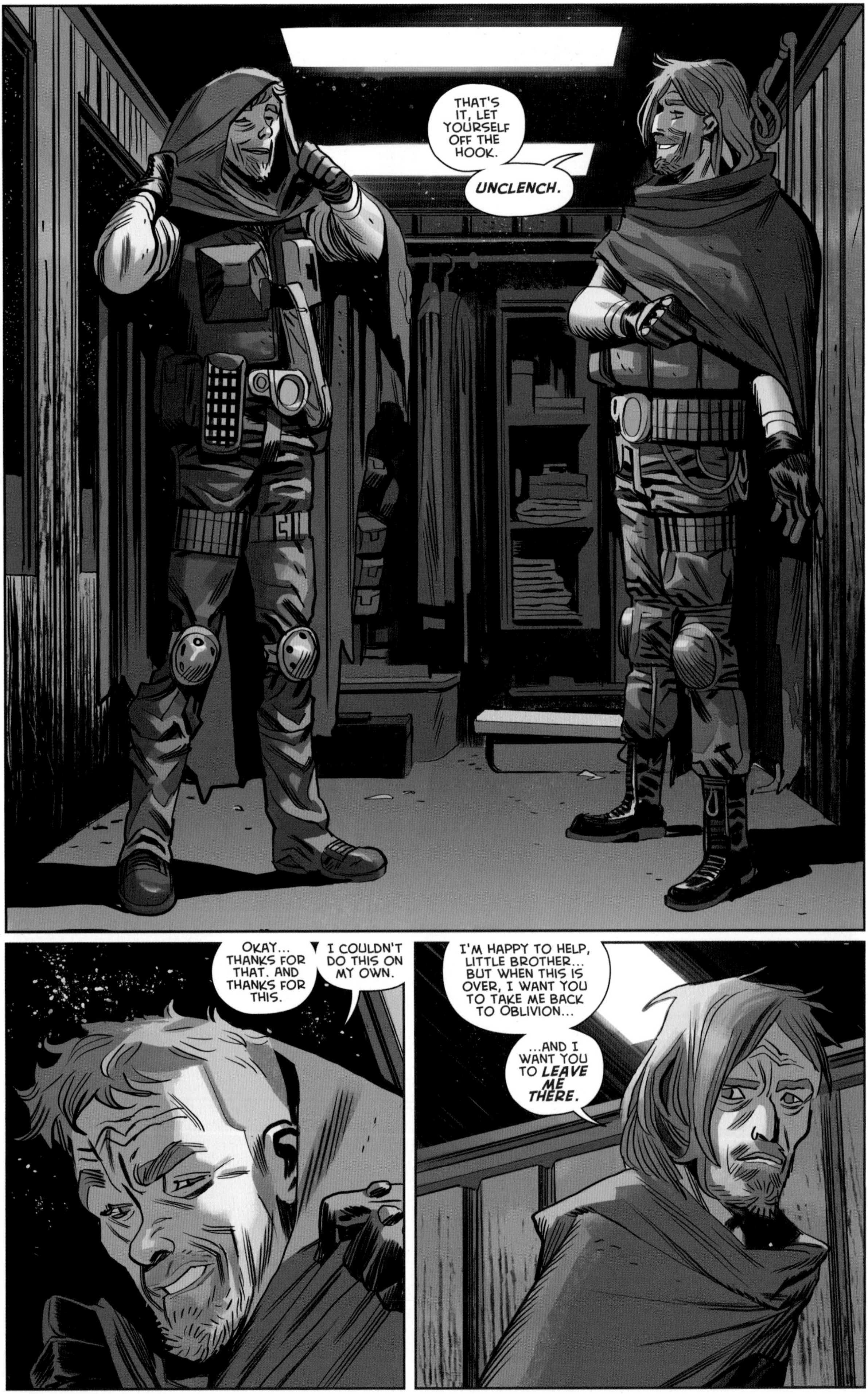
THAT'S IT, LET YOURSELF OFF THE HOOK.
UNCLENCH.
OKAY... THANKS FOR THAT. AND THANKS FOR THIS.
I COULDN'T DO THIS ON MY OWN.
I'M HAPPY TO HELP, LITTLE BROTHER... BUT WHEN THIS IS OVER, I WANT YOU TO TAKE ME BACK TO OBLIVION...
...AND I WANT YOU TO LEAVE ME THERE.

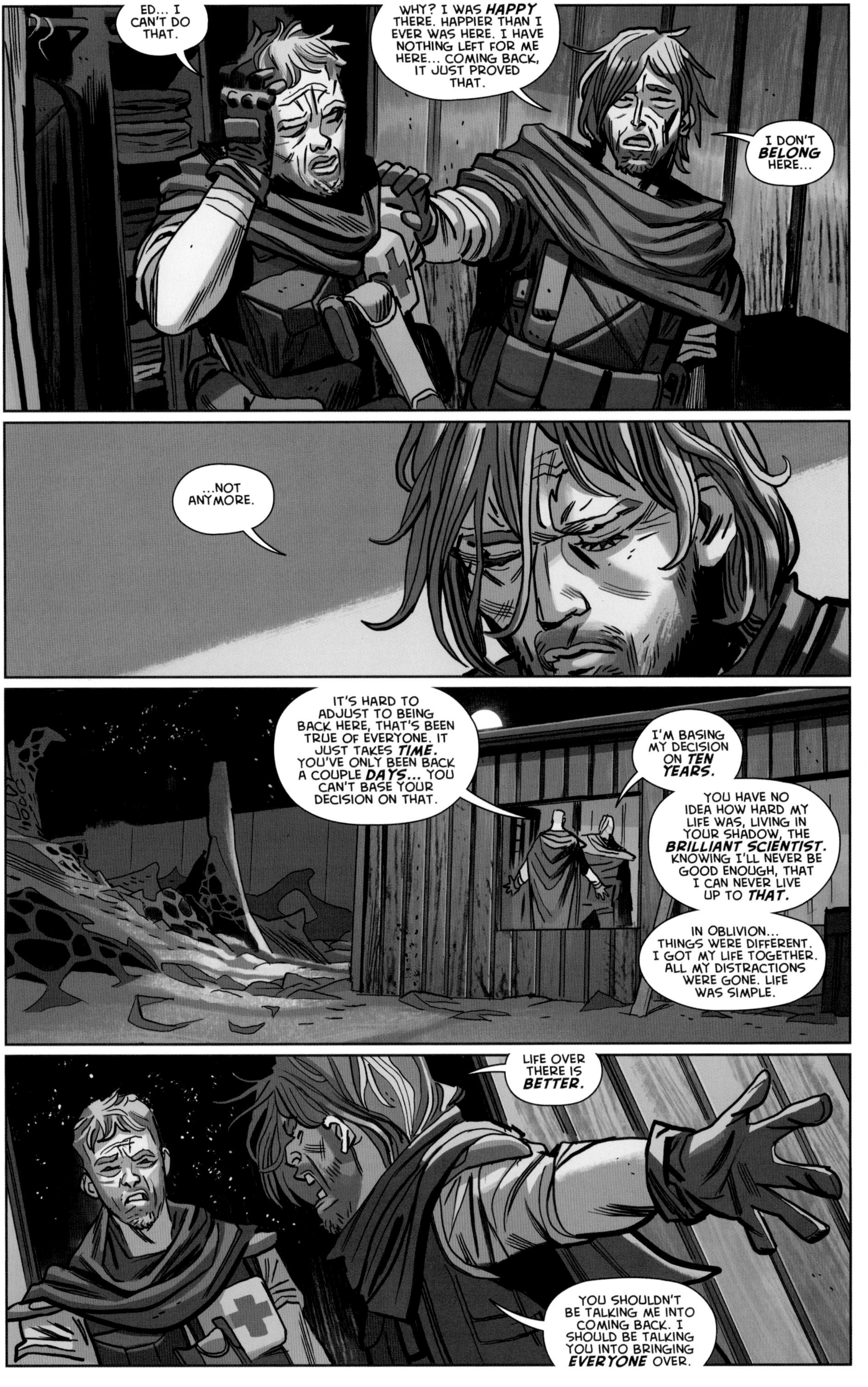
ED... I CAN'T DO THAT.
WHY? I WAS HAPPY THERE. HAPPIER THAN I EVER WAS HERE. I HAVE NOTHING LEFT FOR ME HERE... COMING BACK, IT JUST PROVED THAT.
I DON'T BELONG HERE...
...NOT ANYMORE.
IT'S HARD TO ADJUST TO BEING BACK HERE, THAT'S BEEN TRUE OF EVERYONE. IT JUST TAKES TIME. YOU'VE ONLY BEEN BACK A COUPLE DAYS... YOU CAN'T BASE YOUR DECISION ON THAT.
I'M BASING MY DECISION ON TEN YEARS.
YOU HAVE NO IDEA HOW HARD MY LIFE WAS, LIVING IN YOUR SHADOW, THE BRILLIANT SCIENTIST. KNOWING I'LL NEVER BE GOOD ENOUGH, THAT I CAN NEVER LIVE UP TO THAT.
IN OBLIVION... THINGS WERE DIFFERENT. I GOT MY LIFE TOGETHER. ALL MY DISTRACTIONS WERE GONE. LIFE WAS SIMPLE.
LIFE OVER THERE IS BETTER.
YOU SHOULDN'T BE TALKING ME INTO COMING BACK. I SHOULD BE TALKING YOU INTO BRINGING EVERYONE OVER.

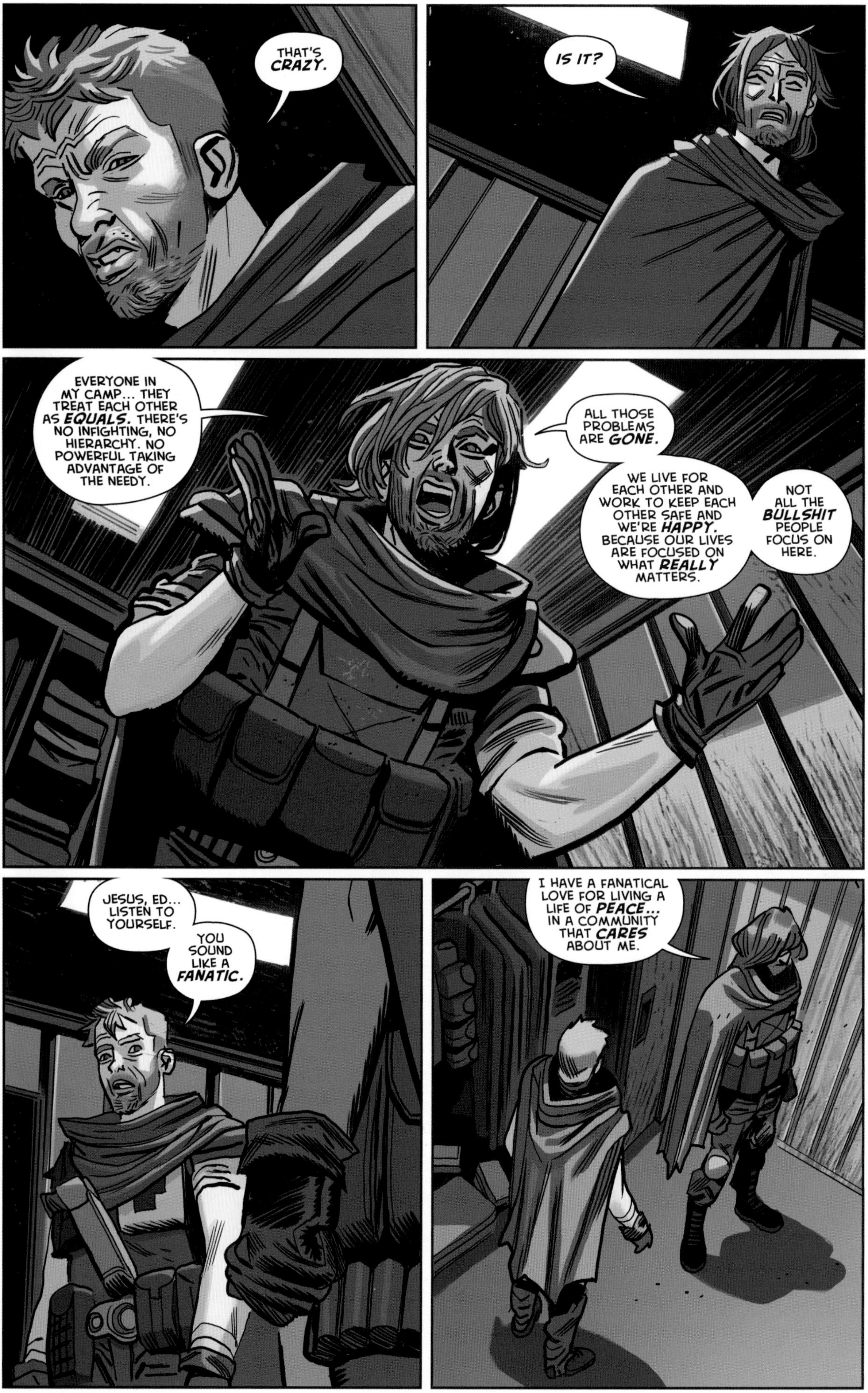
THAT'S CRAZY.
IS IT?
EVERYONE IN MY CAMP... THEY TREAT EACH OTHER AS EQUALS. THERE'S NO INFIGHTING, NO HIERARCHY. NO POWERFUL TAKING ADVANTAGE OF THE NEEDY.
ALL THOSE PROBLEMS ARE GONE.
WE LIVE FOR EACH OTHER AND WORK TO KEEP EACH OTHER SAFE AND WE'RE HAPPY. BECAUSE OUR LIVES ARE FOCUSED ON WHAT REALLY MATTERS.
NOT ALL THE BULLSHIT PEOPLE FOCUS ON HERE.
JESUS, ED... LISTEN TO YOURSELF.
YOU SOUND LIKE A FANATIC.
I HAVE A FANATICAL LOVE FOR LIVING A LIFE OF PEACE... IN A COMMUNITY THAT CARES ABOUT ME.

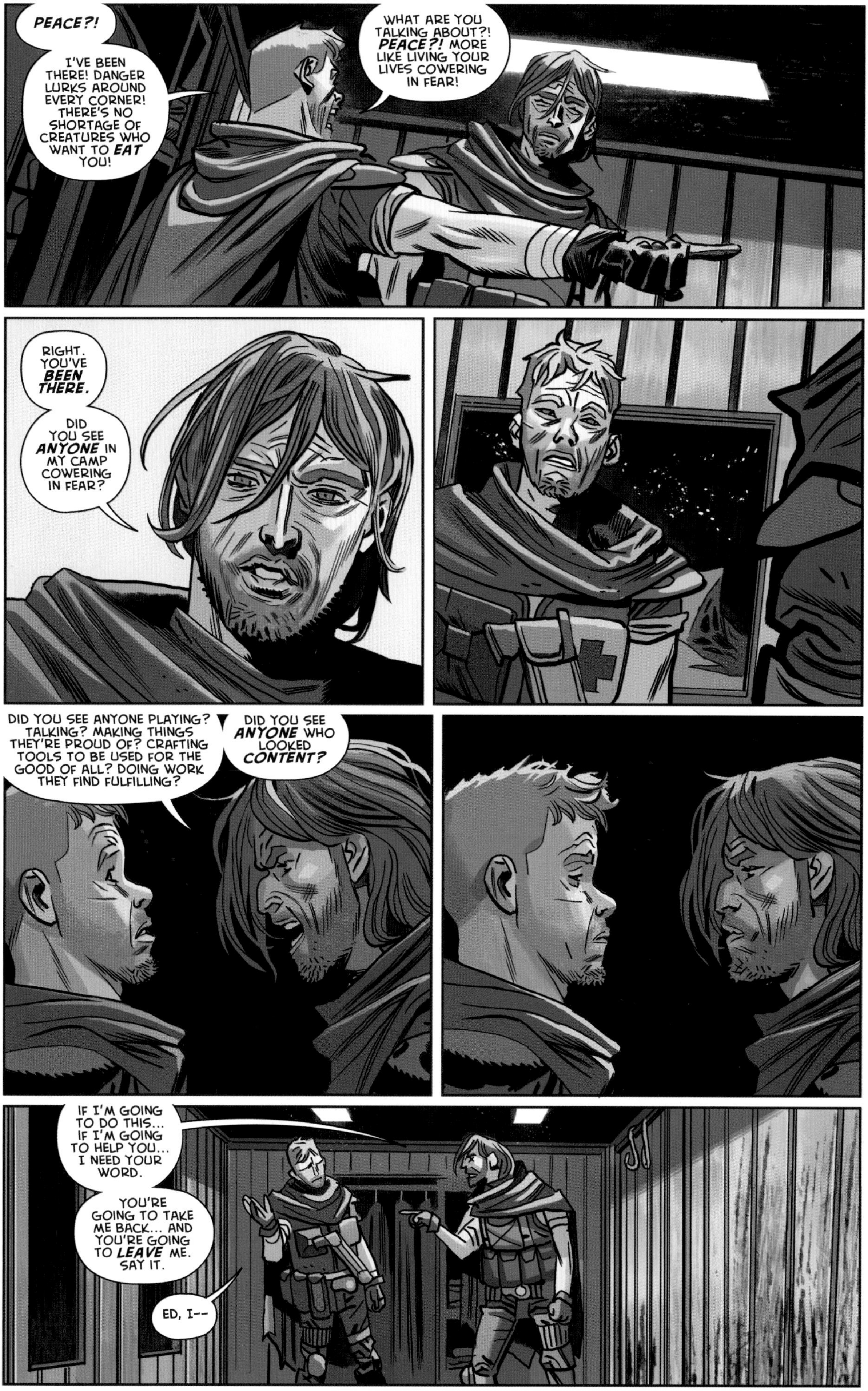
PEACE?!
I'VE BEEN THERE! DANGER LURKS AROUND EVERY CORNER! THERE'S NO SHORTAGE OF CREATURES WHO WANT TO EAT YOU!
WHAT ARE YOU TALKING ABOUT?! PEACE?! MORE LIKE LIVING YOUR LIVES COWERING IN FEAR!
RIGHT. YOU'VE BEEN THERE.
DID YOU SEE ANYONE IN MY CAMP COWERING IN FEAR?
DID YOU SEE ANYONE PLAYING? TALKING? MAKING THINGS THEY'RE PROUD OF? CRAFTING TOOLS TO BE USED FOR THE GOOD OF ALL? DOING WORK THEY FIND FULFILLING?
DID YOU SEE ANYONE WHO LOOKED CONTENT?
IF I'M GOING TO DO THIS... IF I'M GOING TO HELP YOU... I NEED YOUR WORD.
YOU'RE GOING TO TAKE ME BACK... AND YOU'RE GOING TO LEAVE ME. SAY IT.
ED, I--

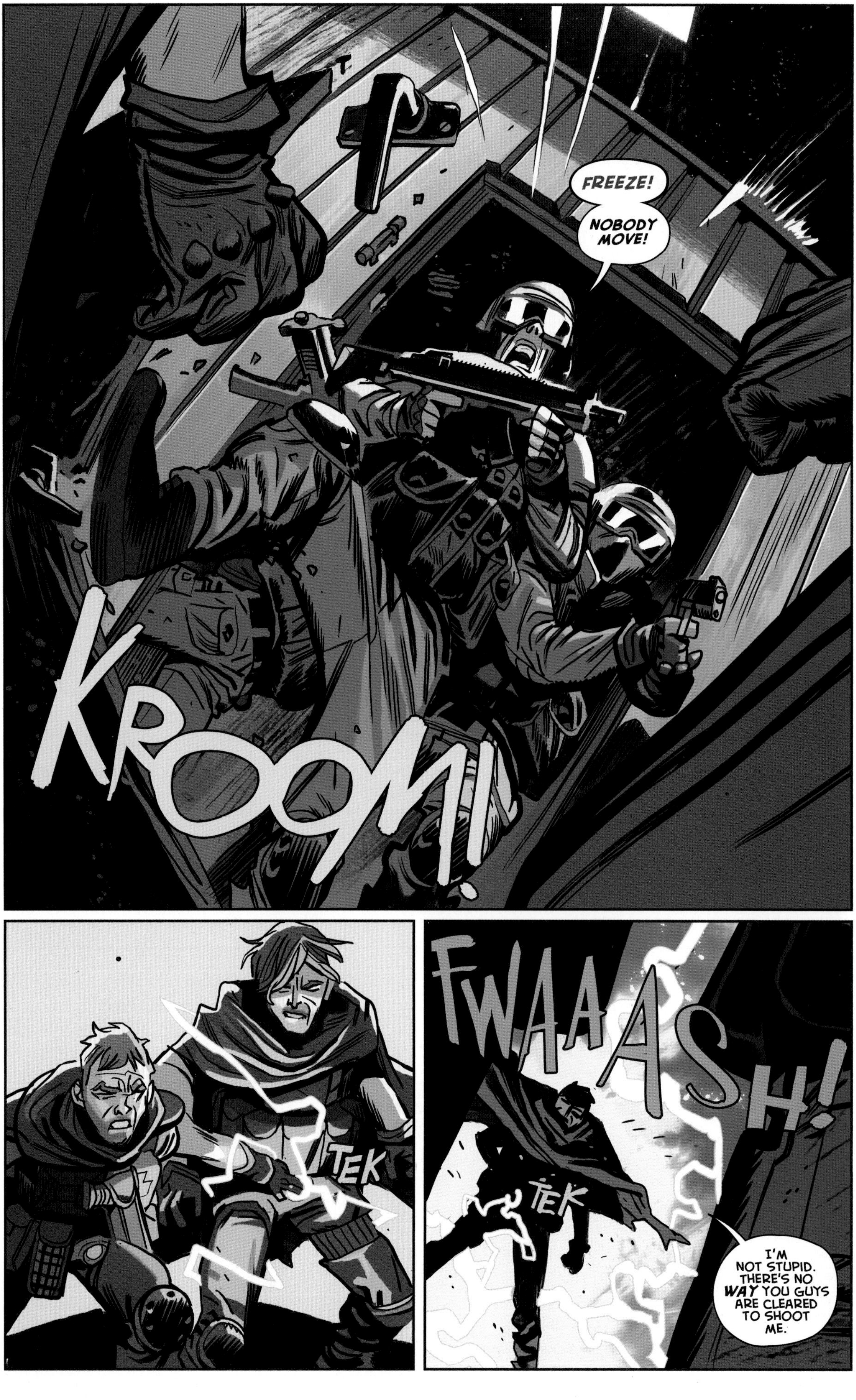
FREEZE!
NOBODY MOVE!
KROOM!
TEK
FWAAASH!
TEK
I'M NOT STUPID. THERE'S NO WAY YOU GUYS ARE CLEARED TO SHOOT ME.

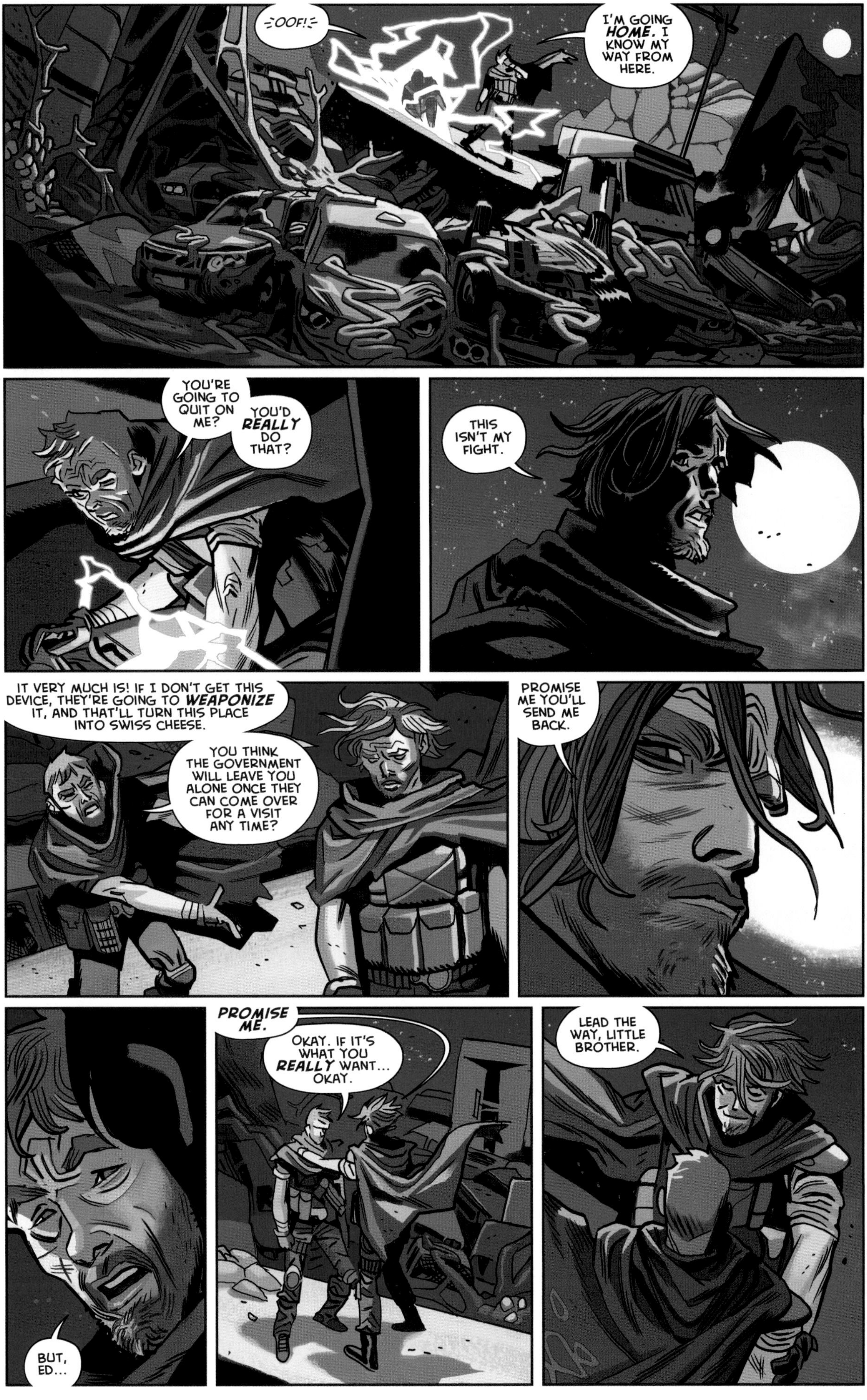
=OOF!=
I'M GOING HOME. I KNOW MY WAY FROM HERE.
YOU'RE GOING TO QUIT ON ME?
YOU'D REALLY DO THAT?
THIS ISN'T MY FIGHT.
IT VERY MUCH IS! IF I DON'T GET THIS DEVICE, THEY'RE GOING TO WEAPONIZE IT, AND THAT'LL TURN THIS PLACE INTO SWISS CHEESE.
YOU THINK THE GOVERNMENT WILL LEAVE YOU ALONE ONCE THEY CAN COME OVER FOR A VISIT ANY TIME?
PROMISE ME YOU'LL SEND ME BACK.
BUT, ED...
PROMISE ME.
OKAY. IF IT'S WHAT YOU REALLY WANT... OKAY.
LEAD THE WAY, LITTLE BROTHER.

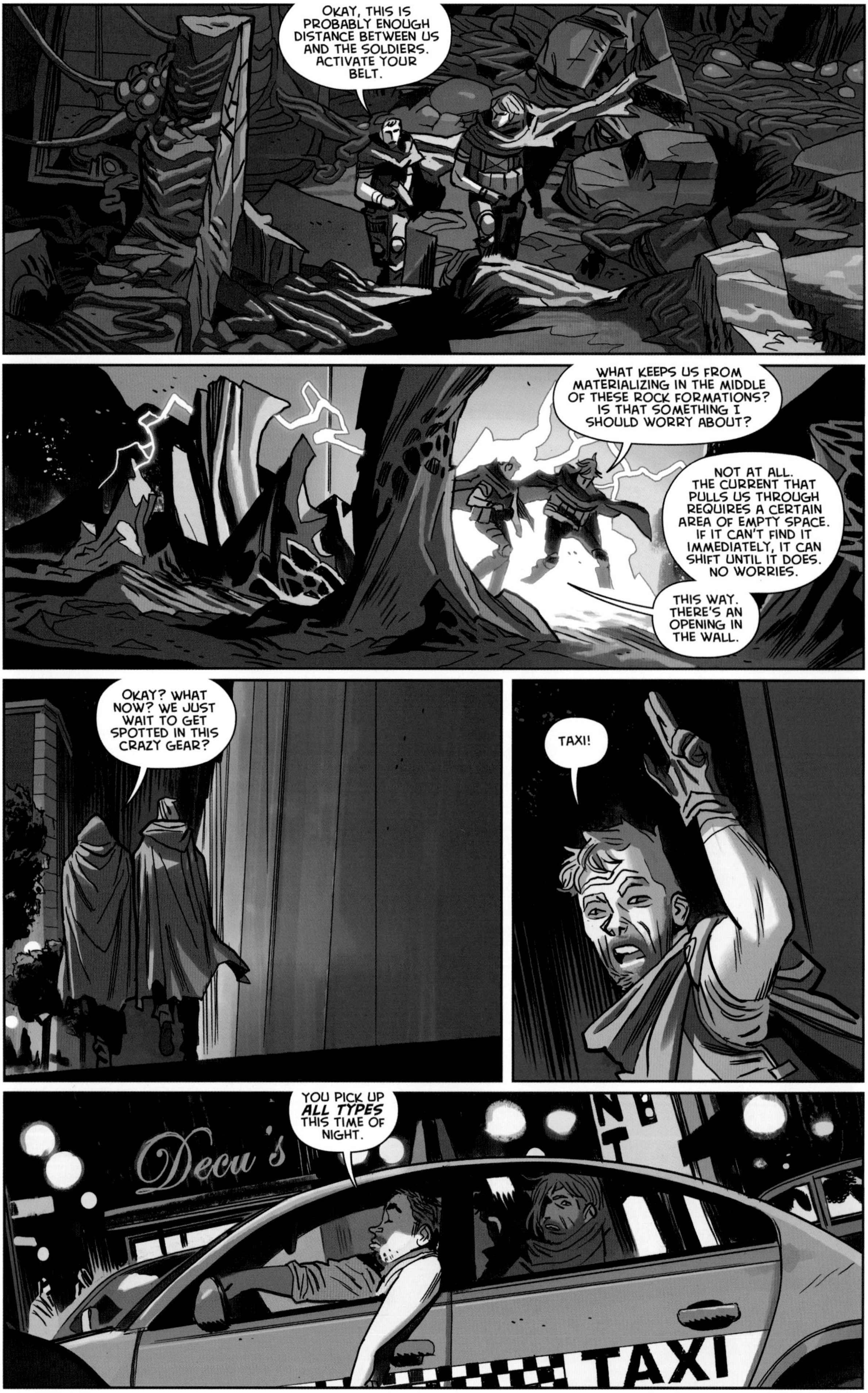
OKAY, THIS IS PROBABLY ENOUGH DISTANCE BETWEEN US AND THE SOLDIERS. ACTIVATE YOUR BELT.
WHAT KEEPS US FROM MATERIALIZING IN THE MIDDLE OF THESE ROCK FORMATIONS? IS THAT SOMETHING I SHOULD WORRY ABOUT?
NOT AT ALL. THE CURRENT THAT PULLS US THROUGH REQUIRES A CERTAIN AREA OF EMPTY SPACE. IF IT CAN'T FIND IT IMMEDIATELY, IT CAN SHIFT UNTIL IT DOES. NO WORRIES.
THIS WAY. THERE'S AN OPENING IN THE WALL.
OKAY? WHAT NOW? WE JUST WAIT TO GET SPOTTED IN THIS CRAZY GEAR?
TAXI!
YOU PICK UP ALL TYPES THIS TIME OF NIGHT.
Decu's
TAXI

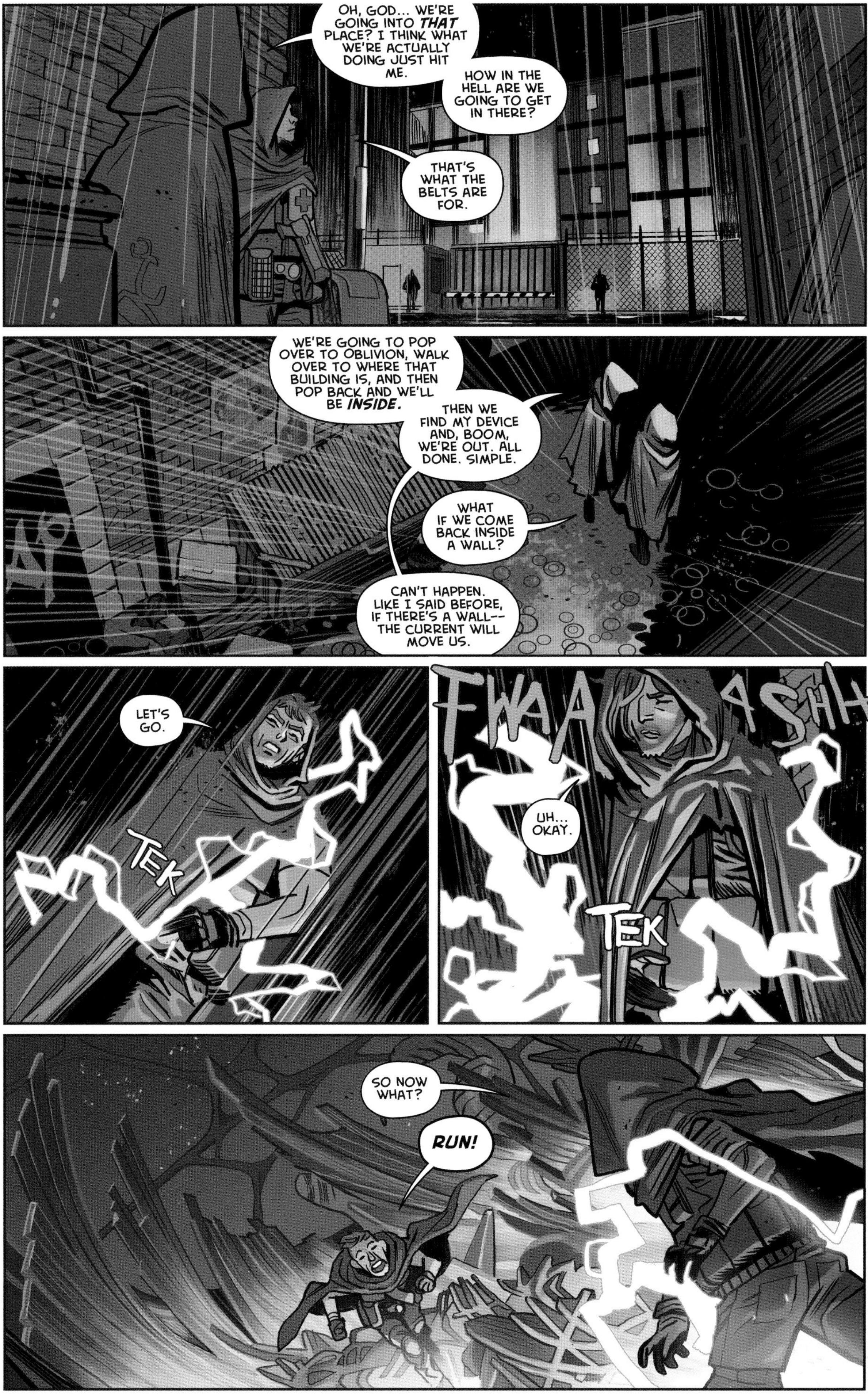
OH, GOD... WE'RE GOING INTO *THAT* PLACE? I THINK WHAT WE'RE ACTUALLY DOING JUST HIT ME.
HOW IN THE HELL ARE WE GOING TO GET IN THERE?
THAT'S WHAT THE BELTS ARE FOR.
WE'RE GOING TO POP OVER TO OBLIVION, WALK OVER TO WHERE THAT BUILDING IS, AND THEN POP BACK AND WE'LL BE *INSIDE.*
THEN WE FIND MY DEVICE AND, BOOM, WE'RE OUT. ALL DONE. SIMPLE.
WHAT IF WE COME BACK INSIDE A WALL?
CAN'T HAPPEN. LIKE I SAID BEFORE, IF THERE'S A WALL-- THE CURRENT WILL MOVE US.
LET'S GO.
TEK
FWAAASHH
UH... OKAY.
TEK
SO NOW WHAT?
RUN!

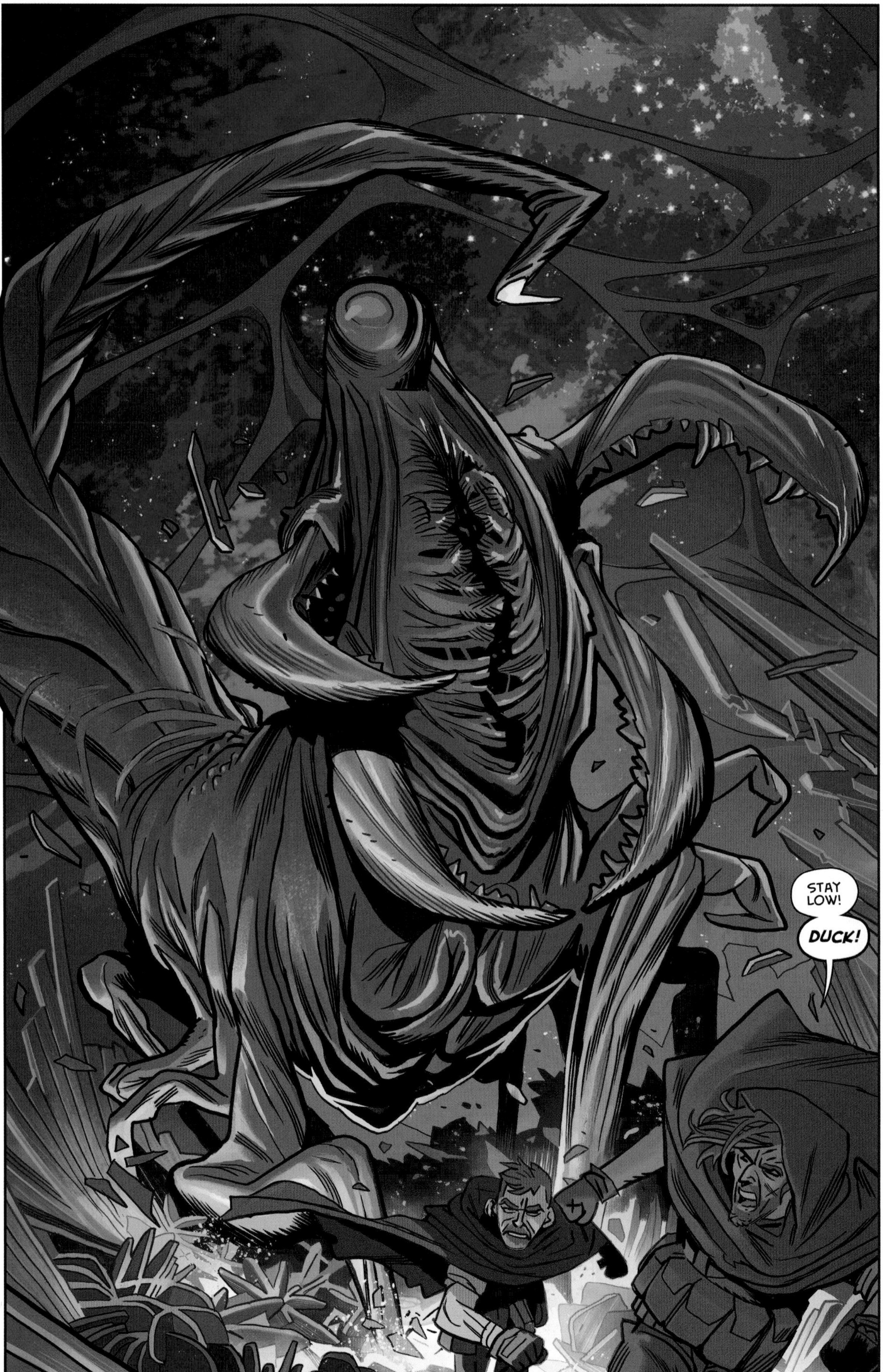
STAY LOW!
DUCK!

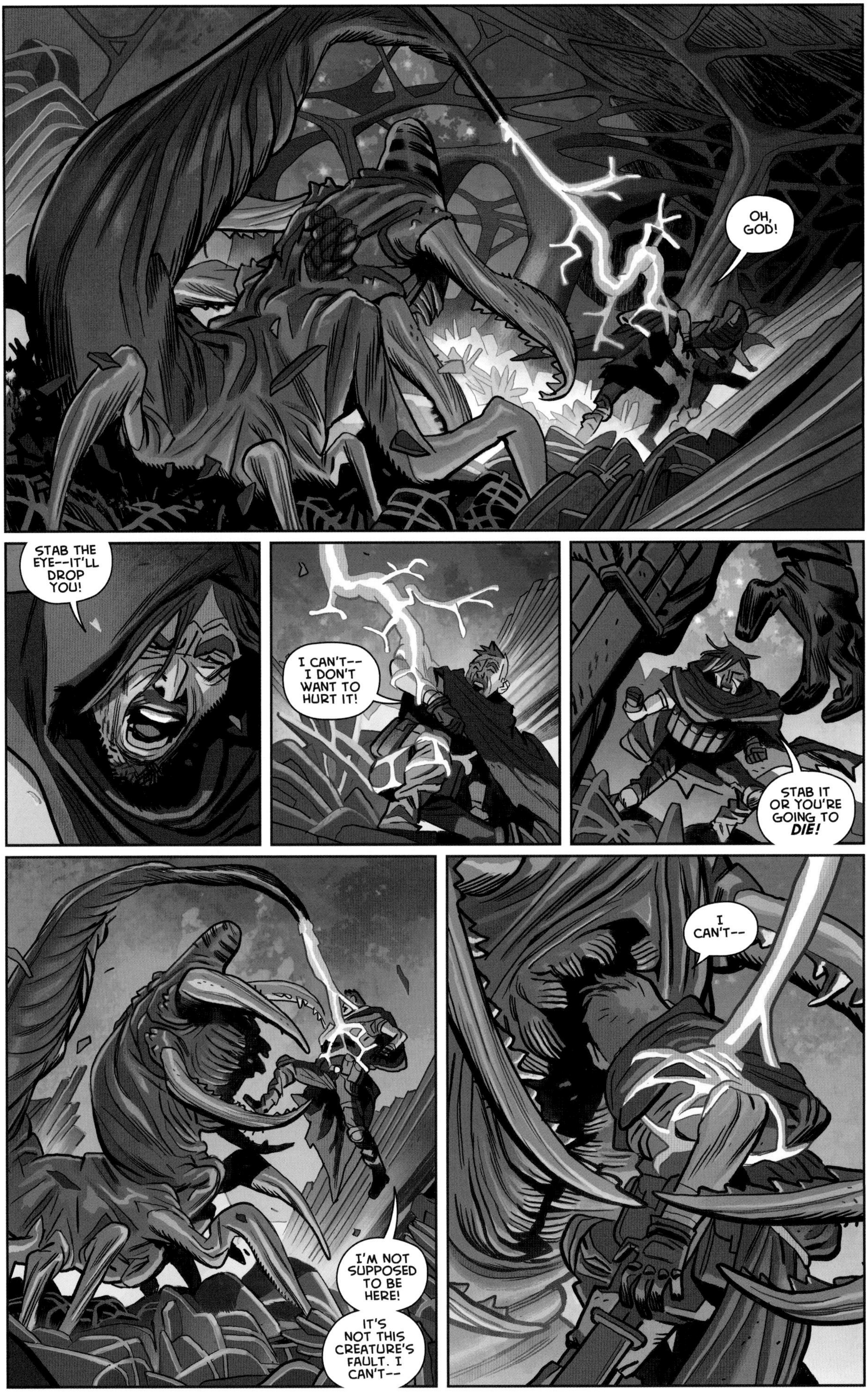
OH, GOD!
STAB THE EYE--IT'LL DROP YOU!
I CAN'T-- I DON'T WANT TO HURT IT!
STAB IT OR YOU'RE GOING TO ***DIE!***
I'M NOT SUPPOSED TO BE HERE!
IT'S NOT THIS CREATURE'S FAULT. I CAN'T--
I CAN'T--

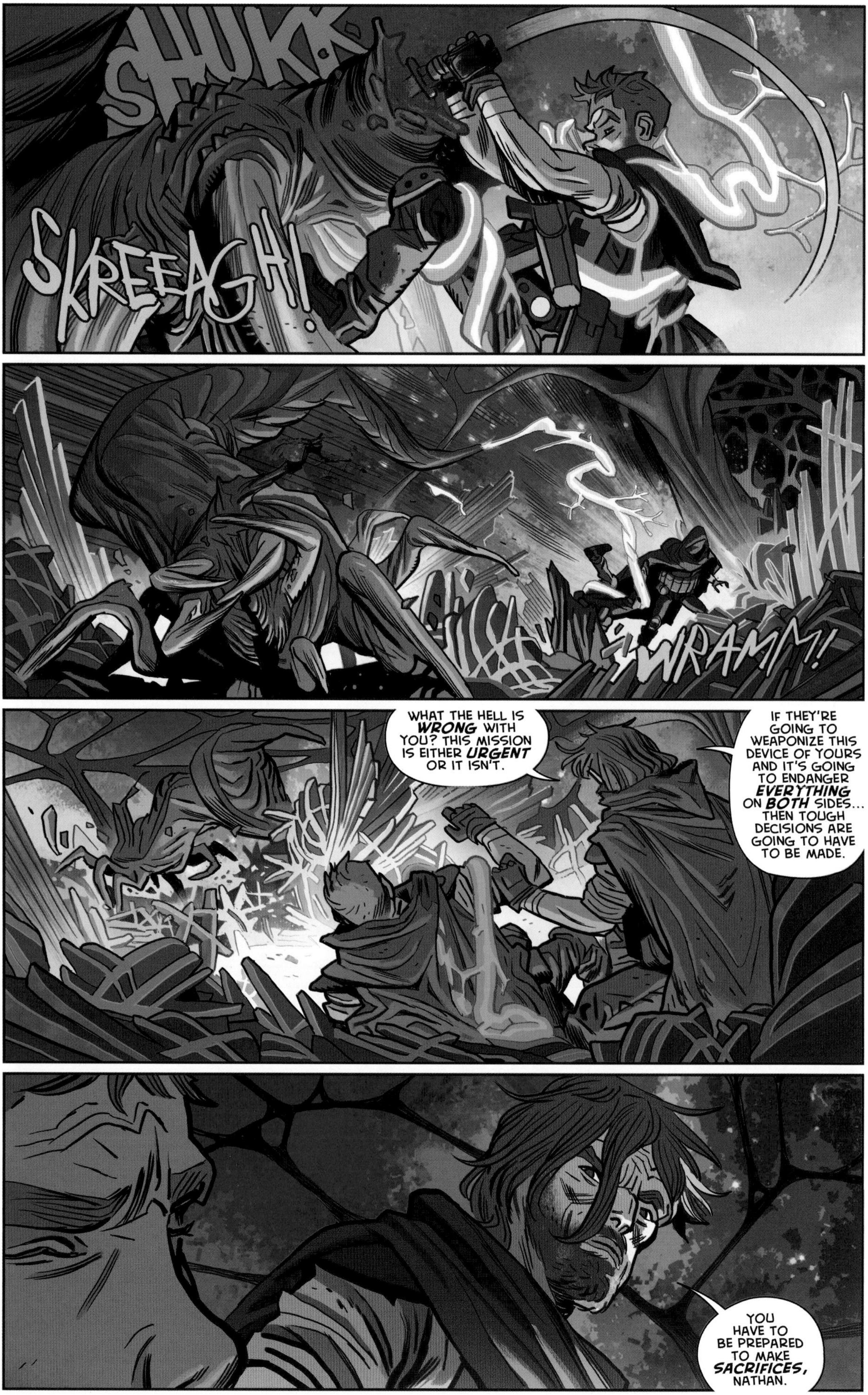
SHUKK
SKREEAGH!
WRAMM!
WHAT THE HELL IS WRONG WITH YOU? THIS MISSION IS EITHER URGENT OR IT ISN'T.
IF THEY'RE GOING TO WEAPONIZE THIS DEVICE OF YOURS AND IT'S GOING TO ENDANGER EVERYTHING ON BOTH SIDES... THEN TOUGH DECISIONS ARE GOING TO HAVE TO BE MADE.
YOU HAVE TO BE PREPARED TO MAKE SACRIFICES, NATHAN.

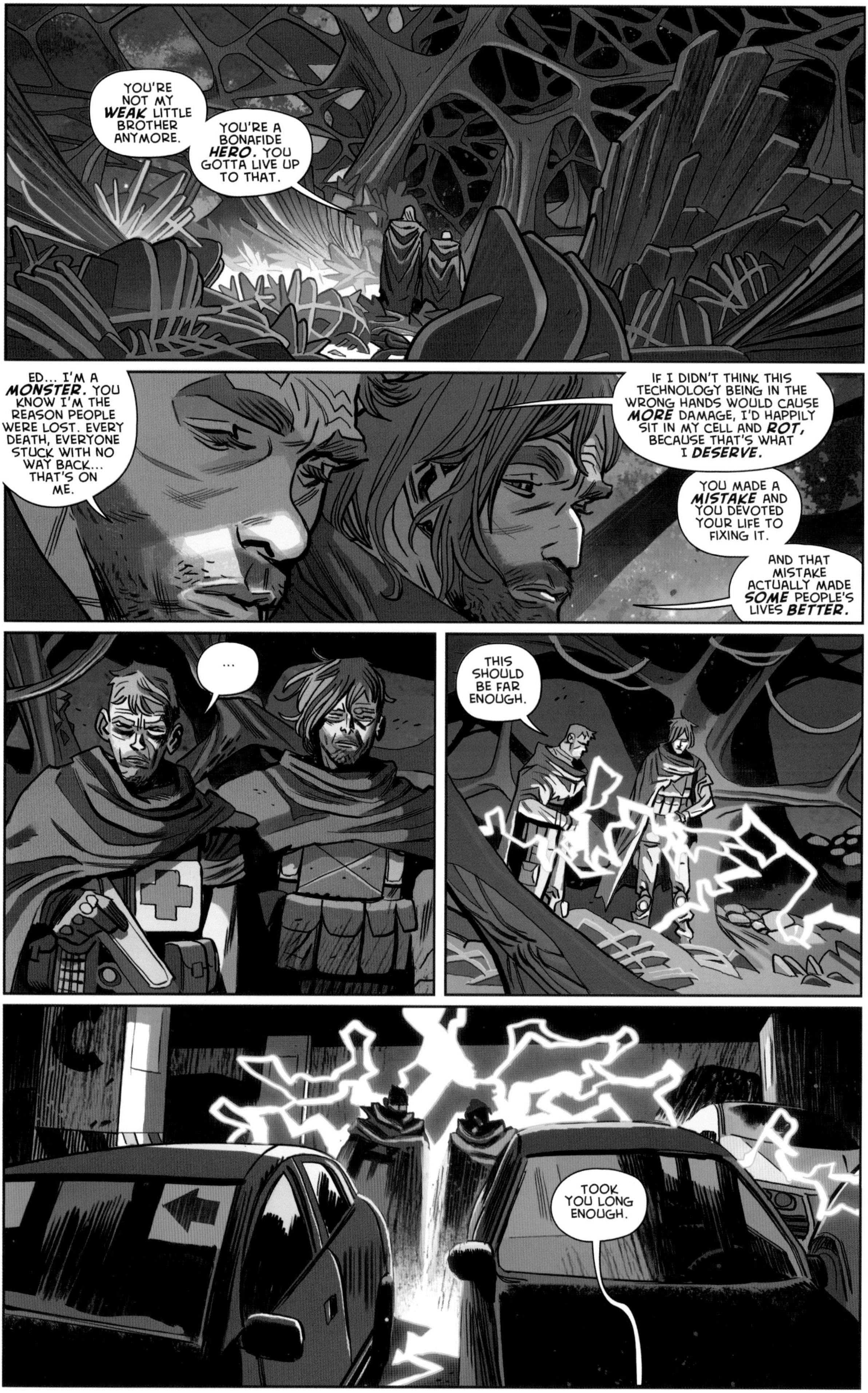

YOU'RE NOT MY WEAK LITTLE BROTHER ANYMORE.
YOU'RE A BONAFIDE HERO. YOU GOTTA LIVE UP TO THAT.
ED... I'M A MONSTER. YOU KNOW I'M THE REASON PEOPLE WERE LOST. EVERY DEATH, EVERYONE STUCK WITH NO WAY BACK... THAT'S ON ME.
IF I DIDN'T THINK THIS TECHNOLOGY BEING IN THE WRONG HANDS WOULD CAUSE MORE DAMAGE, I'D HAPPILY SIT IN MY CELL AND ROT, BECAUSE THAT'S WHAT I DESERVE.
YOU MADE A MISTAKE AND YOU DEVOTED YOUR LIFE TO FIXING IT.
AND THAT MISTAKE ACTUALLY MADE SOME PEOPLE'S LIVES BETTER.
...
THIS SHOULD BE FAR ENOUGH.
TOOK YOU LONG ENOUGH.

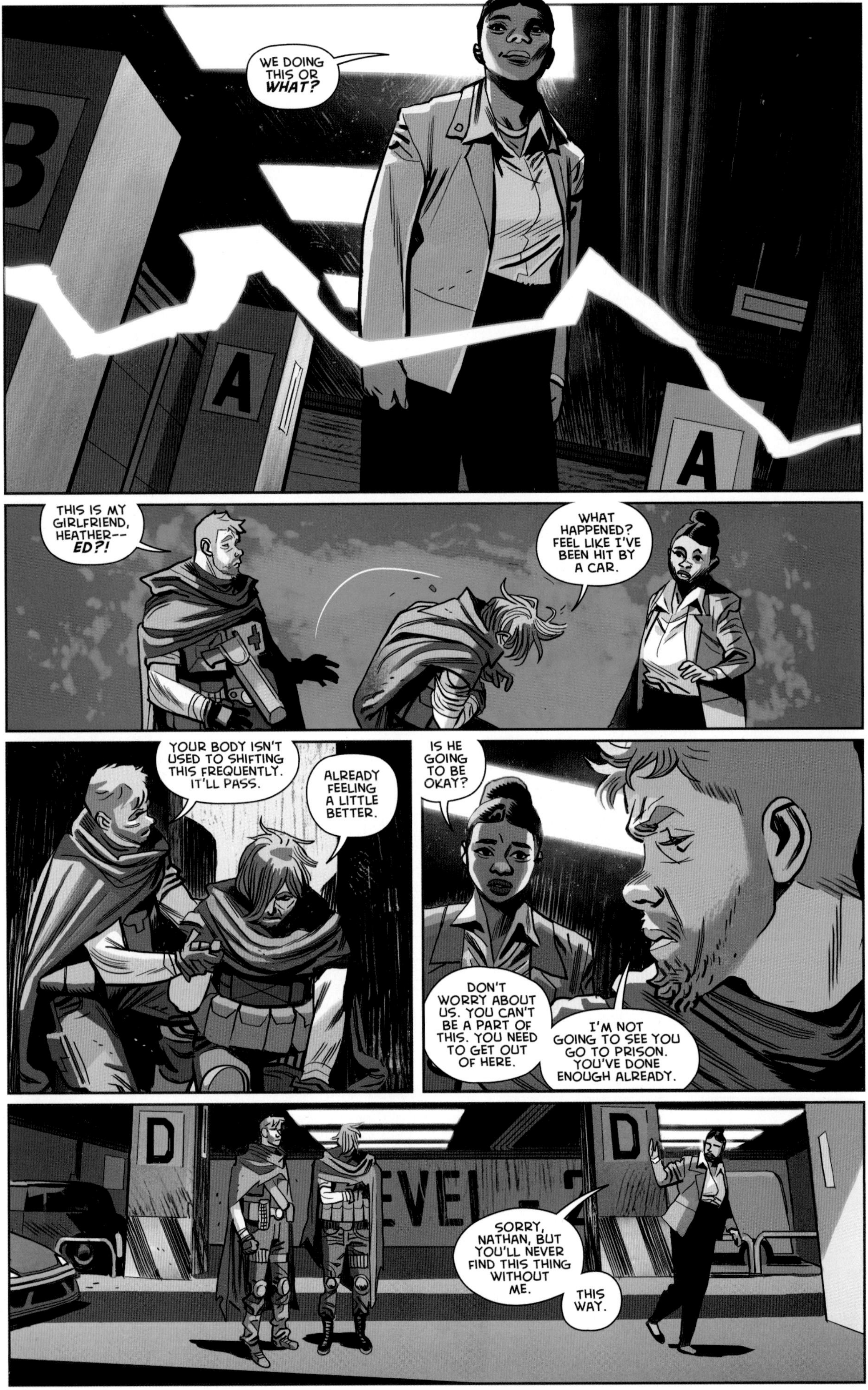
WE DOING THIS OR WHAT?
THIS IS MY GIRLFRIEND, HEATHER-- ED?!
WHAT HAPPENED? FEEL LIKE I'VE BEEN HIT BY A CAR.
YOUR BODY ISN'T USED TO SHIFTING THIS FREQUENTLY. IT'LL PASS.
ALREADY FEELING A LITTLE BETTER.
IS HE GOING TO BE OKAY?
DON'T WORRY ABOUT US. YOU CAN'T BE A PART OF THIS. YOU NEED TO GET OUT OF HERE.
I'M NOT GOING TO SEE YOU GO TO PRISON. YOU'VE DONE ENOUGH ALREADY.
SORRY, NATHAN, BUT YOU'LL NEVER FIND THIS THING WITHOUT ME.
THIS WAY.

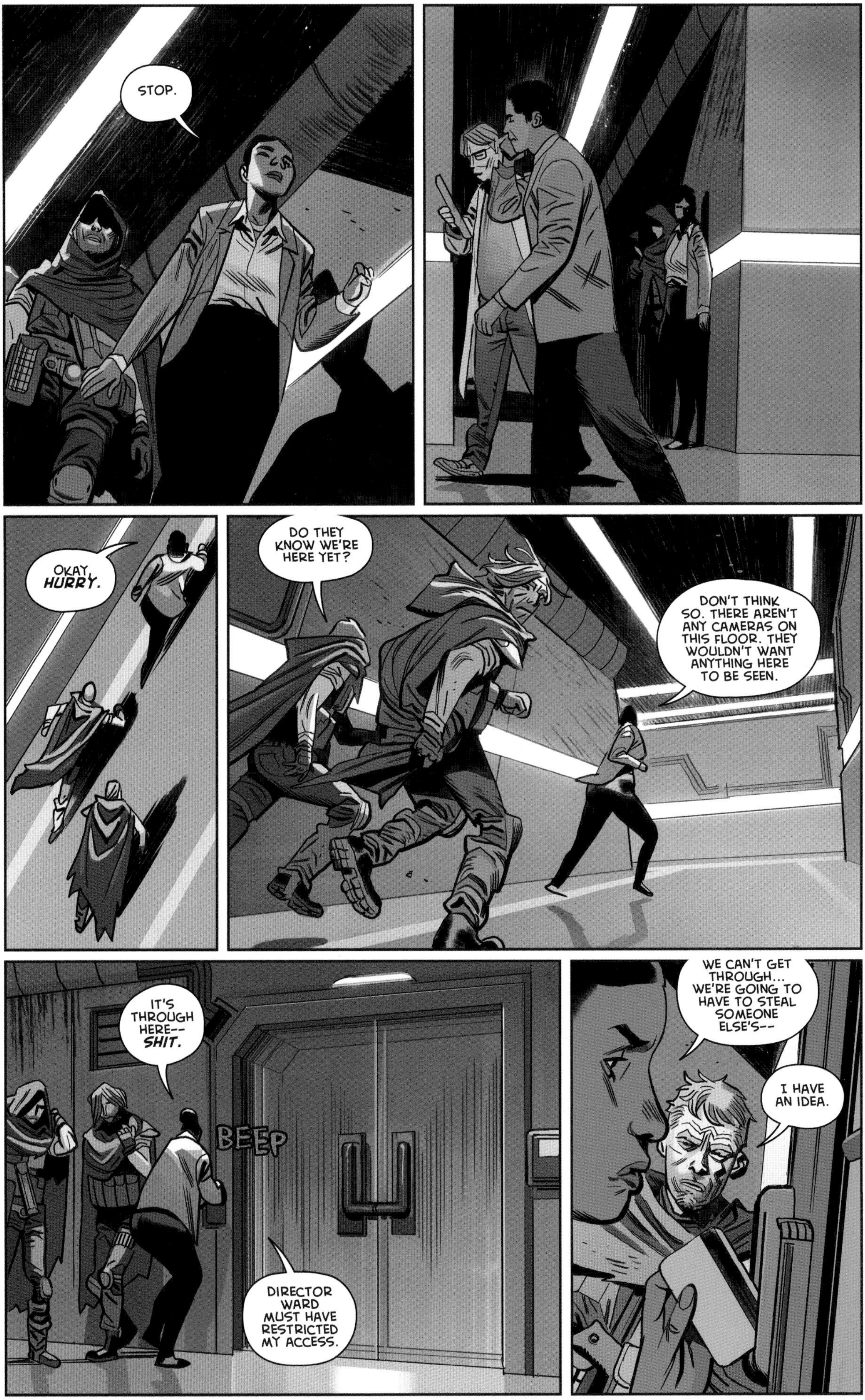
STOP.
OKAY, HURRY.
DO THEY KNOW WE'RE HERE YET?
DON'T THINK SO. THERE AREN'T ANY CAMERAS ON THIS FLOOR. THEY WOULDN'T WANT ANYTHING HERE TO BE SEEN.
IT'S THROUGH HERE-- SHIT.
BEEP
DIRECTOR WARD MUST HAVE RESTRICTED MY ACCESS.
WE CAN'T GET THROUGH... WE'RE GOING TO HAVE TO STEAL SOMEONE ELSE'S--
I HAVE AN IDEA.

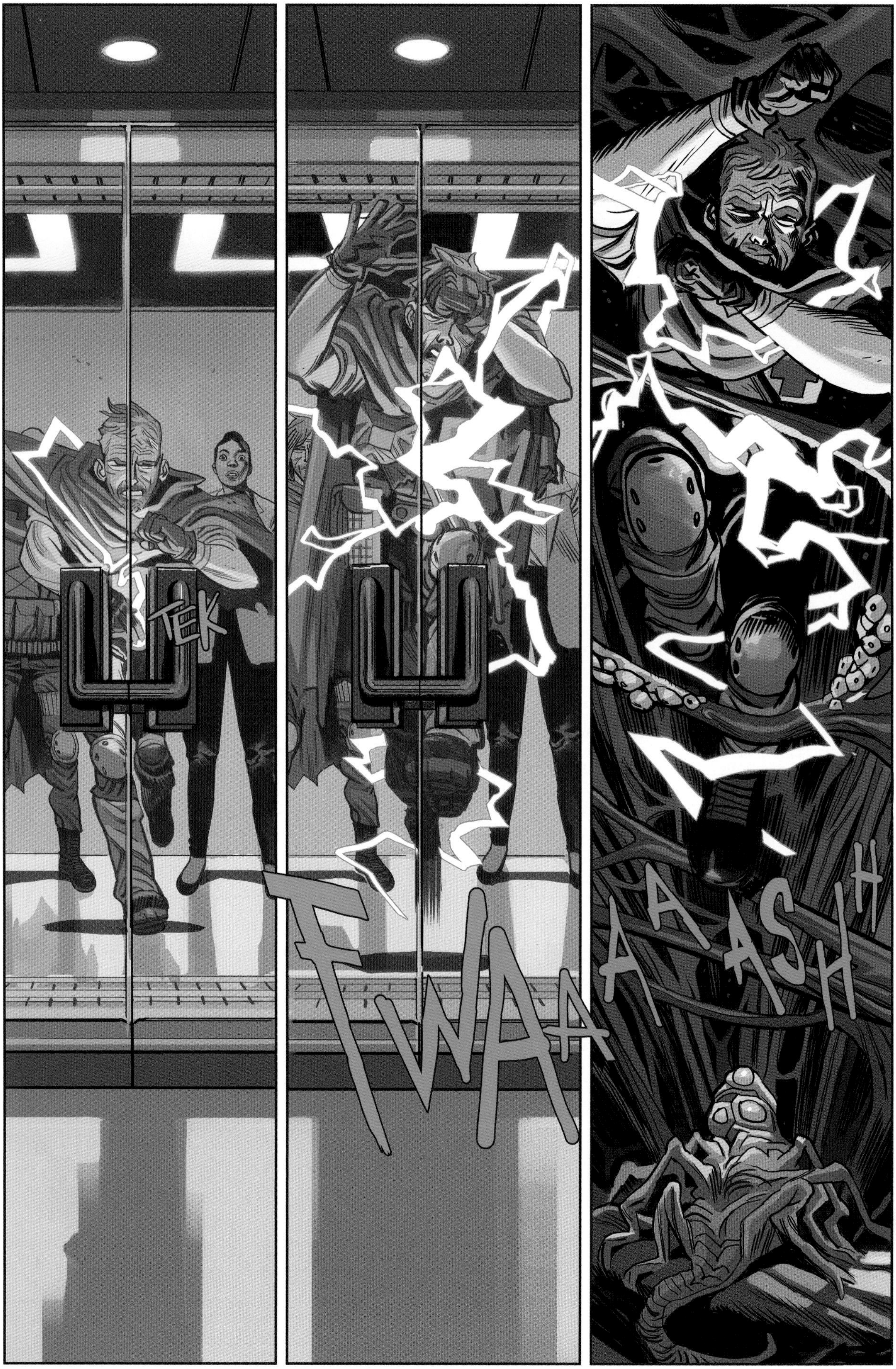

TEK
FWAAAAASH

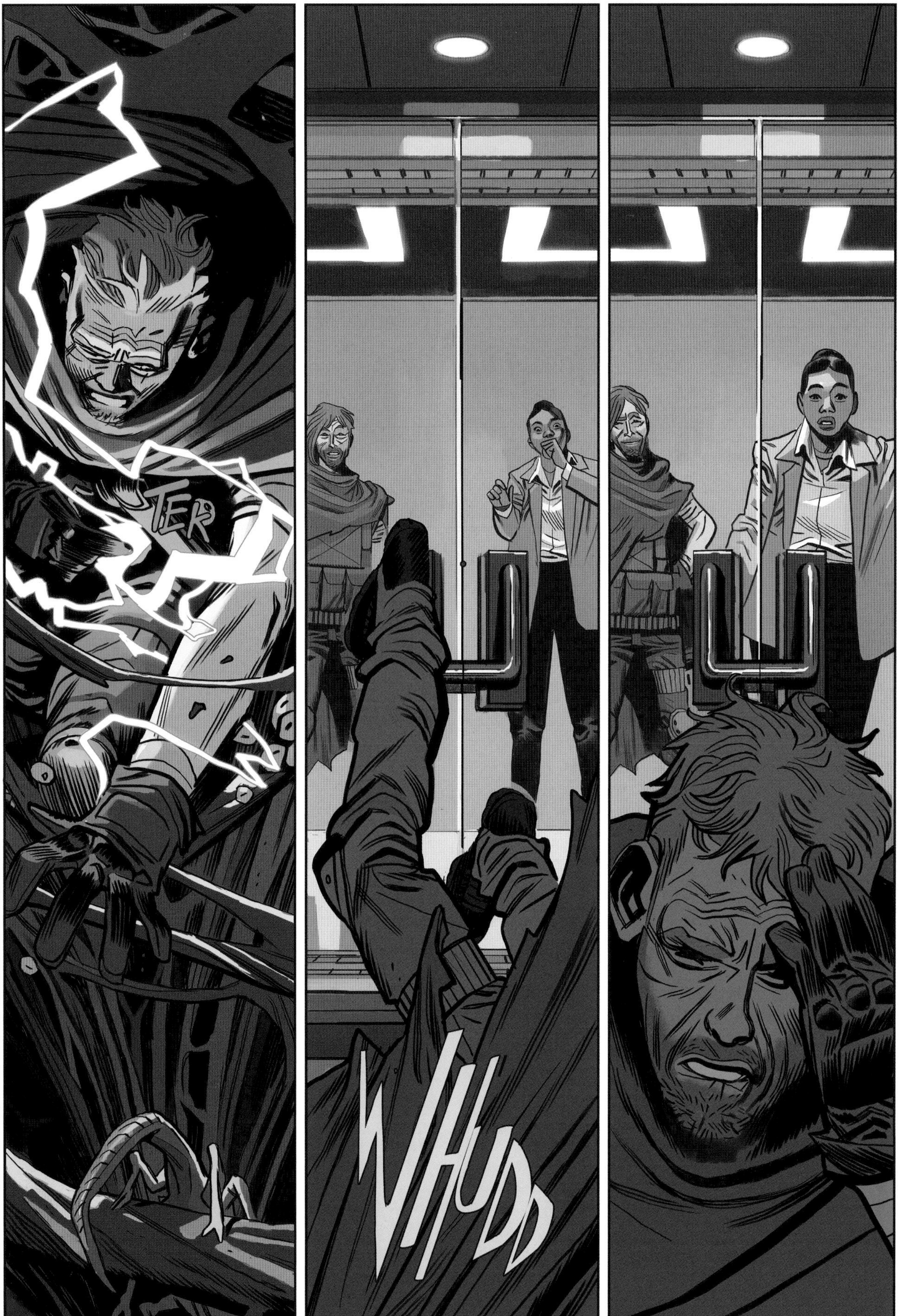
WHUDD

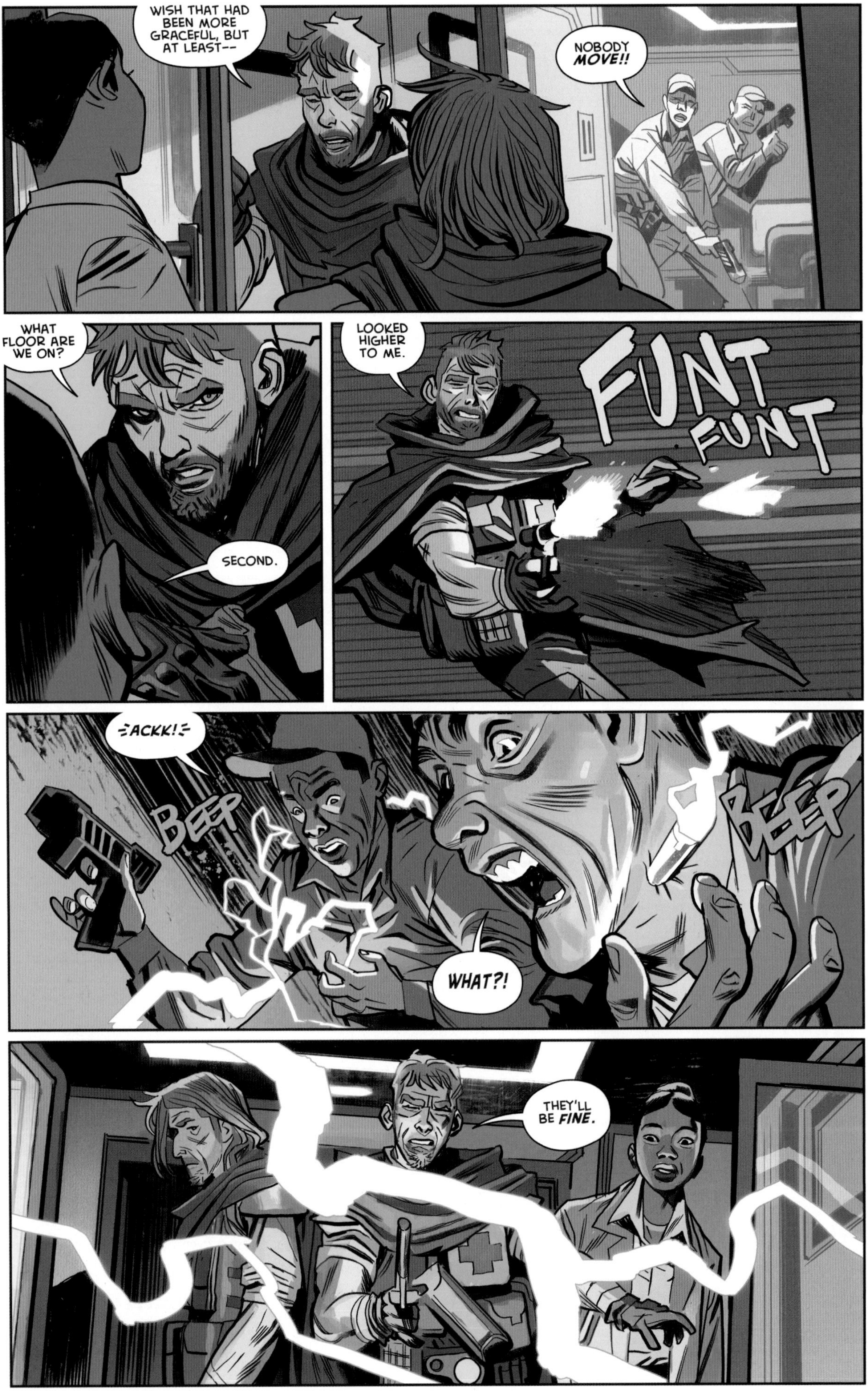
WISH THAT HAD BEEN MORE GRACEFUL, BUT AT LEAST--
NOBODY MOVE!!
WHAT FLOOR ARE WE ON?
SECOND.
LOOKED HIGHER TO ME.
FUNT
FUNT
ACKK!
BEEP
BEEP
WHAT?!
THEY'LL BE FINE.

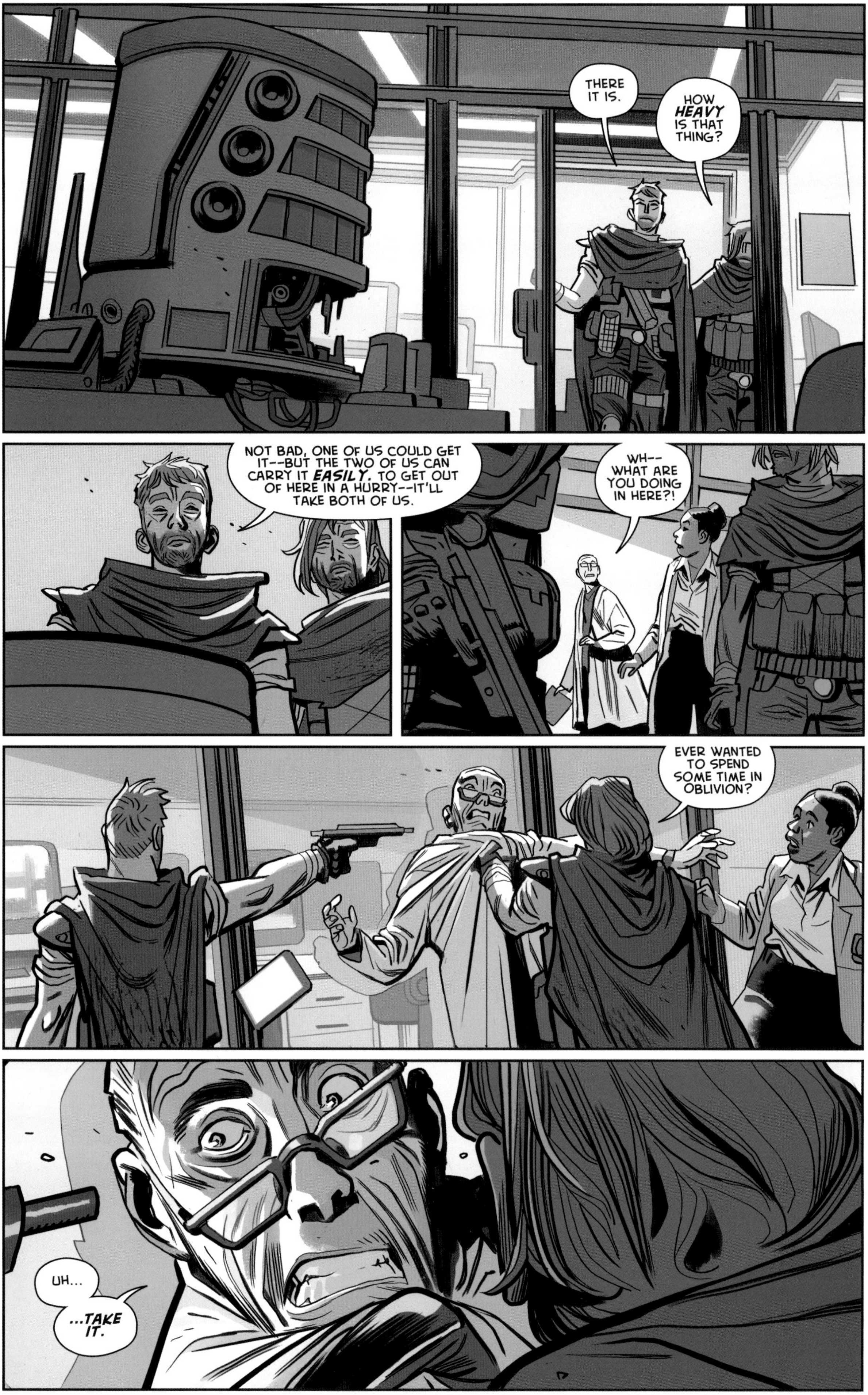
THERE IT IS.
HOW HEAVY IS THAT THING?
NOT BAD, ONE OF US COULD GET IT--BUT THE TWO OF US CAN CARRY IT EASILY. TO GET OUT OF HERE IN A HURRY--IT'LL TAKE BOTH OF US.
WH-- WHAT ARE YOU DOING IN HERE?!
EVER WANTED TO SPEND SOME TIME IN OBLIVION?
UH...
...TAKE IT.

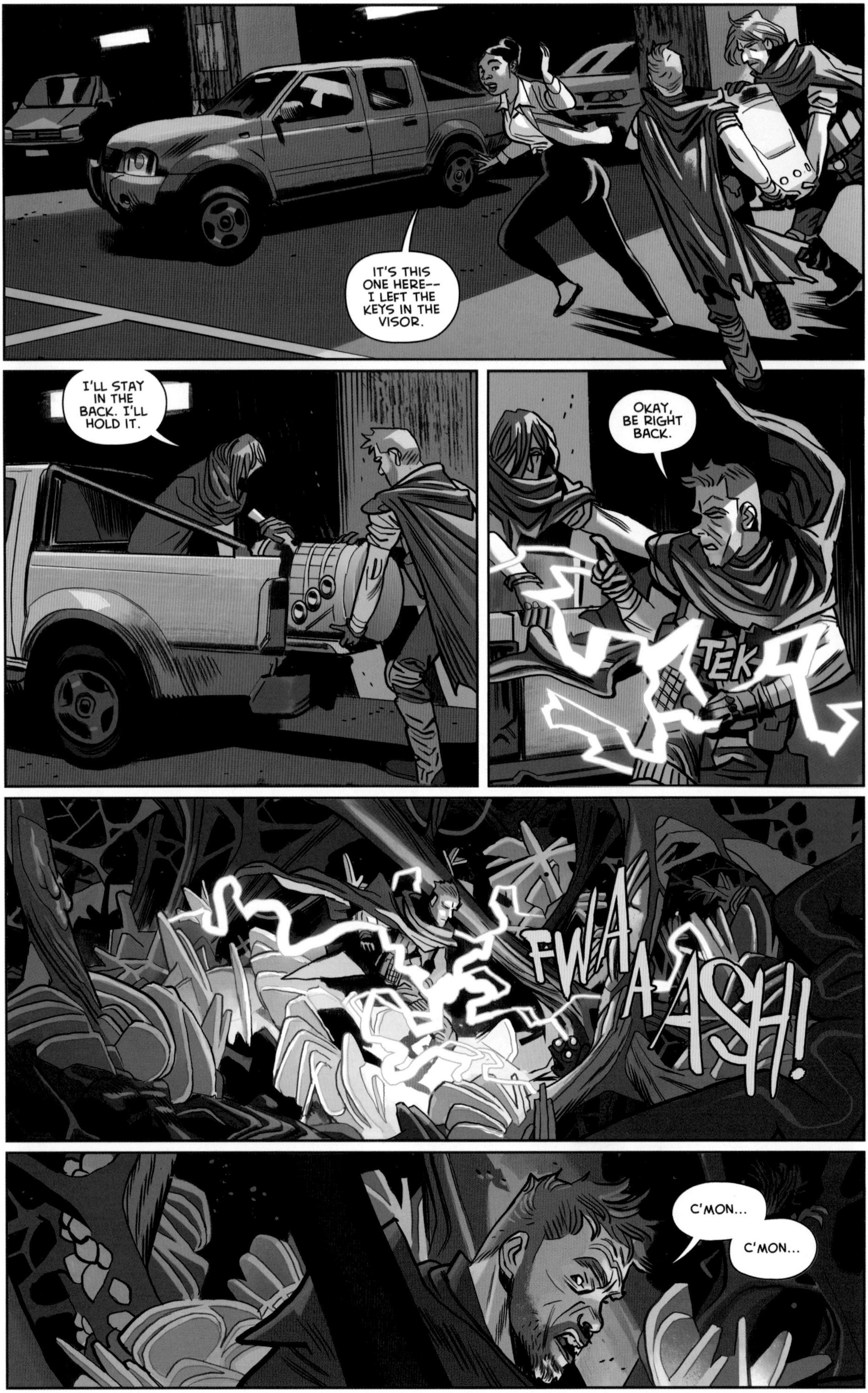
IT'S THIS ONE HERE-- I LEFT THE KEYS IN THE VISOR.
I'LL STAY IN THE BACK. I'LL HOLD IT.
OKAY, BE RIGHT BACK.
TEK
FWAAASH!
C'MON...
C'MON...

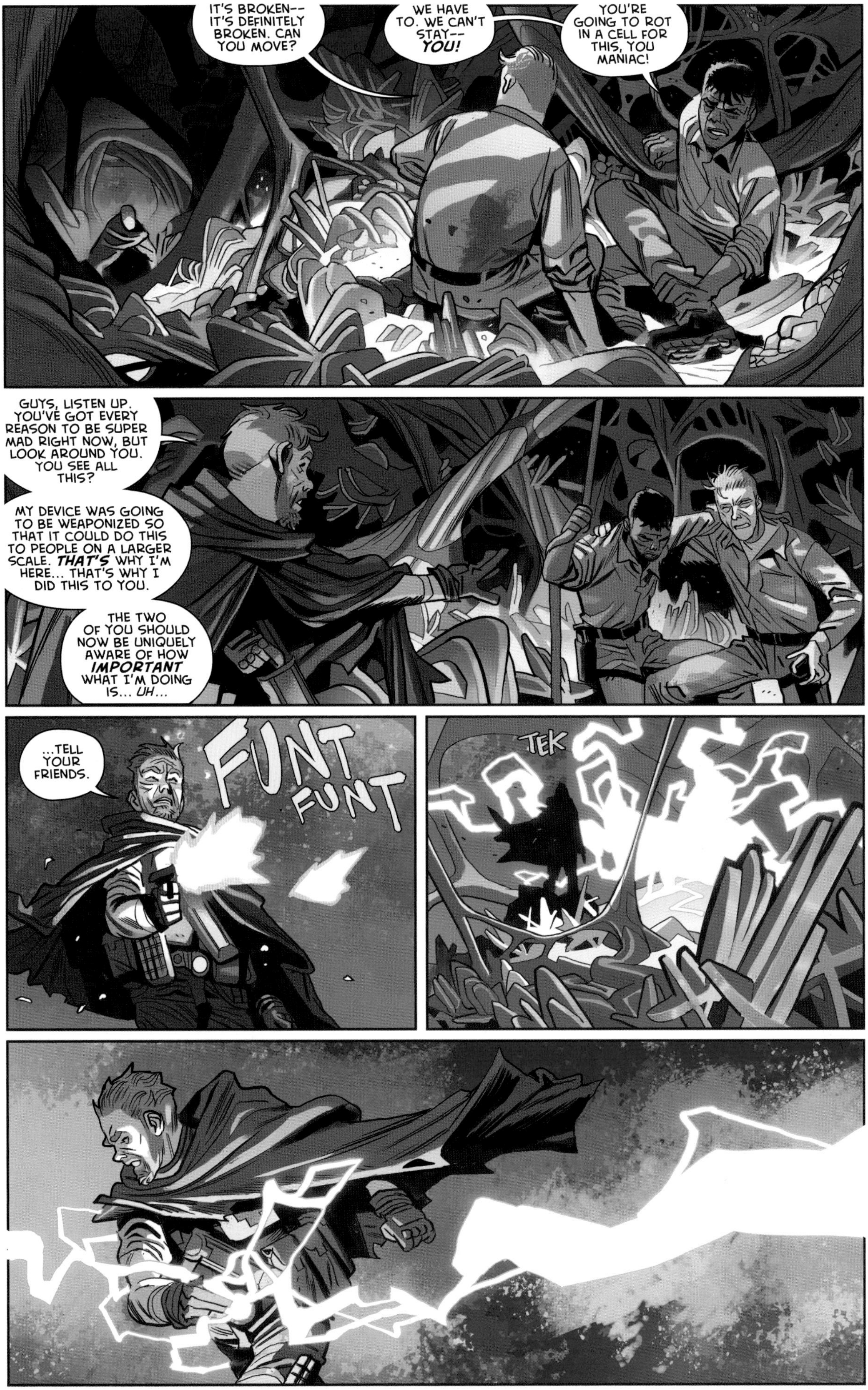
IT'S BROKEN-- IT'S DEFINITELY BROKEN. CAN YOU MOVE?
WE HAVE TO. WE CAN'T STAY-- YOU!
YOU'RE GOING TO ROT IN A CELL FOR THIS, YOU MANIAC!
GUYS, LISTEN UP. YOU'VE GOT EVERY REASON TO BE SUPER MAD RIGHT NOW, BUT LOOK AROUND YOU. YOU SEE ALL THIS?
MY DEVICE WAS GOING TO BE WEAPONIZED SO THAT IT COULD DO THIS TO PEOPLE ON A LARGER SCALE. THAT'S WHY I'M HERE... THAT'S WHY I DID THIS TO YOU.
THE TWO OF YOU SHOULD NOW BE UNIQUELY AWARE OF HOW IMPORTANT WHAT I'M DOING IS... UH...
...TELL YOUR FRIENDS.
FUNT
FUNT
TEK

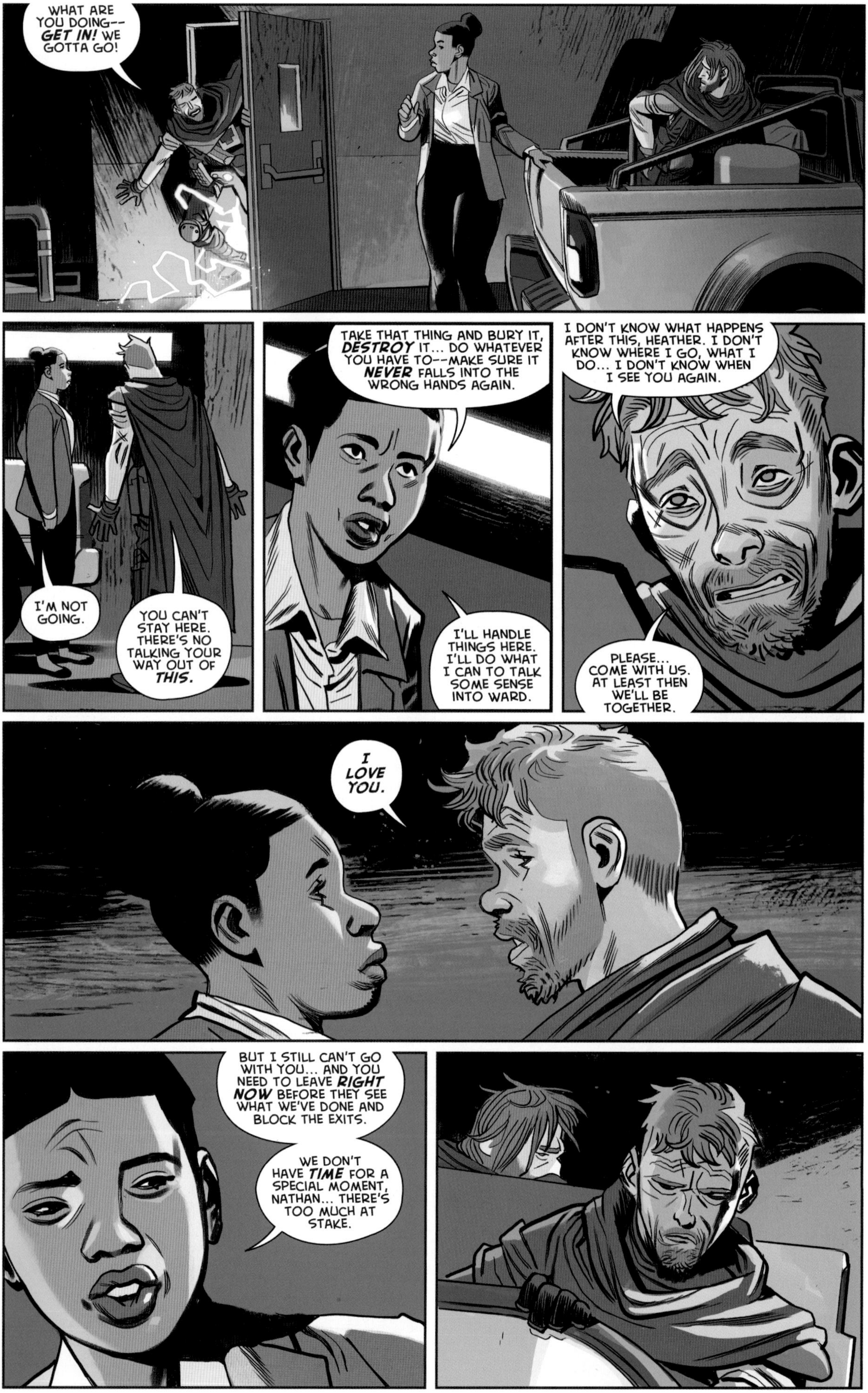
WHAT ARE YOU DOING-- GET IN! WE GOTTA GO!
I'M NOT GOING.
YOU CAN'T STAY HERE. THERE'S NO TALKING YOUR WAY OUT OF THIS.
TAKE THAT THING AND BURY IT, DESTROY IT... DO WHATEVER YOU HAVE TO--MAKE SURE IT NEVER FALLS INTO THE WRONG HANDS AGAIN.
I'LL HANDLE THINGS HERE. I'LL DO WHAT I CAN TO TALK SOME SENSE INTO WARD.
I DON'T KNOW WHAT HAPPENS AFTER THIS, HEATHER. I DON'T KNOW WHERE I GO, WHAT I DO... I DON'T KNOW WHEN I SEE YOU AGAIN.
PLEASE... COME WITH US. AT LEAST THEN WE'LL BE TOGETHER.
I LOVE YOU.
BUT I STILL CAN'T GO WITH YOU... AND YOU NEED TO LEAVE RIGHT NOW BEFORE THEY SEE WHAT WE'VE DONE AND BLOCK THE EXITS.
WE DON'T HAVE TIME FOR A SPECIAL MOMENT, NATHAN... THERE'S TOO MUCH AT STAKE.

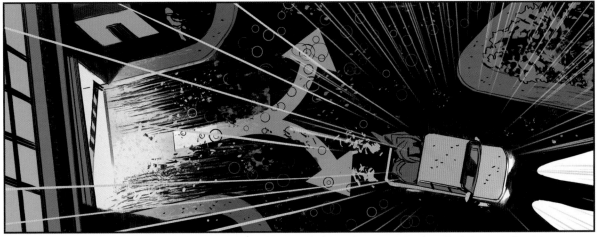

THAT PART WAS EASIER THAN I THOUGHT IT WOULD BE.

THEY WERE FOCUSED ON KEEPING US OUT, NOT IN. LET ME KNOW IF YOU SEE ANYONE FOLLOWING.

HOW DANGEROUS IS THIS THING? DID YOU COMPLETE IT? DOES IT WORK RIGHT NOW?

I REPAIRED AND REBUILT IT. I WAS GOING TO REVERSE THE TRANSFERENCE--BUT AS TIME WENT ON, I REALIZED THAT WOULD PROBABLY JUST MAKE THINGS *WORSE*.

BUT YEAH, IT SHOULD WORK. I EVEN ADDED BATTERIES TO IT SO IT COULD WORK WITHOUT BEING CONNECTED TO A DEDICATED POWER SOURCE.

THAT'S WHY WE HAD TO GET IT BACK-- AT ANY POINT THAT THING COULD BE ACTIVATED AND SEND ANOTHER CHUNK OF THE CITY INTO OBLIVION.

AFTER WE GET IT OUT OF THE CITY, I'LL FIGURE OUT WHAT WE'RE GOING TO DO WITH IT.

LOOK AT ALL THESE PEOPLE... STUCK IN THESE LIVES, UNABLE TO SEE THIS *PRISON* AROUND THEM.

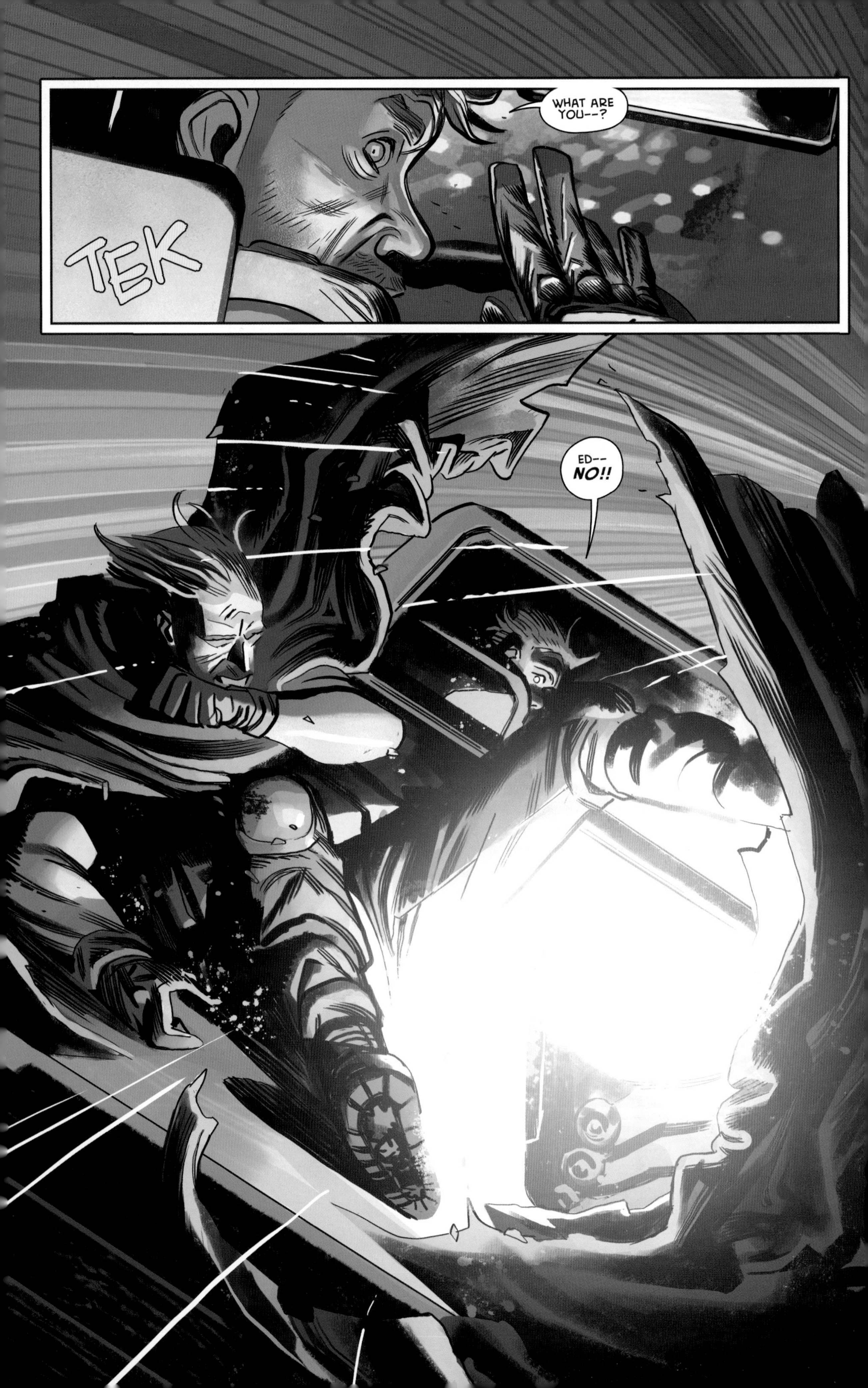
WHAT ARE YOU--?
TEK
ED-- NO!!

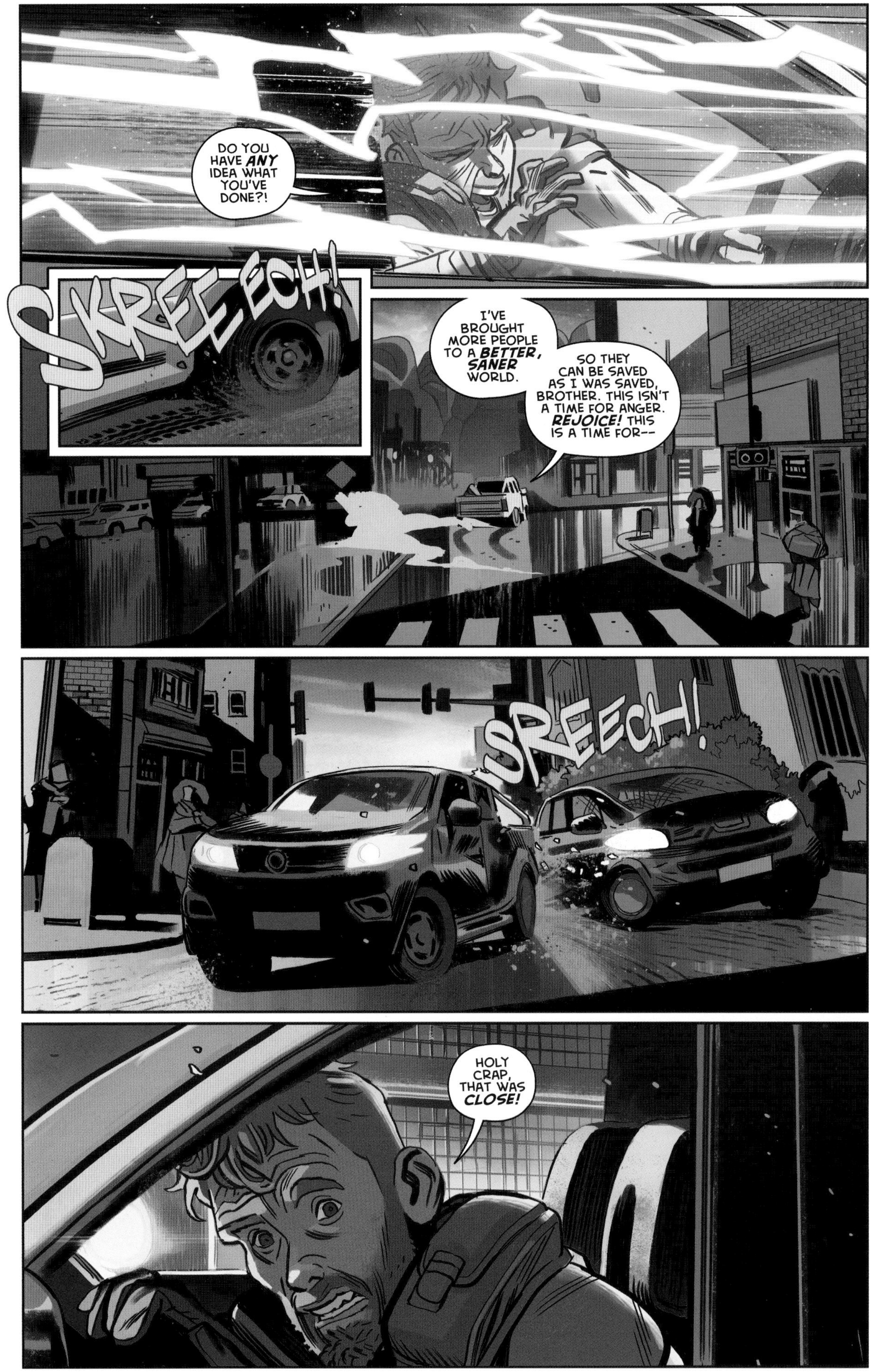
DO YOU HAVE ANY IDEA WHAT YOU'VE DONE?!
SKREEECH!
I'VE BROUGHT MORE PEOPLE TO A BETTER, SANER WORLD.
SO THEY CAN BE SAVED AS I WAS SAVED, BROTHER. THIS ISN'T A TIME FOR ANGER. REJOICE! THIS IS A TIME FOR--
SREECH!
HOLY CRAP, THAT WAS CLOSE!

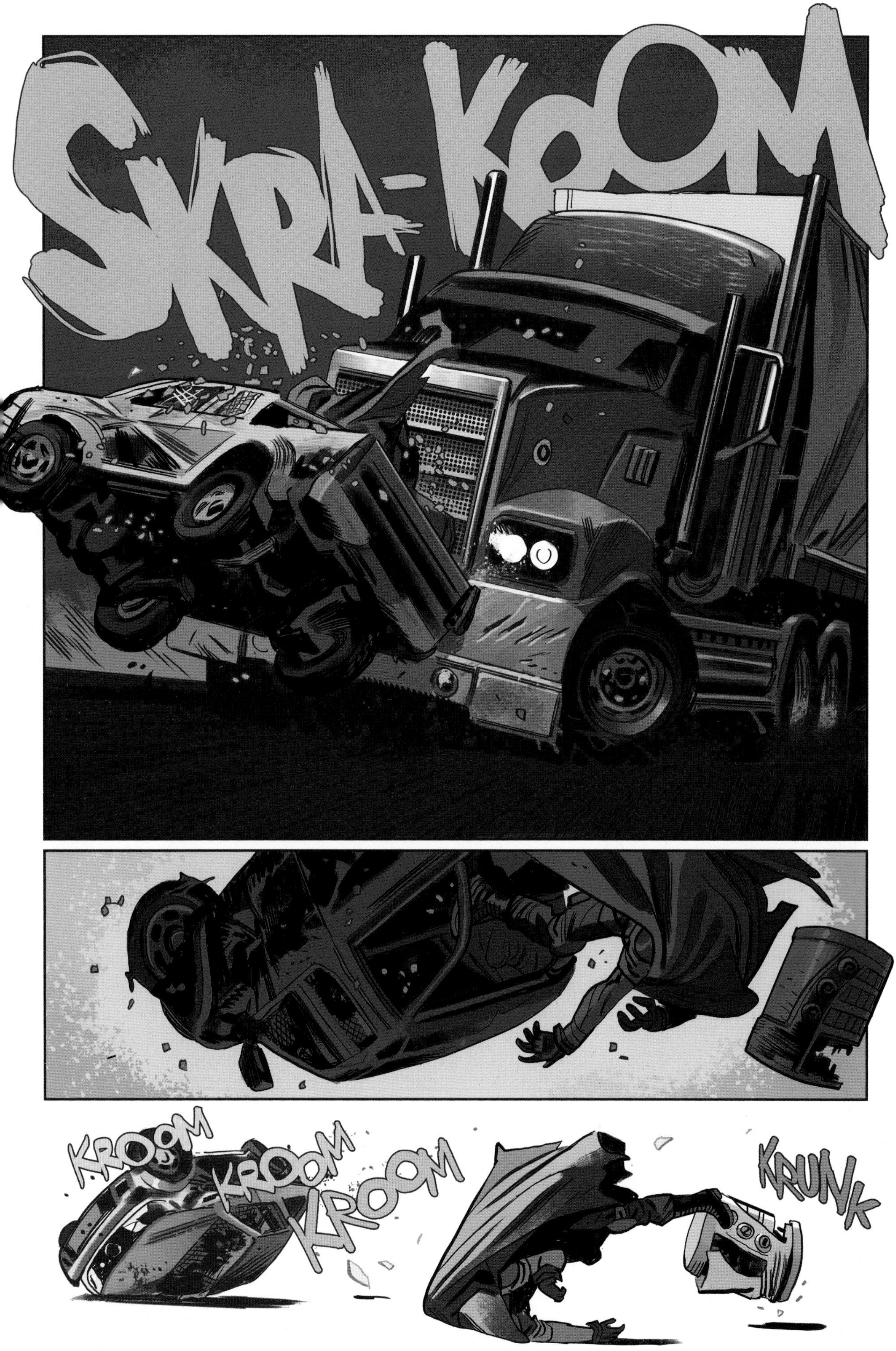
SKRA-KOOM
KROOM
KROOM
KROOM
KRUNK

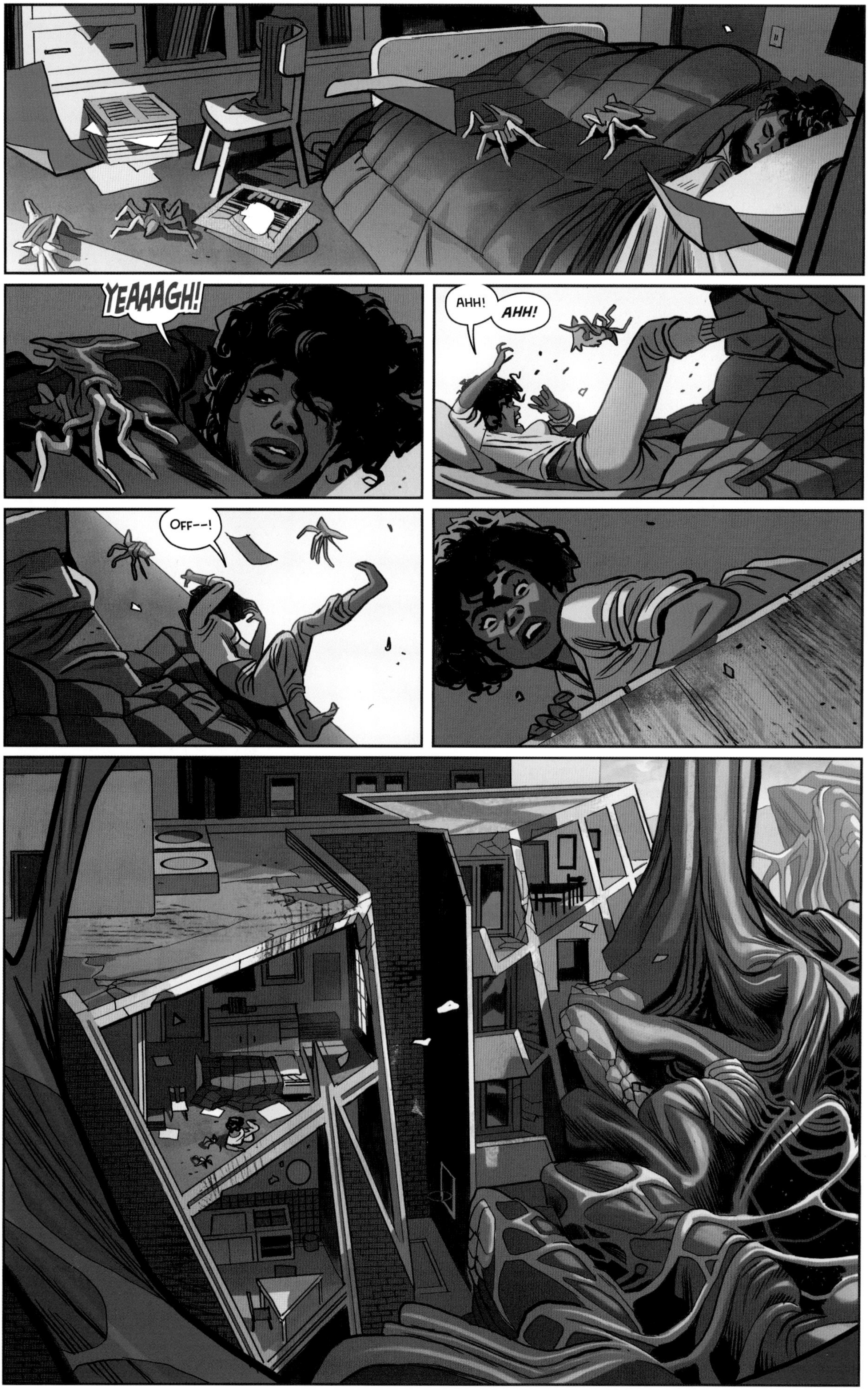
YEAAAGH!
AHH!
AHH!
OFF--!

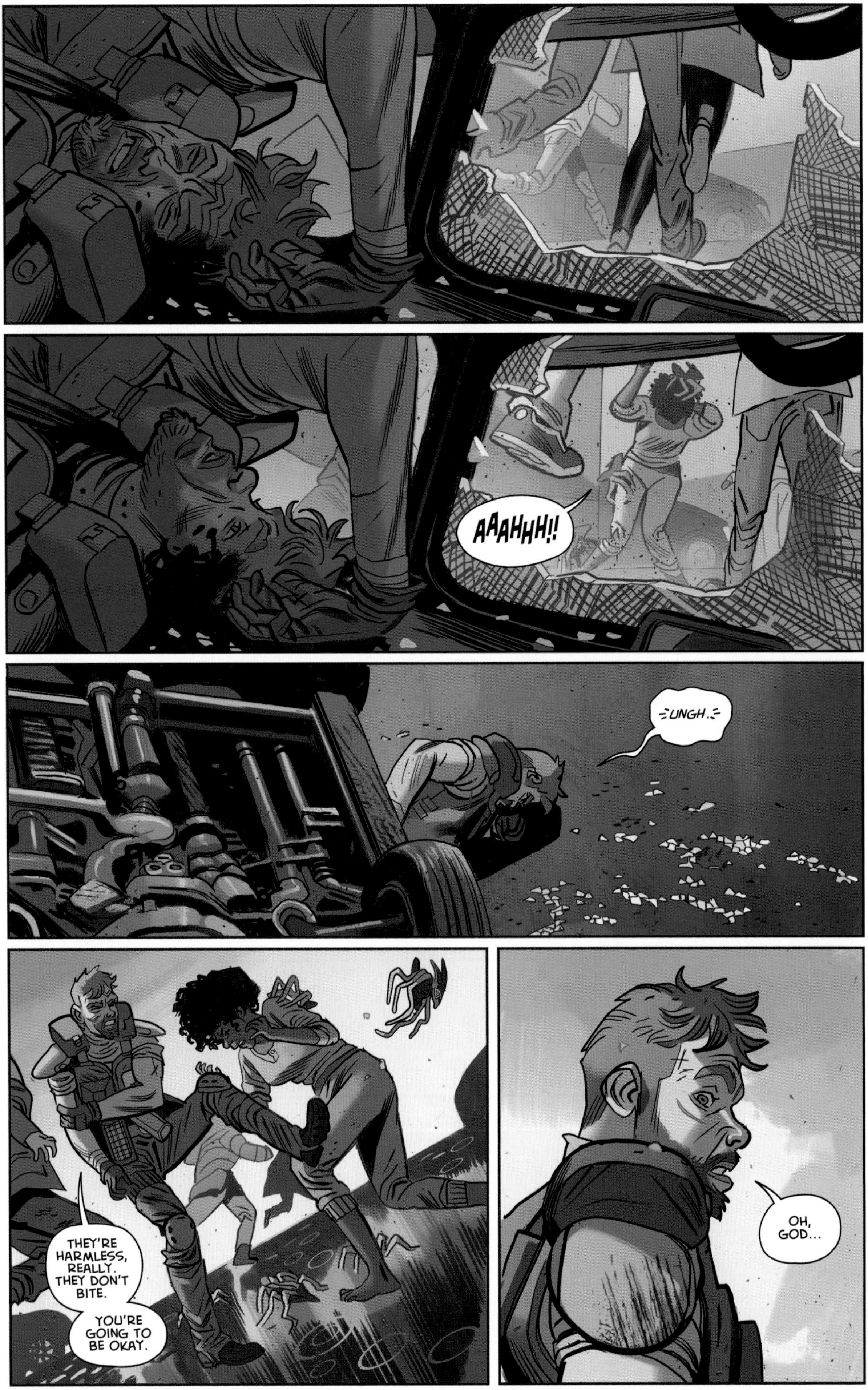
AAAHHH!!
UNGH..
THEY'RE HARMLESS, REALLY. THEY DON'T BITE.
YOU'RE GOING TO BE OKAY.
OH, GOD...

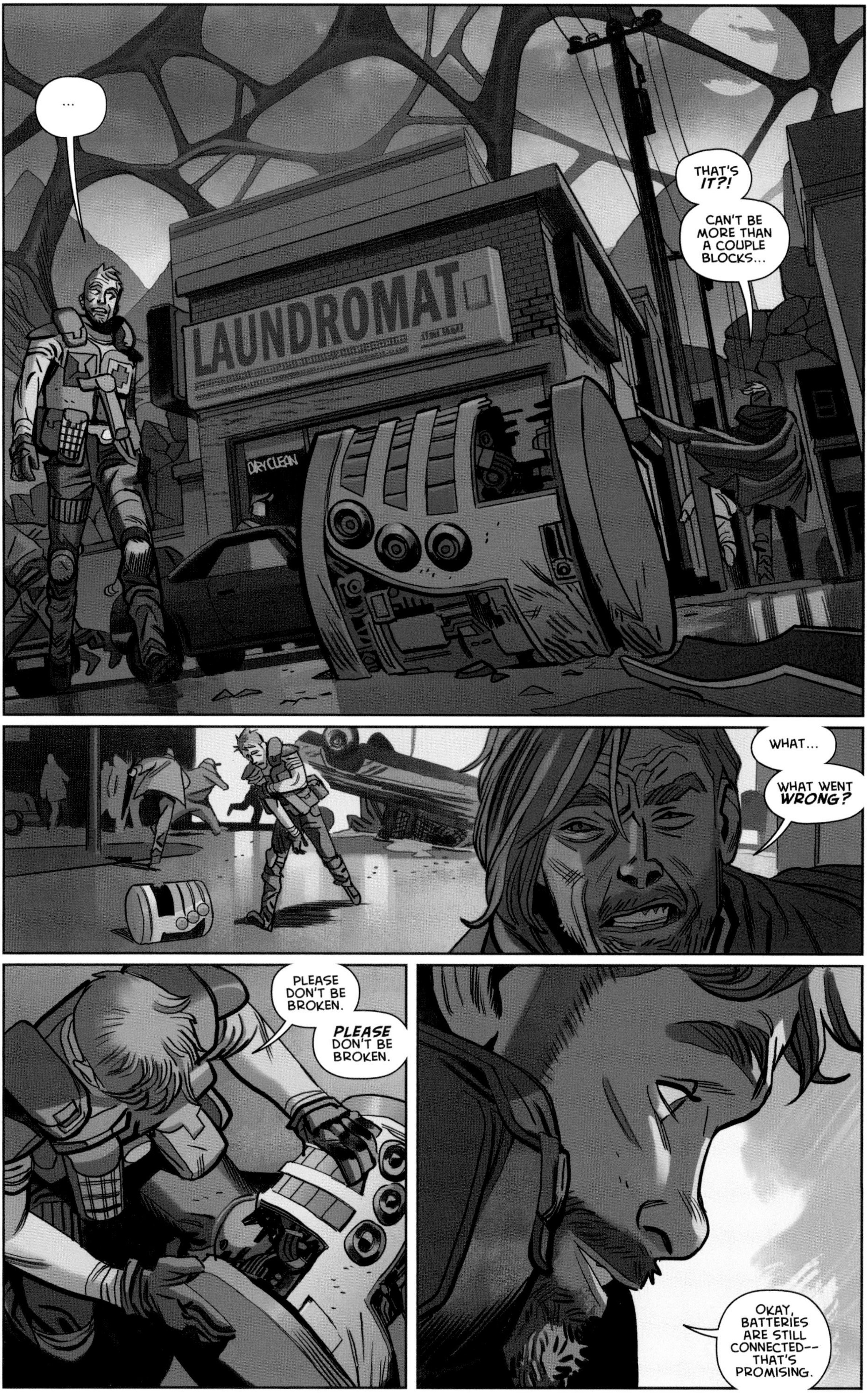
...
THAT'S *IT?!*
CAN'T BE MORE THAN A COUPLE BLOCKS...
LAUNDROMAT
DRY CLEAN
WHAT...
WHAT WENT ***WRONG?***
PLEASE DON'T BE BROKEN.
PLEASE DON'T BE BROKEN.
OKAY, BATTERIES ARE STILL CONNECTED--THAT'S PROMISING.

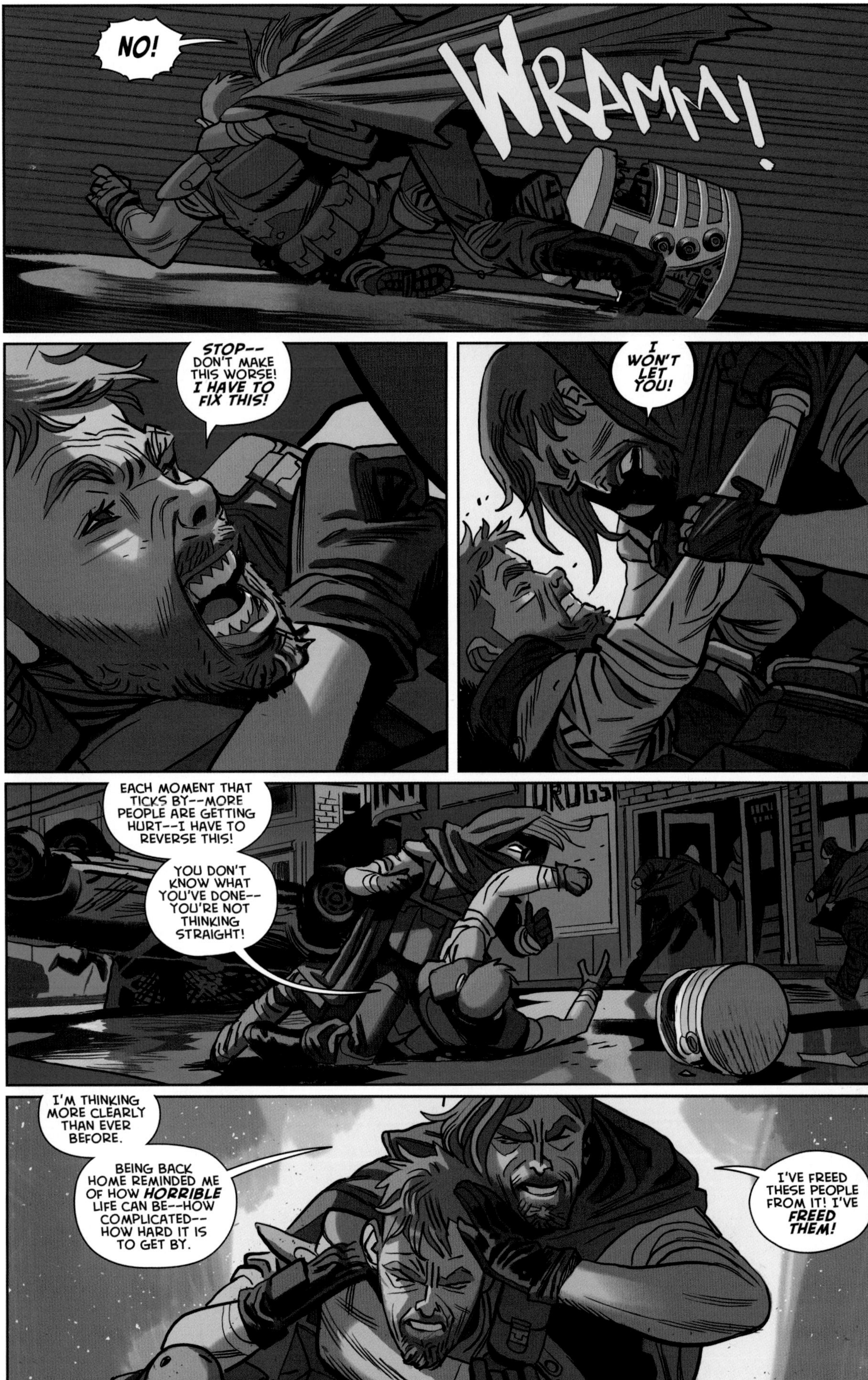
NO!
WRAMM!
STOP-- DON'T MAKE THIS WORSE! I HAVE TO FIX THIS!
I WON'T LET YOU!
EACH MOMENT THAT TICKS BY--MORE PEOPLE ARE GETTING HURT--I HAVE TO REVERSE THIS!
YOU DON'T KNOW WHAT YOU'VE DONE-- YOU'RE NOT THINKING STRAIGHT!
I'M THINKING MORE CLEARLY THAN EVER BEFORE.
BEING BACK HOME REMINDED ME OF HOW HORRIBLE LIFE CAN BE--HOW COMPLICATED-- HOW HARD IT IS TO GET BY.
I'VE FREED THESE PEOPLE FROM IT! I'VE FREED THEM!

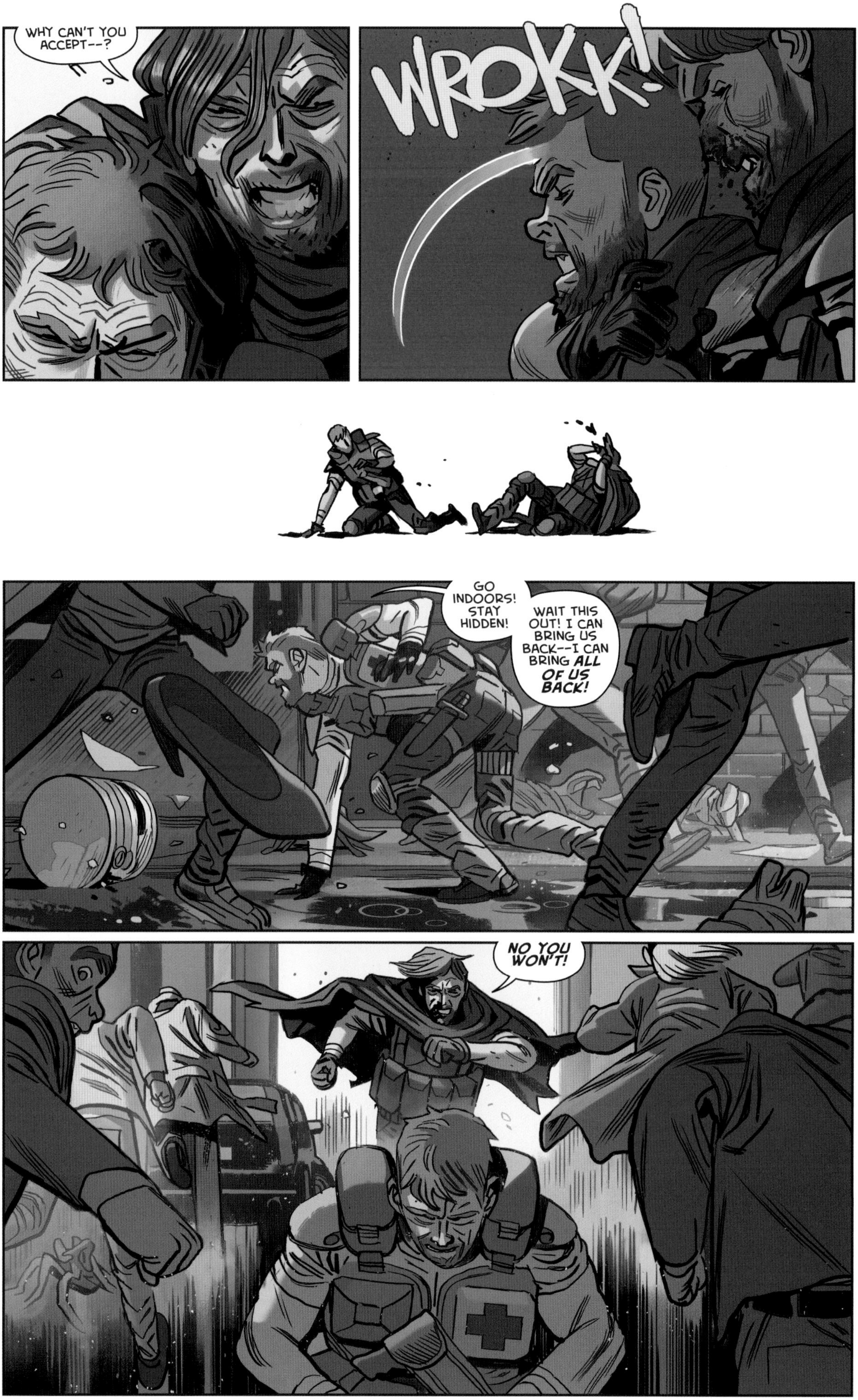
WHY CAN'T YOU ACCEPT--?
WROKK!
GO INDOORS! STAY HIDDEN!
WAIT THIS OUT! I CAN BRING US BACK--I CAN BRING ALL OF US BACK!
NO YOU WON'T!

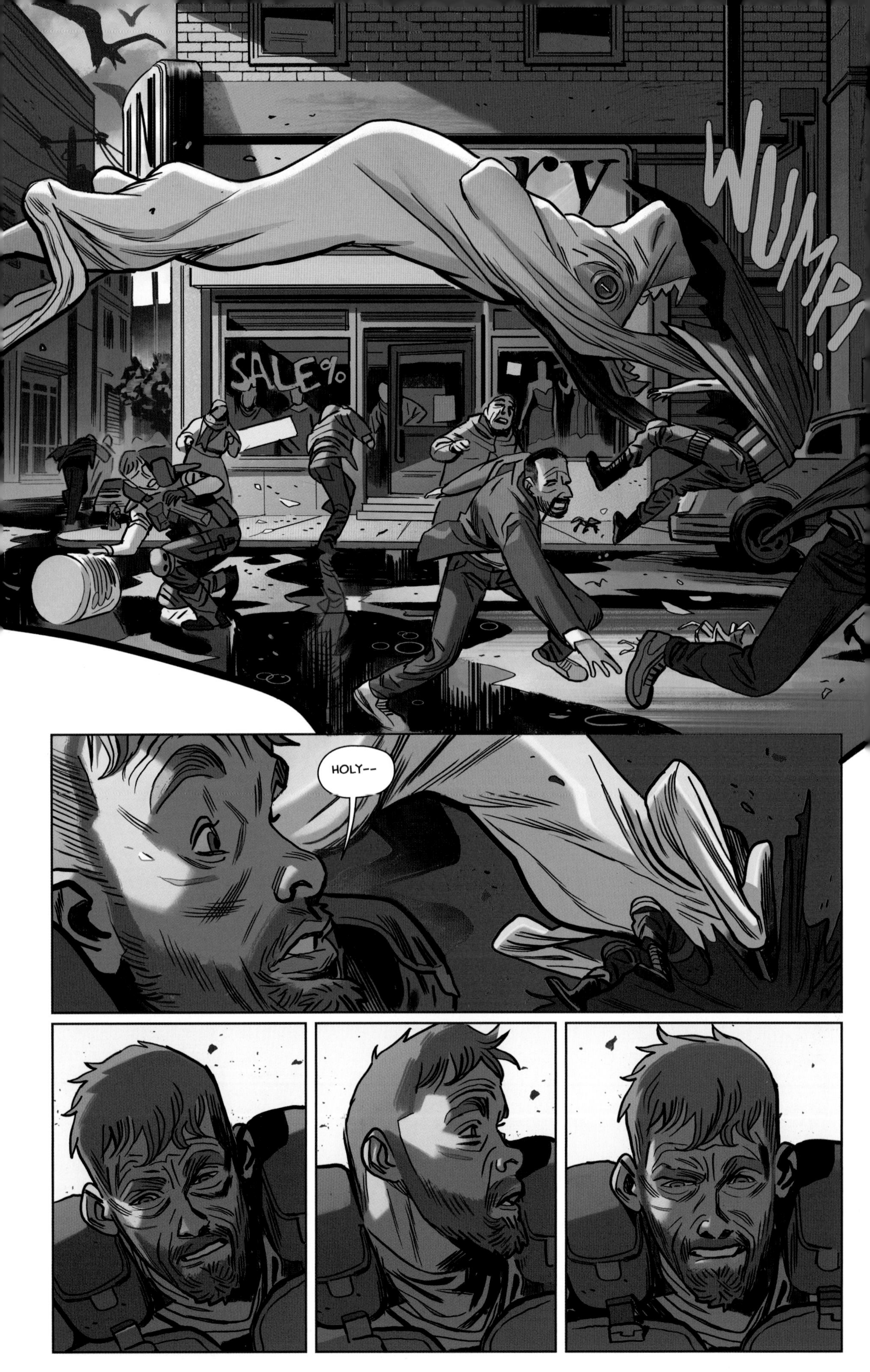
WUMP!
SALE%
HOLY--

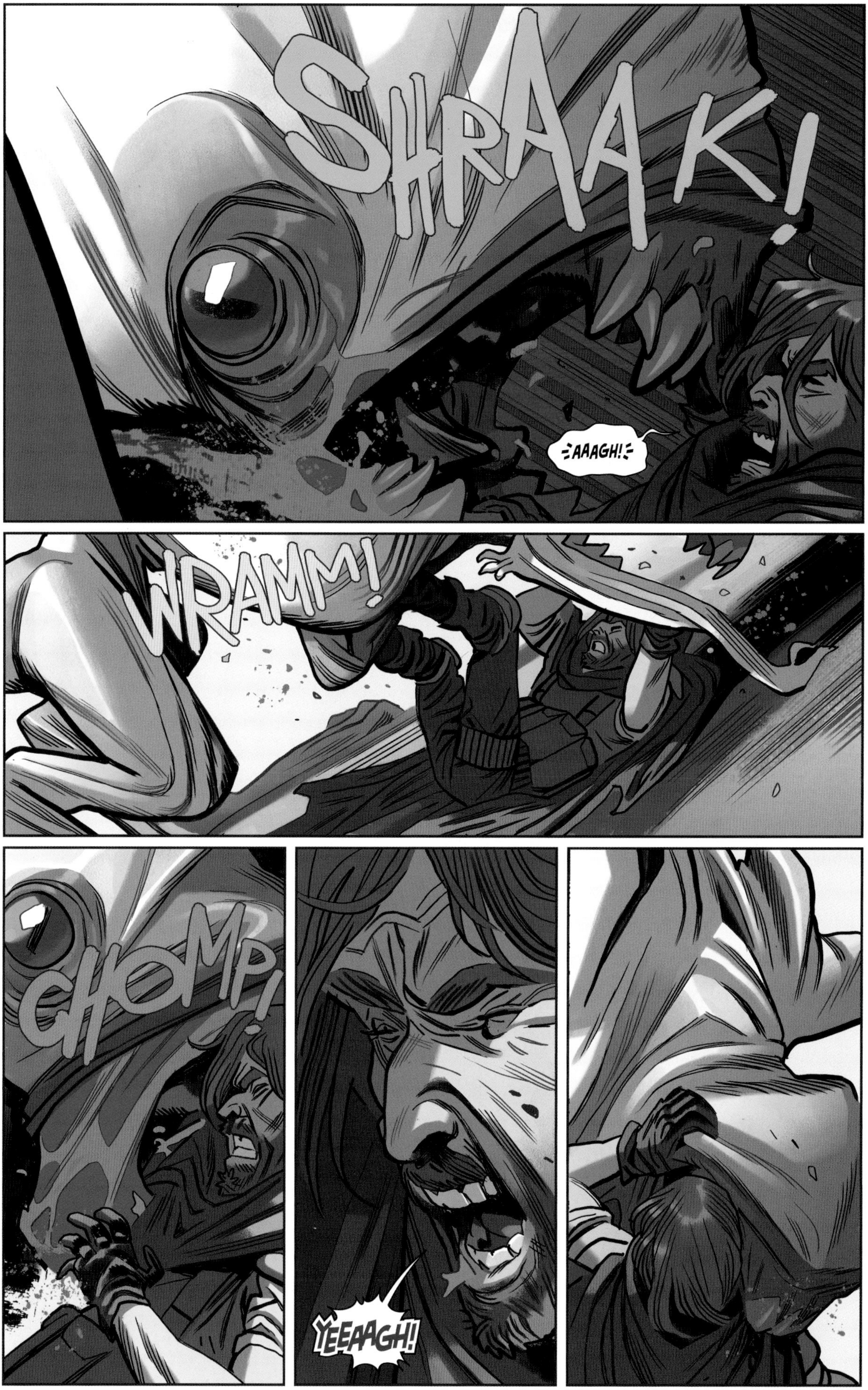
SHRAAK!
AAAGH!
WRAMM!
CHOMP!
YEEAAGH!

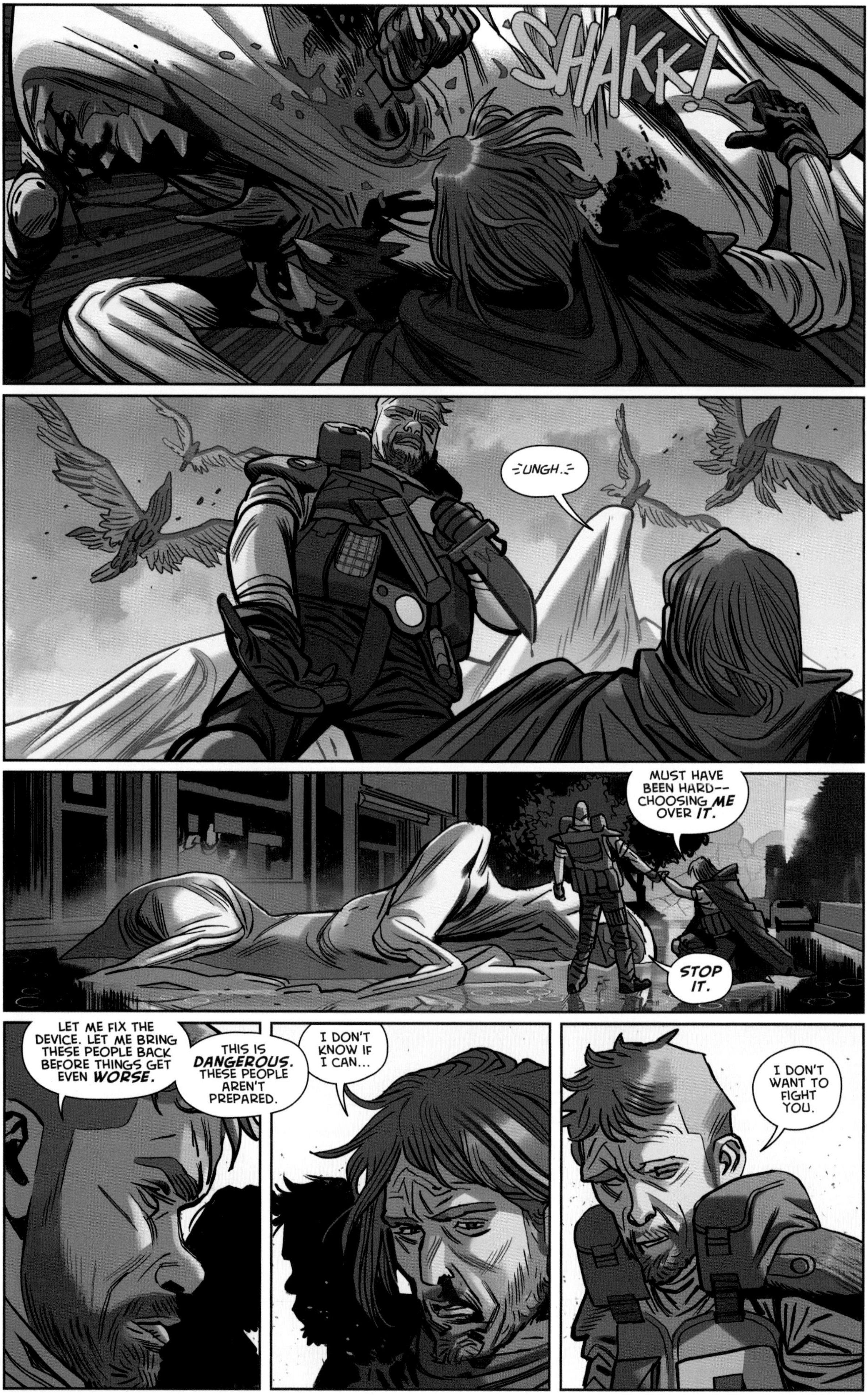
SHAKK!
UNGH.
MUST HAVE BEEN HARD-- CHOOSING ME OVER IT.
STOP IT.
LET ME FIX THE DEVICE. LET ME BRING THESE PEOPLE BACK BEFORE THINGS GET EVEN WORSE.
THIS IS DANGEROUS. THESE PEOPLE AREN'T PREPARED.
I DON'T KNOW IF I CAN...
I DON'T WANT TO FIGHT YOU.

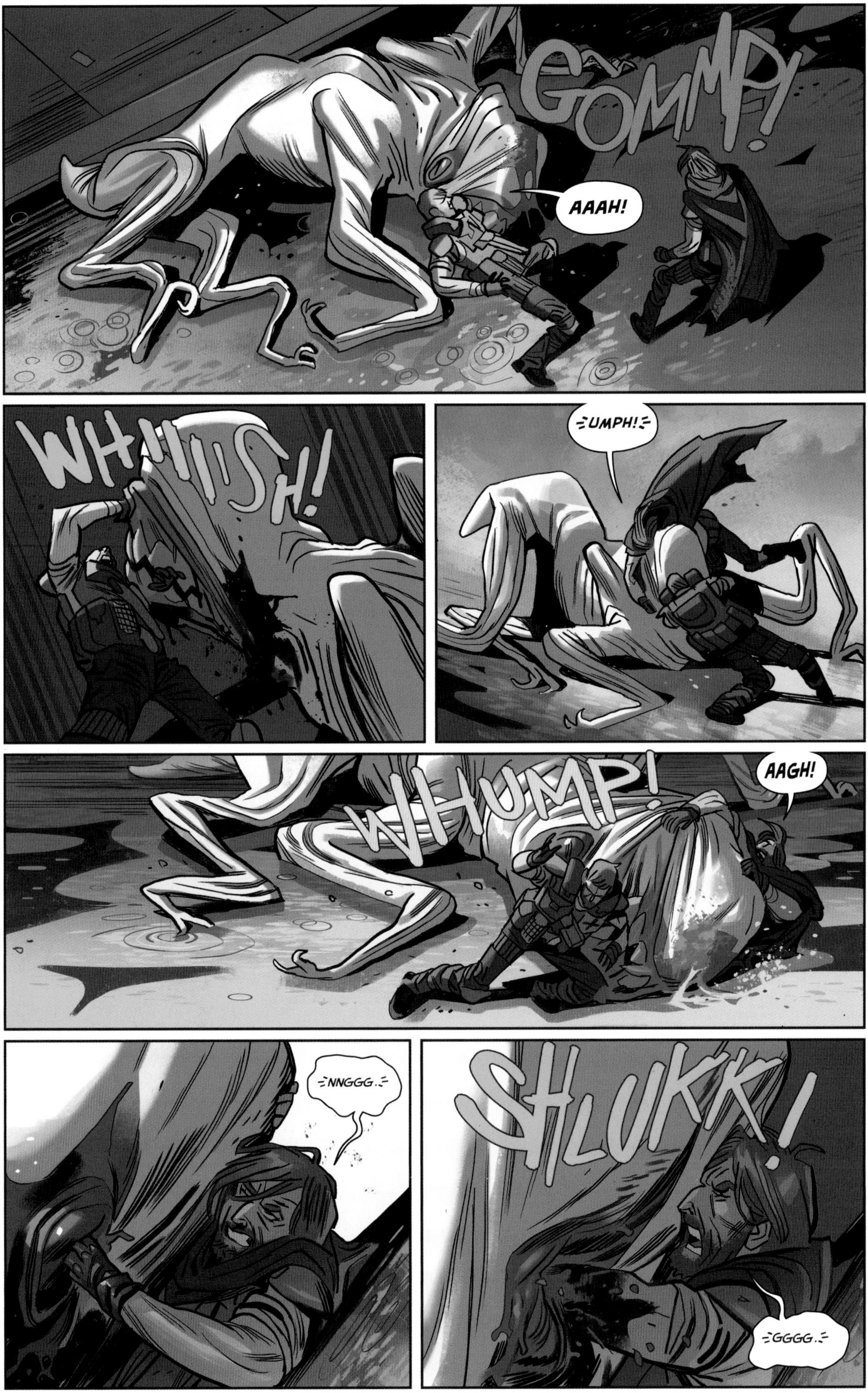
GOMMP!
AAAH!
WHIIIISH!
UMPH!
WHUMP!
AAGH!
NNGGG..
SHLUKK!
GGGG..

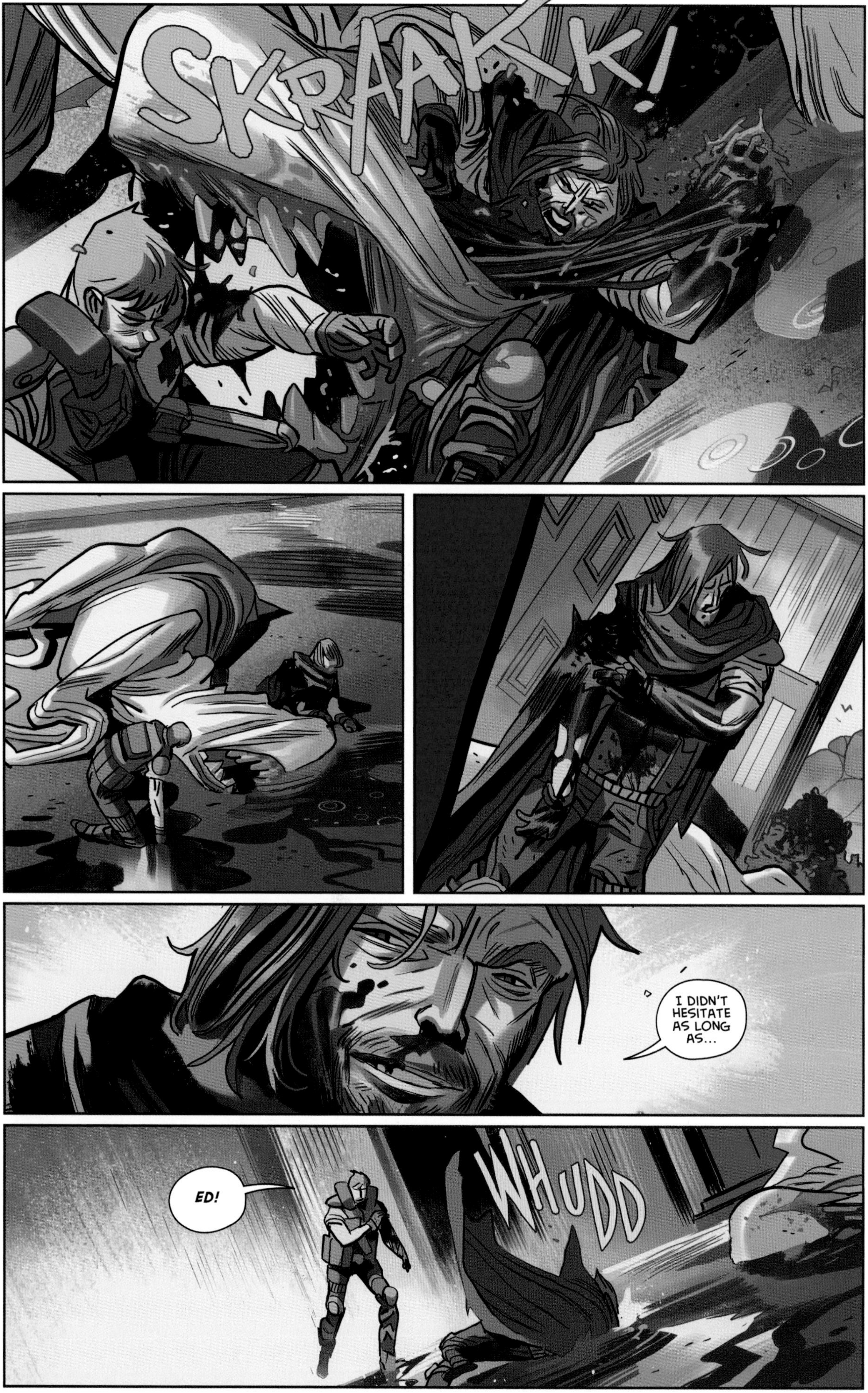
SKRAAKK!
I DIDN'T HESITATE AS LONG AS...
ED!
WHUDD

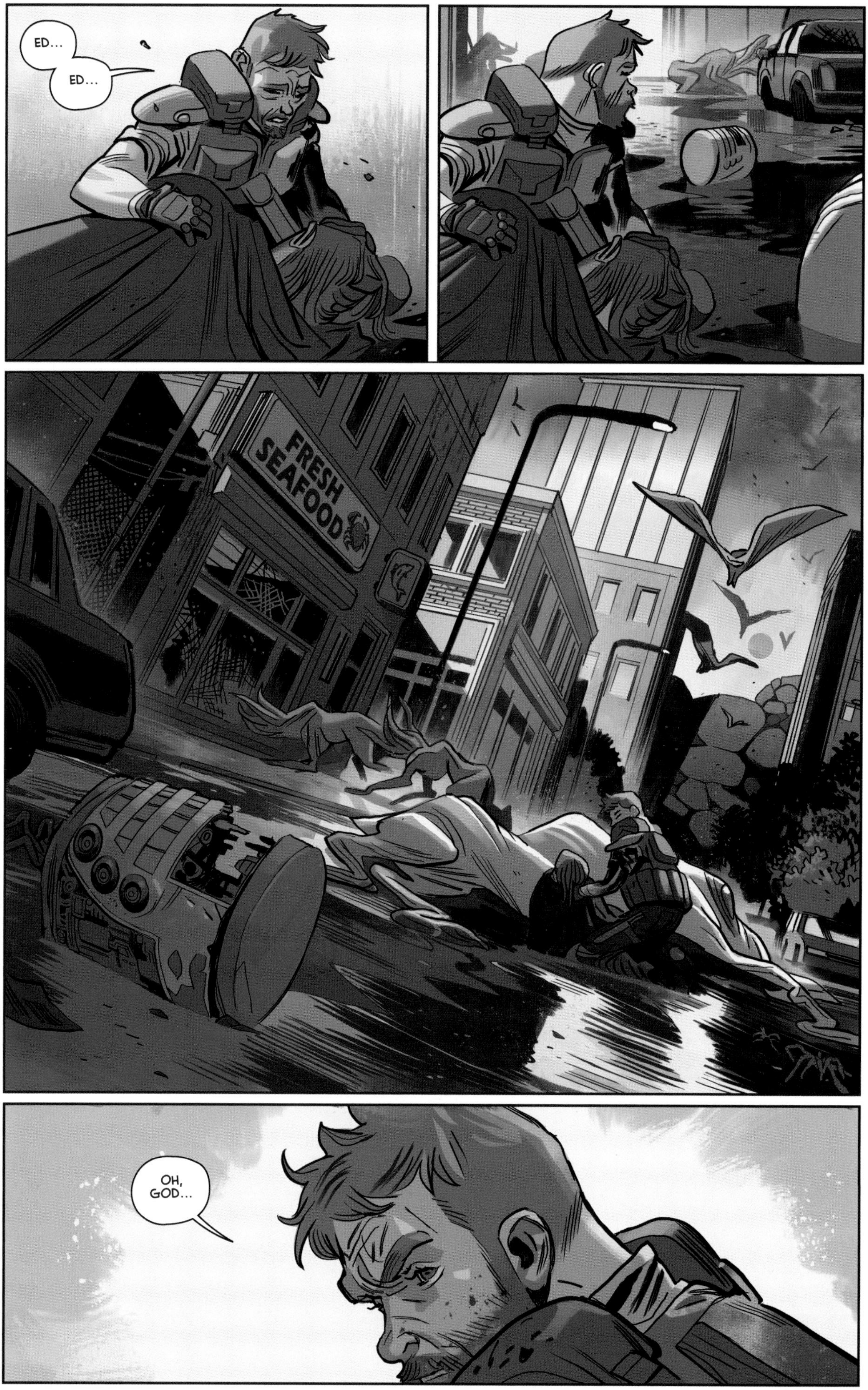
ED...
ED...
FRESH SEAFOOD
OH, GOD...

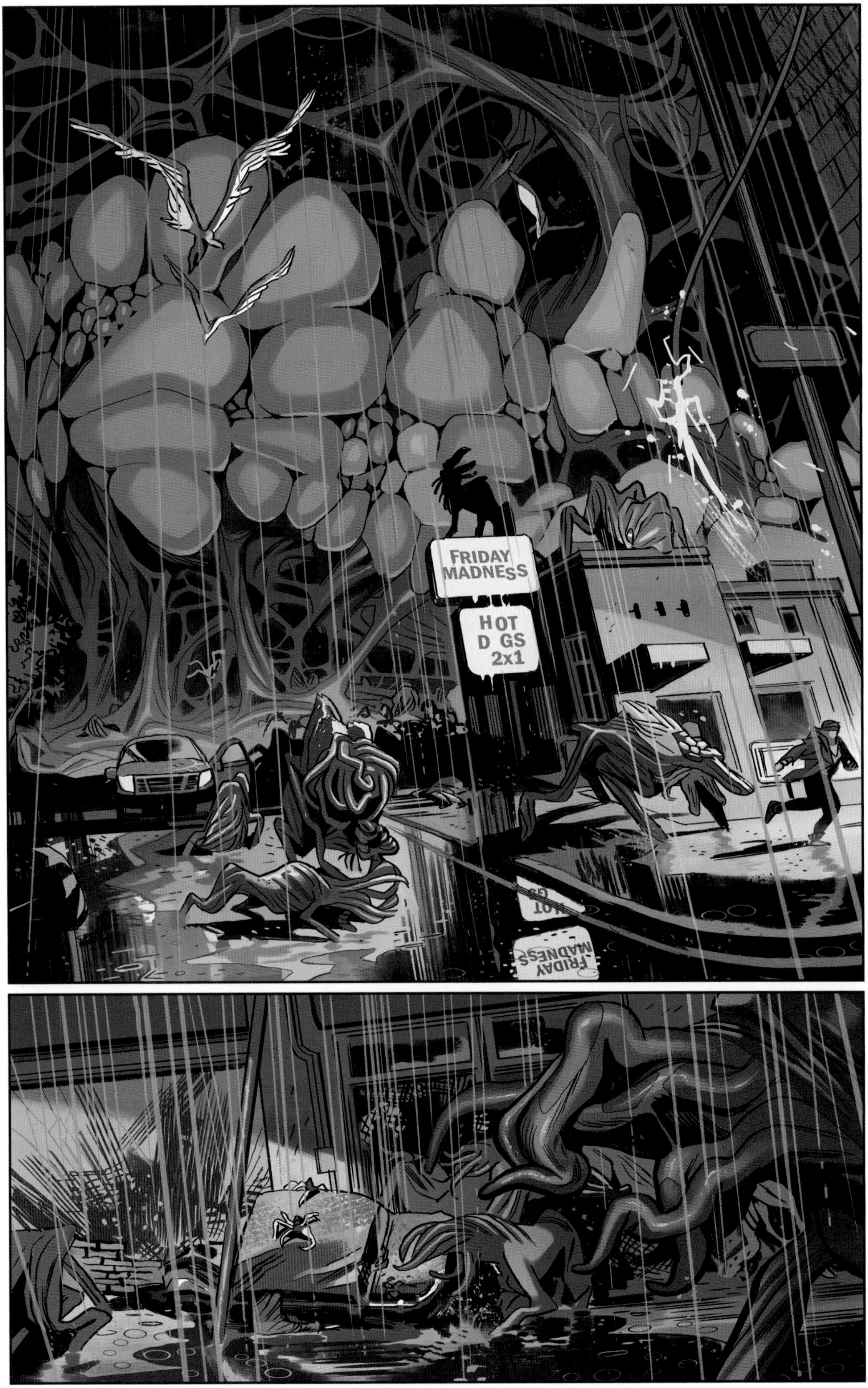
FRIDAY
MADNESS
HOT
D GS
2x1

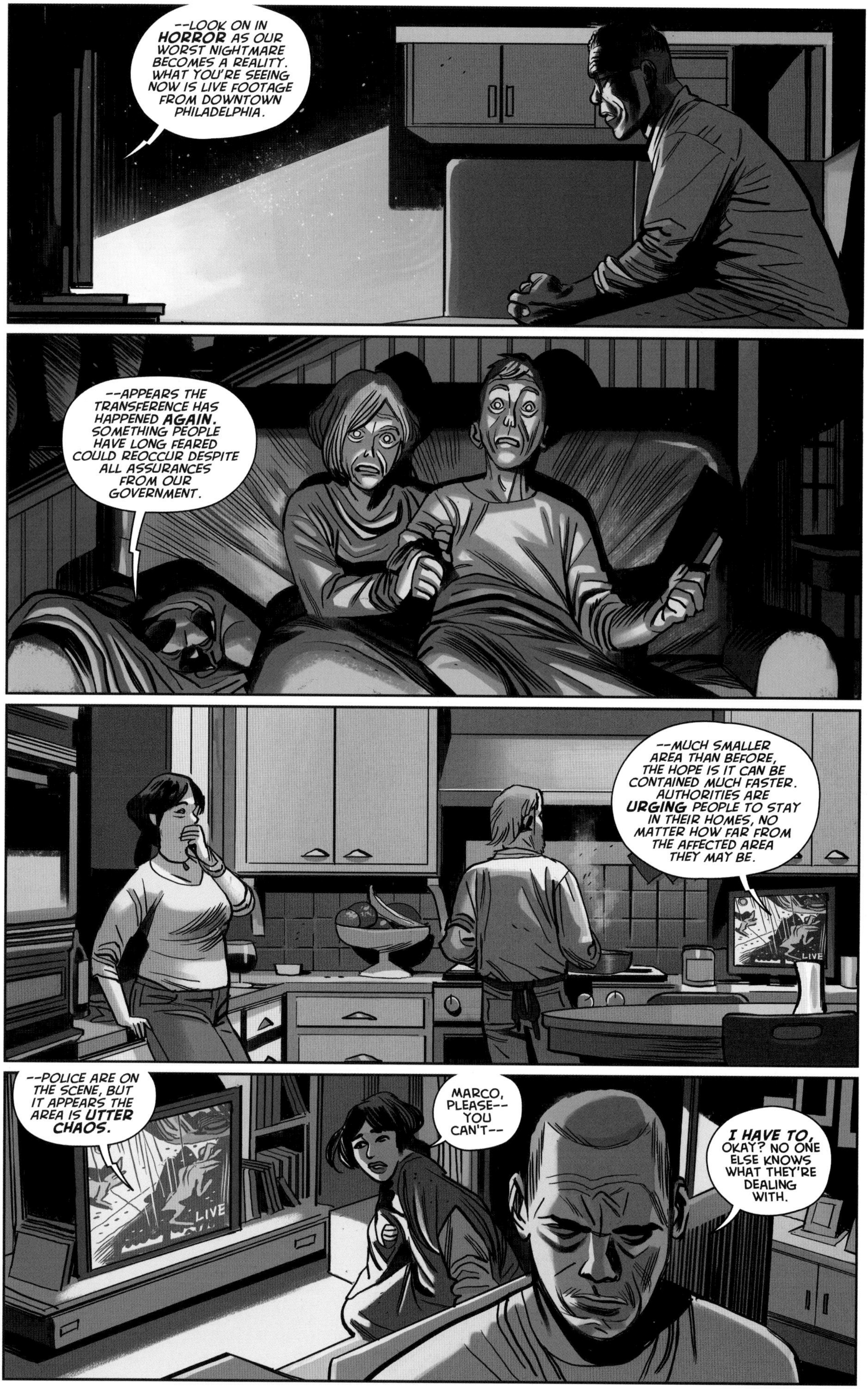
--LOOK ON IN HORROR AS OUR WORST NIGHTMARE BECOMES A REALITY. WHAT YOU'RE SEEING NOW IS LIVE FOOTAGE FROM DOWNTOWN PHILADELPHIA.
--APPEARS THE TRANSFERENCE HAS HAPPENED AGAIN. SOMETHING PEOPLE HAVE LONG FEARED COULD REOCCUR DESPITE ALL ASSURANCES FROM OUR GOVERNMENT.
--MUCH SMALLER AREA THAN BEFORE, THE HOPE IS IT CAN BE CONTAINED MUCH FASTER. AUTHORITIES ARE URGING PEOPLE TO STAY IN THEIR HOMES, NO MATTER HOW FAR FROM THE AFFECTED AREA THEY MAY BE.
LIVE
--POLICE ARE ON THE SCENE, BUT IT APPEARS THE AREA IS UTTER CHAOS.
LIVE
MARCO, PLEASE-- YOU CAN'T--
I HAVE TO, OKAY? NO ONE ELSE KNOWS WHAT THEY'RE DEALING WITH.

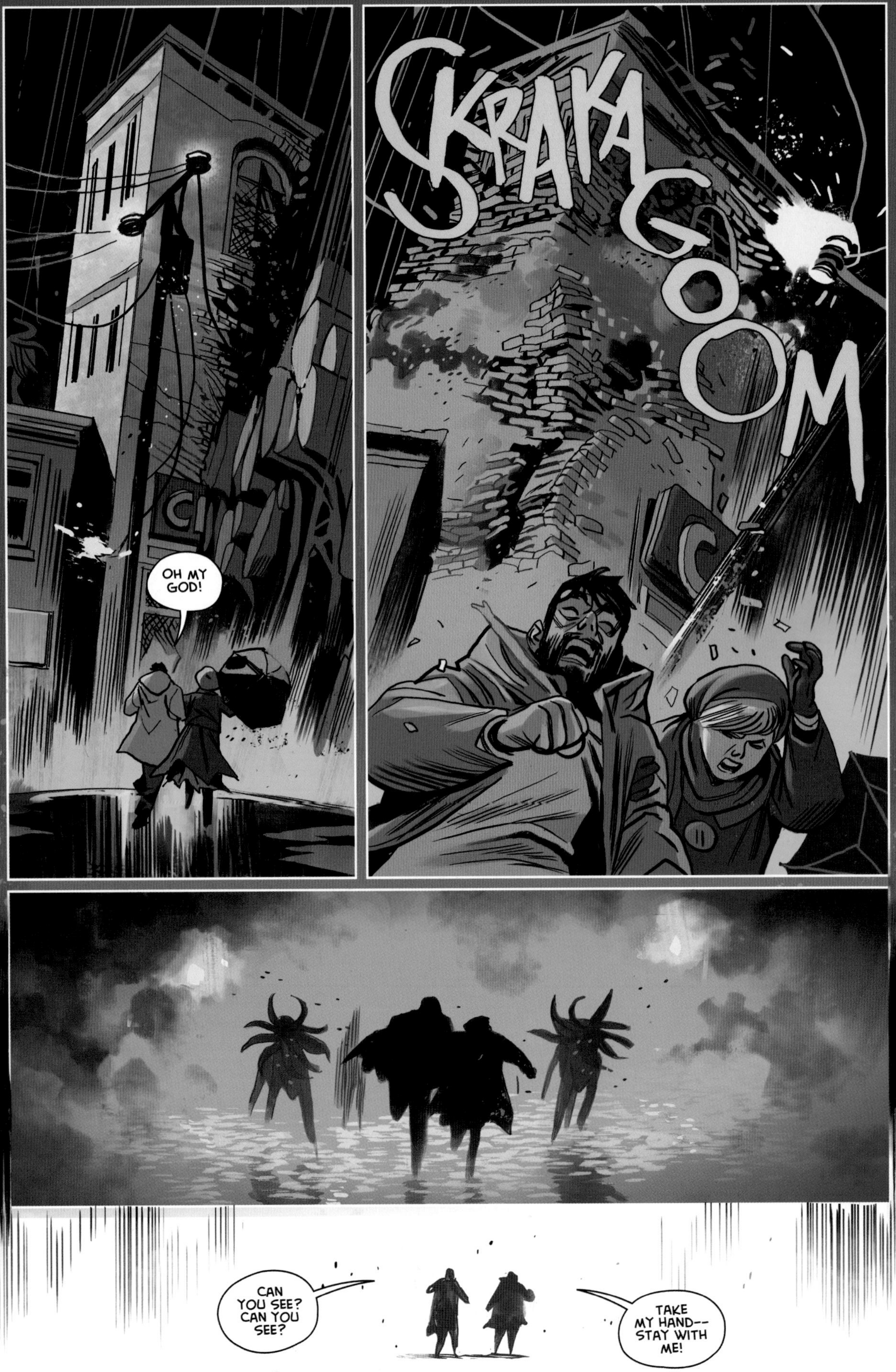
OH MY GOD!
SKRAKAGOOM
CAN YOU SEE? CAN YOU SEE?
TAKE MY HAND-- STAY WITH ME!

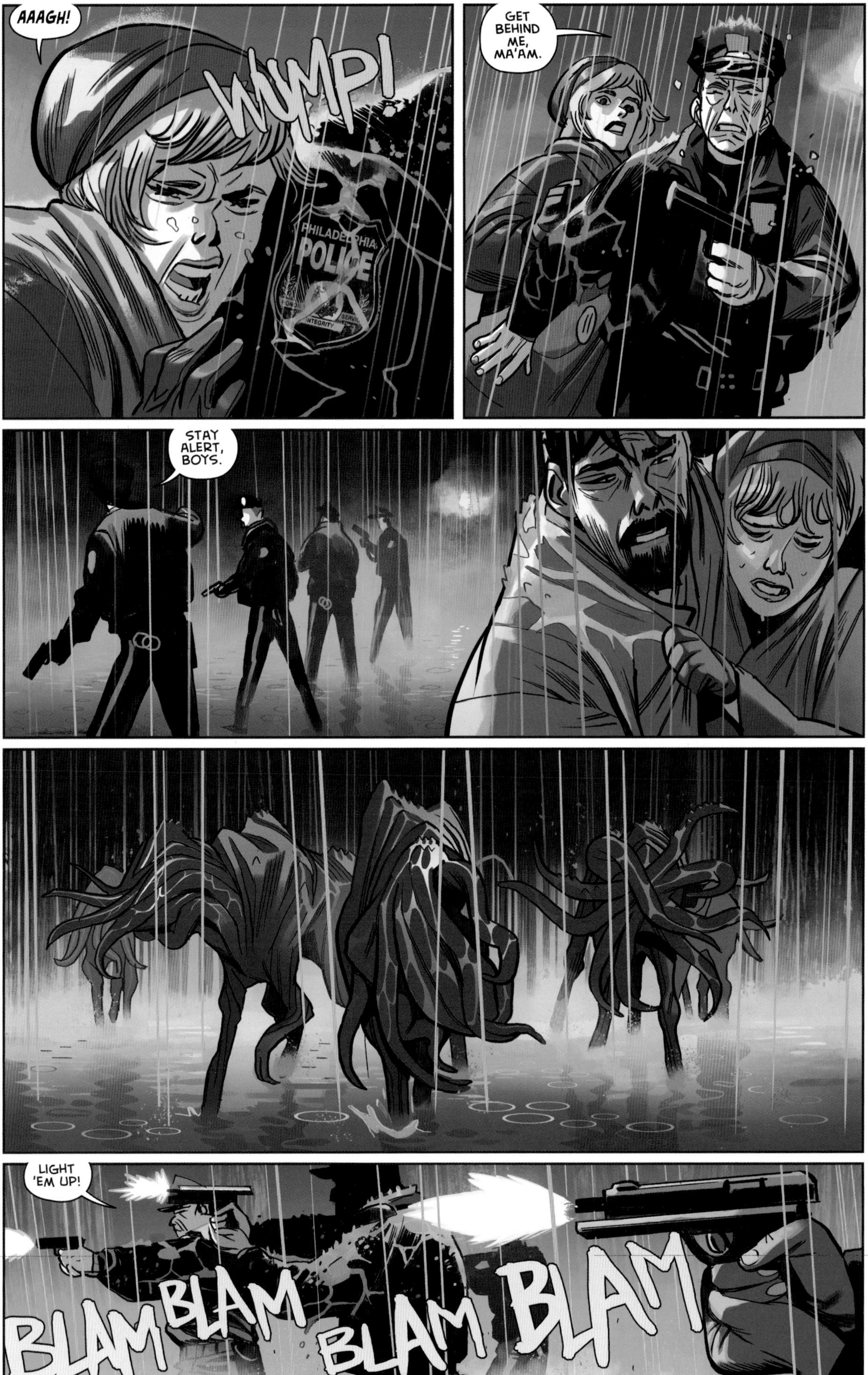
AAAGH!
WUMP!
PHILADELPHIA POLICE
INTEGRITY
GET BEHIND ME, MA'AM.
STAY ALERT, BOYS.
LIGHT 'EM UP!
BLAM BLAM BLAM BLAM BLAM

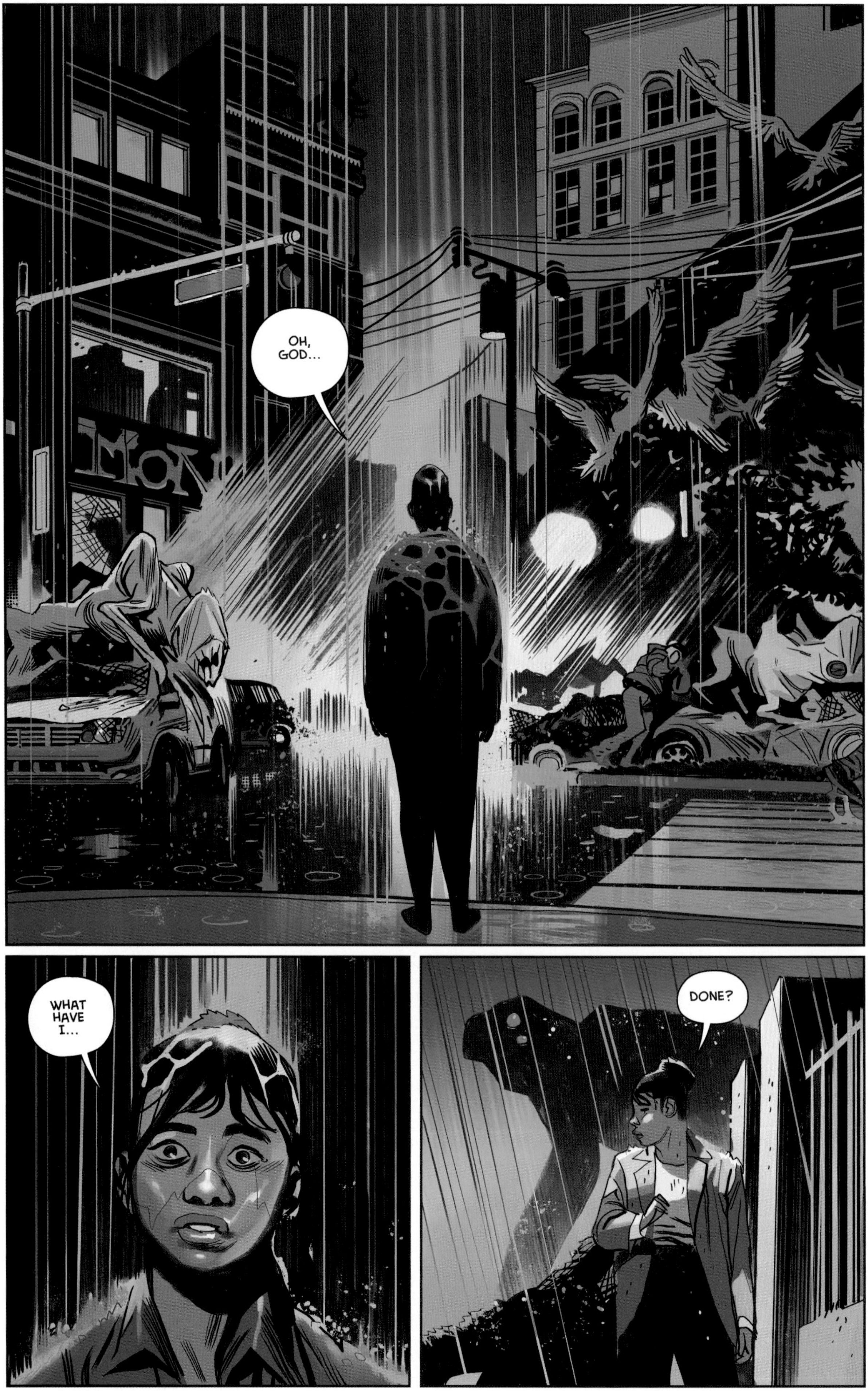
OH, GOD...
WHAT HAVE I...
DONE?

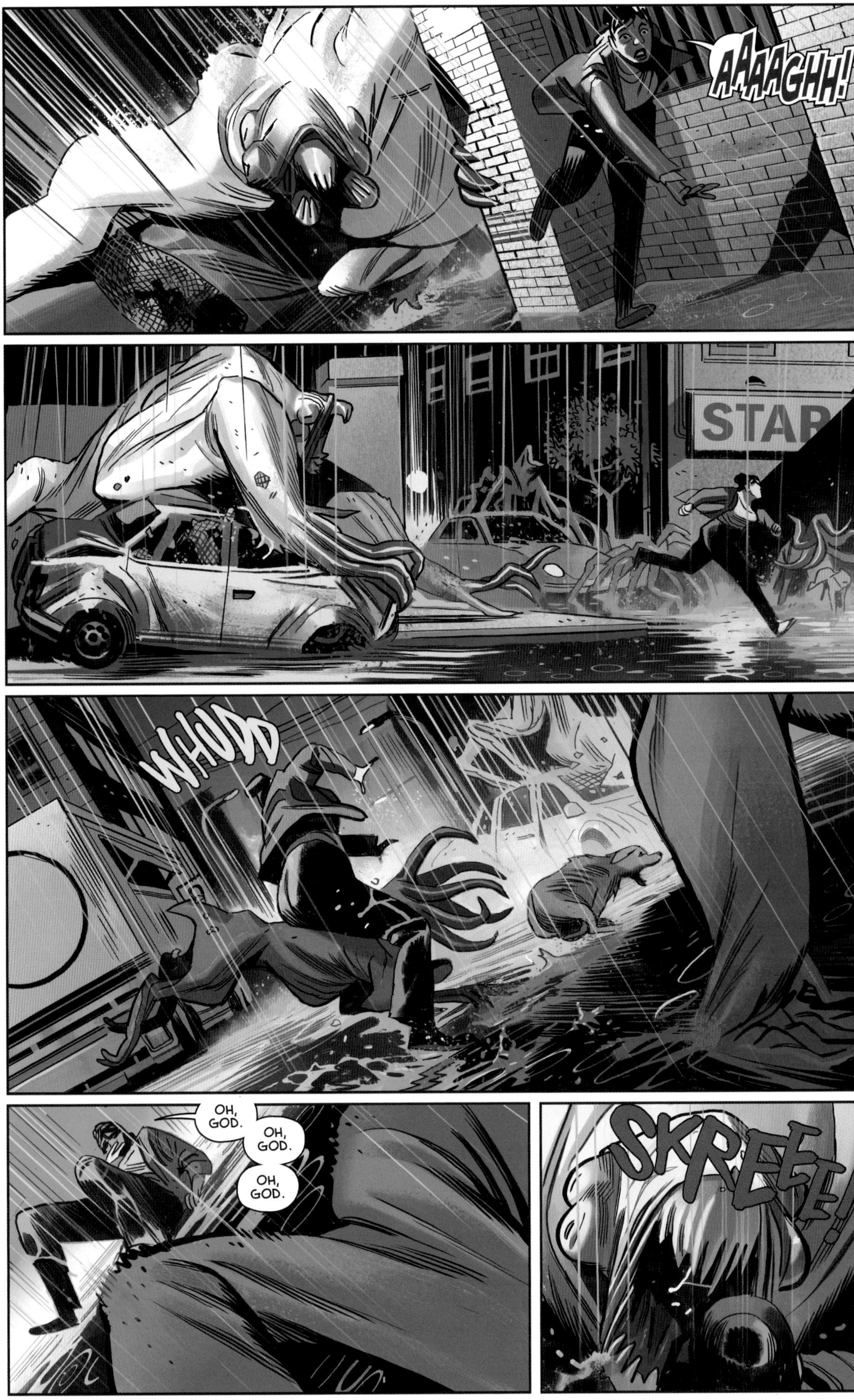
AAAAGHH!
STAR
WHUDD
OH, GOD.
OH, GOD.
OH, GOD.
SKREEEE!

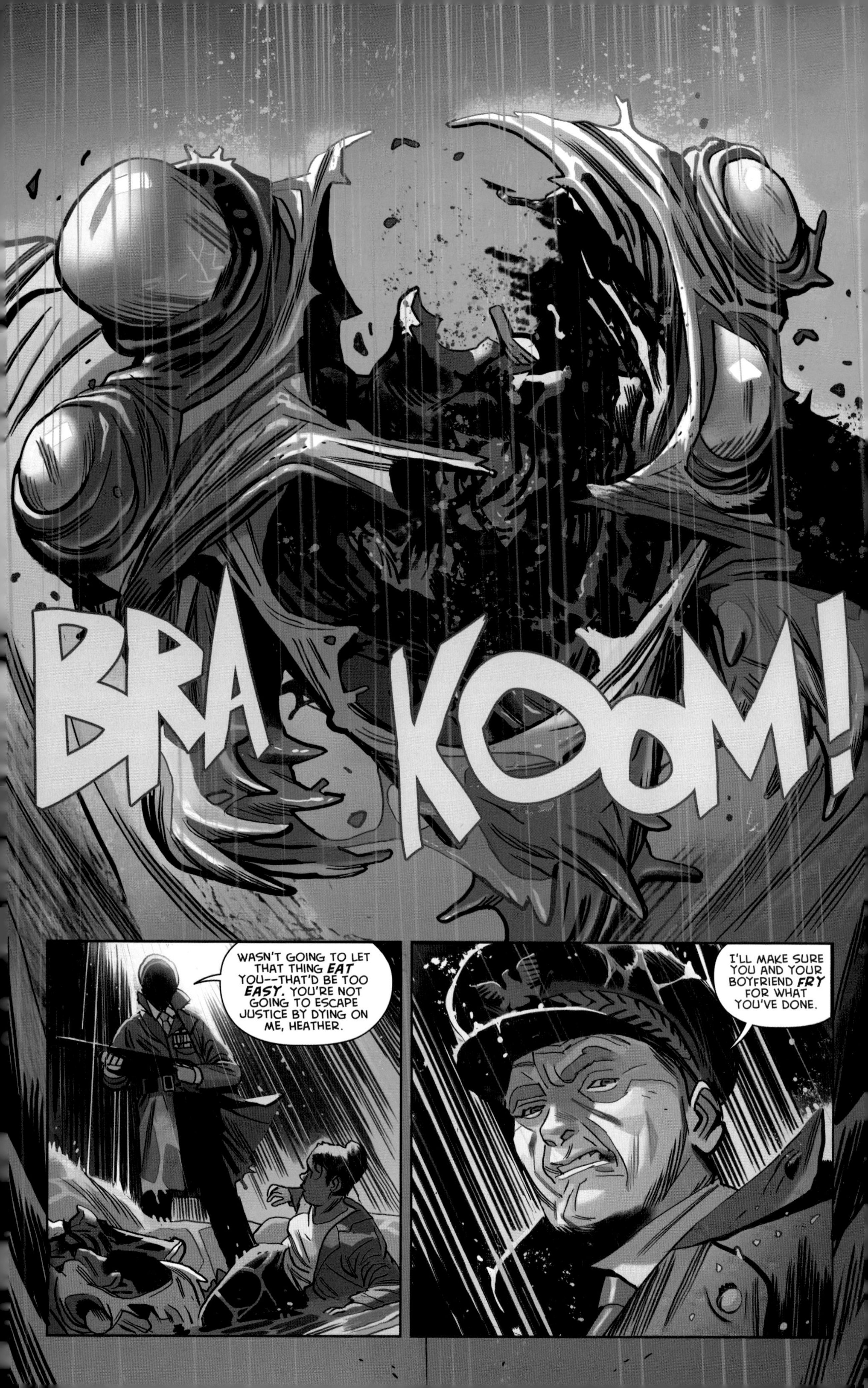
BRA KOOM!
WASN'T GOING TO LET THAT THING EAT YOU--THAT'D BE TOO EASY. YOU'RE NOT GOING TO ESCAPE JUSTICE BY DYING ON ME, HEATHER.
I'LL MAKE SURE YOU AND YOUR BOYFRIEND FRY FOR WHAT YOU'VE DONE.

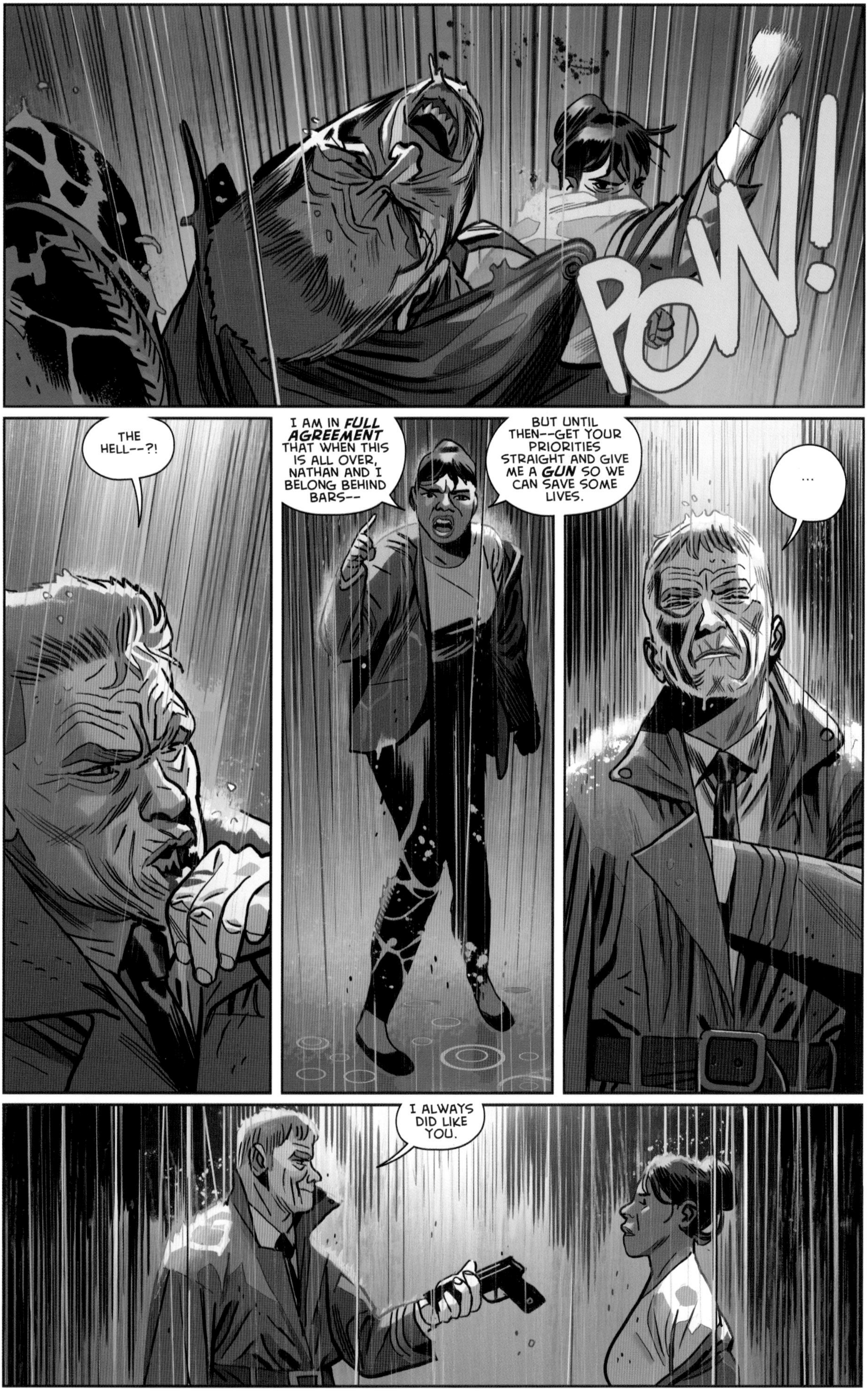
POW!
THE HELL--?!
I AM IN FULL AGREEMENT THAT WHEN THIS IS ALL OVER, NATHAN AND I BELONG BEHIND BARS--
BUT UNTIL THEN--GET YOUR PRIORITIES STRAIGHT AND GIVE ME A GUN SO WE CAN SAVE SOME LIVES.
...
I ALWAYS DID LIKE YOU.

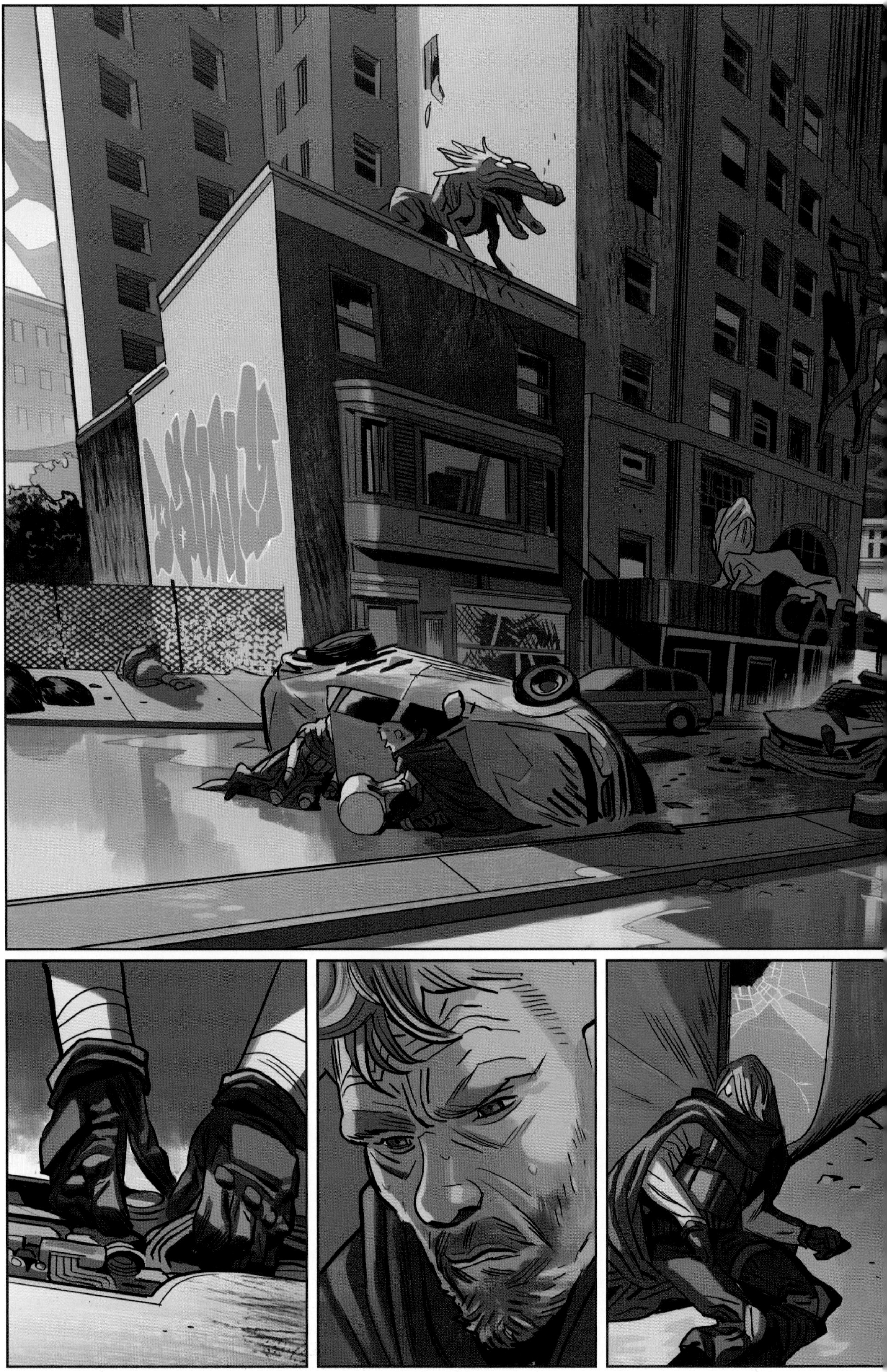

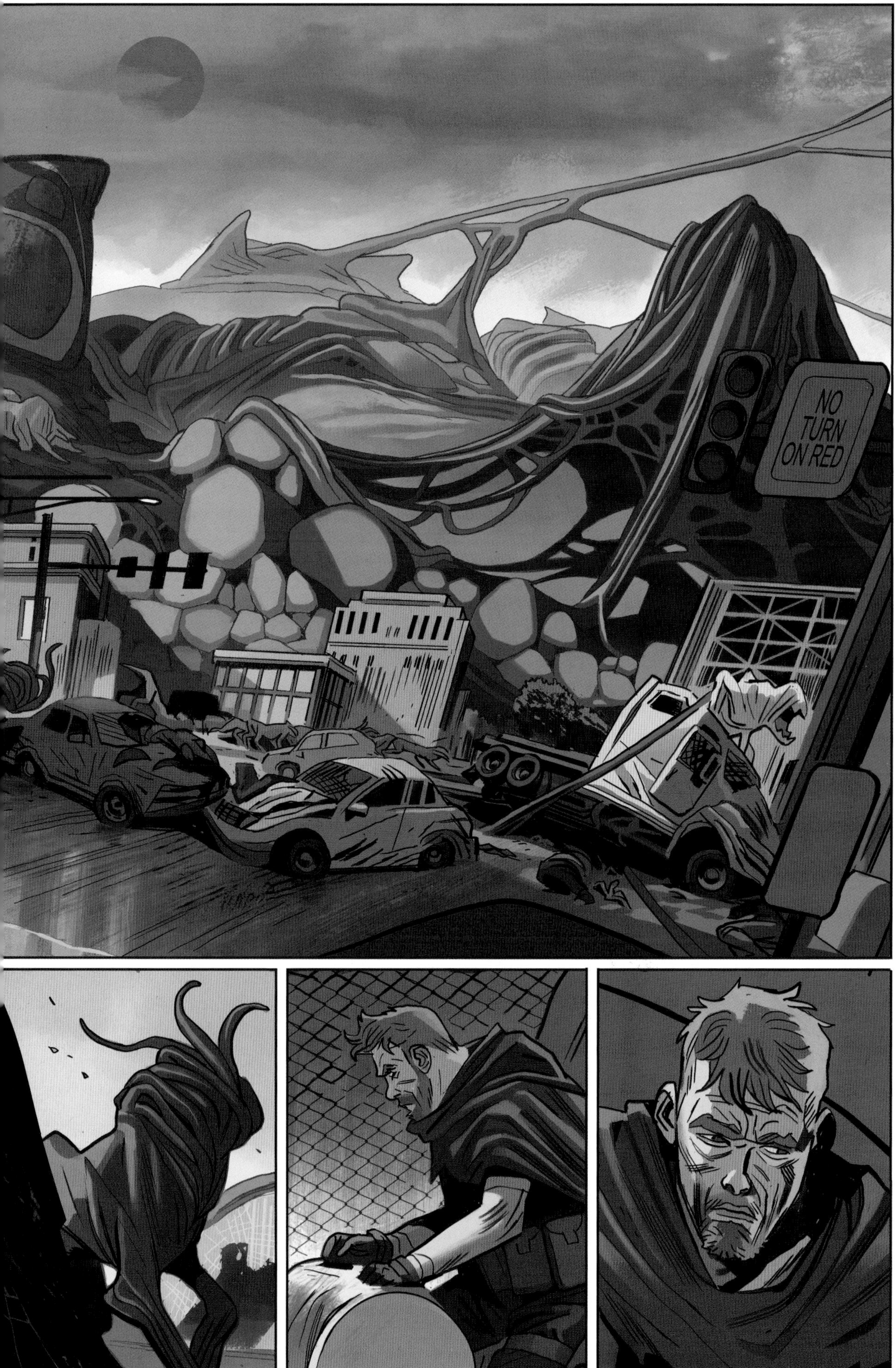
NO
TURN
ON RED

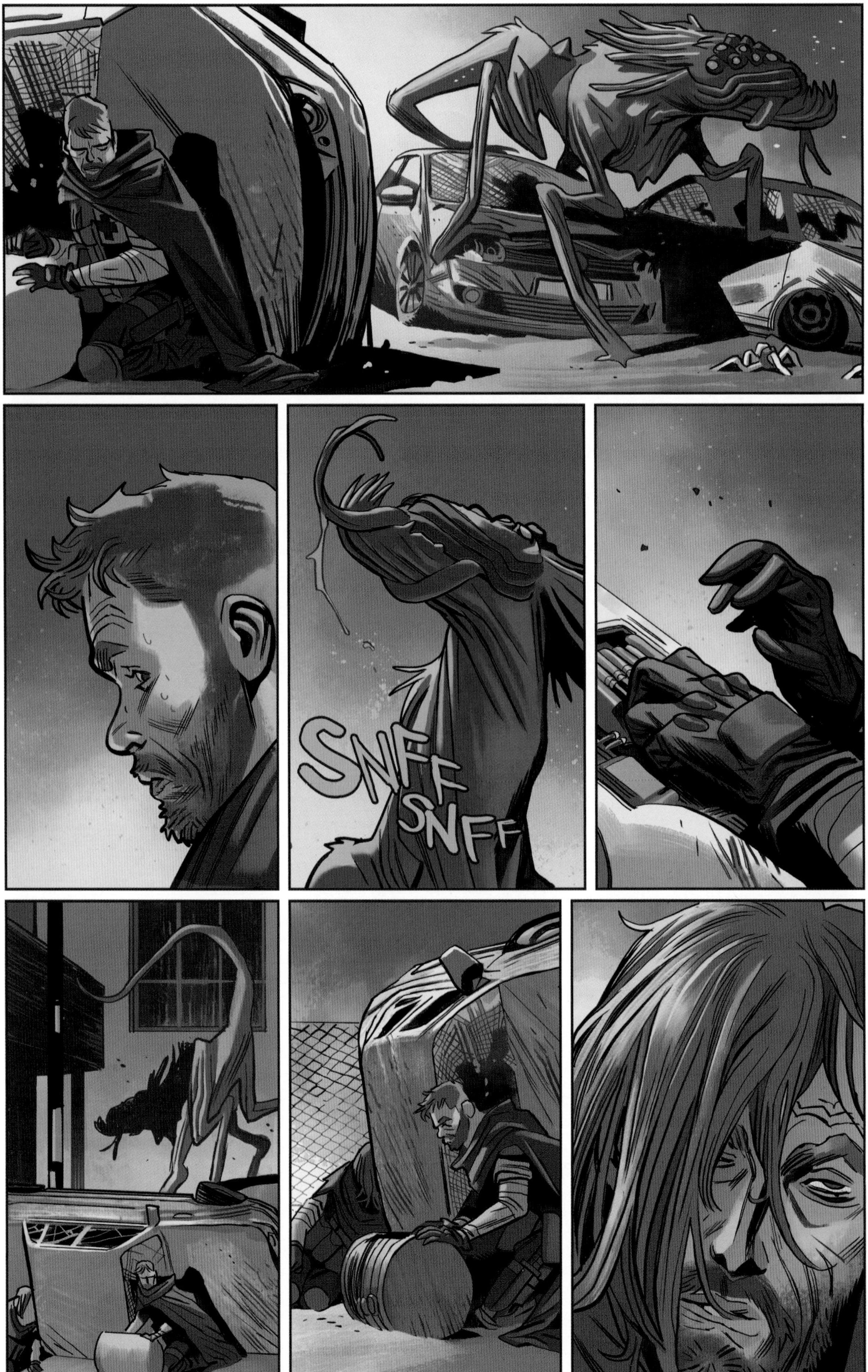
SNFF
SNFF

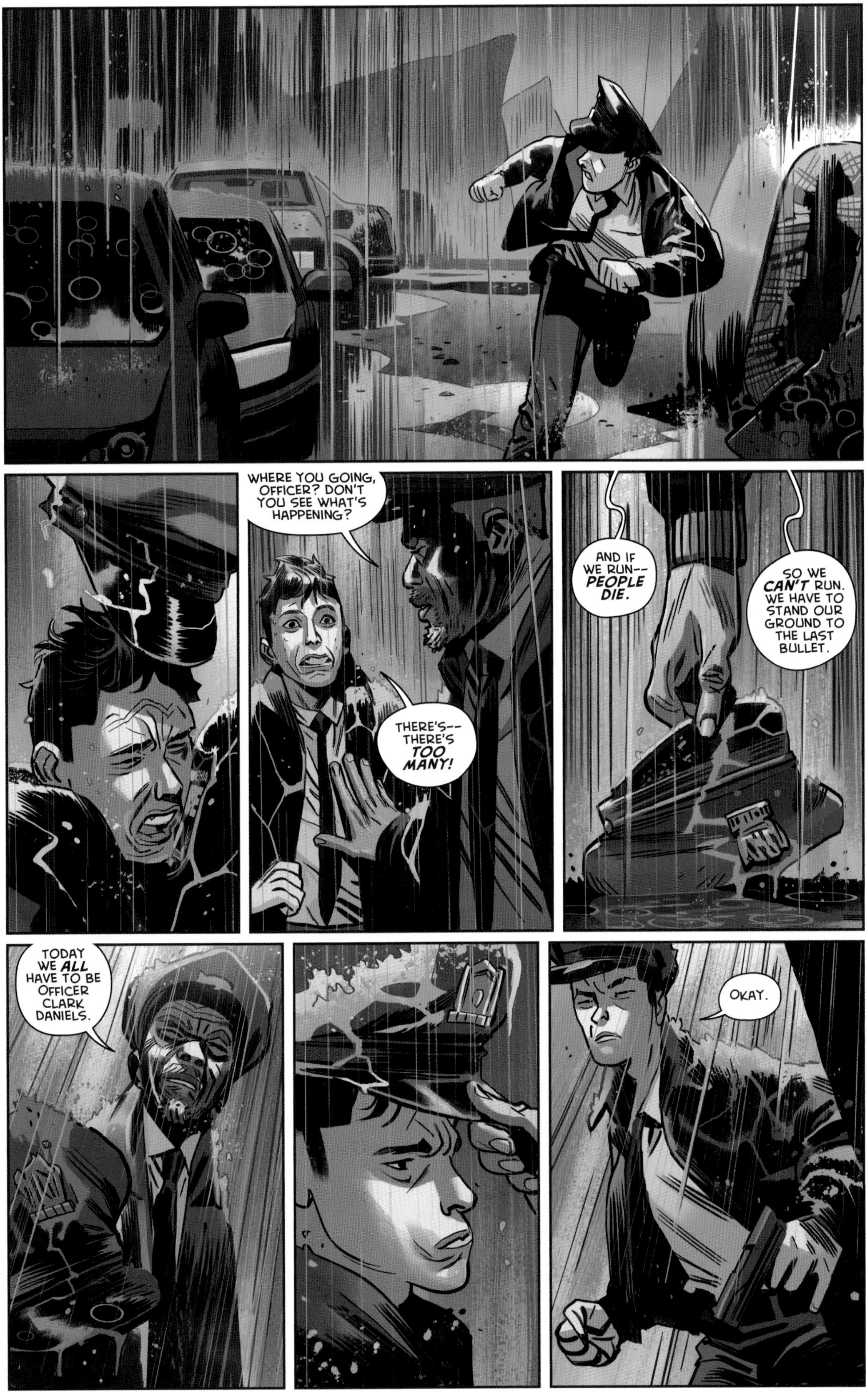
WHERE YOU GOING, OFFICER? DON'T YOU SEE WHAT'S HAPPENING?
THERE'S-- THERE'S TOO MANY!
AND IF WE RUN-- PEOPLE DIE.
SO WE CAN'T RUN. WE HAVE TO STAND OUR GROUND TO THE LAST BULLET.
TODAY WE ALL HAVE TO BE OFFICER CLARK DANIELS.
OKAY.

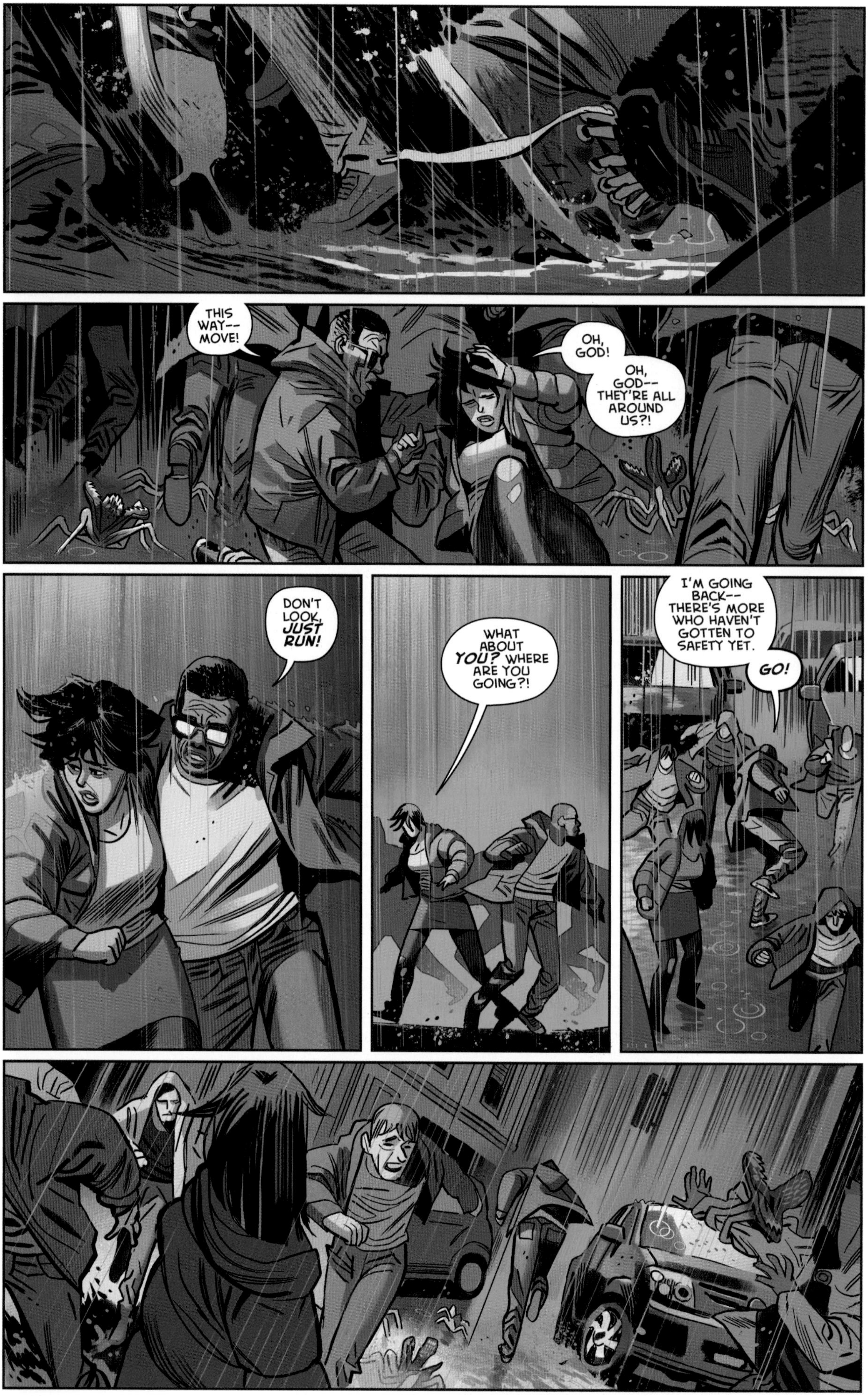
THIS WAY-- MOVE!
OH, GOD!
OH, GOD-- THEY'RE ALL AROUND US?!
DON'T LOOK, JUST RUN!
WHAT ABOUT YOU? WHERE ARE YOU GOING?!
I'M GOING BACK-- THERE'S MORE WHO HAVEN'T GOTTEN TO SAFETY YET.
GO!

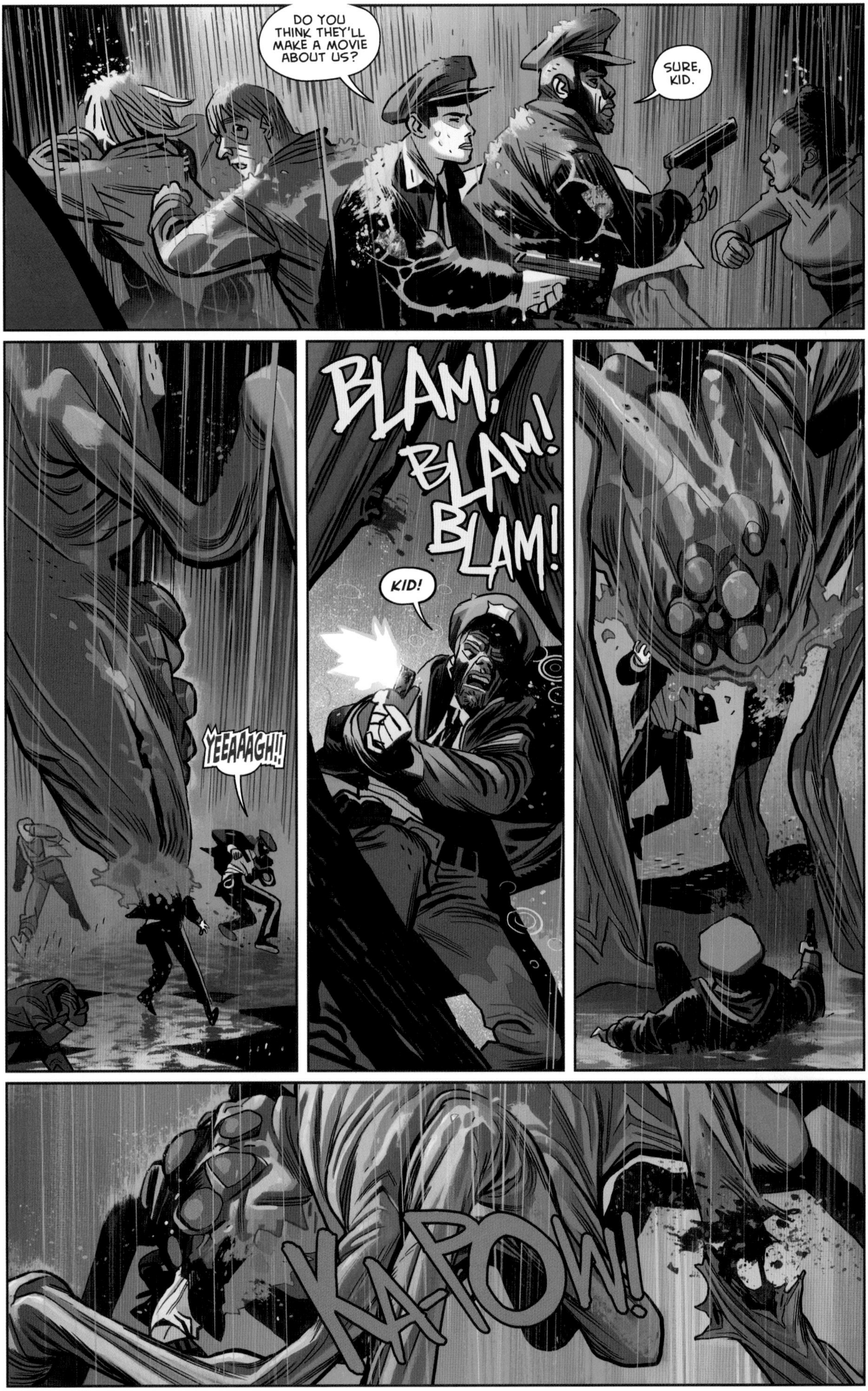
DO YOU THINK THEY'LL MAKE A MOVIE ABOUT US?
SURE, KID.
YEEAAAGH!!
BLAM! BLAM! BLAM!
KID!
KA-POW!

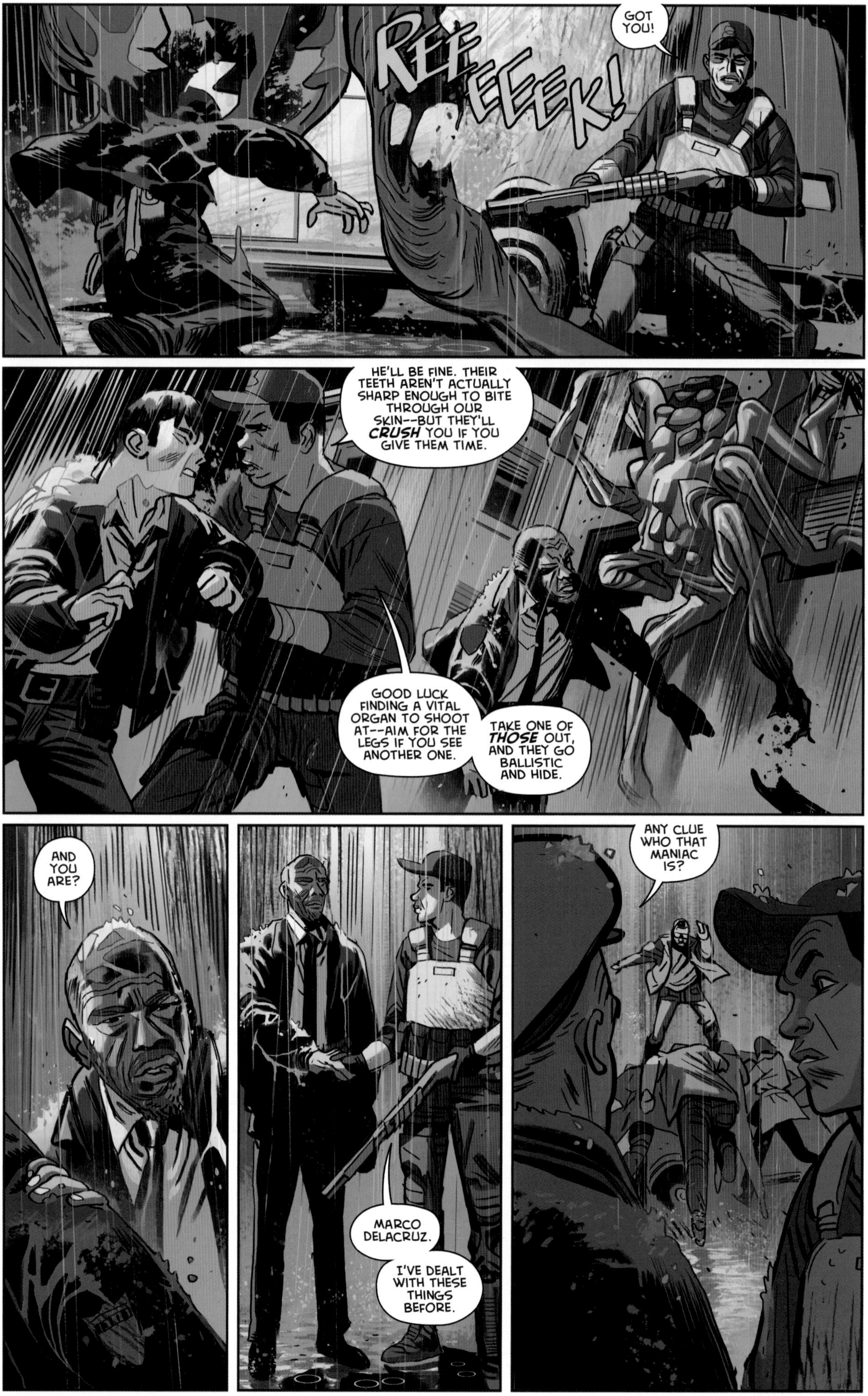
GOT YOU!
REEEEEK!
HE'LL BE FINE. THEIR TEETH AREN'T ACTUALLY SHARP ENOUGH TO BITE THROUGH OUR SKIN--BUT THEY'LL CRUSH YOU IF YOU GIVE THEM TIME.
GOOD LUCK FINDING A VITAL ORGAN TO SHOOT AT--AIM FOR THE LEGS IF YOU SEE ANOTHER ONE.
TAKE ONE OF THOSE OUT, AND THEY GO BALLISTIC AND HIDE.
AND YOU ARE?
MARCO DELACRUZ.
I'VE DEALT WITH THESE THINGS BEFORE.
ANY CLUE WHO THAT MANIAC IS?

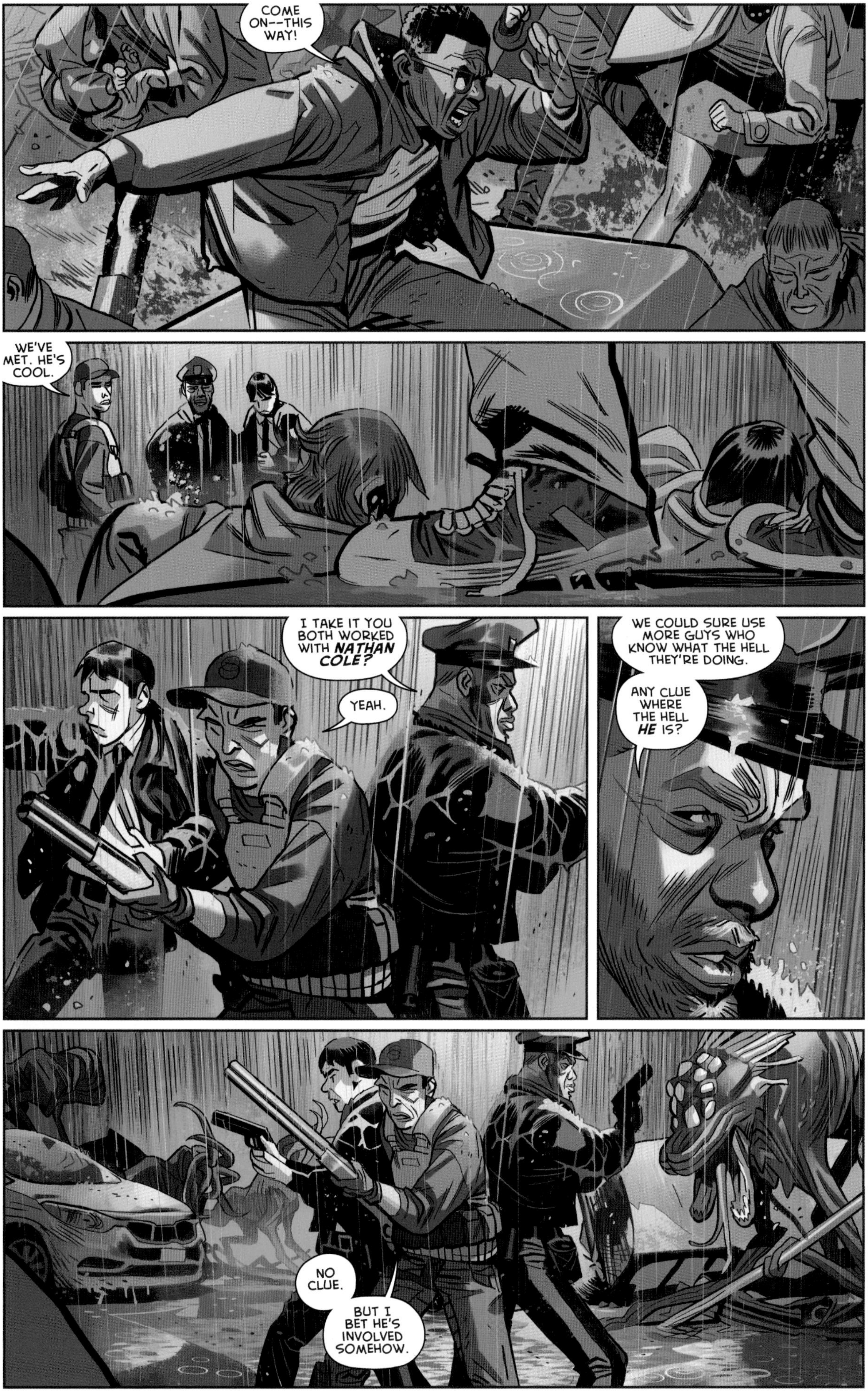
COME ON--THIS WAY!
WE'VE MET. HE'S COOL.
I TAKE IT YOU BOTH WORKED WITH NATHAN COLE?
YEAH.
WE COULD SURE USE MORE GUYS WHO KNOW WHAT THE HELL THEY'RE DOING.
ANY CLUE WHERE THE HELL HE IS?
NO CLUE.
BUT I BET HE'S INVOLVED SOMEHOW.

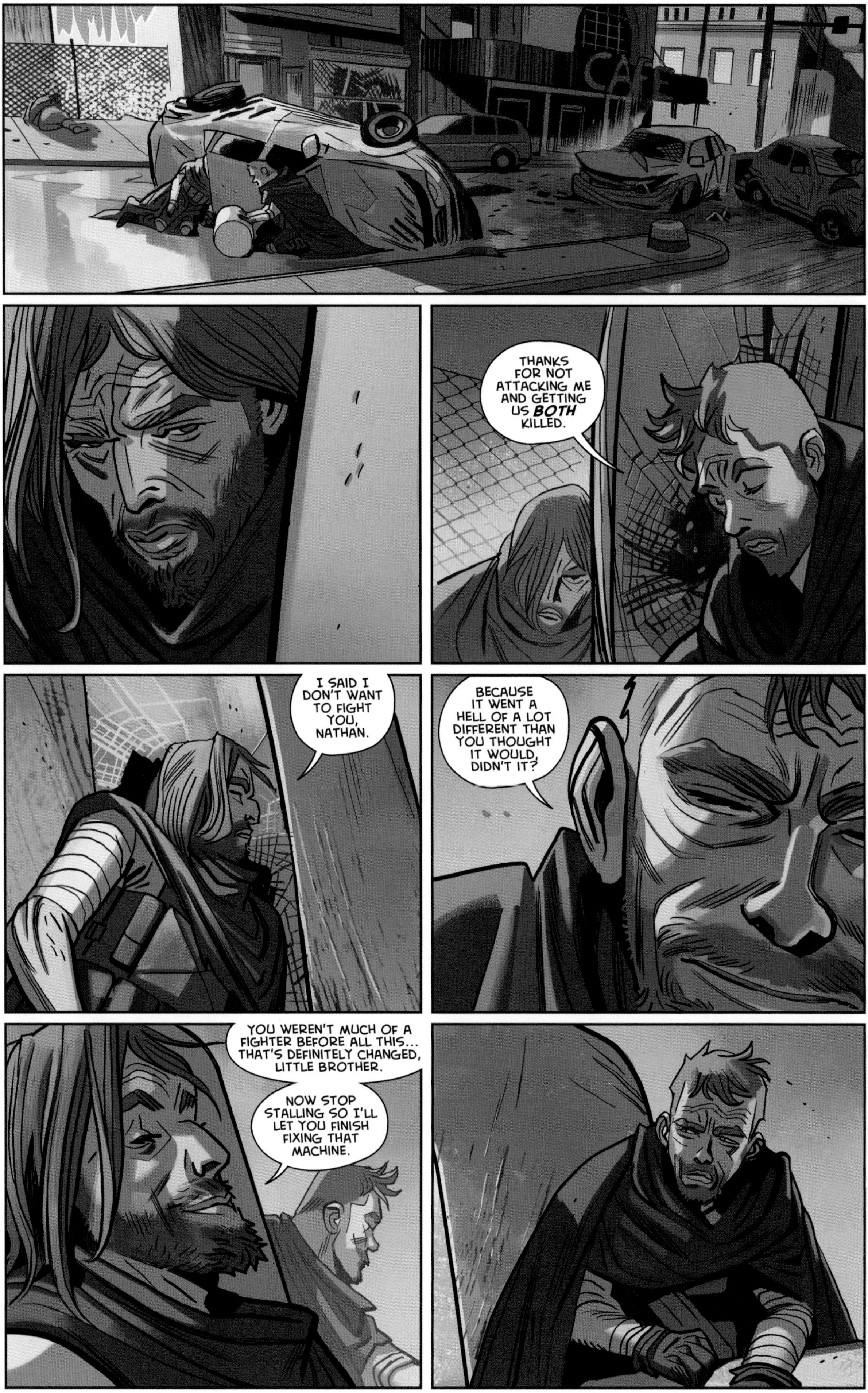
THANKS FOR NOT ATTACKING ME AND GETTING US BOTH KILLED.
I SAID I DON'T WANT TO FIGHT YOU, NATHAN.
BECAUSE IT WENT A HELL OF A LOT DIFFERENT THAN YOU THOUGHT IT WOULD, DIDN'T IT?
YOU WEREN'T MUCH OF A FIGHTER BEFORE ALL THIS... THAT'S DEFINITELY CHANGED, LITTLE BROTHER.
NOW STOP STALLING SO I'LL LET YOU FINISH FIXING THAT MACHINE.

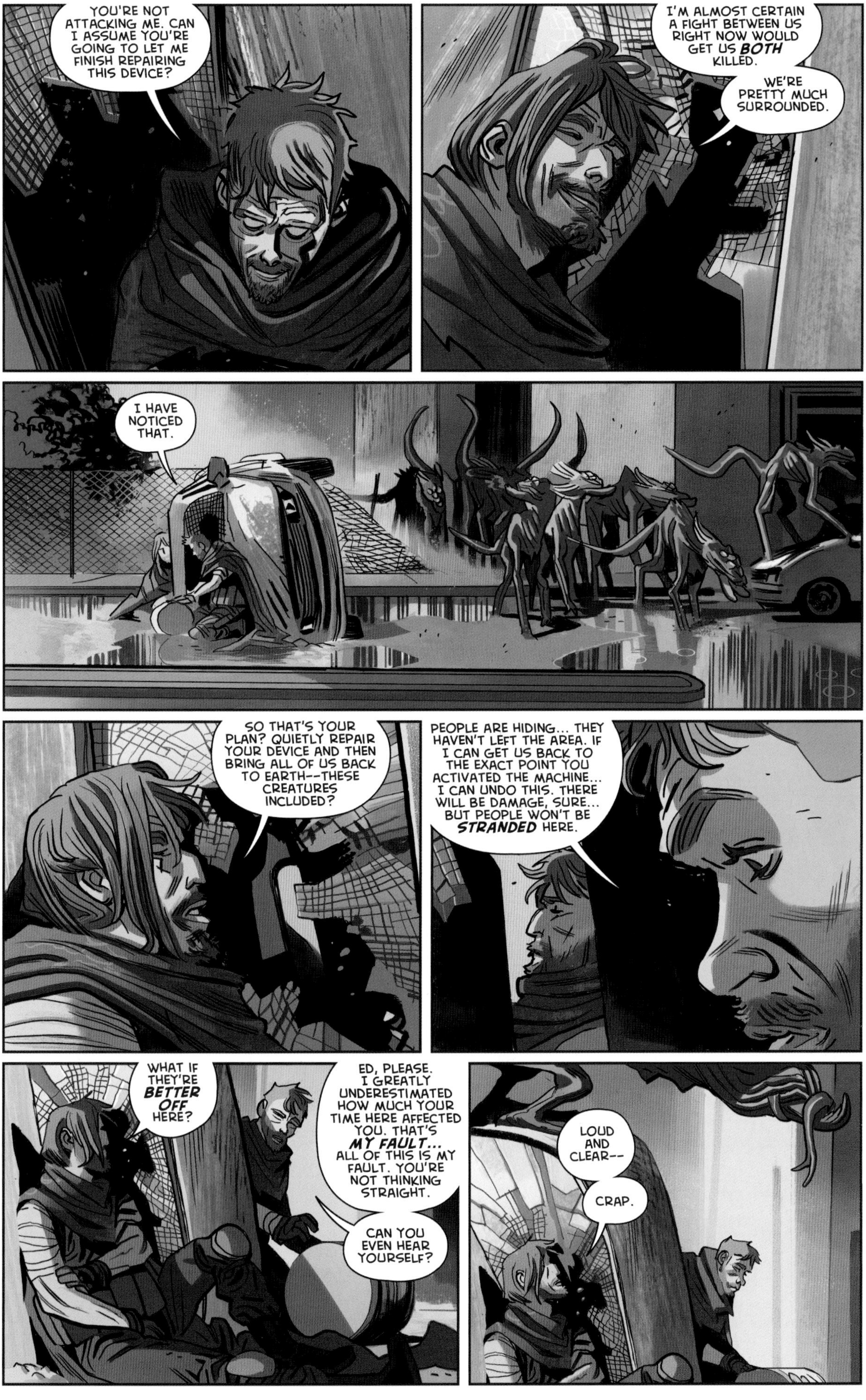

YOU'RE NOT ATTACKING ME. CAN I ASSUME YOU'RE GOING TO LET ME FINISH REPAIRING THIS DEVICE?
I'M ALMOST CERTAIN A FIGHT BETWEEN US RIGHT NOW WOULD GET US BOTH KILLED.
WE'RE PRETTY MUCH SURROUNDED.
I HAVE NOTICED THAT.
SO THAT'S YOUR PLAN? QUIETLY REPAIR YOUR DEVICE AND THEN BRING ALL OF US BACK TO EARTH--THESE CREATURES INCLUDED?
PEOPLE ARE HIDING... THEY HAVEN'T LEFT THE AREA. IF I CAN GET US BACK TO THE EXACT POINT YOU ACTIVATED THE MACHINE... I CAN UNDO THIS. THERE WILL BE DAMAGE, SURE... BUT PEOPLE WON'T BE STRANDED HERE.
WHAT IF THEY'RE BETTER OFF HERE?
ED, PLEASE. I GREATLY UNDERESTIMATED HOW MUCH YOUR TIME HERE AFFECTED YOU. THAT'S MY FAULT... ALL OF THIS IS MY FAULT. YOU'RE NOT THINKING STRAIGHT.
CAN YOU EVEN HEAR YOURSELF?
LOUD AND CLEAR--
CRAP.

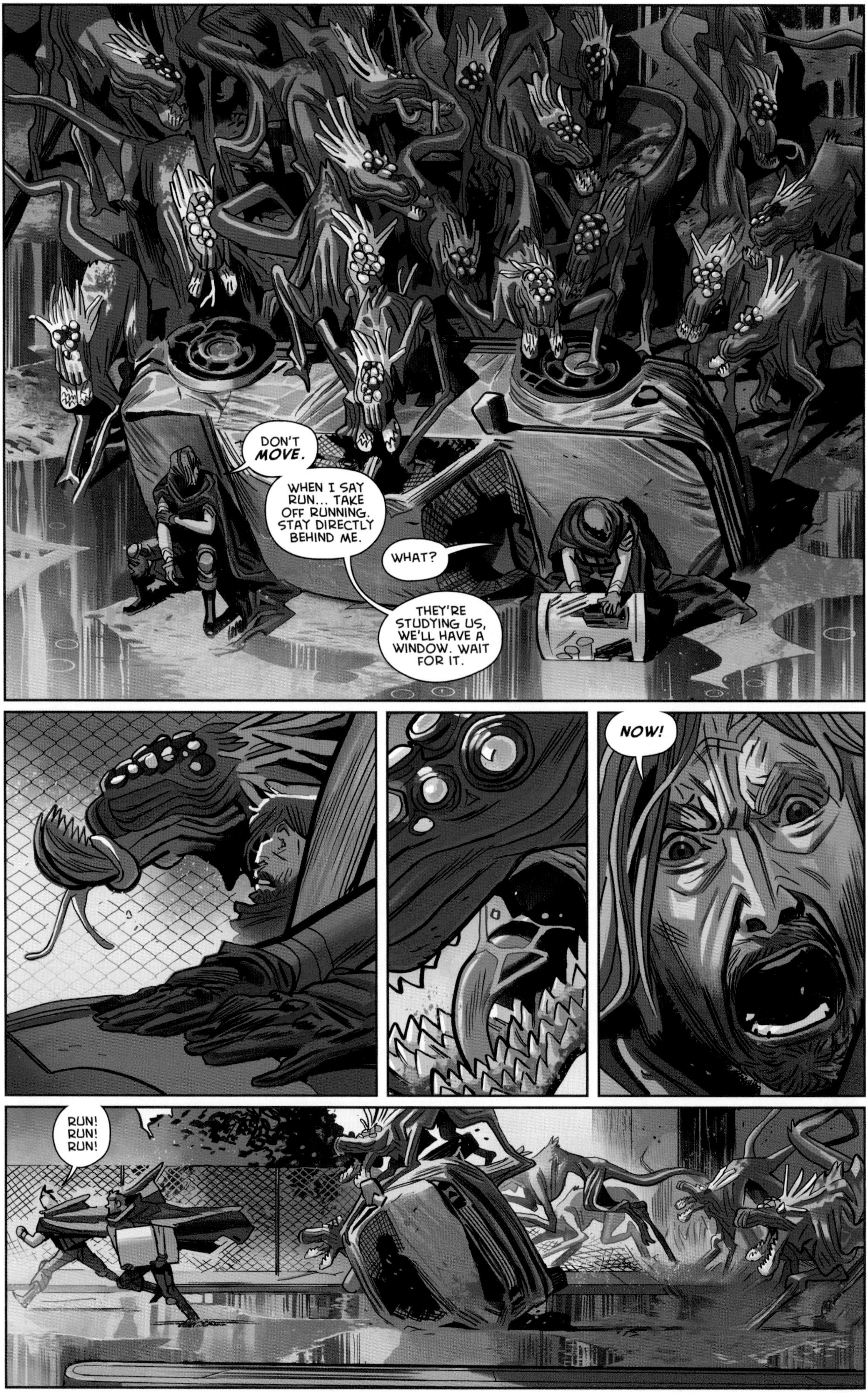
DON'T *MOVE.*
WHEN I SAY RUN... TAKE OFF RUNNING. STAY DIRECTLY BEHIND ME.
WHAT?
THEY'RE STUDYING US, WE'LL HAVE A WINDOW. WAIT FOR IT.
NOW!
RUN! RUN! RUN!

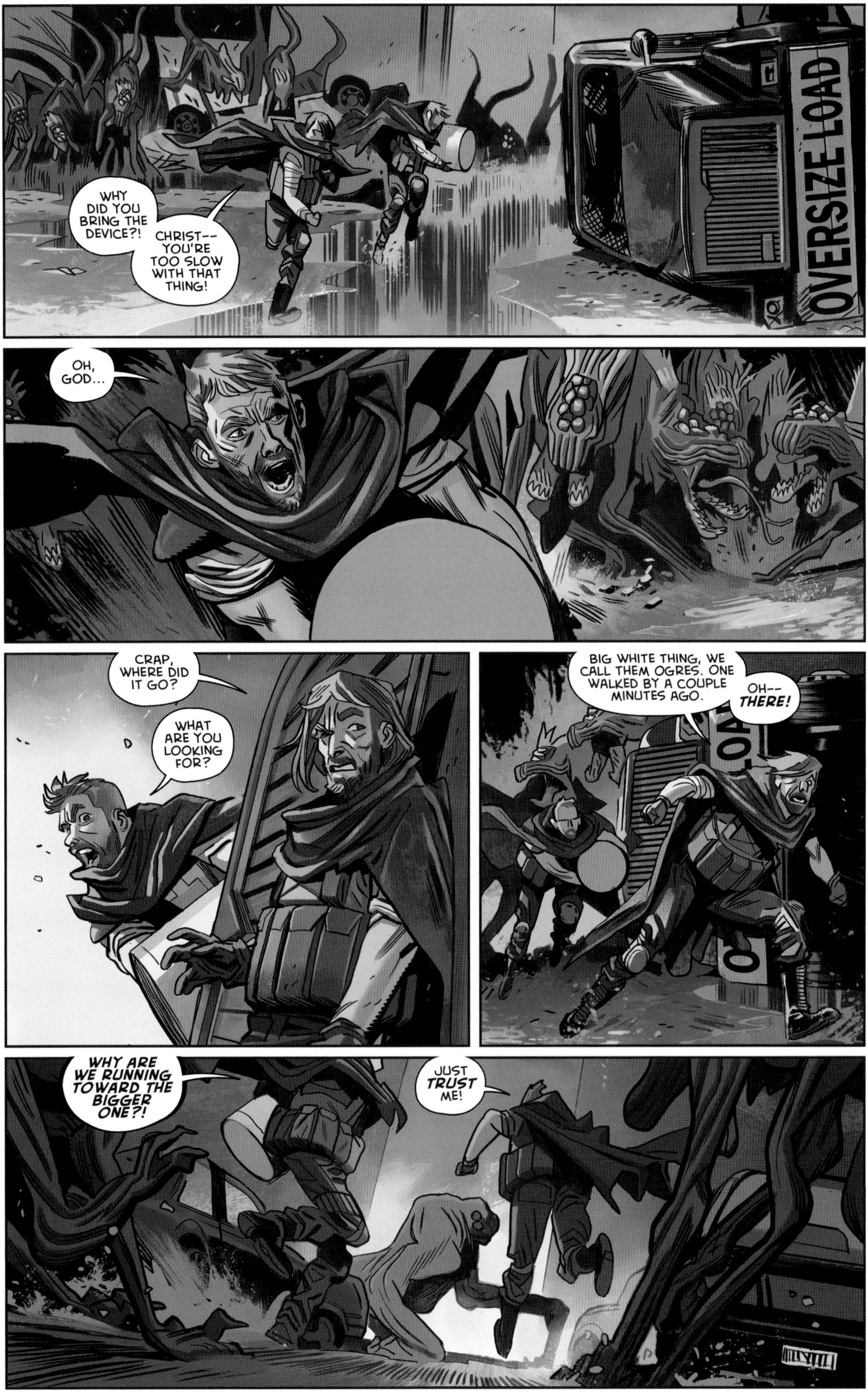
WHY DID YOU BRING THE DEVICE?!
CHRIST-- YOU'RE TOO SLOW WITH THAT THING!
OVERSIZE LOAD
OH, GOD...
CRAP, WHERE DID IT GO?
WHAT ARE YOU LOOKING FOR?
BIG WHITE THING, WE CALL THEM OGRES. ONE WALKED BY A COUPLE MINUTES AGO.
OH-- THERE!
WHY ARE WE RUNNING TOWARD THE BIGGER ONE?!
JUST TRUST ME!

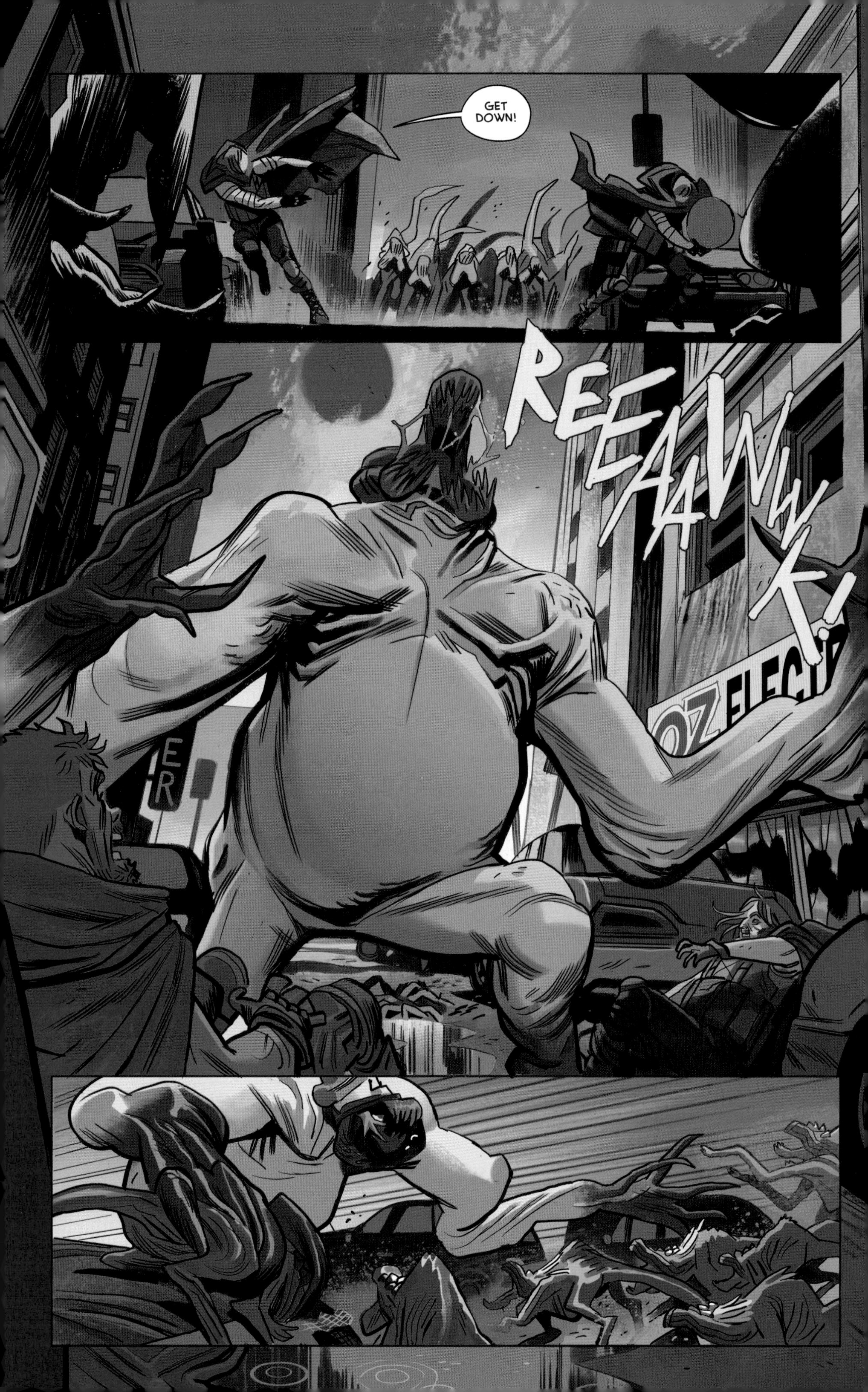
GET DOWN!
REEAAWWK!
OZ ELEC
ER

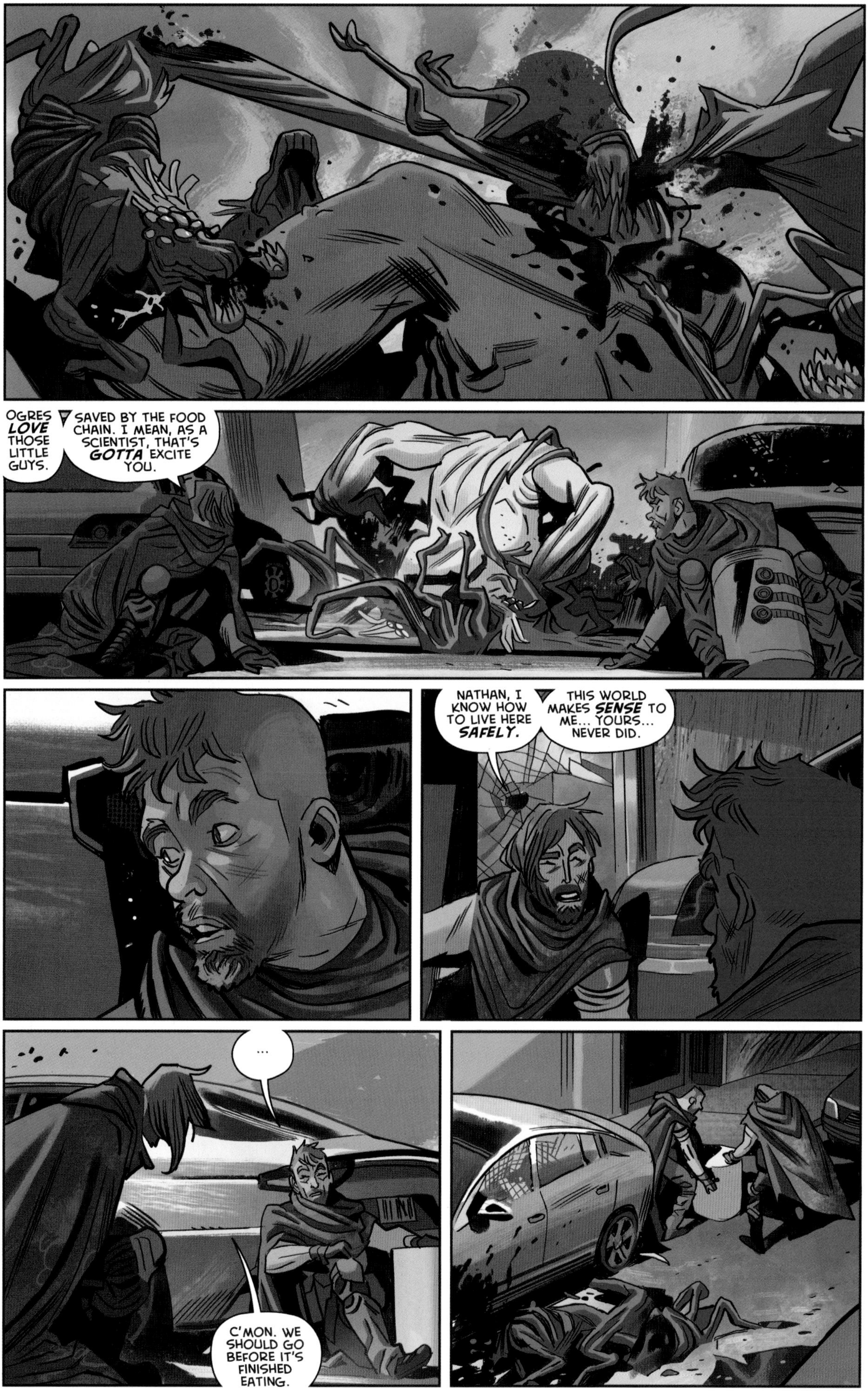
OGRES LOVE THOSE LITTLE GUYS.
SAVED BY THE FOOD CHAIN. I MEAN, AS A SCIENTIST, THAT'S GOTTA EXCITE YOU.
NATHAN, I KNOW HOW TO LIVE HERE SAFELY.
THIS WORLD MAKES SENSE TO ME... YOURS... NEVER DID.
...
C'MON. WE SHOULD GO BEFORE IT'S FINISHED EATING.

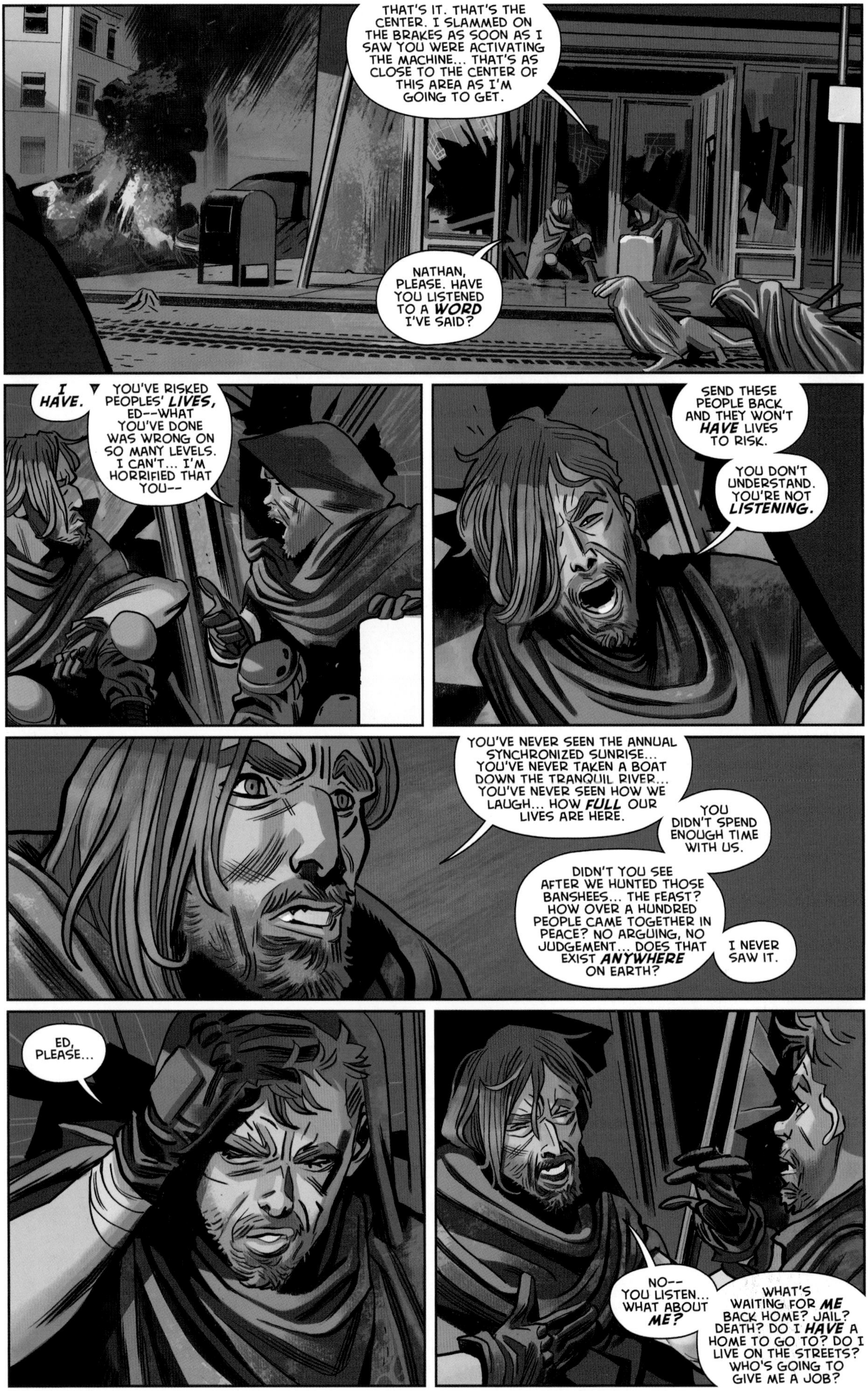
THAT'S IT. THAT'S THE CENTER. I SLAMMED ON THE BRAKES AS SOON AS I SAW YOU WERE ACTIVATING THE MACHINE... THAT'S AS CLOSE TO THE CENTER OF THIS AREA AS I'M GOING TO GET.
NATHAN, PLEASE. HAVE YOU LISTENED TO A *WORD* I'VE SAID?
I HAVE.
YOU'VE RISKED PEOPLES' *LIVES,* ED--WHAT YOU'VE DONE WAS WRONG ON SO MANY LEVELS. I CAN'T... I'M HORRIFIED THAT YOU--
SEND THESE PEOPLE BACK AND THEY WON'T *HAVE* LIVES TO RISK.
YOU DON'T UNDERSTAND. YOU'RE NOT *LISTENING.*
YOU'VE NEVER SEEN THE ANNUAL SYNCHRONIZED SUNRISE... YOU'VE NEVER TAKEN A BOAT DOWN THE TRANQUIL RIVER... YOU'VE NEVER SEEN HOW WE LAUGH... HOW *FULL* OUR LIVES ARE HERE.
YOU DIDN'T SPEND ENOUGH TIME WITH US.
DIDN'T YOU SEE AFTER WE HUNTED THOSE BANSHEES... THE FEAST? HOW OVER A HUNDRED PEOPLE CAME TOGETHER IN PEACE? NO ARGUING, NO JUDGEMENT... DOES THAT EXIST *ANYWHERE* ON EARTH?
I NEVER SAW IT.
ED, PLEASE...
NO--YOU LISTEN... WHAT ABOUT *ME?*
WHAT'S WAITING FOR *ME* BACK HOME? JAIL? DEATH? DO I *HAVE* A HOME TO GO TO? DO I LIVE ON THE STREETS? WHO'S GOING TO GIVE ME A JOB?

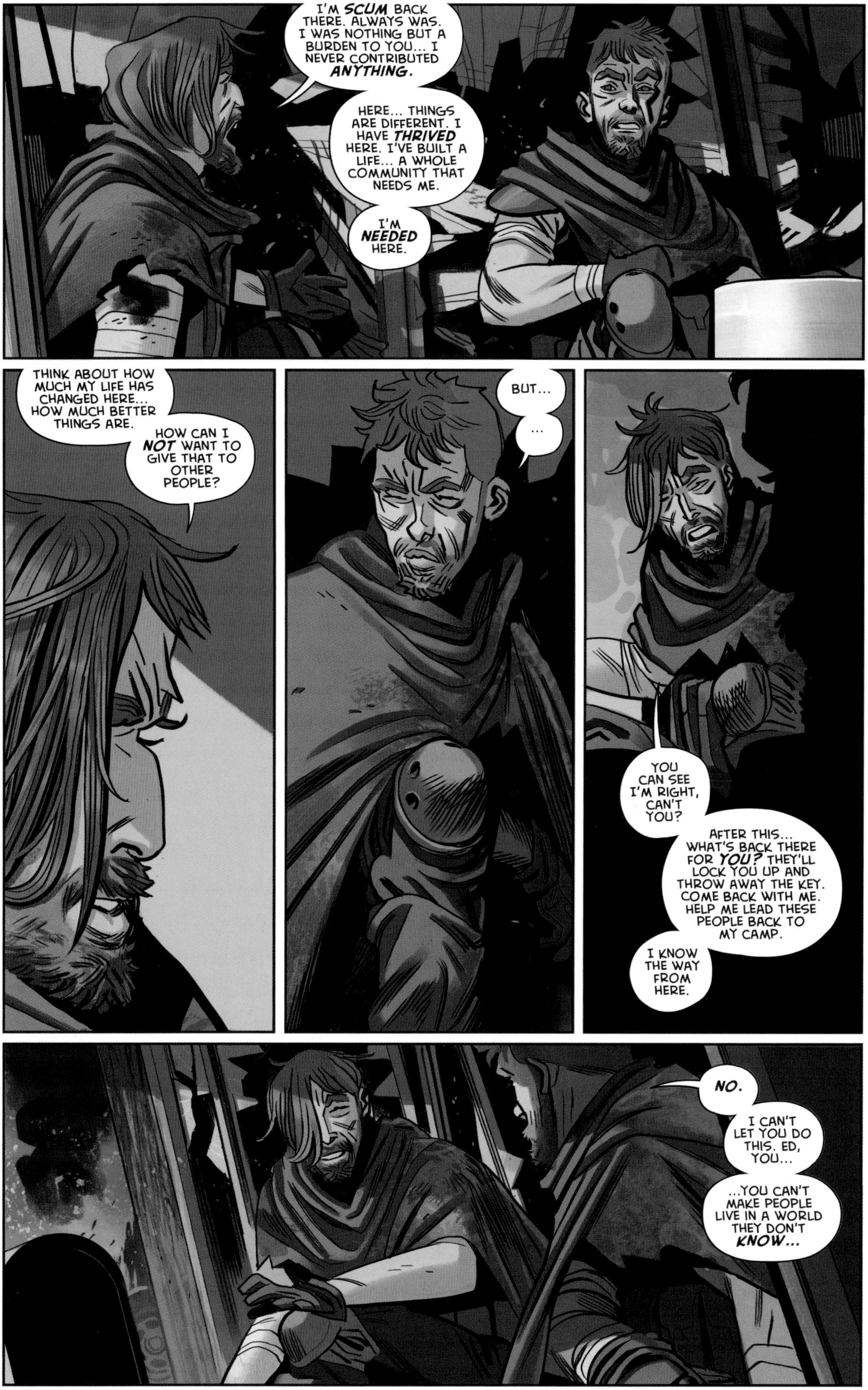
I'M SCUM BACK THERE. ALWAYS WAS. I WAS NOTHING BUT A BURDEN TO YOU... I NEVER CONTRIBUTED ANYTHING.
HERE... THINGS ARE DIFFERENT. I HAVE THRIVED HERE. I'VE BUILT A LIFE... A WHOLE COMMUNITY THAT NEEDS ME.
I'M NEEDED HERE.
THINK ABOUT HOW MUCH MY LIFE HAS CHANGED HERE... HOW MUCH BETTER THINGS ARE.
HOW CAN I NOT WANT TO GIVE THAT TO OTHER PEOPLE?
BUT...
...
YOU CAN SEE I'M RIGHT, CAN'T YOU?
AFTER THIS... WHAT'S BACK THERE FOR YOU? THEY'LL LOCK YOU UP AND THROW AWAY THE KEY. COME BACK WITH ME. HELP ME LEAD THESE PEOPLE BACK TO MY CAMP.
I KNOW THE WAY FROM HERE.
NO.
I CAN'T LET YOU DO THIS. ED, YOU...
...YOU CAN'T MAKE PEOPLE LIVE IN A WORLD THEY DON'T KNOW...

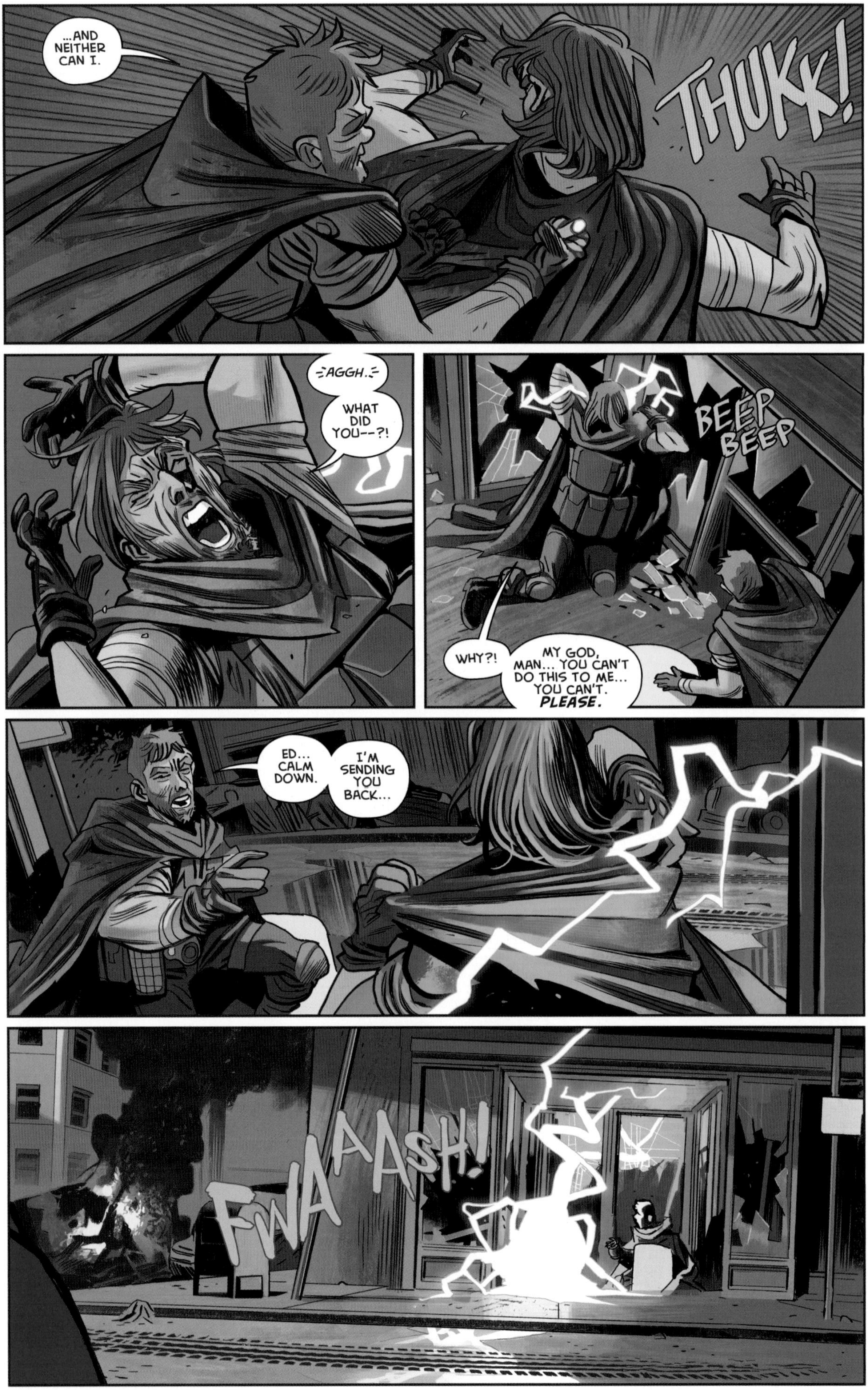
...AND NEITHER CAN I.
THUKK!
AGGH.
WHAT DID YOU--?!
BEEP BEEP
WHY?!
MY GOD, MAN... YOU CAN'T DO THIS TO ME... YOU CAN'T. PLEASE.
ED... CALM DOWN.
I'M SENDING YOU BACK...
FWAAASH!

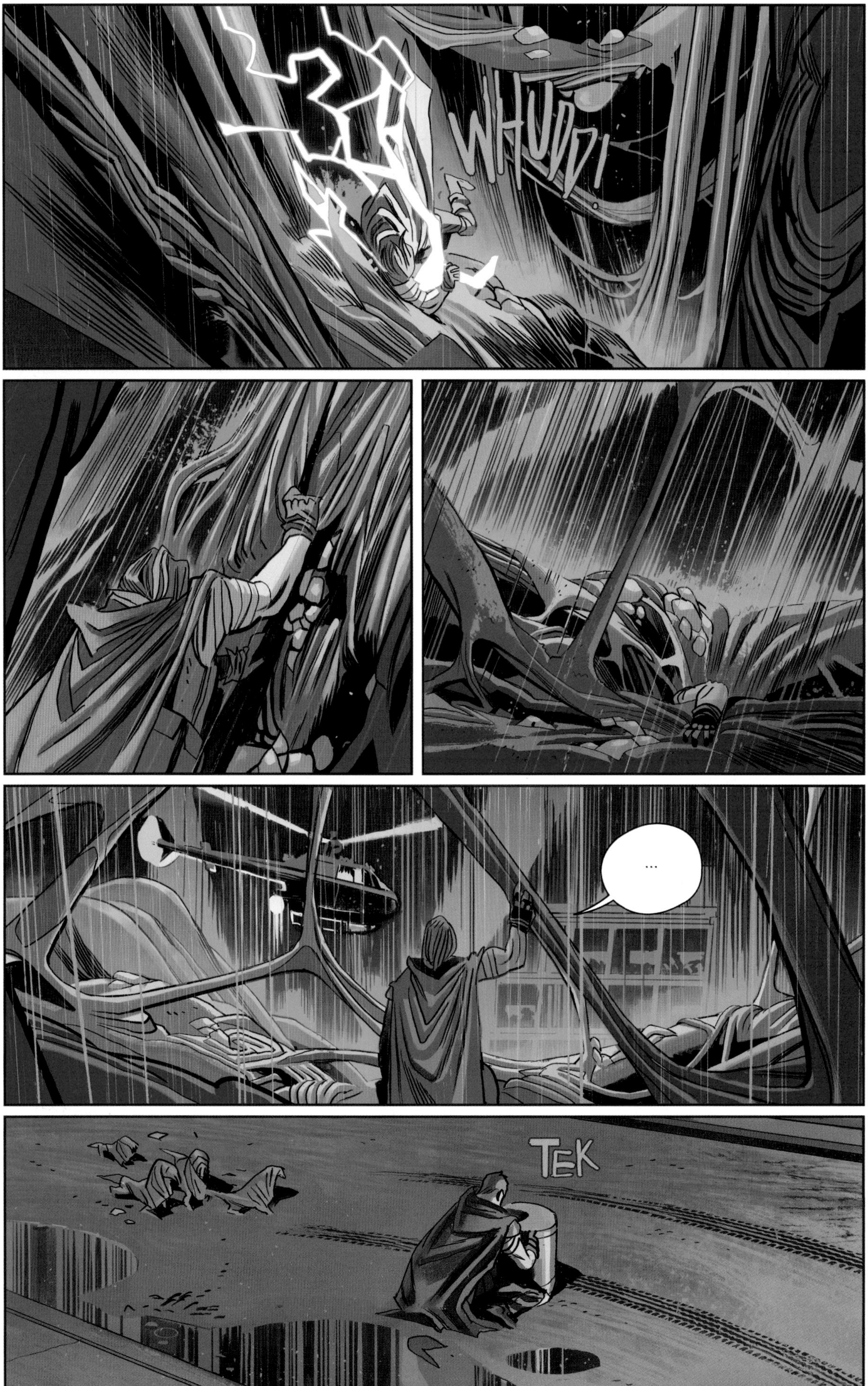
WHUDD!
...
TEK

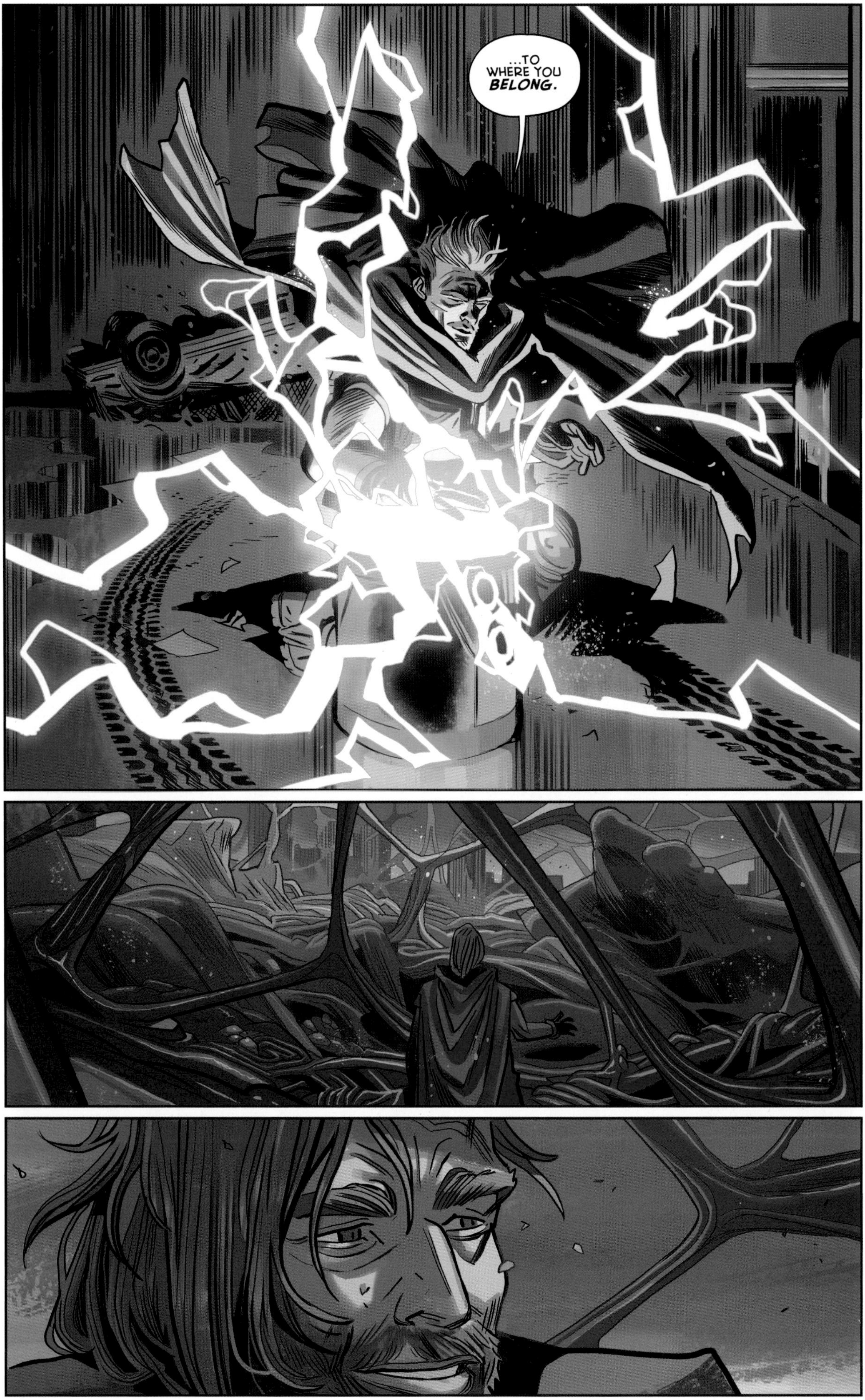
...TO WHERE YOU BELONG.

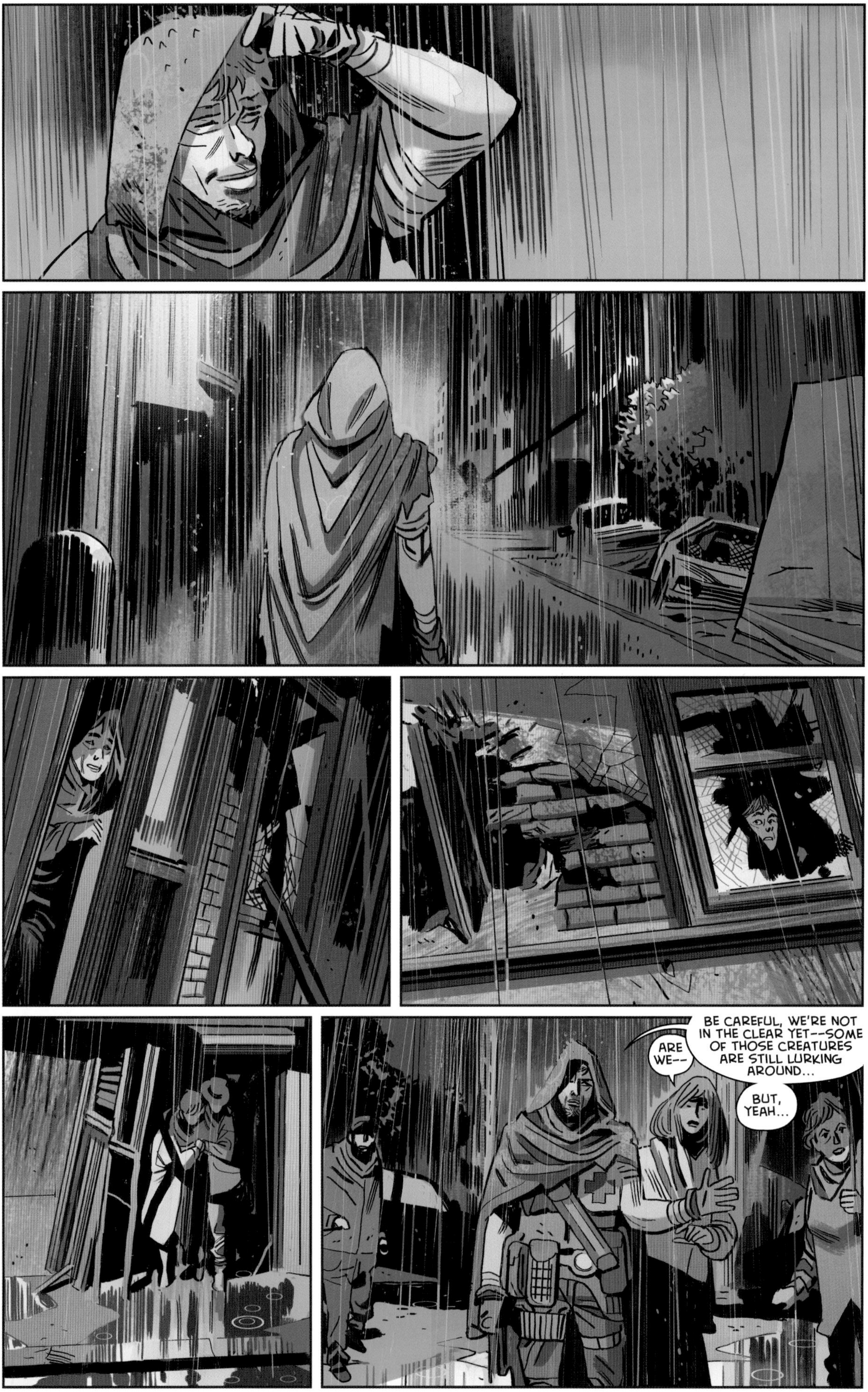
ARE WE--
BE CAREFUL, WE'RE NOT IN THE CLEAR YET--SOME OF THOSE CREATURES ARE STILL LURKING AROUND...
BUT, YEAH...

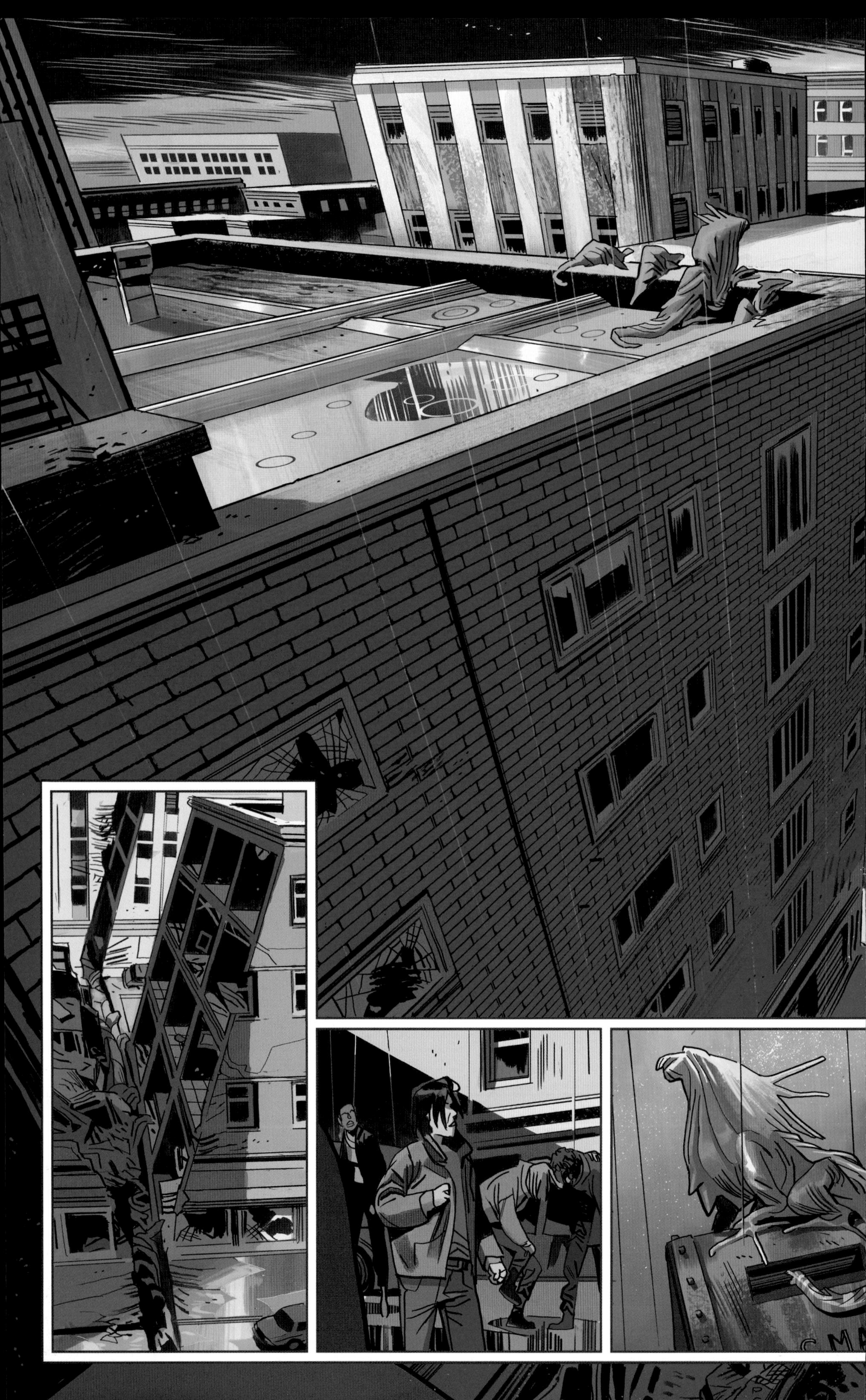

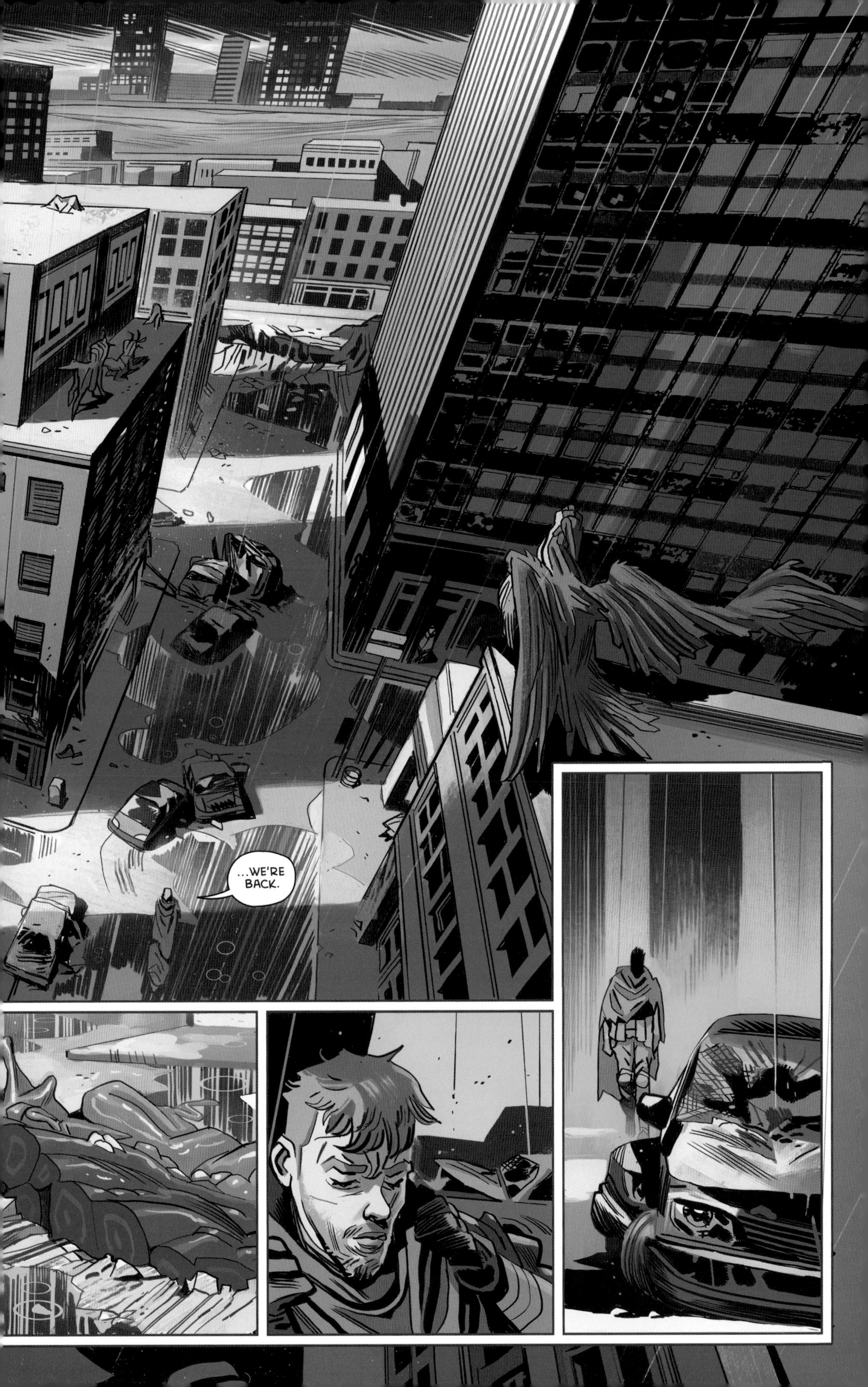
...WE'RE BACK.

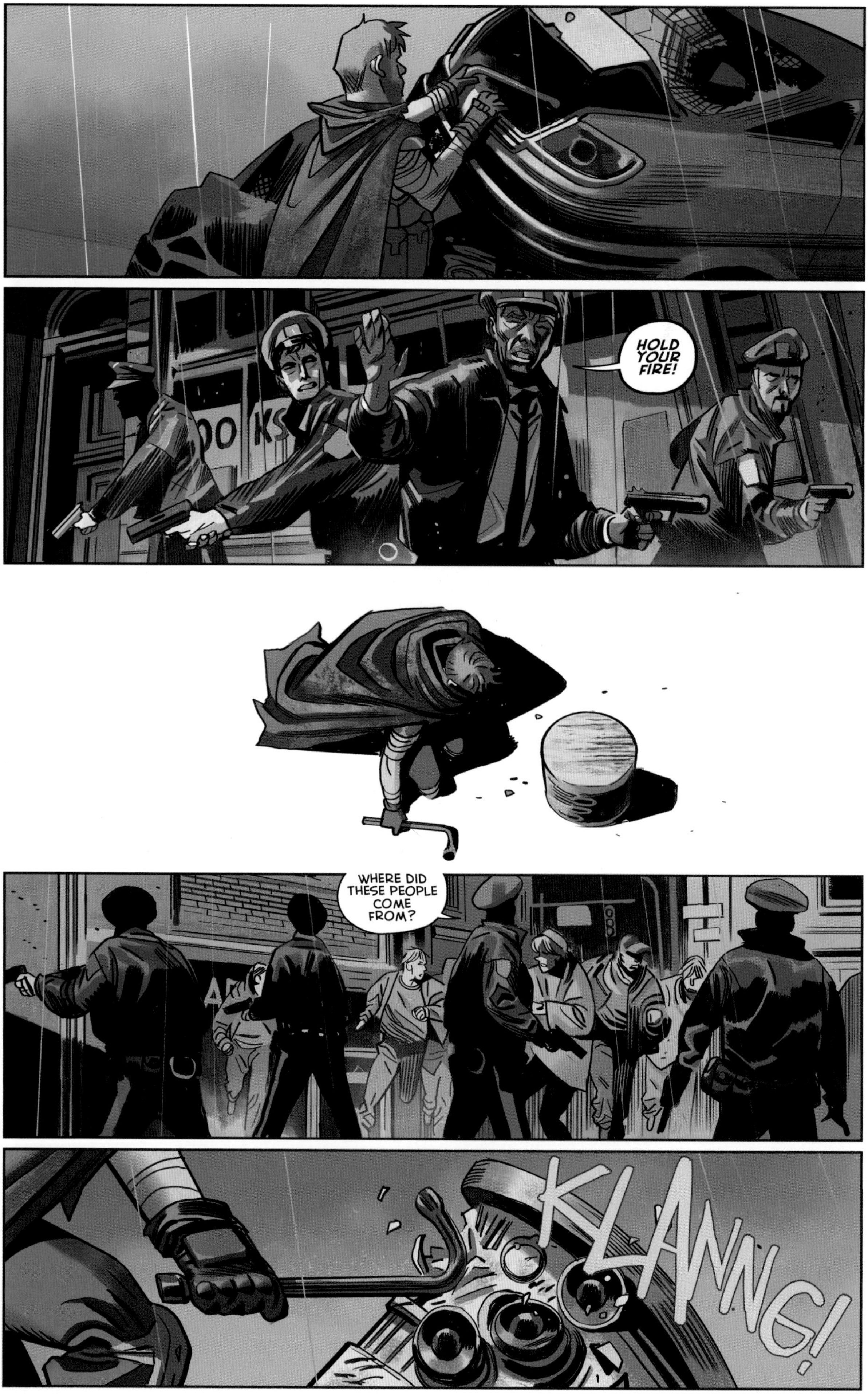
HOLD YOUR FIRE!
WHERE DID THESE PEOPLE COME FROM?
KLANNG!

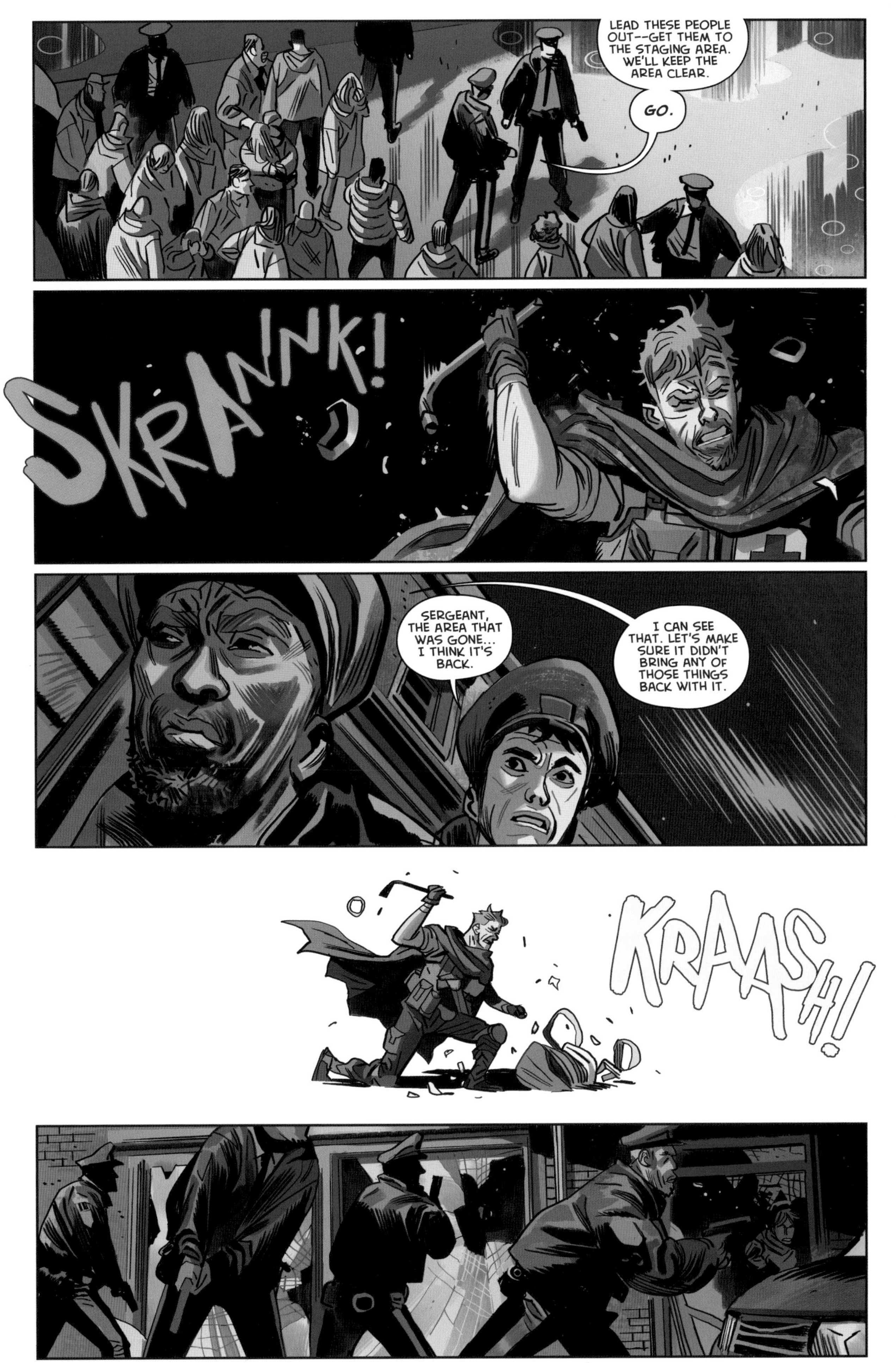
LEAD THESE PEOPLE OUT--GET THEM TO THE STAGING AREA. WE'LL KEEP THE AREA CLEAR.
GO.
SKRANNK!
SERGEANT, THE AREA THAT WAS GONE... I THINK IT'S BACK.
I CAN SEE THAT. LET'S MAKE SURE IT DIDN'T BRING ANY OF THOSE THINGS BACK WITH IT.
KRAASH!

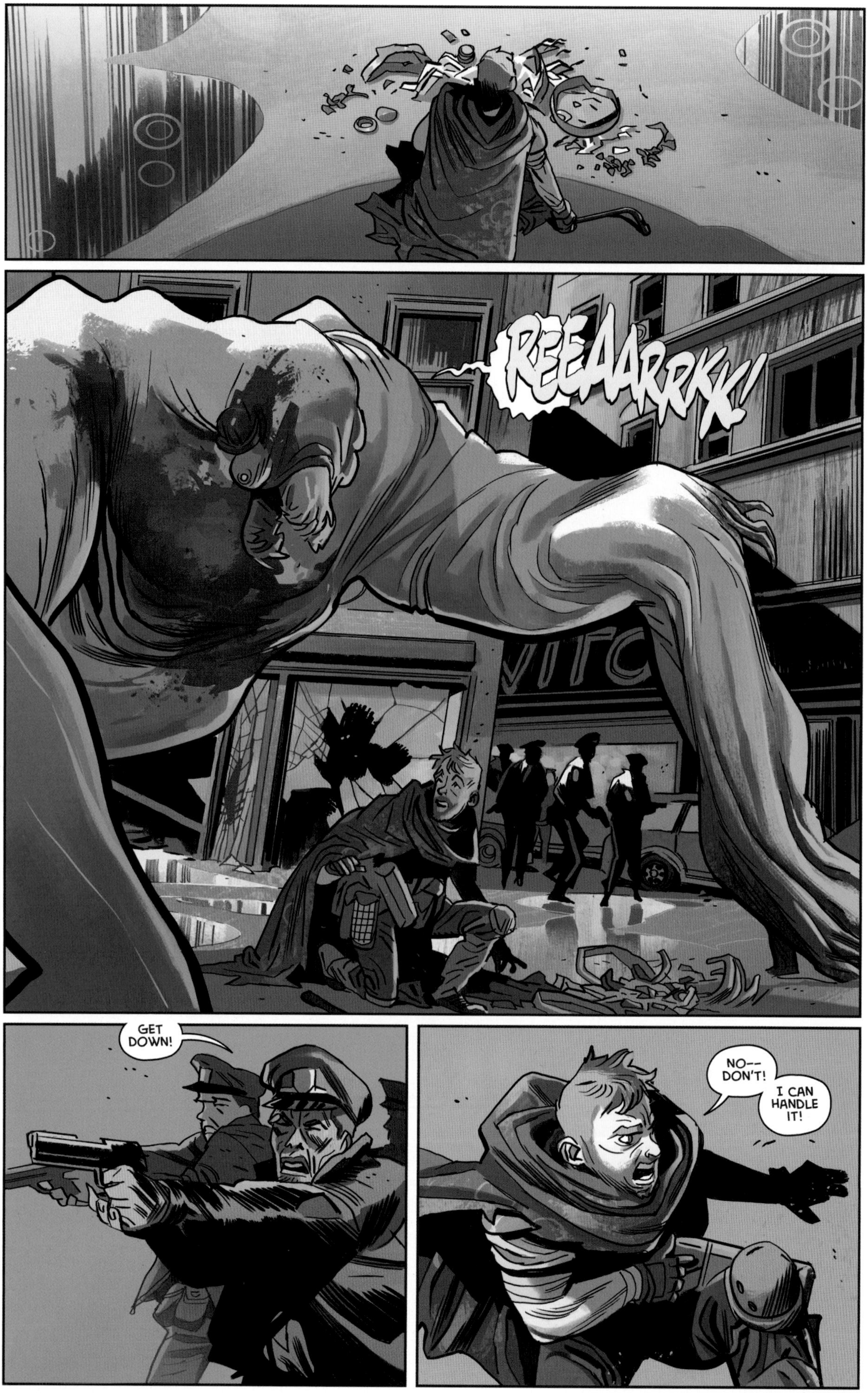
REEAARRKK!
GET DOWN!
NO-- DON'T!
I CAN HANDLE IT!

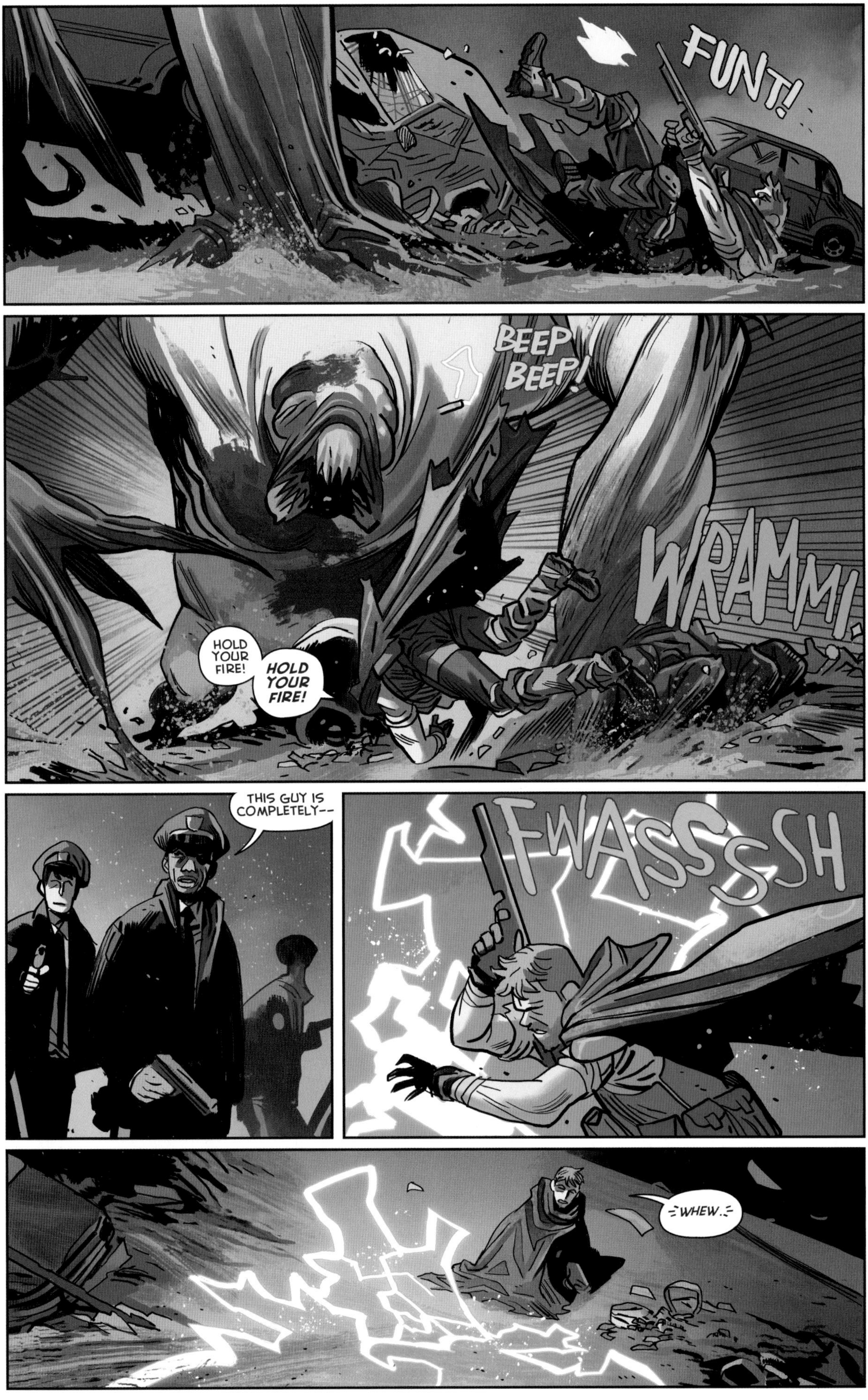
FUNT!
BEEP BEEP!
WRAMM!
HOLD YOUR FIRE!
HOLD YOUR FIRE!
THIS GUY IS COMPLETELY--
FWASSSSH
WHEW.

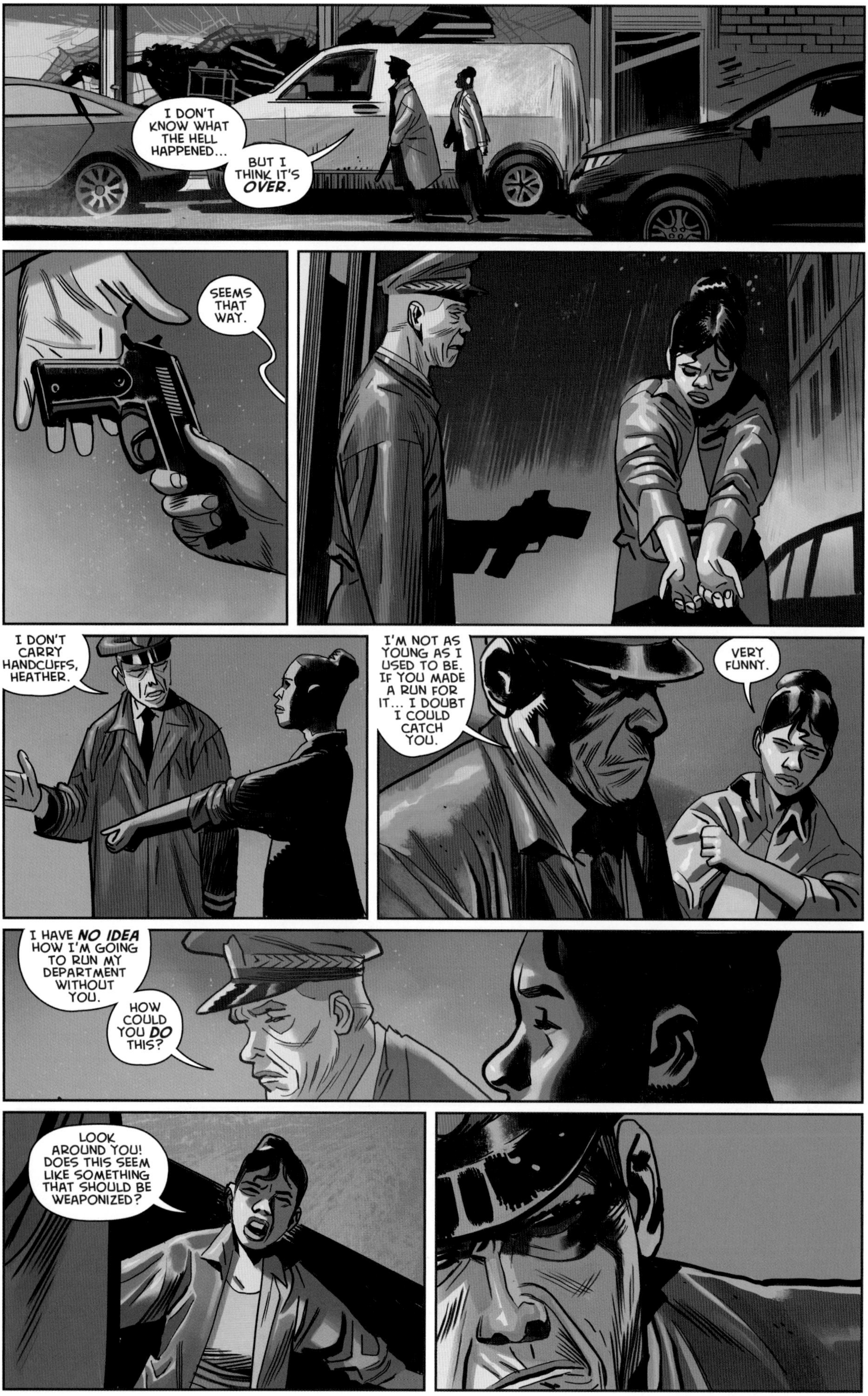
I DON'T KNOW WHAT THE HELL HAPPENED...
BUT I THINK IT'S OVER.
SEEMS THAT WAY.
I DON'T CARRY HANDCUFFS, HEATHER.
I'M NOT AS YOUNG AS I USED TO BE. IF YOU MADE A RUN FOR IT... I DOUBT I COULD CATCH YOU.
VERY FUNNY.
I HAVE NO IDEA HOW I'M GOING TO RUN MY DEPARTMENT WITHOUT YOU.
HOW COULD YOU DO THIS?
LOOK AROUND YOU! DOES THIS SEEM LIKE SOMETHING THAT SHOULD BE WEAPONIZED?

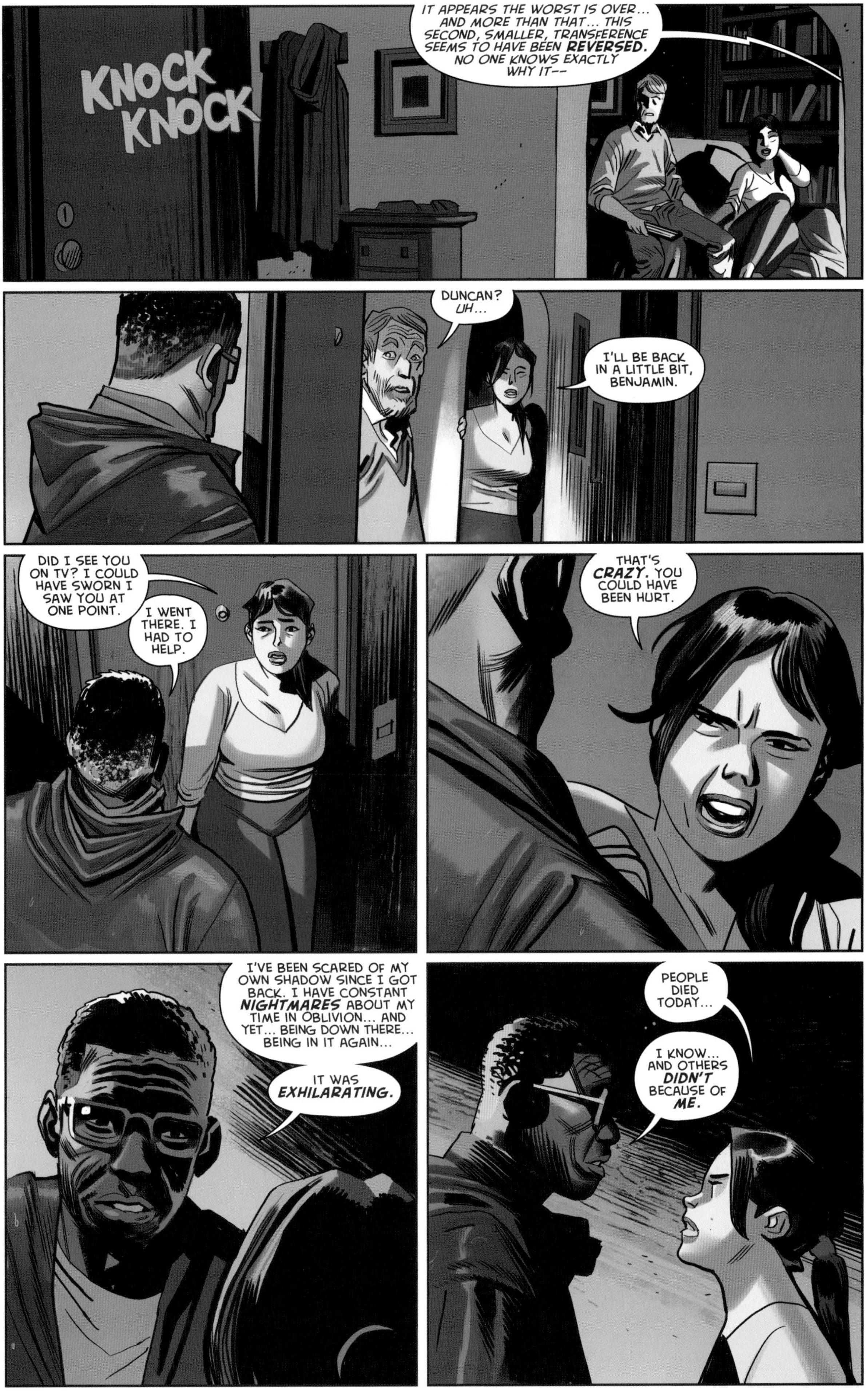
KNOCK KNOCK
IT APPEARS THE WORST IS OVER... AND MORE THAN THAT... THIS SECOND, SMALLER, TRANSFERENCE SEEMS TO HAVE BEEN REVERSED. NO ONE KNOWS EXACTLY WHY IT--
DUNCAN? UH...
I'LL BE BACK IN A LITTLE BIT, BENJAMIN.
DID I SEE YOU ON TV? I COULD HAVE SWORN I SAW YOU AT ONE POINT.
I WENT THERE. I HAD TO HELP.
THAT'S CRAZY. YOU COULD HAVE BEEN HURT.
I'VE BEEN SCARED OF MY OWN SHADOW SINCE I GOT BACK. I HAVE CONSTANT NIGHTMARES ABOUT MY TIME IN OBLIVION... AND YET... BEING DOWN THERE... BEING IN IT AGAIN...
IT WAS EXHILARATING.
PEOPLE DIED TODAY...
I KNOW... AND OTHERS DIDN'T BECAUSE OF ME.

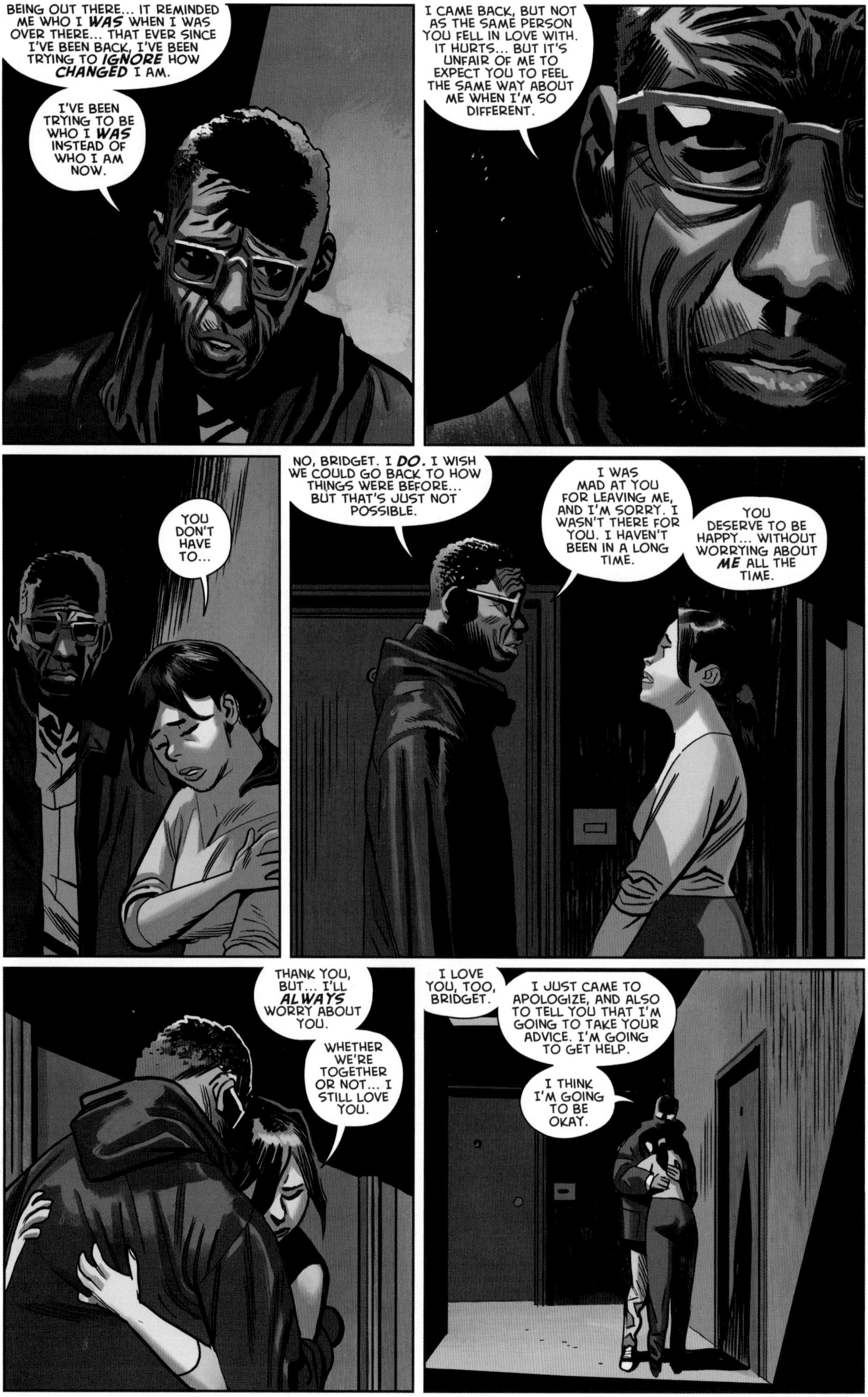
BEING OUT THERE... IT REMINDED ME WHO I WAS WHEN I WAS OVER THERE... THAT EVER SINCE I'VE BEEN BACK, I'VE BEEN TRYING TO IGNORE HOW CHANGED I AM.
I'VE BEEN TRYING TO BE WHO I WAS INSTEAD OF WHO I AM NOW.
I CAME BACK, BUT NOT AS THE SAME PERSON YOU FELL IN LOVE WITH. IT HURTS... BUT IT'S UNFAIR OF ME TO EXPECT YOU TO FEEL THE SAME WAY ABOUT ME WHEN I'M SO DIFFERENT.
YOU DON'T HAVE TO...
NO, BRIDGET. I DO. I WISH WE COULD GO BACK TO HOW THINGS WERE BEFORE... BUT THAT'S JUST NOT POSSIBLE.
I WAS MAD AT YOU FOR LEAVING ME, AND I'M SORRY. I WASN'T THERE FOR YOU. I HAVEN'T BEEN IN A LONG TIME.
YOU DESERVE TO BE HAPPY... WITHOUT WORRYING ABOUT ME ALL THE TIME.
THANK YOU, BUT... I'LL ALWAYS WORRY ABOUT YOU.
WHETHER WE'RE TOGETHER OR NOT... I STILL LOVE YOU.
I LOVE YOU, TOO, BRIDGET.
I JUST CAME TO APOLOGIZE, AND ALSO TO TELL YOU THAT I'M GOING TO TAKE YOUR ADVICE. I'M GOING TO GET HELP.
I THINK I'M GOING TO BE OKAY.

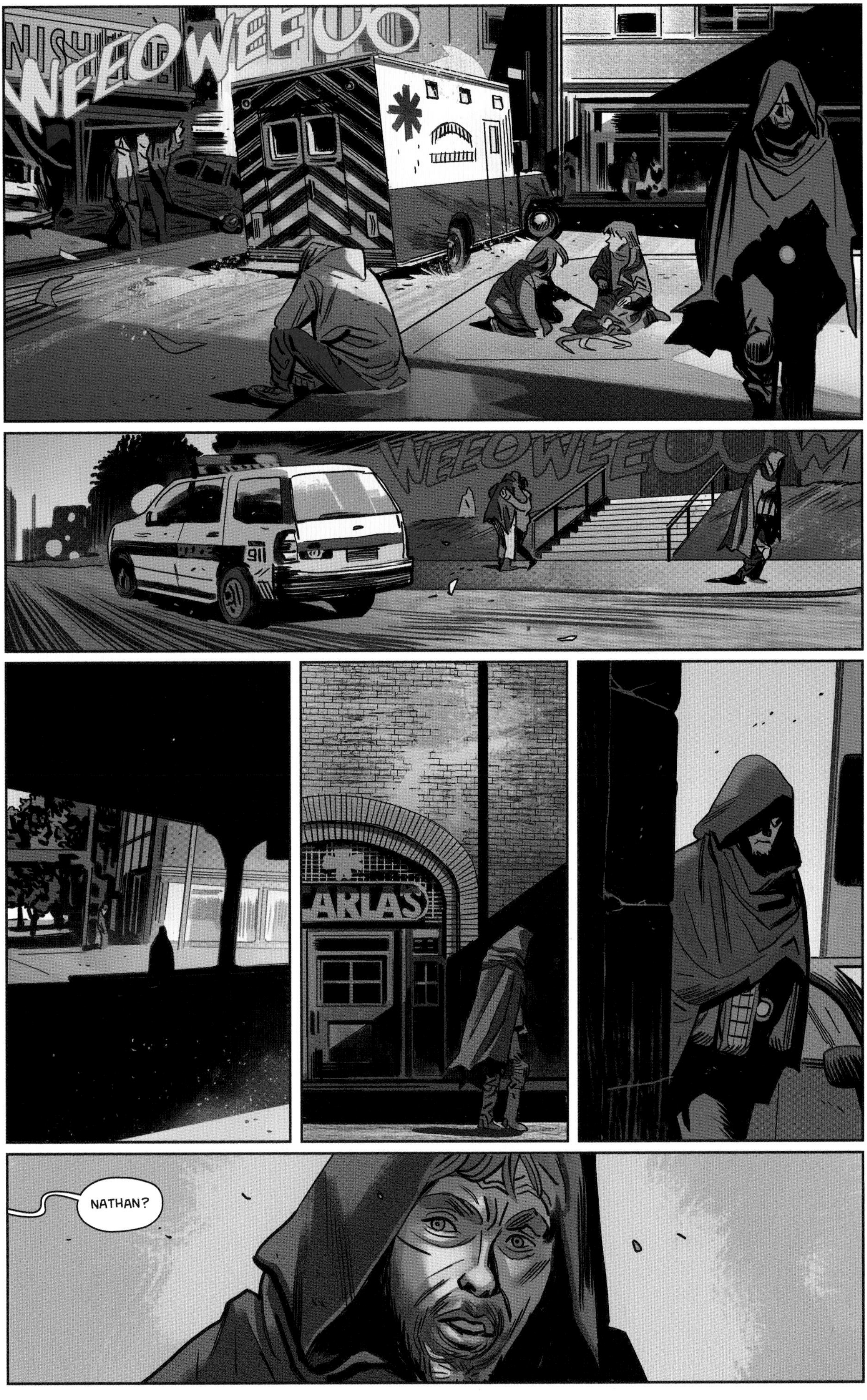
WEEOWEEOO
WEEOWEEOOW
CARLA'S
NATHAN?

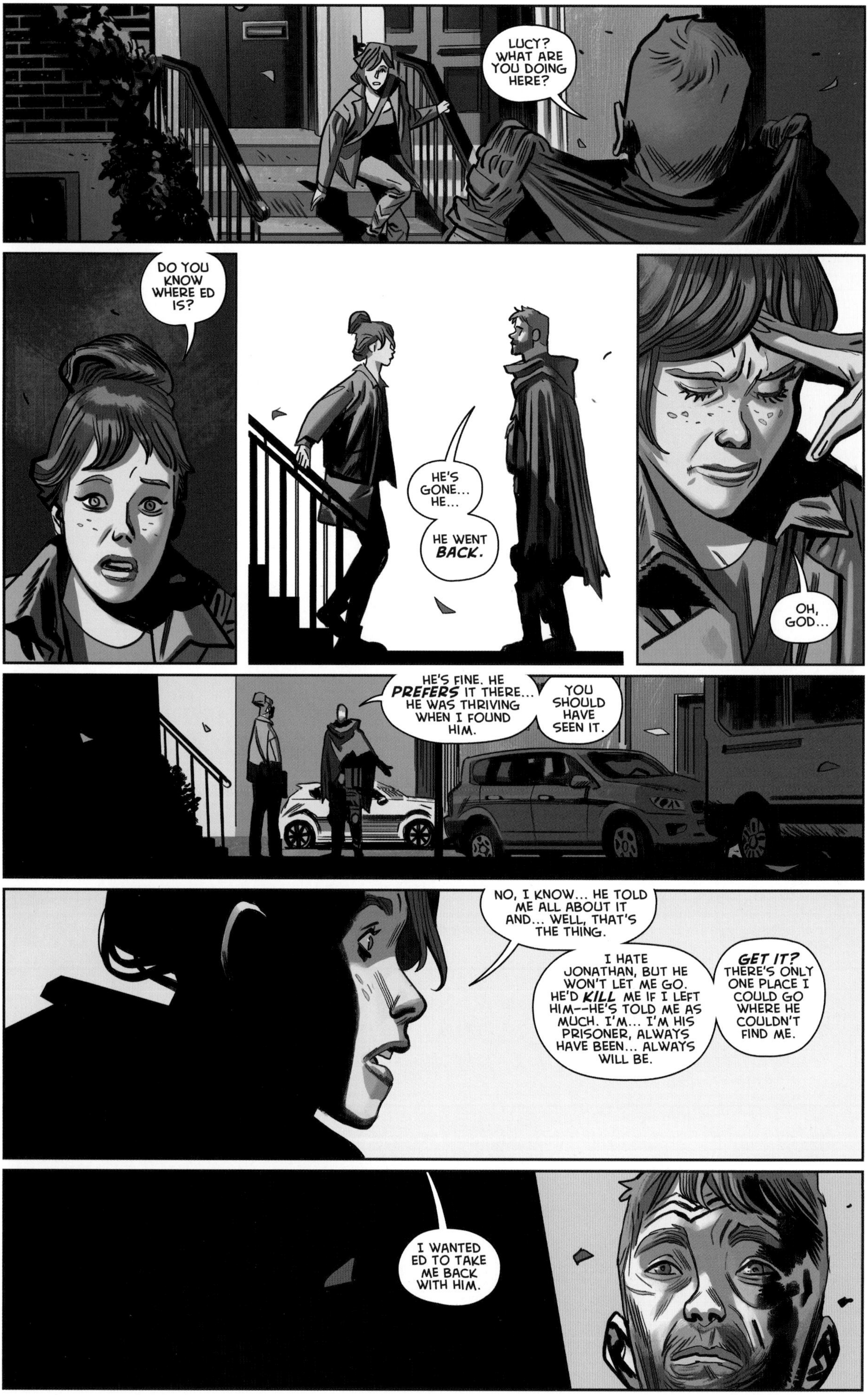
LUCY? WHAT ARE YOU DOING HERE?
DO YOU KNOW WHERE ED IS?
HE'S GONE... HE...
HE WENT *BACK.*
OH, GOD...
HE'S FINE. HE *PREFERS* IT THERE... HE WAS THRIVING WHEN I FOUND HIM.
YOU SHOULD HAVE SEEN IT.
NO, I KNOW... HE TOLD ME ALL ABOUT IT AND... WELL, THAT'S THE THING.
I HATE JONATHAN, BUT HE WON'T LET ME GO. HE'D *KILL* ME IF I LEFT HIM--HE'S TOLD ME AS MUCH. I'M... I'M HIS PRISONER, ALWAYS HAVE BEEN... ALWAYS WILL BE.
GET IT? THERE'S ONLY ONE PLACE I COULD GO WHERE HE COULDN'T FIND ME.
I WANTED ED TO TAKE ME BACK WITH HIM.

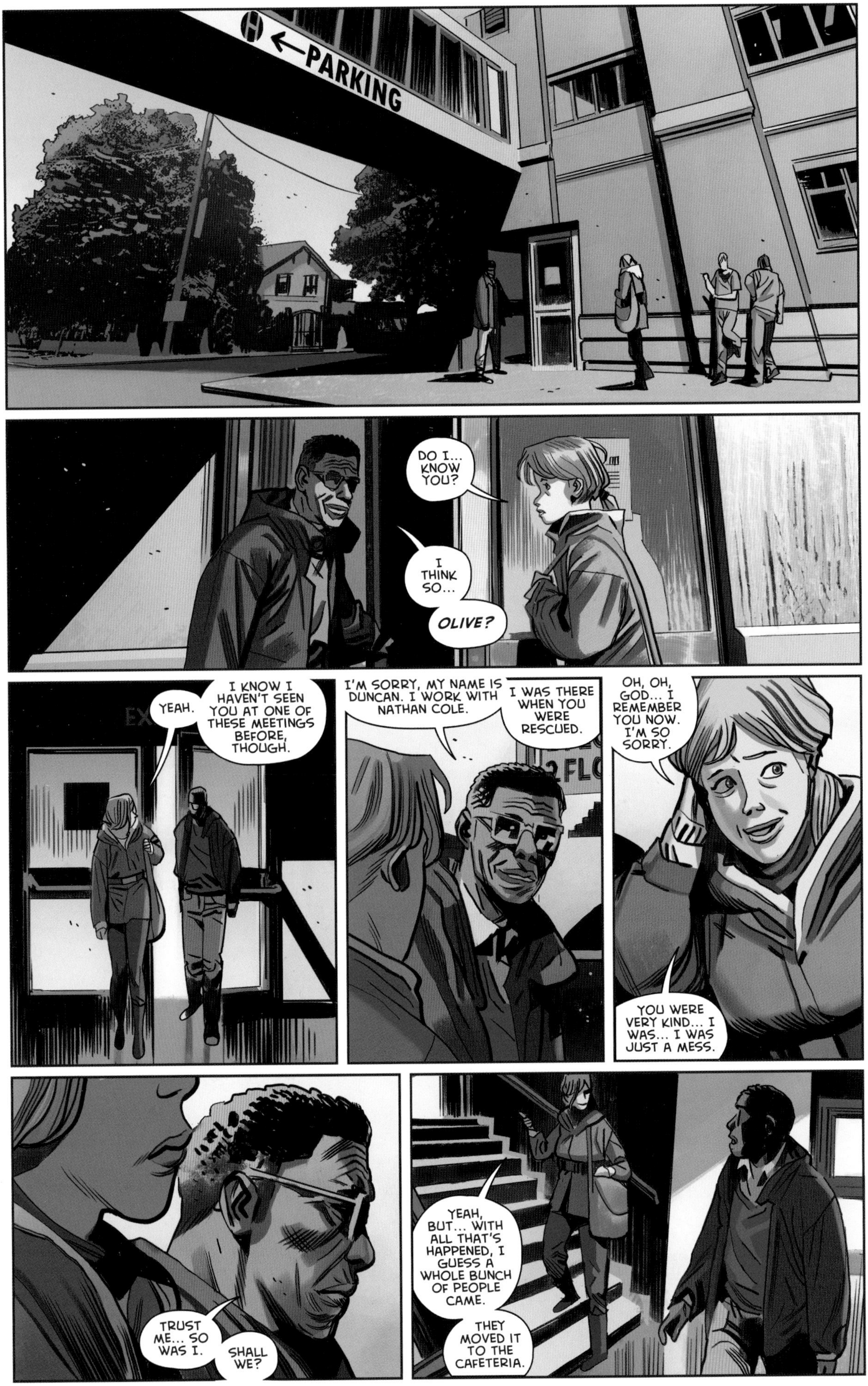
PARKING
DO I... KNOW YOU?
I THINK SO...
OLIVE?
YEAH.
I KNOW I HAVEN'T SEEN YOU AT ONE OF THESE MEETINGS BEFORE, THOUGH.
I'M SORRY, MY NAME IS DUNCAN. I WORK WITH NATHAN COLE.
I WAS THERE WHEN YOU WERE RESCUED.
OH, OH, GOD... I REMEMBER YOU NOW. I'M SO SORRY.
YOU WERE VERY KIND... I WAS... I WAS JUST A MESS.
TRUST ME... SO WAS I.
SHALL WE?
YEAH, BUT... WITH ALL THAT'S HAPPENED, I GUESS A WHOLE BUNCH OF PEOPLE CAME.
THEY MOVED IT TO THE CAFETERIA.

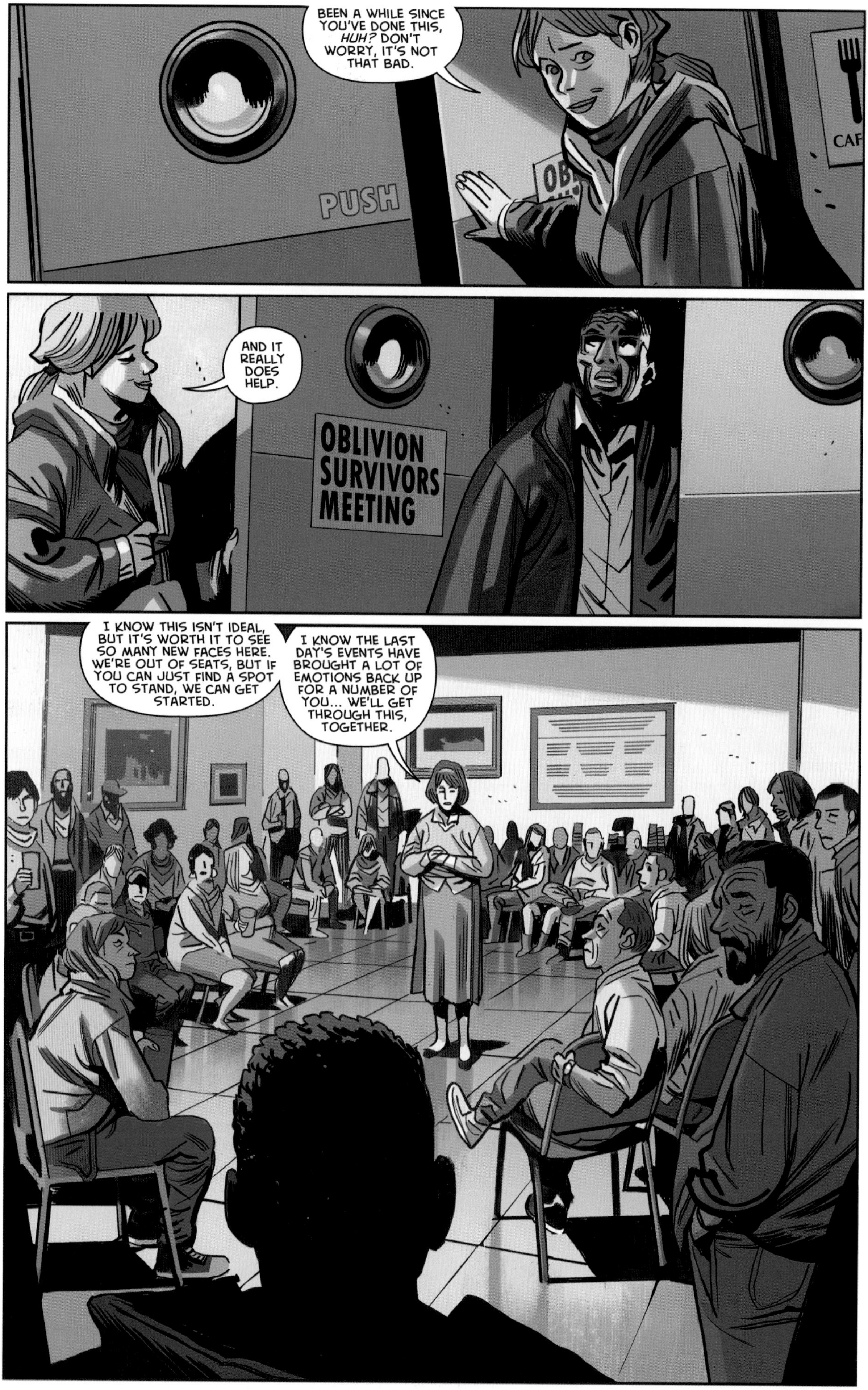
BEEN A WHILE SINCE YOU'VE DONE THIS, *HUH?* DON'T WORRY, IT'S NOT THAT BAD.
PUSH
CAF
AND IT REALLY DOES HELP.
OBLIVION SURVIVORS MEETING
I KNOW THIS ISN'T IDEAL, BUT IT'S WORTH IT TO SEE SO MANY NEW FACES HERE. WE'RE OUT OF SEATS, BUT IF YOU CAN JUST FIND A SPOT TO STAND, WE CAN GET STARTED.
I KNOW THE LAST DAY'S EVENTS HAVE BROUGHT A LOT OF EMOTIONS BACK UP FOR A NUMBER OF YOU... WE'LL GET THROUGH THIS, TOGETHER.

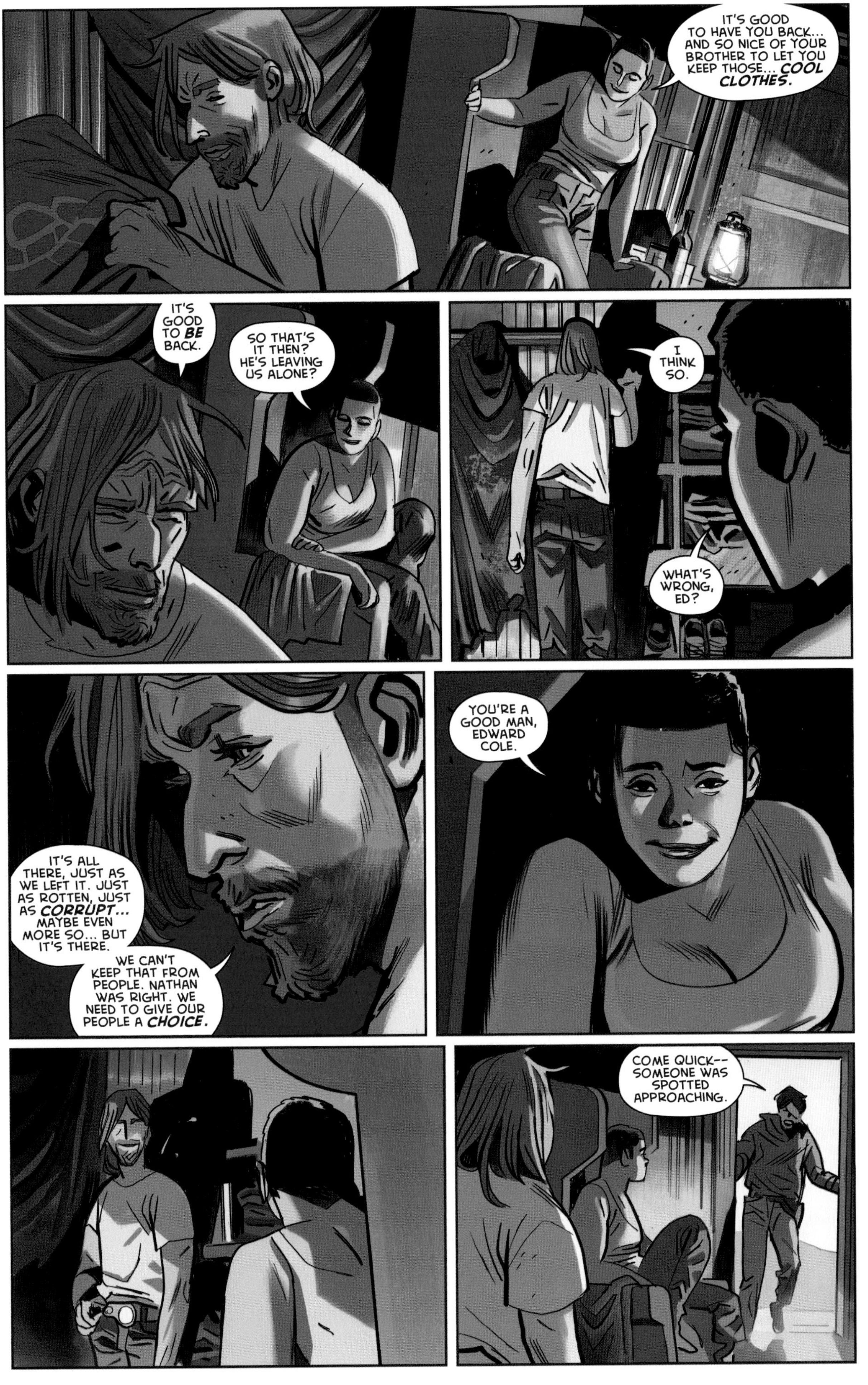

IT'S GOOD TO HAVE YOU BACK... AND SO NICE OF YOUR BROTHER TO LET YOU KEEP THOSE... COOL CLOTHES.
IT'S GOOD TO BE BACK.
SO THAT'S IT THEN? HE'S LEAVING US ALONE?
I THINK SO.
WHAT'S WRONG, ED?
IT'S ALL THERE, JUST AS WE LEFT IT. JUST AS ROTTEN, JUST AS CORRUPT... MAYBE EVEN MORE SO... BUT IT'S THERE.
WE CAN'T KEEP THAT FROM PEOPLE. NATHAN WAS RIGHT. WE NEED TO GIVE OUR PEOPLE A CHOICE.
YOU'RE A GOOD MAN, EDWARD COLE.
COME QUICK-- SOMEONE WAS SPOTTED APPROACHING.

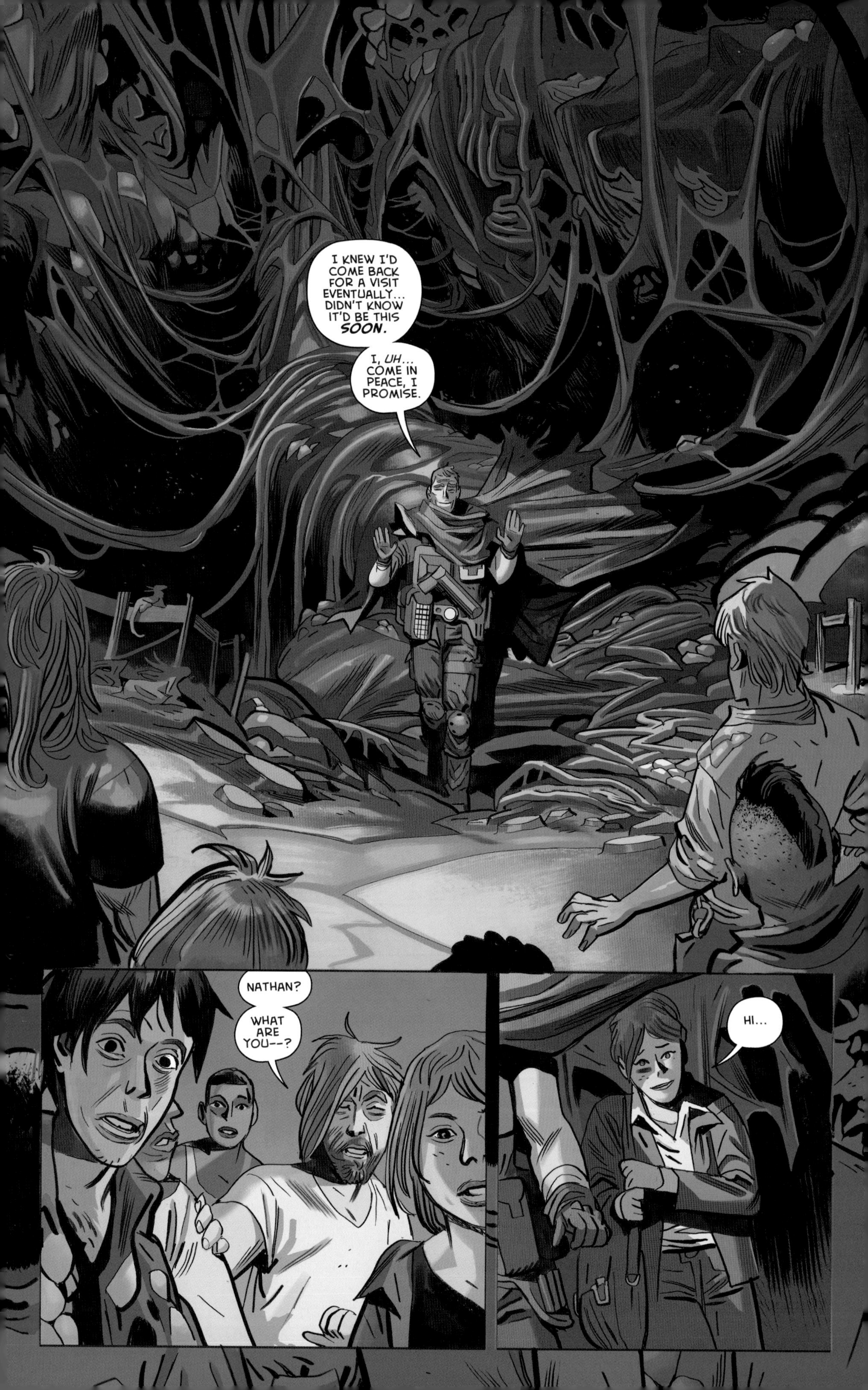
I KNEW I'D COME BACK FOR A VISIT EVENTUALLY... DIDN'T KNOW IT'D BE THIS SOON.
I, UH... COME IN PEACE, I PROMISE.
NATHAN?
WHAT ARE YOU--?
HI...

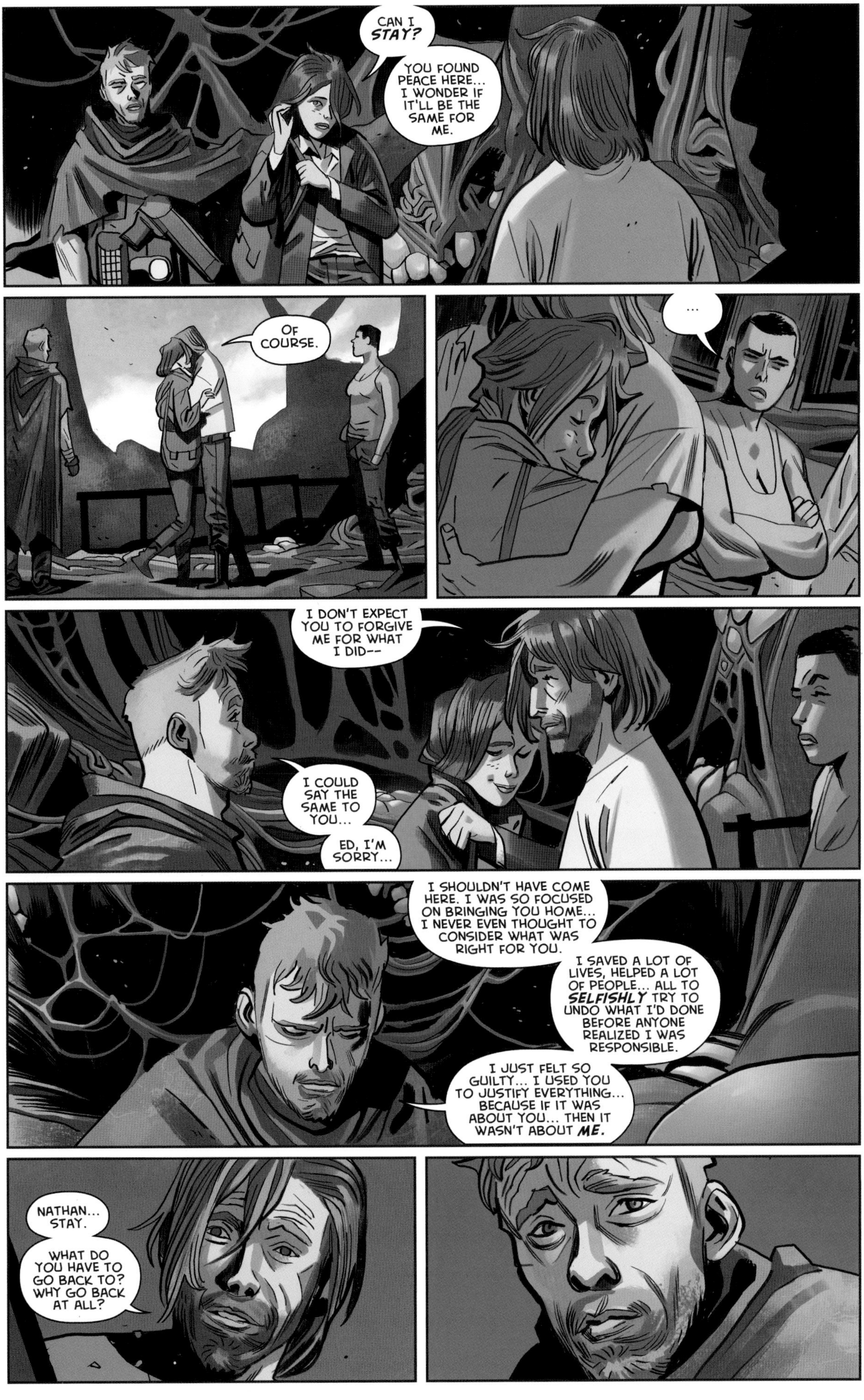
CAN I STAY?
YOU FOUND PEACE HERE... I WONDER IF IT'LL BE THE SAME FOR ME.
OF COURSE.
...
I DON'T EXPECT YOU TO FORGIVE ME FOR WHAT I DID--
I COULD SAY THE SAME TO YOU...
ED, I'M SORRY...
I SHOULDN'T HAVE COME HERE. I WAS SO FOCUSED ON BRINGING YOU HOME... I NEVER EVEN THOUGHT TO CONSIDER WHAT WAS RIGHT FOR YOU.
I SAVED A LOT OF LIVES, HELPED A LOT OF PEOPLE... ALL TO SELFISHLY TRY TO UNDO WHAT I'D DONE BEFORE ANYONE REALIZED I WAS RESPONSIBLE.
I JUST FELT SO GUILTY... I USED YOU TO JUSTIFY EVERYTHING... BECAUSE IF IT WAS ABOUT YOU... THEN IT WASN'T ABOUT ME.
NATHAN... STAY.
WHAT DO YOU HAVE TO GO BACK TO? WHY GO BACK AT ALL?

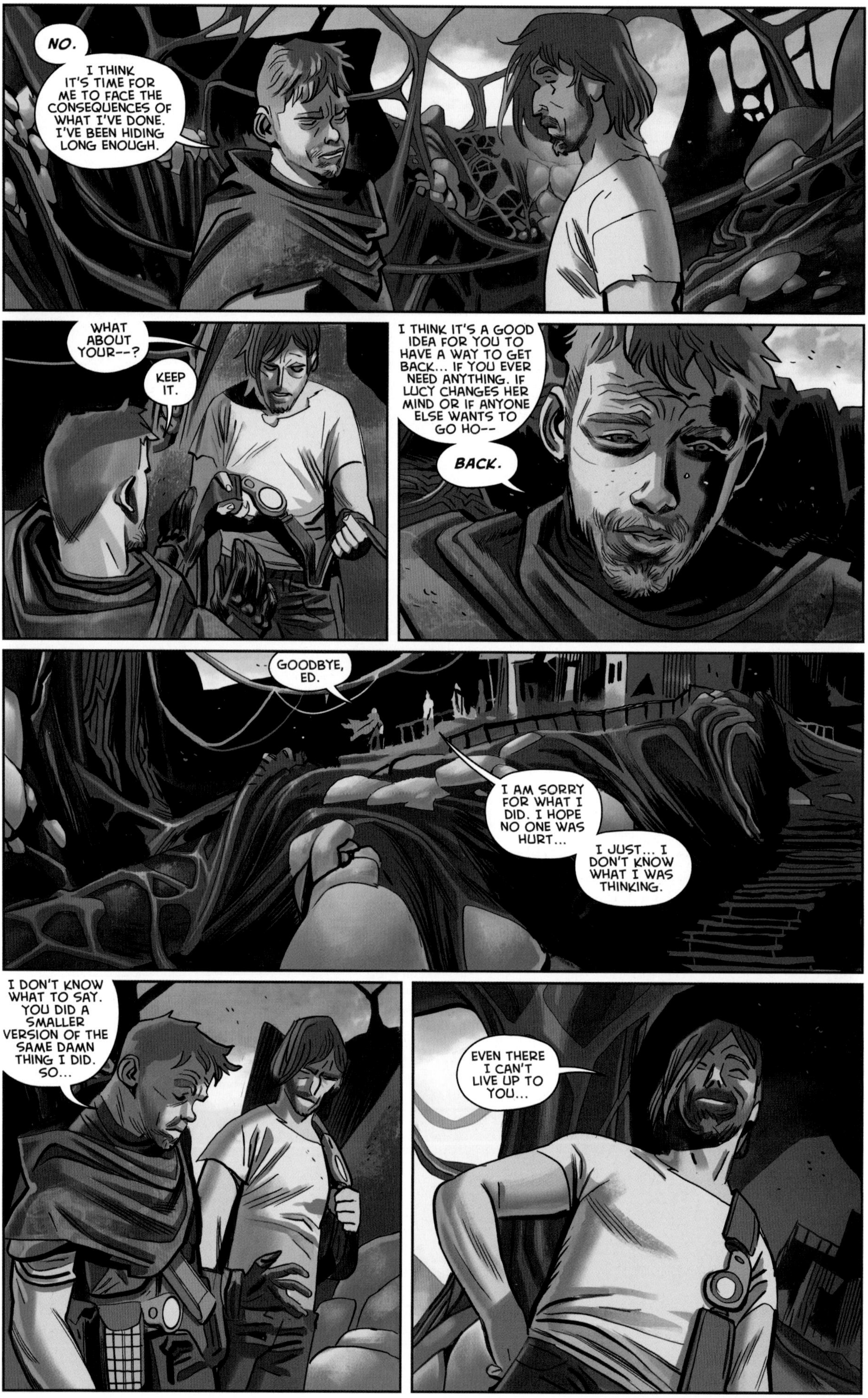
NO.
I THINK IT'S TIME FOR ME TO FACE THE CONSEQUENCES OF WHAT I'VE DONE. I'VE BEEN HIDING LONG ENOUGH.
WHAT ABOUT YOUR--?
KEEP IT.
I THINK IT'S A GOOD IDEA FOR YOU TO HAVE A WAY TO GET BACK... IF YOU EVER NEED ANYTHING. IF LUCY CHANGES HER MIND OR IF ANYONE ELSE WANTS TO GO HO--
BACK.
GOODBYE, ED.
I AM SORRY FOR WHAT I DID. I HOPE NO ONE WAS HURT...
I JUST... I DON'T KNOW WHAT I WAS THINKING.
I DON'T KNOW WHAT TO SAY. YOU DID A SMALLER VERSION OF THE SAME DAMN THING I DID. SO...
EVEN THERE I CAN'T LIVE UP TO YOU...

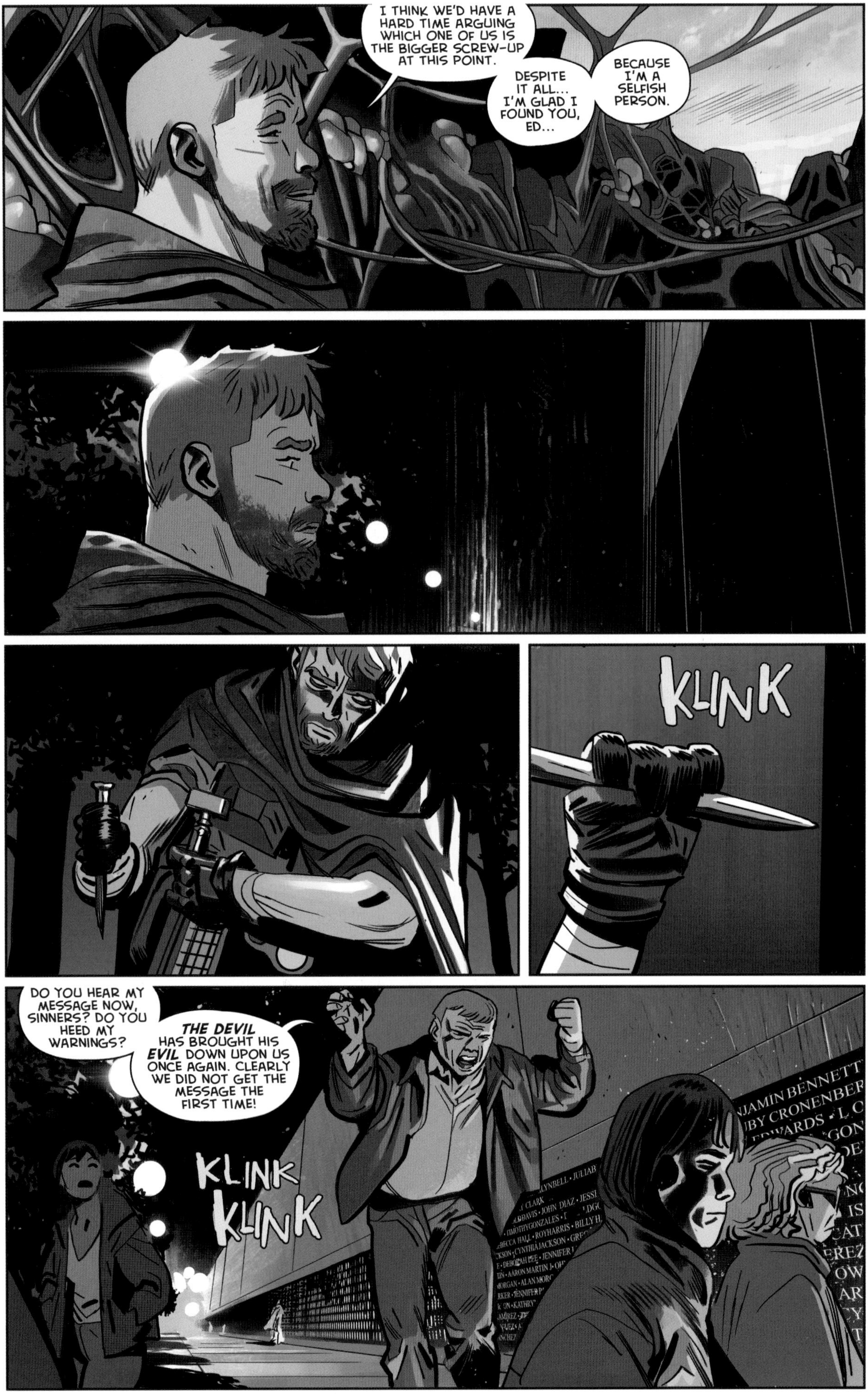
I THINK WE'D HAVE A HARD TIME ARGUING WHICH ONE OF US IS THE BIGGER SCREW-UP AT THIS POINT.
DESPITE IT ALL... I'M GLAD I FOUND YOU, ED...
BECAUSE I'M A SELFISH PERSON.
KLINK
DO YOU HEAR MY MESSAGE NOW, SINNERS? DO YOU HEED MY WARNINGS?
THE DEVIL HAS BROUGHT HIS EVIL DOWN UPON US ONCE AGAIN. CLEARLY WE DID NOT GET THE MESSAGE THE FIRST TIME!
KLINK KLINK

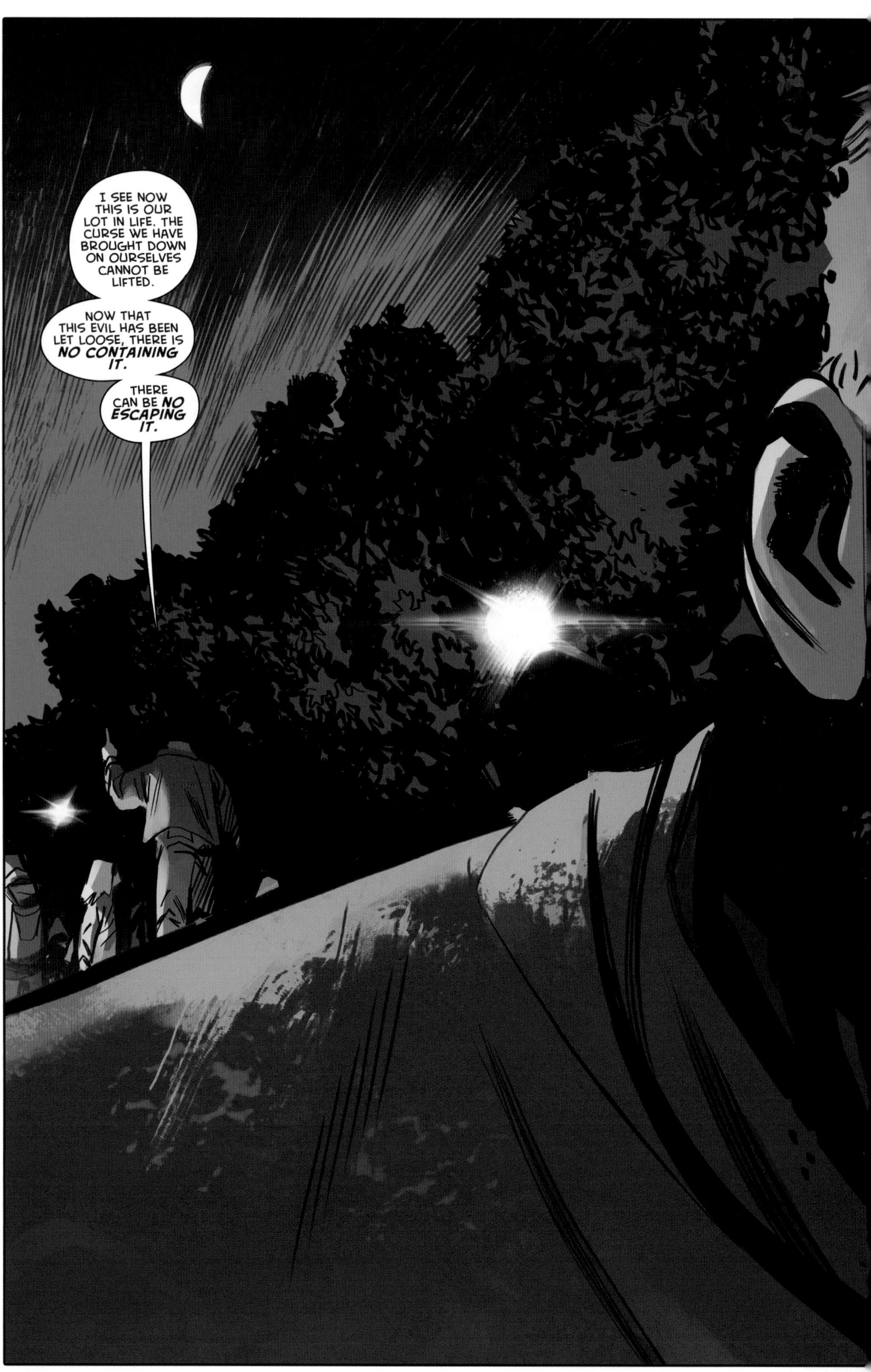
I SEE NOW THIS IS OUR LOT IN LIFE. THE CURSE WE HAVE BROUGHT DOWN ON OURSELVES CANNOT BE LIFTED.
NOW THAT THIS EVIL HAS BEEN LET LOOSE, THERE IS *NO CONTAINING IT.*
THERE CAN BE *NO ESCAPING IT.*

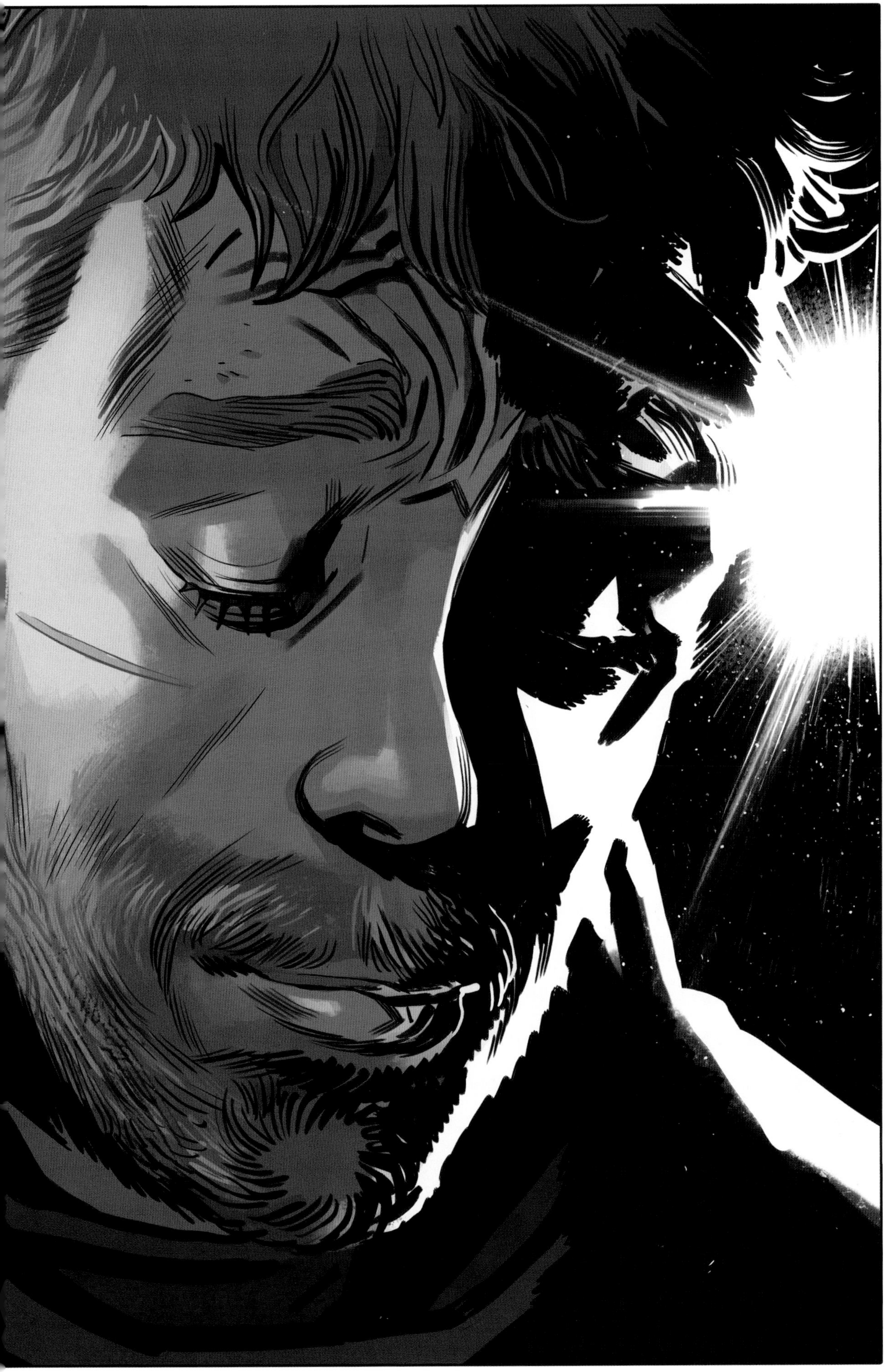

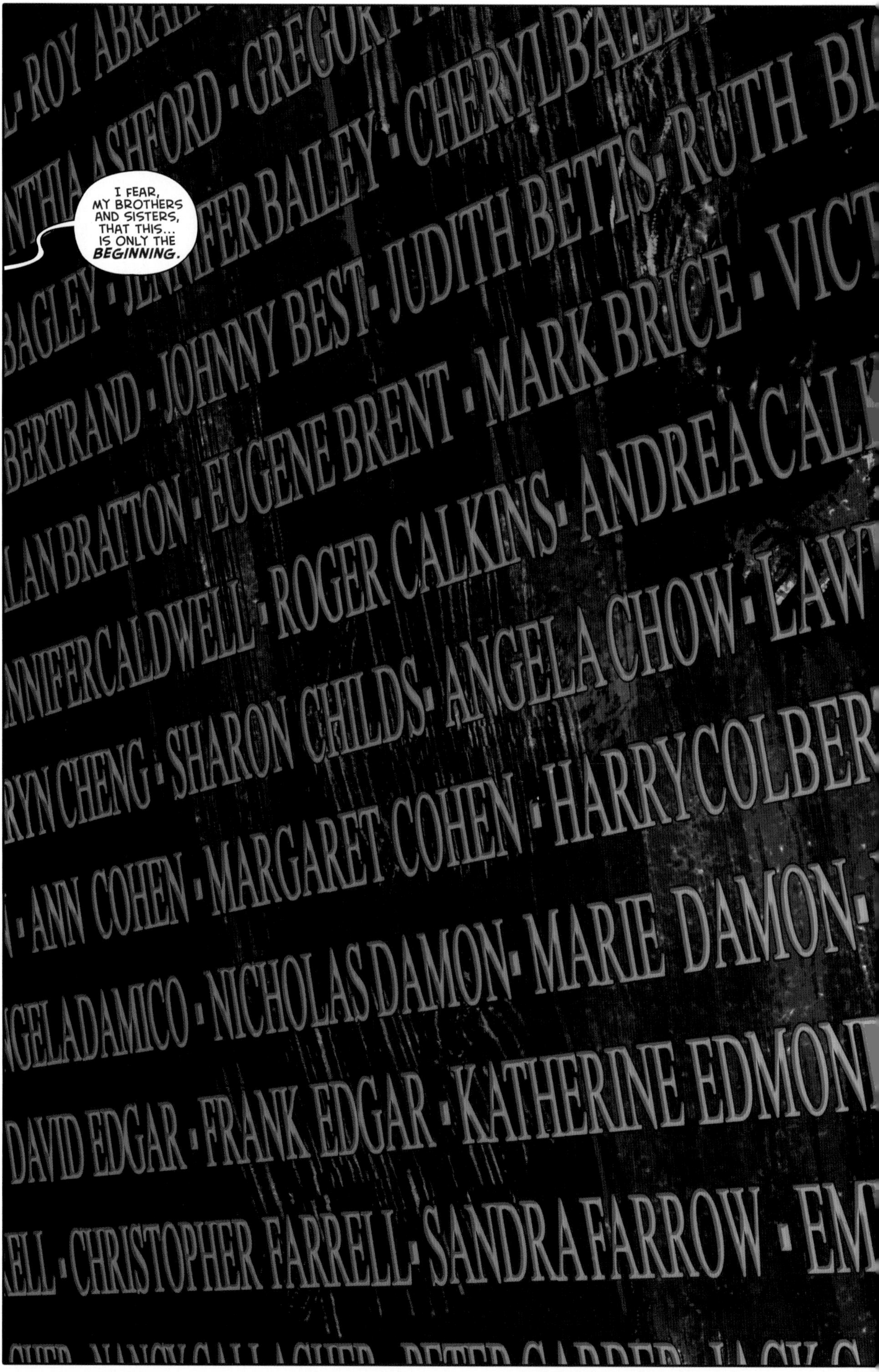
I FEAR, MY BROTHERS AND SISTERS, THAT THIS... IS ONLY THE ***BEGINNING.***

FOR
BRIDGES · CATHE
S · ROBERT CALLAWAY ·
NCE CHRISTENSEN · BREN
EDWARD COLE · CHARLES
AN DAMON · CYNTHIA DAN
LAURA EDWARD · DENISE
FENNER · RONALD FERGUS

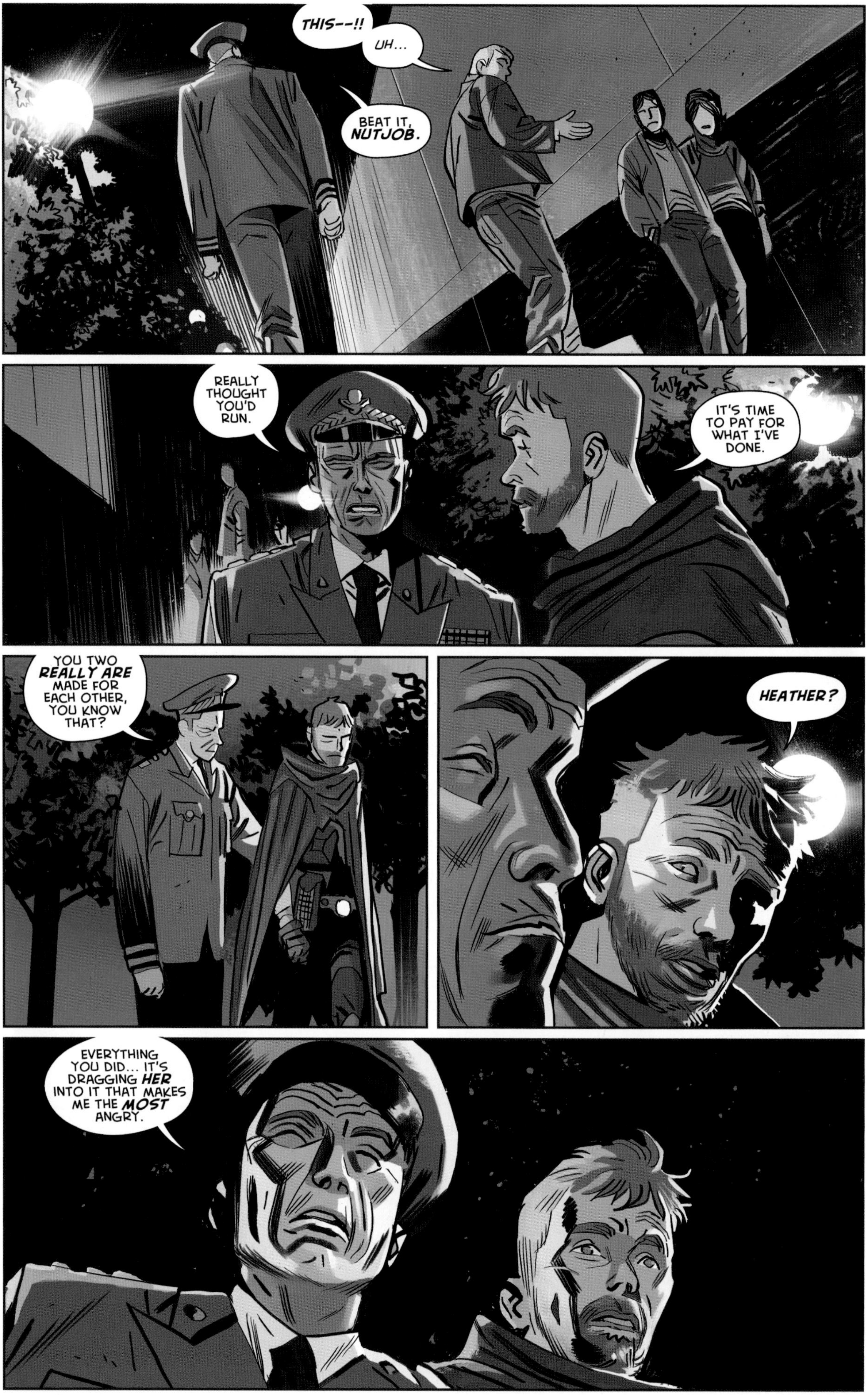
THIS--!!
UH...
BEAT IT, NUTJOB.
REALLY THOUGHT YOU'D RUN.
IT'S TIME TO PAY FOR WHAT I'VE DONE.
YOU TWO REALLY ARE MADE FOR EACH OTHER, YOU KNOW THAT?
HEATHER?
EVERYTHING YOU DID... IT'S DRAGGING HER INTO IT THAT MAKES ME THE MOST ANGRY.

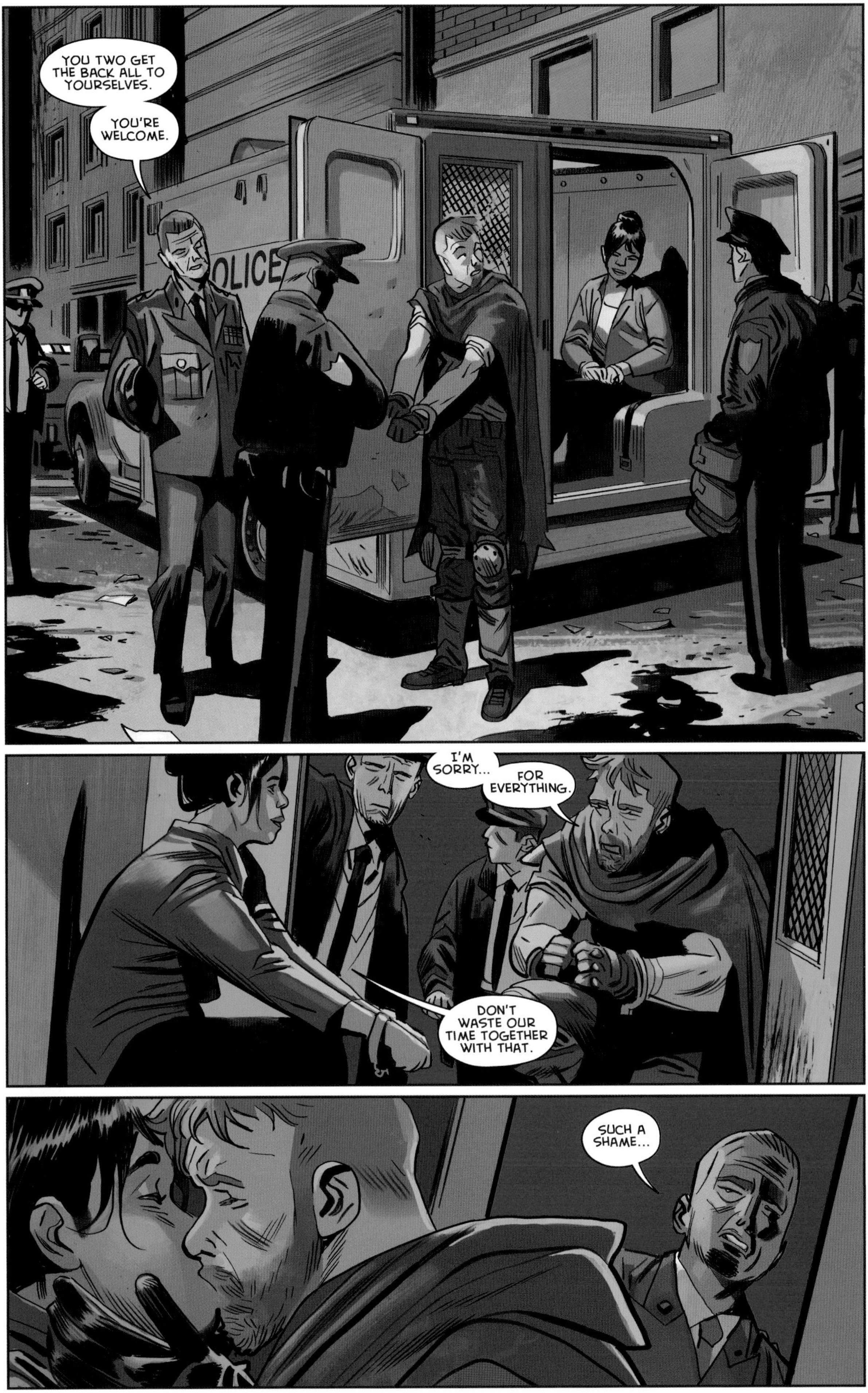
YOU TWO GET THE BACK ALL TO YOURSELVES.
YOU'RE WELCOME.
POLICE
I'M SORRY...
FOR EVERYTHING.
DON'T WASTE OUR TIME TOGETHER WITH THAT.
SUCH A SHAME...

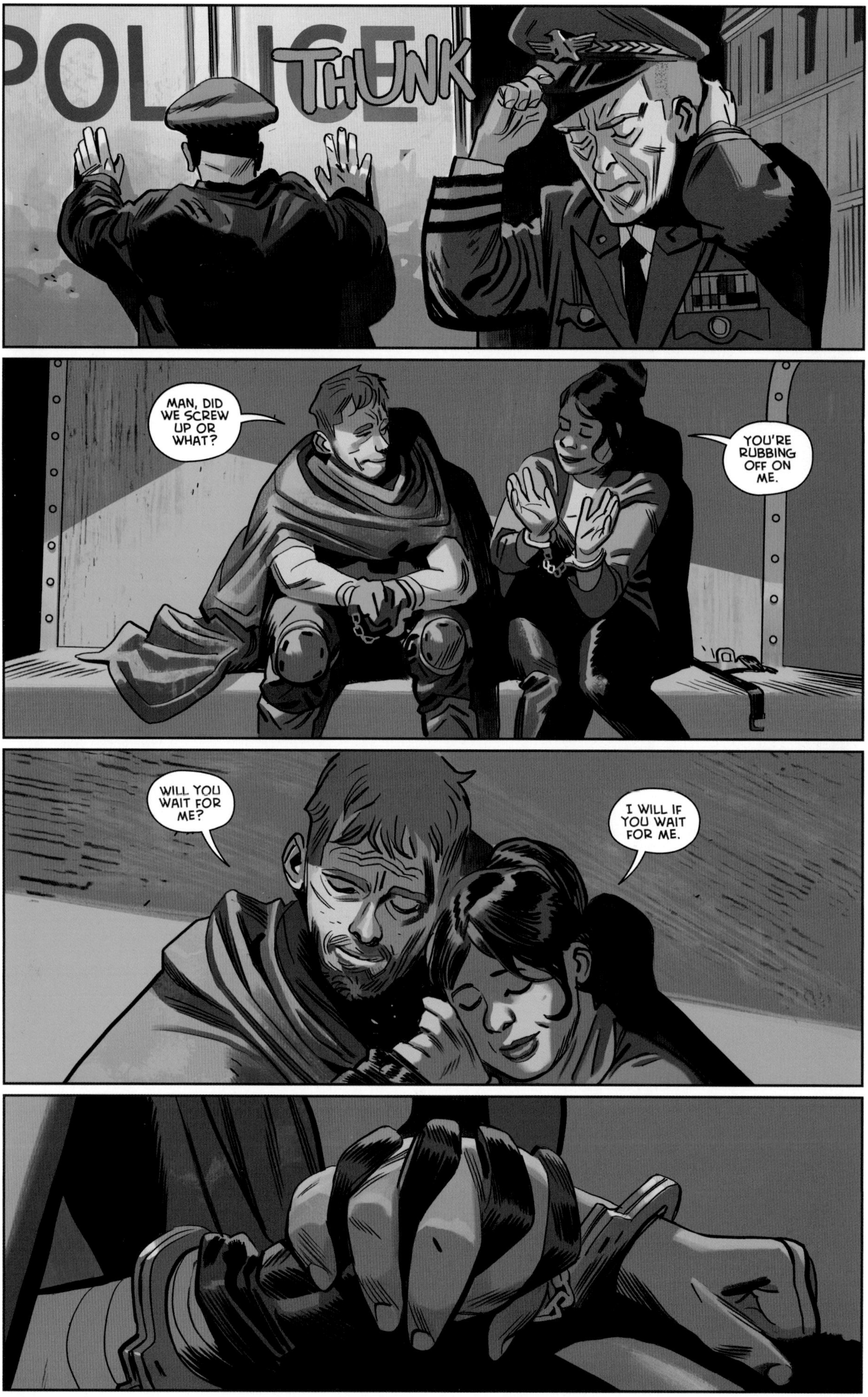
POLICE
THUNK
MAN, DID WE SCREW UP OR WHAT?
YOU'RE RUBBING OFF ON ME.
WILL YOU WAIT FOR ME?
I WILL IF YOU WAIT FOR ME.

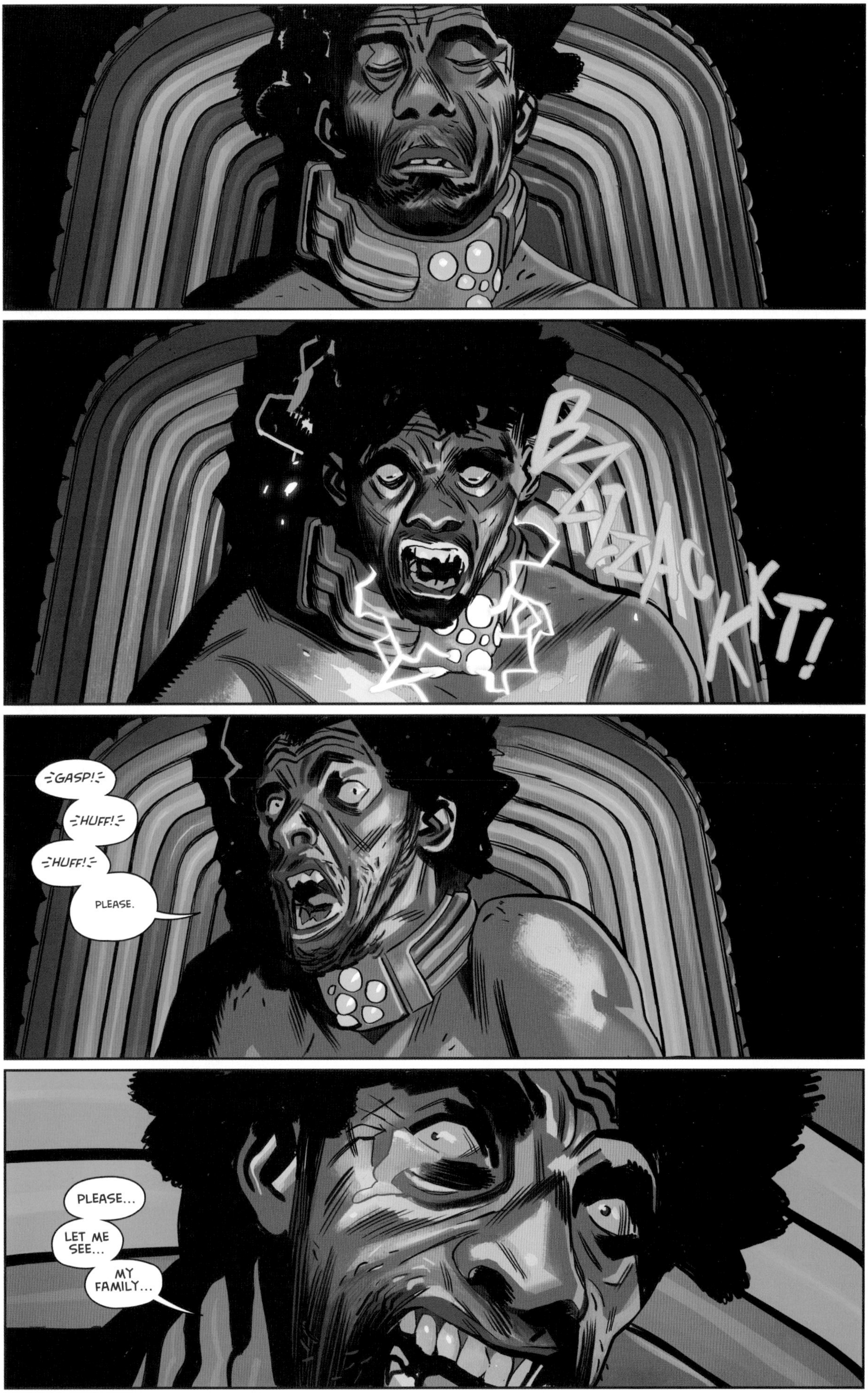
BZZZACKKKT!
GASP!
HUFF!
HUFF!
PLEASE.
PLEASE...
LET ME SEE...
MY FAMILY...

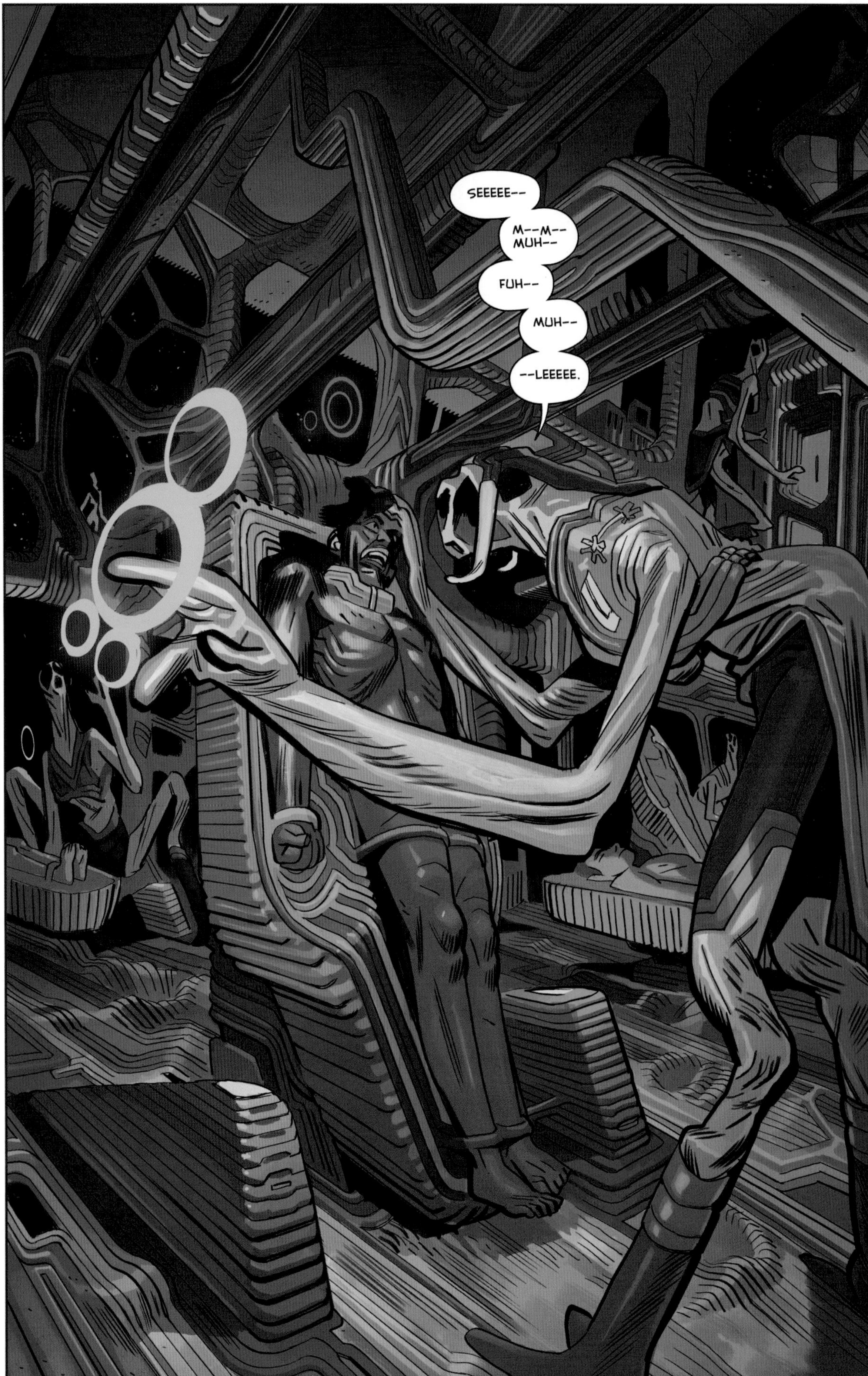
SEEEEE--
M--M--
MUH--
FUH--
MUH--
--LEEEEE.

CONTINUED

TO BE

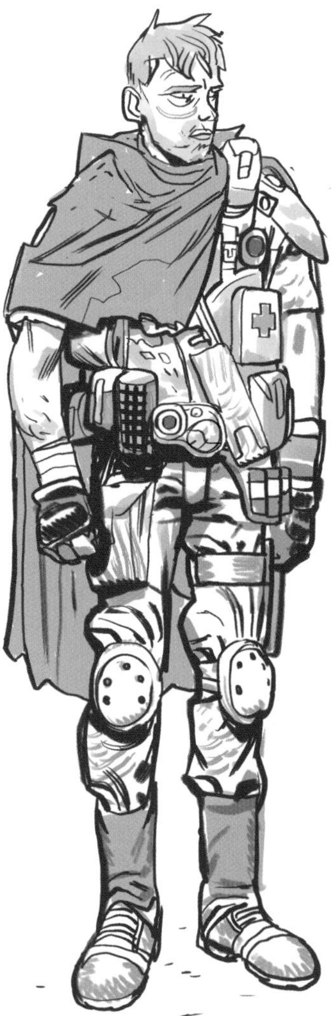

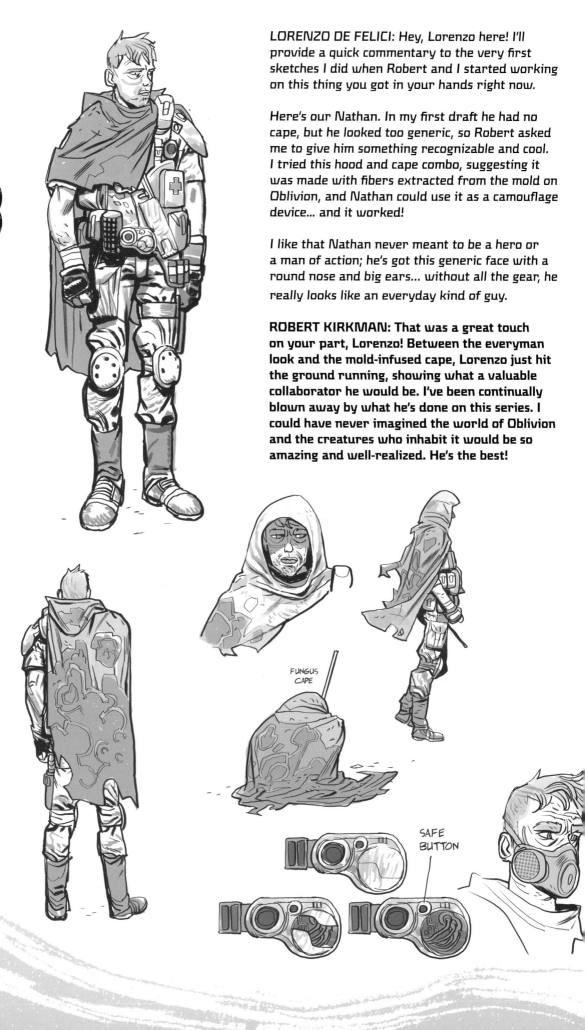

LORENZO DE FELICI: *Hey, Lorenzo here! I'll provide a quick commentary to the very first sketches I did when Robert and I started working on this thing you got in your hands right now.*

Here's our Nathan. In my first draft he had no cape, but he looked too generic, so Robert asked me to give him something recognizable and cool. I tried this hood and cape combo, suggesting it was made with fibers extracted from the mold on Oblivion, and Nathan could use it as a camouflage device… and it worked!

I like that Nathan never meant to be a hero or a man of action; he's got this generic face with a round nose and big ears… without all the gear, he really looks like an everyday kind of guy.

ROBERT KIRKMAN: That was a great touch on your part, Lorenzo! Between the everyman look and the mold-infused cape, Lorenzo just hit the ground running, showing what a valuable collaborator he would be. I've been continually blown away by what he's done on this series. I could have never imagined the world of Oblivion and the creatures who inhabit it would be so amazing and well-realized. He's the best!

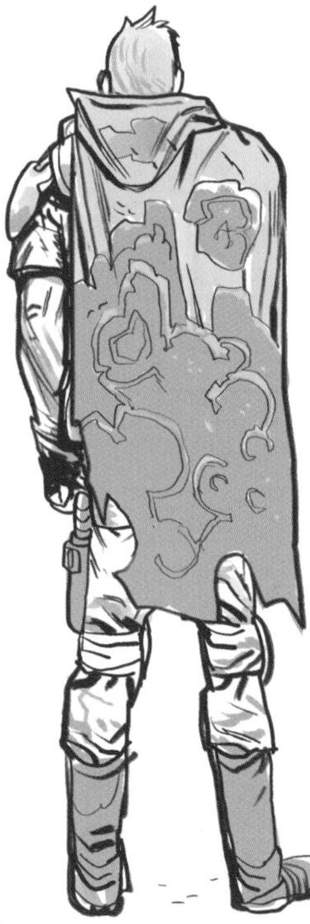

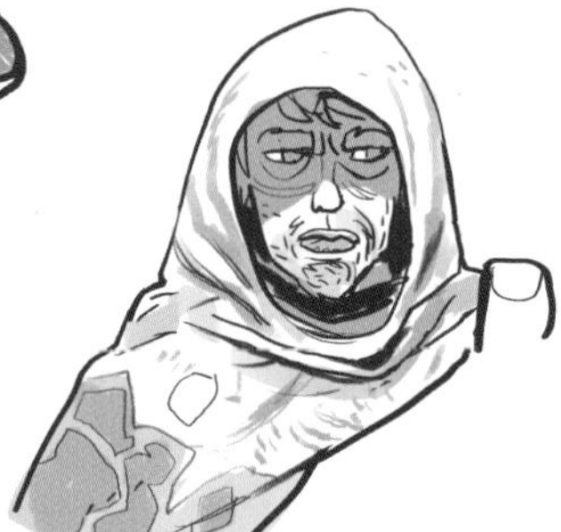

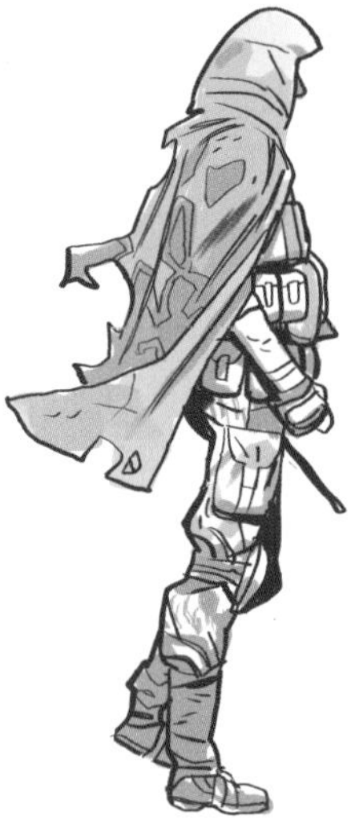

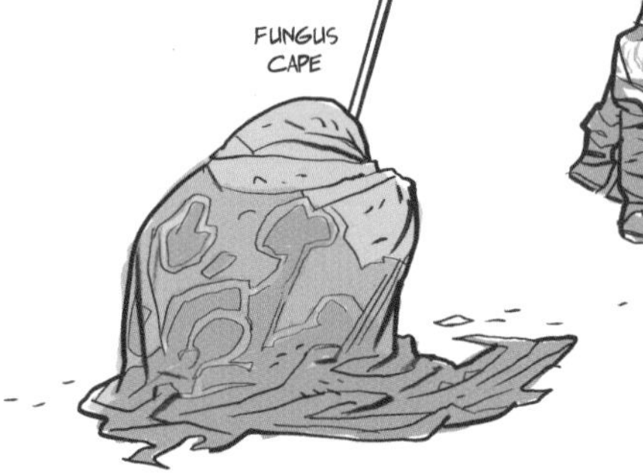
FUNGUS
CAPE

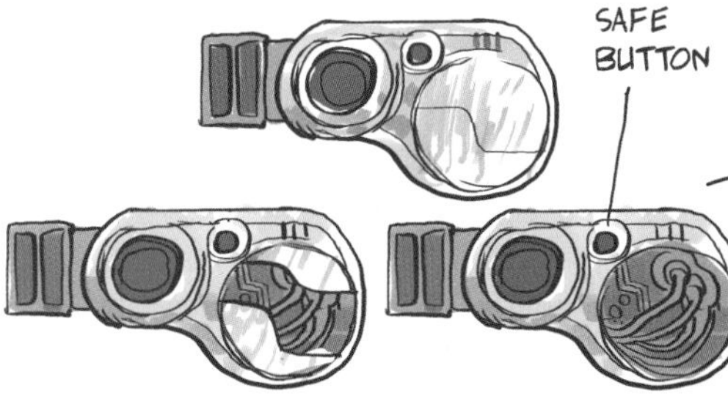
SAFE
BUTTON

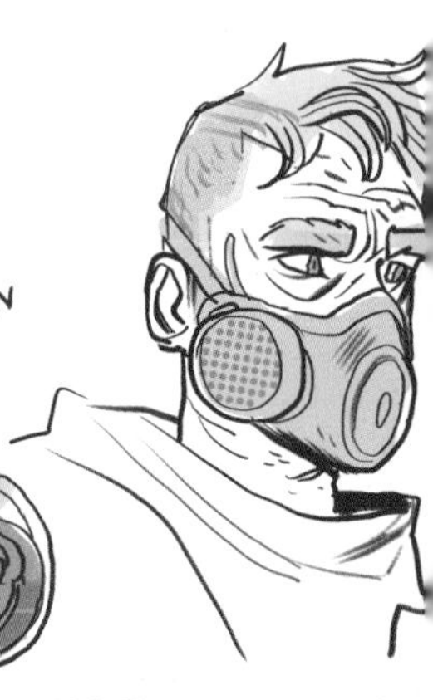

LORENZO: *Living in Oblivion really shows up on your face, and Duncan's face is no exception. He's got all these lines, he rarely smiles, and his eyes are always hidden behind glasses. I came up with the worn-out shoes because I thought it would be cool if he had something to symbolize his trauma. He never talks about it, but he can't get rid of it.*

ROBERT: Crap, did I come up with any ideas for this book? I forgot the worn-out shoes were your idea as well.

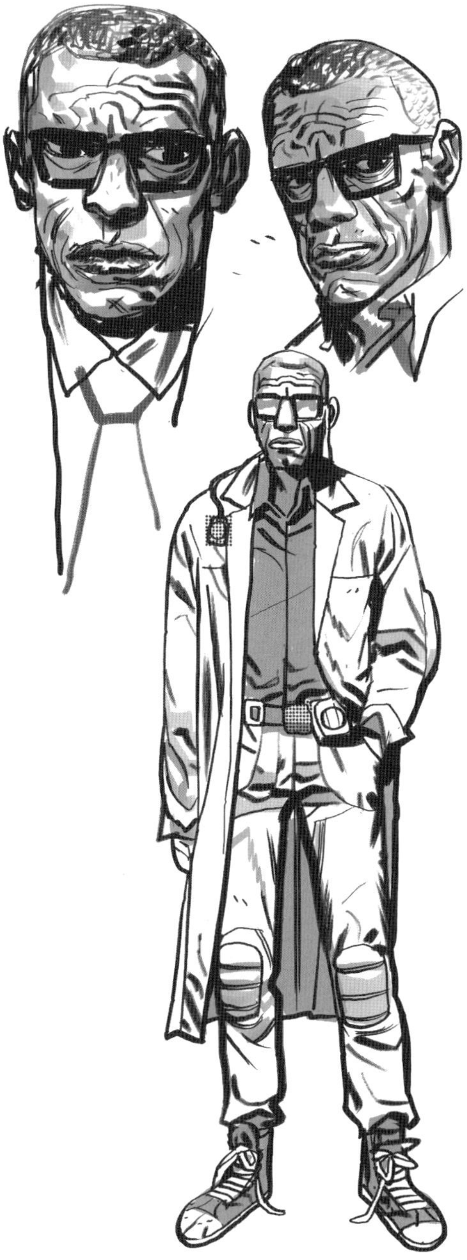

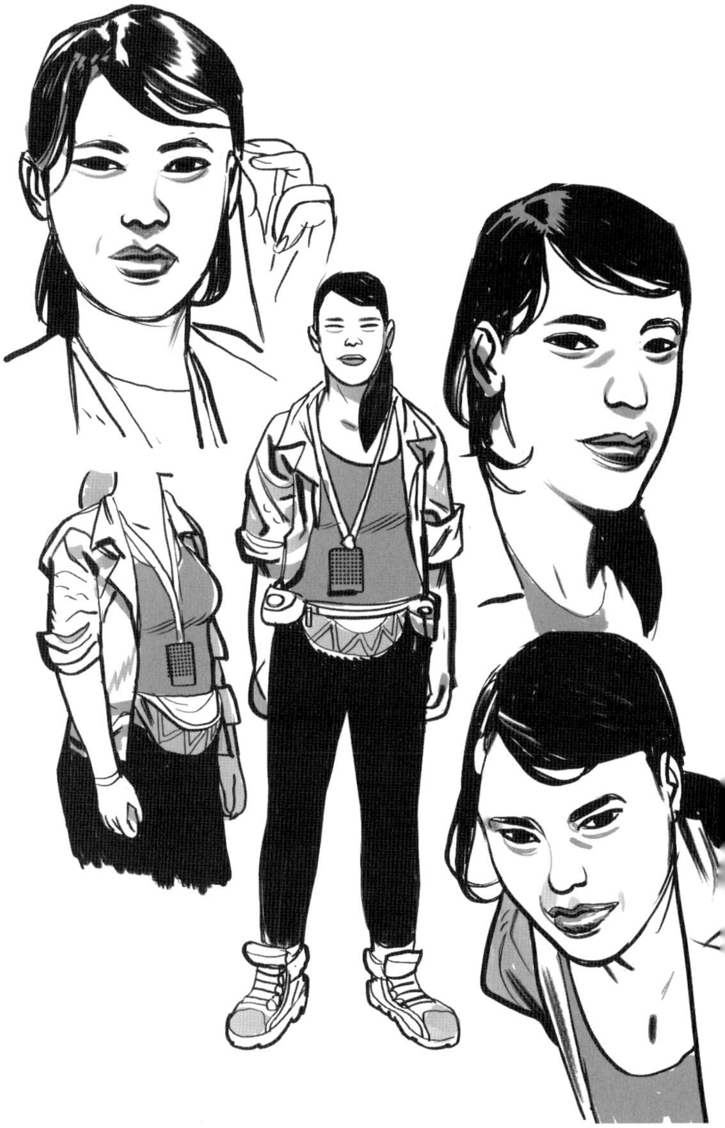

LORENZO: *I really love Bridget. It was clear that her spirit should be in contrast with Duncan's, so I figured she had this fresh and adventurous look a la Jurassic Park's Ellie Sattler, and she's also brave enough to have a fanny pack. That's badass right there.*

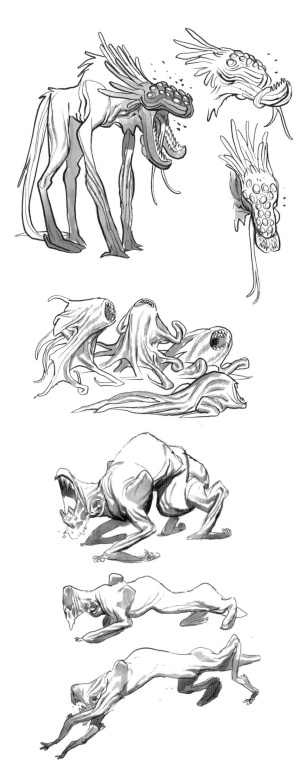

LORENZO: Monsters! I mean, creatures! I love coming up with those. I tried to imagine what kind of beings could survive in a habitat such as Oblivion's. I find that the most difficult thing when you design a creature is getting rid of the things you instinctively would put on an animal... like a head, for example. I usually start from a suggestion Robert gives me, "Yeah like a squirrel, but two stories high!" or "A freakish gorilla with fangs" or something fancy like that. Sometimes I just follow my imagination, especially when it comes to some creature you see in the background (like those tentacle fellas down there).

ROBERT: In the script I would literally write "I don't know, giant alien gorilla" or "this monster should be like an alien tiger or something." I would just lazily pick an Earth animal and put the word "alien" in front of it... and just sit back and watch Lorenzo spin it into gold. We eventually came up with the naming system where the Oblivion animals have the names of mythical creatures: Ogre, Harpy, Banshee, Griffin, etc. But I honestly can't remember if I came up with that or if Lorenzo did. What do writers even do?

LORENZO: For this one I just tried to take a lion, turn it upside down and stretch it. Something you definitely don't want to do in the real world (believe me).

LORENZO: This is just disgusting, I'm sorry. To make it better just imagine his saliva tastes like very good French cheese.

ROBERT: You made it worse!

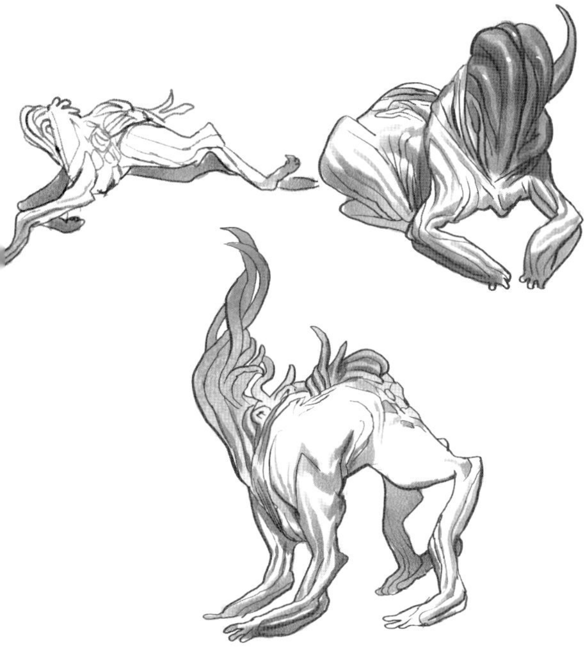

LORENZO: This is one of the creatures I'm most attached to, it's so fun to draw those tentacles! I guess this is just Oblivion's take on a dog.

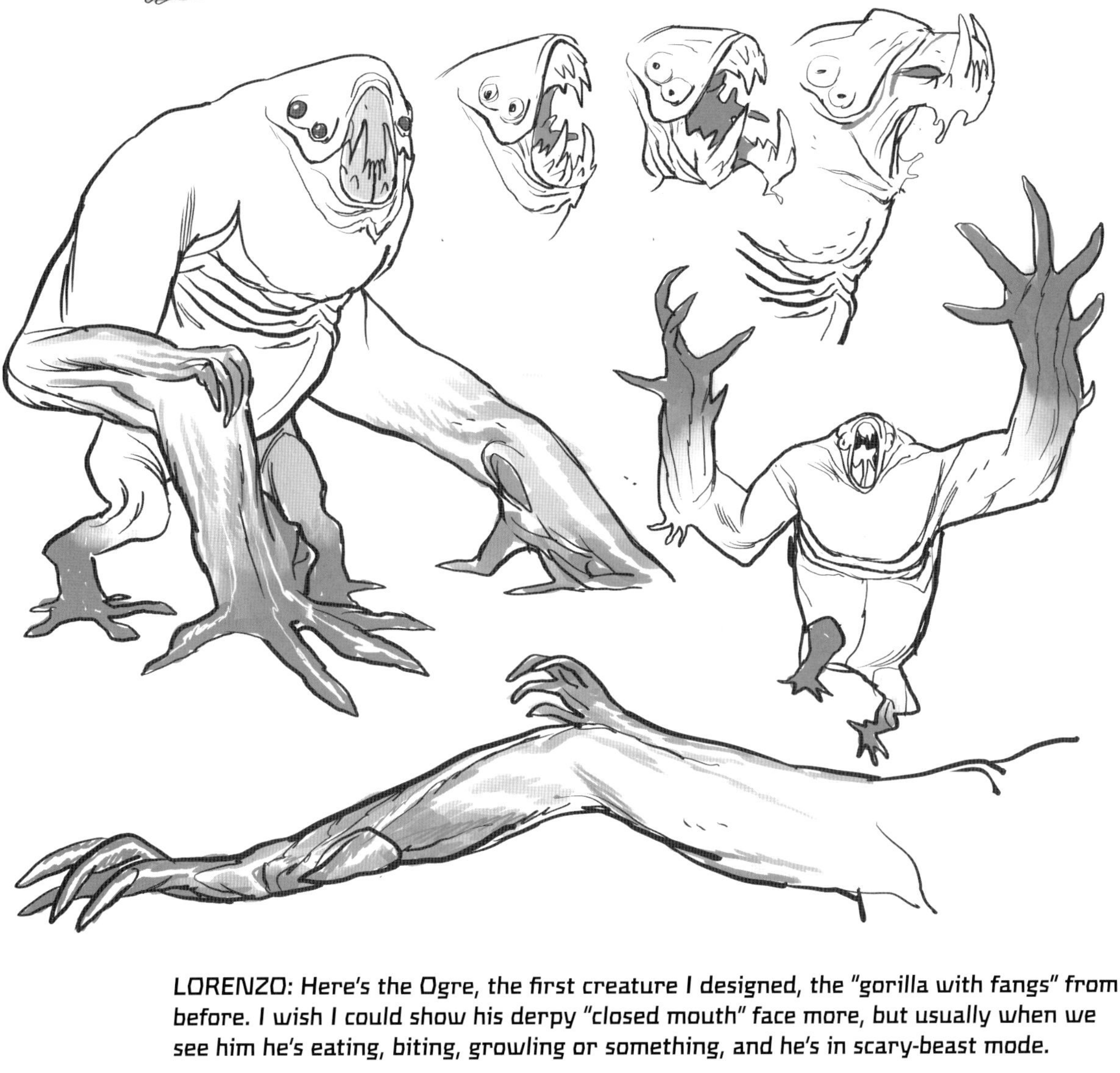

LORENZO: Here's the Ogre, the first creature I designed, the "gorilla with fangs" from before. I wish I could show his derpy "closed mouth" face more, but usually when we see him he's eating, biting, growling or something, and he's in scary-beast mode.

ROBERT: All you have to do is ask, man. I'll try to work that into future issues.

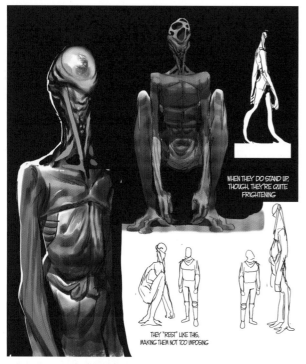

WHEN THEY DO STAND UP, THOUGH, THEY'RE QUITE FRIGHTENING

THEY "REST" LIKE THIS, MAKING THEM NOT TOO IMPOSING

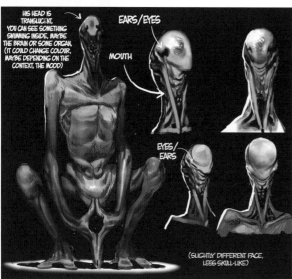

HIS HEAD IS TRANSLUCENT, YOU CAN SEE SOMETHING SWIMMING INSIDE, MAYBE THE BRAIN OR SOME ORGAN. (IT COULD CHANGE COLOUR, MAYBE DEPENDING ON THE CONTEXT, THE MOOD)

EARS/EYES

MOUTH

EYES/ EARS

(SLIGHTLY DIFFERENT FACE, LESS SKULL-LIKE)

LORENZO: For the Faceless Men, Robert told me he had in mind something mostly featureless – particularly the eyes, since not being able to spot them on a living thing is naturally unsettling. So I went all in, removed ALL the features and tried a couple of approaches. At first I made the head round and semi-transparent, so that you can barely see something inside moving and squirming. Unsettling in theory, but also difficult to convey through still images. So I moved on and tried something different, making their head a hole. I knew it was better since it looked less "already seen" and it allowed more variations. Also I immediately started thinking about how they work, like how they live, how they communicate, how they are born, how they get old, etc. Most of this stuff won't see the light of day (or... will it?), but it was like an alarm going off in my head saying, "This works!"

ROBERT: SUCH a great visual. You also came up with the creepy crouching position and making them all long and gangly. Very cool stuff. It's hard coming up with something that's a bipedal living creature from another dimension that doesn't read as "human in a mask". I wanted something human-like so that you can relate to them in some way, see them as equals to us, but I wanted them to look truly alien. Lorenzo delivered on all fronts.

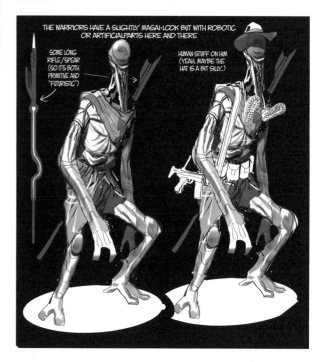

THE WARRIORS HAVE A SLIGHTLY MASAI-LOOK BUT WITH ROBOTIC OR ARTIFICIAL PARTS HERE AND THERE

SOME LONG RIFLE/SPEAR (SO IT'S BOTH PRIMITIVE AND "FUTURISTIC")

HUMAN STUFF ON HIM (YEAH, MAYBE THE HAT IS A BIT SILLY...)

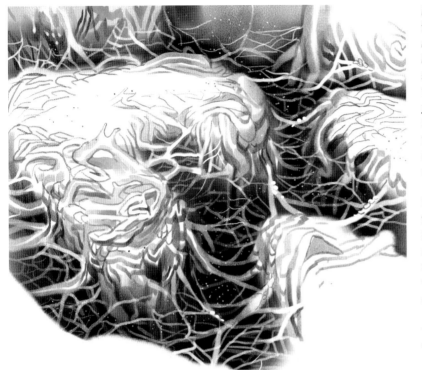

LORENZO: Starting from the idea of Oblivion being basically a giant ball of vines and jungle, having no "floor" outside some sporadic plain formation of the vines, the look of this bottomless jungle came out pretty naturally. Moving further and further from the vine formations, we end up seeing something that resembles a brain.

ROBERT: This take was just nuts! I only asked for crazy-dense vegetation, like a crazy alien fungus and mold-based rain forest. The idea being that the Transference happened, and on the Oblivion side of things, Philadelphia lined up with a remote, uninhabited part of the planet (except for the Kuthaal/Faceless Men). So it took a while for intelligent life to even find it.

LORENZO: The surface of Oblivion is just a bottomless, endless tangle of vines and lianas, but occasionally you can stumble upon some plains with an actual surface. Here you can meet the larger, heavier creatures and, occasionally, bodies of water. Also, you can rest your legs.

LORENZO: This is the first Oblivion Song picture that was colored! Annalisa tried different approaches and palettes, and finally came up with this reddish-brown/green combo for the fungus that looks natural, and at the same time alien. Her colors have been (and still are!) a huge part of the making of the world itself.

ROBERT: Annalisa is the best!

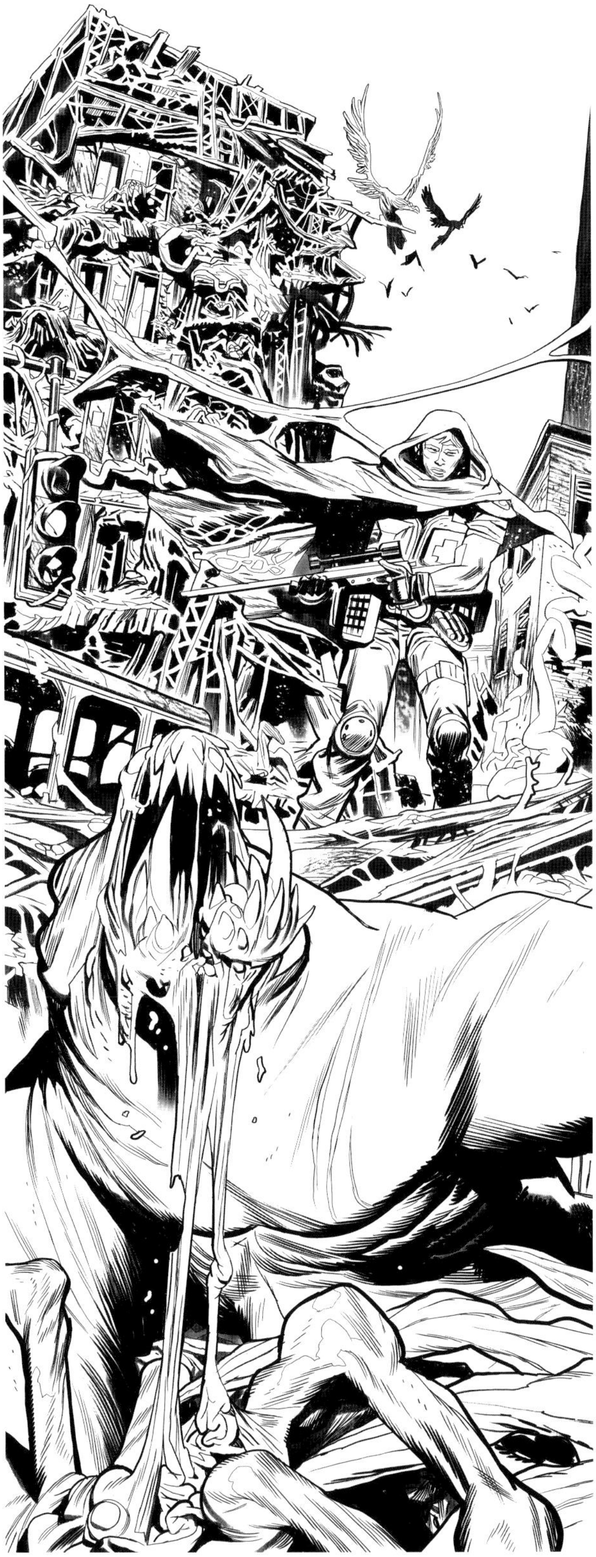

ROBERT: This image was done by Lorenzo for a MASSIVE retail poster we sent out to promote the launch of the series. I was worried it was a little too violent at first, since really, this book isn't all that violent, but it looks so dang cool I knew it would be very effective. Being able to see this image, four feet tall or so hanging on a wall is glorious. I highly recommend you hit eBay and snag one for yourself!

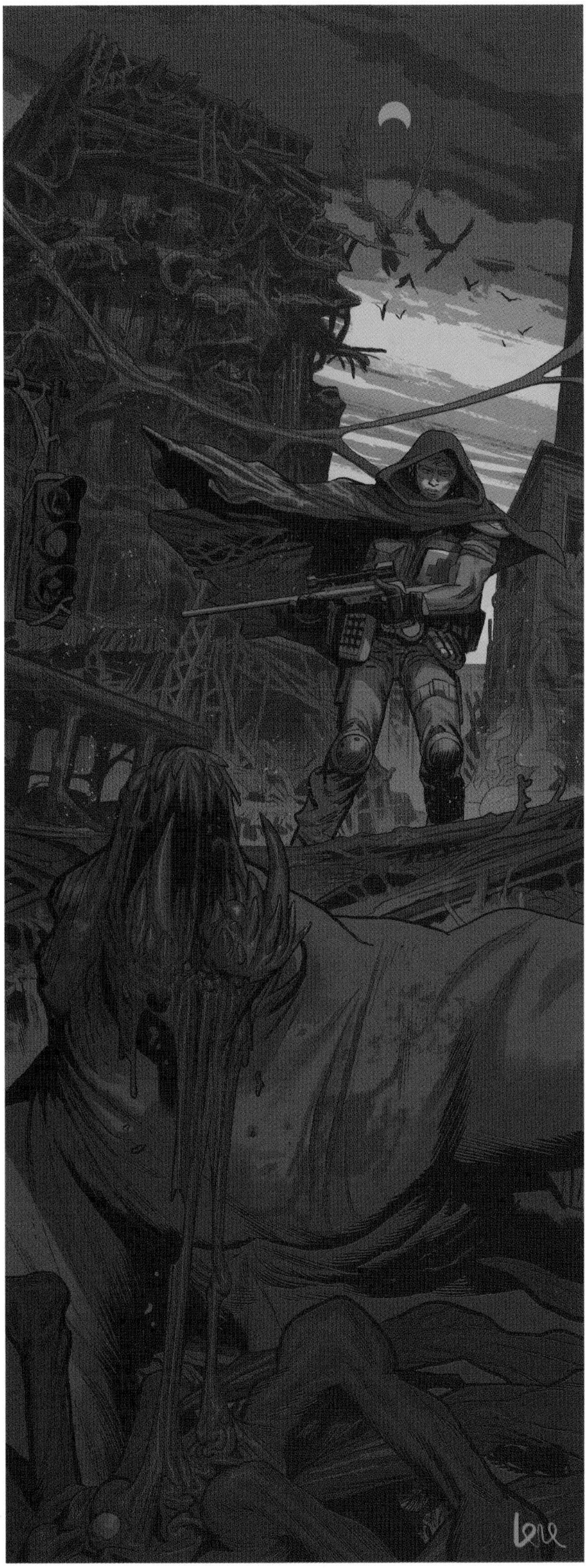

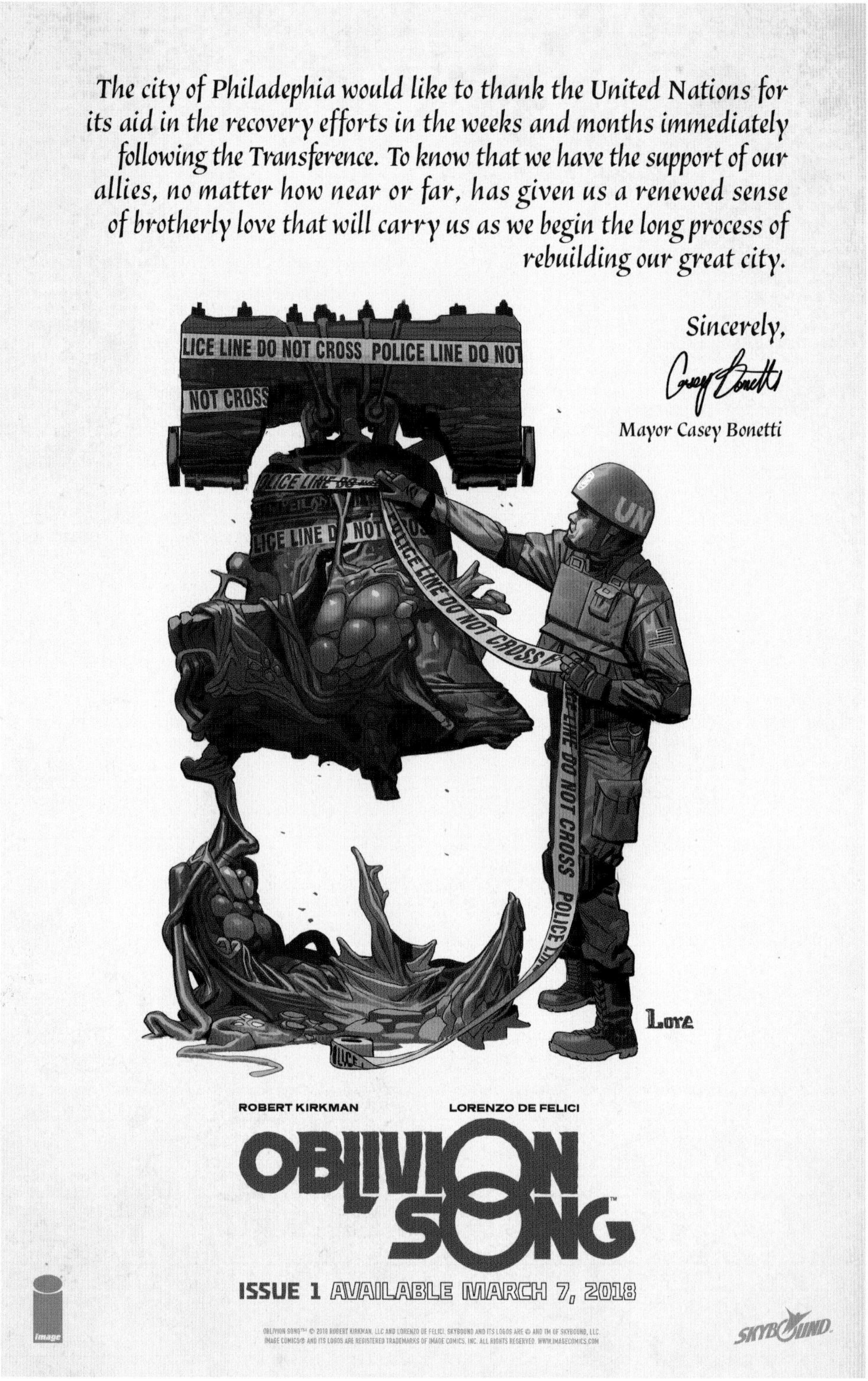
The city of Philadephia would like to thank the United Nations for its aid in the recovery efforts in the weeks and months immediately following the Transference. To know that we have the support of our allies, no matter how near or far, has given us a renewed sense of brotherly love that will carry us as we begin the long process of rebuilding our great city.
Sincerely,
Mayor Casey Bonetti
LICE LINE DO NOT CROSS POLICE LINE DO NOT
NOT CROSS
POLICE LINE DO NOT CROSS
LINE DO NOT CROSS
UN
Lore
ROBERT KIRKMAN
LORENZO DE FELICI
OBLIVION SONG™
ISSUE 1 AVAILABLE MARCH 7, 2018
OBLIVION SONG™ © 2018 ROBERT KIRKMAN, LLC AND LORENZO DE FELICI. SKYBOUND AND ITS LOGOS ARE © AND TM OF SKYBOUND, LLC. IMAGE COMICS® AND ITS LOGOS ARE REGISTERED TRADEMARKS OF IMAGE COMICS, INC. ALL RIGHTS RESERVED. WWW.IMAGECOMICS.COM

LORENZO: I was SO stoked about doing this! I wanted to do something involving the Liberty Bell, and I was looking around for references when I found Norman Rockwell's painting of him wrapping the Bell with a "Happy Birthday" sash, "Liberty Bell (Celebration)", 1976. I had to do it.

ROBERT: I was wanting to try something a little different for the ads for this book. I'd been seeing a lot of 1950s ads for shaving cream and cologne and things like that that had tons of text and kind of told little stories as part of the ads. We've all seen Mad Men, you know what I'm talking about. So I wanted to try those type of things for this book. This Liberty Bell illustration worked perfectly for one of those ads. You can see the other ads we did on the next couple pages. I thought they'd be a great way to introduce potential readers to this world we were building before the series launch.

WHY CAN'T SHE BE ENOUGH?

Nathan never would have found Heather if it weren't for the Transference. When he was brought in by the government to help figure out what had happened, she was his direct contact. They spent hours together, strategizing on how to convince her bosses to provide more time and funding for his research. After many months without a breakthrough, there were times when his work was nearly shut down. But together they persevered, so when Nathan's belt technology showed he could pass safely between dimensions, and rescue teams were being formed, it was a win for both of them.

Ironically, it was Heather who was able to talk her bosses into allowing Nathan to lead the rescue teams. He'd already spent so much time in Oblivion testing the technology. He knew more about the area than almost anyone. It wasn't until his first day of leave, in the middle of boot camp, that they first became intimate. They were both taken off-guard by the fact that neither of them saw it coming.

Their relationship began at the worst possible time. Nathan was part of the rescue mission, dropping into Oblivion, tracking down those lost there, bringing them home. It was more than a full-time job, that left no room for anything else. As time went on, they found fewer and fewer people. Eventually, after a dry spell of more than three months where no one was rescued, the program was permanently shut down.

A chapter in Nathan's life was closed, or rather, it should have been. He'd done all he could, they'd rescued... most... of the people lost in Oblivion... but most wasn't enough. Not when Nathan's own brother, Edward Cole, was counted among the lost. Despite Nathan's love for Heather, Oblivion and those lost there are a shadow he can't get out from under.

Instead of settling down, putting all this behind him and marrying the woman he loved, Nathan became a fugitive, using his technology to illegally go into Oblivion and continue looking for those lost there. Now, every day, he leaves her, to risk his life traveling alone to Oblivion, searching for any sign of life, any hope he might save someone who knows something about his lost brother. Despite his love for Heather, he can't resist the siren call of the

ROBERT KIRKMAN   LORENZO DE FELICI

ISSUE #1
AVAILABLE
MARCH 7, 2018

In the hours after the Transference, more than twenty thousand people lost their lives. The alien life of the dimension that came to be known as Oblivion ran rampant on the streets of Philadelphia. No one could have been prepared for what happened. Somehow in the chaos, a young girl, Nadia Abbasi, was able to take this photo as she fled. She would later reveal that she didn't even see the man who saved her. She had no idea how or why she'd survived that day.

In the years since, this has become one of the most viewed photographs of all time. What the young Ms. Abbasi was able to capture is remarkable. So much fear and terror on the faces of everyone present, including Officer Clark Daniels. Yet where others flee, Daniels stands his ground. He fires blindly at the approaching creature, managing to wound it, driving it away, but not before it took his life. Every single person captured in this photograph survived that day, save for one.

Officer Clark Daniels. His sacrifice will never be forgotten.

ROBERT KIRKMAN   **LORENZO DE FELICI**

ISSUE 1 AVAILABLE MARCH 7, 2018

LORENZO: This was an idea for a cover that we liked so much that I finalized it, even though we didn't know what to make of it. We finally used it on a promotional card. Also, I think it also became the cover of the first OBLIVION SONG trade paperback here in Italy. You can see writing on the wall just behind Nathan saying, "Where are we?" My idea was that the survivors stuck in Oblivion started writing stuff on the buildings like slogans, cries for help, or just the biggest questions they had. You can spot some of those writings in the pages, too. I don't really know if something like that would occur in a post-apocalyptic situation like that, and I hope I won't find out anytime soon.

ROBERT: People would definitely be writing messages all over the place in this situation, but I tried to avoid that in this series because we did it so much in that mostly unknown, forgotten series I wrote, THE WALKING DEAD.

LORENZO: There was no doubt about this cover to #1. I remember Robert being so excited about this!

ROBERT: I was! Still am!

LORENZO: The front! Definitely less epic than the back. I drew it with and without mask, since we also used it as a starting point for the statue. Nothing goes to waste.

ROBERT: This cover was used for the special #1 variant cover that CAME WITH A STATUE! So cool!

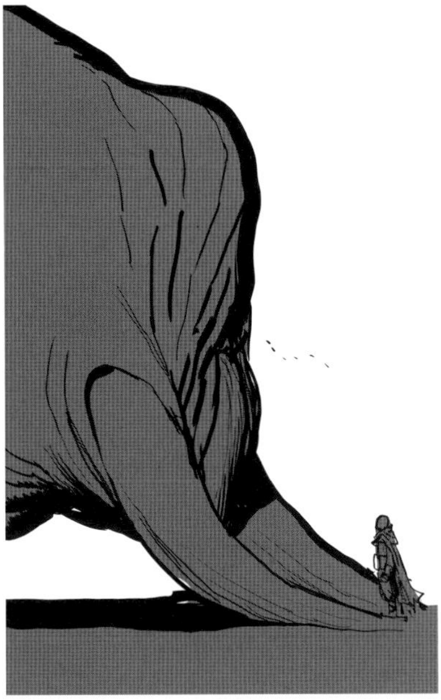

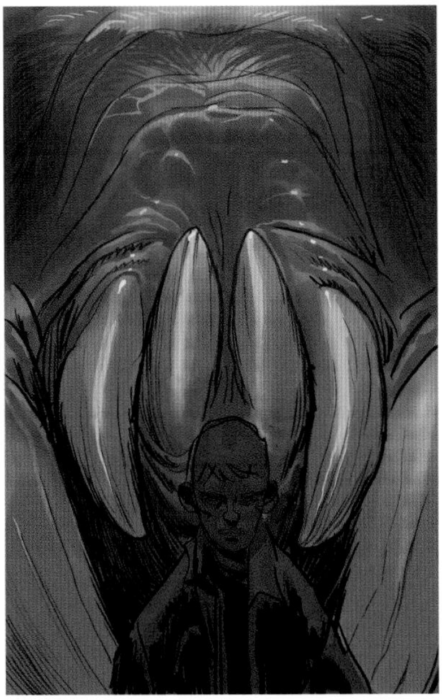

LORENZO: Sketches for the cover of #2. I wanted to use the HUGE guy we see in the museum, but Robert had something else in mind.

ROBERT: It was a cool idea, but I wanted to do a cover that was more personal and character-based. Don't hold a grudge!

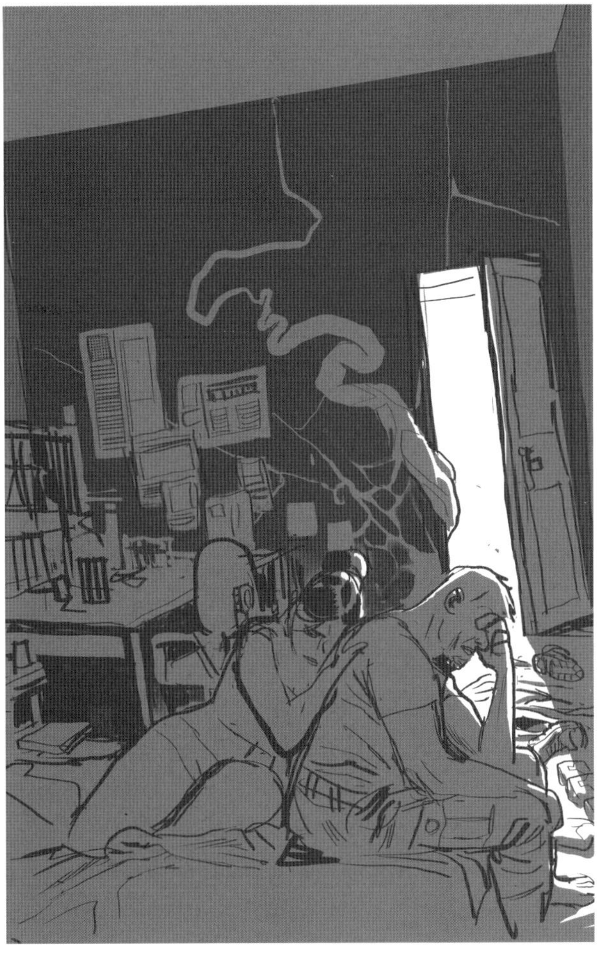

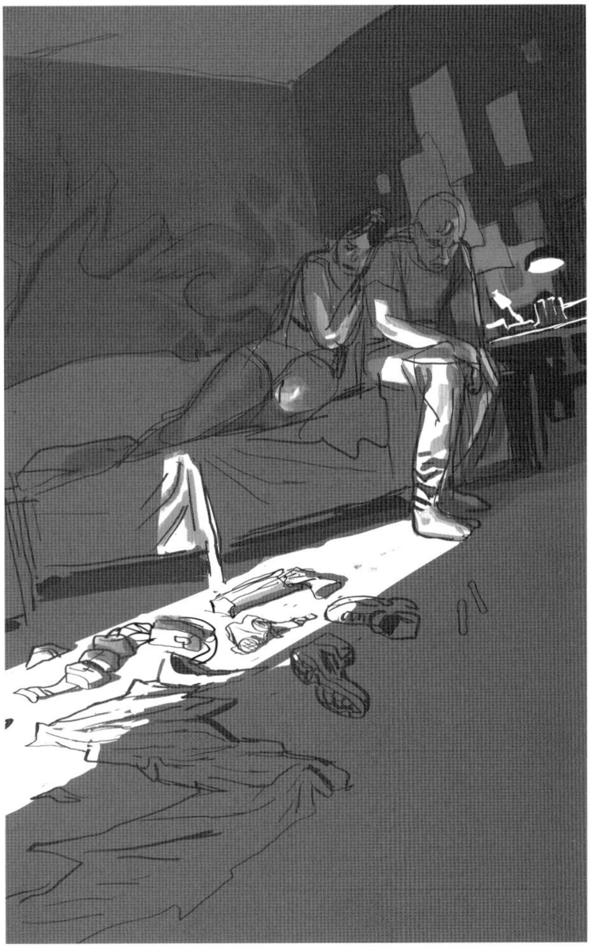

LORENZO: Robert wanted to see an intimate moment, to counter the heroism and epicness of the first one. I tried to frame it in an interesting and dramatic way. These are a couple of rejected sketches.

LORENZO: The frog variant to #4!

ROBERT: I really like the idea of there being variants that are kind of stealthy, so you don't even notice them. I got the idea when I noticed that *Youngblood #2* has a variant where the logo and the background are different colors... and I never noticed!

LORENZO: Here I paid homage to René Magritte's "The Blank Check", a painting that's always hypnotized me. We went with a different sketch though, since this one was a little bit too static.

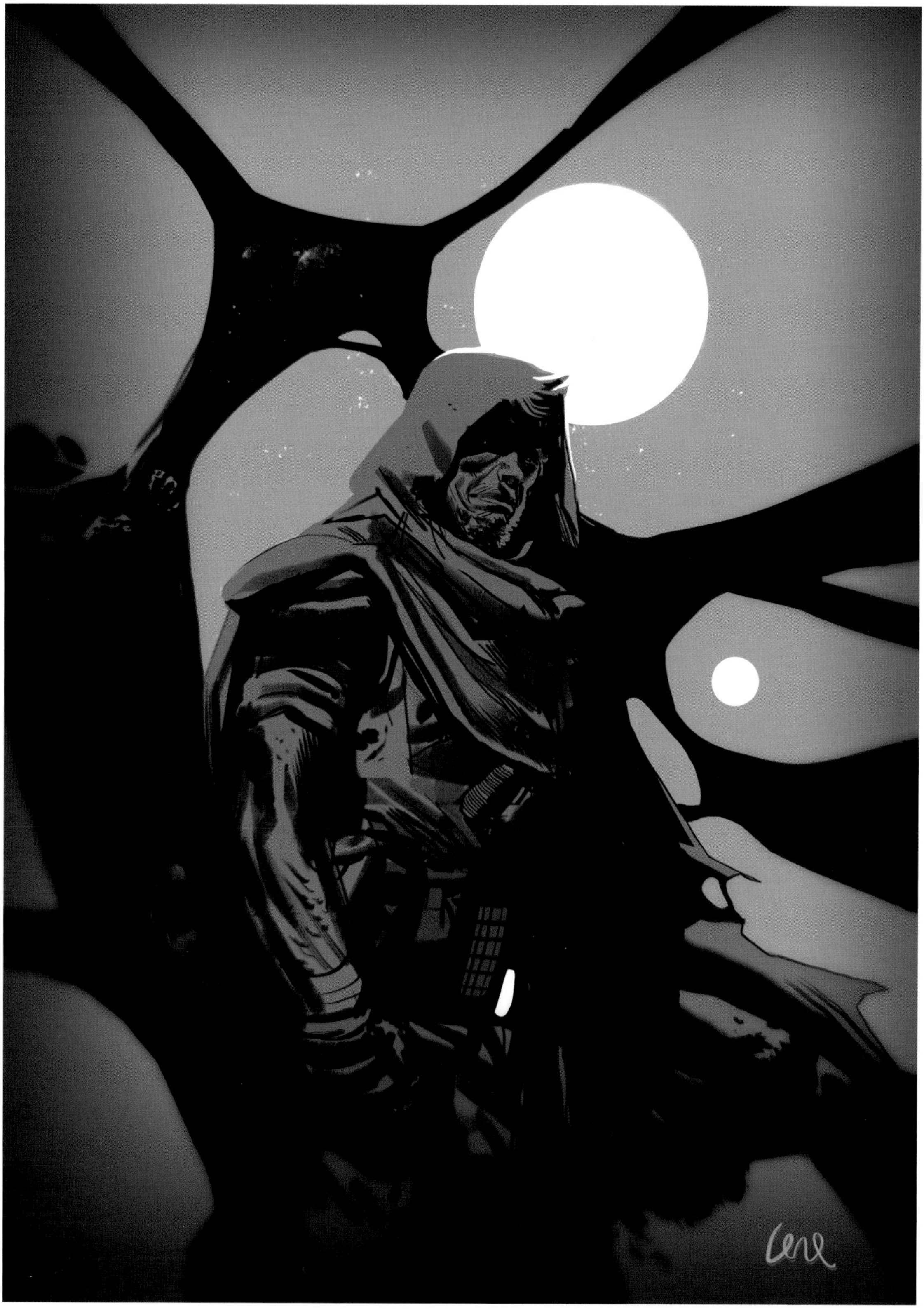

LORENZO: This very menacing Nathan just crawled out of my hand.

ROBERT: And it's magnificent!
That'll do it for this installment of sketchbook section! See you all back here in a year or so for Book 2!

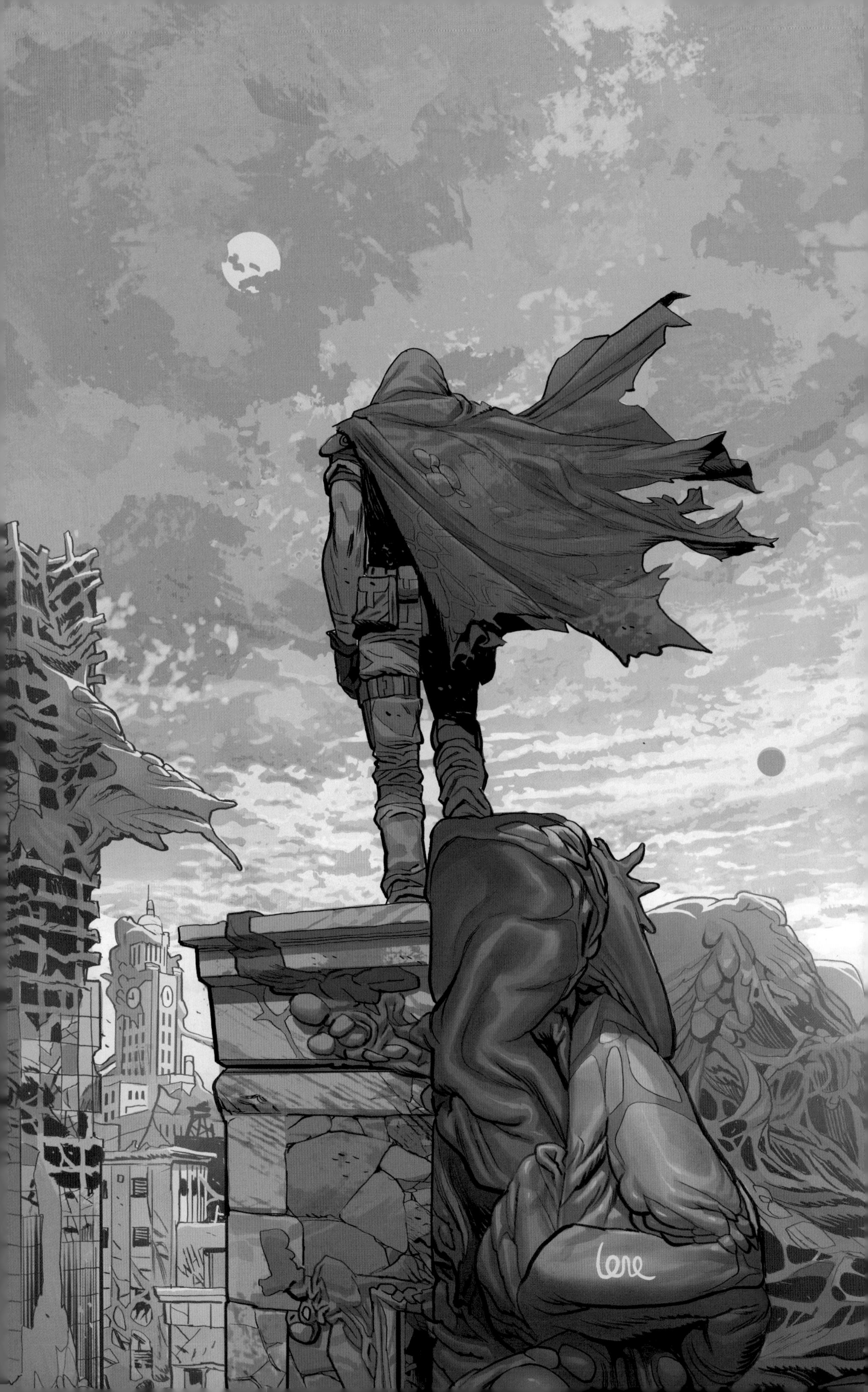

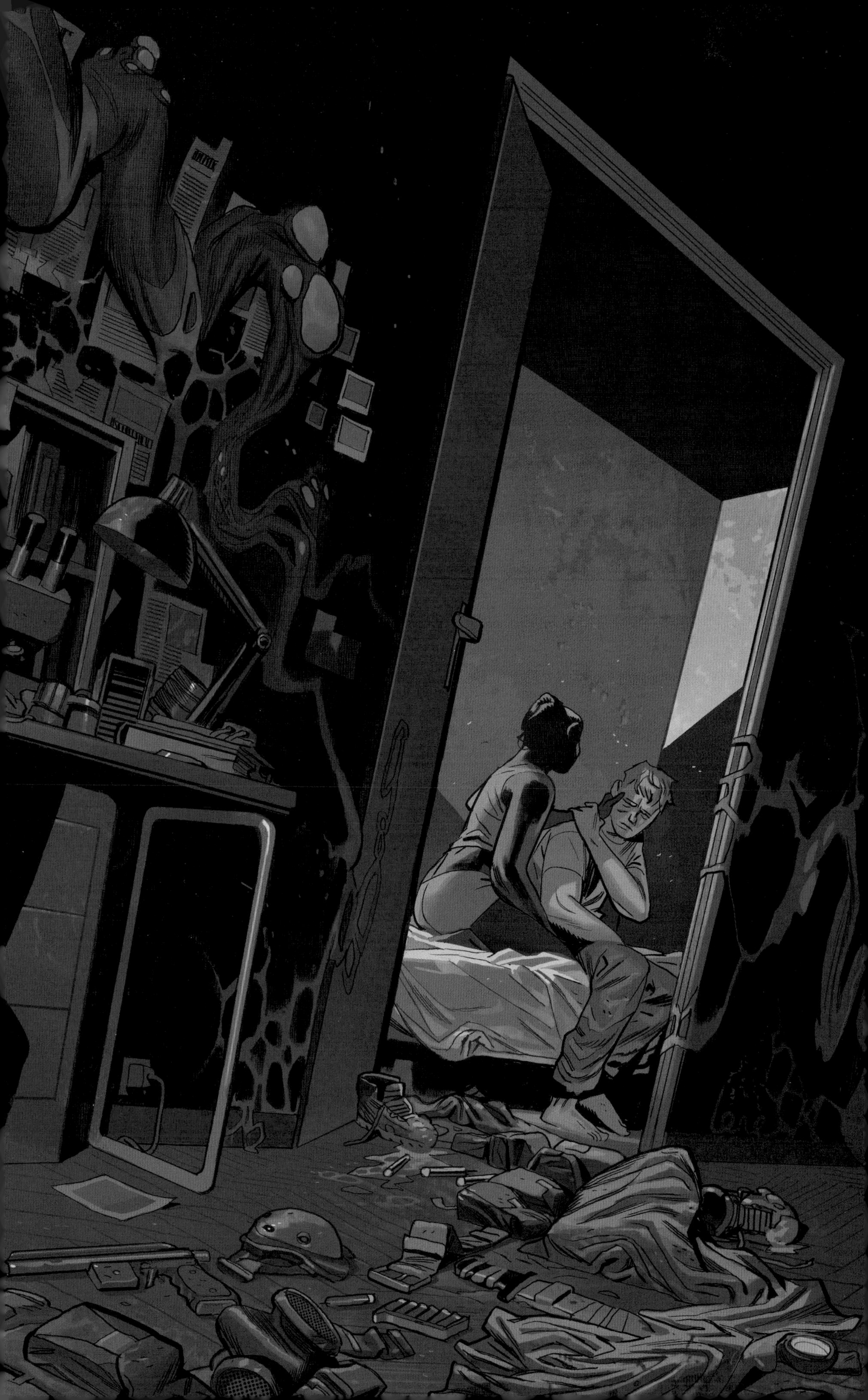

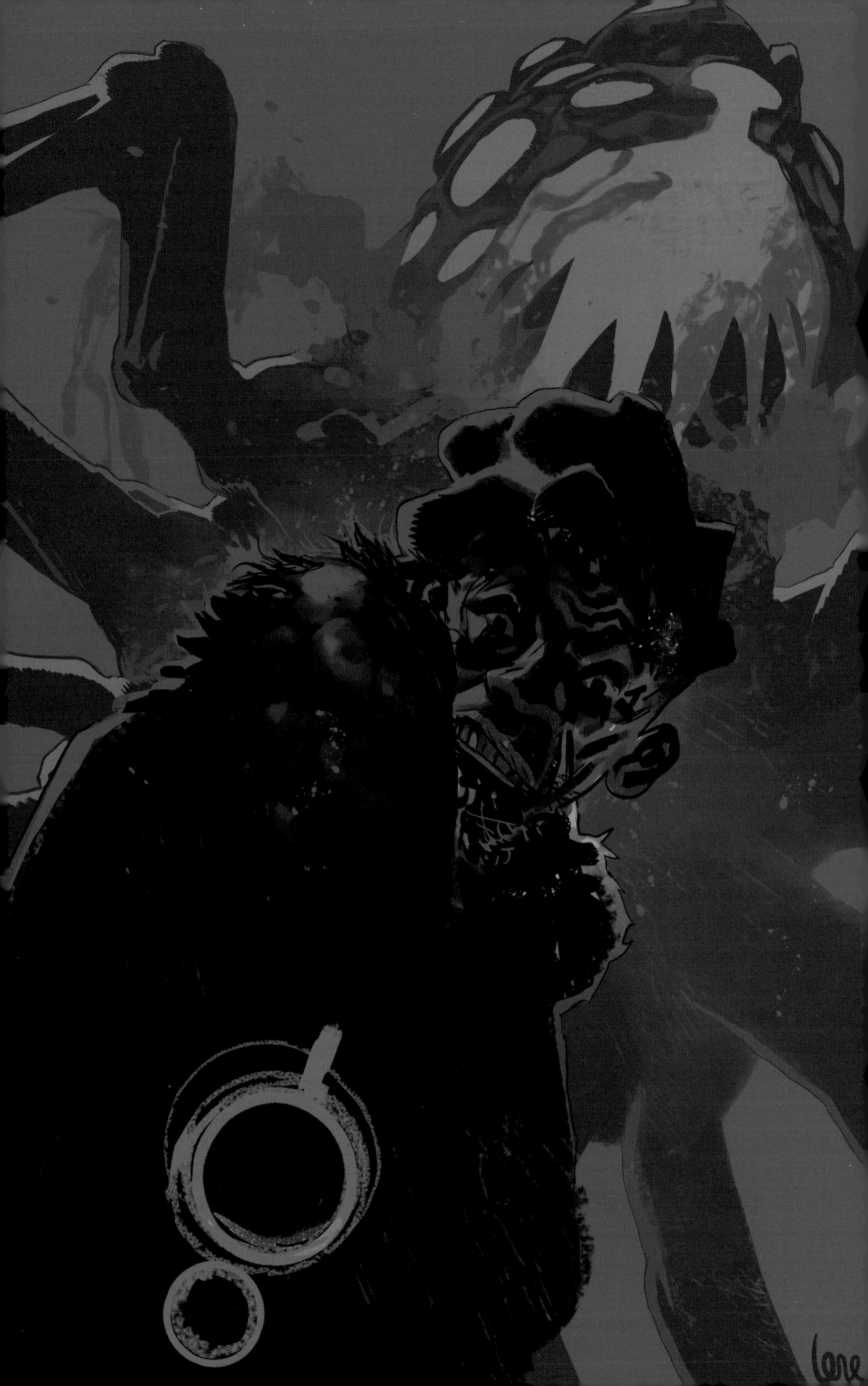

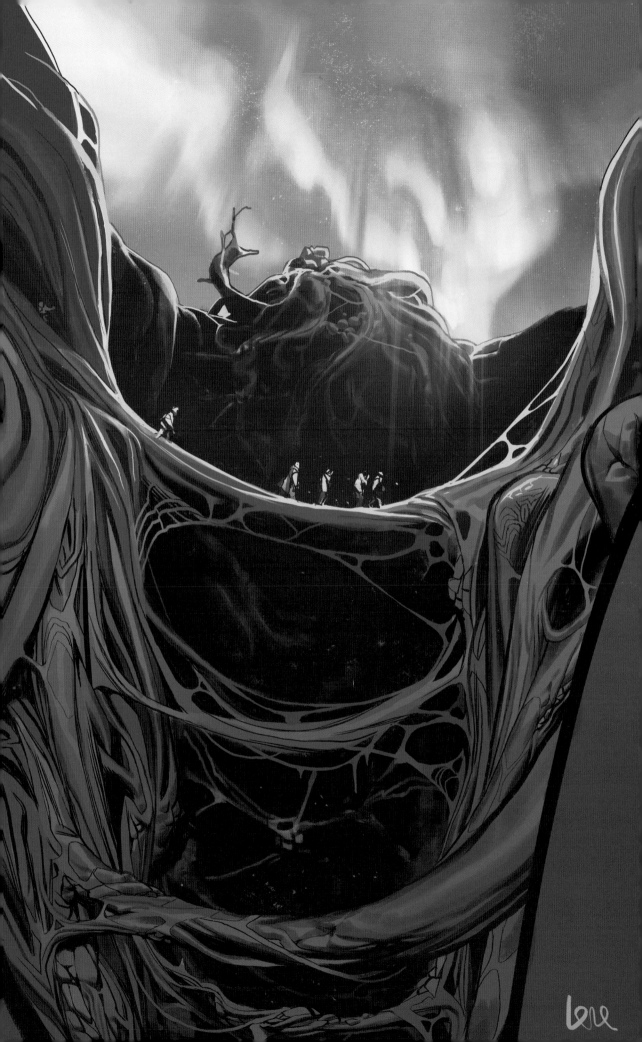

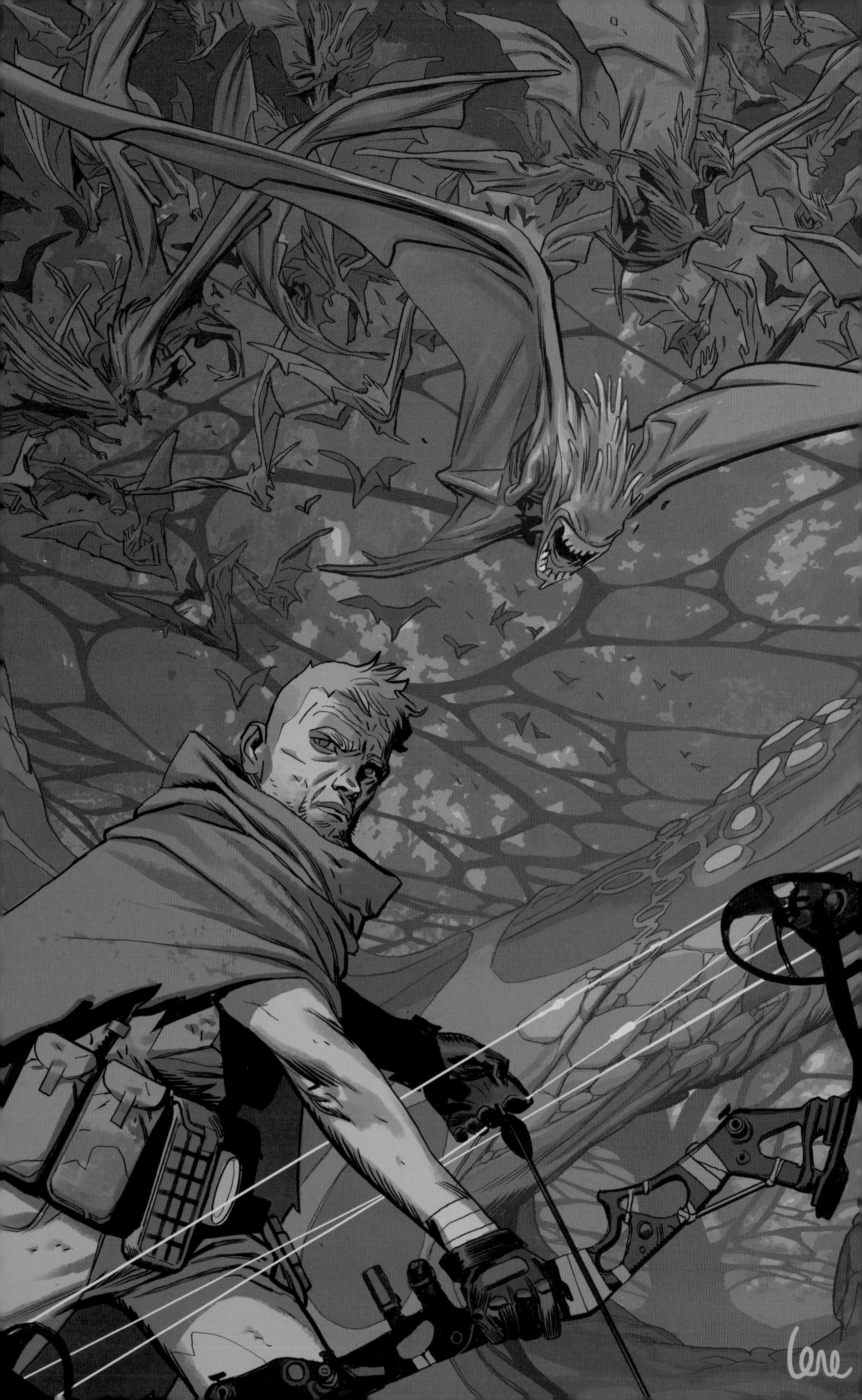

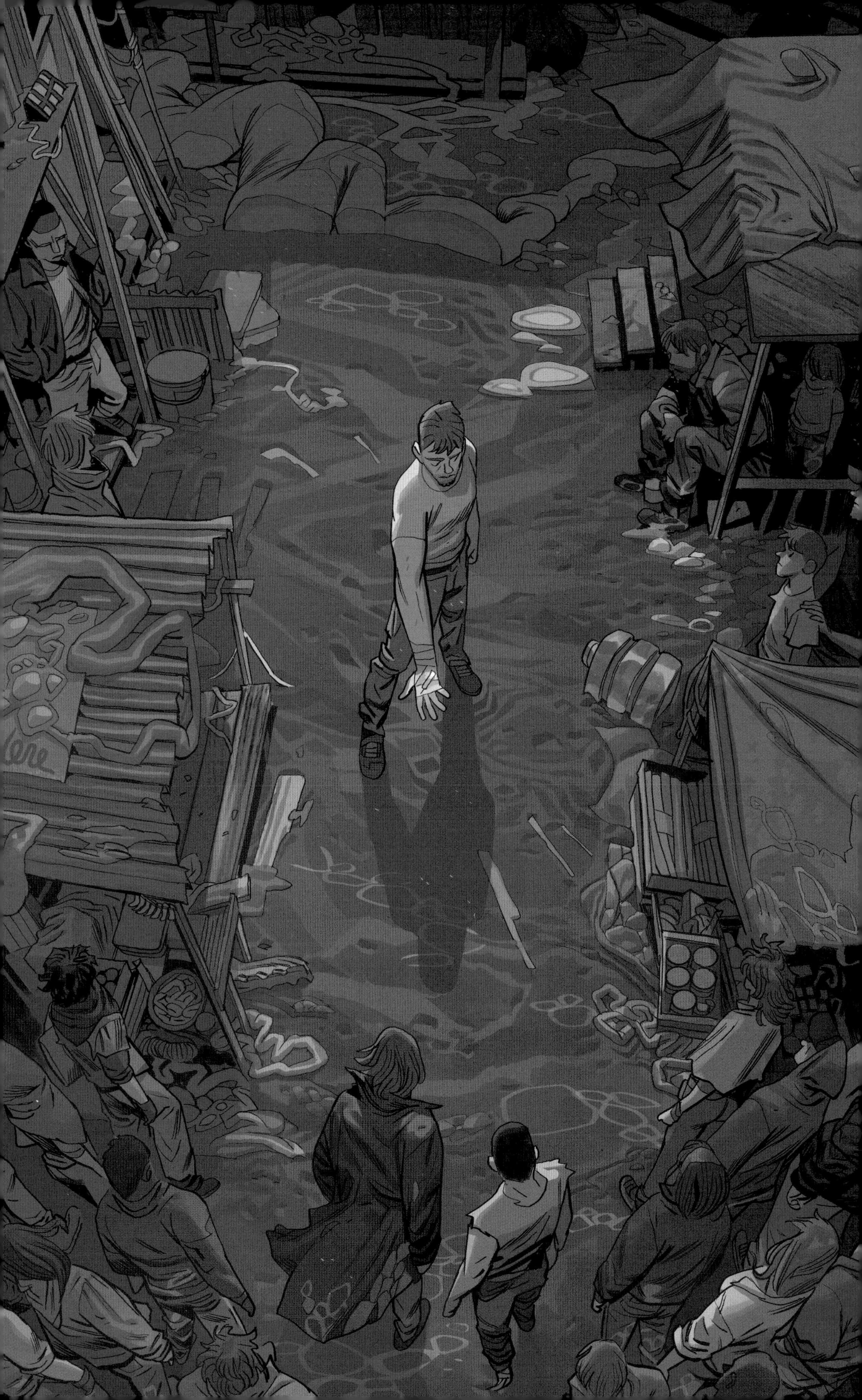

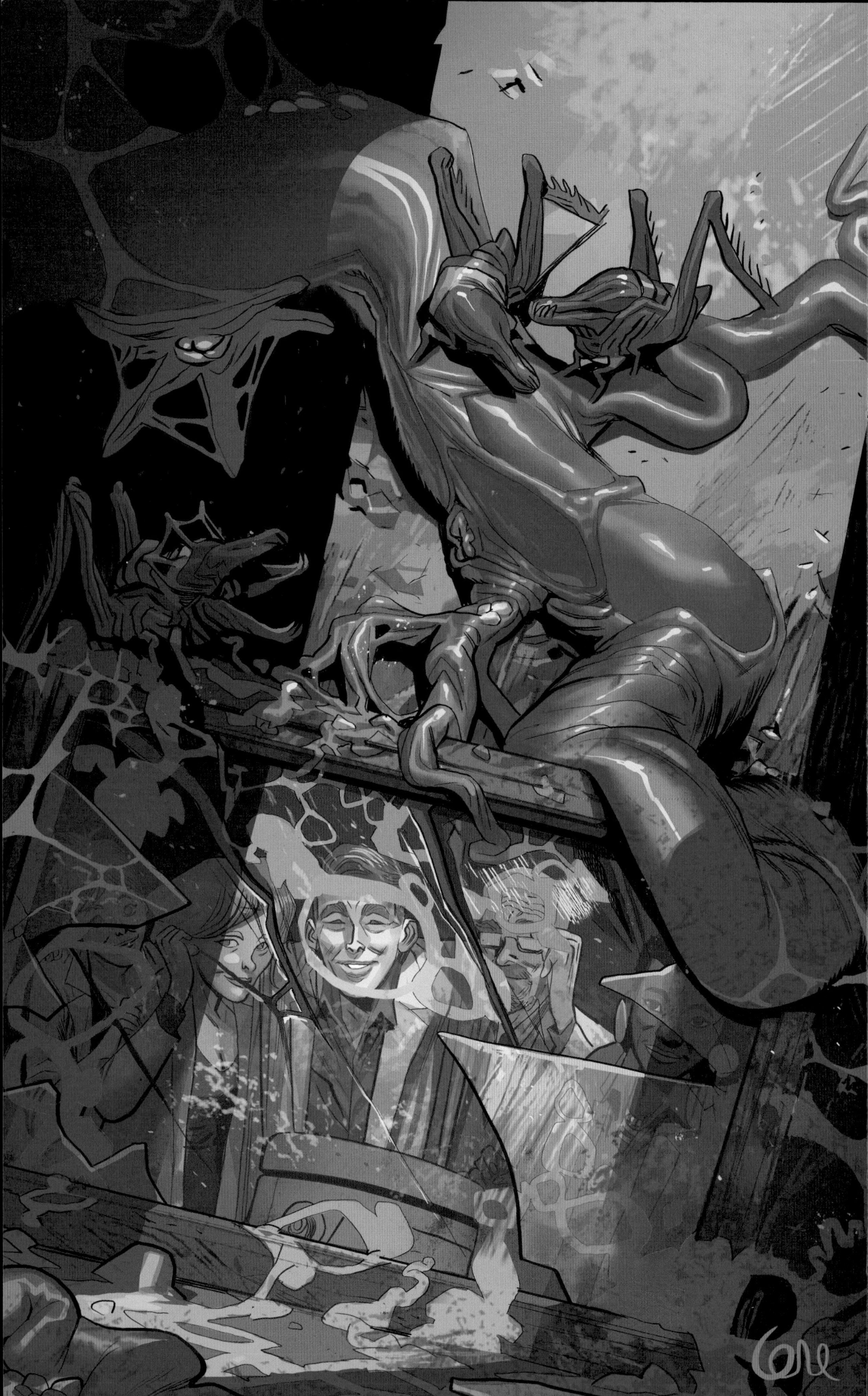

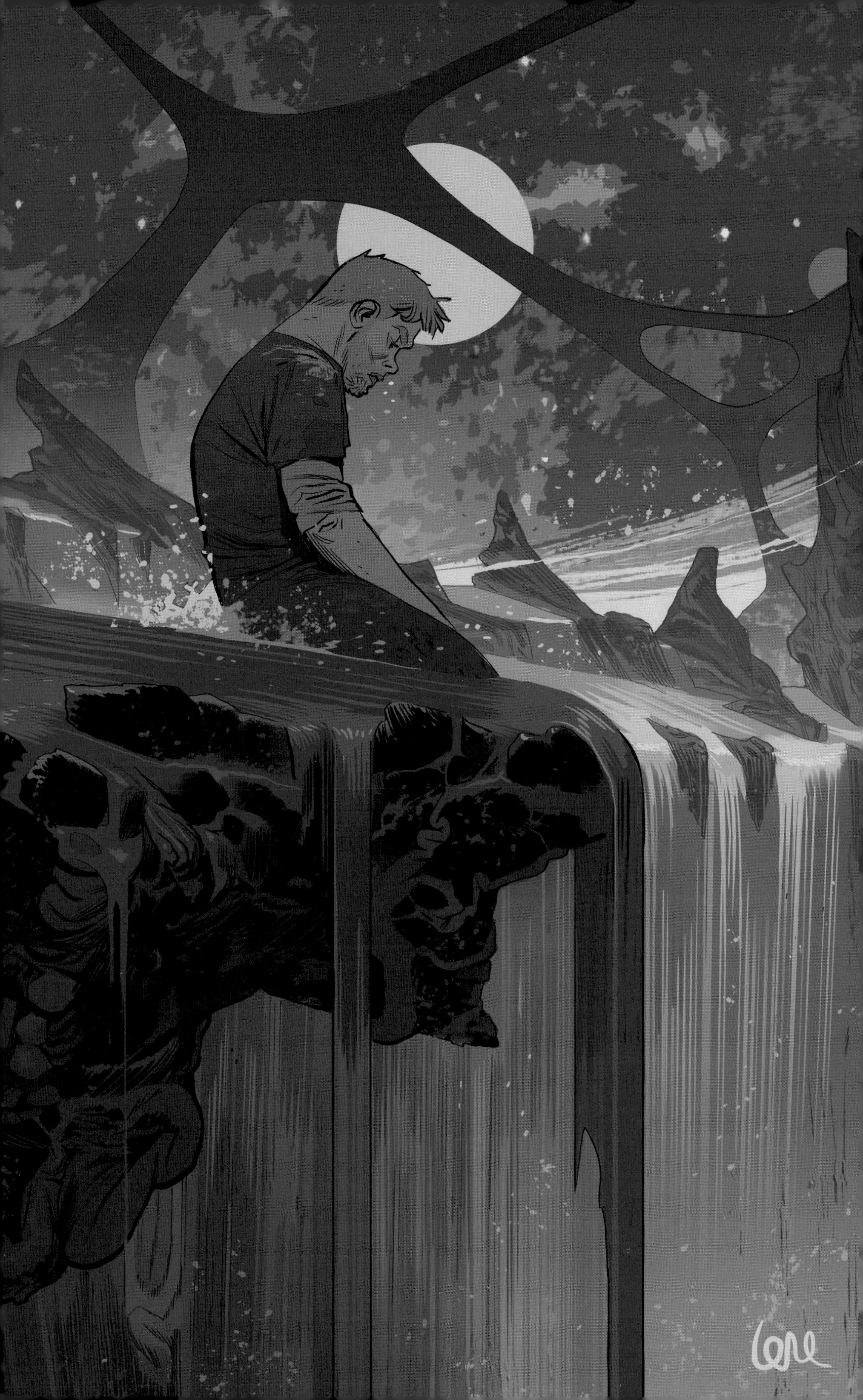

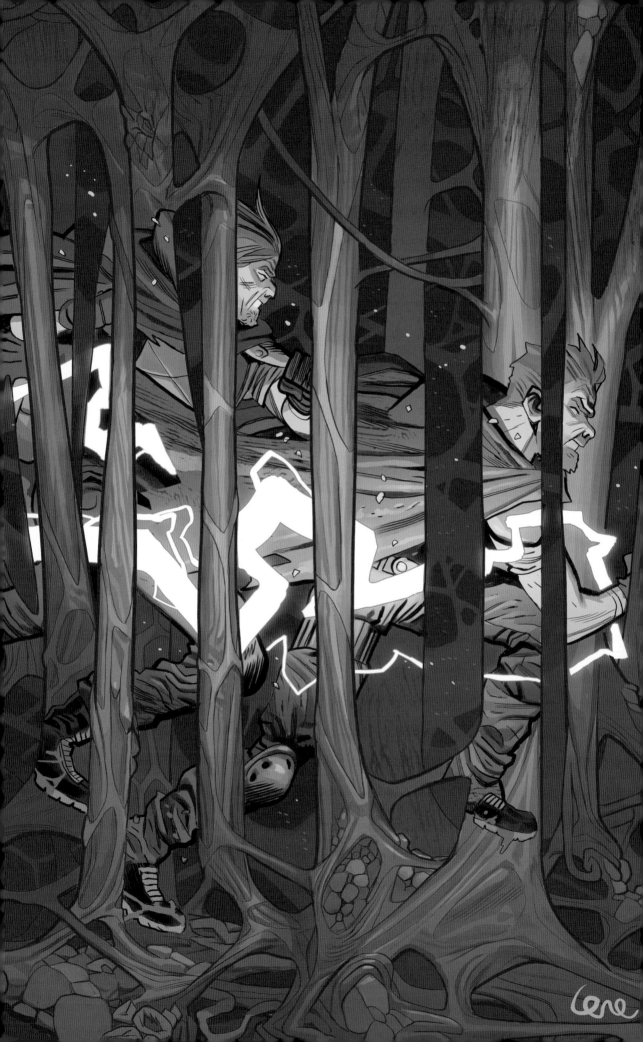

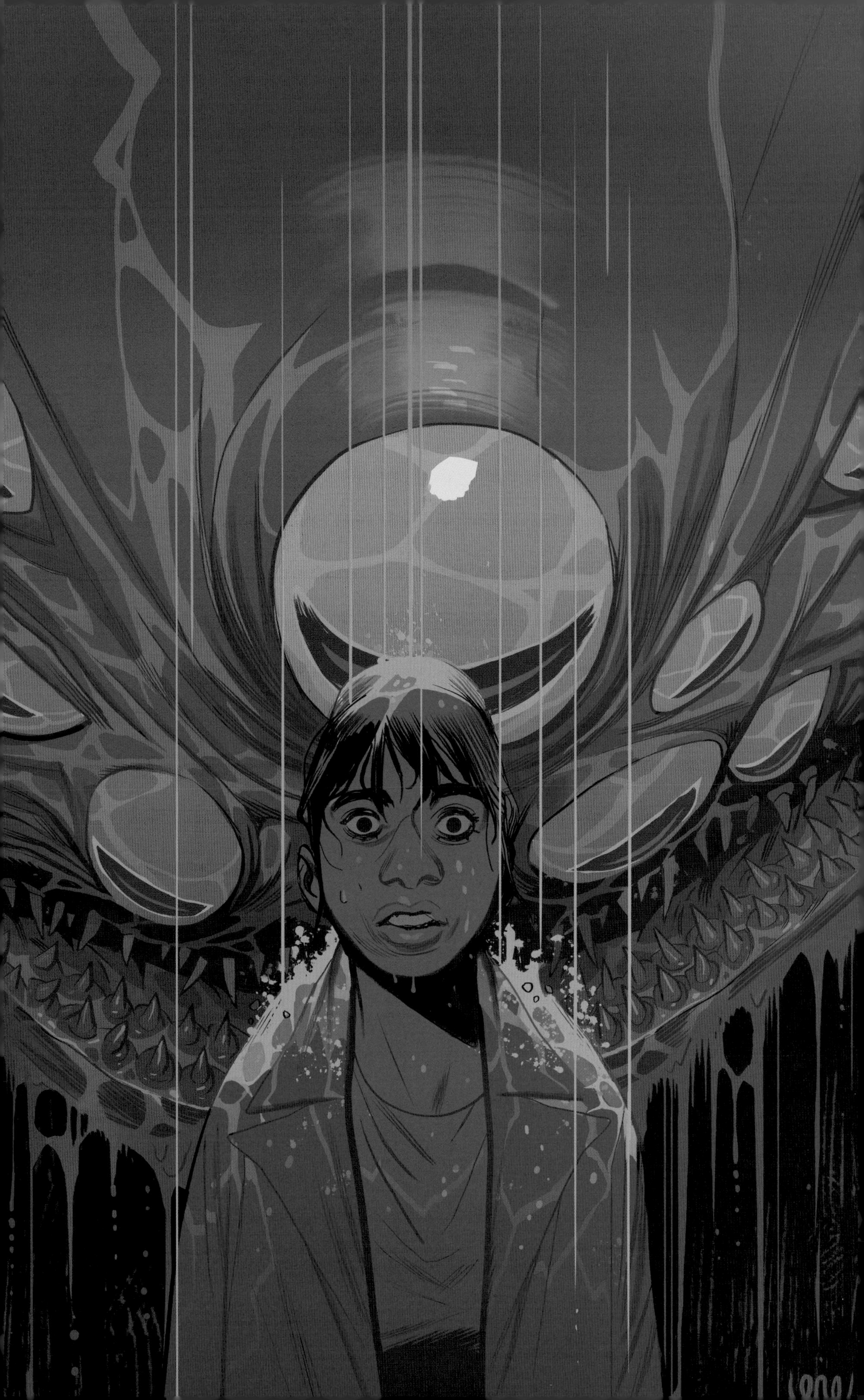

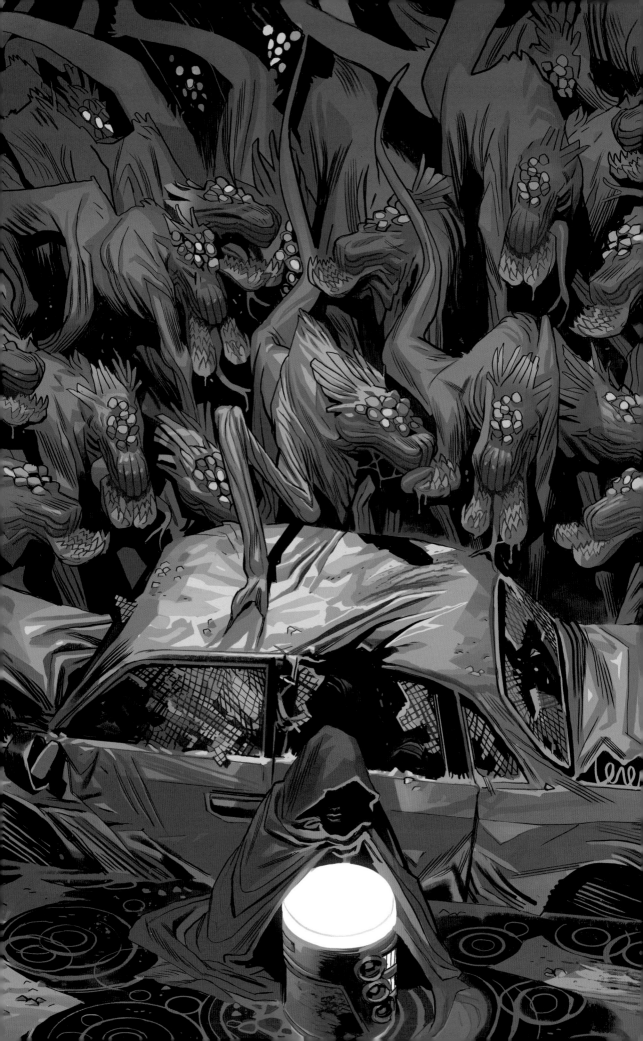

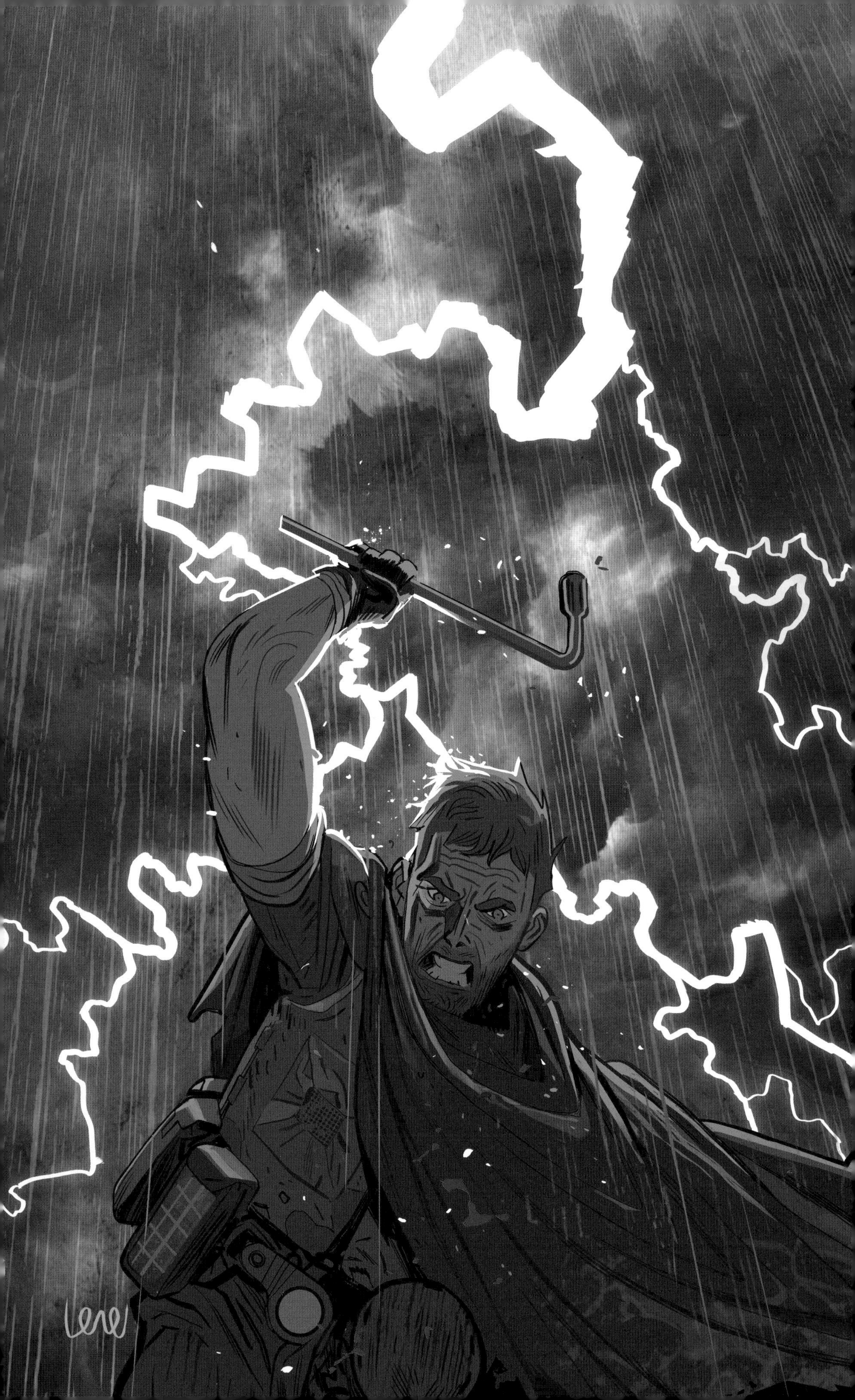

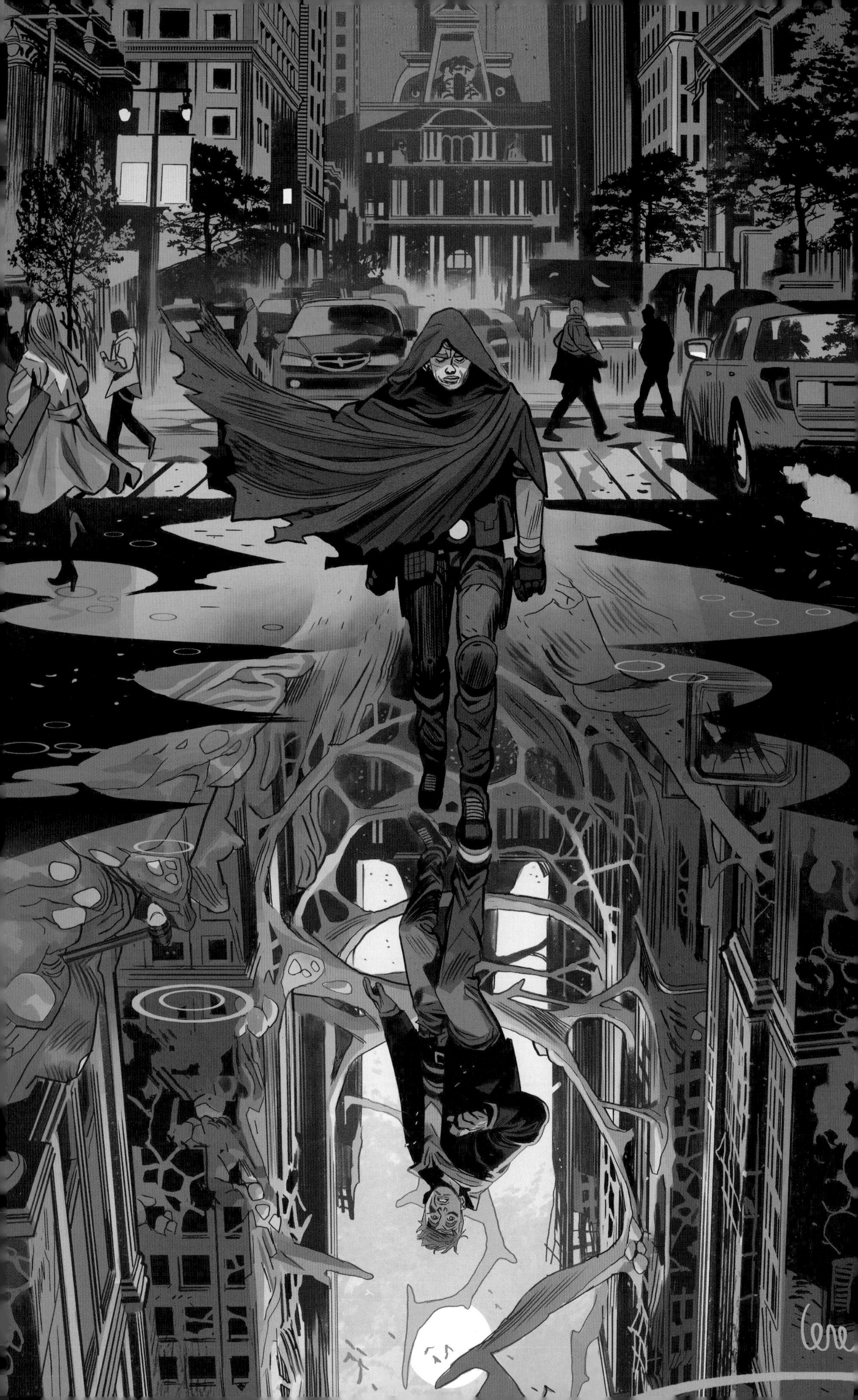

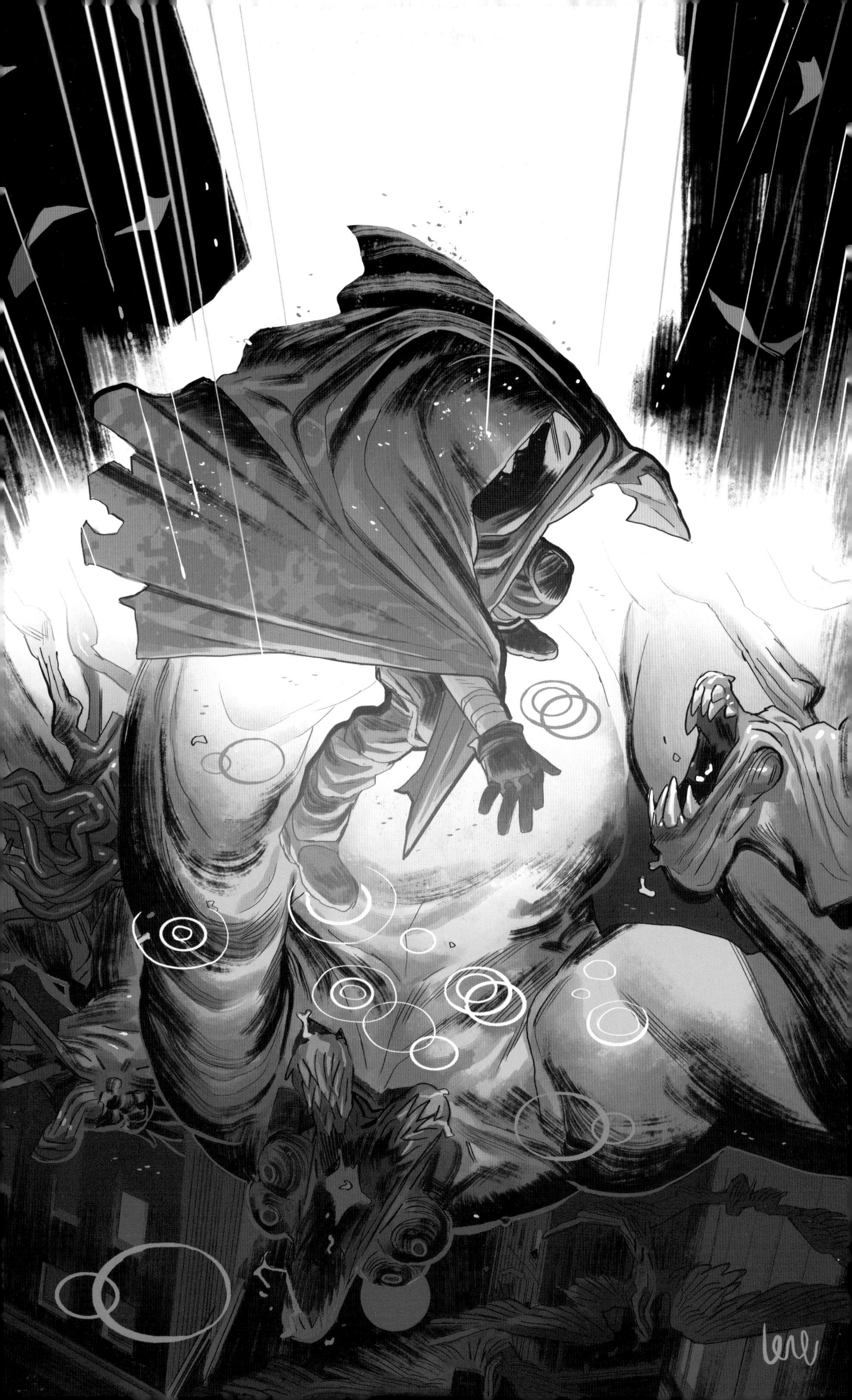

FOR MORE TALES FROM **ROBERT KIRKMAN** AND **SKYBOUND**

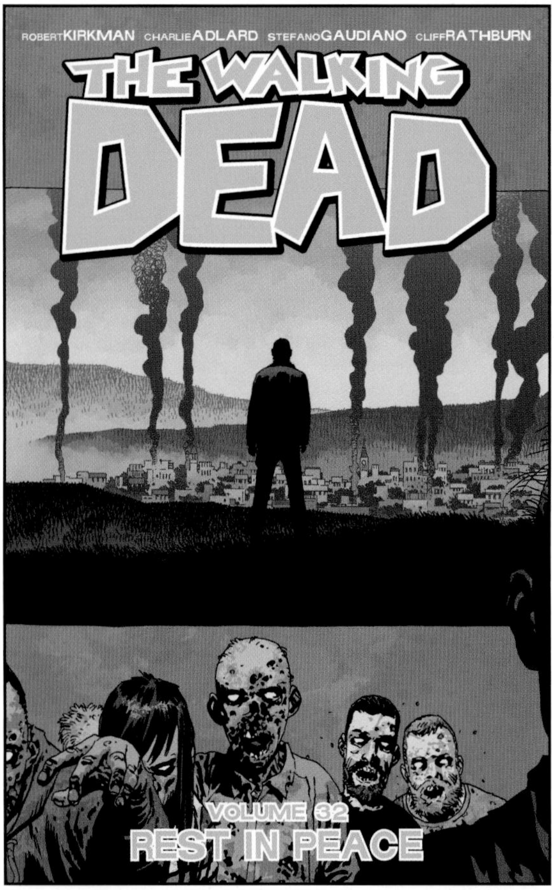
ROBERT KIRKMAN CHARLIE ADLARD STEFANO GAUDIANO CLIFF RATHBURN
THE WALKING DEAD
VOLUME 32
REST IN PEACE

VOL. 1: DAYS GONE BYE TP
ISBN: 978-1-58240-672-5
$14.99

VOL. 2: MILES BEHIND US TP
ISBN: 978-1-58240-775-3
$14.99

VOL. 3: SAFETY BEHIND BARS TP
ISBN: 978-1-58240-805-7
$14.99

VOL. 4: THE HEART'S DESIRE TP
ISBN: 978-1-58240-530-8
$14.99

VOL. 5: THE BEST DEFENSE TP
ISBN: 978-1-58240-612-1
$14.99

VOL. 6: THIS SORROWFUL LIFE TP
ISBN: 978-1-58240-684-8
$14.99

VOL. 7: THE CALM BEFORE TP
ISBN: 978-1-58240-828-6
$14.99

VOL. 8: MADE TO SUFFER TP
ISBN: 978-1-58240-883-5
$14.99

VOL. 9: HERE WE REMAIN TP
ISBN: 978-1-60706-022-2
$14.99

VOL. 10: WHAT WE BECOME TP
ISBN: 978-1-60706-075-8
$14.99

VOL. 11: FEAR THE HUNTERS TP
ISBN: 978-1-60706-181-6
$14.99

VOL. 12: LIFE AMONG THEM TP
ISBN: 978-1-60706-254-7
$14.99

VOL. 13: TOO FAR GONE TP
ISBN: 978-1-60706-329-2
$14.99

VOL. 14: NO WAY OUT TP
ISBN: 978-1-60706-392-6
$14.99

VOL. 15: WE FIND OURSELVES TP
ISBN: 978-1-60706-440-4
$14.99

VOL. 16: A LARGER WORLD TP
ISBN: 978-1-60706-559-3
$14.99

VOL. 17: SOMETHING TO FEAR TP
ISBN: 978-1-60706-615-6
$14.99

VOL. 18: WHAT COMES AFTER TP
ISBN: 978-1-60706-687-3
$14.99

VOL. 19: MARCH TO WAR TP
ISBN: 978-1-60706-818-1
$14.99

VOL. 20: ALL OUT WAR PART ONE TP
ISBN: 978-1-60706-882-2
$14.99

VOL. 21: ALL OUT WAR PART TWO TP
ISBN: 978-1-63215-030-1
$14.99

VOL. 22: A NEW BEGINNING TP
ISBN: 978-1-63215-041-7
$14.99

VOL. 23: WHISPERS INTO SCREAMS TP
ISBN: 978-1-63215-258-9
$14.99

VOL. 24: LIFE AND DEATH TP
ISBN: 978-1-63215-402-6
$14.99

VOL. 25: NO TURNING BACK TP
ISBN: 978-1-63215-659-4
$14.99

VOL. 26: CALL TO ARMS TP
ISBN: 978-1-63215-917-5
$14.99

VOL. 27: THE WHISPERER WAR TP
ISBN: 978-1-5343-0052-1
$14.99

VOL. 28: A CERTAIN DOOM TP
ISBN: 978-1-5343-0244-0
$14.99

VOL. 29: LINES WE CROSS TP
ISBN: 978-1-5343-0497-0
$16.99

VOL. 30: NEW WORLD ORDER TP
ISBN: 978-1-5343-0884-8
$16.99

VOL. 31: THE ROTTEN CORE TP
ISBN: 978-1-5343-1052-0
$16.99

VOL. 32: REST IN PEACE TP
ISBN: 978-1-5343-1241-8
$16.99

BOOK ONE HC
ISBN: 978-1-58240-619-0
$34.99

BOOK TWO HC
ISBN: 978-1-58240-698-5
$34.99

BOOK THREE HC
ISBN: 978-1-58240-825-5
$34.99

BOOK FOUR HC
ISBN: 978-1-60706-000-0
$34.99

BOOK FIVE HC
ISBN: 978-1-60706-171-7
$34.99

BOOK SIX HC
ISBN: 978-1-60706-327-8
$34.99

BOOK SEVEN HC
ISBN: 978-1-60706-439-8
$34.99

BOOK EIGHT HC
ISBN: 978-1-60706-593-7
$34.99

BOOK NINE HC
ISBN: 978-1-60706-798-6
$34.99

BOOK TEN HC
ISBN: 978-1-63215-034-9
$34.99

BOOK ELEVEN HC
ISBN: 978-1-63215-271-8
$34.99

BOOK TWELVE HC
ISBN: 978-1-63215-451-4
$34.99

BOOK THIRTEEN HC
ISBN: 978-1-63215-916-8
$34.99

BOOK FOURTEEN HC
ISBN: 978-1-5343-0329-4
$34.99

BOOK FIFTEEN HC
ISBN: 978-1-5343-0850-3
$34.99

BOOK SIXTEEN HC
ISBN: 978-1-5343-1325-5
$34.99

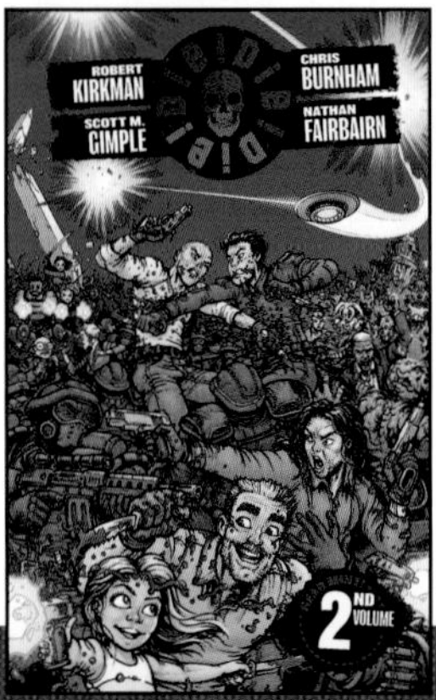
ROBERT KIRKMAN
SCOTT M. GIMPLE
CHRIS BURNHAM
NATHAN FAIRBAIRN
2ND VOLUME

VOLUME 1 TP
ISBN: 978-1-5343-1214-2
$19.99

VOLUME 2 TP
ISBN: 978-1-5343-1707-9
$16.99

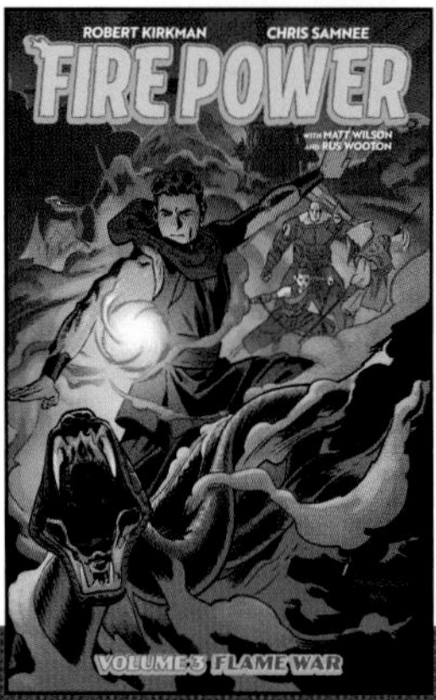
ROBERT KIRKMAN
CHRIS SAMNEE
FIRE POWER
VOLUME 3 FLAME WAR

VOL. 1: PRELUDE
ISBN: 978-1-5343-1655-3
$9.99

VOL. 2: HOME FIRE
ISBN: 978-1-5343-1718-5
$16.99

VOL. 3: FLAME WAR
ISBN: 978-1-5343-1908-0
$16.99

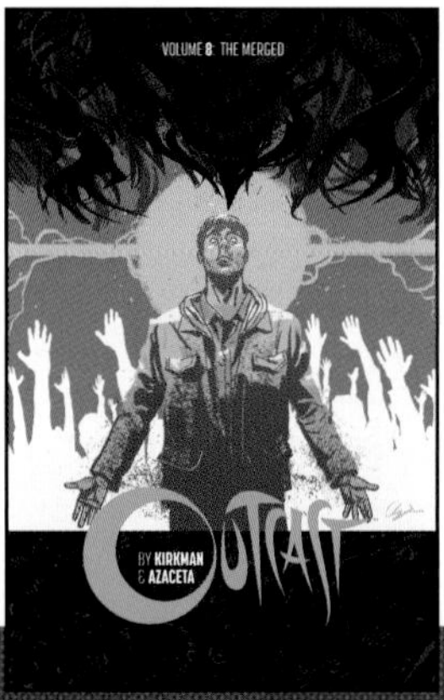
VOLUME 8 THE MERGED
BY KIRKMAN & AZACETA
OUTCAST

VOL. 1: A DARKNESS SURROUNDS HIM
ISBN: 978-1-63215-053-0
$9.99

VOL. 2: A VAST AND UNENDING RUIN
ISBN: 978-1-63215-448-4
$14.99

VOL. 3: THIS LITTLE LIGHT
ISBN: 978-1-63215-693-8
$14.99

VOL. 4: UNDER DEVIL'S WING
ISBN: 978-1-5343-0050-7
$14.99

VOL. 5: THE NEW PATH
ISBN: 978-1-5343-0249-5
$16.99

VOL. 6: INVASION
ISBN: 978-1-5343-0751-3
$16.99

VOL. 7: THE DARKNESS GROWS
ISBN: 978-1-5343-1239-5
$16.99

VOL. 8: THE MERGED
ISBN: 978-1-5343-1604-1
$16.99

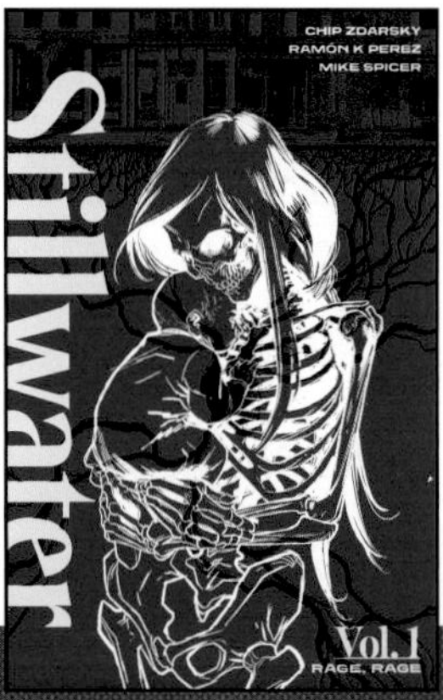
CHIP ZDARSKY
RAMÓN K PEREZ
MIKE SPICER
Stillwater
Vol. 1
RAGE, RAGE

VOL. 1: RAGE, RAGE
ISBN: 978-1-5343-1837-3
$16.99

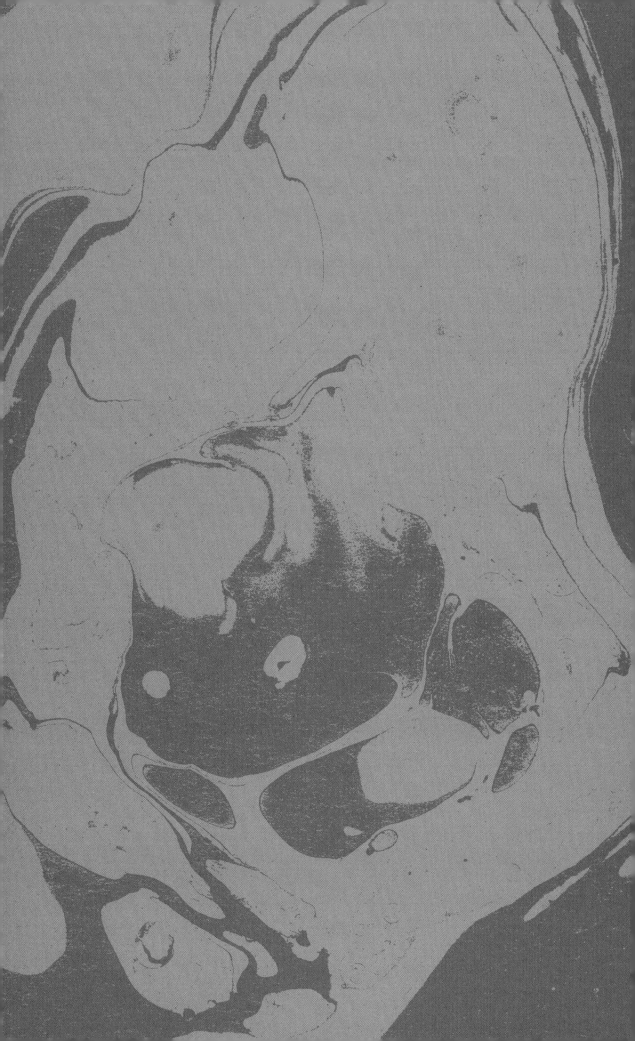

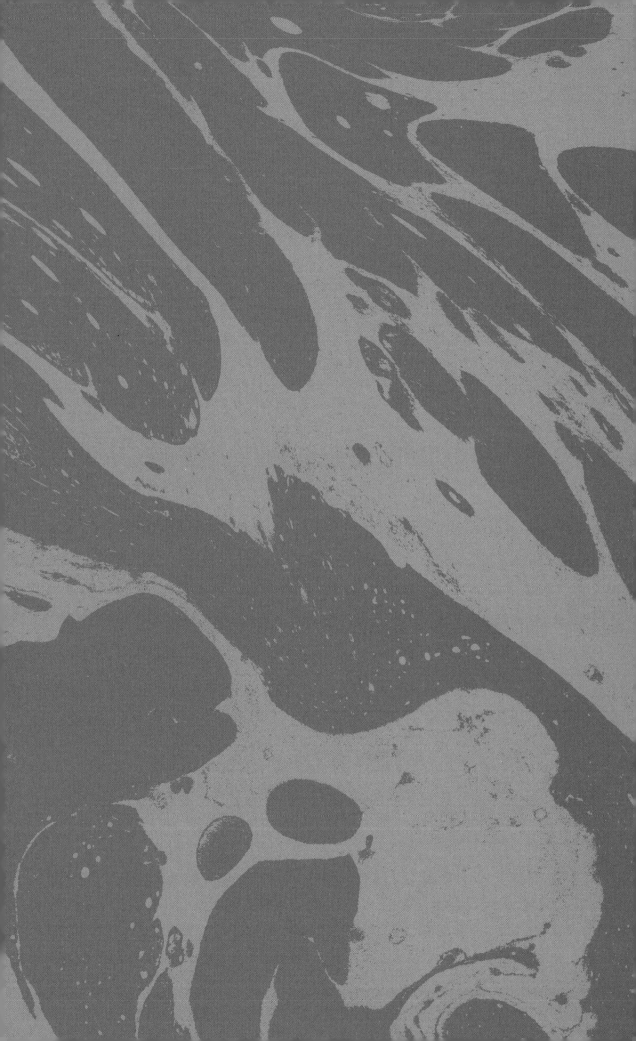